Badge of Honor: Texas Heroes
Collection One

BADGE OF HONOR: TEXAS HEROES

BOOKS 1-4
COLLECTION ONE

By Susan Stoker

Edited by Kelli Collins and Missy Borucki
Cover Design by Chris Mackey, AURA Design Group

Manufactured in the United States

Table of Contents

JUSTICE FOR MACKENZIE

BADGE OF HONOR
TEXAS HEROES
BOOK 1

By Susan Stoker

Dedication

The Badge of Honor Series is dedicated to every law enforcement officer out there. Every day you put your lives on the line to try to uphold the law and keep the rest of us safe. Every day you may be yelled at, spit on, or shot at. People see you and immediately wonder who you're looking to arrest or get into trouble. But there are also those of us who see you and sigh in relief. Who know you're there to make sure we get home safely, who see the time you spend on the streets and away from your families. So thank you. From the bottom of my heart. Thank you for all you do.

And to the *families* of law enforcement officers everywhere. You're the strongest men and women I know. You kiss your loved ones as they walk out the door, never knowing what they might be walking into that day on the job. Thank you for letting your loved ones look after us.

You all have my utmost respect. I have taken some creative license with police procedures for the sake of the story, so if I've mangled something in this series that isn't quite right, please know I mean no disrespect to you or to your profession.

Chapter One

————◆————

DAXTON CHAMBERS BARELY concealed his impatience with his friend and fellow law enforcement officer, Thomas James "TJ" Rockwell.

"Shut up, TJ. The only reason I agreed to come tonight is because I lost that ridiculous bet."

"Yeah, only *you* were stupid enough to bet the SAFD would win that basketball tournament. You should've gone with the boys in blue rather than those hose jockeys."

"Hey, I've played against some of those guys and they're killers on the court, that's why I thought they'd win. They just had a bad day. Driftwood and Crash played in college, and Squirrel and Taco played in high school. The rest? Doesn't matter, they're usually just there to cause havoc so the others can handle the ball."

TJ laughed. "Yeah, you might be right, but whatever happened, they still lost, so suck it up. This charity thing is only gonna last for a couple of hours. Just be thankful they didn't decide to have a bachelor auction. I think that's been way overdone and is totally cliché, but it's easy and kinda fun in a warped way. But for tonight, we just have to show up, flex our muscles a bit, then leave." TJ ran a hand through his dark, wavy hair.

Dax watched as a tableful of women nearby checked TJ out and then giggled, whispering softly to each other. He chuckled. "Don't look now, but I think you've got an entire table of admirers over there."

Of course TJ looked, but immediately turned back to his friend. "Jesus, Dax. They're barely out of college. No thank you. That time in my life is over. I'm looking for a woman who's serious about a relationship, not a badge bunny who only wants to sleep with as many cops as she can. Been there, done that, got the T-shirt."

"Well, when you find one, hopefully she has a best friend or a sister for me." Dax slapped TJ on the shoulder. "Come on, let's go get a beer and hide out in the corner until this shindig is over. What kind of shifts you got this week? Want to go to that new steak place the guys have been talking about?"

"Let me check and get back to you. They're changing the shifts around and I'm not sure what I'll be doing after next week."

TJ was an officer with the Highway Patrol and Dax was a Texas Ranger. They'd met at a crime scene, and had been friends ever since. Now they were able to collaborate more readily on cases and hang out at law enforcement conferences.

"Are Cruz and Quint coming to this thing tonight?" Dax asked. Cruz Livingston was an FBI agent who worked at the San Antonio Station and Quint Axton was an officer with the San Antonio Police Department.

"Yeah, I think so. Calder, Hayden, and Conor are also supposed to show up. The nonprofit group tried to get law enforcement from all over the city to attend. I haven't seen them in a while and it'll be great to catch up."

Calder Stonewall was one of the medical examiners for San Antonio. Both TJ and Dax had gotten to know him through their cases. Hayden Yates was a sheriff's deputy, the only woman in their tight-knit group, and she'd earned all their respect in a recent rape case. Rape was never easy to investigate or prosecute, and Hayden had worked hard to get justice for the teenager who had been violated by three college men while she'd been attending a party.

The last man in their law enforcement posse was Conor Paxton.

He was also probably the person they all knew the least. He worked for the Texas Parks and Wildlife Law Enforcement Division, a member of the SCOUT team that assisted in critical incidents. There were only twenty-five SCOUT members in the entire state of Texas. Conor was quiet and focused, but made a hell of a partner in emergencies.

"Well, we might as well get settled in. There are some speeches first, right? Then the kids are coming out for the talent show?" Dax asked TJ.

"Yeah, our table's off to the side. I asked the organizers not to put us in the middle in case any of us get called away."

"Good thinking."

The men walked around until they found the table with their names on the seating cards. As requested, Cruz, Quint, Calder, Hayden, and Conor had also been assigned seats at the same table.

"As much as I bitched about this tonight, I'm glad I'm here. The kids are always so cute singing and dancing, and it's not often all of us get to be in the same place at the same time, especially when it's for fun and not for work," TJ said after they'd gotten comfortable at the table.

"Agreed," Dax said while nodding.

TJ and Dax settled into their seats and waited for their friends to show up and for the entertainment to start.

"SANDRA, MAKE SURE the kids and their parents know what order everyone is performing. We can't have too much of a break between the acts. We gotta keep this moving." Mackenzie Morgan put her hands on her hips and surveyed the crowd mingling in the large ballroom. This was the second year she'd almost single-handedly organized the annual charity event. It was a rewarding experience, and the law enforcement personnel who showed up were mostly easy on the eyes.

Mackenzie worked for a nonprofit agency called San Antonio Cares (SAC). The company helped all sorts of people in the city, from children to the elderly. They held auctions, charity events, and generally raised money for the less-fortunate people living in the large metropolitan city in Texas. Sandra was the administrative assistant, and one of Mackenzie's biggest helpers for the event. There was no way she'd be able to pull it off without her.

This event was one of their biggest. SAC invited law enforcement officers from all over the city and they usually had a phenomenal turnout. Tonight was no exception. Mackenzie had always liked working with law enforcement. The men and women were almost always very polite and courteous. It was a fallacy that they were all good-looking, though. Mack had seen her share of policemen and women who wouldn't win any beauty contests anytime soon.

However, tonight for some reason, everywhere her gaze landed, she saw almost nothing but good looking officers. Most were in uniform, many wore cowboy hats and boots. Even though the women were also in uniform, Mackenzie was a little jealous of how strong and, yes, beautiful many looked. Mack had always wanted to be svelte and muscular, but she'd been blessed with her mother's genes. She was short, about five feet four, and had too many curves to ever be the type of woman men noticed and fell immediately in lust with.

At a hundred and forty pounds on a good day, Mack was lush. She wasn't embarrassed by her weight or her looks, but with every year that passed without finding someone who she wanted to spend the rest of her life with, she'd begun to worry she never would. At thirty-seven, Mack had dated her fair share of men, and while she'd honestly loved one or two, she'd never felt an all-consuming love; one in which she didn't think she'd be able to live without the other person.

Mackenzie looked around the room once more, her trained eye straining to pick up any problems so she could fix them before they got too big to handle. Her eyes stopped at a table off to the side of the room.

There were two men standing to greet a group of other officers who'd just arrived. They caught her eye because every single person was wearing a slightly different uniform. Usually the men and women tended to clump together in groups of their own kind, for lack of a better word. The SAPD members sat with each other, the FBI agents sat together, and so on. As Mackenzie watched, the six men and one woman sat down after shaking each other's hands and entered into what seemed like a lively conversation.

The man holding a cowboy hat caught Mack's attention and held it. While the other men were all extremely good-looking, Mack made a mental note to suggest to her boss that they revisit the law enforcement calendar for a fundraiser next year. For obvious reasons, this man with the cowboy hat stood out. He had short brown hair. He was tall, but then again, almost every man seemed tall to Mackenzie. She couldn't tell his exact body type, as she was across the room and he was wearing a long-sleeve uniform, but she liked the way he looked people in the eyes as he greeted them, making sure each person knew he was paying attention to them.

Hell, Mackenzie had no idea what drew her eyes to the man, especially since there were handsome men all around her. But there was an attraction, and it was instant and baffling at the same time. She'd never felt a zing like the one she felt looking at this man.

A shout drew her attention past the table to one of the little girls who was supposed to be performing later on. She was shouting at one of her friends as she ran, not paying attention to what was going on around her. A waiter carrying a tray full of empty beer bottles and glasses was right in her path.

Mackenzie immediately started across the room, knowing she

wouldn't be able to prevent the accident, but hoping she'd be able to keep the little girl from being hurt.

The little girl crashed into the waiter just as Mackenzie reached them. Performing what had to be an award-winning snatch-and-grab, Mackenzie caught the little girl around the waist just as she bounced off of the waiter's legs.

Mack watched as he teetered and then lurched to the side, trying to avoid dropping the tray on the little girl's head. Inevitably, the tray slid, unbalanced by his sudden movement, and all the glasses fell to the floor in a loud, very noticeable crash.

Mack took a few steps away from the mess on the floor and kneeled down to speak to the child, wanting to make sure she'd gotten there in time to keep her from getting cut by the glass.

"Are you all right?" Mackenzie looked at the nametag attached to the startled girl's sparkly dress. "Cindy? Did the glass hurt you?"

Cindy sniffed and shook her head, putting her thumb in her mouth and sucking hard.

Mackenzie looked up to see a woman striding toward them, and Cindy reached up for her as she got close.

"I'm so sorry, Ms. Morgan," Cindy's mom said as she comforted her daughter.

Seeing Cindy's mom relieved Mackenzie. She liked kids, but wasn't very good with them. "It's okay; I'm just glad Cindy's not hurt. Go ahead and take her to where the other kids are getting ready, I'll take care of this and we'll start the show in a bit. All right?"

"Sure. And thanks. I've never seen someone move so fast before."

Mackenzie nodded absently, already turning back to the waiter. Relieved, she saw two of the caterers there, already cleaning up the mess.

"Are you all right, miss?"

Startled, Mackenzie looked up—right into the eyes of the man she'd been admiring earlier.

Wow. He was even better-looking up close. She briefly noticed the Texas Ranger star on his chest and nodded her head in answer to his question. Damn, Rangers were the best of the best in the state. They had a great reputation and she knew he was way out of her league. Besides, as much as she might want to, she didn't have time to chitchat.

"Yeah, I'm good. It's inevitable that something like this happens with this many people around. You're okay too, yeah? Was anyone hit by the glass? Crap, I gotta make sure they put up a 'wet floor' sign, I don't want anyone slipping. Just what I need, to have a cop slip and hit his head. I'd probably get sued or something. That would be bad karma for sure. Anyway, yeah, I'm good, I gotta get going. Got a shit-ton of stuff to do. Glad you're okay too."

Mackenzie shifted away from the Ranger, knowing she was babbling but not able to stop. She had a tendency to go on and on, especially when she was nervous. She moved away from the man with a pang of regret. She wasn't being coy, she really *didn't* have time to talk to him. She had a show to get started and a mess to make sure was cleaned up.

Dax watched as the brunette walked away from him and over to a woman in black pants and white shirt, who looked as though she worked for the catering company. He smiled, not taking his eyes from the curvy woman's backside. She'd adorably talked on and on, not quite looking him in the eye. It was a refreshing change from the women he encountered on a daily basis. They either flirted shamelessly with him solely based on his looks and the fact he was a Ranger, or they were shifty and elusive, lying their asses off to get out of whatever crime they'd committed.

"Come on, Dax. Get your ass back over here. Calder wants to know what the hell you were thinking, siding with the firefighters over the officers last week," Cruz yelled from the table.

Dax took one last look at the woman, now talking with the lady from the catering company, and sighed. He didn't know her, and had really only said a couple of words to her, but she was cute babbling on with him. Not only that, she had the kind of body he was most attracted to. But he'd had issues in the past with women not wanting to put up with his crazy schedule, and figured with his luck, this woman would probably not be any different.

He turned and headed back to the large table with a deep breath. It would be a long night, taking the good-natured ribbing from his friends. He wouldn't change it for the world.

Chapter Two

D AX LOOKED ACROSS the police vehicle at TJ. He'd never forget when he met the Highway Patrolman for the first time. TJ had called in the Rangers when the report of a dead body had been made off one of the many rural highways that snaked around San Antonio. Dax met TJ at the scene and they'd immediately clicked. After a long investigation, the men had become friends.

At the moment, TJ was technically off duty, although they were in his official vehicle and they were driving to a steak place that had just opened and had gotten rave reviews. They'd finally synched their schedules and were headed for dinner.

"How's that serial case you've been working on?"

Dax sighed. They'd talked about it for a bit at the charity talent show they'd attended a couple of weeks ago, but it'd gotten worse since then. "Sucks. This guy is good."

"How many bodies have been found so far?"

"Five. All buried alive and called in. Who knows how many more there are, because it's not like we'd ever find the bodies if the bastard didn't let us know where they were."

"What does Calder say about cause of death?"

As one of the medical examiners for Bexar County, Calder was responsible for figuring out the cause of death for all persons who died suddenly, unexpectedly, or violently.

"Asphyxiation, of course. The bastard buries them alive and Calder estimates they stay alive for anywhere from two to ten hours.

Fucking torture."

TJ didn't have much to say. It was inevitable that their talk turned to work whenever they got together. Both men were committed to their jobs and getting bad guys off the streets, one way or another.

Just as Dax was about to try to change the subject to something a little less depressing, a blue Honda Civic going the opposite direction flew by them. TJ flipped on the rear-facing radar just in time to clock the car going eighty miles an hour in a sixty zone.

"Hang on."

Dax held on and didn't bother to protest as TJ slowed just enough to make a safe U-turn and then stepped on the gas to catch up to the speeding car. While technically off duty, every law enforcement officer knew they were never *really* off duty. Someone going that fast could easily kill someone, and it was TJ's duty as an officer to stop them.

Dax grinned as they quickly made up the distance between them and the car. Dax didn't get to work patrol anymore, so it was adrenaline-inducing to be involved in a high speed chase once again. The Honda was no match for the Crown Victoria with its powerful engine, and TJ quickly caught up. He flicked on the police lights while simultaneously radioing the license plate to dispatch. The driver in the car immediately pulled over to the side of the road after seeing the flashing lights in her rear-view mirror.

"Thought you were off duty, TJ," the dispatcher on the other end of the radio said with laughter in her voice.

"Yeah, well, you know how it is."

Dax and TJ pulled over to the shoulder behind the vehicle waiting for dispatch to get back with the vehicle information. They didn't have to wait long.

"Blue, 2011 Honda Civic. Registered to a Mackenzie Morgan, age thirty-seven. Five feet four, one hundred-forty pounds. San

Antonio resident. No priors, no record."

"Ten-Four. Thanks." TJ told the dispatcher he'd be out on the traffic stop and put down the mic.

"Sorry, Dax. I'd love to let her off with a warning to speed this up, but I'll have to play it by ear. I'll try to keep it short so we can be on our way. I'm starved. Be right back."

Dax watched as TJ eased out of his patrol vehicle and carefully made his way to the driver's door. The most dangerous part of any traffic stop was making the initial contact with the occupants in a vehicle. There was no way to know if the person or people in the car had weapons and if they would open fire on an officer as he or she came up to the car.

Dax could see the woman in the car holding on to the steering wheel with both hands, as she'd probably been taught.

TJ stood a foot or so away from the door and leaned over a bit, talking to the woman. Dax watched as she reached over to the glovebox and handed some papers out the window to TJ, most likely her license and registration.

Dax couldn't see much of the woman from his vantage point in the front seat of TJ's cruiser, but he could imagine how she looked from the description relayed by the dispatcher. Short and probably curvaceous. Just his type. Oh, Dax had dated all shapes and sizes of women, but he always came back to what he liked best. At an inch over six feet, Dax liked the feeling of being taller and bigger than the woman he was dating. He liked it when she fit into the bend of his arm. Dax hated when a woman was skin and bones. There was nothing like being able to have some flesh to hold on to while pounding in and out of her body.

Dax shifted in his seat. Jesus, he had to get ahold of himself. He was too old to get an erection imagining what the anonymous woman might look like. It'd obviously been way too long since he'd gotten laid. He'd have to see what he could do about that.

TJ turned and came back to the vehicle after a lengthy conversation with the woman in the car. He sat back down and pulled the laptop mounted in the center console to him. He quickly punched in the information from the driver's license in his hand.

"So?" Dax asked, "What was her sob story?"

TJ grinned. "You wouldn't believe it. She was actually really cute."

"Cute?"

"Yeah, she started babbling like I don't think I've heard anyone do before. She wasn't really trying to get out of the ticket, and she wasn't trying to excuse herself...she was just spilling her guts."

Dax tilted his head. What did TJ's words remind him of?

"She babbled about how she'd had a terrible day at work with her boss from hell. Then she explained she had to go home and be tortured by her family for being single and childless. *Then* she went into the cutest fucking rant about how she hated when people would zoom by her on the highway and not even care they were going so fast. Somehow she then changed the topic and began to talk about eighteen-wheelers on the roads before I cut her off."

"What was her name again?" Dax asked, the niggling feeling even stronger. He still couldn't figure out why he had it though.

"Mackenzie Morgan. She's clean. She's never even had a parking ticket before, at least not here in San Antonio. I'm going to let her off with a warning."

"A warning? That's not like you. You must've *really* thought she was cute."

Laughing, TJ handed over the driver's license to Dax while saying, "Yeah, she's cute, but that's not why I'm letting her off. She was honestly mortified she'd been going so fast."

"Suuuure that's the reason." Dax laughed then looked down at the license he held in his hand. Surprisingly, the picture actually wasn't as horrible as most tended to be.

Mackenzie A. Morgan. Just as the dispatcher said, she was nine inches shorter than he was. She had brown hair in the photo and was smiling crookedly. Dax had the thought that even her eyes were smiling. Why did she look so familiar to him?

TJ just shook his head at Dax and held out his hand for her license. After Dax handed it over, TJ got out of the car. Before going back to the Honda, he said, "Besides, it's just too much trouble to write up the ticket. We have reservations."

Dax laughed out loud as TJ headed back to tell Mackenzie the good news. TJ had always been a sucker for a pretty face, and Ms. Morgan was certainly one of those.

TJ was gone a bit too long to deliver a simple warning to the woman, and Dax frowned, not liking the feeling in his gut.

Fuck, it was jealousy. He was jealous of his damn friend. It looked as if they were in another in-depth conversation and Dax saw the woman shaking her head several times. His leg bounced up and down with impatience. How could he be jealous of his friend? Fuck, it was just a traffic stop, one of thousands TJ had made over his career. It wasn't as if he was arranging a date with the woman...was he?

Dax himself had pulled over his share of people before he became a Ranger, so why was this one different? Dax didn't want to admit it, but it was because of the woman behind the wheel. He hadn't seen her face in person, just the image on her driver's license, but he still had a feeling he knew her. His gut was screaming at him, but he didn't know why.

TJ finally nodded at the woman and came back to the patrol car. He sat down and pulled the laptop over to him to close out the traffic stop. Dax watched as the Honda pulled sedately away from the side of the road and continued on until it was out of sight. Feeling as if he'd somehow lost something important, and that he should've at least gotten out and met the woman—even if that would've been highly unusual—Dax frowned. It was too late now.

"What was that about?"

"Damn. Did I say she was cute before? Because she was even more adorable the second time. I told her she was off the hook and gave her the warning and she broke into another long soliloquy about how relieved she was and how I'd protected her clean record."

"So she was flirting with you?" Dax asked sharply.

TJ looked over at his friend. "That's not how it was."

"Then how was it?"

"Look, I don't pick up women I pull over, Dax, Jesus. Besides, she's not my type. She just started babbling again about how thankful she was. Oh, she also mentioned she'd just helped with the same charity event we were at the other week. She told me she always knew cops weren't the hardasses we tried to portray and she thanked me for all the money her group raised that night."

"Holy shit, that's it!" Dax exclaimed.

"What's it?" TJ asked, his face scrunched up in confusion.

"That's where I recognized her from. I saw her that night, at the charity thing. Remember when the waiter dropped the tray?"

"Vaguely."

"She was the one who came over to help."

"And? I don't get your point, Dax."

Dax remembered how the woman had babbled on and on with him before abruptly turning away to take care of business. He smiled. "Can I have her number?"

TJ looked at his friend in disbelief. "What?"

"Her number. I know it's in the computer. Give it to me."

"You can't call her out of the blue and ask her out, Dax."

"Why not?"

"She's gonna think you're a stalker."

"No, she won't."

"Besides, it's against the law for me to give it to you, and you know it."

Dax tried to smile at his friend charmingly. "Come on, man. Please? I never got her name at the thing the other week, but I think it's fate that you pulled her over tonight. I had no way of finding her before, but now I do."

"You have it bad."

Dax just kept smiling.

"Oh all right, but if I get in trouble, I'm siccing the review board on your ass."

"Cool."

"Jesus, I feel like a dating service. She really got to you, huh?"

"Yeah. There's just something about her. I'm not sending out wedding invitations. Hell, I'm not even saying I want to date her. But I'm interested enough to call her up and see if anything comes out of it."

TJ started the car and, after looking both ways to make sure no cars were coming, did a U-turn in the road and headed back the way they were going before pulling Mackenzie over.

"Ready for food?" TJ was obviously trying to change the subject.

"Oh, hell yeah. Think you can avoid pulling anyone else over in the next thirty minutes so we can actually get something to eat?"

"Funny guy."

Dax smiled. He loved being part of the brotherhood of law enforcement. It didn't matter that he was a Texas Ranger and TJ was a Highway Patrol officer. Law enforcement was law enforcement and they all worked together on cases. Neither he nor TJ had ever been married, and they liked it that way. Dax knew it was tough to be married to a cop and he hadn't been able to find a woman who could handle it yet. At forty-six years old, he figured he never would. He mentally shrugged. He didn't care. He had his career and his friends. Life was good.

But for the first time in a really long time, he was excited about the prospect of a date. He hadn't lied to TJ. There was something about Ms. Mackenzie Morgan that got to him. He hoped he could find out what it was and either get it out of his system, or see where it could lead.

"Pedal to the metal then. Let's go eat."

Chapter Three

———◆———

MACKENZIE SIGHED HEAVILY as she made her way up to her apartment. Getting pulled over was the icing on the cake to a very long, craptastic day. She couldn't believe she'd been so lost in her head she'd been going twenty miles over the speed limit. Thank God the officer decided to give her a warning instead of a ticket.

After opening the door, Mackenzie slipped her keys back into her purse and dumped it on the small table in the entryway. She shut and locked the door, then hung her coat on the hook on the wall in the small hallway.

She then kicked off her shoes and padded down the hall to her living room. Mackenzie collapsed on her sofa, put her head back, and closed her eyes. Damn, she was glad to be home.

The day had started out all right. Mackenzie had arrived at work with plenty of time to spare and settled into her chair at her desk. She'd had a lot of paperwork to reconcile after the charity event, even weeks later, and had been well into it when her horrible boss had called her into her office.

Nancy Wood was one of a kind. She was around four inches taller than Mackenzie, but was about thirty pounds lighter. She was scary skinny. Not only that, but her hair was long and black, like down-to-her-butt long. It swished around her as she walked because she refused to wear it up or braid it. With her hair, her pointed nose, and long face, Nancy was an odd looking woman. She never smiled and loved ordering everyone in the office around. Everyone made fun of her behind her back and called her the "wicked witch of the SAC."

The woman thought she was much more important than she really was. Nancy had spent two hours going over the spreadsheets of the donations they'd received and the money that had been spent. It drove Mack crazy because ultimately the finances were her responsibility. She hated having her boss double-check her work as if she was a fifth grader.

Not long after she'd finally gotten out of the meeting with her boss, the phone rang. It was her mom wanting to invite her over for an impromptu family dinner.

Mackenzie loved her mom and her brothers, but they simply didn't understand her. First they'd started on her choice to live in an apartment instead of buying a house. She knew at her age she should have probably bit the bullet and invested in a property by now, but she liked living in an apartment. She liked being able to call the manager when something went wrong and not have to deal with it herself. She wasn't very handy, so it was nice that she could put the responsibility for fixing whatever was wrong on someone else. Mackenzie was also especially grateful she didn't have to worry about any kind of yard work.

Nevertheless, every time she got together with her family—every single time—they harped on her for being thirty-seven and unmarried. It wasn't that Mackenzie didn't want to be married; she just hadn't found someone who she wanted to spend the rest of her life with.

She sighed. Mackenzie knew she was picky. It wasn't a secret. Every time she thought she'd found the perfect guy, he'd do something or say something to make her reconsider. Then she'd grab hold of that one little thing and eventually it would grow bigger and bigger and she'd become more and more discontent and the relationship would end. Mackenzie's best friend, Laine, told her all the time she was like Seinfeld, finding stupid reasons to dump men. Most of the time her relationships would end with the man throwing up his hands in disgust and walking out the door.

Mackenzie wasn't an idiot; she knew it was her fault for nitpicking the men she dated to death and making them not want to stay, but she had no idea how to stop. And if a little voice inside her wanted the man to stay despite her being a bitch, she'd never admit it.

She had some bad habits, she knew it, but she didn't think they were horrible enough for a guy to break up with her over them. One boyfriend told her he thought her habit of rambling on and on was cute, but toward the end of their relationship, he'd admitted it was embarrassing for him when she said whatever she was thinking around others with no filter, and that if she ever wanted to keep a man, she'd better rein that in. Jerk.

She recalled the conversation she'd had tonight with her brothers. They'd been unusually blunt with her, and their words had struck home all the more because Mackenzie knew they were right on most counts.

"Mack, what do you expect a guy to do when you're going at him every day for stupid shit? Take it? No way."

"But Mark, if he loved me, he'd see how upset I am and change."

"I love you, sis, but no. First of all, I've heard you complain about how the men you date want you to change some of the things you do, so I don't see how you can stand there and say that if someone loved you, they wouldn't ask *you* to change, but you can turn around and bitch that *he's* not doing things the way you think he should. You can't expect a guy to alter the way he does the dishes, for Christ's sake, just because you want him to put the plates in the dishwasher one way and he does it another. It's ridiculous. You're *looking* for ways to push them away and you harp on them over and over until they decide you're just not worth it."

Mackenzie lowered her head. She knew Mark was right. Then

Matthew had started in on her.

"Seriously, I've seen the way you are with them. Remember that one Thanksgiving when we all had to sit around and listen to you bicker with…whatever his name was? It was crazy. You wouldn't let anything go. Hell, the man couldn't even sit and watch football without you telling him he was doing it wrong."

Mackenzie's mom joined in as well. "All we're saying, sweetie, is lighten up. You'll never find a guy who's perfect. You just have to learn to give a little more when you're in a relationship."

Mackenzie sighed and grabbed the pillow next to her on the couch, held it to her stomach, and buried her face in it. She was such a headcase. She didn't know why she was this way…strike that, she did, but she hated to admit it to herself, or anyone else. Her first real adult boyfriend had done the exact same thing to *her*, nitpicked everything she'd done, and apparently, she'd committed everything he'd done to memory and decided it was how relationships were supposed to work. It was a self-fulfilling prophesy apparently, because every man she'd dated since that first man, she'd done the same thing to. Nitpicked stupid little things he did, until he got fed up and left.

Mackenzie knew it was stupid, knew *she* was being stupid. Her brother was right, it didn't really matter if a man left his shoes in the closet, or on the bathroom floor. But now that she was used to doing things the way *she* thought they should be done, it was hard to stop. Hell, her mom had told her often enough that she'd been an extremely stubborn child, now she was a stubborn adult.

But she was a romantic. Always had been. As a kid, she'd made her mom buy her every Disney movie and she'd watched them over and over. *Cinderella, Snow White*…it didn't matter. As long as the fairy princess ended up with the prince, Mackenzie had loved it. It'd probably skewed her thinking.

Mackenzie turned her mind from her family—as well-meaning as they were, they still depressed her—and back to the incident on her way home.

She'd been horrified when she'd been pulled over. Mackenzie was a good girl, never had even a parking ticket before, so being pulled over was not a fun experience. She'd been speeding because she wanted nothing more than to get home and into some comfy clothes and relax.

The police officer had actually been very nice, all things considered. He'd taken her license and registration and she'd felt humiliated waiting for him to come back and give her a ticket. Of course she'd babbled on and on to him. She even saw him laughing with the man who'd been in the car with him.

Mackenzie had glanced into her rear-view mirror and watched as the officer and whoever the man was sitting next to him laughed with each other. She'd felt the blush rise on her face, hoping they weren't laughing at her. But the other man was definitely good-looking. Mackenzie had always had a thing about men in uniform. There was just something about seeing a crisp shirt, a pressed pair of pants, a badge, and all the accoutrements that came with whatever the man's profession was, that pushed her buttons.

She had no idea how tall the man in the passenger seat was, but he had dark hair and a nice smile. Mackenzie shook her head. Sad that that was all it took to get her interested.

Suddenly Mack sat up straight on the sofa and said out loud to her empty apartment, "Holy shit!"

The man in the car had been the Ranger she'd lusted after at the charity event!

At least she thought it was the same man. She couldn't be sure, but she remembered how she'd talked about the event the other night with the officer outside her car and he'd mentioned he'd been there. If he was there, the man sitting next to him in his car most likely was too. It probably really *was* the man she'd briefly spoken to at the charity event.

She buried her face in her hands. How freaking humiliating. Great. Just great. This was all she needed on top of everything else that had happened today. Mackenzie had spilled her entire lunch in her lap when she'd misjudged the table and put her plate down too close to the edge. She'd always been a klutz and was constantly spilling and breaking things, as well as tripping over her own feet.

All in all, it'd been a shitty day and she hadn't been able to stop the tears from falling while she'd waited for the officer to come back with the ticket she knew she deserved. He'd been very nice to her. Mackenzie didn't have any excuses for speeding; she'd just wanted to get home and wasn't watching how fast she was driving.

Getting a warning instead of a ticket had been one of the only good things about the day. Mackenzie took a deep breath. Thank goodness today was finally over. She got up off her couch and headed into her bedroom, not bothering to check the mail she'd picked up.

She stripped off her shirt, threw it into the laundry hamper and took off her bra, just dropping it on the floor where she stood. Her pants came next, along with her panties. Mackenzie walked naked into her bathroom, where she got ready for bed. It was early, but she didn't care.

Mackenzie had always preferred to sleep naked. She had expensive fifteen hundred thread count sheets that felt smooth and silky next to her body. Mackenzie once had a boyfriend who chided her for her penchant to sleep without anything on, telling her she didn't have the type of body that looked good naked and she'd be sexier if she covered it up with a nightie. She'd dumped his ass the next day. Fuck him.

Mackenzie knew she wasn't beautiful, and that was okay. She wasn't a troll, she had great legs, but she was too short to ever be considered classically pretty. She liked to eat, she liked her sweets and loved pasta and hated to work out as well. She'd never be stick thin, and that was perfectly all right with her. Rather than wishing to be thin, Mackenzie always wished to be taller instead. It was tiring always looking at people's chests or necks instead of being able to look them in the eye. Not to mention the way men would try to look down any shirt she wore. Jerks. Mackenzie had also hated wearing heels, she was way too clumsy to pull off a sophisticated look in them, so she was stuck at her five feet four.

She climbed into her queen-size bed and under her comforter and fleece blanket and snuggled in for the night. Mackenzie didn't bother picking up her e-reader to finish the romance she'd been reading. She wasn't in the mood to read about how some lucky woman got her happy ever after with a hunk of a man…even if it was only fiction.

She closed her eyes, trying not to relive the day, and surprisingly fell asleep quickly. She dreamed of a dark-haired policeman backing her against a police car and leaning down to kiss her.

Chapter Four

A FTER WHAT SEEMED like the longest week in the history of her life, Mackenzie sat on her couch with a cup of double-dark hot chocolate, watching one of her favorite movies of all time, *Ever After*. The acting wasn't the best, and the accents were horrendous, but since it was a version of *Cinderella*, Mackenzie loved it.

Laine was supposed to have come over to watch movies with her, but she had a date. Mackenzie and Laine had made a deal a long time ago that if they had plans and one of them got asked out, they'd go on the date, with no hard feelings. Of course, they'd made the pact when they were in middle school, and certainly didn't have to honor it all these years later, but since they were both still hoping their prince was out there, the pact was still in force today.

Mackenzie's cell phone rang, startling her, and when she jerked, of course the drink she'd been holding spilled all over herself. Cursing and wiping the hot drink off her pants, Mackenzie reached over and swiped the small screen to answer the phone without looking at the number, figuring it was Laine calling to dish about her date.

"Hello?"

"Hello. Is this Mackenzie Morgan?"

"Yeah, who is this?"

"My name is Daxton Chambers. I'm a Texas Ranger and was calling to follow up with you after your traffic infraction earlier this week."

Mackenzie's blood ran cold. *Oh my God. Was she in trouble? Was she supposed to get a ticket after all? Was she not supposed to drive away when she did? She didn't know the protocol when you'd been given a warning...Wait, she was given a warning, wasn't she? Fuck.*

She did what she usually did when she was nervous, she talked—fast. "I'm so sorry. Was I not supposed to leave when I did? I thought it was a warning. I didn't mean to break any laws. Shit. Do I have to turn myself in somewhere or something? I really didn't mean to be speeding, I'd had a horrible day, and that was just the icing on the cake. Seriously, Officer, I swear I'm not like that usually."

"Ma'am—"

Mackenzie kept talking. "I didn't think there was a fine with a warning, but I admit I didn't really look at the paper that closely. I was too relieved I didn't get an actual ticket and I just stuffed it into my bag and forgot about it. I'd look at it now, but it was in my purse and my stupid nail polish busted open inside my purse and it got all over it and I had to throw it away. Hell, I had to throw away the whole purse because the lining was completely ruined, but I swear—"

"Ma'am." The Ranger's voice was stronger now.

"Seriously, it was my own fault. I don't know why I had the stupid nail polish in there in the first place. I'm extremely clumsy and I thought I'd bring it with me and do my nails at lunch, which is stupid, because my nails just break anyway, the polish wouldn't really do any good, but I thought that maybe I'd make the effort because my mom and brothers have been on me to try harder with my appearance—"

"Mackenzie, shush for a second."

Mackenzie closed her eyes, mortified. Jesus. She'd been going on and on, but she was so nervous. This guy must think she was a complete idiot. "Sorry," she whispered, waiting to hear what he wanted.

Mackenzie waited, but the line was silent. She felt sick. "Hello?"

"I just wanted to make sure you were really going to be quiet and let me talk." His voice was low, rumbly, and full of humor.

"Um…"

He continued, and Mackenzie could tell he was completely amused with her. At least he was amused and not pissed.

"You're not in trouble, and it *was* just a warning. I was there that night when Officer Rockwell pulled you over. I don't know if you remember me, but I met you briefly at the charity event a couple of weeks ago. I just wanted to check in with you and make sure you were all right after getting pulled over."

Mackenzie was stunned into silence, and that was highly unusual for her. Was this really the guy she'd met and lusted over? It couldn't be. There was no way he wanted to check to make sure she was all right. Something else had to be going on. "You wanted to check to make sure I was all right?" She couldn't help the question.

"Yeah."

"Uh, why?"

"Because I was worried about you."

"You were worried about me."

The man chuckled on the other end of the line. "You gonna repeat everything I say, Mackenzie? Yeah, I was worried about you, but more than that, I wanted to call because I remembered you from the charity event."

Mackenzie didn't really know what to say. This was just so odd. "You said you were a Texas Ranger? You're not a Highway Patrol officer, right? Why were you there, too?"

"Officer Rockwell and I were on our way to dinner when you zipped by. We made the stop, then continued on to the restaurant."

"Oh my God," Mackenzie whispered, disconcerted. "He was off duty and had to stop me? And, you were on the way to dinner?"

Dax was enjoying the hell out of his conversation with Mackenzie. She was incredibly entertaining and just as interesting as she was that night he'd met her. Besides that, he'd never had a conversation like this with a woman before. She zipped from one topic to another without seeming to breathe. "Yeah, I was there."

"Okay, that's it. I'm never driving again. I'm going to throw my license away and become a hermit who never leaves my house."

Dax chuckled. "I don't think I'd go that far. But you want to answer my original question now? Everything okay?"

Mackenzie huffed out a breath and leaned back against the couch, one hand holding the phone to her ear and the other still holding the cup of cocoa in her hand. "I'm fine."

"You're fine." His words weren't stated as a question, but Mackenzie could tell they were a question nevertheless.

"What was your name again?"

"Daxton Chambers."

"Well, Daxton Chambers, I don't know if you are really who you say you are, but I'm going to give you the benefit of the doubt here. If you must know, I'd had a really crappy day when I was pulled over. I know, everyone has crappy days, but that was a *really* crappy day. To top off a crappy day at work, where I spilled my lunch and didn't have any chance to get anything to eat to replace it, and where I got yelled at by my horrible boss for something stupid, I had just spent two hours at my mom's house where I was told I was basically a dried-up old maid and it was all my fault because I'm too picky and I chase every guy away. So yeah, when I got pulled over, I can't say I was in a happy place. But the day ended with a warning instead of a ticket, so my felon-free life is still squeaky clean and I've moved on."

Mackenzie forced herself to stop talking. She was such a dork.

"In case you're wondering, I'm not easily chased away."

"Shit!" At his surprising words, Mackenzie had spilled her mug of hot chocolate—again—and it was now seeping into the cushions of her couch as well as dripping off onto the floor. "Shit. Shit. Shit! Hang on. Fuck." Mackenzie threw the phone down and frantically looked around for something to mop up the drink. Seeing nothing, she sighed and whipped off the T-shirt she was wearing. It was already stained with who-the-hell-knew-what, so she might as well use it as a towel. She held it to the couch, trying to clean up the bulk of the mess. She kneeled on the floor and tried to mop up the liquid on the couch as well as what was dripping over the side.

Mackenzie reached over with her free hand and brought her phone back up to her ear. "Hello? Are you still there?"

"What happened? Are you hurt?" Dax's voice was hard and urgent.

"Sorry! No, I'm fine. I spilled my drink. That's all. I told you I was clumsy."

Dax relaxed back against the counter where he'd been standing. For a second, he was afraid Mackenzie had been hurt and he'd have to call 911 for her. He grinned. "I gotta say, this has to be one of the most fascinating phone calls I've ever had with a woman."

"Oh Lord." Mackenzie rested her head on the cushion in front of her. The couch muffled her voice when she mumbled, "I'm seriously never leaving the house again."

"I hope that's not true, since I'm coming over tomorrow night to pick you up and take you to dinner."

Dax waited for a response, but didn't get one. He knew Mackenzie hadn't hung up because he could still hear her breathing on the other end of the phone. He hadn't been this interested in a woman since…well, in a really long time. Mackenzie was cute as hell and he knew she wasn't even trying to be. That was what drew him in the most.

"Mackenzie? You still there?"

"Yeah, but I think I'm having hallucinations. Maybe the cocoa was bad or something."

"You're not hallucinating and I don't think hot chocolate *goes* bad. I'm coming over tomorrow night. I'll be there around six to take you out to dinner. It'll be casual, so don't wear anything fancy."

"I don't think I own anything fancy. I'd just ruin it anyway; I'd probably drop my fork in my lap or something and mess it up."

Dax noticed Mackenzie hadn't tried to get out of the date. He smiled again. "Good. You gonna be there tomorrow at six when I get there?"

"I don't think this is how it works."

"How what works?"

"I don't think you can just tell me you're coming to get me and you're taking me out to eat."

"Why not?"

"Why not what?"

"Why isn't it how it works?

"I don't know you."

"I'm trying to change that."

Mackenzie tried to get the conversation back on track. "How do you know where I live?"

"Mack, I'm a Ranger. I was in the car when TJ stopped you and ran your information. I know where you live."

"Are you really a Texas Ranger?"

"Yeah."

"Are you gonna kidnap and kill me like that psycho has been doing to women around here?"

"No."

"This is weird."

"It's not weird," Dax put every ounce of sincerity in his voice that he could. "I met you a few weeks ago and thought you were cute. Hell, I haven't met anyone like you in a long, long time. I watched you walk away from me with regret. I didn't know your name. I didn't know anything about you, but I liked what I saw and what I heard, anyway. Then it was as if fate took hold, because there you were…again. What are the odds you'd be on the road you were, speeding, and I'd be on that same road? I'd like to take you out to

33

dinner and get to know you more. Maybe we won't get along. Maybe we'll go out once and decide, mutually, that we should be friends, or not at all. Give me a chance, Mackenzie. I'll be there tomorrow night at six. Will you be there?"

"I'll be here."

Every muscle in Dax's body relaxed. He hadn't realized how tightly he was holding himself until after Mackenzie had accepted his date. He hadn't planned on asking her out, but there was no way he could sit there and listen to how incredibly adorable she was, rambling on about nail polish and how clumsy she was and *not* ask her out. TJ was going to give him a rash of shit, but Dax didn't care. For the first time in a long time, he was looking forward to a date.

Most of the time women hit on *him*, simply because of the uniform he wore. It was nice, for once, to be the pursuer instead of the pursued. Mack wasn't going to know what hit her.

"Good." Dax lowered his voice. "I'm looking forward to it."

"But, seriously, don't get your hopes up, Daxton. I don't do one-night stands."

"I don't recall asking you to sleep with me."

Mackenzie buried her head even farther into the couch cushion, embarrassed. "Shit. See? I'm totally awkward and shouldn't really be out with actual people in public. I should be locked away so people can point and laugh at what an honest-to-God dork looks like. What I meant was that I'm not good at relationships. Seriously. You know how old I am, you know my height and weight…I told you what my own family thinks…I'm just…me."

"And I like 'just' you, Mackenzie. At least what I've seen and heard so far. We'll go out and see what happens. I promise I won't propose tomorrow if you won't jump my bones in the parking lot. Deal?"

Mackenzie laughed out loud. "I think I can agree to that."

"Great. Then I'll see you tomorrow at six."

"Okay, Daxton. See you then."

"Bye."

"Bye."

Mackenzie clicked off her phone and sat up on her haunches in front of her couch for a moment before leaning over and stuffing her face into one of the cushions and screaming at the top of her lungs.

She sat up with a smile on her face. A date. A real live date. Wow. She couldn't wait to talk to Laine.

Chapter Five

————— ◆ —————

THE NEXT AFTERNOON, Dax met TJ for lunch. They were sitting in a local diner that had amazingly good food for a place that looked like a broken-down building.

"You did it? Shit, Dax. I thought you were just messing with me," TJ said incredulously.

"Well, I wasn't. And yes, I did call her. I checked, she said she was fine, then I asked her out."

TJ shook his head and finally smiled at his friend, slyly, testing him. "And if I wanted in there?"

Dax didn't even flinch. "Too late my friend. You snooze, you lose. You should've said something when I asked you for her number. You knew I was gonna call her."

TJ threw his head back and laughed, then shook his head at Dax. "You're crazy. Asking out a woman you don't even know."

Dax got serious. "I'd changed my mind since we talked that night. I knew it was crazy to ask her out. Seriously. I was just gonna call her up and make sure she was okay, but then she opened her mouth. She was rambling on and on about nail polish and being so…real…that I couldn't resist. You know how it is, most women try to act serious and proper around us when they think they're in trouble, then flirt and bat their eyes when they think that will work in their favor. Mackenzie was just so fucking *cute*."

"Yeah, I remember that from when I pulled her over. But you can't ask a woman out because she says cute shit, Dax."

"I'm not explaining it right, but seriously, TJ, admit it. There was something about her that even you noticed."

TJ nodded. "Okay, I'll give you that. But I definitely want a report tomorrow."

"You know I don't do that shit."

"I didn't mean a blow-by-blow, but give me somethin'!"

Dax finally grinned at his friend. "All right, I'll let you know how it goes."

TJ shook his head and slapped his friend on the back as they walked out of the diner after finishing lunch. "I hope it works out for you, Dax. Lord knows with the shit you deal with on a daily basis, you deserve it."

"Thanks, man, you'll find a woman for you too. I know it."

TJ shrugged his shoulders. "If it happens, it happens. I'm not worried."

Dax climbed into his government-issued vehicle and pulled out of the crowded parking lot. He had one hell of a meeting to get through this afternoon before he could even think more about his date tonight. The Lone Star Reaper, as the press had dubbed him, had struck again.

A sixth body had been found recently and the Rangers still had no reliable leads. They'd called in the FBI, and the lead agent, who happened to be Cruz Livingston, had called a meeting to discuss the particulars of the case. Dax pulled into the parking lot of the San Antonio Police Department, where the meeting was going to take place. Dax was glad Cruz was on the case. It'd be nice to have an officer he knew, trusted, and respected helping him try to figure out what was going on and hopefully they'd close down the case before the fucker killed another innocent woman.

Dax strode into the building and told the receptionist he was there for a meeting with Lieutenant Quint Axton and Agent Livingston. Dax was shown into a room where Cruz and Quint were already waiting.

"Dax." Quint nodded at him as he entered. "Thanks for coming down. This shit has gotten way out of control."

Dax nodded in agreement. "Cruz and I have had a few conversations already, and we're glad to bring you into the fold. What do you have on the newest case?"

Quint settled back into his seat and shuffled the file filled with pictures and reports in front of him. Finally he found the pictures he was looking for and, with a flick of his wrist, sent them across the table to Dax.

"Same as the others. A call was received with the details on where to find her. Untraceable and short. Voice was unrecognizable because he used one of those voice-altering devices. She was found in a wooden box, buried about five feet underground at the edge of another rural graveyard. Guy's smart, I'll give him that. No one would question a coffin being buried in a cemetery, for Christ's sake."

Dax looked down at the pictures he was holding. The first was of the disturbed ground at a cemetery. The next was after the ground had been dug up with a backhoe, the coffin visible. The third was of the coffin sitting on the ground next to the hole, its lid pried open. The woman inside was in the beginning stages of decomposition. She hadn't been in there for too long. Dax could see her long blonde hair and the clothes she was wearing were still in good shape. Just as with the other victims, it didn't look—at first glance, at least—as if she'd been raped before being put inside the box. She was completely dressed, her clothes were on straight, and she had no visible marks on her body. She was covered in dirt and the fingernails on her hands had bled profusely. She'd obviously tried with every breath left in her to claw her way out of the crude wooden box she'd been entombed inside.

Dax shuffled to the next photos. They'd been taken off-scene: the inside lid of the box had claw marks on it, showing how desperately the woman had fought for her life, the inside of the coffin, the picture taken after the woman's body had been removed, showing body-fluid stains and an empty water bottle. Dax swore and looked up. He hadn't noticed it in pictures of the killer's other crime scenes.

"He put a bottle of water in with this one?"

The FBI agent nodded grimly.

Dax ground his teeth together. The Reaper was getting more sadistic as time went by. He wanted to provide some "comfort" to his victims, even though he knew they'd never get out alive. It was a complete mind-fuck on the part of the Lone Star Reaper. Dax quickly finished looking through the rest of the pictures.

The hole in the ground, tire tracks in the soft grass, the victim lying on the coroner's table. Dax paused. She'd been pretty. She was slender and had a small tattoo over her left breast, some sort of oriental writing. There was a close-up picture of her hands; her nails had been ripped off in her struggles. Dax put the pictures aside and picked up the medical examiner's report.

Dax was impressed with Calder Stonewall's work. He was thorough and impartial. He'd seen some horrible things, but his reports were easily understood, factual, and to the point.

Calder's report said the woman had been killed by asphyxiation; basically she'd run out of air. Her pupils were fixed and dilated. Dax couldn't think of a more horrifying way to die than to be buried alive.

He turned to his friends. "Anything new this time…besides the water?"

"Nothing with the evidence, or the way he disposed of the body, but he *did* send a note this time." Agent Livingston held up a piece of paper. "He sent it directly to the SAPD. Quint opened it and immediately bagged it. The original is being analyzed as we speak for fingerprints and whatever else they can get off of it."

Dax reached for the note, but Cruz held it out of his reach. "He's making it personal, Dax. You're not going to like it."

"I don't like anything this asshole does, Cruz. Let me see it."

Cruz handed over the piece of paper as he waited for Dax to read it.

By now youve found my latest prezent. I hope you like it. Im impressed you brought in both the FBI and the Rangers. I must be doing something right. Im watching you. Agent Livingston, Ranger Chambers and Officer Axton. Your in my sights. You better hold tight to your loved ones.

"You have *got* to be shitting me." The words came out of Dax's mouth without thought. "This fucker is threatening us? How in the hell did he get our names?"

"Hell, Dax, you know the papers are all over this shit. They don't give a damn about protecting our identities." Quint's statement was matter of fact.

"Dammit!" Dax didn't have any words. He knew his job was intense, but he never wanted to bring danger to any of his friends in the process. All he'd ever wanted to do was get into the elite Texas Rangers. There were only about a hundred and fifty Rangers in the entire state. There were a ton of specific qualifications an officer had to have to even be able to *apply* for one of the coveted positions. Dax had worked his butt off and loved what he did, but this…this was something he had no experience with.

"Okay, so this guy knows us. Fine. What's our next step?"

"We find out if there are prints or anything else we can go off of on the note. The crime scene guys are examining the coffin. We're interviewing anyone who might have seen anything in the cemetery over the last week and we're telling the public to be alert and careful. *We* also need to be careful. I know none of us are dating anyone, but we need to be sure to alert our families to be extra vigilant until this guy is caught."

"Fuck." Dax knew it wasn't enough. They all knew it was only a matter of time before he kidnapped some other unsuspecting woman and did it again.

Dax thought about Mackenzie. For a split second he considered calling off their date. If the killer was serious about targeting their loved ones, he could easily misinterpret a dinner date and target Mackenzie. Dax dismissed the thought almost as soon as he had it. It was just a date. And he wasn't willing to give up getting to know Mackenzie for a threat that was most likely bogus anyway.

"I'm going on TV tonight to update the public on what we know. We're hoping someone saw or knows something and will call us."

"We're not going to catch this guy with a few random tips, Quint, and you know it," Dax said quietly, frustration lacing every word.

"I know, but we literally have nothing else."

Cruz spoke up. "The FBI has a profiler going over the details and will share a profile tonight. It should hopefully generate some new leads. *Someone* knows this guy."

Dax just nodded his head, lips pursed together tightly. This was the part of his job he hated. He hated waiting for a serial killer to strike once more. Most of the time the only way they could get new evidence was for him to kill again, and that sucked.

"That's all we got for now. I just wanted to bring you up to speed," Cruz told Dax softly.

"What was her name?"

Knowing whose name Dax was asking for, Cruz said evenly. "Sally Mason. Married with two kids. Twenty-six years old."

Dax shook his head sadly. Such a fucking waste.

"Go home, Dax. We'll be in touch if we hear anything else. You're off for a few days, right?"

Dax nodded. "Yeah. I've worked a ton of overtime lately, so the

Major ordered me not to show my face in the office again until next Tuesday."

"Lucky dog." Quint's words were heartfelt.

"But that doesn't mean you don't call me the second you hear anything new on this asshole," Dax warned.

"Ten-four. No worries. I've got you on speed dial."

Dax nodded at Quint and Cruz. "We have to catch this motherfucker."

"We will."

Dax stood, gave each man a chin lift, and walked out the door. He had three hours to get into a better frame of mind before he picked up Mackenzie for their date.

MACKENZIE PACED HER little living room nervously. She'd decided that morning she must've been under the influence of some drug last night when she'd agreed to this date. Hell, she didn't really even *know* this guy, had only seen him once...why in the hell had she agreed to go out to dinner with him? It was absolutely crazy.

Laine had been ecstatic for her, and threatened bodily harm if she even *thought* about calling it off, but Mackenzie was still nervous as hell about it.

She'd picked up the phone to call Daxton to tell him she'd changed her mind and realized she didn't even have his number. He'd called her yesterday from a blocked number. Mackenzie had thought about bailing and going somewhere outside of her apartment until way after six so she wasn't home when Daxton got there, but she couldn't. That would be really rude, and she hated to be rude. Besides which, she'd never hear the end of it from Laine if she did something so cowardly.

So here she was, going on a date with a man she didn't know, had only lusted after, and seen briefly through tears in the rear-view mirror of her car and at the charity benefit event and who knew way more about her than she knew about him. Crazy.

Mackenzie rubbed her hands on her thighs, trying to calm herself down. She could do this. It was just a date. That's all. Dinner. If she could keep from dropping or spilling anything on herself, or Daxton, she'd be fine. He'd see she wasn't anything special and bring her home and she'd never see him again. No problem.

Mackenzie was wearing a faded pair of jeans with a pair of black flip-flops with a small heel. She'd always loved them, even if her feet usually hurt by the end of the day. She wasn't used to wearing heels at all, but she figured she'd need every inch of the two inches in height they gave her.

Her shirt was a basic black short-sleeved pullover with a scoop neck. Nothing fancy, and she'd purposely chosen black so if she did drool on herself, which was likely with her track record, it wouldn't show as easily. The shirt did show off her breasts though. Her chest was one of her best assets, and she hadn't met a man yet who could resist checking it out.

Mackenzie had pulled her hair back in a twist and secured it to the back of her head with a barrette. She knew by the end of the night it'd probably mostly be falling out, but for now she thought it looked okay.

She continued to pace until her doorbell rang. Mackenzie looked at her watch. Dang, he was right on time. He was one of *those* people. Mackenzie couldn't manage to be on time if her life depended on it...although today was apparently an exception. She'd been ready for half an hour, a record for her.

Mackenzie walked over to the door and looked through the peephole. Damn. The man standing there was so good-looking, she felt a zing shoot through her body, ending between her legs. She'd gotten the same reaction the night of the charity event. He was looking directly at the peephole, as if he knew she was on the other side looking at him. Mackenzie took a deep breath and opened the door until the chain stopped it from opening any farther.

"Daxton?"

"Yup. That's me."

Mackenzie shoved her hand through the small opening of the door and said, "ID please."

Dax chuckled, not offended in the least. "Good girl." He reached behind him, took his wallet out from his pocket, pulled out his driver's license and put it into Mackenzie's outstretched hand. "There you go."

Mackenzie looked down at the plastic card in her hand. Daxton Chambers. Forty-six years old. Six feet one and two hundred thirty pounds. She gulped. Damn, almost a hundred pounds heavier than she was. She went to hand it back and dropped it.

"Shit, sorry."

Dax just laughed quietly and kneeled down to pick up the license. "No problem."

Mackenzie held out her hand again. "Ranger ID now, please."

Dax smiled even more broadly. "Damn, woman."

Mackenzie faltered a bit, but bravely said, "IDs are easy to fake nowadays, I just want to make sure."

"Oh, I wasn't complaining. No fucking way. I'm pleased as hell you don't trust me. I'd be more worried if you did. Good thinking. Here you go." Dax held out his Texas Ranger badge that he'd pulled from his other pocket. "I don't go anywhere without it, just in case." She took it from his hand and Dax could see her hands shaking.

"If it's okay...I'll just—" Mackenzie gestured back inside her apartment.

"Take your time, Mackenzie. I'll be right here."

Mackenzie shut and locked her apartment door and quickly walked over to her phone. She snapped a picture of Daxton's Ranger badge and texted it to Matthew, Mark, and Laine. Laine knew she was going out with Daxton, but she wanted to inform her brothers as well. She told them she was going to dinner with Daxton, who was a Texas Ranger, and she'd be back later. She trusted Daxton was who he said he was, but she wanted her brothers to know who it was she was going out with and what time she expected to be home. Even though she was thirty-seven years old, she wanted to be safe. She'd call Laine after the date. It was their ritual whenever one of them went out.

Mackenzie thought hard about calling the local Rangers' office and checking on Daxton that way as well, but then decided she was being an idiot. She'd seen him at the charity event with a table full of other officers. Hell, he'd been with the Highway Patrolman when she'd been pulled over. If Daxton was lying, he was an expert. Mackenzie went back to the door, took off the chain and opened it all the way.

"Hi, Daxton. It's great to meet you." Her smile was bright and welcoming, as if this was the first time she'd opened the door that night and she hadn't demanded he show his IDs to her and treated him like a criminal.

Dax chuckled. Damn, she was charming. She pulled him out of his bad mood easily. "Hey."

"Here's your ID back. Sorry about that."

"Don't be sorry. You have no idea how hot that was."

"Uh, what?"

"Yeah, hot. I see all sorts of shit in my line of work. I love knowing you're cautious. I just wish more people were like you."

"Oh, well, okay." Mackenzie handed Daxton his Ranger ID.

"What'd you do with it when you were in there?"

"Uh…" Mackenzie was unsure if she should tell him. "I don't know…um…I've never dated a cop before."

Dax stood there watching Mackenzie with an amused glint in his eye. "Okay."

"And I've never been in trouble before. I mean, really in trouble. I got detention in high school once, but it wasn't my fault. Stupid Darci Birchfield decided to pick on one of the guys on the chess team and I told her if she didn't lay off him she'd answer to me, and she didn't lay off him, so she answered to me and I got a full week of detention for it. But she never messed with him again. I had to endure Bobby thanking me for the rest of our high school years, and shit, he *still* sends me a Christmas card every year, but still…it was totally worth it."

Daxton leaned against the wall next to the door, loving how fucking cute she was. He crossed his arms over his chest, holding his cowboy hat in one hand, and settled in to listen to Mackenzie babble.

"Okay, I also got in trouble at work last year for telling one of the other managers to go fuck himself, but *that* wasn't my fault either. He was totally harassing one of the lesbian women I work with. Calling her a dyke and shit like that. That's just not cool. I mean really, in today's day and age, that crap is totally uncalled for. So I told him off, explaining how a dyke was actually an artificial wall used to regulate water levels, and called a levee here in the States. Okay, I probably also used some other not-so-nice words as well, but he turned around and complained to HR about *me*, when *he* was the one being an asshat. I was sent home for a week, paid, while an investigation was conducted, but was called back after only three days because Ginger totally told HR what a dick Peter was and that I'd been defending her, and since everyone in the office backed Ginger, they ended up letting Peter go and not me."

Mackenzie paused, biting her lip. Shit. She'd done it again. She tried to finish her thought quickly. "So, I've never really been in trouble, or even been around any cops, other than the charity thing each year, so I have no idea what's legal and what's not, so I'll tell you what I did if you promise not to arrest me. I'm claiming ignorance here."

"What'd you do, Mackenzie?" Dax asked with no animosity in his voice.

"I took a picture of your ID and sent it to my brothers and best friend so if I end up dead in a ditch somewhere tonight, they'll know who it was who took me out. I totally planned on deleting the picture when I got home, though. It's not like I was gonna put it on the Internet for someone to make a fake ID from or anything."

"Good for you."

"Really?"

"Yeah. But you know, that name could be totally fake. If I *did* want to kill you and dump your body, and your brothers or friend checked me out, they might not ever find me if I used a fake name."

"Damn." Mackenzie liked this guy. "So what should I have done instead?"

"Called the Ranger Station and checked me out. Told them you're about to go on a date with a man who claims to be a Ranger and that you have a badge and you want to know if it's legit or not."

"I totally was going to do that!" Mackenzie exclaimed excitedly.

"Why didn't you?" Dax asked.

"Well, because it felt like a shitty thing to do…not trusting you when you gave me your ID without giving me crap about it."

"Do it now."

"What?"

"Do it now. Call. Check me out."

"But you're standing right here. And I believe you."

"Do it." Dax's voice was unrelenting.

"Oh all right. Jeez." Mackenzie turned to head into her apartment and pick up her phone she'd left on the counter—

When her arm was suddenly grasped tightly and pulled behind her back and she was turned and pushed up against the wall in her hallway.

Mackenzie looked up at Daxton in surprise and with a little fear.

"What the hell?"

"Don't turn your back on someone you've just met, Mackenzie. If I wasn't who I said I was, I could have you flat on your back by now. You're such a little thing, you wouldn't be able to move, and I could do anything I wanted to you. I could tie you up and haul you out to my car. Don't *ever* let anyone get you in their car. Yell, scream, fight. Your chances of survival drop by fifty percent if you let yourself get taken away."

Mackenzie could feel her heart thudding in her chest. Daxton was holding her against the wall with one of her wrists held tightly behind her back. He'd crowded in until he was pressing against her with his body, holding her immobile. One of his legs was between hers, holding her completely immobile.

The top of her head came to about his chin and she had to tilt it back to look into his eyes. Daxton was wearing a polo shirt with the top two buttons undone. She could see no chest hair, but she could smell him. He was wearing some sort of cologne, nothing too strong, but it smelled divine. Mackenzie knew it was entirely inappropriate to want to bury her nose into the hollow at his neck, but damn.

Mackenzie's breasts rubbed against Daxton's chest as she breathed in and out and she could feel her heart pounding. God, had she ever felt this way in the arms of any of her previous lovers? Hell no. And she and Daxton were both fully clothed.

She wiggled against him, testing his hold on her. It was solid. Her free hand gripped the shirt at his waist tightly, wondering what his next move would be.

"Are you listening to me?"

"Uh…yeah?"

Dax laughed and brought the hand that had been holding her shoulder to the wall to the side of Mackenzie's head. He looked down at her semi-glazed eyes and smiled. "You aren't afraid of me." It wasn't a question.

Mackenzie shook her head.

"Why not? I could do everything I just told you without breaking a sweat."

"Because a bad guy wouldn't tell me those things, he'd just do them." Mackenzie didn't know how she was conversing in a normal way with Daxton, when all she wanted was for him to do the things he'd just described, including throwing her down on the ground and having his way with her. "And you called me 'little.' I've never been described that way by anyone in my entire life."

"Fuck." Dax couldn't help himself. He leaned down and placed his lips over hers. Brushing over them once, then again, this time sweeping from one side to the other with his tongue. When she opened her mouth under his and touched her tongue to his bottom lip, he straightened up before things could go any further. Mackenzie's lips were soft and tasted slightly of apples. Daxton felt ten feet tall. He wasn't alone in whatever this weird attraction was.

"Go make that phone call, sweetheart. I'll wait right here." Daxton slowly let go of Mack's wrist he was holding behind her back.

"Okay." Mackenzie made no move to leave the hall.

Dax took a step back, pulling Mack with him. He then turned her physically with his hands on her shoulders and gave her a little push at the small of her back. "Go on."

Dax waited in the hall by her front door as Mackenzie went back into her apartment. He heard her on the phone doing just as he'd told her, apparently learning he really was a Texas Ranger and his legal name really *was* Daxton Chambers. She came back, this time carrying her purse and a light jacket.

"Okay, Daxton Chambers. You came back clean. You're good."

"It's Dax. You can call me Dax."

"Is it a deal breaker?"

"Is what a deal breaker?"

"I like Daxton. I don't know; you don't look like a Dax. Not that

I've ever met anyone named Dax or Daxton before though. You'll have to tell me how you got that name. That's another reason why I figured you were who you said you were. No one would call himself Daxton if he was using a fake name to get a woman to date him. He'd call himself John Smith or something. Not some sexy-as-hell name like Daxton fucking Chambers."

Mackenzie looked up at the strangled sound Daxton was making. "Fucking hell. Sorry."

"Do you know, I've laughed more in the last twenty minutes than I have in the last week? Don't be sorry. And yes, you can call me Daxton."

"Does anyone else call you that?"

"No."

"No? Not even your mom?"

"Nope, and my parents passed away ten years ago."

"Oh shit, I'm sorry. There I go again, putting my foot in my—" Mackenzie's words were cut off when Dax put his hand over her mouth.

He leaned in close. "It's fine. I like my full name coming out of your mouth. I like it a hell of a lot."

Mackenzie waited, holding her breath. Was he going to kiss her again? The brief touch of his lips earlier made her girl parts sit up and take notice. She hadn't thought she'd be that easy, but apparently three years with only her vibrators for company made her ripe and ready for this man.

Dax took his hand off Mack's mouth and said easily, "You can call me Daxton if I can call you Mack."

"Only my family and friends call me Mack." Her voice was low.

"Since I want to be your friend…now I do too…if that's okay."

"Yeah, it's okay."

"Great. Now shall we go?"

"Where are we going?"

"It's a surprise."

"Really?"

"Yeah, Mack. Really. That a problem?"

"No, not at all. But no one has ever taken me on a date before and not told me where we were going."

"I'm glad I'm your first." Dax laughed as Mackenzie blushed. "Damn, you're cute. Come on, I'm starved. Let's go."

Mackenzie locked her apartment door behind them and followed beside Daxton as he led the way to his car. It was nothing special; in fact, it blended in with all the other cars in the lot quite easily. It was a black four-door Ford Taurus. It was almost a shame. A sleek sports car seemed more his speed. Daxton held the passenger-side door as Mackenzie got in and then shut it behind her once she was safely in the car.

He walked around the front of the car quickly and settled into the driver's seat. He pulled on his seat belt and turned on the engine without a word. He backed out of the space he'd parked in and headed out of the neighborhood.

"So…" Mackenzie's voice was hesitant. She had no idea what to talk about.

"So…" Dax echoed.

"You've laughed more tonight than you have in the last week?"

Dax glanced at Mack. She'd turned so her back leaned against the car door and crossed her legs. She'd put her purse on the floor in front of her and was watching him with her head cocked. Dax liked how all her attention was on him. She wasn't asking to be polite; it honestly looked as if she cared what he had to say.

"Yeah, I can't talk particulars, but the cases this week have sucked."

"The Lone Star Reaper?"

Dax looked sharply at Mack again, showing his surprise at her comment.

"Daxton, I'm not an idiot. Every time I turn on the TV, the news is talking about it. I know another woman was found this week. He's been the leading story for the last month or so. Hell, I think I remember them saying there was a Special Response Team that had been assigned to the case. I don't know if you're on the case or not, but I just assumed you were. I'm sorry if you want me to be a good little girl and not ask about that shit, but I can't be. I might not know anything about the police, but when this story is in the news every damn day and I'm a single woman, I can't help but pay attention."

It wasn't funny, but Dax struggled to keep from smiling anyway. Mack was so easily riled. It was a good thing he wasn't. "Sorry, Mack. You're right. I don't think you're an idiot. And yes, the case has been weighing on my mind a lot this week."

"Okay, I know this is our first date and all, but I'll listen if you want to talk about it…at least what you can."

"Thanks, but no. Can we agree to put all talk of work behind us for the night? I'd rather get to know you than talk about that asshole."

"Deal."

Dax did smile at that. So far, Mackenzie was perfect. He enjoyed being around her, and enjoyed talking to her. She was funny and didn't seem to care about saying the "right" thing, but preferred to blurt out whatever she was thinking.

He also enjoyed her body. He was a man, after all. Holding her against him had solidified that. She was soft in all the right places. Looking down at her while he'd held her in her front hall was almost painful. He'd tried to be careful not to pull her into him too closely; otherwise she'd have felt for herself how attractive he found her. Having her breasts rub against him was one thing, but if he'd pulled her hips into his, it would've been obvious how much he enjoyed holding her against him.

Dax had about lost it when he'd looked down and seen her little nipples tight under the black shirt she was wearing. Because he was so tall, he could practically see down her shirt. He'd known it was rude as hell, but seeing her breasts pushing up into the scoop neck of her shirt made him want to squeeze them in both his hands. They were obviously more than a handful, and he wanted nothing more than to learn the feel, texture, and taste of them.

Fuck. He had to concentrate, otherwise he'd get hard again. Not something Dax wanted to do on their first date. He thought about a safe topic of conversation.

"Okay, so if we're getting to know each other, tell me about your family."

Mackenzie rolled her eyes. "You would start off there, wouldn't you? Okay, but don't blame me if you decide to ditch me at the nearest street corner when I'm done."

Dax could hear the laughter in her voice and merely shook his head at her and gestured for her to continue.

"So, you know I have two brothers, Mark and Matthew—"

"Wait."

Surprised at Daxton's interruption, Mackenzie halted immediately. "What? What's wrong?"

"You have two brothers named Mark and Matthew? And your last name is Morgan…and your name is Mackenzie?"

Seeing where Daxton was going, Mackenzie laughed. "Yeah, apparently my parents thought it was trendy to have the M theme carry on throughout all their kids."

"Do their names start with M as well?"

"Of course." Mackenzie chuckled at the incredulous look on Daxton's face. "Myra and Milton Morgan. So anyway. I'm the middle kid. Matthew is forty and Mark is thirty-five. I'm sure we were a handful, being so close in age. We're all pretty close. My dad died three years ago of a heart attack. It was sudden, and we miss him a lot, but we're doing okay. I get together with my mom and brothers at least every other week. They love me a lot, but don't really understand me. I'm stubborn and they think I'm way too picky. My mom wants me to get married and hurry up and squeeze out a gazillion grandbabies for her."

"Are your brothers married?"

"Yup, and they each have three kids. You'd think the six grandkids she already has would be enough for my mom, but nope. She wants more. I really like my sisters-in-law, who, by the way, don't have names that start with M. Salena and Kathy are great, but we aren't that close."

"What doesn't your family understand about you?"

Mackenzie tried to get her thoughts together to try to explain what she meant without sounding like a complete loser or headcase.

"And don't hold back now. Seriously, tell me what you're thinking."

"I'm thinking I want you to like me, Daxton, I don't want to chase you away on our first date."

Dax took his right hand off the steering wheel, placed it on Mack's knee, and squeezed briefly. "Mack, I already like you. I go through my day talking to people who are only telling me lies. When they get caught in one lie, they tell another to try to get out of it. I have to dig and dig to try to find out the simplest things. You have no idea how refreshing it is to me that you don't play any games...at all. You lay it all out there. At this point, nothing you can say now will make me not want to see you again. Okay?"

"Even if I said I had the hots for my brothers' wives?"

"Okay, maybe that." Dax smiled at Mack again and put his hand back on the steering wheel, even though he wanted to keep it on her knee, and waited for her to continue.

"I'm picky. I like things done a certain way and I'm stubborn. I think when I start dating a guy, I wonder about what *he* thinks about *me*, and it freaks me out. Am I chewing too loud? Do my clothes look okay? Should I wear more makeup or less? And you might have noticed I have a bad habit of blabbering on and on about nothing. So after I stress when I wonder what he might be thinking about me, I start to find things wrong with the way *he* does stuff and I call him on it. Incessantly. Until he can't take it anymore and he leaves."

Mackenzie decided she'd rather Daxton end this now once Dax knew how she really was, than fall in love with him and have him leave.

"Holy shit."

The words came out without Mackenzie meaning them to. What had she just thought? Had that been her problem all along? That wasn't really what she was going to tell him, but now that she thought it, she couldn't *un*think it.

"What?"

"I..."

"What, Mack? Go on."

"I think I've pushed guys away in the past because I knew it'd hurt less for them to leave me before I fell in love with them and they decided to leave anyway."

Instead of the censure Mackenzie was sure would be sent her way, Daxton's voice was level and understanding. "That makes sense. You must have been hurt that way in your past."

"Are you a mind reader?" Mackenzie asked, only half kidding.

Dax chuckled. "No, sweetie, but I don't think you're all that abnormal. Most people want to protect their hearts. It's never any fun to love someone and have them leave you anyway."

"Did that happen to you?" Mackenzie asked before she could think about it.

"Yeah."

"I'm sorry, Daxton. That sucks."

"Yeah. I fell head over heels in love with her and had planned the rest of our life all out in my head. I got a promotion and was supposed to move from El Paso to Austin. Stupidly, I accepted the job without consulting with her about it. I know it was a dick thing to do, but I honestly thought she'd be thrilled for me. She knew how hard I'd been working for the promotion, and she even knew I'd flown to Austin to interview. But when I told her I accepted the job, she flatly refused to leave. She grew up in El Paso and all her family was there. Ultimately, she chose them over me."

"What a moron."

Dax just shook his head and smiled. Mack never said what he thought she would.

"I mean seriously. To give you up for her family? It's not like her family would disown her or anything if she moved...wait...would they?"

"No, they wouldn't have."

"Right then, so she made you choose between her and your career. Sorry to say, but you made the right choice, Daxton. I know I've been a bitch to some of the men I've dated, but I never, not once, made them choose between their job and me. Besides, look where you are today. You're a Ranger! I don't know anything about anything, but I've heard how the newscasters talk about you guys and I don't live in a hole, I know about Rangers. You're amazing! There's no way I'd choose my brothers over you, I mean, seriously. I love them and all, but why would I give up a hot guy and great sex for the rest of my life for my *brothers*? No freaking way! And another thing..."

Mackenzie was on a roll and didn't even seem to notice how Dax's body had gotten tight upon hearing her words.

"She couldn't have loved you. Not really. Not a real true-to-the-marrow-of-your-bones love. If you had that kind of love, there's no way she would've made that decision. Yeah, I get it. El Paso and Austin are far apart, but it's not like they're in different countries."

Mackenzie's voice softened for the first time since her tirade. "If she truly loved you and knew it was what you wanted and what was best for you, she would've moved with you in a heartbeat. It sucks to hear that, I'm sure, but I believe it. Shit, even though you aren't married, I still think you made the right decision. What if you'd married her and tried to make it work and she pulled the same kind of thing later? You'd be stuck in a job knowing you could've had better and would regret not taking the Austin job. That would eat at you and you'd be miserable. So yeah, that sucks, but I think you're better off."

Mackenzie looked up at Daxton, startled because the car wasn't moving anymore. They'd pulled into a parking lot and Daxton had cut off the engine. He was staring at her with a weird look on his face.

"Shit, I overstepped, didn't I? Dammit, I told you I was like this."

"No, Mack, you didn't overstep. You're right. It *was* probably for the best."

"I didn't mean to insinuate that you didn't love her."

"I know you didn't."

Mackenzie closed her eyes and put her forehead in the palm of her hand. "My family also says I have a tendency to talk too much."

"You don't talk too much, Mack. Promise." Dax leaned over and pulled Mackenzie toward him with one hand behind her neck. He kissed her on the top of the head and leaned back. "Ready for some food?"

"Yes, please. Food sounds good. Anything at this point, other than me going on and on about your love life, sounds good."

"Come on then. I hope you'll like this place." Dax had already thought all the things Mack had said at one time or another, but the fact that'd she'd immediately been able to sum up all the reasons why Kelly and he didn't end up together was very insightful…especially for them just having met. It boded well for their budding relationship; at least what he hoped was a budding relationship.

Mackenzie looked up and saw they were at a restaurant on the south side of the city she'd never been to before. Mood lightening, embarrassing conversation forgotten, Mack exclaimed, "Oooh, I've always wanted to eat here!"

"Good. Today's your chance."

Dax exited his side of the car and started to walk around to help Mack out, but she met him before he'd gotten half way around the vehicle.

"I know, I was supposed to wait for you to come open my door, right? I can't. Sorry, Daxton, but seriously, I don't get that. I'm just supposed to sit there with my hands in my lap waiting for you? I feel stupid just sitting there like a helpless little woman. I have two hands. I can open the door just fine by myself."

"It's the gentlemanly thing to do."

"I know, I *know*, but I still think it's weird. I mean, I know you're a gentleman. Hell, the entire embarrassing episode at my apartment told me that."

"How about we make a deal?"

"What kind of deal?"

"The kind of deal where if I tell you it's important to me to come around and assist you out of the car so you don't fall over or when I want to be a gentleman, you'll agree. And if I don't bring it up, you can get out on your own and meet me here, in front of the car, just like you did today."

Mackenzie thought about it for a second and smiled, liking that Daxton thought there'd be times in the future they'd be driving somewhere together. She liked it a lot. "Okay, deal. If it's important to you, tell me and I'll wait. Otherwise I'll do my own thing."

"Good, let's go." Dax took Mackenzie's hand and laced their fingers together, liking the feel of her hand in his. He had a good hunch about Mackenzie and dinner. He hoped this was the beginning of a long relationship.

Chapter Six

———◆———

T HE CAR WAS silent on the way back to Mackenzie's apartment
after dinner. Dax had a great time, Mackenzie was a hoot, and
he couldn't remember when he'd enjoyed a date more. Granted, he
hadn't been on many dates in the recent past, but he still didn't think
any of them had been as fun as this one had been.

The restaurant was one of Dax's favorites. It was a cross between
a bar and grill and a diner. Around ten each night, the owners
stopped serving food and the ambiance changed to more of a bar-type
atmosphere.

Dax and Mackenzie had eaten, then sat talking until Mack suggested they play darts. The funniest part was that she'd never thrown
a dart before in her life. She was awful at it, but she laughed at herself
every time she missed the bull's-eye by a mile.

And Mackenzie *was* clumsy. She hadn't been lying. At one point,
she'd reached across the table and knocked over his water glass. She'd
apologized profusely, but Dax had waved it off. Since the seat on his
side of the booth had been wet, it'd given him an excuse to move over
to sit next to her, so it had all worked out in his favor anyway.

Then when they were playing darts, she'd dropped one and it
barely missed landing on her foot. One throw also went way wide
and luckily had bounced off the wall and landed on the floor, instead
of about a foot to the left, to the man standing next to the wall
drinking a beer. Mackenzie decided she'd had enough darts at that
point.

They'd laughed and Mack had giggled as their date continued. She hadn't been pissed or thrown a hissy fit when a woman, out having drinks with friends, came up to him and gave him her business card and said, "Call me." Mackenzie had thought it hilarious instead.

It was a refreshing change from the last woman Dax had dated, who'd been pissed when another woman had slipped him her phone number while they were out on a date one night. Even though he hadn't done anything to encourage the waitress in any way shape or form, his date got upset at *him* and insisted that he must've done something to make her think he was into her. It was the last time Dax had asked her out.

Now Dax was taking Mackenzie back to her apartment. He didn't want the night to end, but it was late and Mack was yawning in the seat next to him. He pulled into the parking lot and turned off the engine. Dax waited until Mackenzie turned to look at him.

"Wait there, I'll come around." He paused until Mack smiled and nodded at him.

Dax went around the car, opened the passenger door, and held out his hand. Mack put her hand in his and allowed him to help her up and out. Dax held Mack against him as he shuffled them out of the way so he could shut the door. He could feel her heat through the light jacket she wore.

"Thanks for letting me help you. It's dark. It makes me feel better to have my hands on you as we head for your apartment. Okay?"

"Yeah, okay."

"Come on, let's get you inside."

Mackenzie smiled as Daxton led her across the parking lot to her door. She'd had a great night. "I almost ditched you, you know," she told Daxton out of the blue.

Dax smiled. "Yeah?"

"Yeah. I was going to call you and let you know I'd changed my mind, but I didn't have your number, you had it blocked."

"Yeah, I don't like my number out there, especially when I'm following leads on cases."

"I get that. Anyway, then I thought I'd get out of my apartment and wait for six o'clock to pass, then go back home, but I knew that'd be rude and Laine would've kicked my butt. So I decided I'd just tell you when you arrived that I didn't want to go, but I couldn't do that either. So I took a chance. I've only been on one other blind date in my life, and Laine set us up, so I felt pretty safe. The only other time in my life I took a chance that huge was when I moved here to San Antonio. I was living in Houston and got the job offer here. It's not like I make a ton of money, but I knew it'd bring me closer to my family, so I did it. It scared the hell out of me at first, to have to move and make new friends and stuff, but in the end, it turned out all right. Then luckily Laine decided she missed me too much and she moved here, too."

Dax knew he'd never tire of Mack's rambling way of talking to him. It was cute as hell. She had no idea how much information she gave him with her seemingly unrelated ramblings. He loved it. "So, I take it you're not sorry you took the chance on me?"

"Uh, no." Mack said it as if she was saying "duh". "I was a bit freaked that I didn't even really know you. I mean, I saw you at the charity event and thought you were hot as hell, but I didn't *know* you. I've only been on one blind date before, and it was a disaster. And you know, some cops are assholes. I would've been so disappointed if you were one of those, but so far, you've been cool. I've never really liked the whole cowboy-hat thing; I mean a cowboy hat is just funny looking. A lot of men can't pull it off, but on you? I'll just say, you can pull it off just fine. And you're in shape. I'm sure you know that, I mean, you see yourself naked all the time, and I haven't, but seriously, I can tell you're muscular as hell and don't have a beer belly. Why don't you? I mean, you drink beer, you had one tonight, but you're not fat at all."

Dax's lips twitched as he tried to keep his laughter inside. They'd arrived at Mackenzie's door. He turned her so her back was to the door and he was towering over her. He caught Mack's hands in his and brought them up to his chest. He placed her palms flat on his shirt and pressed, indicating she should keep them there. He then framed her face with his hands and tilted her head up.

"You approve of my body, Mack?" He was amused to note that she seemed speechless for the first time tonight. "Because I sure as hell approve of yours."

At the roll of her eyes, Dax continued.

"You fit me perfectly. You're a little thing next to me, and all I can think about is caging you in my arms and having my way with you." He watched Mack swallow.

"Uh…"

"And your curves have been driving me crazy all night. There's nothing sexier than a woman with curves. When I stood behind you tonight and helped with your form as you tried to throw that damn dart, you have no idea how hard it was for me not to push myself up against you to show you how I felt about your hips, and legs, and tits."

"Uh, seriously, Daxton…"

"And your mouth. Hell, woman. Watching you talk to me tonight, watching you lick your lips when they were dry…it took all my willpower not to haul you over the table and into my lap and lick your lips myself."

Dax paused, enjoying the flush that came over Mack's face and her shifting movements against him, before continuing.

"I've had a wonderful time. Not only do I like your delectable little body, I like what's inside it. I've enjoyed talking to you. You're refreshing, especially compared to my friends and the criminals I talk to day in and day out. Don't ever change."

"Uh. Okay."

"And I want to see you again. I'm going to give you my number so you can call me—not to blow me off, but because you want to talk to me. Because you want to know when I'm taking you out again. Because that's what you do with the man you're dating. You good with that?"

"We're dating?"

"Yeah, we're dating."

"Oh. Okay."

"Good. So first things first. I'm going to kiss you. I'm going to taste those lips again. That one taste I got before we left wasn't enough, and I'm going to make it the best kiss you've ever received. After that, I'm going to let you go, because I know if I don't, I'll haul you inside and take you in your hallway until I empty myself inside you and can't stand up anymore. You good with *that?*"

Mackenzie stared up at the man in front of her in bewilderment. He'd been fairly easygoing all night. He was certainly an alpha man, but he hadn't really let it show until just now. Mack flexed her hands until her fingernails were digging into the shirt over his rock-hard chest.

"I'm not sure why you see all that in me, but I'd be an idiot to disagree with you. I'd also be lying if I said I didn't want the same thing. Please, Daxton. Kiss me before I have to tackle you to the ground and have my wicked way with you."

Dax smiled. "You've managed to keep me on my toes all night tonight, Mack. Hold on to me."

He leaned down, tilting Mack's head back even more as she tried to keep eye contact. She really was tiny compared to him. Liking the power he had over her, just because of his height, Dax swooped down and took her lips with his, without any preliminaries. He plunged his tongue inside her mouth and loved it when Mack immediately countered his thrust with her own. There was no way she'd ever just lie under him and take whatever he wanted to give her. She'd fight to give it right back.

Dax moved one hand from the side of her head to the small of her back and hefted her up against him until her feet left the ground and they were touching from groin to chest. He felt her wrap both hands around his neck to help hold herself up. She tilted her head to the side to give him greater access as he continued his onslaught on her mouth.

He sucked her tongue into his mouth and bit down gently. Dax could feel Mack shift against him restlessly and one of her legs came up hesitantly beside his hip. She couldn't hold it there, but tightened her hold on his neck.

Dax thrust his tongue back into Mack's mouth and took his time learning each and every contour and memorizing the taste and feel of her. Finally, knowing he had to stop, or he wouldn't be *able* to stop, Dax drew back and leaned over to put Mack back on her feet. He moved to lick at the corner of her mouth, he nipped at the side of her jaw, then sucked on her earlobe before moving down to her sensitive neck. Dax felt goose bumps rise against her skin as he licked and nibbled at a sensitive spot.

"Uh, Daxton, I've never had a one-night stand in my life, I'm just not the kind of girl who can imagine something so intimate with someone I don't really even know. But I think you should be aware; I'm seriously reconsidering the type of girl I am right now." Mackenzie's voice quivered with the intensity of her lust.

Dax smiled against Mackenzie's skin, running his hands up and down her spine and backside. He finally lifted his head to look down into Mack's eyes. "We aren't rushing this, Mack. There's no need for a one-night stand. This is gonna last a hell of a lot longer than one night anyway. Let go of me and let me give you my number."

Mackenzie realized she hadn't let go of him since he'd put her on her feet and she reluctantly forced her fingers to unclench at the back of his shirt, and to lower her arms. She licked her lips, liking how Daxton's eyes followed her movements.

"Give me your phone, Mack."

Mackenzie reached into her purse and pulled out her cell. She entered the password and put it into Daxton's hand. She watched as he clicked buttons as he added his contact information.

"I programmed in my cell, my work number, as well as the number at Company F...which is my Ranger Company. If you can't reach me, leave a message. If it's an emergency, call the company and tell them it's you. I'll make sure the admins know you're with me and if you call, they can interrupt me. They can get in touch with me no matter what I'm doing. Okay?"

"Wow. Okay, but I'm not the kind of woman who needs to call if she runs out of milk or something, Daxton. I can go and get the damn milk myself. You should get that about me."

"And I'm not the kind of man who expects or wants you to call me if you've lost your purse. But I *do* expect if you truly need me, that you'll call. I won't be happy to find out you've driven yourself to the emergency room or clinic if you fell and broke something."

"Really? That's the example you have to give me?"

Dax liked her spunk. "Yeah. You were the one who told me you were clumsy, remember?"

"Okay, okay, you're right."

"Good. So you'll call."

"Yeah. I'll call if I need something. But, Daxton, you should know something."

"What's that?" Dax fingered the hair by Mack's ear that had come loose from her clip and was wisping around her face.

"I'm a text kinda girl. I have the unlimited package. I like texting, sending and receiving. Is that a problem?"

Dax smiled and leaned down and kissed her hard, and way too briefly, before pulling back. "It's not a problem. I'll get used to it."

The smile he got in return was worth his response. Dax knew he'd do what he could to see it again and again. "Okay, I'm really going now. Lock your door and stay safe."

"You'll…" She paused, not sure if she'd sound too needy if she asked what she was thinking.

"What, Mack?"

"You'll call? We'll go out again?"

"Fuck yeah. I said we were dating, I didn't lie. We're going out again."

When he didn't say when, Mackenzie mentally shrugged. "Okay."

"Okay. Inside. Lock the door."

"Thanks for a fun night. I'll talk to you later."

"Yes, you will. Good night, Mack."

The last thing Mackenzie saw when she shut the door was Daxton's upward chin lift as he stood and watched, making sure she barricaded herself inside her apartment. She slid down with her back to the door. Her butt landed on the floor and she wrapped her arms around her drawn up knees. She smiled. Holy freaking hell she was in trouble.

Chapter Seven

"**D**ON'T BE NERVOUS, ma'am. Just tell me what you remember seeing that afternoon." Dax tried to sound calm and reassuring. Interviewing witnesses was a delicate balance between being sympathetic, but pushy, when it came to trying to pry the right information out of them.

"I'd gone to the cemetery to lay flowers on my dear Harold's grave and I saw a big tractor digging a hole in the back corner of the lot. I thought it was odd because that part of the cemetery hadn't had a funeral held in it in a long time, but what do I know about how cemeteries do business? Maybe they were starting a new plot."

"What color was the tractor?"

"Yellow."

"Did it look old? New? Did you see anyone?"

"Well, I don't know my tractors, but it was very shiny. There was someone in the cab, but I couldn't see him at all. The windows were tinted and it was so far away."

"What time was it?"

"It was around three in the afternoon. I remember because I had a hair appointment at three thirty and I didn't want to be late."

"Thank you, Mrs. Sutton. You've been a big help." And she had. They knew the killer used a yellow tractor and the time he buried his victim. Dax would check with the cemetery staff and see if it was theirs. If they were lucky, it wasn't, and they could do a check of the Department of Motor Vehicles on anyone that owned a yellow tractor. He'd also be sure to tell Cruz to alert the caretakers of the local cemeteries to be on the lookout for any unusual activity in their areas. The local police agencies could also increase patrols around the rural cemeteries as well. It wasn't full-proof, after all they hadn't been able to catch this guy yet, but it was something. The killer hadn't called in to brag about this victim until apparently a week after he'd put the coffin in the ground. The timeline fit what Conor had said about time of death.

"Do you think you'll catch him? What a terrible man, to do those things."

"Yes, ma'am. We'll catch him. We're doing everything possible to catch him sooner rather than later."

"Well, thank you for what you do, young man. The world needs more people like you in it."

Dax helped the woman out of the chair and to the door. "I advise you to keep your visits to Harold at a minimum, at least until we catch whoever this is. If you need to visit, don't go alone."

"I can do that. I'll have my son, David, come with me next time."

"You do that. Thanks again, Mrs. Sutton." Dax nodded at the woman as she left his office. He sighed and sat back down in his chair and looked over the pictures strewn in front of him. Dax had heard back from Cruz. The FBI analysts hadn't found anything useful on the note the killer had sent. There weren't any usable fingerprints and the only trace evidence that had been on the note was a single hair, which seemed to have come from a cat.

So Dax had a lot of information, but it was all disjointed. Their killer was a man who owned, or had come into contact with, a cat, he either owned a yellow tractor or had the know-how to hotwire one. The coffins were a dead end because they were homemade. They could try to track the hardware used to assemble them, but that was a long shot. Fuck. They had information, but it still seemed like they were still at square one.

The phone on his desk rang; it was Quint from the San Antonio Police Department.

"Hey, Dax. Got time for lunch today?"

"Actually, Mack is supposed to come to my office today for a quick lunch, want to join us? I can ask her to pick up an extra sandwich on her way in."

"Sure, if you don't mind."

"Yeah, I've actually been wanting you to meet her anyway. I know it's soon, but I really like her."

"You seem serious about this one. How long have you been seeing her?"

"I *am* serious about her. It's been about two weeks."

"Great, what time then?"

"How about twelve fifteen?"

"See you then."

Dax put the phone back in its cradle and leaned back with his arms behind his head. He knew Quint probably wanted to talk about the Reaper investigation, but Dax needed some Mack time before he'd be able to dive back into the horror that was the case. Burying women alive was some sick shit and Mack helped him keep everything in perspective.

The two weeks since they'd been dating had been great. They'd met up several times for dinner and had advanced their kissing at her door to kissing in his car, and even once on her couch while they were watching a movie.

Dax was trying to take things slow, but the more time he spent with Mack, the more he knew in his gut she was the woman for him. He'd been instantly attracted to her, but it wasn't just that he wanted her sexually. She was funny. She was polite. She didn't get riled up when something went wrong, it just rolled off her back. During one of their dinners, she'd bumped the plate the waitress was clearing from their table and a full cup of ranch had spilled down the front of

Mack's shirt. Mack had merely laughed. Dax shook his head remembering. Mack had almost bent double guffawing at herself and how clumsy she was as she dabbed at her shirt trying to mop up the mess. She'd been more concerned about the waitress, who'd been absolutely mortified. Mack had smiled and told the poor waitress it was an accident and it was fine. Of course they'd gotten their meal free, along with a complimentary T-shirt from the restaurant, but Mack hadn't been upset in the least.

Mack also wasn't afraid to admit when she screwed up, something Dax had rarely seen in the women he'd dated in the past. She laughed at herself when she tripped over nothing, or dropped something. She really was accident prone, but it didn't seem to faze her. It was refreshing to be with a woman who said what she thought most of the time, but still wasn't quite as confident in her own skin as she might try to portray to the world. It was that dichotomy that drew him to her. She also didn't seem to be full of the drama that so many women were these days, which was a relief.

Dax had been on a lot of dates, and had even thought he'd loved a woman once or twice, not including the woman he'd almost married back in El Paso. He'd participated in a couple of one-night stands, and usually felt used. But Mack, she was different. He felt it to the very marrow of his bones.

Mackenzie hadn't lied that first night they'd gone to dinner. She did have a habit of trying to boss him around and make him do things the way she wanted them done. They'd had dinner at her place one night and she'd spent ten minutes lecturing him on the best way to wash dishes. For the most part, Dax went along with it, because he honestly didn't give a shit if he put the dishwasher soap on the sponge thingie or directly on the dirty dish when he was washing it, but apparently, Mack did.

However, he called her on some things. When he did, Dax could see her stop and really think about them and the times she gave in seemed to cement his feelings for her all the more. Mack wasn't being unreasonable for the sake of being unreasonable. Dax hoped the fact that she'd occasionally back off something she wanted done her way, and let him do it however he wanted, meant she liked him and was really trying to make their relationship work.

Like the time she pulled out her credit card to pay for dinner one night. Dax had told her that as long as they were out together, whether it was at a restaurant, gas station, or a department store, she'd never pay.

Mack had puffed up like a banty rooster and had insisted and cajoled and pouted, but in the end, when he'd explained that it made him feel like less of a man when she paid, she'd caved. Of course, later that night she'd told him in no uncertain terms that if he *wasn't* with her, and she was buying food, or whatever, for both of them, *she'd* pay for it. Dax had tickled her unmercifully until giving her what she needed…his agreement. Compromise was the backbone of any relationship and Dax loved that Mack was sincerely trying to compromise for him.

Dax didn't really mind that Mack wanted to pay her way; it was actually refreshing. His relationship with Mack was a complete one-eighty from his relationship with Kelly, the woman who refused to move to Austin with him. She'd never paid for anything, never even *offered* to pay for anything. She'd always expected Dax to pay for everything, from the rent and electricity to the credit cards she'd maxed out. Looking back Dax knew he'd been a sucker, but he'd honestly believed she was the woman he'd spend the rest of his life with.

Dax quickly texted Mack and told her Quint would be joining them for lunch and asked her to pick up a third sandwich. She texted back immediately—another thing Dax loved about Mack, she never made him wait and wonder if she got his message—and agreed without a fuss. She was text crazy, as she'd warned. But it kept the communication open between them, and even Dax had to admit it made him feel good inside to know she was thinking about him when she sent random silly texts just to say hi.

An hour later, Dax heard a knock on the door.

"Come in."

Mack sauntered into his office with a smile on her face and two large bags in her hand.

"Hey, Daxton. How's your day been?"

"Better now that you're here. Come here, sweetheart."

Mack plopped the bags on the little table off to the right of Dax's desk and went to his side, shrieking when he pulled her into his arms in the chair.

Mackenzie immediately straddled Daxton's lap, fitting her knees into the small spaces next to his hips.

"How come you never wear a skirt?"

Mackenzie scrunched up her nose in disgust. "Ugh. I hate them."

"Why?" Even as Dax asked, he knew he'd get an earful. Sometimes he purposefully asked her things that he knew she'd ramble on about because he loved to hear her talk.

"Because they're sexist. I mean really. Back in the dark ages, it was the *men* who wore skirts...or togas or kilts, or whatever they were called. *Their* legs were sticking out, showing off their knees, exposing their backsides if they fell over. Sometime in the last thousand years, some *man* came to his senses and decided he'd rather see a woman's knees and backside."

"Thanks for the history lesson, Mack. Now...why do you really not wear skirts?"

Mackenzie smirked at Daxton. "Do you know, I actually like this position. I can look you in the eye and don't have to worry about you getting a crick in your back from leaning down to me, and I don't have to worry about getting a cramp from looking up at you."

At his raised eyebrow, Mackenzie sighed, knowing she'd been trying to avoid answering his question. "So there was this one time right after I graduated from college and had my first job. I was extremely proud of myself and felt very professional. I bought myself a bunch of new suits to wear to work. I thought I looked very sharp. The first day of work, there were three men who, when they met me, looked me up and down and their eyes stayed fixated on my legs. The second day, I had a woman tell me, politely, that if I needed help shopping for professional clothes she'd be happy to go to the mall with me to pick out more appropriate clothes. On the third day, when I was wearing my favorite of the three skirt sets I'd bought especially for my new job, I slipped in the lobby. My legs went flying out from under me and my skirt came up around my waist as I fell and gave everyone standing around a cooter shot. I heard the security team had it on the security cameras and passed it around to everyone in the company. That was the last time I wore a skirt to work."

"That shit is illegal."

Mackenzie put her hand on Daxton's cheek, not in the least perturbed at her story, or at his ire. "I know. I turned them in and HR fired everyone who they could prove participated in the sharing of the video."

"I should've known you wouldn't have let that pass."

"Of course not. Assholes. That was the last time I wore a skirt to work. I'm just too clumsy to risk it again. Not to mention I don't need anyone making me the butt of their jokes because they don't think I've got the right kind of body to wear a short skirt."

"Wrong," Dax rebutted immediately.

"Huh?"

"You're wrong, Mack." Dax's hands went from resting at her waist down to her ass and he hauled her closer to him. Close enough that he knew she could feel his erection up against her woman bits. "You have the perfect body for wearing a skirt. Imagine if you were wearing one now. Think about what we could do during our lunches together if you wore one every day."

Mackenzie didn't hesitate, but shoved her hands next to Daxton's body until they were resting over his shirt under his arms. She leaned in and whispered, "Daxton, you think a pair of pants would really prevent me from taking you in this chair and riding you until we were both piles of goo if I really wanted to?"

"Hello!"

Dax and Mackenzie both jerked in surprise and turned to the door. Quint stood there, one hand on the doorjamb, smiling at them.

Mackenzie laughed and moved her arms out from Daxton's sides. Dax reluctantly eased Mack back a bit so she wasn't pressed up against him and took his hands off her ass. "We'll continue this conversation later," Dax whispered before returning Quint's greeting.

"Hey, Quint, it's good to see you."

"Uh-huh, sure."

Dax smiled at his friend and helped Mack to her feet, steading her when she stumbled. "Come over here and let me introduce you to Mack, otherwise known as Mackenzie."

"It's nice to meet you, Quint," Mackenzie said politely, holding out her hand.

"I think the pleasure's all mine." Quint brought Mackenzie's hand up to his mouth and kissed the back of it.

Daxton reached up and took Mackenzie's hand out of Quint's. "Enough, Quint."

Quint laughed. "It's just too easy. So...how did you guys meet again?"

Dax opened his mouth to give his friend the short version when Mackenzie piped in.

"Well, I saw him for the first time at that charity event over a month ago. We didn't really meet there though, we just talked briefly. Then I was speeding because I had a crap day, and Daxton's friend pulled me over. But he was nice enough to ignore the fact I'd had a crap day and was crying my eyes out, and gave me a warning instead."

"I don't know what that story has to do with meeting Dax here," Quint said in confusion.

"Oh, well, apparently they were on their way to dinner when I zoomed past them and Daxton was in the car with the Highway Patrol guy and he saw my license, realized he'd met me at the charity thing, called to make sure I was all right after being pulled over and then demanded I go to dinner with him. He came over, I embarrassed myself, as usual, and we went out. He kissed the hell out of me on my doorstep and now here we are."

Quint smiled in amusement and looked at Dax. "How come I didn't see her at the charity thing? Dammit, you Rangers always get the good ones."

Dax laughed and pulled Mack over to him and kissed the side of her head, refusing to rise to Quint's bait. "Hungry, sweetheart?"

"Starved."

Dax loved that Mack wasn't afraid to show that she was human and hungry. Too many women he'd been around tried to pretend that a leaf or two every other day was enough to live on. "What'd you get us?"

"I got you a turkey and cheese sandwich with all the trimmings—yes, including jalapenos. I still don't know how you can eat those, but whatever. I got myself a BLT, minus the mayo and double the T, easy on the B. And I didn't know what your friend would want, so I got both a ham and cheese with the normal condiments, and I also went outside the box, in case he was like you, and ordered a meat-lover's sandwich with every kind of meat and topping they had. Chips for all of us and waters as well."

"Will you marry me?" Quint asked with a smile and his hand over his heart.

Mackenzie giggled at him and rolled her eyes. "Whatever."

The trio settled themselves at the small table and Mackenzie passed out the sandwiches, smiling when Quint chose the meat-lover's sandwich. She knew Daxton would eat the ham and cheese later. It seemed as if he had a bottomless stomach; he could always eat.

After they'd made small talk for a bit, Quint broke the lighthearted mood.

"The Lone Star Reaper stuck again."

Mackenzie gasped and Dax put down his sandwich abruptly. "What the fuck, Quint? Not in front of Mack."

Mackenzie put her hand over Daxton's on the table. "It's okay, really. I'm actually interested."

Dax looked at Mack closely, seeing she was serious, and didn't seem concerned at all. He looked back at Quint and warned, "Nothing deep, got it?"

"Yeah." Quint understood what Dax meant. He'd keep the talk general and not share any of the extreme details until he could talk to Dax alone. "He called it in again, he didn't write a note. She was found on the north side of the city, again in a small rural cemetery. She was buried off to the side as usual, not in the main part of the lot."

Mackenzie interrupted, her curiosity overcoming her reticence to butt into the conversation when she didn't really know Quint. "So this guy kidnaps women, then buries them alive? Right?"

"Right."

"Why?" Her question was short and to the point.

"What do you mean, why?" Quint asked seriously.

"I mean, what does he get out of it? Are the women raped?"

If Quint was surprised at Mackenzie's question, he didn't show it. "No, not as far as the medical examiner can tell."

"So, why is he doing it?

"Well, besides being an asshole, we aren't sure, Mack," Dax answered, picking up Mackenzie's hand and playing with her fingers absently. "We can't find any connection between the women at all. As far as we can tell, they didn't know each other. They didn't live in the same part of the city. They all had different jobs. We can't find the connection."

"Okay, but again, I guess I'm confused about why is he's doing it."

"Who knows why any psycho does the things they do?" was Quint's response.

Mackenzie's brow furrowed in concentration. "But there has to be a reason. Nobody does things without having a reason. Is he pissed at the government? Was he abused as a child? Does he have Mommy issues? Why? If he's not raping the women, he has to get something else out of it. When I was in middle school, I remember a kid kicking a stray dog. I confronted him about it and asked what the dog had ever done to him to deserve to be kicked. The kid said he'd been bitten by a stray dog when he was younger and hated them ever since. So okay, I didn't like his answer and told him he was an idiot, but my point is, he had a reason to want to kick every stray dog he saw. I know that's way too simplistic and I don't mean to say that every guy who has ever been hurt or dumped by a woman would turn into a serial killer, but I still wanna know what *this* guy's reason is."

"Fuck, Dax. If she wasn't already yours—"

"She is." Dax cut off Quint's words immediately and continued as if he and Quint didn't have the short but intense side conversation. "We don't know, Mack. The profilers have some guesses, but we don't really know why he's doing it. We're trying to find out why he's burying the women alive. If we can do that, we might be able to search the databases and find out who he is."

"I suppose it can be hard to really figure out why anyone does anything nowadays. I mean, why do I harp on Daxton when he insists on putting the knives in the dishwasher with the points up? I know it's better to put them pointy side down so you don't cut yourself when you're emptying the stupid thing, but Daxton just can't seem to get that. I mean really, if he wants to risk stabbing himself every time he puts anything in or takes anything out, that's on him, but ultimately it's really not a big deal. Right?"

Dax leaned over and kissed Mack on the side of the head, as he was wont to do. "Right, sweetheart." He leaned back over to his seat and picked up what was left of his sandwich.

"Well, the first time you slice your palm when you're emptying the dishwasher, you'll see I know what I'm talking about."

Quint and Dax both laughed at her and they finished their lunch.

Dax walked Mack to the door and turned back to Quint, knowing he wanted to speak to him alone as much as Quint probably wanted to speak to him. "I'll be back in just a sec."

"I know you need some time to talk to your friend without me there, Daxton, I'm sorry I was in the way," Mackenzie said in a low voice as they got to the door.

"You weren't in the way."

"Well, I hope you know that I realize your work comes first. So if you have to text me at the last minute and let me know you need to cancel, that's okay. Even if I've already picked up lunch, I can find someone who will eat it. Hell, I swear the people I work with are professional mooches. I never leave anything in the fridge there anymore because it'll disappear faster than ice cream on the Fourth of July. All I'm saying is, I know what you do is important and that you can't talk about some of it with me, and that's okay. Hell, I don't *want* to know the details on most of the things you do, but I've been on my own for a long time now and won't be hurt if you have to do other things instead of eat lunch with me."

"Come here, Mack." Dax pulled Mackenzie into his arms and leaned down to her. "You're amazing."

Mackenzie smiled. "Naw, just too old to get sucked into the drama shit that happens in a relationship when two people don't trust each other. I trust you'll let me know if I drive you crazy or if you don't want to see me anymore."

Dax leaned up and looked Mack in the eyes. "That's not gonna happen anytime soon."

"Okay."

"Okay. Be safe today. I'll talk to you later."

"I had a nice lunch. I like your friend."

"Me too, Mack. And as long as you like me better than him, I'm okay with you liking Quint."

"I like you more than him," Mackenzie reassured him with a smile.

Dax kissed Mack hard on the lips and set her away from him. "Get back to work, sweetheart."

Mackenzie waved as she turned around—and ran right into one of the other Rangers who was coming in the door. Luckily he caught her by the arms before she fell over.

"Sorry! Shit, sorry!" She smiled sheepishly at Dax and was gone.

Dax simply shook his head, realizing he'd happily spend the rest of his life catching her when she tripped over her own feet, or someone else's, and headed back to his office to see what it was that Quint wanted to tell him about the Reaper case.

Quint didn't waste any time. "This one had a walkie-talkie in the coffin with her."

"What the holy fuck?" Dax's mellow mood from spending time with Mack disappeared in a heartbeat.

"Yeah, the batteries were dead, and when they were replaced in the lab, it wasn't on a channel that would connect with anyone. The best we can figure, the Reaper wanted to be able to talk to her, or for her to be able to talk to someone else. We have no idea if it actually worked or not so far though."

"Has the next of kin been notified?"

"Not yet, we're still working to identify the victim."

"Fucking hell. He's escalating. He wants to torture his victims. If he's the one talking to them, he can say all sorts of shit to them while they're dying. If he wants them to be able to talk to someone else…what's his purpose behind that?"

"It's as your Mackenzie said, we have to find out why. Find out what his trigger is."

As much as he liked the words, "your Mackenzie", Dax's mind was stuck on this latest development from the psycho targeting helpless woman. "I'm on it. I'll look again and see what I can find in the records for boys ages five to fifteen and see if I can't find something, anything, in someone's past that might trigger something like this. It's an extreme long shot though, and we'll probably get more from surveillance of the cemeteries, but it's worth a shot. I'll get in touch with Cruz and see if he can't hurry up the profilers to give us more to go on."

"Good idea. We're gonna catch him, Dax," Quint tried to reassure his friend.

"I sure hope so. This could keep getting uglier and uglier if we don't."

"I like Mack." Quint changed the subject so abruptly, Dax had a hard time switching his mental gears.

"I like her too."

"She's spunky and quirky and down-to-earth."

"I know."

"You're a lucky man. Don't fuck it up."

Dax smiled for the first time. "I'll try not to."

"You do that. You gonna eat that ham and cheese sandwich, or can I take it?"

"You touch it, you die."

Quint merely laughed. "Okay." His voice turned serious. "Let me know what you find. I don't have a warm and fuzzy feeling about this."

"Will do. Me either."

Chapter Eight

THE LAST MONTH had been quiet; at least, the Lone Star Reaper had been quiet. Other cases, of course, took precedence, so it wasn't as if Dax was sitting around doing nothing all day, but there had been no more dead women found buried alive in coffins, and the Reaper hadn't communicated with anyone at all.

Dax didn't like it. He preferred action over inaction. He felt in his gut the Reaper was still out there killing, he was just biding his time before bragging about it.

Daxton and Quint had gotten with Cruz and he'd hooked them up with the profilers in the San Antonio office of the FBI. After many hours of research and discussion, they finally had a profile.

The Lone Star Reaper was most likely a man in his mid-thirties, unmarried, and a loner. He'd probably be highly intelligent, but not with a high education. He most likely went through some sort of psychological abuse when he was a child. He'd likely experienced a head injury when he was young, which affected the pre-frontal cortex, the area of the brain that controls judgment. The profile also suggested that he lived and worked in San Antonio and had probably had several blue-collar jobs throughout his life.

Further analysis by the profilers revealed that the Reaper probably had a domineering mother who was very strict and a father who wasn't around. He most likely had never had a steady relationship with a woman, and if he had, it was almost certainly dysfunctional.

The profilers warned that he undoubtedly had an unnatural fascination with death, perhaps even attended funerals and visitations of people he'd never met. He may or may not be concerned with his personal grooming habits, and therefore could have dirt under his fingernails from the burials. It'd be a reminder of what he'd done, and he'd like that reminder. The Reaper would also in all likelihood be what most people would consider "strange" or "weird.""

The communications liaisons from the FBI and the Rangers had teamed up to go on the local news to share the profile. Since then, every law enforcement agency in the greater San Antonio area had been busy fielding phone tips about every weirdo people believed could be the killer. Hell, even the Highway Patrol officers were on the lookout for men who fit the profile when they pulled anyone over.

So far nothing had panned out, and the fact that the Lone Star Reaper had gone quiet didn't sit well with Daxton, Quint, Cruz, and every other officer in the city. Everyone was simply holding their breath waiting for the next body to be found. It wasn't a good feeling, knowing someone had to die in order to get more clues to the killer's identity.

The best thing going on in Dax's life was his relationship with Mackenzie. He was more than ready to move it to the next level. They got along great, she made him laugh, and every time his phone dinged, letting him know he'd received a text, he hoped it was from Mack. She'd gotten in the habit of texting him throughout the day to tell him completely random stuff. He loved it.

He picked up his phone when he heard the signal letting him know he had an incoming text.

Would it be inappropriate if I throat punched my boss?

Dax laughed out loud, thankful no one was around to hear him. He typed out a quick response.

Yeah, most likely. And you probably shouldn't tell your Ranger boy-friend you are considering assault and battery.

Expecting Mack to respond right away, Dax was surprised when it was over an hour before he heard from her again.

Okay, you can't do that shit to me, Daxton.

Concerned, Dax texted back immediately.

What shit?
Tell me you're my boyfriend.

Dax smiled and typed out a quick response.

Wanna go steady?

She responded with,

Do you like me? Check Yes ___ or No___

Dax loved Mack's sense of humor. She never ceased to surprise him.

Where's the 'Hell Yes' box?

Dax's phone rang not too much later after his last text. "Hey, Mack."

"Don't you think it's too soon?"

"What's too soon?"

"For us to be labeling what we have as boyfriend and girlfriend?"

Dax got serious. He thought this might be coming. "Mack, we've been out every weekend since we met. I can't count the number of dates we've had, because we've had too many. One of which ended with both of us on your couch, me with one hand down your pants and the other under your bra. I've had my tongue practically down your throat every time we've seen each other and you've inspected every inch of my bare chest with your hands *and* your mouth. Did you seriously just ask me if it was too soon for us to be calling each other boyfriend and girlfriend?"

"Daxton!"

Dax smiled, knowing Mack was blushing. "Mack!"

"Okay, yeah, you have a point, but I just...we haven't...I don't know what this is."

"You're coming over tonight, yeah?"

"If you still want me to."

"You're coming over tonight. Bring a bag. You're staying the night." Dax could hear her breathing, but she didn't say anything. He eased his tone back a bit. "Mack, I want you to stay the night. If you're not ready for more than what we've done, no problem. I want to hold you in my arms as you sleep tonight, sweetheart. I've spent too many days in my shower thinking about you in my bed and jacking off. Sorry if that's too crude, but it's the truth. I want you in my arms. It's time."

"I sleep naked." Mackenzie blurted out the first thing that came to mind after his words.

"What?"

"I sleep naked. I always have. I don't like the feel of a shirt or pants on when I sleep. I don't sleep calmly. I toss and turn and my clothes always end up wrapped around me and I feel like I'm being strangled. I'd like to say I'll try to put something on, something sexy and lacy, but I can't, it's just not comfortable. I'm sorry. I know it's weird, but I've always been that way."

"Mack—"

"And it's weird that we haven't even slept together yet and I'm blurting this out, but I don't think I can spend the night. It'd be weird if I wasn't ready and you wanted me to sleep over and I took all my clothes off. It wouldn't be fair to you, I'd be leading you on or something, and I don't want to do that. I'm not a tease and I don't want you to think that I am."

"Mack, seriously, shut it, I—"

"And, you have a fourteen-pack. Seriously, you work out every morning and all I want to do in the mornings on the weekends is lay in bed until like ten. I hate working out, and I know I should, that would help my love handles, but I get all sweaty and gross then I'm sore and I'd rather keep my body the way it is—a bit big, but okay— than work out and hate every second of it."

"Mack, swear to God, shut up and listen to me."

Dax's words seemed to echo across the connection. Mackenzie swallowed and bit her lip. "Sorry, Daxton. Shit. Sorry…go ahead."

"I'm not sure even where to start after all that, but here goes. I wasn't kidding when I told you I jacked off to the thought of you. I have and I do. I wanted you the second my tongue touched yours in your apartment that first day. Your nipples got hard against your shirt and I looked down at your tits and got an erection. I'm forty-six, Mack, I don't spontaneously get hard anymore. But looking at you? Thinking about easing into your hot folds? Yeah, I'm hard right now just talking about it. Mack, I love your body. It's not perfect, but whose is? You know what? I hate my legs. Seriously, my abs and arms are good, but my legs have always been too skinny. I can't bulk them up no matter what I do. I'm telling you this so you know that we all have hang-ups about our bodies."

Dax took a deep breath and pushed hard on his erection. Fuck, he was hornier than he could remember being in a long time.

"I wish you could see how hard I am listening to you talk about how you sleep nude. Fuck, woman. Thinking about you spread out on my sheets, naked as the day you were born, you have no idea what that visual is doing to me. I swear to Christ, if you aren't ready, I'll be as good as a choirboy. You aren't a tease. You're about as far from a tease as any woman I've ever met. You say exactly what you're thinking all the time. You let it all hang out. I never have to guess what you're thinking. That's my favorite thing about you. Seriously. So please, come over tonight. Stay the night. Sleep naked in my bed, in my arms. If we make love, we make love. If not, it's okay. We'll get there when we're both ready and not a moment before."

Dax waited a beat and when Mackenzie didn't respond, he said, "Mack?"

"My family wants to meet you."

Dax laughed again. "See? You don't hold anything back. And I want to meet them too, sweetheart."

"But it's weird. My mom called last night and browbeat me for twenty minutes until I agreed to bring you over next week for dinner."

"Okay. That sounds good." Dax let Mack talk, let her work through his words at her own speed.

"My mom likes flowers; you'll have to get her some. Don't let Mark and Matthew badger you into saying anything you'll regret later."

"No one bullies me into saying anything I don't mean, Mack. No one."

She finally worked herself back around to his earlier words. "I want you to touch me. I want you inside me, Daxton. I've dreamed about it too. My vibrator has had more action since we've been seeing each other than it's ever had before…and I'm not ashamed to admit that's saying something. I lie in bed naked at night wishing you were next to me, but not knowing how to make that happen. If I asked you to stay, I'd feel like a slut. Hell, not a slut, it's not like I put out…at all…but it'd be weird. But I swear, just about every night I get myself off thinking about you."

Dax sighed in relief. He'd gotten what he wanted. Loving the thought that she'd gotten herself off while thinking about him, but knowing he couldn't go down that road while he was working, he changed the subject. "You want me to pick you up tonight, or will you meet me at my place?"

"Will you pick me up?"

"Of course. I'll be there around five thirty. Will that give you enough time to get home and get ready after work?"

"Yeah."

"Okay, I'll see you then. And Mack…no pressure. Okay?"

"No pressure. I'll see you later, Daxton."

"Later, sweetheart." Dax hung up the phone and smiled, not knowing how he'd make it through the rest of the day. It was bad enough he woke up with a hard-on every morning, but he didn't want to walk around the Ranger Station as he was right now.

Dax put his head back on his office chair and tried to think about something other than Mack naked in his bed.

Chapter Nine

MACKENZIE SHIFTED NERVOUSLY and turned to face Daxton. "Thanks for dinner. It was delicious."

"You're welcome. You're easy to cook for. You eat anything I make, no matter how awful it is."

"That's not true. I didn't eat the rolls you made that one night."

"That's because they were completely black on the bottom and I almost burned the place down."

Mackenzie smiled at Daxton and changed the subject abruptly. "I'm nervous."

Dax leaned over and hauled Mack into him. He leaned back against the sofa and cradled her in his arms. "I know you are. You have no reason to be, but I know you are."

"I'm not fifteen. I've done this before. I know how it all works, but I'm still nervous."

"It's our first time, Mack, I'm nervous too."

"You are?"

"Yeah."

"You shouldn't be."

Dax smiled. He knew she'd say that. "One time in my early twenties, I thought I was all that and a bag of chips. I sauntered into the bedroom, completely naked, ready to impress my girlfriend, and she took one look at me and started laughing hysterically. I had no idea what she was laughing at. She couldn't even breathe, she was laughing so hard. I lost my erection and went back into the bathroom to put my pants back on, humiliated. It wasn't until I was removing the condom that I'd put on in preparation of our night that I noticed it was glowing. I'd accidentally grabbed one of the novelty condoms I'd picked up at a bar earlier that month. I'd walked into the bedroom ready to impress her, with a glow stick attached to my body. No wonder she laughed."

Mackenzie giggled at the picture Dax put in her head. "It still wasn't nice of her to laugh at you like that."

"I deserved it."

"Even so, I wouldn't laugh at you."

Dax pulled Mack closer into his body and leaned down so he could speak right into her ear. "One of the things I like most about you, Mack, is your ability to laugh at yourself and at me when I deserve it. My job isn't the happiest in the world, but I've found myself smiling more at random times of the day when I think about something you've said or done than I ever have before. So laugh at me, laugh at *us*. It's all good. Because I know you. I know you're not laughing *at* me. Even if I do something stupid, you're still not laughing maliciously *at* me. You'll laugh, then share the joke with me so I can laugh too."

"Glow-in-the-dark condom? Got any more of those?"

"Sorry, I'm fresh out…but I do have some of the regular ones."

"Thank you."

"For what?"

"For not making this weird. For bringing up the subject of condoms so I don't have to. For wanting me. Just…for all of it."

"Mack, we're not teenagers anymore, birth control isn't something to be embarrassed about. I don't know about you, but I'm not sure I want to have kids this late in life. I'm not ready to say 'never' just yet, but we both know it's too early to even have that conversation together."

"I'm on the pill. I started it when I was sixteen and my mom dragged me down to her doctor and told him to 'get me started.' It was embarrassing for both of us, but it was the right thing to do. I've never gone off them. I don't think we'll have to worry about babies."

"That's good, sweetheart. But I'm still going to use protection for our peace of mind."

"I haven't slept with anyone in three years."

Dax watched as Mack's blush went from her ears down into her shirt. He moved one of his hands to her stomach and under her shirt until it rested on her bare skin.

"Three years?"

"Yeah. At first I was just busy. I didn't really think about it much. I had my…toys…and wasn't interested in men too much anyway. Then when I did get interested again, I couldn't find anyone who fit the bill. I mean, I know I'm getting older and my prime time is ticking away, but I couldn't find the energy that was required to put into any kind of relationship. It all seemed so pointless anyway."

"Then you met me."

"Then I met you." Mackenzie agreed softly.

Dax moved his hand even farther up under her shirt until it rested directly on her breast. He ran his thumb rhythmically over the side of her soft mound over and over until he felt her nipple come to life under his hand.

"I'm clean, Daxton. I'd tell you if I wasn't."

"I know you would, Mack. I'm clean too, but it hasn't been three years for me. I'll wait until I can get in to a see a doctor to make sure. Believe me, there's nothing I want more than to get inside you bare. I've only had sex without a condom a handful of times, but somehow I know with you, it'll be nothing like my other experiences. I can't wait to fill you up with my come and watch it slide out of your body when I pull out."

Silence surrounded them for a while, until Mackenzie broke it.

"Okay, I'm just going to throw this out there and you can do with it what you want…I'm not that good at sex."

Dax's hand at her breast stopped moving, and Mackenzie hurried on. "I mean, I can do the basics, but I've never been able to orgasm very quickly or easily, and that's irritated men in the past. Usually, I end up getting the guy off and then worrying about myself later. Or I'd be with a guy who thought he could 'get me past my issues' and he'd be all cocky and think that he could bring me to orgasm without any problem. Then when he couldn't, it somehow became my fault…so when I told you I was nervous earlier it wasn't just because this will be our first time. It's because I know I'm not good at it, and I want you to enjoy it, enjoy *me*, more than I've ever wanted to please anyone before in my life. But I'm scared you'll be disappointed."

Dax moved before Mackenzie could figure out what he was doing. She was on her back under him as he pressed his hips into hers. His head was higher than hers since their hips were lined up, and Mackenzie had to tilt hers back to see him.

"I have no doubt we'll be good at this together, sweetheart. No pressure. Seriously. If you can't orgasm with me, we'll experiment with your toys. We'll get you off first, then me. Or I'll go first, then take care of you. It's not a contest. I hope like hell I can watch you explode in my arms, but if not, we'll figure it out together. What do you fantasize about?"

"Huh?"

"Fantasize, Mack. What are your fantasies? What do you think about when you're using your vibrator?"

Mackenzie looked anywhere but at Daxton. She shouldn't be embarrassed. Sex was a normal thing, a healthy thing, but it was still awkward.

Dax put his hands on Mack's waist and slowly brought them upward, taking her shirt with it. "Arms up." She immediately moved, allowing him to tug her shirt off over her head. Dax looked down and put his hands on her breasts, caressing and squeezing as he spoke.

"What positions have you made love in? Did one position feel better than another? What about erotic pain? Has anyone pinched your nipples as they were pleasuring you? Have you tried anal play? Some people are more sensitive than others back there and it can bring a lot of pleasure if done right. Do you like to tell your lover what to do or have him tell you what to do?"

"Are you going to let me answer any of those questions or are you going to keep firing them at me all night?"

"Sorry," Dax said with a sheepish grin. "Just thinking about doing those things with you made me lose my mind for a moment, Please, carry on."

"If I can remember what you asked correctly…doggy and missionary, no, don't know, no, no, and the latter not the former."

Dax smiled down at Mack and pulled her bra down under her breasts. Without looking away from her face, he took both nipples in his hands and pinched lightly until Mack squirmed under him. "Do you like that, sweetheart?" At her nod, Dax let go, rubbed his palms over her nipples, then took them between his fingers again, pinching harder than he had before, until Mackenzie arched into him, moaning and digging her fingernails into his biceps. "I'm not into pain myself, but there's something to be said for a little bit of…discomfort to make you concentrate on the pleasure."

Mackenzie's hands moved up his arms to grip Daxton's wrists. She wasn't stopping him, but she had to hold on to something. "Daxton…"

Dax's gaze left Mack's for the first time and looked down at his hands. "I love the way you say my name, and fuck, you are beautiful. Seriously. Look at these beauties. Your nipples are red and standing straight up, begging for my touch. Your breasts are soft and fleshy and I can't wait to hold them together as I thrust between them. I can feel you squirming under me, are you wet, Mack? Does this feel good?"

"You know it does."

"You aren't going to have any problem getting off with me, sweetheart. I'm not being arrogant like the other men you've been with. If I can make you squirm with just my hands on your nipples, I can make you come. I promise you that." Dax let go of her breasts, leaving her bra where it was, pushing up her mounds. He stood up and held his hand out. "Come on. It's time."

Mackenzie swung her legs to the side and let Daxton help her up.

"Come up here." Dax held Mack by the waist and urged her to jump up into him. She didn't hesitate and hopped up and wrapped her legs around his waist. Her naked breasts were sensitive and she squirmed against him as they rubbed his shirt as he stalked out of the TV room.

Dax walked with one hand under Mackenzie's ass and the other holding her at the small of her back. When he got to his bedroom, he put her down by the bed and said simply, "Strip."

Dax could tell Mack was unsure, but she immediately put her hands behind her back and unhooked her bra, letting it fall to the ground. Her hands then moved to her pants and undid the button and unzipped them. Without breaking eye contact with Dax, she pushed until they fell to a heap on the floor and she stepped out of them. Mackenzie put her hands to the sides of her panties and Dax took a step toward her.

"Let me."

Mackenzie's hands froze and she pulled them away from the cotton at her hips.

Dax put his own hands where hers had just been, but he hesitated, saying in a low, reverent voice, "Fuck, sweetheart, you are my ideal woman. Look at you. Lush and curvy. Breasts that overflow when I hold them. Soft skin that pebbles under my hand." Dax ran his hand up Mackenzie's side then back down, proving his words true as goose bumps rose on her skin everywhere he touched. "No matter what happens tonight, I'll always remember this moment. You, standing naked next to my bed for the first time, giving yourself to me so unselfishly, even though you're unsure."

Dax eased his hands under the cotton on the sides of her hips and slowly pushed down, not taking his eyes away from her for a second. Suddenly dropping to his knees in front of her, Dax held her in place with one hand while he pushed her underwear to the floor with the other.

Mackenzie took a deep breath. She didn't mind being naked usually, but Daxton's gaze was intense and she could feel herself growing wetter. She jerked in surprise when Daxton leaned forward and put his forehead on her belly. She looked down. All Mackenzie could see was the top of Daxton's head. His nose was...right there. She moved to step back and Daxton's hands tightened on her hips.

"Don't move, sweetheart," he mumbled into her flesh. "I'm soaking up the moment here."

"Daxton—"

"Shhhhh."

Mackenzie giggled, she couldn't help it. "Okay, don't mind me. I'll just wait for you to finish...soaking."

Her giggle cut off when Mackenzie felt Daxton's fingers graze over the hair between her legs. "Holy mother of..."

"You trim yourself down here."

It wasn't a question, but Mackenzie answered anyway. "Yeah."

His hand moved lower.

"And you shave down here. I can feel how wet you are. You're coating my hand with your juices. Fuck, Mack." Dax lifted his head and looked up at Mackenzie. "I want to touch you. I want you to come for me, but even if you don't, I can make sure it feels good for you, so no pressure. I want to learn you from the inside out. Touch you. Feel you. Taste you. But I won't if it doesn't feel right or you don't want it. We'll climb in the bed and simply hold each other all night. Your choice, Mack."

"I want you."

"Good."

"Can you please get naked now?"

Dax laughed and stood up slowly, running his hands up her sides as he did. Mackenzie could feel her own wetness being spread on her skin as his hand made its way upward. It should've been weird, but instead it was sexy as hell. She *felt* sexy as hell.

"Get on the bed, Mack. Tonight we'll probably keep it simple, but I plan on introducing you to a whole new world of positions later."

Mackenzie smiled as she sat on the mattress and then scooted back until she was in the middle of the bed. She watched as Daxton tore off his shirt, not even trying to prolong it or make his striptease sexy. He undid his belt and didn't bother taking it out of his pants. He unzipped and unbuttoned and suddenly he was standing there completely nude. He'd pushed his boxers down with his pants. He stepped out of the material and, without taking his eyes off of Mackenzie, lifted one leg, and took off one of his socks. He did the same to the other foot and suddenly he was on the bed with Mack.

"I can tell you with one hundred percent honesty that I have absolutely no desire to laugh right now."

Dax smiled and crawled up Mack's body until he was hunched over her on his hands and knees. "Like what you see, sweetheart?"

"Is the Pope Catholic?"

A laugh burst out of Dax. "Fuck, I love that you can make a joke right now. Lie back. Let me make you feel good."

Mackenzie did as Daxton asked. She lay back and pulled a pillow under her head. She knew she'd never forget this moment. She wanted to watch every second.

"Put your hands over your head and don't move them. This is my job right now. I don't need your help. You don't have to do anything, or think about anything but how I'm making you feel. Relax, sweetheart." Dax nodded in approval as Mack slowly raised her arms and put them over her head. He bent his head and nipped the side of Mack's breast. Running his hands over her body as he continued to move downward, he kept up a running commentary.

"Your body was meant for my loving." He squeezed both breasts in his hands as he nuzzled her belly button. "I can hold on and feel *you*, no matter what my mouth may be doing." Dax moved his hands down to her belly, caressing and massaging. "You aren't skinny, you're right, but this is so fucking sexy. I love your body. You're so soft."

Then finally, Dax's mouth was over her folds.

His thumbs moved down to hold the lips of her sex open. He blew lightly against her skin. "Fuck. Seriously. You are beautiful here. Your skin is bright pink and I can see your juices glistening, beckoning me. You're wet for me, Mack. *Me*." Dax lowered his head and nuzzled against her inner thigh. Mackenzie heard him inhale loudly.

"And your smell. Fucking divine." One of his thumbs moved until it was rubbing against her bundle of nervous.

"Oh my God, Daxton. What are you…yeah…right there."

"Here, Mack? Right here?" Dax pushed down harder and laughed as she squirmed under him. He eased a finger on his other hand into her tight sheath. "Or here?"

"Daxton!" Mackenzie couldn't get any other words out. She inhaled as Daxton's finger brushed against something inside that sent shockwaves shooting up through her body. "Oh my God."

"Yeah, Mack. That's it. Relax, feel it. Just enjoy my touch." Dax continued, taking his time, learning Mackenzie's body. He let her get used to him, his touch. He'd stroke her clit, then move his hand and caress her inner thigh. He used his mouth to suck and lick. Mackenzie writhed on the bed beneath him and Dax had never felt so masculine. He hadn't been completely sure he'd be able to make her come; hell, she knew her body better than he did, but he'd hoped. Now, running his hands and tongue over her folds, he knew she was on the verge of a monster orgasm.

Dax eased his finger back inside her sheath, loving how hot and wet she was. He curled his finger and brushed against the front wall of her body, stroking and fingering the bundle of nerves inside her body.

"Daxton...I—"

"That's it, baby. That's it. Let it happen. Right there...just a little more."

Mackenzie wasn't hearing Daxton anymore. All she heard was a ringing in her ears. She pushed her hips up and down, jerking in Daxton's grasp. She had no control over her own body. Mackenzie didn't even realize when her hands came down from over her head and grasped Daxton's shoulders hard enough to leave ten little indentations with her fingernails.

Just when Mackenzie didn't think she was going to make it over the edge, Daxton lowered his head and sucked her clit into his mouth as his free hand went up and pinched her nipple tightly. She'd never had a man handle her as roughly as Dax was, but the slight pain, combined with the fast flicking of his tongue on her clit and his finger thrusting in and out of her body, was all it took.

"Oh my God, Daxton! I'm coming!" Mackenzie gasped in disbelief. She threw her head back and whimpered as her first orgasm at a man's hand coursed through her body. She thrust up again and again, clenching on Dax's finger as she went over the edge. It seemed to last forever and Mackenzie couldn't stop her body from shuddering with aftershocks as Daxton removed his hand and stroked her body lightly.

When Mackenzie came back to herself, she found Daxton's face right next to hers. He'd pulled himself up and was resting his head on his right hand and his left was running up and down her body, stroking and caressing as he went.

"Welcome back."

Mackenzie could feel herself blushing. "Hi."

"Forgive me if I'm remembering wrong, but I thought you said you weren't good at this sex thing." Dax smiled as he said it.

Mackenzie moved her hand and stroked over Daxton's belly, caressing his hard abs, much as he was doing to her own body. "That's the first time... thefirsttimeamanhasmademecome." Her words were said quickly so they all bunched together. Then she continued in a more normal voice, not giving Dax time to say anything. "I know, it's ridiculous, right? I'm thirty-seven years old, you'd think at some point in the last, oh, twenty years or so someone would've gotten lucky and done just the right thing, touched just the right spot at the right time, but it never happened. Don't get me wrong, I've gotten myself off while I've...uh...you know, but a guy...all on his own? No. I've never had an orgasm with a guy where I didn't have to help."

Dax leaned in and whispered in her ear a bit cockily, "It won't be the last."

Mackenzie smiled up at him. "Can I touch you?"

"Nothing would please me more, sweetheart." Dax rolled over until he was on his back and put his hands behind his head as if he was lying down for a nap. Mackenzie sat up, got on her knees next to him, and looked down in awe.

"Whoa, Daxton. I know I've seen this before, but hiding this under your uniform has to be a crime. You really do have a fucking fourteen-pack. When I try to keep you from getting up to work out, just ignore me, will ya?"

Daxton chuckled. "Glad you approve, sweetheart."

"Oh, I approve all right."

Mackenzie ran her eyes up and down his body, stopping at his shoulders. She ran a finger over the small puncture wounds on the tops of his shoulders. "Did I do that?"

Dax moved one hand from under his head and caught Mackenzie's hand in his. He brought it up to his mouth and kissed her palm, running his tongue over the long line after kissing it. "Yeah, and it felt awesome. Remember when I talked about erotic pain? Yeah, I wasn't feeling anything. I was too busy enjoying the hell out of watching you come."

He put his hand back under his head and lifted his chin to her. "Go on, make yourself at home."

Mackenzie did what Daxton asked. She started by leaning over and licking each of the ten little wounds she'd put in his skin with her nails. Then she moved her head lower and sucked on Daxton's nipples, while running her hands up and down his body. Slowly, enjoying the feel of his stomach muscles jerking under her ministrations, Mack shifted to his erection. He was long and thick, and Mackenzie could see fluid shining on the head.

Maneuvering between his legs, and grunting in approval when he widened his stance so she could kneel between them, Mackenzie gripped his balls with one hand and used the other to caress his shaft. She spread his wetness over her palm, making it easier to glide up and down.

Not able to stop herself, Mackenzie leaned over and licked the head of his shaft so she could taste him. She looked up from between Daxton's legs to see him staring down at her with an intense look on his face.

"I want to be inside you, Mack. I can't wait much longer."

"But I'm just getting started," Mackenzie pouted.

"Oh, you'll have your chance, it just isn't right now."

"Condom?"

Dax indicated with his head to the table next to the bed. "There."

Mackenzie had to let go of Daxton and crawl up to where he'd gestured. When she leaned over him, Daxton guided her nipple into his mouth with a hand and sucked hard, making Mackenzie whimper in need.

"Let go, Daxton. I need you too."

Dax let go of Mack's breast with a small popping sound and allowed her to reach forward for the condom on the side table.

She eased back with the packet in her hand.

"Put it on me," Dax growled.

Mackenzie nodded and without losing eye contact, she put the packet up to her mouth and ripped it open with her teeth. She finally had to look down so she could see what she was doing. She pinched the tip, eased the condom over Daxton's erection, and smoothed it into place.

Before Mackenzie could think about what to do next, Daxton had her flipped over and she was on her back looking up at him. He paused above her, not saying anything, not moving, just watching her intently.

"Please, Daxton." Mack tried desperately to pull him down to her, to rub against him. She wanted him inside. Now.

He moved slowly, taking himself in his hand and pressing against her wet heat, easing himself into her tight sheath inch by inch. He didn't stop until he was all the way inside, then he lowered down until they were touching from toes to chest. "Perfect."

Mackenzie closed her eyes briefly against the small bite of pain she'd felt as Daxton entered her. It'd been a while and her body needed to adjust to having a man inside again. When the pain faded, she opened her eyes and held on tightly to Daxton's biceps as he slowly withdrew from her body, then pushed back in. He held her eyes the entire time. He slowly increased his speed as he moved in and out of Mack's body.

"You feel good, Daxton. I love how you fill me up. Faster. Go faster."

"You'll take it how I give it, Mack. You like this?"

"Yeah."

"You're hot and slick around me. I can feel your heat through the condom. As much as I love how you feel, I can't wait to get inside you without anything between us. Ah…you like that, don't you? I could feel you clench around me."

"Yeah, I want to feel you. Just you."

"You'll get me, babe. I'll pump you so full, as soon as I pull away from your tight body, our juices will leak out. When I take you standing up, you'll feel us dripping down your leg."

"Oh God, Daxton. That's so uh…realistic and slightly gross, but honestly, I can't wait."

Dax sped up his thrusts until he was pounding into her.

Mackenzie watched as Daxton closed his eyes and his muscles tightened. He was on the verge of losing it. "Yeah, that's it, Daxton, come for me. Don't wait for me. I want to watch you come." Mack tightened her inner muscles as hard as she could, squeezing him from the inside out. "Do it. Fuck me. You feel so good."

At her words, Dax couldn't hold back anymore. He reached down and pulled up Mackenzie's thighs until he could hook his elbows under her knees. "Hold on, Mack. Let me know if I hurt you."

"You won't hurt me, Daxton. Do it. I love when you pound into me. The friction of your skin against mine feels awesome."

Dax let go of his iron control, using Mack's permission to fuck her like he'd dreamed of for so long. He hammered into her, and when he felt Mackenzie pinch his nipples, he couldn't hold his orgasm in any longer. He ground into her, holding himself inside as tightly as he could and let go. His hips undulated against her once, twice, and then three times. He groaned loud and long.

Finally, feeling empty, he eased down next to Mack, holding her to him so he didn't slip out. He hiked her leg up over his lap, keeping their connection intact. "Holy shit. You killed me."

Mackenzie giggled, and Dax loved the sound. "I think that was my line."

"Nope, definitely mine." Dax picked up his head and looked Mackenzie in the eyes. "Just so you know. I'm going to make it my mission in life to make you come with me."

"Daxton, I told you—"

Dax put his finger over Mack's lips to stop her words. "Shhh, I know what you said, and I don't believe it for a second. Anyone who came as hard as you did with just my finger and the brief touch of my mouth to your clit...can orgasm with penetration. We just need to keep practicing. And I'll enjoy the hell out of that practice in the meantime."

"You're crazy. We're too old for this shit."

"No, we're not. I don't feel too old and I'm nine years older than you. So if I can do it, you can too."

"Whatever." Mackenzie's words were muffled against his chest.

"Let me take care of this condom, and we can get some sleep."

Mackenzie watched as Daxton rolled away from her and went into the bathroom. He came out not long after.

"You need to use the bathroom?"

"No, I think I'm good."

"Okay, lift up so I can get you under the sheet."

Mackenzie lifted up one butt cheek enough so Daxton could pull the sheet out from under her. He climbed in next to her and hauled her into his arms.

"You don't have to—"

"Shut it. I want to. I'll go absolutely insane if I can't hold you in my arms."

Mackenzie didn't say a word, but dipped her chin and fit her head under Daxton's chin. She put her arm around his chest. One leg came up and wrapped itself around his thigh.

"Comfy?"

Mackenzie could hear the laughter in Daxton's voice, but didn't care.

"Yeah, extremely."

"Go to sleep, sweetheart."

"I don't have to get up early tomorrow, do I? It's Saturday. It's against my religion to get out of bed before nine on the weekend."

"You don't have to get up early, Mack. Just sleep."

"Okay. Thank you for making this easy and not weird."

"You're welcome."

Mackenzie fell asleep almost immediately. Dax stayed awake a bit longer, enjoying the soft breaths Mack made as she slept and wondering how in the hell he'd gotten so lucky.

Chapter Ten

TWO WEEKS AFTER Mackenzie had spent the night for the first time, Dax knew for sure she was the woman for him. They'd settled into a regular routine. They'd leave together each morning for work, and over the course of the day figure out whose place they'd spend the night at, then they'd meet there after work. They'd make or go out for dinner, then head to bed, making the most of their time together.

Dax had several sets of uniforms over at Mackenzie's apartment, just as she had plenty of work clothes to choose from at his. Not one night had gone by that they hadn't spent together, and Dax couldn't be happier.

Mackenzie was just as cute now as Dax had thought she was on their first date, perhaps more so. She was who she was and didn't have a devious bone in her body...something that was refreshing to Dax.

The day Mackenzie met TJ again was one of Dax's favorite memories. He'd taken Mack out to dinner, knowing TJ was going to meet them there. TJ slid into the booth across from them and Dax laughed until his stomach hurt at the look on Mack's face. She'd blushed a fiery red and stammered a bit before getting her wits about her.

"Daxton Chambers, I can't believe you didn't tell me Officer Rockwell would be here tonight!"

"TJ, babe. Call me TJ."

"TJ then. Am I allowed to thank you for not giving me a ticket?

Or is that bad cop karma and I'll end up getting six tickets in the next month as a result?"

TJ and Dax laughed. "You're welcome, and as long as you don't decide to be a speed demon or start stealing from the neighborhood grocery store, I think you're good."

"So does that mean I can drop your name—yours too, Daxton— and I can get out of any tickets in the future?"

"Mack, how many times had you been stopped before we pulled you over? Or since? I don't think you have anything to worry about. You usually drive like an old granny," Dax said, picking on Mackenzie.

"Shut up. Maybe I'll take up street racing now that my boyfriend is a Texas Ranger and I know not only an SAPD Officer, but a Highway Patrolman too!"

"I don't think so, sweetheart. If you get stopped you'll have to take your chances just like everyone else."

"Don't you guys have like some secret sticker I can put on my car that's like a 'get-out-of-a-ticket-free' card?"

"Sorry, Mackenzie, there's no such thing." TJ was smiling broadly, resting his elbows on the table.

"Well, poo. There should be one. I should get *something* out of dating a police officer!"

That night, Dax had reminded Mack what she was getting out of dating a police officer…him. He'd brought her to the edge of orgasm several times, pulling back right before she'd been about to explode. He'd gotten his test results back from the doctor the day before, and Dax couldn't tease her for long before he had to be inside her. Having pity on her, he'd finally pushed her over the edge, loving how she shuddered and shook in his arms.

After she'd come apart, Dax had hauled her out of the bed and pushed her face down, leaning over the mattress. He'd taken her from behind as she moaned and thrashed on the covers. While she'd technically done it doggy style before, that had been completely different. They'd snuggled together afterwards and Dax didn't think either one of them had moved a muscle all night.

Dax looked over at Mack standing in his kitchen. It was Friday morning and they were about ready to head to work. Mackenzie was leaning on the counter in front of his toaster, gazing at the bagel within as if it would cook faster if she glared it into submission while it cooked.

Dax walked up behind her and pulled her into the front of his body.

"I'm on call this weekend again."

Mackenzie turned and put her arms around him as far as they'd go. "Okay. You want me to stay here, or are you coming to my place?"

Dax shook his head, loving how Mack didn't give him any grief for having to work on the weekend. Kelly had hated if he had an overnight shift when he'd worked at the El Paso Police Department, and had made his life miserable every time he came home from those shifts.

"Whatever you want, Mack."

She thought about it for a second, then finally said, "Okay, my place. I'll make dinner and put it in the fridge and if you're hungry when you get home, you can eat. You have clothes over there?"

"Yeah, I'm good."

"Okay then."

"Okay then."

"Just so you know, in case you were wondering. Sleeping alone, waiting for you to get home, sucks. I'm not complaining, just saying...I've gotten used to your warm body next to mine and I actually feel cold in my bed until you get home. I've never felt that way before. I even contemplated putting on a T-shirt the last time you worked late."

"You better not put anything on. I like you naked and waiting when I get to you."

"What if someone breaks in?"

"No one is breaking in. Make sure the doors are locked and you'll be fine."

Mackenzie smiled at Daxton. The first thing he'd done after the first time he'd spent the night was go to the hardware store and buy new locks to upgrade what she already had. She hadn't minded; she'd always rather be safe than sorry.

"Okay, Daxton. Can I ask you something?"

"Of course."

Mackenzie ignored the ding of the toaster indicating her bagel was ready and soldiered on. "I know you can't talk about your cases, but I worry about you. I know the crap you have to do sucks, and I don't want you to think I'm some wilting wallflower who can't take hearing some tough stuff from you every now and then. If you need to talk about a case or something that happened, I'm here for you. I think we're past the get-to-know-you stage where all we talk about is hearts and flowers."

"Hearts and flowers?" Dax smiled at Mack, she was so fucking adorable. He thought that about her about a thousand times a day.

"Yeah, hearts and fucking flowers. You know how I feel about my boss. She's a bitch. She doesn't care about anyone in the office and makes us do work over, just because she can. The other day she actually complained that I'd found a mistake in one of the spreadsheets she'd already checked over. She'd prefer the work she did be wrong, just so she didn't 'look bad' in front of her bosses. It's ridiculous. And you know about Mark and Matthew and how they drive me crazy. You know a million other things about me that aren't things people who are trying to impress each other know. I just want you to know you can share right back."

Dax turned with Mack in his arms and pulled her up until she was sitting on the island in the middle of the kitchen and they were face-to-face. He stepped into her and she spread her legs so he was right up in her space. He hauled her hips to the edge of the counter and held her against him. "I know I can share with you, Mack. I haven't done it, not because I don't trust you, or because I'm trying to hide anything…okay, that might be a lie. I don't *want* to tell you some of the shit I see and hear in my job because I like you just the way you are. You have a unique take on life and I don't want to see your light dim because of the shit that happens in my world. I like that you're naïve about the seedier side of life and my job."

"But you need to talk about it."

"And I do. I talk with Quint, and Cruz, and TJ, and other very good men and women who are in law enforcement. We have lunch together. We go to conferences together. We see each other in the field and in task-force meetings. I promise you, sweetheart, I'm not holding shit in that will make me lose it. I'm forty-six years old and have been in this job for a hell of a long time. If I hadn't learned to deal before now, I'd have had a heart attack. Okay?"

Dax watched as Mackenzie processed what he'd just told her. He loved that she never agreed with him just to shut him up. She'd been known to argue with him about something for hours on end, if she truly believed what she said or thought was the right way.

Mackenzie brought her hands up to the back of Daxton's neck and laced her fingers together. "Okay, I believe you. I don't know what's normal for a cop's girlfriend to know and not know. I'd never want you to think I wasn't interested in what you did for a living."

"I know it, sweetheart. Swear."

"Good. I have something else to tell you, since we're having this deep chat and all."

Dax smiled. "What's that?"

"Sunday we're going over to my mom's for lunch. I hope that's okay. She understands that you had to cancel both times we tried to arrange it before, after I told her you were a big bad Texas Ranger and you had to save the world. But mom's decided it's time. Hell, they decided it was time about a month ago, but they're not going to let us out of it for much longer. And to be honest, I'm glad we haven't been able to make it over there yet, I've been trying to make you so infatuated with me that no matter what they throw at you, you'll ignore it and not break up with me."

"Do they have any bodies buried in their backyards?"

"Daxton!"

Ignoring Mack's tone of outrage and smiling as he continued, Dax said, "No? Then relax, Mack. I know how families are. It'll be fine. You certainly don't have to try any harder to make me infatuated with me. I'm already there."

Ignoring his words that made her insides flutter, Mackenzie retorted, "Well, I appreciate that, however you haven't actually met my family yet and I don't want you to decide after tonight that I'm a loon and rather than deal with my crazy family after breaking up with me, you change your name and move out of the state.

Daxton laughed, and she told him she was only half-way kidding, "Daxton, you have no clue. I'm the only girl in our family. Now that dad's gone, Mark and Matthew won't care that you're forty-six and I'm in my upper thirties. They'll probably take you out back for a birds-and-the-bees chat. And mom will probably have the pastor there and he'll be ready to perform a wedding ceremony over tea and crackers. You have no idea how insane they are. I just wanted to warn you ahead of time."

Dax leaned in and moved one of his hands from Mackenzie's hip to her back and up to her neck. He held her still in his arms by tightening his hold. In a low, serious voice, without a trace of humor, he told her, "I wouldn't be opposed to a wedding."

"Holy shit, you did not just say that." Mackenzie could feel her heart beating a million miles an hour, she curled her hands and unconsciously dug her blunt nails into Daxton's neck.

"I said it. I'm not proposing, Mack. Not right now. But I sure as hell can see you in my future. I like you in my life, in my bed, in my space. I like it a lot. You're cute as all get out, we're more than matched in bed, and we're practically living together already. I'll meet your family this weekend, they'll like me, and I'll like them. I'm not sure either of us is ready for 'I love yous' yet, but it's coming, sweetheart."

"Daxton."

Dax waited for Mack to say something. When she didn't, he smiled at her. "Mackenzie."

"I…dammit. I don't want to go to my job and deal with the bitchface I work for. I don't want you to go and talk to scumsuckers. I want to barricade us in your room, get naked, and not leave for the rest of our lives."

"I think we'd get hungry eventually."

Mack smiled, glad the extreme-emotion sharing seemed to be over. "And stinky."

"And we'd eventually get kicked out because we couldn't pay the rent."

"And my family would come over wondering where we were."

"I'll miss you tonight, sweetheart. Stay safe for me. I'll come to you as soon as I can."

It looked as though the emotional part of the morning wasn't quite over yet. "I always miss you too, Daxton."

"Okay, I'm going then. I'll see you tonight. I have a new position I want us to try. I think you'll like it. I read about it in a book once and I think you're flexible enough. Sunday we'll go to your mom's house. Text me today and let me know how your day is going."

Shivering at the lustful look in his eyes, Mackenzie said simply, "I will. Bye, Daxton."

"Bye, Mack."

Dax kissed Mackenzie swiftly, knowing if he lingered, he might just get carried away and lock them in his bedroom as she suggested. He backed away, headed away from the temptation she offered, and out the front door.

Mackenzie hopped down off the counter, not smiling, and headed for the toaster. If she wasn't mistaken, Daxton had just told her he loved her…not in so many words, but he might as well have.

Finally, she smiled to herself as she dug the cream cheese out of the fridge. Daxton loved her. Holy shit. It was gonna be a good day.

DAX ROLLED HIS head and tried to work the kinks out of his neck. His morning chat with Mack notwithstanding, his day had not started out well. He'd arrived at work to find three letters addressed to him sitting on his desk with a note from the administrative assistant. She'd apologized and said the letters had been delayed in getting to him. She'd been on vacation for a week and a half and no one had bothered to hand the mail out to the appropriate Rangers in her absence.

He'd opened the first, and dropped it immediately seeing who had sent it. Dax had leaned over his desk, being careful not to touch the paper any more than he already had, read the extremely alarming words, and called the Major. It was from the Lone Star Reaper. This time the letter was addressed specifically to Dax. The thought didn't give him warm-fuzzies. While Dax didn't know if the other two letters were from the Reaper, he wasn't taking any chances.

Three hours later, he'd received a call from Quint and had been asked to come to a joint task-force meeting. Knowing he wouldn't like what he was about to find out, Dax braced himself.

The meeting included the Chief of Police at the SAPD, Quint, Cruz, the Major from his Ranger Company and a few other high-ranking officers.

"Dax, thanks for coming, and thanks for the quick response with those letters. They're being worked over now and preliminary thoughts are that we might have a partial print on one of them this time," the Major said.

"So all three were from the Reaper?" Dax asked.

"Yeah."

Silence fell over the room and Dax knew they weren't telling him something important. "What did the other letters say? Did he give the locations of more victims?"

"Yeah, we have three separate teams checking out the cemeteries he mentioned in the notes."

"Why did he change his M.O. now?" Dax wondered out loud. "He used to call in the body locations, but now he's writing me a letter like he's my fucking pen pal?"

"The Reaper is escalating his game and changed the rules in the middle," The Chief of Police said unnecessarily.

"Yeah," Dax agreed in a tight voice. "He's made it way more personal now. He sent these notes specifically to me," Dax said, stating the obvious.

Cruz ran his hand over his face, then up and over his short-cropped black hair. "It's more serious than that." Cruz shuffled through the piles of various reports and evidence sitting in front of him and handed over three sheets of photocopied paper. "I'm sorry, Dax."

Dax clenched his teeth. Fuck. He pulled the copies toward him and read the notes the Reaper had left. He'd already read the first one, but the others were just as horrifying.

Daxton Chambers, you might be a tough ol Ranger, but id like to see you catch me. You can find a present ive left you in Johnson cemetery. I thnk youll find her to your liking. 5'4, curvy and brunette. Sounds like just your type.

So, you decided to ignore my last letter. Fine. Maybe you wont ignore this one. Check out my latest beauty in White Oak cemetery. She fought valiantly, but in the end she succumbed just like all the others. I nicknamed her M&M.

The last note was the most chilling.

Fuck you Chambers. You think im joking? You think shes safe? Shes not. I hope youre enjoying fucking your new girlfriend. No one is safe from the Reaper. Do you know where Mackenzie is right this second? I wonder how long shed last in one of my coffins. Im sure shell be my favorite yet. Ive got big plans for your little cutie. In the meantime check Shadows End cemetery to see how that Mackenzie fared.

Dax stood up so abruptly the chair he'd been sitting in fell backward with a crash. He stalked over to the side of the room and punched the wall. Ignoring the pain in his fist, he leaned over, grabbed the windowsill with both hands, and panted, trying to control the need to beat the shit out of someone.

The fucker knew about Mackenzie. Had threatened her. Was choosing women who looked like Mack, who were even *named* Mackenzie. Dax felt sick. Knowing he was going to lose his breakfast, he strode over the trashcan in the corner of the room and threw up. He stayed crouched in front of the plastic container, hands on his thighs, using everything he'd learned in his training to regulate his breathing and get his equilibrium back.

He was a Texas Ranger. He didn't act like this. Then again, the woman he loved hadn't ever been threatened and targeted by a psychotic serial killer either.

He loved Mack. He'd been pretty sure of his feelings before, but thinking of this psycho getting his hands on her solidified it.

"When were the letters sent?" Dax's voice was low and brittle. He was proud his voice only cracked once. He stood up, and wiped his face on his sleeve and faced the other officers in the room, not embarrassed in the least by his break in control. He knew they all understood. He stalked over, grabbed a bottled water off of the conference table, and chugged half of it waiting on Quint's response.

"The last one was postmarked five days ago."

"Jesus fucking Christ." Dax said the words under his breath and pulled out his phone. He had to get ahold of Mack now. He couldn't wait for the meeting to be over. He had to reassure himself that she was at work and fine. He looked down and wanted to cry at the silly little texts she'd left him over the last couple of hours.

> Can we rewind and make a different decision? Bitchface is being extra bitchy today.
>
> Is it too late for me to join up and become a cop?
>
> Are you sure there are no secret stickers that will get me out of jail free?
>
> I just wanted to let you know I was thinking about you. Miss you.

Dax hit Mackenzie's name and brought the phone up to his ear, waiting for her to pick up. He turned his back to the room and stood next to the wall looking down at his feet.

"Hey Daxton! What's up?"

"I just wanted to call and see how you were doing."

"I'm good, except for you-know-who. But that's nothing new."

"Change of plans tonight, sweetheart."

"Yeah?"

Dax knew the way Mackenzie stretched out the word, she was thinking sexy thoughts, but he couldn't bring himself to banter with her as he usually would.

"Yeah, I still have to work late, but TJ is gonna pick you up from work and take you back to my place. He'll stay there with you until I get home." Dax hadn't asked TJ, but he knew he'd protect Mackenzie until Dax could get home, no questions asked.

"Is everything okay?" Mackenzie's voice was serious, and no longer teasing. She'd obviously picked up on the fact that something was seriously wrong.

"No. But it will be. Trust me, sweetheart. Okay?"

"With my life, Daxton. What about my car?"

"Leave it. It'll be fine. If we need to move it later, I'll get one of the other Rangers to help me out with it."

"Are you all right?"

Dax lowered his voice. "I'm okay, Mack."

"Swear?"

"I'm okay."

"You didn't swear."

"Mackenzie—"

"Okay. I'll stop. Just…be safe all right? I can't lose you."

"You aren't losing me." Dax didn't know what else to say to reassure her. He knew she was freaked out. She wasn't rambling on and on as she usually did. Dax knew it was his fault. "There's some shit going on at work, and unfortunately there could be some blowback on you and me. We've got it under control, but in the meantime I need you to be smart and safe. Okay, Mack? Don't be one of those 'too stupid to live' women you bitch about in those romances you read. Be safe. Be alert. Don't leave work for lunch or on breaks. Wait in your office for TJ to come inside for you. All right? Can you do that for me?"

"Yes." Mackenzie's answer was immediate and strong. "Blowback?"

"I'll explain tonight."

"All right, Daxton. I…fuck…okay here goes. Ready? Iloveyou." Her words were fast and jumbled together. "I've only loved one other boyfriend before in my life and that was when I was eight years old. He'd chase me around the playground, corner me, and kiss me. Then he'd run away again. He brought me bubble gum as presents and even let me have the Little Debbie oatmeal cream pie from his lunch one day. I told him I loved him and he freaked out. He never chased me again and made it a point to sit on the other side of the lunchroom after that. He moved away the next year and I never saw him again, but I've never told any guy that I've loved him since then.

"I don't know what's going on, but I want to make sure I tell you now. I'd hate for something to happen and not be able to tell you. Okay? You don't have to say it back, because I know you're stressed, I can hear it in your voice, and you're probably surrounded by a hundred other cops and shit and they're probably staring at you and you can't say anything anyway, cos it'd make you look like a wuss. So it's okay, but *you* stay safe. Don't do anything crazy, wear your bulletproof vest, even though it's hot and you don't like how you can't move that well with it on. I'll wait for TJ and won't do anything stupid. I swear."

Dax closed his eyes. Fuck, he loved this woman. How the hell she'd managed to make him smile when there was abso-fucking-lutely *nothing* to smile about was beyond him. "I love you too, Mack."

"You said it." Her words were whispered. "Are you alone?"

"Nope." Dax turned around and looked at the men around the table, all of whom were watching him curiously. None were hiding their eavesdropping. "There are about eight guys from four different agencies sitting here staring at me."

"Daxton—"

"I gotta go, sweetheart."

"Okay." Mackenzie was still whispering.

"I'll still be late tonight, but I'll be home. There's an extra T-shirt in my top drawer."

Dax smiled as Mack chuckled. "Guess I'm not sleeping naked tonight?"

"Not while TJ is there."

"Okay, Daxton. Love you. Be safe."

"Love you too. See you later. Bye." The words felt natural and right.

Dax clicked off the phone and shoved it back into his pocket. He strode to the table and grabbed his chair, setting it back on its feet. Sitting down, he looked around the room and asked gruffly, "What the hell are we doing to catch this asshole?"

The men around the table began strategizing. No way in hell would they allow the Reaper to get ahold of Dax's woman. She was one of them now. Period.

Chapter Eleven

————————◆————————

MACKENZIE LAY IN bed wide-awake. TJ had arrived to pick her up with about fifteen minutes left to go in the workday. He hadn't said much, just sat in her office waiting for her to be done. Mackenzie hastily finished up and didn't put up a fuss at all when TJ put his arm around her waist as he guided her to his patrol car.

It was obvious there was something terribly wrong, and Mackenzie didn't know what to do or say, so she did as TJ asked, and moved beside him without hesitation to his car. When they'd arrived at Daxton's apartment, TJ didn't waste any time, but guided her to the door, telling her to wait just inside the apartment as he entered and made sure it was clear before allowing her inside.

Mackenzie made spaghetti for dinner. It was quick and easy. TJ thanked her and they ate in relative silence. She really *really* wanted to know what was going on, but Mackenzie figured TJ probably wouldn't tell her.

They watched some silly reality show set in Australia with lots of extremely catty and bitchy women all fighting for the man to pass the time. Mackenzie had asked once if they could turn it to the news, and when TJ had refused, she knew whatever was happening was probably being talked about on the local news stations. She let it drop; preferring to hear what it was straight from Daxton.

Around nine o'clock, Mackenzie told TJ she was going to bed. He didn't say anything other than, "Sleep well." As if.

Mackenzie put on one of Daxton's Ranger T-shirts, as he'd requested, knowing she probably wouldn't be able to sleep nude again until whatever was happening was over, and huddled under the comforter waiting for Daxton to get home. She turned on her side and hugged the pillow he usually used to her chest, burying her nose into it, inhaling Daxton's comforting smell.

Two hours later, Mackenzie was still wide-awake, jumping at every sound she heard outside, when she heard TJ and Daxton talking to one another in the other room. She didn't move. She lay still, waiting for Daxton to come to her.

Mackenzie watched as the bedroom door opened quietly and saw Daxton enter the room. He didn't hesitate, but came straight to the bed as if he knew she wouldn't be asleep. He laid himself out on top of the covers and pulled Mackenzie into his arms, pillow and all.

Dax wrapped his arms around Mack with one hand at her nape and the other around her waist. He dipped his head and snuggled his nose into the crook of her neck. He sighed when he felt her arms snake up between them to come to rest around his shoulders. They were as close as they could be, and still be fully clothed.

"I'm sorry, Mack."

"Don't."

"But—"

"No. This isn't your fault. I don't know whose fault it is yet, but I know it's not yours. So don't apologize for something someone else is doing to us…whatever it is they're doing."

"If I wasn't a Ranger—"

Mackenzie lifted her head and tried to squint in the darkness at him. "Seriously, Daxton. Stop it. You *are* a Ranger. You're a fucking awesome Ranger. I love you because of the man you are. If you weren't a Ranger, we might not be together. I don't know what's going on yet, but the way I choose to look at it is that you've worked your entire life to get to this point. You've learned what you needed to learn, you know what you need to know to stop whatever it is. I believe in you. I love you."

"Fuck, sweetheart." Dax didn't say anything else, just held the most important thing in his life tightly in his arms. "I love you too." Dax's words were soft and heartfelt.

Mackenzie pulled back. "Did TJ go?"

"Yeah."

She pushed at Daxton. "Are you hungry?"

"No."

"All right. Go get ready for bed, I'll be right here waiting. You can tell me whatever you can or need to when you get back."

Dax took a deep breath, inhaling the unique smell that Mack always seemed to carry with her. It was sweet. Some sort of sugar smell. Vanilla? He didn't know, but he loved how it mixed with the natural essence of her skin. He forced himself to loosen his arms and roll out of bed. He quickly got ready in the bathroom and stripped off his pants and shirt on the way back to bed.

Dax left on his boxers for the first time since they'd started sleeping together. He'd noticed Mack had on his shirt, as he'd requested, but figured she felt as vulnerable as he did being completely nude...and she didn't even know what was going on.

He climbed under the covers and pulled the pillow out of Mack's arms. He turned her on her back and propped himself up next to her with his head resting on one hand and the other on her belly under the shirt she was wearing. He didn't beat around the bush.

"The Lone Star Reaper struck again. Three more bodies were found today."

"Oh, Daxton. That sucks."

"Yeah. He sent the notes to me, telling me where to find them."

"What?"

Dax continued, wanting to get the worst over with so they could talk through what their next steps were.

"He sent the notes to me personally. He inferred that he's been watching me. He knows about you, Mack. He mentioned you specifically in the notes, by name."

"Oh my God."

"It gets worse. Can you handle it, or do you want to wait until later?"

"Worse?" Mackenzie's voice was soft. Dax heard her take a deep breath. "I can handle it. Tell it all to me now, we'll deal together."

"His last two victims looked like you, and the last woman was named Mackenzie." Dax didn't pause to let her process his words, he kept going. "He fucked up though, Mack. We got prints this time. We're going to get him. He won't touch you." Dax knew he was stretching the truth a bit. Even with this guy's prints, if he hadn't been arrested and his prints weren't in the system, they wouldn't do any good, but he'd say just about anything right now to reassure Mack.

"O-o-okay, Daxton. Okay."

"You've got to be vigilant though, sweetheart. I'm afraid going to your mom's on Sunday is out. I don't know if he knows about your family, but I'd rather not involve them right now, or have us go there and have him somehow use them against you. I'd love for you to stay home from work for a while, but I don't know if that will be possible. If not, okay, but you'll have to do some basic things for me. Can you do that?"

"I can't stay home. There are like, three big projects coming up due. Nancy would flip her shit if I wasn't there to do them for her and for her to take credit for them."

"All right, can you listen to what I want you to do to stay safe then?"

"Of course. I don't want to be buried alive, Daxton. I'll do whatever you tell me to."

Dax stopped long enough to lean over and kiss the side of Mackenzie's head, then he leaned back. "I'll drop you off at work each morning, and either one of the guys or I will pick you up each night. I know you've only met TJ and Quint, but I swear to you that you can trust Cruz, Conor, and Hayden, and even the other Rangers, as much as you do me. I'll be sure to introduce you so you'll feel more comfortable around them. Don't leave the office, not even for a quick errand. That's going to be a pain in the ass, I know it, but it's important. I don't want him snatching you when you're in the grocery store or something."

"No problem. I can do that."

"You'll never be home alone. I want you to stay here. My place is more secure than yours. I'm assuming he knows where I live, but he definitely knows about you. We need to come up with a plan in case he does something crazy like set a fire or something."

"Set a fire? Holy shit. Daxton—"

"Yeah, I know, stay with me, baby…" Dax could feel how freaked Mack was because she was gripping his biceps so hard, he knew she'd leave marks.

"Okay. Okay, go on."

"If something happens and we have to leave the apartment because of a crisis, don't panic. Stick close to me, or whoever I have here to watch over you. Don't leave my side. If someone calls you and says I'm hurt or killed or whatever, do *not* rush off on your own. It'd be a ploy to get you away from whatever protection you've got. You text me every hour and let me know you're okay; even if I don't answer, know that I'm watching and waiting for your text."

"I'm scared. No, I'm fucking petrified."

"I know, and I'm so sorry. Do you know what I did when I first read the notes he'd sent me, threatening you?"

"What?"

"I threw up. Literally. I puked my guts out in front of a room full of cops. I'm scared for both of us, sweetheart."

"Oh, Daxton." Mackenzie took a deep breath. She had to get herself together. It was obvious Daxton had thought a lot about how to keep her safe, and he'd gone to great lengths to arrange everything. "I swear I won't be stupid. You said you got his prints. Why can't you just go pick him up if you know who it is?"

"Forensics doesn't work in real life like it does on television. It doesn't take an hour or two to get results back, unfortunately. It can take weeks. This case is taking precedence, so hopefully it won't take that long, but we have to wait. Fingerprints don't typically take as long as DNA samples, but the bad thing is that his prints might not be in the system. If he's never been arrested or had his prints taken for a job and put in the database, we won't know who he is."

"How long do you think this will go on?"

"I don't know, Mack. I simply don't know."

"Should I leave town? I mean, I can go on an extended vacation somewhere. Or something. I know I said I needed to be at work, but fuck it. I'd rather lose my job and be alive than get caught by this guy."

"I love you, Mack. I love that you're completely practical and haven't thrown a hissy fit over your job or having been thrown a curve ball. The man in me wants to agree and to ship you off to some far-flung, out-of-the-way cabin in the woods where you can be safe, but the Ranger inside knows that probably wouldn't help. This guy is crazy. He could just follow you and get ahold of you wherever you went. I'd rather you be here, with me, so I can keep you safe, than to send you off by yourself where he might be able to track you. Besides, it gives me a chance to hold you in my arms every night."

"I'd rather be in your arms every night as well."

"Okay, so one more thing."

"Oh God, something else?" Mackenzie took a deep breath. "Sorry, sorry...okay, go ahead."

"Fuck." Dax's voice was low and tortured, but he plunged ahead. "We need a code word. Something that, if said, via text or over the phone, will alert us to the fact that something's wrong. How about if you say 'I'm so clumsy' to me, I'll know you're in trouble and I'll do everything in my power to get to you. If you hear me say, 'I'm busy,' you'll know something is wrong on my end and you need to hunker down and get to safety, no matter what getting to safety means. You know I'm never too busy for you, Mack, so if I say it, or text it, you'll know it's our code word. Yeah?"

"Yeah."

Dax dropped his head and put his forehead against Mackenzie's. "We're going to make it through this. I can't have met you after all these years, only to lose you now."

"Damn straight."

Dax smiled, even though he didn't really feel like it.

"You really puked in front of all your friends?"

"Yeah, Mack. I couldn't handle him threatening you and it made me physically sick to my stomach."

"I've never had someone throw up over me before. I mean, not because they were worried about me. I had a guy throw up *on* me before though. I was in college at a party and I was sitting next to this guy, minding my own business, and he didn't say anything just leaned over and, *buulllahh*, his dinner and most of the alcohol he'd drank in the last hour, was in my lap. Seriously, it was gross, and he didn't even know me. My brothers have been worried about me before. Once when I was on a trip with some friends to Amistad National Recreation Area west of San Antonio, the group decided they wanted to go to Cuidad Acuna to shop and my brothers about lost it. They were calling and texting me, but I'd turned my phone off, because, hello, I was in Mexico, and international rates are so expensive, and when I finally got back across the border I had to endure them yelling at me for hours...okay, well what seemed like hours. But no one, in my entire life, has been so worried about me that they actually threw up."

Dax took a breath to respond, but Mackenzie put her finger over his lips.

"As much as I like the sentiment behind you losing your lunch, I don't like it. Don't do it again, Daxton."

Dax loved that, even freaked and scared, Mack could still lapse into her cute-as-hell ramblings when it'd really only take a sentence or two to say the same thing. "I can't say I liked it much either, sweetheart. But I'll tell you this. I'll always worry about you. Every moment you're not in my arms, I worry. I'll worry about a short trip to the store, or a simple walk to the mailboxes because I've seen too much shit in my life. I'll try to curb it, but you should know I'm going to be über-protective. Probably annoyingly so."

"You know what? Before today, I probably *would* have been annoyed. But not now. I know you have reasons to be. So I'll deal."

"I love you, Mack."

"I love you too."

"Whatever happens, know I'll do whatever I have to, to keep you safe."

"I know you will."

As the night lengthened, they held each other tight. Mackenzie finally fell asleep a couple hours later. Dax didn't sleep until the sky started brightening with the morning sun.

Chapter Twelve

MACKENZIE HAD A hard time concentrating on the spreadsheet in front of her. It'd been a long week and a half since the Lone Star Reaper had basically declared her his next victim. She'd spent most of that time scared to death, but trying not to show it. Daxton had enough stress on his plate, so she tried to hide her fears as much as she could. Mackenzie figured he knew she was scared, but was allowing her to have her delusion that she was hiding it from him.

He'd done just what he said he would. He'd dropped her off at work every morning and he, or one of his law enforcement friends, picked her up every day. Laine had freaked when Mackenzie had told her what had been going on. She'd met Daxton several times, but let Mack know in no uncertain terms how she felt about the fact that because of Dax's job, her friend had been targeted by a serial killer.

Mackenzie couldn't get pissed at Laine. If Laine had called Mack to tell her that her new boyfriend's job was dangerous and someone had threatened her life, Mack knew she'd be beyond worried about Laine as well. All Mack could do was try to reassure her friend that she was being careful and not taking any chances.

Mackenzie had watched the news...once. It was enough to wake her up in the middle of the night with a horrendous nightmare. She hadn't tried to watch it again and hadn't asked Daxton anything about the case since then either. Mackenzie knew he'd tell her if the threat was gone...or if it'd gotten worse.

The newscaster had droned on about the profile the FBI had

done on the killer and warned the viewers to be careful and safe. Then they'd abruptly shown pictures of the latest victims. Three women; all short and overweight, all brown-haired. It was their names that had gotten to Mackenzie the most. The second woman's name was Monica Miller, first and last names starting with an M, just like hers. However, it was the last woman's name that sent chills down her body. Mackenzie McMillian.

It hadn't really hit home to Mack that she was the target of a serial killer until she'd seen those names on the screen, next to pictures of women who had the same body type and look as her; that she could actually be in extreme danger. She'd believed Daxton, but hearing him say it and seeing it were two completely different things.

After she'd woken up shaking and crying and completely freaked-out, Daxton had asked her not to watch the news unless he was either there with her, or until everything had played itself out. Mackenzie had no trouble agreeing immediately. Things were a bit too real for her right now and she didn't know if she ever wanted to watch the local news again.

Mackenzie picked up her phone and sent a short text to Daxton, letting him know all was well. She'd done just what he'd asked, to the letter. She hadn't been anywhere other than work and Daxton's apartment. When they'd needed groceries, Daxton had stopped on his way home from work one night. Mackenzie knew she should feel suffocated, but if she was honest with herself, she didn't.

The phone on her desk rang and Mackenzie picked it up after only one ring.

"Hello?"

"Hey, Mack, it's me."

"Hey, Daxton. How are you?" The simple phrase had a whole new meaning now; one Mackenzie knew she'd never take for granted again.

"Good. Everything's good. You?"

"Same. No news?"

"No new news on the case, sorry. But I *do* have some news I think you'll like."

"I could use some good news, Daxton. Sock it to me."

"I'm getting off early today. Thought you might want to go on a mini-vacation with me."

"Yes."

"You don't know where we're going."

"I don't care where, as long as you're with me."

Dax's voice gentled. "Fuck, woman. How'd I get so lucky?"

"Where are you taking me, Daxton? Tahiti? Fiji? The Swiss Alps?"

"Nothing so grand, I'm afraid, but I'll put those on our bucket list. How about Austin?"

"Austin? What's in Austin?"

"I thought we'd take a long weekend and get out of here for a bit. I've reserved us a suite at Hotel Ella. It's a five-star hotel not far from the University of Texas campus. We can stay holed up all weekend and not have to worry about anything that's been going on."

"That sounds awesome, but if I'm going to be able to take a day off, I have to get a lot of work done this afternoon. I'm not sure I'll be able to call or text you again...will that be okay?"

Dax thought about it for a moment, then agreed. "Okay, but don't leave your building. In fact, better yet, stay in your office all afternoon."

"But Dax," Mackenzie protested, "I can't sit here for another four hours! What if I have to use the bathroom? What if I get thirsty?"

"Don't leave your floor then. It's important, Mack."

"That I can do. I can't wait for the weekend. I've missed you."

"I know, sweetheart. I've missed you too. I want nothing more than to be able to put everything aside and concentrate on you again." Dax's voice turned teasing. "There are about three new positions I want to introduce you to, and some toys as well."

"Daxton! You can't say that stuff while I'm at work!"

"You love it."

"Maybe so, but still!"

Dax chuckled. "Okay, I'll be there to pick you up around five and we'll head straight up there."

"But I don't have any of my things with me."

"We'll stop at a store and grab some bathroom stuff. You won't need any clothes, Mack. I plan on keeping you naked the entire weekend."

"Okay. I like that plan."

"I love you, Mack."

"Love you too. I'll see you in a few hours."

"Okay, babe. Bye."

"Bye."

Mackenzie hung up the phone and smiled. She couldn't wait to get away from San Antonio with her man. She hadn't lied. It had been too long since they'd taken their time in bed together. They'd made love, but it'd been rushed, both of them feeling vulnerable with the threat hanging over their heads. She couldn't wait to be with Daxton with no worries between them, other than pleasuring each other.

DAX ENTERED MACK'S office building with large strides. He hadn't heard from her in a couple of hours, which wasn't too concerning since she'd told him at lunch she had a lot of work to do before they could leave. He didn't want to rush to conclusions, but after a week and a half of nothing remotely concerning happening, he'd told himself that Mack was fine at work. He'd tried calling once, but her phone went to voice mail. Dax rationalized it by telling himself she was working extra hard to be able to get away for the long weekend.

But now, as he strode into her building, he felt very uncomfortable about his decision to not check on her earlier.

The other employees knew who he was by now and greeted him easily as he walked through the office. Dax didn't see Mack's boss anywhere around. He stopped at Mack's office and looked inside. Empty. He turned around and headed for the administrative assistant who sat a couple of cubicles away.

"Hey, Sandra, have you seen Mack?"

"Actually, no. She told me she was going to take a quick break and she didn't come back. I figured she'd called you and decided to leave early. We all heard about the awesome weekend you have planned. Mackenzie told us all about it."

Dax frowned. "When did she take the break?"

Sandra looked down at her watch. "Probably about two hours ago, I guess."

Fuck. Two hours. Dax turned and strode quickly back to Mackenzie's office. He rounded her desk and opened the drawer where he'd seen her stash her purse. It was there. He looked around her desk. Mack's cell phone was sitting next to her keyboard. He wiggled the mouse, the monitor came to life, and Dax could see that Mackenzie had locked her computer, following proper office protocol. It looked as though she'd simply left her office for a quick break as she told Sandra she was going to do.

Dax's stomach churned. He tried to hold himself together. No, this wasn't anything. Mackenzie knew to be careful. She was fine. Dax pocketed her cell phone and went back to Sandra's desk.

"Where would she go to take a break?"

Sandra got up immediately. "Let me show you, it'll be quicker."

Dax nodded and followed behind Sandra as she led the way down a hall into a small break room. It was at the end of the building. Dax looked around. There were three small tables in the area, each with four chairs. Against the wall were two soda machines and a snack machine. Against the wall perpendicular to the vending machines was a sink, cabinets, a water cooler filled with water, and a plastic bin filled with plastic forks and spoons and a handful of napkins. A trash can sat, half-filled, next to the sink. Nothing looked out of place.

Dax stepped out of the room and looked around. To the right was a hallway leading to another room full of cubicles. To the left were two doors. He stepped to the first and opened it cautiously. It was a janitor's closet. Inside was a bucket and a mop as well as a cleaning cart. The room was tidy and neat. Dax closed the door and walked to the other door.

It opened to a stairwell.

The uneasy feeling inside Dax bloomed until it filled his throat. While there was security in the lobby on the first floor of the building, Dax hadn't been able to get 24/7 security for Mack. He'd been cocky, thinking he'd covered the main entrance and exit and she'd be fine. He'd been stupid. Dax turned to Sandra. "I need you to find me *anyone* who saw Mackenzie this afternoon. I need to know the last time anyone saw her and what they saw her doing."

"Yes, sir." Sandra could obviously feel the waves of danger emanating from Daxton as he went into full Ranger mode. She turned around immediately to do as he'd asked.

Dax took out his phone and swiped it on and hit Cruz's name. As soon as Cruz picked up, Dax started talking.

"He's got Mack. I don't know how yet, but dammit, Cruz. I need you."

"Where are you?" Cruz didn't waste time asking how he knew Mackenzie had been taken. He got right to business.

"I'm at her office. No one has seen her in a couple of hours. The secretary said Mack told her she was going to take a break. The break room is next to a set of stairs."

"I'm on my way. Don't let anyone touch anything. If the Reaper did get to her, that place is now a crime scene."

"Fuck."

"Stay with me, Dax."

"That fucker has her."

"Dax." Cruz said his name as a warning.

Dax took a deep breath, knowing he had to keep his emotions in check. "I'm fine. Just get here."

"On my way."

The line went dead. Dax knew Cruz would call Quint and there'd be people crawling all over the office before too long. Knowing if he stopped to think too much, he'd lose it, Dax headed back to Sandra.

She'd done what he'd asked her to do and there was a large crowd of people standing around her desk.

One of the women spoke in a nasally voice. "Look, I'm sorry Mack skipped out on you, but my employees have work to do. They can't just drop everything just because you told them to."

Knowing this was Mack's boss he'd heard so much about, Dax said curtly, "Nancy, right?" At her nod, he continued in a pissed-off voice. "Mackenzie is missing. I'm very sorry if your first concern isn't for her, but for work. Shit, woman, you work in a nonprofit organization that's supposed to help people. Shut the hell up and help me help Mack. If you haven't seen her, fine, get the fuck out and let me talk to everyone else. I'm sure after I talk to them, they can go back to doing the precious work that you take credit for. Now, can I continue, or do you want to keep antagonizing me when Mack could be suffering at the hands of a psycho serial killer?"

The room was silent. No one said a word as they watched Nancy try to think of something to say to backtrack. Finally she said quietly, "Please continue," and then she turned around, her hair swishing around her, and went back to her office, shutting the door behind her. Not stopping to think about how much Mack would've loved seeing her boss eat a slice of humble pie, Dax turned to the employees.

"Listen, everyone. Please. First, don't touch anything unnecessarily. Keep away from the break room. The FBI and the SAPD are on their way. I'm sure the officers will interview you, but please, think hard. When was the last time you saw Mackenzie today? Did anyone see anything that seemed out of place?"

Dax watched as each of the employees shrugged and shook their head. From what he could gather, the last time anyone saw Mack was around a quarter past three that afternoon. It was now half past four.

Two fucking hours. That bastard had had her for two hours. It was time enough for him to have her long gone from the area.

The phone in Dax's front pocket buzzed. It was Mackenzie's cell, not his own.

Dax pulled it out with clenched teeth, dread filling his gut. He swiped it, not needing the password to see the text that had just been sent. The three words seared themselves onto his brain and Dax couldn't hold back a small whimper.

Game on Ranger

Chapter Thirteen

Two o'clock AM

DAX PACED THE small office in the Ranger Station, barely holding himself together. It was probably about eleven hours after the Reaper had kidnapped Mackenzie. Quint, Cruz, and TJ, as well as Hayden, who worked for the Bexar County Sheriff's Office, were all there with him. Conor, a Game Warden and a member of the SCOUT team, had also heard about Mack's disappearance and had shown up. Also present were about five other random employees of the FBI office and the SAPD. Papers were strewn over the large conference table, the voices were low and rumbled as the men and women frantically tried to find something, anything, that they might have missed that would lead them to the killer, and the man who'd kidnapped one of their own.

Dax stopped in front of the large picture window overlooking the parking lot, putting his hands on the sill and leaned over, staring out into the night, but not seeing anything. The only thing he could picture was Mack's smile. Scenes flitted through his mind as if he was watching a movie.

Mack in bed smiling up at him. Mack in his car, holding his hand while gesturing wildly with the other as she rambled on about something. Mack in his shower. Mack at his kitchen table. Mack. Fuck.

Dax jerked when TJ put his hand on his shoulder. He turned eagerly to his friend. "Got anything?"

TJ just shook his head. "Nothing more than we had a few hours ago."

Dax turned back to the window. "I never thought I'd find the woman who was meant for me, TJ. I'd resigned myself to being alone. Mack came barreling into my life with her oddball charm and her quirky sense of humor and I haven't been the same since. I've lost her."

"No! Don't fucking say that, Dax. You haven't lost her. Don't give up now. For Christ's sake, man, Mackenzie *needs* you. You can't give up on her."

Dax turned in frustration and threw his hand out, indicating the table and all the people. "We've been at it for hours, and we have nothing. *Nothing.* How in the hell are we supposed to catch this guy when we don't know jack shit about him? He's been two steps ahead of us the entire time. It's been around eleven hours, TJ. Eleven. Fucking. Hours. She could be buried five feet underground by now. We'll never find her unless he wants to fuck with me."

TJ, for once, didn't have any words of comfort for his friend. "Come on back to the table; let's look over the cemeteries where the other women were found again, we have to be missing some sort of pattern."

TJ watched as Dax nodded and turned away again, but not before TJ saw a tear fall over Dax's cheek. He squeezed his friend's shoulder and went back to the table, leaving Dax to get control over his grief.

Seven Thirty AM

DAX STARED BLEARY-EYED at the transcripts of tips sitting in front of him that had been called into the various law enforcement offices. The sun was peeking over the horizon, making for a beautiful sunrise. Dax could feel the heat on his face through the window, but didn't bother looking up. He only cared about Mackenzie right now. Not eating, not sleeping, not a fucking sunrise.

Quint and Cruz were snoring in the seats next to him. Quint had succumbed to sleep around four thirty and Cruz not much later. They were the only ones left in the big conference room at Ranger Company F. Dax knew his fellow Rangers would soon be arriving, and they'd put all their other cases on hold for him...for Mack...but his skin was crawling. He was on the verge of something, but he couldn't quite grab ahold of it. It was there. He'd read something in the hundreds of pages of transcribed phone calls and tips they'd received after the FBI profilers had gone to the media and reported on the profile of the Lone Star Reaper.

Dax flipped through the page and scanned the information he was seeing through blurry eyes. He needed coffee, but it'd have to wait. The feeling hadn't started until recently, so he went back and looked at the latest couple of tips.

My neighbor has to be the Lone Star Reaper, because he's extra creepy. I wish he'd move.

I've seen this guy at the grocery store and he seems to fit the profile the guy on television talked about. He's middle age and he always buys olives. I mean cans and cans of olives. That's crazy! I bet he's the killer.

I worked with a guy who just seemed off. We were the night custodians for this big building and even though we used cleansers all the time, his hands were always dirty. He didn't socialize with any of the rest of us at all. It was weird.

I'm afraid the Reaper could be my husband. He works late every weekend but gets texts at weird times and won't let me see them. He smells like perfume too. I bet it's those missing women's perfume.

Dax slammed the notebook shut and threw it across the table, watching as it came to rest on the other side, just shy of tumbling over the edge. He shut his eyes and leaned back in his chair. The leather creaked under him as the chair rocked back with his body weight. He put the heels of his hands into his eyes and rubbed.

People just didn't get it. Mackenzie's life was held in the palms of their hands, and they were reporting cheating husbands and creepy co-workers as the Reaper. It was maddening. Wait a minute…

Dax suddenly shot forward in his chair, his hands hitting the top of the table with a loud smack, waking up both Cruz and Quint. Dax quickly leaned up out of his chair and across the table, snatching up the notebook he'd just thrown.

"Oh my fucking God. That has to be a clue."

"What? Dax? What time is it?"

Dax ignored Quint's drowsy murmurings and frantically flipped back through the tips, trying to find the one he wanted.

He stopped at the one he was looking for and flipped it over to Cruz. "Read that."

Cruz didn't hesitate, and seemed to come awake immediately. He leaned over and read the tip Dax was referring to. He looked up. "Maybe."

Dax stood and started pacing again. "I know you think I'm desperate and am seeing clues where there might not be any. But this seems promising. He worked nights. He was a janitor. He had time to get to those women during the day when he wasn't working. We need to go back through and see if we can't match up the victims with this guy. And Mack. No one notices the cleaning crew in buildings. What if he was there yesterday? Mack is nice to everyone. She would've taken the time to talk to this guy, to try to befriend him. He could've done something and sneaked her out of the building by the stairs next to the break room. Hell, he probably has a van or something that wouldn't seem out of place either."

Cruz pulled the tip sheet closer to him, thinking out loud. "His dirty hands could be because of the dirt and burying the boxes, and it matches the profile." He stood up and took the notebook with him.

"I'll get the tipster on the line right away. We need to get more information. We need to know what this guy's name is."

"Once you get the name, I'll see if I can't get the forensic team to research where he might have worked as well. It could lead to a pattern of where he got his victims from," Quint added, standing up himself, all signs of being sleepy gone from his face. "It could take awhile, but I'll see what I can do to get them to put a rush on it."

Dax took a deep breath before following his friends out of the room. It might be nothing, but it was more than they'd had an hour ago. He put his hand in his pocket and pulled out Mack's cell phone. He absently tapped the screen and glared down at the words, still showing on the opening screen. He knew Mack's password, but couldn't bring himself to use it.

Game on Ranger

The words sat on the screen, mocking Dax.

What was the bastard waiting for? Why hadn't he contacted him? Dax figured the Reaper knew where he was and probably had all of his own personal contact information as well. If he wanted to play a fucking game with Mack's life, why hadn't he started it already?

Dax shoved the phone back into his pocket and strode out of the room behind his friends. He had some research to do. He'd catch this motherfucker if it was the last thing he ever did. If he killed Mackenzie, and at this point it was a likely ending to the whole fucked-up mess, Dax knew he'd make the Reaper pay. The Reaper would wish he hadn't laid his eyes on Dax or Mackenzie.

It wouldn't bring her back, but it'd make Dax feel better...maybe.

Ten o'clock AM

QUINT BURST INTO Dax's office holding a piece of paper. "Jordan

Charles Staal. Age thirty-nine. Has a high school education. Was married for two years to a second cousin. She disappeared and her information is sitting in the cold-case files. What do you want to bet he killed her? We're still working on finding out about his childhood, looking for signs of abuse or any kind of juvenile record."

Dax sat up straight in his chair and drilled Quint with his eyes. "Jobs?" he barked.

Quint sat on the edge of the wooden chair in front of Dax's desk and continued. "He's held six different custodian jobs in the last eight years. All like the tipster said, third shift. We're cross-referencing the victims now, but I recognize at least one of the buildings off the top of my head as where the fourth victim worked." Quint looked up. "We've fucking got him, Dax."

"It seems too easy."

"Don't think that. We'll get him, and Mackenzie too."

Two o'clock PM

THE RANGER SPECIAL Response Team spread out around the ramshackle house in western San Antonio. The neighborhood looked as though it once used to be pretty, but now the houses mostly appeared abandoned and almost all needed some sort of major repair.

Dax didn't see any of that. He was fixated on the door in front of him. They'd tracked Staal's address through his employment records and as soon as they'd gathered the SRT, they were on their way.

Dax had agreed not to be at the forefront of the assault; he was too close to the case. He watched as the door was broken in and the team rushed into the house. He followed behind, gun drawn, hoping against hope they'd find Staal cowering in a back room and he'd tell them what he did with Mack.

It was quickly clear that no one had lived in the house in a very long time. It smelled stale and there were cobwebs everywhere. Some kids had obviously broken in and partied in the house at one point, as there were beer cans strewn all over the floor.

The address Staal had given his employers was false. No one was there. Not Staal, and not Mackenzie.

Dax's stomach churned. Mack wasn't here and he had no idea where she was. He wasn't sure he'd ever see Mack alive again. He'd promised he'd keep her safe and he'd let her down.

Four Thirty PM

DAX WATCHED THE news correspondent review the facts of the Reaper case dispassionately.

And now an update to the killer the press has dubbed the Lone Star Reaper. It's being reported that another woman is missing. Mackenzie Morgan, age thirty-seven, disappeared from her workplace yesterday afternoon. The San Antonio Police Department, the Texas Rangers and the FBI are working on a joint operation to follow any leads.

We've been told they have a person of interest in the case. Jordan Charles Staal. If you have any information about Mr. Staal's whereabouts, or if you have information that might lead to finding him so he can be questioned, please call the police department's tip line at...

Dax clicked off the television, not able to stomach the sight of Staal's face. The third place the man had worked was able to provide them with his picture from the employee ID computer system. He truly was a creepy-looking man. He had black hair that was too long. His jaw was tight and he wasn't smiling in the photo. There was a scar running along the right side of his face, from the corner of his mouth all the way up to disappear into his hairline.

Dax closed his eyes. He was so tired, but didn't know if he could sleep. He knew he couldn't go back to his apartment. He'd see Mack's stuff, see the indentation in the pillow where she'd last lain her head, he'd smell her perfume and soap in the bathroom, smell her vanilla scent all over his apartment. Nope, he'd have to see if he could catch a few hours of sleep here at his desk instead.

Even though it wasn't even five in the afternoon yet, Dax crossed his arms and put them on his desktop. He put his head down and closed his eyes, willing the tears back. If he let them out now, he didn't know if he'd be able to stop.

Six Thirty PM

DAX JERKED UP from his awkward position and looked around in confusion. He hadn't slept well; visions of Mackenzie crying out for him in a dark room haunted him. He couldn't find her and she needed him. He rubbed his hand over his eyes, trying to orient himself.

The cell phone in his back pocket vibrated again. Dax pulled it out and saw the number was blocked. Normally he'd let the call go to voice mail, but while Mackenzie was missing, he wasn't taking any chances.

"Chambers."

"Daxton?"

Dax straightened his spine then stood up suddenly and headed out of his office. He had to get someone...anyone. Holy fucking shit. Mack was on the phone.

"Mack? Where are you, sweetheart? I'm on my way to you right now, just tell me where you are and I'll come get you."

Her voice was low and strained and the connection was crap. The air crackled and dropped in and out as she spoke the words Dax somehow knew, from the very fiber of his being, were coming.

"I don't know. I'm buried alive."

Chapter Fourteen

D AX HAD BEEN on the move before Mackenzie had spoken, but he halted for a moment, holding himself upright in the hallway of his office building with a hand on the wall. He lowered his head in despair. He then took a deep breath and strode down the hall with purpose. It might be evening, but the building was never empty. He wasn't hanging up with Mackenzie to try to get ahold of someone; he'd just have to multitask.

"Mack…" Dax stopped. He didn't really know what to say. What the hell *did* you say to someone who was in her situation? He tried to think. He had to pull his head out of his ass and *think*.

"I love you." First things first. He had to tell Mack how much he cared about her.

"I love you too, Daxton. I…know how it happened…drink…woke up."

"You're cutting in and out, baby. Try again."

Dax burst into the Major's office and put his hand over the speaker on his phone. "Mack's on the phone. She's underground somewhere. Get Cruz and Quint on the line, now."

The Major didn't hesitate. He immediately picked up the phone on his desk and dialed.

Mackenzie's voice was small and wobbly in Dax's ear. He'd never heard her sound so unsure. "I know how he got me. I was…work, the janitor…a glass of water, and I woke up…the dark. It's so dark, Daxton."

Dax backed away from the Major's desk and turned toward the window. Not seeing anything but Mackenzie's face, he tried to reassure her. "It's not your fault. It's mine. I shouldn't have let you keep working. I should've been there."

"No, Daxton. Don't do that. You couldn't know, there's no way…known this would happen."

"You're wrong, Mack. He knew about you, I should've protected you better."

"I know you told me never to get in a car with someone who wanted to…but does it count if I didn't…what was happening?"

The connection was crap, but Dax could get the gist of what Mack was saying. "I think you get a pass, baby. He probably roofied your water."

"Yeah, I figured that too…seemed so nice. I hadn't seen him around…but he was getting his own cup of…he offered me one too, I said sure. I'm sorry, Daxton, I'm so fucking sorry."

"It's okay. It's okay. I'm going to find you. We know his name. Do you hear me? We know who he is."

"Good. You'll find me?"

Dax heard Mack's voice crack. He gripped his phone so hard he thought he'd break it. He breathed in through his nose trying to get his composure back. "I'll find you, baby. No matter what. I'll find you and bring you home."

Dax looked over at the Major. He was gesturing to his office door. Dax followed him out and back toward the conference room.

"Look at the phone in your hand, Mack. Take it away from your ear for a second and tell me if you can see a phone number on it. The number was blocked from my end, so I can't call you back if we lose the connection."

"Don't go, Daxton! Oh God, please…don't—"

"Mackenzie!" Dax's tone was harsh. He was losing her and he needed her focused on helping him find her. "Listen to me. You there? You listening?"

"I'm here."

"Take a deep breath, sweetheart. Don't panic. If you panic, you'll lose too much air. Do you understand? You have to stay as calm as you can. If we lose the connection, don't freak. You called me, right? All you have to do is call me back. I'll be here."

"Yeah, okay, you're right. I'm...hang on and let me...if I can see the number."

There was a pause and Dax figured Mack was looking at the face of the phone; he turned to the Major. "What's their ETA?"

"They're on their way, lights and sirens, and I put the SRT on standby. As soon as we get *any* information, we're ready to roll."

Mackenzie's voice came back over the line. "I don't see the number. I clicked buttons but...light. It's so dark. I can't find...I can't find it."

"Okay. Don't worry about it. If we lose the connection, you can just call me back. I'm not going to hang up. You might hear me talking to others in the background, but I'm still here. Okay?"

"Okay."

"I'm going to get to you, Mack. I need you to tell me everything you can about what you remember, what you see, smell, hear, and what you feel around you. Everything, Mack. No matter how small you think it is. How insignificant. Every single thing will help me get to you."

Mackenzie's description of her surroundings was completely heartbreaking and Dax couldn't hold back the tears that had been at the back of this throat since he'd answered the phone and heard Mack's voice. She was trying to be so brave and he couldn't fucking stand it.

"I'm pretty sure...in a coffin. There's no material, it's all wood, but...only a couple inches above...head but it seems like...room at my feet. For the first time...glad to be short."

Dax grabbed a tissue from the box in the middle of the conference table and turned his back to the Major. He held the tissue to his
eyes, willing himself to keep silent. Mackenzie didn't need to hear
him losing it.

"It's crude...I think. There's no material...I admit I freaked out
when...and in places...nails. I found this phone
and...when...it...later."

Dax cleared his throat. "Mack, say again. That last part cut out."
He was proud at how normal his voice sounded.

"The phone was here and two bottles of water. I thought I'd save
them for later."

"Good thinking, Mack. What do you hear?"

Mackenzie's voice lowered. "Nothing. There's nothing. It's so
quiet all I can hear is the ringing in my ears."

"What about smell? What do you smell?" Dax knew even the
most insignificant thing could be the difference between finding Staal
and thus, Mack...or not finding either of them.

"Dirt. Daxton, I smell dirt. I'm so scared...I thought I'd be
brave, but I can't..."

Dax's heart felt as if it was being pulled out of his body, it hurt so
badly. Hearing Mackenzie break down into sobs was completely heart
wrenching.

"Shhhh, baby. Deep breaths. I know you're scared. I am too. I'm
doing everything I can to find you. You hear me? Don't give up on
me."

As Mackenzie tried to control her sobs, Dax heard the door open.
Quint and Cruz stalked in, crazed looks in their eyes.

"That her?" Quint asked.

Dax nodded.

"That your cell? The guys are seeing if they can trace it," Cruz
told Dax matter-of-factly.

Dax nodded again, relieved as fuck his friends were there.

"She give you anything yet?"

Dax held up his finger to tell Quint to wait a second. He spoke into the phone again. "Mack? Quint and Cruz are here; can you give me a moment to talk to them?"

"Yeah. I'm okay. Talk…them." Mackenzie's voice was a bit stronger this time.

"I'm so fucking proud of you, sweetheart. I can still hear you, but I'm going to put you on mute a second. I'm not hanging up. Okay? Hang on."

Dax kept the phone against his ear, not willing to be out of hearing distance from Mackenzie for even a second, just in case she needed him.

"She's in a homemade wooden box, sounds like the others, two water bottles, cell phone. She can't hear anything, but can smell dirt. Bastard must've drugged her. She saw him in the break room and he got her a glass of water. It's about the last thing she remembers. I don't think she's going to be able to give us anything." Dax paused, meeting his friends' eyes. "Help me. For God's sake, help me."

"Tips are rolling in from tonight's news. We're following up on them now."

"It needs to be faster, Quint."

Quint simply nodded, went to the table, pulled out his phone and punched some buttons.

Dax didn't see what Cruz was doing, but turned his attention back to Mack and clicked the mute button so she could hear him again. "I'm back, sweetheart."

"Daxton?"

"Yeah, Mack. I'm here."

"Does my family know…?"

"Yeah, they know." Dax had fielded a call from her brother Mark before he'd taken the short catnap. He'd been furious, rightly so, and Dax had promised him they were doing everything they could to find his sister. Dax knew his words weren't comforting in the least to the man, because they weren't to his own ears.

"Don't let them see...scene photos. I don't want them...me looking...this."

"Fuck, baby."

"Promise," she demanded.

"I promise."

"Do you remember...first kiss?"

"How could I forget?"

"You pushed me up against the wall and were trying...scare me. I told you I wasn't...and you leaned down...kissed me. I didn't tell...that if you'd asked, I would've...dragged...hall to my...and made love to you right then. You smell fantastic...I ever tell you that before? Well...do. I love the way...smell. Like man and...you should bottle that shit, you'd...a mint on it. But I want to keep it...myself. I'd give anything...smell you...now."

Dax shut his eyes, loving how Mack could ramble even when she was scared out of her mind and buried underground. "I remember that night. I couldn't have stopped myself from kissing you if my job depended on it. You were so cute, and not scared of me in the least. And Mack, you might think I smell good, but you...you corner the market on that. Every morning before I get out of bed I lean into you and bury my nose in your hair. It's vanilla or something. I don't know exactly what it is, but it's you. And I love it."

"Really?"

"Really."

Dax noticed Cruz gesturing to him frantically from the table.

"Hang on, Mack. Okay? I gotta talk to Cruz."

"Okay. It's not like...going anywhere."

Dax chuckled, even though there wasn't anything to laugh about, and took the four steps over to Cruz. He held his hand over the speaker on the phone.

"What you got?"

"One of the tips came from a funeral director. He'd been watching the news and recognized Staal. Said he's seen him a few times at various visitation services to 'pay his respects.' I'm figuring Staal doesn't even know the people in the visitations, he just goes to get off on seeing the dead bodies in the coffins laid out."

Dax saw where Cruz was going. "So we just narrowed down the area where he might live."

"Right."

Quint was speaking into his phone, ordering whoever was on the other end to "hurry it up."

"Daxton?"

Dax turned his attention away from his friends and back to Mackenzie immediately. "Yeah, sweetheart?"

Her words were coming in pants now. Dax tried not to panic. He was running out of time, dammit.

"I don't regret meeting you."

"Baby—"

"No, really. Even if I knew how this would end up when we first met, I'd still...through with it. I've been happier in the last...months than I have in my...life. I know I'm not perfect, hell...a pain in the ass. I hadn't met one...who could put...me. But you, you just ignored...I got bitchy and you smirked at me. It was annoying...first, but you made me really think. I don't...care if you put the...in pointy side up. It's stupid...argue over something...that. I want you to know that I don't regret a...thing about...you. I know what love is now, and...cherish that."

"Mack."

"No, I'm still talking."

Dax smiled sadly again and lowered his head. Fuck. She was killing him.

"Don't let this prevent...trying again. You found love once, you'll...again. And don't tell me...too old. That's bullshit. You should...a chance. Don't stop living just because I did."

"Fuck!" The word was torn from Dax's mouth and he couldn't take it anymore. He took a step to the table, handed his cell to Cruz, and left the conference room.

Chapter Fifteen

MACKENZIE TRIED TO hold back her sobs, but couldn't. She'd meant every word she'd said to Daxton. She didn't regret one second of their relationship, even though it led to her being buried alive. It wasn't Daxton's fault and she wouldn't have given up the feeling of being loved, and loving in return, for anything.

She hadn't meant to upset Daxton, but she knew she had to say the words. She hoped he'd forgive her.

Mackenzie was uncomfortable. She'd been lying in the same position for way too long. She couldn't sit up, she couldn't turn over, the space she was in was simply too small. She'd tried to turn on her side, but couldn't. Her hips hurt, her butt hurt, and she was scared out of her mind. She also knew she was dying.

The air in the coffin was getting thin. Mackenzie could tell because she found herself panting more and more as she spoke with Daxton. She had no idea how long she'd been in there. She'd been completely freaked when she'd come to the first time and found herself unable to move. She'd panicked and whacked her head against the top of the box more than once while she was freaking out. She must've passed out, but once she'd woken up and calmed down, Mack had known immediately what had happened.

The fucking janitor.

He hadn't even given her a chance to fight him. The drugs made her groggy and uncoordinated and he was practically carrying her by the time they'd gotten to the bottom of the stairs. Mackenzie didn't remember anything after that, and she'd come to in the box. It could've been an hour, or three days. Mack simply had no idea.

She'd flailed around in the coffin for way too long before taking a deep breath to calm herself down. She'd fumbled around, trying to feel around her, and had discovered the bottles of water and the phone sitting next to her shoulders. The bastard had known she wouldn't be able to reach them if they were at her feet.

Mackenzie tried to talk to Daxton. "Hello? Daxton? Are you there?"

"Hey, Mackenzie, it's Cruz."

"Where's Daxton?"

"He's taking a break, he'll be right back. How're you holding up?"

"Cruz, I'm not going to make...I'm having a hard time breathing...just know I'm not...survive."

"Don't think that way. We're close to figuring this out. Don't give up on us."

"I'm...practical. Please, promise...don't let Daxton become...hermit. Make him...out and meet...don't let him...alone for the...life. I couldn't stand...please?"

"I won't, Mackenzie. I promise."

"Thank you. I...a question."

"Anything."

"How the hell am I able...to you on a fucking cell...if I'm underground?"

Cruz froze. Holy hell. How the fuck had he overlooked that?

Mackenzie continued. Cruz could understand her through the crappy connection...barely.

"I mean, doesn't dirt...connection? It doesn't make...that I'd be...get a connection...I was underground. Right? Hell, I once...call Mark while I was...car going through...tunnel and...call totally dropped...in the middle...conversation. Of course...blamed me and told me…trying to avoid…to him but I told him…was crap that it was…I was underground. I thought…it now and I don't…it."

"Listen to me, Mackenzie. Are you listening?" At her affirmative response, Cruz continued. "We're on the verge of finding out where this guy lives. We're going to get to his house as soon as we figure it out. We'll get him and he'll tell us where you are. Maybe you're not underground yet; maybe he's stashed that coffin somewhere until he can get back to the cemetery to bury it. That's why you can talk on the cell. I don't know. But even if you're underground, you hold on. Got it? Breathe slowly, do whatever you have to do, but hold the fuck on. You aren't allowed to give up. Not when we're this close. Hear me?"

"You're not…saying that? You really are…the way?"

"We really are." Cruz forgave himself the slight lie. They weren't on their way to anywhere at the moment. They still needed more information.

"I wish there was more I could do to help you guys. I feel worthless…here. If I was a true heroine…all sorts of information to give…that would lead you right to me."

"Don't worry about it, Mackenzie. It's our job to do that. You're only job is to wait for us to get there. And to keep breathing. Nothing else."

"Okay. Is Daxton there?"

"Not yet, but he will be soon."

"Okay."

Quint hung up the phone he'd been on and swore. Cruz turned his head toward him with raised eyebrows. "Where's Dax? He needs to get his ass in here. There's a development."

Just as the words left Quint's mouth, Dax walked back in. The knuckles on his left hand were bloody, but no one said a word about it. It was obvious Dax had heard Quint's words, but he still went straight to Cruz and held out his hand for the phone. Cruz handed it to him immediately.

"Mack?"

"Yeah…here."

"Okay, hang on, I gotta talk to Quint. He's got an update for us. We're getting closer. I swear."

"I know. I'll be here when you find me, Daxton."

Dax muted the phone again and turned to Quint.

"A call just came in on the tip line. I'm going to read you what the caller said." Quint looked Dax in the eyes. "Keep it locked down, Dax. Mackenzie needs you."

Dax clenched his teeth. He had no idea how much more he could take. He nodded.

"The caller's voice wasn't altered this time. It was a man. He said, and I quote, 'Jordan Staal here. I hope Ranger Chambers is having a good time talking with his lover. It really was too easy to get to her. He should watch over those he loves better. And that memory of first kiss is gonna have to be enough to tide him over for the rest of his life. Too bad he didn't fuck her that first night.'"

The room was silent after Quint's voice faded, until Dax broke it. "That fucker is listening. He put the damn phone in there with her so he could listen to her calling me."

No one said anything. The level of Staal's cruelty was becoming clearer as the minutes went by.

The ringing of Cruz's cell phone broke the heavy atmosphere of the room. "Livingston. Yeah. Got it. Meet at Ranger Company in ten. Out."

Cruz kept his voice low. "The SRT is ready. We have an address. Fucker screwed up. Gave a different address to the first company he worked at. It's the same address his wife was reported missing from. It's him this time. I can feel it. We're headed out in ten. We're going to get your woman, Dax."

Dax nodded once and was on the move before Cruz had finished speaking. Ten minutes, it felt like ten hours. He clicked the phone off mute once again. "Mack?"

"...you find me yet?" Her voice was soft, but steely. It was obvious Mackenzie was scared out of her mind, but she was keeping a lock on it. She was hanging in there, believing he was coming for her.

"We're working on it." Dax didn't want to say anything to alert Staal they were on their way right then to get him. He hated knowing that asshole was listening to his conversation with Mack, but he couldn't let her know. Dax knew he had to act like he had no idea. Keeping it from Mack made him feel like shit, but he didn't have a choice. Dax wanted to give her some hope, something to give her so she'd hang on until he could get to her. He took a breath and lobbed a Hail Mary, hoping she'd figure out what he was saying. "Remember when we had that conversation about Christmas, sweetheart?"

"Uh, no."

"You know, you were telling me about the time Matthew brought you downstairs to the closet and told you that your parents were Santa Claus? You said you cried for a bit until he showed you how to unwrap just the end of the packages so you could see what was inside, then you could close it back up and no one would know you peeked?"

Mackenzie closed her eyes and tried to remember back to any conversation she'd had with Daxton about Christmas... Finally she remembered. They'd been talking about anticipation and how Mackenzie had no patience. She hated knowing she had to wait for something. She'd told Daxton she always preferred to be surprised than to know something was coming. Vacations, presents, holidays...they were all torture, knowing they were coming but not there yet.

"Oh, yeah, I remember now."

"Well, this is like that." Dax hoped like hell Mack understood what he so badly was trying to say.

Mackenzie frantically tried to read between the lines of what Daxton was saying. It was obvious he was trying to tell her something. "Okay, Daxton." She thought about it…she thought he was saying that she had to hold on…have patience because he was on his way. It wouldn't be a surprise; he was coming. She got that. Mackenzie decided right then and there anticipation wasn't necessarily a bad thing.

"Okay, Mack. Cruz has his technicians working as hard as they can. We've almost got it. Swear. You just hold on. Baby? I have to put the phone on mute on my end, but I can still hear you. Okay? Just keep talking to me. I can hear you just fine. Whatever you need to say, say it."

Mackenzie didn't want Daxton to put her on mute. She wanted to close her eyes and hear the low rumble of his voice as he spoke with her. The silence pressed in on her when he muted his end of the line, making her tomb seem even smaller than it was, but she answered affirmatively anyway. "Okay."

Mackenzie strained to hear anything on the other end of the line. She heard nothing. The coffin was airtight and completely silent. She started talking to break the silence; she couldn't just lie there in stillness.

Dax kept his phone at his ear, listening to Mack talk about nothing. Her voice still stuttered in and out, but Dax didn't care. She was talking, that meant she was breathing. He'd go with it. He opened the door to the garage, nodding in surprise at both Conor and TJ. They'd obviously been granted permission to be part of the entry team. He looked around in approval at the rest of the men assembled. The SRT was ready to go.

"I've sent the coordinates to Staal's house to your GPSs. We're going in silent. He's got ears on the phone call between Chambers and Ms. Morgan, so when Dax gives the cue, everyone shut the fuck up. We want to sneak up on him. He can't know we're on the way.

Got it?" Cruz told the men waiting for the word to go in and arrest a killer.

There were nods all around. Dax put his cell on the trunk of the car in front of him while he shrugged on the bulletproof vest. He wouldn't be a part of the entry team, once again he'd leave that to Cruz's people, but there was no way he wasn't going with them. He grabbed up the phone again and sat down in the front seat of Quint's patrol car.

Nine minutes. Dax would be able to look Jordan Charles Staal in the face in nine minutes and find out where he'd stashed his woman.

Chapter Sixteen

———◆———

"**D**ID YOU CANCEL...reservations for the hotel in Austin? Cos you can't...waste the money. Make sure they...charge your card. Once I had a vacation planned...mom got sick...forgot to call and I had...dollar charge. They refused...take it off even...produced the doctor's bill...mom was sick. Bastards. So it might...seem like a lot, but you shouldn't let...get away with that shit. When you find me...we go there? It sounded...and I was looking forward...all weekend in bed...you."

Mackenzie paused and panted. She had no idea if Daxton was even listening to her anymore, but she didn't stop talking. Even though she was dizzy and her chest hurt to breathe, she didn't stop.

"I hate math. I don't know...I just do. I know we need...and...use it all the time but...suck at it. It's stupid...not that hard. But I just have never...how to do it in my head. I always...the wrong column and end up...the wrong answer. Thank...calculators. Where would we be without...? I use the app...all the time. It's embarrassing...break it out...day. I must look like...a six...kid."

Dax listened to Mack ramble on with clenched teeth. Her voice had gotten lower and lower and he hated it. He wanted to tell her to stop talking, to save her breath, and conserve the air in her tomb, but he couldn't make himself. Every word out of her mouth was being committed to his memory...just in case.

The vehicle stopped on a street in a nice neighborhood in northern San Antonio. The lawns were all well-kept and Dax could even see some people out playing in the yards. It wasn't the type of neighborhood he expected to see a scumbag like Staal living in. He tapped his phone to unmute it.

"Mack?"

"Daxton! I'm here, I'm here."

Dax's stomach hurt. Of course she was there. Where would she have gone? "I love you. You're doing great."

"I…it hurts to breathe."

Dax shut his eyes. Fuck. "I know, but keep doing it anyway. The forensics team just came in and I'm going to be busy for the next bit, but I'm not hanging up. But don't talk, baby. You need to save your air. Just relax for a bit, okay?"

"It's too quiet…ringing in my ears. I don't…it."

Knowing he wouldn't be able to reassure her for at least the next fifteen minutes or so, Dax suggested, "Would it help if I put my phone up to the radio? Then it wouldn't be quiet and you wouldn't waste your breath with talking."

"Yeah, I'd like that. As long as…not the god-awful silence."

"Okay, sweetheart. You know I love you, right? I'm gonna find you. Soon. You just have to hang on."

"I'll try, but…it's getting hard. If you don't…me, don't blame…I wouldn't change…about loving you. Not one thing. I've heard it doesn't hurt…you know…that I'll…basically fall asleep… The last thing…about is you. I'll remember the feel…hands on my body and…lips on mine. Don't mourn me forever, Daxton. That's an order."

Dax swallowed hard, ignoring the heavy hand Quint laid on his shoulder in silent support. "I'll love you forever, Mack. No one will come close to replacing you in my life and my heart. You're seriously the best thing that's ever happened to me. Ever. Hang in there for as long as you can…but if it gets too much and you need to fall asleep…it's okay. Don't hang on for me if it hurts. You do what you need to do. I don't want you in pain. Got it?"

Dax could hear Mack sniff. Her words were just a wisp of sound. "I don't want to die. I want to live...fifty years with you."

"I know, Mack. I know. God, baby." Dax didn't know what to say. He sure as hell didn't want her to die either, but right this second, he had no idea how to prevent it. He was completely helpless to do anything for her, other than to try to reassure her.

"I love you, Daxton Chambers." Her words fortuitously didn't cut out.

Dax knew he had to get going. "I love you, too. I'm going to let you listen to some eighties music. Okay?" He heard her chuckle.

"Eighties music. What every girl stuck in...coffin wants to hear. It's fine. Anything...be okay, as long as it's not silence. Stay safe, Daxton. Don't...anything stupid."

Dax whispered his words. "I will. I love you, sweetheart." He didn't wait for her response, knowing it would tear his heart right out of his chest if he had to hear one more thing from her. He put his cell on the dash and took Quint's phone that he held out. He clicked on the music app, pulled up the eighties channel, and waited for the music to start. He placed Quint's phone face-down on his own, then closed his eyes, kissed his fingers and pressed them to the phones for a moment.

Abruptly he turned from the dashboard of the car and opened his door. He eased the door shut, making sure no sound could be heard over the phone lines, and nodded in approval as Quint did the same thing.

Neither man said a word as they got in position behind the Special Response Team. It was time to catch a rat in its hole...and hopefully pry the location of where he'd stashed Mackenzie out of him before it was too late.

DAX FOLLOWED THE ten men into the small, nondescript house. They'd used the breaching tool to break down the front door and had swarmed inside, quickly fanning out to find where Staal was hiding. Within seconds, there were shouts from the back of the house. Dax moved that way with Quint and Cruz at his heels and stood in the doorway of what was obviously an office.

Staal was sitting behind three monitors with his hands on his head, grinning. He didn't bother to look at the officers who were pointing their AR15 rifles at him and ordering him to stand up and turn around. Cruz motioned for the officers to wait. Typically they would've grabbed him and cuffed him, but at the moment Staal had the upper hand. They didn't know if he was armed, and they needed information from him. They'd give him space until they had to make a move. At the moment he didn't look like a threat to them. They had to get him to talk.

"Well, well, well. Look who finally tracked me down. Took you long enough, Ranger Chambers."

"Shut the fuck up, Staal. Where is she?"

"Who? Oh…poor little Mackenzie?"

"You know that's who I'm talking about. Stand up and turn around, asshole."

"Tsk, tsk, tsk. You didn't think the game would be over that soon, did you? You really thought I'd stand up quaking in my boots and tell you where she was? That would ruin the fun now, wouldn't it?"

"Why are you doing this?" Cruz demanded, impatience in his voice.

"Why not?"

"That's not a fucking answer, Staal."

Staal's voice lost some of its easiness. "You want to know why? Haven't your precious profilers figured it out yet? Where'd you get them anyway? Profilers-R-Us? They don't know shit."

"Why don't you tell us then?" Dax tried to keep calm, when all he wanted to do was reach across the desk, over the fucking monitors blocking his view, and choke the shit out of the man.

"You ever seen anyone die, Chambers? I mean, not because you shot them from ten feet away, but watched them moment by moment as they took their last breath? It's absolutely fascinating. If you watch closely enough, you can see the life literally drain from their eyes. I didn't understand it at first. My mother did though. She made me see."

"What are you talking about? Come on, stand up, and turn the fuck around." Quint's voice was testy.

"Oh, Officer Axton, you have no patience. My mother always told me I was the most patient little boy she'd ever seen. She taught me everything she knew. First, it was my little brother. He wouldn't shut up, you see. So she had to shut him up. She made me stand in the corner of the room and watch. She put her hand over his mouth and nose. He wiggled a bit and made some grunts, but eventually he quieted. It was beautiful. His little eyes were glazed and staring at the ceiling. I was afraid at first, but mother made me touch him, made me see how beautiful it was."

"Motherfucker." The officer standing next to Dax breathed the words almost tonelessly.

"And it was beautiful, but she showed me that doing it that way was too easy. She trained me. She showed me how it worked. She'd hold me down in the tub, making me look her in the eyes as she held me underwater. Just when I didn't think I could hold my breath anymore, she'd let me up. She went to an estate sale one year and bought a brand-new coffin. It was a piece of beauty. I wish I still had it today...but I'm getting ahead of myself.

"Mother would put me in it and close it up, leaving me there for what seemed like hours on end, but was probably only twenty minutes at a time. She showed me what it meant, how it worked.

How beautiful death could be. The more I struggled, the better it was. She got me a birthday present when I was just six years old. We lived in a crappy neighborhood with crackhead parents who didn't watch their kids. There was a little girl, Dorothy Allen. I'll never forget her. She trusted me. I told her we were playing a game. She climbed into that coffin all on her own. Mother and I listened as she cried and beat on the lid for two hours. Mother walked me through what was happening. She understood. Finally when the fervor died down and no one cared about finding Dorothy anymore, mother let me open the lid. I've never experienced anything like I did with her that first time."

Dax was appalled. Staal was sicker than they'd imagined. "Where. Is. Mackenzie?" Dax bit the words out, not wanting to hear the filth spewing from Staal's mouth anymore.

"Calm down, she's right here, Ranger Chambers." Staal reached out and turned one of the three computer monitors around until Dax could see what Staal had been watching. It was grainy, and had a greenish hue to it, but everyone in the room could see what it was. It was Mackenzie. Inside a box.

"She's beautiful. So much more than any of the others. And I've come so far since Mother taught me what she knew. When she couldn't teach me anything else, I put *her* in our coffin and listened as *she* died a beautiful death. I've honed my craft. The water gives them hope, makes them hold on just a little bit longer. Prolonging their deaths. I tried using a walkie-talkie, but that didn't work at all, not enough range. I then found that using a special satellite phone, with extra strength, used by the toughest military teams in the world, was the key."

Staal leaned over and pushed a button on a small console on his desk. The haunting notes of Bonnie Tyler's "Total Eclipse of the Heart" sounded loud in the room. "Your last words to each other were beautiful. Epic. That's what I'd been missing with all the others.

They died, but no one knew. With Mackenzie, you knew. She knows she's dying. You know she's dying. You gave her permission to die. Fucking perfect. You told her to die, Chambers. It's my masterpiece. A beautiful death. I've recorded every second so everyone around the world can watch it as well. Once the media gets ahold of it, I'll be famous. Mackenzie will be famous. My beautiful death will be famous."

Staal finally stood up, holding a small pistol pointing straight at Dax.

Dax knew what was going to happen seconds before all hell broke loose. He screamed out, "Nooooooo, hold your fire!"

Just as the men around him opened fire on Jordan Charles Staal.

The smoke in the air was thick and choking. Dax coughed once, then twice as the air slowly cleared around them.

"Steady. Hold your positions!" Cruz yelled out. "Hold your fucking positions!"

Dax moved as if in a trance. He walked past the officers standing with their rifles now pointed at the ground, and around the side of the large desk Staal had been sitting behind. Dax felt as if he were having an out-of-body experience, he couldn't hear or see anything but Staal's dead body. He'd fallen backwards with the force of the bullets hitting his body, knocking the chair over in the process. He was lying on his back, arms outspread, blood slowly seeping into the light-blue carpet under Dax's feet. His legs were propped up on the seat of the tipped-over chair and his eyes were open, staring straight up. The gun, which Dax could now see was a fucking water pistol, lay next to his open hand, mockingly.

Dax moved his eyes to the desk top, turned the monitor Staal had twisted to face the doorway back to its original position, and groaned. He leaned over and propped himself on the desk with both hands and stared, not believing what he was seeing. The song coming through the speakers changed to the upbeat tones of the B-52s singing "Love Shack". The song so incongruent to what he was seeing, Dax could barely process it all.

There were three views of Mackenzie in the coffin. One was a viewpoint from the top corner of the small box. Another monitor showed a view from Mack's feet upward. Dax could see how small the box really was. Her breasts were almost brushing the top of the box and he could see her shift restlessly.

But it was the third view, on the monitor that Staal had turned to the room, that hit Dax the hardest. It was a close-up of Mack's face. It looked as though Staal had used a wide-angle lens and mounted it in the lid of the coffin, over her head.

Her eyes were huge, open wide as she struggled to see something, anything. Her pupils were dilated as far as they could go. Dax could even see the tear tracks on her face from where she'd sobbed in fear. She had a dark spot on her forehead, where a bruise from hitting the lid of her tomb was forming. She was holding the satellite phone up to her ear with a death grip. He could see her struggling to breathe. Her mouth was open as if she was gasping for air, and not getting any. Every now and then she'd tilt her head back, as if doing so would mean what little air was left in her tomb could get into her lungs more easily.

Dax could hear some of the SRT members walking through the house, making sure there was no one else lurking around waiting to ambush them and that Staal really was working alone. A door opened, footsteps sounded on the floor above them, the low murmurings of the officers clearing the rooms as they searched. Dax figured it was useless. Staal wouldn't have Mack stashed here. He'd already buried her somewhere, he was sure of it.

TJ came up beside Dax and put his hand on his shoulder. "Fucking hell, Dax. Come on, you don't need to watch that."

Dax shrugged off TJ's touch violently. "Don't touch me!"

"Let the guys get into the hard drives to see what they can get.

There's still time to find her, Dax."

Dax just shook his head. "It's too late. Look, TJ." He turned to his friend, throwing out a hand. "Fucking *look*! Without Staal here to tell us where she is, it's too late. We'll take too long. We'll never find her in time." Dax said the words, but readily moved when two officers came up behind him. One immediately started typing, careful not to blacken the screen with Mackenzie's face on it, knowing Dax would lose it if he lost sight of her.

"Maybe we can track the feed," one of the officers said to the other, entirely focused on what he was doing.

"Yeah, see if you can pinpoint where it starts. If it's within a few miles we can be there in minutes."

Ignoring the two men frantically trying to use their computer knowledge to find out where Staal had stashed Mackenzie, Dax ran his finger over the screen as if he was actually touching Mack's cheek. "God." The word was spoken with such angst, it was obvious to everyone in the room Dax was suffering.

TJ had no words for his friend, and finally backed off, leaving Dax to his grief.

"Dax, your phone." It was Quint. He'd run out to his patrol car and retrieved their phones. "The last words she hears should be yours."

Dax took the phones Quint held out with shaking fingers. There was still music coming from it. Mack was still hearing the sound of cheesy eighties melodies in her coffin. Dax didn't know if he could do it. He looked back at the monitor.

He didn't have a choice. For Mack. She should hear his voice, the voice of the man she loved, and who loved her back with his entire being.

He tapped off the music on Quint's phone and brought his own phone up to his ear.

"Hey, sweetheart. I'm back." Dax's voice was low and soothing and eerily echoed out of the speakers on the desktop.

"Daxton."

Dax took a deep breath. He loved hearing his name come from her mouth. He watched as Mackenzie shut her eyes and opened her mouth wider, trying to get air that wasn't available into her lungs.

"Please be quiet and listen, Mack. Relax. Close your eyes and let it happen. I'm right here with you. I have a story for you. This is a story of a boy who dreamed of a girl made just for him. This boy had the same dream every night. Every single night of his life, he dreamed of a special woman. Not a princess, not a millionaire, but a plain ol' hardworking woman. As the years went by, and he grew older, he continued to have the dream. He lived his life, made friends, dated, but not one woman he met was the one of his dreams. He dreamed about how she wasn't perfect. She made mistakes, but owned up to them immediately. She was clumsy and silly and had a tendency to pratter on when she was telling a story or when she was nervous. The man wanted that dream woman more than he could say, but she never appeared."

Dax cleared his throat, and tried to control the tears gathering in his throat and his eyes. He watched as a tear came out the side of Mack's eye as she lay gasping for breath and he dug deep to find the strength to continue. To give her this. Her last moments should be filled with the sound of his voice, not the sound of silence or some fucking pop song from years ago.

"One day the man met a woman, he said hello politely and went on his way, not knowing he'd just met the woman he'd dreamed about his entire life. Luckily, fate had pity on the couple, as they met again not long after. One day led to the next and before he knew what hit him, the man realized he hadn't dreamed of his special dream woman in weeks. He mourned the loss, until he realized there was no need to dream about her anymore, she was standing right in front of him.

"Mack, sweetheart. You're that woman. I've dreamed of you my entire life. I might not have had you for long, but I'll treasure every second you were in my arms, my bed and in my life. I love you, Mackenzie Morgan. You will not be forgotten. Not by me. Not by your family, not by any-fucking-body. Relax now, baby. Stop fighting. It's okay. I'm here with you now."

Dax watched through the tears in his eyes as Mackenzie's hand went lax and the phone she'd been holding fell by her head. Her mouth stopped gaping open and shut and she lay still, her eyes staring up at the camera, not blinking.

Dax clicked his phone off and put his hand on Mack's face on the monitor. She was gone.

A single tear coursed down Dax's cheek and he felt hollow inside. "I love you, Mack. There'll never be another like you."

Chapter Seventeen

—————◆—————

"**D**AX! MOVE YOUR ass!" Cruz's words were sharp and urgent and came from somewhere in the house.

Dax could tell his friend was shouting the words, as he heard them come from another room, but they also seemed to be coming from the speakers on the desk in front of him. Dax looked at the officers working on the computer next to him, they gazed back at him, eyes wide with disbelief.

Dax didn't want to go anywhere. He didn't care that Staal's dead body was on the floor behind him. He didn't care about anything but staying right where he was, being with Mackenzie. He didn't know how he'd get through the rest of the night, or the following day, or the next. He had a million things to do. He had to get ahold of Mackenzie's family and Laine. He had to... Hell, he had no idea *what* he needed to do.

"Seriously, Dax. Get your ass down here. Right fucking now!"

The words, louder in the room now that the officer next to him had turned up the volume on the speaker, made Dax stand up abruptly. Now that he was beginning to be able to think again he knew there was only one reason he'd be hearing his friend through the speakers of the computer Staal had been sitting in front of.

"Where the hell are you?" Dax roared, already on the move.

"Basement. Now, Dax!"

Dax jogged through a room with a sofa and TV to an open door, following the pointing finger of the officer standing next to it.

Obviously while he was saying good-bye to Mack, Cruz had been searching the house with the other officers. On auto-pilot, Dax pulled out his weapon and moved down the stairs, having a feeling he knew what he'd find.

Dax stopped dead in his tracks at the bottom of the stairs.

In the middle of the room was a large wooden rectangular box. It was sitting on a pedestal and there were four wires leading from the box up into the ceiling. He had a hard time processing what he was seeing. Dax's mind was still up in the office with Mackenzie.

Dax met Cruz's eyes.

"Look around, grab anything you can to help me get the lid off. It's nailed shut with about a million nails. We need something to help us get in there." Cruz's words were frantic as he and two other officers did their best to force the lid up by brute strength alone, with no luck.

Dax shoved his pistol into the holster at his back and looked around quickly, realizing what the hell was going on. His heart beat fast in his chest. How long had it been since he'd seen Mack take her last breath? If he was lucky, she might still have a chance. Dax spied a metal pipe leaning against a wall and grabbed it. He shoved it into Cruz's hands, hoping it would work. Dax continued to scan the room to see what else he could find.

There! A crowbar. Exactly what he needed.

Dax grabbed it and rushed over to Cruz's side. He put the end under the lid and pushed. At first he didn't think it was going to move, but finally Dax felt the lid move a tiny bit. With one more heave, getting help from Cruz and the others around the coffin and putting pressure on the metal tool, the lid finally shifted an inch.

"Grab it. Get it off!" Cruz's words were barked to the other officers. Every man around the box forced their fingers under the rim of the make-shift coffin, and pulled with all their might.

Dax held his breath as the lid was pushed open.

Mack.

She lay still, not moving, not breathing. She looked exactly like she did on the damn monitor. Her eyes were open, staring sightlessly up, her mouth parted, her hand lying lifeless next to her head. At her feet were piles of dirt. Staal had obviously dumped it into the coffin, ensuring she'd smell it and believe she was actually underground. Fucking bastard.

Dax didn't hesitate, but leaned over and scooped Mack up into his arms and lifted her from the damn tomb she'd been ensconced in and immediately laid her on the floor.

"Call the paramedics," he ordered Cruz.

"Already on their way, Ranger," one of the other officers said quickly.

Dax turned back to Mackenzie. He couldn't lose her now. Not when he'd been so close. She'd held on for too long for two damn minutes to make a difference between tearing his heart out or making his life complete.

Dax put two fingers on Mack's neck and felt a faint pulse. "She's got a heartbeat," he announced to no one in particular. She wasn't breathing though. He needed to get air into her lungs. He tilted her head back. Dax put one hand on her bruised forehead and the other on her chin, pulling her lip down. He leaned over and breathed twice into her mouth, pushing much-needed oxygen into her lungs.

"Come on, Mack. Come on, baby."

He breathed into her again.

"You can do it. Come on. Don't let him win."

He leaned over and breathed into Mack's mouth again.

"Come back to me, sweetheart. I need you."

Dax did it again, then again.

He firmed his voice. "Breathe, Mack. Fucking breathe already!"

Finally, Mackenzie coughed once, low, and Dax held his breath. "That's it, Mack. You can do it. Breathe, baby."

Dax wanted nothing more than to take Mack into his arms, but knew it wouldn't be smart. He kept his hands on her head and kept encouraging her. She slowly coughed harder and harder and finally Dax could see her gulping in air on her own.

He leaned down into her. "I'm so proud of you. You did it. Thank God. Thank you, Jesus." Dax sobbed into Mack's hair until the paramedics arrived.

DAX HELD MACKENZIE'S hand, refusing to let go, all the way to the hospital. Cruz brushed aside his thanks, telling him to "go with your woman." Dax didn't have to be told twice.

Mackenzie hadn't fully woken up yet. She had regained consciousness twice, but was obviously still confused about where she was and what had happened. She had an IV inserted and was being given oxygen. Dax hadn't seen any wounds on her, other than the bruise on her forehead, but wasn't taking any chances.

He'd refused to leave her room, telling the doctors she was under the Texas Rangers' protection, which wasn't exactly a lie. The nurses had changed her out of her soiled clothes and put her into a gown. After the doctor had examined her, they'd stuffed her under the covers, and Dax was finally alone with her.

He sat down next to the hospital bed and picked up Mack's hand. Her nails had been ripped and broken in her initial struggles when she'd awoken in the coffin and tried unsuccessfully to claw her way out, but otherwise she looked fine. Dax kissed each finger gently and rested his head on top of her hand on the mattress.

Now that the adrenaline was wearing off, and he knew Mack was safe and unharmed, Dax was exhausted. He quickly fell asleep, with one hand clasping Mack's and the other laying possessively and reassuringly on her stomach.

Mackenzie woke slowly and shifted, feeling something heavy on her belly. Suddenly remembering everything, she opened her eyes, then closed them immediately against the harsh light in the room.

Light. That's all she needed to know.

She wasn't buried alive anymore. Dax had found her, gotten to her.

She knew she'd had a close call. She recalled every second of straining to breathe, and not being able to get any oxygen into her lungs. She had no idea what had happened and how she'd been rescued, she just thanked God Daxton had done it.

Mackenzie moved a hand to her stomach and covered the hand that was laying there. Daxton's. She'd know it anywhere.

Mackenzie turned and squinted her eyes open this time, being more cautious now that she knew she was safe and with Daxton. All she could see was his hair. He was sound asleep, trapping her left hand under his head. Mack closed her eyes again.

Safe and with Daxton, that was all she needed to know. She fell asleep again without a further thought.

⁓

"SO YOU'RE TELLING me I wasn't buried alive at all?"

Mackenzie was sitting with Cruz, Quint, TJ, Calder, Conor, Hayden, and Laine in Daxton's apartment. She'd been released from the hospital a few hours ago and all of Daxton's friends, and Laine, had come over to see how she was doing.

"Nope. Fucker didn't actually bury anyone until after they'd died."

"Seriously? Man, that is fucked up."

Everyone laughed, even though it really wasn't funny.

"He'd run cameras into the coffin and was upstairs watching you. He was also listening to your phone call to Dax, getting off on it." Cruz laid it out for Mackenzie. He'd had a talk, privately, with Dax and asked what he thought Mackenzie should know. Dax had told him to say what he wanted, but if Dax thought Mack wasn't dealing, then he'd cut it off. So far, Mack was dealing just fine. She was amazing.

"I mean, really? It's one thing to kidnap women. It's another to want them for sexual shit. But he didn't even touch me. He didn't hurt me in any way. For him, it was all psychological torture? What a sick, sick man." Mackenzie held on to Daxton's hand tightly. It was hard to believe she'd made it through what she had, but she refused to dwell on it. She wouldn't give the Lone Star Reaper that.

"Apparently his mom taught him all he needed to know about killing when he was a young child. She made him watch as she suffocated his little brother, helped kidnap a little girl in the neighborhood, and they killed her the same way he ended up killing all those other women. But karma always wins; she taught him so well, Staal ended up killing his own mother, and then couldn't stop. We figure he killed his wife, but I'm not sure her body will ever be found. If he buried her coffin somewhere, it's probably better she's allowed to rest in peace. Somehow along the way, he fixated on law enforcement, specifically Dax here, and the rest is history."

Mackenzie turned to Daxton. "He was filming me in there?"

"Yeah, baby. He was."

"Are the tapes...will others see them?"

Dax turned to Mack and put his hands on her face. "Look at me, Mack. No one will see those tapes. I swear to you. Cruz took them. They're at the FBI. They won't go anywhere."

"I—"

"You're safe. The things you said to me. The stuff I said back. They're between us. No one else gets that. It's ours. Okay?"

"Okay. I get it. But, Daxton. If someone can learn from what he did, from what's on those tapes, I think we should let them see them. I don't remember some of the stuff I said, and I'm sure I was a big dork, but if somehow the FBI or whoever can use something to prevent this from happening again, I'm okay with that. Or maybe doctors somewhere can use them to see what happens during asphyxiation. Calder, do you think the medical examiner's office could use them?"

Dax pulled Mack into his arms. "Don't answer that, Calder. My Mack. Always thinking about others, aren't you?"

"Well, I'm not doing cartwheels that my last breaths—well, my almost-last breaths—are on tape in some deep dark vault somewhere, and I certainly never want to see it, and I don't want *you* to have to see that again, but Daxton, I'd feel bad to ask to have them destroyed if some good could come out of them."

"I love you, Mackenzie Morgan."

"And I love you, Daxton Chambers, but you *are* hearing what I'm saying, aren't you?"

"I hear you, baby. But trust me when I say, you taking your last breaths of oxygen, is not something anyone else can ever learn from."

Mackenzie snuggled into Daxton's arms, ignoring the others around them. "I hate him."

"Me too."

"But I hate him for what he did to *you* more than what he did to me. It's one thing to know, abstractly, that I'm dying, it's another thing altogether to see someone you love dying. I hate that he did that to you. I wish I could make you unsee it."

"Mack—"

"No, really. It's like when I was thirteen and I accidentally walked into the bathroom when Matthew was in there. I can never unsee that. Seriously. Seeing your brother's you-know-what when you're on the verge of womanhood is never a good thing. I thought I'd be scarred for life. I'm surprised I even let Donny what's-his-name get to second base at prom when I was a junior. All I'm saying is that some things can't be unseen, and that's one of those things that should never have been seen in the first place. Damn Jordan whatever, for doing that to you. It sucks, and I hate it. I'm glad he's dead. I'm glad he got blown away. Fucker."

"Bloodthirsty little thing, isn't she?" Conor commented from the chair across from the sofa.

"Yeah." Dax's agreement was soft and heartfelt. "All I see now is you, here in my arms. Alive, breathing, and making me want to laugh and roll my eyes at the same time, Mack. Go with it."

"Okay. Are you guys hungry? I'm hungry. They wouldn't give me anything at the hospital and Daxton wouldn't stop to get me fries on the way home. Anyone want pizza? Maybe we can order some pizza. Oh and Daxton, you heard Mark and Matthew are coming over right? We never did get to that family get-together we had planned. Between your job and me being kidnapped by a psycho serial killer, we haven't made it over there yet. There was no way I could say no when they said they wanted to see me. Don't be surprised if mom comes over with them."

"I knew they were coming, Mack. No worries."

"Okay, but remember what I said about them. They're a little crazy."

Laine piped in at that. "They *are* a little crazy. Mack, remember that time we wanted to go to that party and Matthew busted us? I said I'd be at your house and you said you'd be at mine. He came home from college and wanted to see you and called over to my house. My mom told him we were at *your* house. He knew where the party was usually held, and pulled us out of that hotel room kicking and screaming.

Mackenzie smiled at her friend. "Yeah, how embarrassing." She looked back at Daxton. "See? Even my best friend thinks my family is crazy."

"Okay, sweetheart."

"Good. Oh, and are we still going to Austin? Because I think I could go for that. Hotel Ella sounded so awesome. I looked it up and did you know some of the suites are bigger than my apartment? Don't get one of those, though, what a waste of space, especially if we're going to spend all our time in bed. Oh shit, I didn't mean to say that out loud. Please forget you heard that, guys. Oh, and you should know, I'm not a Longhorn fan. I know, it's sacrilegious, but I thought you should know in case you wanted to walk around the UT campus oohing and ahhing about everything. I'm weird and couldn't really give a crap about football or basketball or anything related to college. I went, got my degree, and I'm really proud of that, but I'm not into all the hoopla with the sports. Sorry."

"It's okay, Mack."

"But I *am* a fan of law enforcement. I've always loved a man in uniform and I think I love them even more now that my rescue went down with like four different agencies participating. It's a girl's dream come true, no offense, Hayden. You're hot in your uniform too, though I don't go that way, but it's okay if you—"

Dax had enough. He leaned over, cutting off Mack's passionate babbling with a gentle hand on her mouth. "You mean, *I'm* your dream come true."

Mackenzie turned her serious eyes up to Daxton. When he moved his hand she said, "I vaguely remember you telling me a story about a little boy dreaming about the girl of his dreams. Didn't I?" At Daxton's nod, she continued. "I had the same dream. I knew I'd find you, it just took longer than I wanted it to."

"I love you, Mack."

"I love you back, Daxton."

"Enough snutaling on the couch, you two. Mack's family is coming over, you better not be naked when they get here," TJ warned with a laugh.

"Snutaling? Is that a word?" Mackenzie asked chuckling.

"Who cares? You get what I mean."

"Okay, Daxton will stop snutaling. I need to get up and get ready to see my family."

Dax kissed Mack on the lips hard. "You look fine the way you are, Cruz will get the door when they get here."

Without a word of protest, Mackenzie eased herself back into Daxton's arms. If she didn't have to get up, she wouldn't. There was no place she'd rather be than right there, safe, in Daxton's arms, surrounded by their friends.

Chapter Eighteen

———◆———

MACKENZIE STRETCHED, FEELING delicious. She felt a hand on her stomach and then felt Daxton lick at her folds. She groaned in delight. "Oh my God, Daxton. Seriously?"

"I can't get enough of you…of us."

"Aren't you tired? What time is it?"

Dax grinned up at Mackenzie. He'd left the table lamp on next to the bed so he could see Mack as he made love with her. "It's around three."

"Daxton," Mackenzie moaned and squirmed in his grip as he ran his hands over her stomach and down to her thighs, parting them so he could fit more comfortably between them. "It's only been two hours since you last made love to me. You can't possibly be ready to go again."

"Mack, I'm not fifteen anymore, of course I'm not ready to go again yet, but I can't resist you. And women aren't made like men are. You can come over and over."

"Daxton…" The word came out as a whine.

"This time we're coming together, sweetheart. No, don't protest. I haven't pushed, and you're so primed, you'll be screaming my name before too long. It'll take me longer to get there so we'll have time to work you up, this won't be a problem. Trust me."

"Touch me, Daxton. Please. I need you."

Dax pushed one finger into Mackenzie's folds and felt her clench down on him. "This is just as sexy as I knew it would be. You are fucking soaked with both our juices. I wish you could see yourself. My cum is slowly seeping out of you, and the more worked up you get, the faster it comes out." Dax knew he was being crude, but he couldn't help it. He scooped up some of their juices with his fingers and brought it to his mouth. "Fucking fantastic."

Before Mack could say anything, Dax moved so he was on his back and Mackenzie was straddling his stomach. He held on to her hips with his hands until she was steady.

Mackenzie looked down at Daxton with heavy-lidded eyes, ready for whatever he wanted. They'd been adventurous in bed, and if he wanted her to ride him, she was ready. They'd done that before and he'd made her explode right before he'd taken her hard.

"Come up here, I want more of that."

"Oh my God, Daxton, no."

Ignoring her embarrassment, Dax grabbed Mack by her hips and encouraged her to scoot up his chest until she was kneeling over him. He looked up at her folds before moving. "Yes. Can you feel us, Mack?"

She could. Mack could feel their fluids dripping from inside her to dampen her inner thighs. "Daxton…" She tried again to move.

"Oh no, stay right where you are." Dax pulled Mack down to him and got to work building her up to another orgasm. He used his lips and his mouth to lick and suck until she was shaking and he knew she was on the verge of exploding.

Mackenzie had never, in all her sexually active years, had a man want to taste her after he'd come inside her. She thought it'd be weird, or even gross, but if she was honest with herself, it was hotter than hell.

Dax pushed Mack down his body, loving the feel of her wetness smearing over his chest and stomach. Finally she rested on his lower abs. "Take me in your hand, baby. Feel how much I love this, love you. Put me in. Take me."

He didn't have to say it twice. Mackenzie rose on her knees just far enough to reach under herself and grab him. She fit him to her, scooted back into place and sank down with a groan.

"That's it. Now ride me, Mack. Take what you need. Take me."

Mackenzie concentrated on the amazing feeling of Dax inside her. She could feel him flex within her and she squeezed him as she pulled up, then slammed back down. She placed her hands on his chest to brace herself, and did it again, then again. Each time she came down on him, she clasped him with her inner muscles with all her strength.

Dax reached up, took Mack's breasts in his hands, and grasped her a little harder than he would if they were just getting started. He pinched her nipples. "Harder, Mack. Do it. Fuck me, baby."

At his words, Mackenzie did as he asked. She slammed herself up and down on Dax, lost in the exquisite sensations.

"Touch yourself, Mack. Rub your clit. Do it. Now. Make yourself come all over my dick."

Lost in the moment, and not feeling any embarrassment, Mackenzie trailed one hand where they were joined and rubbed against her bundle of nerves, hard. She immediately felt the orgasm building.

"It's coming, Daxton. Almost…"

"Keep riding me, baby. There you go. You're beautiful. Fucking beautiful, and mine. Keep going, harder. That's it."

Mackenzie let Daxton's words wash over her. She *felt* beautiful. In his arms, in his bed, she felt like the prettiest woman in the world. She wasn't thinking about what had happened to her with Staal or of how awkward sex had been previously for her. Her orgasm was coming, and coming fast.

She touched herself one last time and hunched forward as she felt her orgasm start to move through her. "Oh God, yes, Daxton!"

Dax felt the fingernails of Mack's left hand digging into his chest and ignored them. He slammed Mack down on himself twice more then held her there as she shook and trembled in his arms through her climax.

Finally, he eased her down, still twitching. "Easy, Mack. That's it. Just relax. I've got you. Good girl." Dax continued to murmur to her until she finally came back to herself and her surroundings.

"You killed me, Daxton. Seriously. But you didn't—"

"I did."

"What?"

Dax chuckled. "We came at the same time, sweetheart."

Mackenzie sat up and braced herself on Daxton's chest. "No we didn't."

"Yeah, we did." Dax rubbed one thumb over Mack's sensitive clit and she shuddered. "Can't you feel me inside? You drained me dry, Mack. We came together."

Mackenzie burst into tears and collapsed on his chest. Dax simply wrapped his arms around the woman he loved and smiled, waiting for her to get it all out, knowing why she was crying.

"I d-d-didn't think I'd ever be able to—"

"Shhhh, I know. I knew you could. You just needed to get out of your head to do it."

"I love you. I fucking love you so much."

"I love you too, Mack. And just so you know, that wasn't a one-off. It's gonna happen again. Not every time, no. But it will happen again."

"Good. I liked it."

"Good. Sleep, baby."

"Are you gonna let me sleep? Or are you gonna wake me up in twenty minutes to go again?"

Dax chuckled. "Sleep for now. We'll play it by ear and see how it goes."

Dax held Mackenzie close, still inside her, as she slid into sleep. He brushed her hair back behind her ear and listened to her breathe.

He'd never take such a simple thing for granted again. Seeing Mack take her last breath would haunt him for the rest of his life. He was very grateful he'd been able to get to her in time to breathe life back into her, but it'd been close, too close.

Thank God for Cruz searching Staal's house so quickly after everything had gone down. If it hadn't been for him, they wouldn't have found Mack in time. If they'd found her twenty minutes, ten minutes…hell, even five minutes later than they did, he would've had to stand at the side of her grave in a cemetery. He owed Cruz everything.

Dax had driven to Austin with Mack to Hotel Ella to hide out after the press had hounded them. Everyone wanted an interview with the woman who'd been kidnapped by a serial killer, and died, but then been brought back to life. Mackenzie had given a few interviews then called it quits. She'd told Dax she understood why people were curious, and she'd told her story, but enough was enough.

They'd been in Austin for three days, and just like they'd originally planned, hadn't left the hotel room and hadn't worn any real clothes for the entire time they'd been there. They'd just enjoyed being with each other, alive and well.

Dax leaned down and kissed the top of Mack's head. He was the luckiest man in the world.

Epilogue

—— ◆ ——

"I DON'T LIKE it, Cruz." Daxton tried to reason with his friend. "Why the hell do you have to be the one?"

"Look, it's only for a couple of months, then I'll be back. There simply isn't anyone else who can do it."

"Bullshit. Going undercover for months isn't healthy. I've known too many people who get completely fucked up in the head by being under for too long."

"I appreciate your concern, Dax, but I'm doing it."

Dax sighed and ran his hand through his hair. "Tell me again what you can."

"You know as well as I do the drug situation is getting out of control. We do everything possible, but they won't stop. I'm going undercover to try to see if I can find out where they're coming from. We keep getting the low-level players, and they don't matter. We need to find the source."

"And how do you think you'll be able to infiltrate the drug ring in a month or so without drawing suspicion to yourself?"

Cruz sighed, knowing his friend wasn't going to like what he had to tell him. "We think we know who the mid-level man of one of the drug rings is. He's the leader of a motorcycle gang. Word is that he has a girlfriend who doesn't know anything about what he's doing. I don't believe it. I'm going to see if I can—"

"Fuck, Cruz!" Dax exploded. "You can't bring a woman into this. You know as well as I do how fucked-up that is. Not to mention, cozying up to an MC president's girlfriend isn't the smartest move."

"Look, first, she's *already* in it, I'm not bringing her into anything. Innocent or not, whether she knows what's going on or not, she's in there. All I'm going to do is see if I can't get her to open up to me. I want to check it out, see if she's as innocent as the other agents think she is. Personally, I think she's hiding something. How the hell can she not know her boyfriend is a fucking drug runner? Do you know how many people have been killed by this shit?"

"You're using her." Dax knew how it worked. He'd done an undercover assignment or two in his time, but he wasn't sure this one was a good idea.

"Yeah, but think of how many lives I'll be saving."

"You'll stay in touch?"

Cruz smiled at his friend. "Yeah, I'll stay in touch."

"If you need help, you'll let me know?"

"Yeah."

"You were there for me when Mack was taken. I'm not taking this lightly, Cruz. You're my brother, I'd do anything for you. Promise me, if this shit goes bad, you'll get out. You know how upset Mack would be if something happened to you. Hell, she's not going to like that she can't talk to you for a couple of months. You'd better find some way to appease her."

Cruz grinned. He loved how Mackenzie and Dax were together. Dax was a completely different person around Mack, and didn't give a fuck how cheesy he acted. They were in love. Truly in love. Cruz was happy for his friend.

"I will. Give her my love, will ya?"

"Yeah, and the others will want to know what's going on as well. If you just disappear for a couple of months, they're gonna notice and question it."

That was another thing that had come out of Mackenzie's kidnapping and Staal's death. The group of friends had gotten even closer. They made it a point now to hang out together. They went out for drinks, and had dinner together all the time. Even though they were all from different law enforcement agencies, with different priorities and missions, they were all on the same side. Working together to find and rescue Mackenzie had solidified their relationships.

"I thought maybe you could let them know what was up once I was gone."

"Fucking hell, Cruz."

"Well?"

"Okay, shit. Yeah, I'll let them know. Only if you check in regularly though."

"You got it."

"Keep your head down. Don't let them catch on. And don't fuck with that woman. If she knows, fine, get out and let your Director know. If she doesn't, do what you can to get her away from him, but if she won't go, fuck it. Don't get caught in the middle."

"This isn't my first rodeo, Dax. I fucking know how this works."

"Okay then. I'll talk to you soon, and see you in a few months?"

"Yeah."

"Stay safe, my friend."

"You too, Dax."

Cruz walked away, his mind already moving to his upcoming undercover mission. He'd take down the drug ring if it was the last thing he did. He didn't care who got in his way; he'd use his own mother, God rest her soul, if it meant getting more drugs off the street. He owed his ex-wife that, at the very least.

It wouldn't change anything for her, or them, but maybe it would for someone else.

Read on for the next book in the series:
Justice for Mickie.

JUSTICE FOR MICKIE

BADGE OF HONOR
TEXAS HEROES
BOOK 2

By Susan Stoker

Chapter One

———— ◆ ————

CRUZ LIVINGSTON TOOK a deep breath and willed himself to relax. He'd been undercover with the Red Brothers Motorcycle Club for a month—no, twenty-six days to be exact—and in his eyes, it was twenty-six days too long. Undercover assignments were never easy, but this had been like taking a fiery trip to hell the entire time.

He hadn't expected the job to be sunshine and roses, but he'd obviously gotten soft, because Cruz knew some of the shit he'd been forced to do to "prove" himself would haunt him for a long time. He hadn't killed or been pushed to rape anyone, thank God, but he'd threatened and beaten men up, and sold drugs. It was the selling of the drugs that had almost broken him.

It was ironic, the very reason he'd gone undercover—to *stop* the sale of drugs—was what he'd been forced to do from the very start of this assignment.

Cruz hadn't seen much of Ransom's supposed girlfriend, the person he was supposed to be getting close to in order to get information about the president. Her name was Angel, but from what Cruz could tell, she wasn't much of a girlfriend, more like a woman he was screwing. Cruz had seen Ransom fuck women in the middle of the clubhouse, not caring who was watching, so he obviously wasn't concerned about being exclusive with Angel.

Cruz's original plan had been to get in tight with the girlfriend and see what he could find out about the operation through her. But he had quickly found out that wasn't going to work. Ransom didn't give a shit about Angel, so it would look extremely odd for him to be cozying up to the woman.

MCs typically had two types of women hanging around—bikers' old ladies and club whores. The old ladies were somewhat respected by the other members of the club, and weren't ever disrespected by the whores or anyone outside the tight-knit group. The whores, on the other hand, were there to fuck and to use. Period. The whores knew their place, and never complained about it, ever hopeful that one day they might catch the eye of one of the members and become an old lady.

Cruz figured many of them continued to hang around for the drugs they were given in return for their services far more than they wanted to be an old lady. It was hard for him to fathom why any woman would allow herself to be mistreated as the whores in this club were, free drugs or not.

In the twenty-six days Cruz had been a prospect of the club, he'd seen some of the worst treatment of women he'd ever had the misfortune to observe in all his life, and that was saying something. His job as a member of the FBI included some pretty gnarly things, but watching as a drugged-out, half-conscious woman got gang-banged by ten members of the Hermanos Rojos motorcycle club, who didn't give a shit how rough they were, was one of the worst. The only reason Cruz hadn't had to participate was because of his prospect status. Until he was deemed "worthy" of the club, he wasn't allowed to participate in the orgies. Thank God.

Cruz knew he couldn't save everyone, but watching the women essentially get raped by the MC members brought to mind his ex-wife. She'd never been raped, but Cruz hadn't been able to save her from other seedy parts of life.

Cruz shook his head, trying to get back into the game. Standing in the middle of the Red Brothers' clubhouse wasn't the time to remember his fucked-up relationship with his ex-wife.

"Yo, Smoke, get your ass over here!" Ransom called from across the room.

Cruz had chosen the nickname Smoke when he'd joined the club. He hadn't bothered to explain it, letting the club members think what they wanted about the name. In actuality, it was his friend Dax who'd come up with the moniker. They'd joked that he was sneaky like smoke…getting into every crevice of the Hermanos Rojos's business and hopefully being the reason they were eventually taken down.

The only reason Cruz was able to infiltrate the MC was because an FBI agent who'd had a long-term undercover assignment at another club, near the border of Texas and Mexico, had vouched for Cruz when Ransom and his vice president had inquired. Simply being allowed in the clubhouse, and being privy to much of what went on there, was a huge step in being able to gather information on the club and hopefully stop one of the many entry points for drugs into the city.

He'd told Ransom and the others he was a part-time mall security cop. He had to have some sort of job, and doing anything directly related to law enforcement was definitely out, but he also needed a reason to look relatively clean-cut and not quite so "bikerish."

Cruz ambled over to where Kitty, Tick, and three other members of the club were standing.

"What's up?" Cruz asked with a chin lift to the guys.

"Got a job for ya," Ransom said with disdain, obviously annoyed at something. "I'm keeping some pussy on the side, but she's getting to be a pain in my ass. You know, demanding and shit, but I've got plans for her, so I can't piss her off. She called and demanded to come over to the clubhouse tonight. I don't particularly like her ass anywhere near here, but if I want to get in there and use her to get more high-class customers, I have to give in. I need you to go and pick her ass up."

Cruz's mind spun. He figured Ransom was talking about Angel, but he hadn't been privy to what customers Ransom thought he could get by using her. Cruz wondered just what other plans the president of the club had.

"Sure thing. What's the bitch look like?" Cruz's words were sneered with just the right amount of attitude.

"She's tall and skinny with big tits, which makes her nice to fuck. She's got long blonde hair and fancies herself in love with a real live MC president." The other guys laughed as if Ransom had said the funniest thing they'd ever heard.

"What's the draw, Pres?" Cruz knew he was pushing his luck, but he wanted to see if he could dig a bit deeper and see if getting in with Angel's friends was the only reason the man was hanging around her.

"The draw is that we're trying to expand business, and Angel is beautiful to look at but dumb as a rock. She's got access to a whole new set of customers...fancy-ass rich women, and we need to draw them in. She's so enamored of my role, and my cock, she'll do whatever I tell her to. I know she wants to continue to suck my MC president dick, so she'll do what I want, no questions asked."

Cruz didn't like what he was hearing, but kept his voice even. "So, I pick her ass up and bring her back here, then what?"

"Then we throw a lame-ass party with the old ladies, no whores around, she sees we're harmless, like a real-live, fucking romance novel or like that stupid-ass TV show, and she goes on her merry way. I get her hooked on me and the lifestyle she wants to believe in, as well as the drugs, and she'll be my ticket to selling to her rich friends."

Cruz's stomach turned. He wondered if this was how his ex had started out. He didn't know Angel, but there was no way he wanted to be a party to anything Ransom had in store for her, never mind her friends.

When he'd volunteered for the assignment, the goal was for him to gain some knowledge the FBI could use to remove just one of the avenues for drugs getting into the city, and if necessary, plant the seed for placing a more long-term agent inside the club. Since Cruz wasn't supposed to be there for months, he was to gather evidence about their drug-dealing so the agency could keep their eye on the club and, if things went as planned, bring down some of their contacts as well. No one knew how deep the Hermanos Rojos were with the big players.

Ransom wanting to use innocent women—although always a possibility; they'd known about Angel going in—was something that would never be all right with Cruz. If he could save Angel in the process of shutting down some of their supply lines before he got out, all the better.

"Sounds easy enough. Pick her up, bring her here. Got it. You got her address?"

"Better. I'm tracking her. Planted a bug in her purse. Bitch doesn't go anywhere without that huge-ass bag." Ransom flicked a small electronic device in Cruz's direction. "You'll see where she is. Bring her ass back here at eight. Not a second before. We'll do the party thing, I'll take her home, fuck her, and be back here by eleven. Then we can *really* party."

The other men around him laughed crudely.

Ransom focused on the other members of his club. "Make sure the whores are back by then. I'm in the mood for a gang bang tonight. Angel's tight pussy just won't be enough. There's nothing like fucking a whore when she's tied down and squirming for more."

Cruz laughed along with the other men at the president's words, while cringing inside.

"One more thing, Smoke," Ransom warned as Cruz started to leave.

Cruz turned back to the president and lifted his chin.

"Angel has a bitch of a sister who doesn't want her to have anything to do with the club. She's been riding Angel's ass, and I'm sick of it. Do whatever it takes to keep her skanky ass away, even if that means you put her out of commission for a while. That bitch had better not fuck with my plans, otherwise she'll find herself hurt in a way so she won't be *able* to mess with me."

Chapter Two

———— ◆ ————

MICHELLE "MICKIE" KAISER sat across from her sister in the small restaurant and tried to reason with her.

"Angel, those guys are bad news, seriously. I've told you this a million times."

"And I keep telling *you* to back the hell off. Ransom already doesn't like you. He knows how you harp on me and he's fed up with it. I was hoping you'd support me, and be friends with my boyfriend, but you haven't ever liked *any* of the men I've dated."

"You know that's not true. I just think you could do better. I honestly think Ransom is using you."

"How is he using me? Huh? Tell me that. He dotes on me, buys me stuff, and he *listens* to me when I talk, which is more than you do."

Mickie tried really hard not to lose her cool. "Think about this for a second, Angel. First of all, he's at least twenty years older than you. It's actually kind of gross. He's also never invited you to his house, wherever that might be. He comes to your apartment, fucks you, then leaves. He doesn't date you at all. No movies, no dinners, no nothing. Buying you skanky, whorish clothes to wear isn't love. He's creepy and scary as hell."

Angel flipped her hair so it fell in waves down her back. She leaned over the table and narrowed her blue eyes at her sister. "He loves me, Mickie. Why can't you be happy for me?"

Mickie threw her hands up and leaned back against the seat with a huff, not surprised Angel ignored everything she'd said. She tried to keep her voice low and reasonable. "I want you to find love as much as you do, but Ransom doesn't love you, Angel. He's using you. I don't know why, or how, but he is."

"He's *not* using me. He likes to hear about all my friends. He's *interested* in me and my life. And for your information, he invited me to his clubhouse tonight for a party. He wants to show me off to his friends. You'll see. He's fine."

"Oh my God!" Mickie was quickly losing patience with her younger sister. "This is *not* a romance novel. He's *not* a good guy, Angel. You aren't going to find hearts and flowers with him. Invited you to his clubhouse for a party? Do you know what goes on in those places? Again, this is not like one of those MC books you read. He does drugs, he probably runs guns—shit, he most likely has a stable full of women he pimps out."

"He does not! Jesus, you're always such a downer!"

"You don't know anything about him, Angel. I've done some research—"

"Oh hell no! I don't want to hear it."

"No, seriously, Angel. He's been arrested—"

Angel stood up from the table and put her hands on her hips and stared down at her sister. "No, I mean it. You've hated every guy I've ever dated. Just because you're embarrassed that you were boring in the sack and your husband left you for another woman, doesn't mean *every* guy is like *him*. Look at you! You'll never catch another man's eye. Your hair is too short—no one likes short hair! You're fat, have no sense of style, and you're a nagging bitch. It's not like you'll ever read one of my romance books and understand what the MC world is like. Under all his gruffness, he's a good guy. I've seen it. So leave me alone. Just because Ransom drinks and smokes and occasionally goes to a strip club, doesn't mean he's a bad guy."

Mickie ignored the hurt her sister's words caused and tried one more time. "All I'm saying is to watch your back. Please, Angel, I know you think MC guys are all marshmallows under their hard exteriors. That they do bad things for the good of the community, but these guys are *not* like that. They're doing bad things for the sake of doing bad things. They're breaking the law and they're scary, sis. Thugs. I don't want you hurt."

"Fuck you, Mickie. *You* aren't happy, so you don't want to see *me* be happy. I don't think I want to talk to you anymore. Good luck with your life. You're lonely and pathetic and you're going to be like that forever."

Angel stormed out of the restaurant, her blonde hair twitching behind her perfect body as she went. Mickie pushed her plate away and dropped her head on her arms dejectedly. "That didn't go well," she mumbled under her breath.

Mickie had no idea why she continued to try to watch over Angel. It was absurdly obvious her sister wanted nothing to do with her. But it wasn't something she could just turn off. She loved her sister, no matter how badly Angel treated her. She held out hope that eventually Angel would grow up and they'd be able to have a sisterly relationship.

Mickie was ten years older than her; Angel had been an "oops" baby, and their wealthy parents hadn't really wanted to start over with another kid when she was born. They'd left a lot of her raising to Mickie, leaving her to do most of the babysitting. When Mickie was ready to head off to college, her parents convinced her to go to the local community college and live at home instead of going away. They hadn't wanted to lose their unpaid babysitter.

Mickie hated thinking badly about her own parents, but by the time she'd realized how they'd made her feel guilty over wanting to go away to school and how much Angel would miss her, she'd made her decision.

By the time Angel had reached middle school, she'd seen their parents manipulate Mickie so much, she'd learned to do it like a pro. Their parents gave her whatever she wanted just to shut her up and keep her out of their hair. Mickie had tried to teach Angel right from wrong but somewhere along the line, Angel had decided her sister was the enemy.

They couldn't look more different. No one ever guessed they were sisters. Where Angel was tall, slender, and light, Mickie was curvy and dark. She kept her black hair short and couldn't care less about makeup, fashion, or pleasing those around her. She said what she wanted to say, and to hell with what others thought. On the other hand, Angel wore full makeup in the sixth grade and had dated more boys than Mickie could even remember.

Angel's words had hurt, but Mickie was sadly used to them. She didn't want to take notice, but she couldn't help it. Anytime Angel didn't want to hear what Mickie was telling her, she'd strike back at her sister's looks or her disastrous marriage. There were days Mickie thought she looked good, but Angel's words could still sometimes hit her where she was most vulnerable, and she'd fall back into believing she wasn't as pretty as her sister.

Angel was also always telling her that she would never talk to her again, but Mickie knew the next time her sister needed something, she'd conveniently forget anything she'd said in the past and call her for help.

Ignoring the hurt in her belly, Mickie thought about this Ransom guy. He completely freaked her out. He was bad news, and she knew she'd never forgive herself if she didn't *try* to warn Angel. Even if they didn't get along, Mickie still loved her. She was her sister. Her younger sister. The girl who'd held her hand when she was small. Who Mickie had mostly raised. Mickie had known going into lunch that it was a long shot to try once more to talk Angel out of dating the president of the motorcycle club, but she'd had to try.

Mickie had to give Angel one thing, Ransom was a good-looking man. He was in his mid-forties and had dark brown hair. He had a beard, but it wasn't one of those beards that were long and straggly looking. Ransom kept it neatly groomed. It hung about an inch below his chin and actually looked soft. He was a few inches taller than Angel, probably a bit over six feet. He wasn't all muscle, he could probably stand to lose about fifteen pounds, but he wasn't obese. The few times Mickie had seen him, he'd been wearing his leather vest with nothing underneath. He didn't have a beer belly, but there was no six-pack present either.

All in all, he wasn't a troll, but it was the look in his eyes that freaked Mickie out the most. They were cold. Cold, hard, and empty, as if he didn't have any morals and didn't give a crap if what he did hurt someone else. And that was the thing. Mickie didn't want Angel to be the one he didn't care about hurting.

Mickie had done a bit of research about Ransom and his motorcycle club. It was really a gang. They called themselves the Red Brothers, or Hermanos Rojos, and one story had claimed it was because of the amount of blood they'd spilt around the city.

If that wasn't enough to scare the hell out of Mickie, she read that they'd been involved in drugs, owned a strip club that had been busted for prostitution more than once, and one member of the gang had been put in prison for murder the year before.

Every man in the gang had a tattoo that said "Loyalty to One," whatever that meant. Mickie had seen a picture of the tattoo on a newspaper exposé of the club. The men in the gang apparently were "honored" with the ink once they were voted in as full members. It was huge, and spanned their entire backs, from shoulder to shoulder and down to just above their butts. It was a takeoff of lady justice, but instead of being a woman, it was a man sitting on a motorcycle. He was holding a pistol in one hand in place of a sword, and rather than the scales of justice, he was holding up the severed head of a man who had been blindfolded. The letters RB were on one side of the vest the man on the motorcycle was wearing, and on the other side was the letter R. Above the image were the words "Loyalty to One" in beautiful scrolled letters.

The entire tattoo was creepy as hell, and Mickie couldn't believe that anyone would voluntarily get it put on their back permanently.

Even the women who hung around the men in the club were hard and scary looking. The same exposé about the gang included the tattoos the women got that read, "Property of...", and listed the man they belonged to. The words were put on the backs of their necks, as well as on their lower stomachs. One woman who was interviewed had proudly claimed they were inked in both places so no matter how their man was "doing them," they could see the brand on their skin.

Mickie shivered. She liked reading romance novels herself, and even liked the ones that portrayed submissive women to their domi-nant men, but she didn't think these MC relationships were like that.

Angel was twenty-four years old; more than old enough to make her own decisions, but Mickie knew this wasn't the *right* choice. But obviously trying to talk sense into her sister hadn't done any good.

Mickie sighed and kept her eyes closed as she rested her head on her hands and tried to figure out what she was going to do next.

CRUZ HELD HIS breath and tried to filter through what he'd just heard. He was sitting in the booth behind Angel and her sister. He'd arrived just after Angel, having followed her with the tracking device Ransom had planted in her purse.

Everything Mickie had tried to tell her sister had been dead-on correct. Ransom had been right in his assessment of Angel, she wasn't very smart, but she *was* beautiful. Cruz felt bad for the sister. He hadn't gotten a good look at her because he'd already been seated behind Angel when Mickie had come into the restaurant, and she'd come at the booth from the opposite direction of the one he was sitting in.

Angel hadn't sugar-coated her words, and Cruz had flinched when she'd laid into Mickie about her looks. No woman liked hearing she wasn't pretty.

While Cruz didn't have any brothers or sisters, he did have good friends he considered his family. If they wanted to warn him about a girlfriend, he might not necessarily agree with them, but out of respect, and due to his history with his ex and, yes, love, he'd listen to what they had to say.

The fact that Angel wouldn't even listen to Mickie was telling. She was used to getting her way and doing what she wanted. Spoiled was how Cruz would characterize her. Ransom wasn't the smartest person Cruz had ever met, but he wasn't stupid either. He couldn't be and have clawed his way to being the president of the MC. He'd chosen well in Angel. She was pretty, stubborn, spoiled, and clueless. She'd most likely do exactly what Ransom wanted her to do, including trying to sell her friends drugs if it came down to it. Damn.

He didn't like Ransom's threat against Angel's sister. It was obvious he had plans for Angel, and if her sister did somehow convince her that Ransom was bad news, the MC President wasn't going to be happy. He didn't even know the woman sitting in the booth behind him, but if her stubborn tone was anything to go by, she wasn't going to let the matter of her sister dating Ransom drop. The president was right to be worried about her.

Ransom's not-so-vague threat about hurting his pseudo-girlfriend's sister echoed in his mind. If Ransom had no issues asking Cruz to hurt her, he wouldn't have any problem ordering any of the other members of the club to do it as well. Cruz knew without a doubt that Ransom would do it too. He'd have her hurt to keep her away from Angel. And that was unacceptable. Cruz couldn't exactly warn her off without blowing his cover, but he could try to stick close to make sure Ransom didn't get near her. It wasn't a perfect plan, but if she got hurt and he didn't do anything to prevent it, he'd feel like shit. If push came to shove, he'd tell Ransom he was tailing the sister and keeping his eye on her. That should buy them both some time. If Ransom thought the sister was under control, maybe he wouldn't sic anyone else on her.

He thought about what his next steps were. He was supposed to meet Angel in a couple of hours and bring her into the lion's den, but he knew what he had to do before then. He'd ditched the idea of getting close to Angel because Ransom had been keeping her far away from the club up until now. He was gathering quite a bit of information without having to involve the woman, which was a relief.

Cruz got up and left the restaurant, going the long way around the table Angel had been sitting at so her sister didn't see him. Not that she'd notice him if he walked right by her. Her head was face down on the table.

He put his leather vest, which the members of the club called a cut, in the trunk of the small black piece-of-shit car the FBI had given him for the assignment. He'd wanted to have a Harley, but he'd been denied by the bean counters at the FBI. Damn the government and their budget cuts. They'd argued the expense was only worth it for long-term undercover assignments, not his short-term one. Cruz could've used his own bike, but didn't want to risk it getting wrecked, confiscated, or stolen while on assignment.

So Cruz had sucked it up and taken the shit from the Red Brothers about his lack of a bike. It wasn't normal for a prospect not to have a motorcycle, but somehow they'd bought it...with the groundwork story laid by the other agent in the southern club about how his previous bike had been stolen.

Cruz took out a pair of sneakers and exchanged his black boots with the zippers and rings on them for the more normal shoes. He also pulled a black T-shirt over his tank top, and even tucked it into his jeans to try to look more respectable. Cruz ran his hand briefly over his short crew cut. There was nothing he could do about the stubble on his face. It was too short to be called a beard, but too long to really be called a five o'clock shadow.

He took a deep breath and headed back into the restaurant toward the sister's table. Here went nothing.

MICKIE DIDN'T KNOW how long she'd been sitting at the table with her forehead resting on her arms when she heard someone talking to her. She lifted her head and saw an absolutely beautiful man standing next to her table.

She looked around, thinking he must have the wrong table, but when she gazed back up at him, he was looking down at her and smiling.

"I'm sorry, did you ask me something?"

"Merely if you were all right. I saw your companion leave and you looked distraught, so I thought I'd check on you."

Holy freaking hell. Mickie looked around again, trying to see if someone was playing a joke on her. When she didn't see anyone, she looked back at the man standing next to her table.

He was tall. So tall Mickie had to tilt her head up to see him clearly. She'd always had a thing about tall men. There was nothing that made her feel safer than a man who towered over her. But then again, most men were taller than her five feet six inches.

He was wearing a tight, black T-shirt that didn't hide his extremely muscular arms. Even his forearms were tight and bulging with muscles. Mickie could just see the tip of a tattoo peeking out from the left sleeve of his shirt. It was done in shades of black, with no other color. Even though she couldn't make out what it was, she suddenly wished she could explore it in depth.

The man's jeans were well worn and tight in all the right places. His crotch was at her eye level and Mickie blushed and quickly brought her eyes back up to his face, trying to ignore the bulge that more than filled out his pants. His hair was black, like hers, but cut military-precision short. He had facial hair that looked rough, and Mickie briefly wondered what it might feel like against her skin. Would it be prickly, or soft?

She shook her head. She had to get herself together. "I'm okay. Thanks for asking."

"Are you sure? May I sit?"

The man gestured at the empty seat across from her. Mickie frowned. She wanted him to, she really did, but what was the point?

"Why?"

"Why what?"

"Why do you want to sit with me? You don't know me. I don't know you. You, looking like you do, can't possibly be interested in me, so why would you waste your time?"

The man shifted, leaned one hip against the table, and crossed his arms over his chest. He didn't look pissed at her words, but instead seemed amused. "I want to sit with you because I've been watching you since you walked in. I noticed you right off. You've got a cute little sway to your walk and I liked what I saw. You're correct in that we don't know each other, but I'm trying to remedy that. I don't know why you think I can't possibly be interested in you, but you're wrong. I'm probably overstepping some social boundaries by telling you so, but there it is. So as I see it, I'm not wasting my time at all. In fact, I can't think of anything I'd rather be doing right now than sitting here talking and getting to know you."

Mickie could only gape at the man. What. The. Hell?

"My name is Cruz. I'm very glad to meet you."

Mickie looked at the hand the man held out to her. She glanced at the other hand resting on the table, no rings. His fingernails were short and well groomed. Mickie mentally shrugged and reached out to him with her own hand.

"Michelle, but I go by Mickie."

"It's great to meet you, Mickie. So, may I sit?"

Mickie found herself nodding. Holy shit. This wasn't like her, but there was no way she could turn this man down. If nothing else, she'd bring this memory back out later and bask in feeling good about herself for the first time in a long time. His attention soothed the hurt feelings from Angel's words.

Cruz eased into the seat across from Mickie. He was surprised by how attractive he found her. After hearing Angel's words, he'd assumed she'd look very different than she did. He was a bit ashamed of himself for thinking the worst. Mickie's hair was cut short, but still managed to frame her face in a way that was very pretty. She had large brown eyes and her lips were plump, especially since she kept nervously chewing on them with her teeth. Cruz couldn't see her body with the table in the way, but what he saw definitely wasn't a turn off. Her breasts were on the full side, way more than the A cup his ex's had been. And he had to be at least a foot taller than her.

She was the complete opposite of her sister...and his ex. Sophie had been slim, and even though Mickie was shorter than him, she was curvy. She probably thought she carried too much weight, but ever since discovering Sophie's slight frame had been the result of years of drug abuse, Cruz much preferred a woman who looked healthy. And Mickie certainly fit that bill.

He continued scrutinizing her. He watched as Mickie brought a hand up and smoothed her short hair back behind one ear nervously. She was wearing a light purple shirt that dipped low in front, showing off a hint of cleavage. Her eyes would meet his, then skitter away nervously. Her modesty and nervousness was endearing...and suddenly the entire undercover mission took a weird turn for Cruz.

He'd only meant to get to know her a bit today so he could accidently run into her again later and talk to her, stick close to her to make sure Ransom didn't get some bright idea to do something drastic to keep her away from Angel. But suddenly Cruz wished he really was sitting here with no agenda and with no other motive than to get to know the woman sitting in front of him. Somehow he knew he could really come to like her.

If he wasn't undercover, and wasn't trying to keep her safe from a psychotic motorcycle club president, he might have seriously considered dating her.

"So, Mickie, you never did tell me if you're all right or not."

"I'm okay. Just a sister thing."

"Ah…"

"You have any brothers or sisters?"

Cruz decided right there to be as honest as he could with Mickie. If he was going to have to deceive her, he wanted to keep things as real as possible as long as he could. "No, I'm an only child. My parents wanted more, but it didn't ever happen. I do have some friends I consider my siblings, but I know it's not the same thing. You? Only one sister?"

"Yeah. She's way younger than me. My parents thought they were done having kids, then she came along."

"Wow, was that tough on you?"

"Yes and no. I was still young enough that I thought it was cool at first. She was my own living doll. Then my parents became less and less interested in raising another daughter, so the job mostly fell to me."

Cruz reached across the table and put his hand on Mickie's. "I'm sorry, that sounds tough." He pulled his hand back and leaned forward on his elbows. He'd wanted to keep his hand on hers, but knew it would be weird since they didn't really know each other. "I'm sure your sister appreciates everything you've done for her."

She gave a quick, short chortle. "I'm not so sure about that, but thanks for being optimistic. So, you from around here?"

Cruz nodded, letting Mickie change the subject. "Yeah, you?"

"Yeah, me and Angel have lived here our entire lives. You like San Antonio?"

"I do. There's culture, there's art, it's a city but if you drive twenty minutes in any direction, you're out of the city and can see longhorns and ranches."

Mickie laughed. "That's about right."

Cruz knew he was asking for trouble with his next question, but he couldn't stop wanting to get to know the woman in front of him. "Since we're learning about each other...what do you do?"

Mickie tilted her head and eyed Cruz critically. There was something about him that seemed...off, but she couldn't really put her finger on it. She mentally shrugged and gave him a vague explanation. She wasn't so stupid that she'd tell him everything about her. She didn't know him, after all. "Nothing too exciting, I assure you. I work at a car dealership in the service department. It's not very glamorous, but it pays the bills."

Cruz looked at Mickie in approval. "Good girl."

"What?"

"You didn't tell me which car dealership. Smart."

Mickie blushed. "I-I didn't—"

"It's fine. I was being honest. You shouldn't go blurting that stuff out to any ol' man who asks to sit with you and flirts shamelessly."

"Is that what you're doing?"

"If you have to ask, I'm obviously not doing it right. I guess I'm rusty."

"I'm just...guys don't usually flirt with me." She blushed again. Jesus, this guy was going to think she was pathetic if she didn't keep her mouth shut.

Cruz thought Mickie was adorable. He leaned farther on his arms and toward her a bit more. "Their loss is my gain."

Mickie shook her head in exasperation at Cruz. Trying to change the subject, she asked, "So, what do *you* do?"

Cruz's stomach dropped, but he didn't show any outward emotion at her words. He'd hoped to distract Mickie enough that she'd forget to ask. Still, he'd learned over the years that keeping his answer truthful but vague was always the way to go. "I'm in security."

There was silence between them for a moment, then Mickie asked, "Security, huh?"

"Yup."

"Hummm. I guess I can see it. You're in shape, unlike a lot of security guards I've seen, so you get points for that."

Cruz swallowed back a laugh. "I'm not sure that's saying much, but I'll take it. Besides, it pays the bills," he intentionally repeated her words, happy when she smiled at him.

Deciding that the best way to make sure Mickie was safe was to stick to her like glue, at least when he wasn't at the club, he blurted, "I like you. Will you let me take you out sometime? Maybe for dinner?"

"Uh...I don't know."

Cruz knew he wasn't being very smooth, so tried to back off a bit. "I know, too soon, right? Okay, at least let me give you my number. You can text me or something. Maybe we can accidently meet for lunch again sometime?"

Mickie laughed. "You don't give up, do you?"

"Not when it's something I want."

She paused for a beat, scrutinizing him. Finally she said. "Okay, give me your number. I'll have to think about it."

Cruz gave her the number to the phone he was using as Smoke. He couldn't keep her safe if she needed him by giving her his personal number, since he never carried that phone with him when he was at the club. When she contacted him, and hopefully she would, he'd add her to his contacts under a fake name so if the phone was compromised by one of the members at the club, *she* wouldn't be.

He looked Mickie in the eye. "I hope you use it. I really do want to get to know you." Cruz stood up reluctantly, knowing it was time to go if he didn't want to freak her out. "It was nice meeting you. I hope your sister comes to see what a treasure she has in you."

Mickie cursed the blush she knew was blooming on her cheeks...again. "It was nice to meet you too, Cruz."

"Bye, Mickie."

"Bye."

Cruz left the restaurant and Mickie noticed that his back view was just as nice as the front. She hadn't ever understood the phrase "you could bounce a quarter on that ass" until now.

She sighed. What the hell was she thinking? She looked down at the number she'd programmed into her phone. She really should just delete it. There was no way a man like Cruz would honestly be interested in her, but damn it felt good.

She clicked the button to turn the screen to her phone off and gathered up her stuff. Fuck it. Why wouldn't he be interested in her? Mickie knew she'd been taking Angel's words to heart more than she should.

She had a job, she was a good person, she might not be a size two, but it wasn't as if she was grotesque either, size twelve was more normal in today's day and age than a size two. So what if she had some fourteens in her closet too? Most women's weights went up and down...and besides, not every store had the same size chart. Whatever.

Mickie made up her mind. She'd text Cruz, see if he was serious. If he was, she'd go for it. She deserved it. Not only that, she wanted it.

The day seemed brighter as Mickie left, even though Angel and the damn MC were still on her mind. She had to do something, but she didn't know what. She'd have to wait and hope like hell Angel would come to her senses after the damn "party" tonight. Hopefully it would be out of control and would scare Angel shitless...and away from the club altogether.

Chapter Three

————•◆•————

CRUZ LOOKED AROUND the clubhouse in barely concealed disgust. The men had been on their best behavior from the moment he'd arrived with Angel. The music was loud, the booze was flowing freely, but it was extremely tame compared to some of the parties Cruz had been to in the last month.

After leaving the restaurant, Cruz had pulled over and donned his biker clothes, essentially putting back on his new identity, one he was beginning to hate. He continued to Angel's apartment and gathered her. He'd tried to be a dick to her as much as he could, while not risking Ransom's ire if she tattled about his actions to the president. Cruz wanted to show Angel that the bikers weren't nice guys. He didn't think his tactic worked, because the rest of the guys at the club were going out of their way to be solicitous and pleasant, at least for them.

Even the few old ladies who were there were taking Angel under their wings. They'd taken her to a back room when she'd arrived, and an hour later when they'd come out, they'd all been acting as if they were best friends.

Cruz learned from Knife and Donkey, two of the more hard-core men in the gang, that the women were slowly going to bring Angel into the fold that night, including getting her high. It was all a part of their plan. They'd supply her with all the weed she wanted, and then eventually Ransom would pressure her into trying the harder stuff.

They were giggling and chummy when they came out of the

backroom. The old ladies went to their men and Cruz watched as Angel weaved her way across the room to Ransom. When she got to him, he hauled her against his side with an arm around her neck. He didn't acknowledge her in any way, but merely kept on talking with Kitty and Tick.

Finally after a few minutes went by, Ransom looked down at Angel and asked, "Have fun tonight?"

"Oh yeah, everyone was so nice!"

"It's time to go."

"But, Ransom, I just got here," she whined.

"I *said* it's time to fucking go. Get your shit and I'll take you home."

"Okay."

Angel teetered her way back across the clubhouse floor on her four-inch heels, not knowing or probably not caring that all eyes were on her ass as she went. When she was out of hearing, Camel, a prospect who'd been voted into the club recently, said, "I gotta tap me some of that."

Cruz half expected Ransom to lose his shit, but it was more verification that the man didn't give a fuck about Angel when he merely laughed and said, "You'll have your chance. Patience, man. Everyone will get their shot at her when I'm done and when we're rolling in the dough her friends give us. I don't give a shit if you all pass her around...*after* I'm done with her and the club gets what it needs."

Everyone laughed and high-fived. Cruz joined in, sick to his stomach thinking about what Ransom had in store for Mickie's sister.

"Hurry up and get back, Pres. Bambi's coming over with a few of her friends after you leave. You know she likes it up the ass," Dirt informed his president with a smirk.

"Oh, hell yeah. I'll get Angel home, fuck her, and get back here. Half an hour, tops."

"You gonna let her orgasm tonight?" Tick asked. They all knew how Ransom used orgasms as a method of control.

"Fuck no. I don't have time for that shit and I don't give a fuck if she gets off or not as long as I do. I'll tell her she didn't pay enough attention to me tonight or some bullshit…how I like it when my woman does her drugs in front of me. She'll be begging for something to smoke the next time I see her."

Once again, everyone around them laughed crudely. "Well, hurry the fuck up. We need you to get the party started," Camel complained, knowing Ransom had one rule when it came to the club whores. He was the first to fuck each night. Once he'd had his fill of who he wanted, they were fair game for anyone and everyone else. No one was allowed to get any pussy until he decided he was done and permitted the other men to have their fun.

"Shut the fuck up, Camel. I'll get back when I get back. Don't piss me off."

"No disrespect intended, Pres."

They watched as Angel clipped her way back to them. Ransom smiled crookedly at her, shoved one hand down the back of her jeans, and grabbed hold of her hair with the other. He yanked her head back and kissed her long and deep. The hand at her ass moved up and squeezed her breast as he kissed her; he was obviously unconcerned with his audience.

As the other men catcalled, he lifted his lips off of Angel's. She had a dreamy look on her face. "Come on, let's go. I need inside that hot cunt."

Ransom led Angel out of the room with his hand at the back of her neck. It could've been a loving gesture; Cruz had seen his friend Dax put his hand on the back of his girlfriend Mackenzie's neck as they walked together sometimes, but he knew Ransom used it more as a controlling action than an affectionate gesture.

"Get on it, assholes. Get Bambi's ass over here. Ransom is gonna be ready to fuck when he gets back. Let's not disappoint him," Bubba ordered. The vice president's words were muted and harsh. He lifted his chin at Cruz. "Smoke, you're on lookout tonight. Make sure the pigs don't crash the party. The Snakes are bringing a shipment tonight. Don't fuck it up."

Cruz gave a short nod to the other man in response. Bubba was a large man—not muscular, but overweight. He looked like a heart attack waiting to happen, but Cruz had seen him take down one of the younger prospects the other day with absolutely no effort. He was big and mean, and took no shit from anyone in the club. He might be the VP, but he was also one of the best enforcers as well.

"No problem, Bubba. Are we expecting trouble?" Cruz wanted to know what he might be up against.

"We always expect problems, Prospect. That's why you're on fucking duty."

Cruz nodded in response instead of taking the other man to the ground for his asshole-ish tone and turned to head outside the big warehouse. It was located in the industrial part of San Antonio. All around them were other warehouses that held everything from vehicles to boxes and crates of merchandise. Inventory that was stored until it was either picked up and driven to the coast and put into shipping containers to be sent overseas, or trucked throughout the States. Eighteen-wheelers were entering and exiting the big complex day and night. It was actually a perfect hideout for the gang and their illegal activities. Of course, motorcycles didn't quite blend in, but it seemed the MC had done their work well, and everyone was either too scared to say anything, or they'd been bought off.

Thankful he didn't have to watch the orgy that was sure to go down that night, Cruz crossed his arms and leaned against the corner of a nearby warehouse. He knew there were other prospects standing around at other key points around the building as well. It wasn't likely anyone would just randomly show up, but it was another bullshit job the president got off on having the prospects do.

Cruz thought about the investigation; it was getting murkier and murkier every day. How the hell he was going to get Angel out of the shitstorm she'd found herself in, keep Mickie safe from Ransom's wrath, and find out who the mysterious new big dealer the club had somehow managed to procure, was all running through his brain.

On top of that, Cruz found his thoughts turning to Mickie. She hadn't been what he'd expected at all. She was spunky...and cute. She was a bit eclectic and obviously wasn't afraid to say what she felt.

On the other hand, Cruz couldn't remember the last time a woman had blushed so much. Every time he'd flustered her, she'd turned a light shade of pink. It was adorable and he was way too jaded for her, but that wasn't going to stop him from sticking close.

Feeling his phone vibrate, Cruz pulled it out, thinking it was one of the other prospects fucking with him. He was surprised to see a message from Mickie, figuring she'd make him wait longer before getting in touch with him.

Hey. Just wanted to say hi. It was nice meeting you today.

The text was short and to the point...a feeler of sorts. There was no commitment to it, so if he didn't answer, she wouldn't be embarrassed. But it also told Cruz a lot. She'd reached out in the hopes he'd answer. He immediately texted her back.

Hi. You too. I'm glad you got in touch. You want to accidently be at the same place at the same time tomorrow to feed ourselves?

Lol. Ok. Where?

Cruz smiled. God. He loved that Mickie didn't play hard to get.

Wherever you want.

The sub shop on Crystal Hill and Wurzbach Rd?

Cruz knew which one she was talking about. It probably wasn't a good idea for him to be seen in his "normal" clothes that close to the Red Brothers' hangout.

Actually, I was thinking Iron Cactus down on the River Walk.

Cruz sweated the ten minutes it took Mickie to respond.

I didn't peg you as a River Walk kind of guy.

Mickie was exactly right. Normally Cruz wouldn't be caught dead at the overpriced tourist trap that was the collection of shops downtown by the river. But he also figured none of the Red Brothers would be there either.

Figured for our first date, I'd treat you right.
A girl can't argue with that. See you there at one-ish?
Yes. Be safe until then.

Cruz stared at the words he'd typed on the screen. He'd told Sophie "be safe" every time they'd parted. Toward the end of their marriage, she'd merely rolled her eyes at him. Cruz didn't know why he'd said the words to Mickie, but there they were, in black and white. *Be safe.*

Thank you. I will. You too. Later.
Later.

Cruz tucked his phone back into his pocket and couldn't hold back the smile that crept across his face.

A bike pulling into the area brought him out of his musings of Mickie with a jolt. Cruz observed Ransom returning after having dropped Angel off, well within his thirty-minute estimate. Shortly thereafter, a car pulled up and three whores Cruz recognized stumbled out of the vehicle, obviously already stoned. The churning in Cruz's stomach wouldn't stop. Even though he wasn't inside, he could well imagine what was going to happen.

The prostitutes had Cruz thinking about his ex and finding her in their bedroom with three men.

The last time Cruz saw Sophie was when the SAPD had arrested her for prostitution and drugs. After their divorce, she hadn't stopped her illegal activities. He'd begged her to get help, but she'd refused, calling him a "fuddy-duddy," claiming she'd been using drugs for their entire marriage and that she'd never been satisfied by him in bed.

Cruz had met Sophie when he'd first joined the FBI. She'd been a senior at Georgetown and they'd met while at a bar one night. He'd fallen in love almost immediately. Sophie was tall and slender and her long blonde hair had blown him away. She'd been funny and gregarious and had made him feel as if he was the most important person in her life.

The reality more than lived up to his imagination. Sophie had been a wildcat in bed and Cruz thought he was the luckiest guy in the world. Eventually they'd made their way to San Antonio, where Cruz was still posted. He'd hoped being in a new city would strengthen their relationship, but instead it seemed to only exacerbate the issues they'd been having.

Sophie was known as the life of the party. She had a friendly disposition and she easily made friends wherever they went. However, it wasn't long before her party-girl attitude started to get old. At company get-togethers, she'd usually end up drinking too much and embarrassing the hell out of Cruz. Eventually it got to a point where he refused to bring her to any of the social functions he went to for work. He needed to maintain some sort of professional persona, and watching his wife flirt shamelessly and have to be carried home didn't cut it.

Sophie didn't seem to care. She'd simply shrugged and went out with her friends instead of accompanying Cruz to work events. By the time they'd moved to San Antonio, Cruz was tired of making excuses and he knew they weren't working out as a couple.

His friends in the FBI were always complimenting him on how sexy his wife was and Cruz took their comments with a smile, but deep down, hindsight being twenty/twenty, he'd known he wanted more out of their relationship. He'd wanted a supportive partnership that was more than sex and parties.

The night Cruz found out about the real Sophie was one he knew he'd never forget as long as he lived. He'd gone to an annual charity event in San Antonio. He'd promised his friends he'd at least show up. He'd worked with various law enforcement offices throughout the city and had become close friends with five officers. They all joked that they were a living, breathing bar joke...a cop, Feeb, game warden, highway patrolman, doctor, and deputy walked into a bar...

But Cruz knew he'd never find closer friends than Dax, TJ, Quint, Calder, Hayden, and Conor. The other men, and woman, had all met during various cases they'd been on, and they'd bonded as a result.

Cruz had been at the charity event and felt like crap. He was coming down with the flu and had left early. He'd tried to text Sophie and let her know he was on his way home, but she hadn't answered. He'd entered their small suburban house and knew immediately something was off. He'd pulled his sidearm out and cautiously searched the house.

When he'd found his wife, he stood in the bedroom doorway, aghast, not able to believe the scene before him. Sophie had been on her knees in the middle of three men, alternating sucking one man and jacking off the other two. She'd been switching between the men, seemingly enjoying what she was doing. Cruz remembered the scene as if it was yesterday...

"What the hell?" He barked the words into the otherwise quiet room.

Sophie took her lips off one man's cock to peer around his leg, never stopping her hands from moving up and down the other two men's dicks. "Hey, Cruzch, I didn't eschpect you home scho early. Come join the fun."

Cruz could only stare at his wife as she went back to what she'd been doing before he'd interrupted, not caring her husband had caught her in the act. He looked over to the table sitting next to their bed and saw three lines of white powder, along with a plastic frequent-shopper card from the local grocery store. There were three used condoms on the floor by the bed and the covers were mussed, as if the group had just moved their sexual orgy to the middle of the room.

Cruz literally felt his heart break as memories careened through his mind and everything clicked into place with extreme clarity. All the nights Sophie came home from partying with her friends, immediately showering before joining him in bed. The weight she couldn't seem to put on. Her excessive frenetic energy and mood swings.

"Get the fuck out," Cruz clipped. When the men didn't move, he cocked his pistol and then warned in a deadly voice, "You have ten seconds to get your asses out of my house before I shoot first and call the cops second."

Even with Sophie trying to hold on to the men by their dicks, they managed to tear themselves away and brush past him on the way out the door. The last straw was when Sophie called, "Leave the money on the table on your way out."

Cruz thought back to Sophie's comment that he hadn't satisfied her in bed. He would've been hurt, except he'd dealt with enough addicts to know the only thing they could think of was their next hit. Besides that, he knew for a fact that they'd been more than sexually compatible...at least at the beginning of their marriage.

The officers at the San Antonio Police Department had known who Sophie was and had tried to go easy on her the first couple of times she'd been arrested, but it hadn't done any good. She'd simply not cared.

There was nothing left of the Sophie he'd once loved. She was lost to the drugs, her new life on the street and her pimp. Cruz had tried calling her parents to get her help, but they'd truly disowned her, as Sophie had told him early in their relationship. It seemed she'd entered a life of drugs while in high school. When her parents had been called to pick her up at a police station when she'd been taken into custody—after being caught in a hotel room with two men thirty years older than she was, naked and drugged out of her mind— they'd refused. One of her friends had been worried about her and had called her parents to try to get her some help. But instead, they'd washed their hands of her altogether. They figured that Sophie had made her bed and they'd had enough.

Cruz just wished they'd said something to him. Granted, he'd only met them once, but it would've been nice for them to have made an effort to reach out to him and let him know about their daughter. He mentally shrugged. The bottom line was that Sophie had put on a great show and he'd bought it hook, line, and sinker.

The backfiring of a car brought Cruz's attention back to the mostly deserted shipping yard. Even with the party going on inside the club, the area was quiet and the night passed slowly for Cruz. He hated knowing there wasn't anything he could do at the moment to help Bambi and the other two women who had been shown inside earlier, but his hands were tied.

The night was one for memories…both good and bad. He hadn't thought about Sophie in months, and after only a few hours of meeting a woman who was his ex's complete opposite, he'd rehashed their entire relationship. Cruz wasn't sure what to think about that. He'd already made the decision to get close to Mickie for her own protection, but he was beginning to think she'd be more than simply another job.

Chapter Four

MICKIE WIPED HER hands on her jeans for the hundredth time as she made her way up the River Walk to the Iron Cactus. She'd waffled back and forth before actually texting Cruz the night before. Finally, talking herself into it, she'd sent him the noncommittal text, hoping he'd been serious about wanting to see her again. Never in a million years did she think he'd respond to her as soon as he had.

She hadn't lied when she'd told Cruz she didn't think he seemed like the type of man who would take a date to the River Walk. He seemed more…rugged or something. The iconic San Antonio River Walk was very touristy and didn't match the image of Cruz in her head. Mickie mentally shrugged. There were bound to be other things she'd learn about him that weren't what she expected.

Mickie couldn't help but think about her ex, and how everything she'd known about him had been a lie. Troy was a piece of work. Mickie had thought she was the luckiest woman in the world. She'd married him when she was around Angel's age. They'd met at the dealership. Troy had brought his car in for service and they'd immediately clicked. He'd seemed so nice.

Troy had been thirty-one and quite wealthy. Mickie had money. Her parents gave her a monthly allowance to try to assuage their guilt over not helping much in raising Angel, but Troy had way more. He wasn't good-looking in the turn-heads-on-the-street kind of way. He was a bit of a nerd, but it was his perceived sincerity that had drawn Mickie.

He'd wined and dined her and had swept her off her feet. He'd even convinced her to wait until after they were married to consummate their relationship. Like a fool, Mickie had been convinced it was the most romantic gesture she'd ever heard of. She wasn't a virgin, but hadn't had a lot of experience either.

So they'd had a huge wedding, paid for mostly by Troy's family. She wore a wedding dress with a six-foot train along with six bridesmaids and six groomsmen, all friends of Troy's. The sex they'd had that night wasn't anything to write home about, but it wasn't awful either.

There hadn't been a honeymoon because Troy had claimed he was in the middle of a huge project at the accounting firm where he worked, but he promised they'd take a trip later. Later had never arrived. Troy had started working past five every day, and six o'clock became seven. Then eight. And slowly but surely, any intimacy between them turned tepid at best.

The lack of a sex life was what Mickie had stressed over more than anything else. She'd never been very adventurous, even before she'd met Troy, but they'd never had sex in anything but the missionary position. Mickie longed for more, but had never gotten it from Troy. They acted like roommates rather than man and wife, and slowly his lack of interest in her eroded any confidence she had in her own sexuality.

It wasn't until they'd been married for two and a half years that she found out the real reason Troy had married her. It had devastated her, and Mickie knew she'd never forget how gutted she'd felt listening to Troy talk on the phone with Brittany, one of the women who'd been a bridesmaid in their wedding, and who'd apparently been the real love of Troy's life all along.

"Yeah, Mickie has no clue. Brit, I promise, in another few months we'll get that divorce. You know I had to marry her in order to get my inheritance. Mum and Pop never liked you. It was a shitty thing to do,

forcing me to marry or lose all that money, but now that I have control over it, I'll make sure Mickie loses interest in me and we can agree on an amicable divorce. I can guarantee the sex already sucks. When I have to fuck her, I don't bother even trying to make it good for her. Once she signs the papers that say she wants no alimony, I'm free for you, baby."

He'd been silent for a moment, obviously listening to Brittany on the other end of the line.

"Oh yeah. She never wants to rock the boat. She'll sign them, no contest. Swear. And yeah, I'll tell Mickie I'm working late again tonight and get to your place around three."

Another pause and Mickie felt the tears rolling down her cheeks, but didn't bother to wipe them away.

Troy's voice deepened as he responded to whatever Brittany had said. *"I can't wait to get you pregnant. Hopefully by this time next year, you'll be having my baby. I can't wait to start our family. As soon as you're pregnant, I'll tell her we've drifted apart and we'll be better off as friends. I have no doubt she'll sign the divorce papers. I love you, baby. See you later."*

Mickie had stood still in the doorway and stared at Troy with no emotion on her face as he'd turned around. All the blood had drained from his face and he'd had the nerve to stammer the clichéd phrase, "Mickie. It's not what you think."

She'd simply said, "You'll have divorce papers delivered within the week instead of waiting for her to get pregnant. I hope you have a good lawyer, because I'm sure as hell asking for alimony."

She'd received a fortune in the divorce, especially after Troy's long-term affair with Brittany was exposed. His parents despised Mickie for dragging their family name through the mud, almost as much as they hated Brittany, but Mickie didn't give a damn. As far as she was concerned, Troy and his parents had brought it on themselves. They hadn't allowed him to marry who he loved in the first place, and Troy didn't have the balls to stand up to them.

Her own parents were disappointed she and Troy couldn't get past "their little argument." Their attitude had saddened Mickie as much as the divorce itself.

Last she'd heard, Troy was now married to Brittany and they'd moved to Seattle. They'd had a little girl and Troy was employed by one of the best accounting firms in the state. "So much for karma," Mickie said out loud to no one in particular.

She sighed and stopped in front of the restaurant. She'd moved on. Older and wiser and all that crap. She was much more cautious now when it came to dating, and hadn't found anyone who had been able to break through her walls after Troy. More importantly, there wasn't anyone who she *wanted* to try with...until now.

Knowing she was running late—traffic had been horrendous because of an accident on the interstate—Mickie quickly opened the door to the restaurant and was hit with a wall of different sounds and smells. There was a large group of people in the bar area and the scent of spices and tequila hit her nose hard. Her stomach growled. Mexican was her favorite thing to eat and Mickie had forgotten just how good the food was here.

"Hello, Mickie. Thank you for not standing me up."

Mickie turned and saw Cruz next to her, as if he'd materialized out of thin air. She shook her head. "I'm sorry I'm late. Traffic was a bitch. And seriously, I don't know who you've been asking out, but any woman would be insane to accept a date with you then not show up."

"Oh, you'd be surprised, honey. Come on, our table is ready."

Mickie melted a bit inside when his fingertips skimmed her lower back, guiding her in front of him, protecting her from the crush of people as they made their way behind the hostess, who led the way to a table.

They were shown to a booth in the back of the restaurant, away from the water. Mickie supposed it wasn't a prime seating arrangement, but sitting away from the people and in the dim light seemed just as intimate as if it'd been a candlelight dinner.

Cruz held her elbow as she sat, then surprisingly, opted to sit next to her instead of across the table.

"Do you mind?" Cruz asked, smiling and gesturing to the space next to her on the bench.

"Uh, no. I guess not," Mickie stammered. She'd never had a date want to sit next to her. Every time she and Troy had gone out, he'd sat across from her and buried his nose in his phone throughout the meal.

He sat and said nonchalantly, "I'd prefer to sit next to you. It feels more like a date that way." He shrugged. "I know…it's weird, right? Sorry, I'll just…" Cruz started to get up from the table to move to the other seat.

Mickie put her hand on his. "It's fine, Cruz. I have to be honest, you surprised me, but not in a bad way. Okay? I'm just not used to it. But I don't mind at all. Promise."

He laughed and settled back down next to her. "It's been a while since I've been out with a woman I wanted to impress. I think I've lost my touch."

"I think you're doing just fine."

"Really?"

"Really."

"Would you two like something to drink?"

The waitress's voice cut into their conversation and they both laughed. After ordering, and after the waitress had walked away, Cruz turned in his seat and looked at Mickie.

"So, come here often?"

Mickie giggled. "I've been here a few times, yes. You?"

"Once." At her lifted eyebrow, Cruz continued. "It was a celebratory dinner. I came with my friend and his woman, and the rest of our friends. She'd recently been through a horrific ordeal, and we were celebrating the fact she was alive, as well as our friendship."

"Wow, I'm glad she's okay. You sound like you're close with your friends."

"Yeah, I told you before they're like my brothers and sister. I don't think people like that are brought into our lives by accident, or very often."

At Mickie's silence, Cruz cursed again. "Shit. Sorry. That's a bit deep for a first date, isn't it? It's just—"

Mickie squeezed Cruz's hand that she still held in hers. "It's fine. Actually it's refreshing. It's real. I feel like most of us go through life being fake and lying so often it's hard to remember who we are deep down inside. I like that you aren't holding back. It's nice."

Cruz shifted uneasily. Suddenly he didn't like that he was getting close to her just to keep her safe from Ransom and the other club members. So far he liked her. She hadn't done anything crazy and he felt comfortable around her. Granted he'd only been in her presence for an hour, but an hour was long enough for some women he'd met in the past to go from interesting to bat-shit crazy. Hearing her compliment him made him feel worse about the reason why he was there, especially since he wasn't being completely honest with her.

Mickie looked at Cruz in confusion. It was as if her words, meant to be a compliment, had made him uncomfortable. "I didn't mean that in a bad way. Being nice is good. I like nice."

Cruz tried to relax and smile. He was doing a piss-poor job of making her want to hang out with him. At this rate, she'd excuse herself to go to the restroom and sneak out. "Sorry, and you should know…I like nice too. And I'll be on my best behavior from here on out, so you won't have to make up an excuse to ditch me."

Mickie smiled back at him. "Deal."

The waitress came back with their drinks and after quickly scanning the menu, they both made their choices.

"How's your sister? Have you had a chance to talk to her recently?" Cruz asked, hating to even bring it up, but wanting to know how much the party last night worked in Ransom's favor. When Cruz had seen him after the party was over early that morning, he'd been mellow and satisfied. Cruz hadn't asked about Angel, knowing it would seem weird for a prospect to be interested in his relationship, but he'd wondered.

Mickie sighed. "I called her this morning and she actually answered, which was surprising. But after listening to her, I knew she only talked to me so she could tell me that I'd been wrong about everything I'd told her yesterday."

"What was your fight over, if you don't mind talking about it?" Cruz asked.

"She's dating this guy who's not good for her, and she won't listen to me."

Cruz shrugged nonchalantly. "She's an adult, right? She's bound to make some dating mistakes as she learns what and who she wants."

"I'd normally agree with you, but not this guy. I'm assuming since you're from around here you've heard of the Red Brothers Motorcycle Club, yeah?" At his nod, she continued. "Well, she's dating the president of the club. She thinks he's misunderstood and a great guy, but he's not. I'm guessing you don't know this, but MC romance novels are very popular now. If you go online and do a search, there are a ton of them. Pages and pages of books with hot, built, tattooed men on the covers. They mostly tout these big scary guys who are pussycats under all their bravado. They do slightly illegal things, but all in the name of keeping their communities safe. They don't deal drugs because that's wrong, and they might prostitute women, but only because they want to give them a 'safe place' to make money and to make sure no men take advantage of them. In the end they all end up together and happy as clams. It makes a good story. Hell, I read some of those books myself, and enjoy them. But my sister thinks *this* guy is straight out of one of those romance books. But he's not. I did some research. I'm scared to death for her. He's bad news."

Knowing he was treading on thin ice, Cruz waded in cautiously. He whistled low. "The Hermanos Rojos *are* bad news."

Mickie didn't even give him time to continue or to elaborate. She leaned one elbow on the table and put her head in her hand as she turned toward him. "I *know*, Cruz. Angel told me this morning that she went to their compound, or whatever it's called, while a party was going on. She said that it was all civilized and normal. She even said it was a bit lame. She told me she met some of the 'old ladies' and they were all very nice to her. They partied in the back, away from the men because that's their place, then Ransom brought her home. Something doesn't seem right about it, but I think she's even more in love with this guy than before. He's scum, and the more I try to talk her away from him, the tighter she holds on."

"I hope you aren't thinking about doing anything crazy."

Mickie sighed. "If I knew what crazy thing to do, I'd probably do it. Angel is spoiled and has said some pretty mean things to me in the past...but she's my sister and I love her. I know for a fact that anything I do to interfere will only make her more stubborn. She's a lot like me in that way." She smiled somewhat sadly.

Cruz hated seeing Mickie so dejected, but it wasn't as if he could break cover and tell her he'd keep his eye on her sister and do what he could to keep her out of danger. Deciding a change in subject was in order, he tried to flirt with her a bit, "So, tell me about yourself. I know you work at a car dealership, have a sister who drives you crazy and that you have hair that makes me want to run my fingers through it, but what else?" He smiled at the blush that bloomed over her cheeks.

"You can't ever ask a simple question, can you?" Mickie laughed and started playing with her napkin as she spoke. "I'm really not that interesting. I know I'm supposed to tell you all sorts of cool things, but I'm really just a nerd. I'm thirty-four years old and prefer to sit at home with a good book than go out and party. I've been married once, no kids, and have lived here all my life. I have my undergrad psychology degree from the University of Texas-San Antonio and I've only been to Mexico…not anywhere else out of the United States."

Cruz's hand lifted, as if it had a mind of its own, and pushed a lock of her hair behind her ear. He fingered the short strands hugging her nape, thrilled when she didn't pull away from his light touch. "I don't think you're a nerd, Mickie. Lots of people don't like the bar scene. I hate it, as a matter of fact. There are too many people, the noise is too loud, and drinking to get drunk never held that much appeal for me. What made you choose psychology?"

Mickie tried not to shiver each time Cruz's fingers brushed against the nape of her neck. Holy hell, if just the slight touch of his fingers made her horny, she was in big trouble. The chemistry between them was off the charts. It was crazy, but felt good at the same time. "I just really enjoyed learning about what made people do the things they do, and after a while I'd taken so many psych classes it just made sense."

"So, you like to know what makes people tick?"

"Yeah, but I couldn't find a job I liked. I know I'm way too picky, but I just couldn't see myself working as a social worker, or school counselor or something. Working at the car dealership isn't exactly my dream job, but it's entertaining sometimes and you'd be surprised how often I use what I learned in school." Mickie laughed, obviously recalling some of the antics of the customers she dealt with. "What about you? What made you go into the security field?"

Cruz took a sip of his drink and tried to figure out what to tell Mickie. He really wanted to tell her the story of how he'd decided to go into law enforcement, but he couldn't go into as much detail as he might've if she knew he worked for the FBI. He'd have to tread carefully.

"To understand why, you have to know a bit about me first. My mom passed away from heart disease when I was young. My dad remarried a couple of years later and I never really knew any mother other than Barb. We moved around a lot when they got married. We lived on the east coast for a few years, then my dad got transferred to Ohio. Then Barb took a job in southern California, so we moved again, but they quickly found out that the fast pace of life there didn't suit them, so we moved to Maine and that's where I finished high school.

"They're still there, retired and loving it. They live in a small, conservative town. Nothing much ever happens. My parents weren't rich, but they weren't poor either. I had everything I ever wanted as I grew up, so did most of my friends. The only real crime I had any experience with was petty theft every now and then." Cruz chuckled. "Well, that and underage drinking."

The waitress interrupted his story with their food. Once she left and they'd both dug into their lunch, Cruz continued between bites.

"My sophomore year in high school, we were in California, the only year we were there. One of my classmates' little sister disappeared. She literally was there one day and gone the next. There was a lot of speculation about what happened to her, but I think we all knew she wasn't going to come home. Avery seemed like a good kid. I didn't know her, but I heard her brother talking on the news one night, begging whoever took her to bring her back. She liked singing, dancing, dogs, and had a gazillion stuffed animals. I watched the news and read the papers about her disappearance. Before too long, the stories changed from interviews with her parents and brother and news about the search parties that had been organized, to other more recent sensational stories, like murders, climate change, and of course, politics.

"I never forgot Avery though. It was only about three weeks later when a couple hiking in the woods, nowhere near our town, found her body. A beautiful little girl, gone. To make a long story short, she'd been killed by a man who'd been kidnapping young women and kids all over the place. He'd been in our town a total of ten hours. Ten fucking hours. That's all it took for him to ruin at least four lives. Avery's parents divorced and her brother ended up joining the Navy."

"That's tough, Cruz. What did that have to do with you getting into security?"

Her question was a legitimate one, and Cruz tried to explain without giving anything about his career as an FBI agent away. "The police officers in our town weren't prepared for an in-depth investigation into Avery's disappearance. Her parents begged for help in finding their daughter, but after a token search, they said there wasn't much more they could do because there just wasn't any evidence. I guess stranger abductions are rare, and some of the toughest cases to solve. I saw firsthand how important it was for everyone to do *something*. Being involved in the search for Avery, and seeing how everyone came forward to help, really struck something in me. I know being in security isn't like being a police officer, but even if it's just helping little old ladies get their purses back after they're snatched away, it makes me feel good."

That last part was pretty lame, but Mickie seemed to buy it.

"That's amazing, Cruz."

He merely shrugged. "The best part of the story was that I saw on social media that Avery's brother recently found the asshole that killed his sister. He'd been hunting for him ever since he'd graduated high school. He'd apparently joined the Navy and become a SEAL and with some of his Navy SEAL buddies, they finally killed him. I never kept in touch with Sam, Avery's brother, but I bet if I'd stayed in California and finished high school there, we would've been good friends."

"That's an awesome story. Seriously. And you shouldn't feel bad about what you do. I mean…I don't know exactly *what* you do; I'm sure it's not like you're a Texas Ranger or anything, but I'm assuming you do your best to keep people safe now."

He let the Texas Ranger comment go, but made a mental note to tell Dax what Mickie had said…he'd get a huge kick out of it. It was obvious she hadn't meant it as it came out. "Stopping shoplifters or patrolling for trespassers is a long way from solving serial-murder cases."

"Yeah, but if there weren't people like you around, then it'd be chaos. Who knows what would be stolen or destroyed? It'd be anarchy." She smiled. "The teenagers would have a field day. Just the other day I saw a security guard make a group of little old ladies walk the correct way around the mall. Without people like you, the world would go crazy, I tell ya."

Cruz smiled. She was adorable, assuming he was a security guard and trying to make him feel good about it. There were some really good men he'd worked with over the years who *were* in the general security field, but he'd been honest when he'd told her it was a long way from solving serious cases.

"What's the craziest thing you've seen?" Mickie asked with her chin propped on her hand and leaning on the table. He loved the way she paid complete attention to him. She didn't seem to care about her cell phone, or what was going on around them. It was refreshing. He decided to feel her out a little bit. He knew she was worried about her sister, but he wanted to prod a bit deeper.

"I saw a drug deal go down one day."

"Oh my God! Really? What'd you do?"

"I called the cops. I followed the guy who sold the drugs, figuring he was probably more involved than the kid who bought them. Drugs. I can't stand drug use and what it does to families and to the user. Using is an insidious thing. At first it seems harmless, it makes people feel good, makes them feel invincible. The kid who bought the drugs didn't look like a hard-core druggie. He was probably getting it for a party or something. But drugs can easily take over a person's life. Each time, the fall gets longer and longer and they'll keep pushing their boundaries when it comes to what they'll do for that high."

Mickie put her now-empty plate to the side and asked earnestly. "It sounds personal for you."

"It is. My ex-wife got mixed up in it."

"I'm sorry, Cruz. That sucks."

"Yeah."

His response was whispered and Mickie could hear the sorrow in his voice. She put her hand on his forearm and squeezed gently.

Cruz sighed and put his hand over Mickie's. He could feel the body heat emanating from her palm through his sleeve and penetrating directly into his blood stream, or so it seemed. "She got hooked in high school, but I had no idea. She portrayed herself to me one way, and all the while she was prostituting herself to get money for more drugs."

"Wow. How long were you married?"

"Too long. I should've seen it."

"Cruz, you loved her. At least I'm assuming you did." Mickie waited until he nodded, then continued. "You gave her the benefit of the doubt. It's what you do when you love someone. You make excuses for them when they do things and you forgive them when they hurt you."

"Like you and your sister."

Mickie snorted. "Yeah, like me and Angel."

Cruz went back to the previous subject. "My ex is still here in San Antonio. Every now and then she gets arrested for prostitution. I feel like I'm the laughingstock of all my friends. They all know about her."

"I'm positive your friends aren't laughing at you, Cruz. They probably feel bad for you, but that's way different than feeling sorry for you or laughing at you."

Cruz brought Mickie's hand up to his lips and kissed the back of it. "Thank you, Mickie. I'm sorry I'm such a downer. I didn't mean to dump all this on you on our first date."

Mickie laughed low in her throat. "This is one of the most interesting first dates I've ever had." At Cruz's skeptical look, she continued quickly. "Seriously. Most of the time the guy wants to talk about how great he is and how lucky I should feel to be with him."

"I don't know how lucky *you* are, but *I* feel lucky as all get out that you're sitting here with me."

"I'm not sure you know me well enough to feel lucky you're here. I have my own sob story when it comes to my ex."

"He was an idiot."

Mickie laughed at his immediate and honest-sounding response. "I'll agree with you on that one."

They smiled at each other. Cruz hadn't let go of her hand since he'd kissed it and he tightened his grip on her fingers. "Seriously, Mickie. I can't imagine what happened to make him decide not to be married to you anymore. From where I'm sitting, you're pretty amazing."

"Thanks, Cruz. That means a lot."

"Enough that you'll go out with me again?"

Mickie laughed. "Probably."

"Just probably?"

"Well, probably leaning heavily on the definitely side."

Cruz's voice got soft and rumbly and Mickie shivered at the promise she could hear in it. "Good. I have to say, I'm looking forward to getting to know more about you, Mickie."

"Me too."

"Can I call you?"

"Yes, I'd like that."

"And you'll keep in touch in the meantime?"

"Yeah."

"Good. Come on, I'll walk you out."

They stood from the table and Cruz helped Mickie up. He stepped back and led her out of the restaurant with his hand at the small of her back. Mickie didn't know what it was about the gesture that made her feel cherished, but it did. Maybe it was because Troy had never really touched her outside of the times they were in bed, but Cruz's hand against her felt wonderful.

They walked side by side down the sidewalk next to the water until they got to a staircase that led up to the street.

"This is me. I'm parked down the street up there," Mickie said.

"I'll walk you all the way to your car."

"Really, Cruz, it's fine, I can—"

"I'll walk you all the way to your car," Cruz repeated, his voice unrelenting.

Mickie looked up at his face and saw he was serious. "Fine, but it's really not necessary, it's the middle of the day."

"It's necessary to me."

Mickie smiled and simply nodded, giving in gracefully. They continued up the stairs and down a street until they got to a small public parking lot, where Mickie had left her car.

Stopping at the driver's side door, Cruz turned to Mickie. He took both her hands in his and brought each one up to his mouth. He kissed the back of her left and turned her right hand over and kissed the palm. "I've had a good time. Thank you for coming, Mickie."

"Me too. I'll text you and we can talk more this week. Okay?" Mickie didn't step away from Cruz, liking the feeling of her hands in his.

"That sounds great." Cruz leaned toward Mickie slowly, giving her time to move back. When she didn't, he briefly touched his lips to hers. He wanted to linger and savor their first kiss, but he didn't. He drew back and squeezed her hands once more before letting go. "Go on and get in. I'll talk to you soon."

"Bye, Cruz." Mickie opened her door and Cruz shut it behind her. She started the engine and turned to see Cruz was still standing near her car. She gave a small wave as she prepared to head out. He gave her a chin lift in return. Mickie pulled out of the space and headed toward the exit of the lot. She looked back once and saw Cruz headed down the street, back in the direction of the River Walk.

It'd been an interesting date. Intense at times, but she'd enjoyed being with Cruz and being the focus of his attention. She definitely hoped he'd call.

Chapter Five

"**O**H YEAH, TAKE that ass. Give it to her."

Cruz threw back the last of the beer in the bottle he was holding and tried to ignore the actions going on behind him. It'd been five days since his date with Mickie and he'd never felt so unclean…maybe except for the time he'd gone to his doctor to be checked for any sexually transmitted diseases after learning the truth about Sophie.

This shit had to end. He had to figure out where and from whom Ransom was getting his drugs, see if he couldn't shut down the Red Brothers and get the hell out before he became a person he couldn't live with anymore.

Cruz was sitting around a table with Ransom, Tick, and two other prospects. Ransom was going over the prospects' new assignments. Every other day they were tasked with some sort of bullshit job, to prove their loyalty to Ransom and the MC.

It was ten in the morning, and behind them were three of the other members of the club and a girl who Cruz hadn't seen around before, but who couldn't have been more than twenty years old. Bubba had her bent over a table while Dirt and Camel cheered him on. They'd each had their shot already, and Cruz knew whoever walked into the room next would most likely take his turn as well.

Almost all of the men in the club were large, either tall and muscular, or overweight, and able to protect themselves and their president. The club whores were probably pretty at one point, but over time, through lack of proper diet, drug use and the abuse they took at the hands of the club members, they'd morphed into shells of the women they used to be. Most were average height, some were almost certainly underage, and because of the drug use, none carried much extra weight on their bodies. It made Cruz's stomach seize to watch as the MC members took their turns with them. Seeing the women helpless underneath the large, unrelenting bodies of the men fucking them was something Cruz knew he'd never forget.

This morning, Bubba and the others had tied the woman's ankles to the table legs, about three feet apart, and her wrists were bound with some sort of cord behind her back. They'd stuffed a ball gag in her mouth and Cruz had seen the drool pooling under her. She wasn't struggling at all, however, merely lying limp on the table as each of the men fucked her.

The woman's eyes were vacant. She was out of her head with drugs and most likely didn't even realize what was going on, or if she did, she didn't care, only waiting until the men were done so she could get paid in more drugs. None of the men wore a condom, and Camel and Dirt had ejaculated all over the woman's back and hands when they'd orgasmed.

The entire scene was disgusting and obscene, and Cruz couldn't help but see in his mind first Sophie, and then Angel, lying across the table instead of the drugged-out woman.

"Got that, Smoke?"

Shit. "Sorry, what?"

Ransom laughed heartily. "You're a bit distracted this morning, Smoke. You're wishing you could join in, aren't you? Well, too fucking bad. You know prospects don't get to fuck. Club pussy is only for the Hermanos Rojos."

Cruz tried to look suitably chastised. "Sorry, Pres."

"Now, fucking pay attention. I don't like to repeat myself. Today you assholes are gonna take Angel out and sweet-talk her and her bitch friends. I gotta move this shit along. She's annoying as fuck and this needs to happen sooner rather than later. I promised my supplier this new market would be hot. It's taking too fucking long."

Thankfully, Tiny, another prospect, asked what was on Cruz's mind. "How will being nice to this bitch move things along?"

Ransom's fist came across the table and landed in Tiny's face almost before Cruz even saw him strike. Tiny, ironically named because he weighed at least three hundred pounds, didn't really move with the force of Ransom's fist. His head went back, but that was about all that budged.

"What was that for?" he whined, holding his palm to his face.

"Because you don't ever fucking question me, prospect. 'Loyalty to One.' And *I'm* the fucking 'one.' If I tell you to take a shit in the middle of the River Walk, you'll do it without fucking asking why or whining about it. That's how this works. Once you prove you're loyal to me, and only fucking me—and part of that loyalty means you don't *question* me—then *maybe* I'll consider patching you in. Until then, you do what the hell I say, whenever the hell I say it. And today, the three of you are gonna pick up Angel, take her to Smoke's fucking mall to meet her rich-bitch friends, and you're going to show them how gentlemanly you can be. As a parting gift, you'll give Angel some joints and encourage her to share with her friends."

"Yes, sir. No problem," Roach answered meekly. Cruz and Tiny followed suit.

The outing seemed like a bullshit one to Cruz, but there was no way he'd say anything now. He'd have to watch it play out and see how it went. Ransom thought he worked security at the mall, and obviously decided it was the perfect place to take Angel and her friends in the name of introducing them to the MC.

Ignoring the group of men, now grown to six, who were gathered around the girl tied to the table, and who were cheering each other on even louder, Cruz and the other two prospects left the clubhouse to pick up Ransom's pseudo girlfriend.

"Fuck. I can't wait until I'm a full member. That there was prime pussy," Roach grumbled as they got into the panel van the club owned.

"I tend to like 'em a bit older," Cruz drawled.

"You're losing out, bro." It was Tiny who chimed in this time. "The younger they are, the tighter the pussy. I'm a big motherfucker and I need tight pussy to get off. Twelve and thirteen is ideal." He laughed at himself. "Don't get me wrong, I'll take pussy and ass no matter how I can get it, but I prefer the girls. They're just starting to get little titties."

Cruz swallowed the bile that rose up in his throat. Jesus fucking Christ, he had to get this job done sooner rather than later. He couldn't wait to bring these assholes down. He only hoped he didn't lose himself in the process.

MICKIE TRIED ONCE again to get through to her sister. "Angel, why don't you come over here? We'll go get manis and pedis together."

Angel sighed heavily into the phone. "No. Ransom is sending some of the guys over and they're taking me to the mall to meet up with Cissy, Kelly, and Bridgette."

"Why would MC guys want to go with you to the mall?" Mickie asked in what she thought was a reasonable tone. The entire thing made no sense to her. There was no way rough-and-tough motorcycle club men would want to hang out at the mall with some spoiled, rich twenty-somethings. They were up to no good and Mickie didn't like it.

"Maybe because they *like* me and want to get to know my friends?"

Mickie knew there was nothing she could say that would sway her sister. There were so many things she *wanted* to say, but nothing that

Angel wouldn't take offense to at the moment.

She settled for asking her sister, "Be careful then, okay? Will you call me when you get back?"

"No. I'm not twelve anymore, Mickie. I don't have to call you when I get back and I don't have to ask permission to do anything either."

"I just worry about you."

"You don't need to. I know you don't approve of Ransom and his friends, so therefore, I don't want to hear anything else you have to say about them."

Mickie stared at the phone in her hand. Angel had hung up.

She sighed. The only bright spot in her life at the moment was Cruz and his texts. They were really funny. Mickie had tried to keep her communication with him to a minimum, they didn't really know each other after all, but he'd made that hard. Cruz was charming, even in his texts. He always told her how nice it was to hear from her and he made her feel special.

Mickie clicked on the app and read the last text from Cruz from the day before.

Green beans or corn on the cob?

Mickie had answered with corn. His next text had made her laugh out loud.

Guess I'm going back to the store this afternoon then. :)
Whatever you get is fine. I can eat green beans.
Nope, you want corn, you're getting corn.

They'd set up their next date. Cruz had invited her over to his apartment for dinner. Mickie supposed she should feel awkward and nervous about going to his place, but she didn't. She knew she'd just met him, but so far he'd seemed pretty sincere. And while their first date hadn't exactly been textbook, considering some of their topics of conversation, she still was interested in getting to know him better.

She enjoyed talking with him and it felt good to be the center of a man's attention again. Even though their relationship, if it could be called that at this point, was new, she really wanted to trust a man again. Troy had ripped her heart out and had really done a number on her, but to not trust anyone ever again was letting Troy win, and she refused to let that happen.

Mickie typed a quick text, letting Cruz know she was thinking about him…and wanting to run something by him. She hoped she wasn't being paranoid, but thought maybe a second opinion would reassure her that's all it was.

Hey. Just thought I'd say hi.

His response took a few minutes, but she smiled when she heard the ding of her phone.

Hey back. How are you?

Good. I think I had some visitors this morning.

Mickie jumped right into what she wanted to ask him.

??

I saw 2 motorcycles leaving my apt complex this am. Never seen them b4. They could've been visiting someone, but it was early and the guys were wearing leather vests. Think they could've been Red Brothers?

Maybe. You have mace?

Yes.

Good, always carry it & have it out when you walk to your car. Call me if you get worried and I'll come and escort you.

U don't have to do that. They didn't do anything, but with Angel and all, it freaked me out a bit.

Your instincts are probably right on. Let me know if anything else weird happens. Ok?

I will. Sorry 2b a downer.

Never apologize for letting me know you're worried.

Talk 2u later?

I'll check back to make sure you're good.

Ok. Bye.

Bye.

Mickie put the phone down and sighed. Darn Angel. Somehow she'd known the bikes were connected to Angel and the MC. She'd have to be extra vigilant just in case.

Cruz's offer felt good. Even though they were still getting to know each other it felt nice that she had someone to contact if something did happen.

CRUZ FELT HIS phone buzz in his pocket and pulled it out. Mickie. After their text conversation this morning he'd had to force himself not to beat the shit out of Ransom. He hated more than anything that the president was messing with her. He'd hoped he'd convinced Ransom she wasn't really trouble, that she and Angel didn't get along, but obviously the man was still keeping her on his radar.

He knew if Ransom was having the members watch her apartment he'd have to make sure if he was seen there, it could be construed as being a part of the role he was playing…keeping his eye on Angel's sister to keep her out of their club business.

Looking down at the phone, Cruz didn't dare let the grin that was dying to come out show on his face in case the assholes he was with wanted to know what he was smiling about.

Just when I think the world has gone crazy, u text me with some-

thing completely normal & innocuous. Thank u. And...I don't look anything like Julianne, but thanks. :) Thinking about u.

Earlier he'd sent a short message:

I just realized who you remind me of...Julianne whats-her-name from that dancing show. Hot.

He'd attached an older picture of the woman when she'd had her hair cut in what the Internet called a "pixie cut." Her hair was blonde, but in Cruz's mind, she and Mickie could've been twins.

Cruz stuffed the phone back into his pocket and tried not to let her words get to him.

Shit, who was he trying to kid; the fact that Mickie was thinking about him had already burrowed deeply into his bloodstream and gotten stuck there.

"There she is. Fuck, she might not be twelve, but I'd still fucking tap that." Tiny's words cut through the warm fuzzies he'd gotten from reading Mickie's text like a knife slicing through butter.

Cruz looked up and saw Angel leaving her apartment as she turned and locked her door. She was wearing a tight pair of jeans that left nothing to the imagination, her thong was clearly visible over the back of her pants. She wore a cropped T-shirt, and as she made her way toward the van, they could all see it was tied in a knot under her breasts. Her belly-button ring was glinting in the sun as she ambled toward them.

"Fuck yeah. I think we'd *all* love to tap that," Roach agreed wholeheartedly.

"Shut the fuck up. We can't get anywhere near her or Pres would have our heads. Keep your dicks in your pants and remember we have to make sure her and her friends have a good time today," Cruz growled out grumpily.

"Yeah, yeah. Shit. Who pissed in your fuckin' Wheaties, Smoke?"

Cruz ignored Tiny's comment and got out of the van just as Angel approached.

"Hey. Ready to go?"

"Yeah. Thanks for coming to get me, Smoke."

Cruz grunted in reply and assisted Angel into the front seat. Roach was driving and Tiny was sitting in the seat behind him. Cruz climbed in and sat behind Angel.

"Hey, Roach, Tiny. How are you?" Angel asked politely, as she settled into the seat.

"Good. How're you?"

Angel giggled as if she was a teenager. "I'm good."

"Ransom sent a present for ya," Roach told Angel. He held out a joint.

"Cool. He's always thinking of me. Got a light?"

Tiny leaned forward from the back and flicked his lighter. The three men watched as Angel lit the marijuana cigarette and coughed as she inhaled.

"Thanks, Tiny."

"Who're we meeting today, Angel?" Roach asked.

The three continued to make small talk as they made their way to the mall. Every time Angel talked too much and let the joint burn, Tiny or Roach would encourage her to take another hit. By the time they got to the mall, Angel was high as a kite. Mission fucking accomplished.

The rest of the afternoon was more of the same. Cruz went through the motions of being nice to Angel's friends and observed Tiny and Roach slowly winning the four women over. They carried their bags and were quick to compliment them.

At one point, when Cissy asked Angel if she was all right—Angel had been giggling uncontrollably at any and everything—Roach threw his arm around the slender woman, leaned into her ear and whispered, "She's feeling awesome. Haven't you ever smoked a joint?" When Cissy had looked up at Roach in shock, he'd told her, "No? Well, shit. We'll have to educate you then."

Cruz had to admit, Roach and Tiny were good. Ransom had picked his prospects well. By the end of the shopping trip, the seven of them were sitting in the panel van in the parking lot. He'd taken them to the employees-only parking area; since he had an employee pass as part of his cover, Cruz figured maybe the cops would pay less attention to the obvious-as-shit van here than if he was parked amongst the Mercedes and more expensive cars that people typically drove to the mall. The women were giggling and laughing after sharing two joints.

"Oh my God, this is so awesome! You guys are the best friends I've ever had!" Bridgette enthused.

"I know. I love you guys!" Cissy joined in. "Angel, you never told us how great this stuff is!"

Trying to sound experienced, Angel huffed, "I wasn't sure you were cool enough to take the chance."

Kelly pouted. "That's not fair. You know we're just as cool as you."

Tiny winked at Roach and Cruz. He leaned over and whispered in Cruz's ear, "And so it begins. Never fails. It's all a competition with these rich bitches."

"When can we do this again?" Cissy asked Angel.

Looking perplexed, Angel looked to Roach and stammered, "Ransom gave me these…"

Roach stepped into the conversation as if he were a puppeteer holding the strings of the marionettes that were Cissy, Bridgette, Kelly, and Angel.

"You know this stuff isn't cheap, Angel. He likes to spoil you, but it's not like it grows on trees."

Bridgette took the bait. "Oh, but we have money, don't we girls? We don't expect to get it for *free*."

"Yeah, I got access to my trust fund last year. I've got lots of money," Cissy said.

Cruz inwardly groaned. Jesus fucking Christ, these women needed a keeper.

"That's good, sweetheart," Roach crooned, leaning into Cissy. He bent down and licked her neck, right by her ear. "You got any right now? I've got some more stuff you could take with you if you wanted. No, wait! I got an idea. You wanna get some more of your friends together? I bet you've got some other cool friends who would be up for it, yeah?"

Bridgette chimed in next. "Oh yeah. Cissy, we could get a group together next weekend! Your parents are leaving the country, aren't they? We could use their house. They have that big room that would be perfect. It'd be like high school!"

All four women giggled hysterically.

"All right. That sounds awesome. But how about instead of having it at one of your houses, you guys all come down to the clubhouse? It's private and secure and all your friends can meet the MC members. We'd love to have you join us for one of our parties."

When the girls nodded enthusiastically, Roach continued reeling them in. "I'll need a down payment. Give me some dough now, and I'll get you the address of the club. You bring some of your friends and the MC will be waiting and we'll have enough cigarettes for everyone," Roach said smoothly.

When the four women opened their purses and pulled out their wallets, Tiny took Kelly's wallet out of her hand and helped himself to two hundred dollars. He closed the wallet and handed it back, leaning into her and nibbling on the lobe of her ear. "That should do it, *ma chère*. I can't wait to hang with you and your friends."

Roach collected money from Cissy, and Cruz reluctantly pocketed five hundred dollars from Angel and Bridgette.

"Because you ladies have been so generous, we're gonna send you home with a few gifts from the Hermanos Rojos MC. Make sure you share with your girlfriends, and remember, only invite the friends you think can handle it and won't go blabbing to the cops or their daddies. If it works out, you can come and party with us all the time." Roach winked at the girls.

After the longest thirty minutes of Cruz's life, the three girls staggered out of the van and into the parking lot. They each had two joints tucked into their purses as they made their way toward their cars. Cruz knew it wasn't safe for them to drive, but there was absolutely nothing he could do about it right now, not while keeping his cover.

With Roach insisting he drive, Cruz climbed into the driver's seat and headed back toward Angel's apartment. She was sitting between Roach and Tiny in the backseat and every time he looked in the mirror, he saw the two men pushing their luck. Tiny had pulled her leg up and over his and his hand was on her thigh, rubbing up and down, getting closer and closer to her crotch with each pass. If she'd been wearing a skirt, Tiny's hand would've been way past neutral territory.

Roach had buried his face in Angel's neck and was licking her like she was an ice cream cone, sucking her earlobe into his mouth each time he reached it. Cruz even saw him push his tongue into her ear once as well. She was giggling but not stopping them, lost in the good feelings of the pot and the sexual tension in the air.

Cruz cleared his throat loudly and said in a threatening voice, "Ransom's."

Tiny's hand stopped its journey upward, but Roach only looked up and smiled evilly.

"Angel, we're here," Cruz announced loudly when they pulled up to her apartment complex.

Without giving her a chance to move, Roach put his hand on her chin and pulled her face toward his. He held her still while he thrust his tongue into her mouth and devoured her. Cruz could see the pressure of his fingers on her chin, even as she struggled lightly in his grasp.

When Roach finally pulled back, he forcefully turned her head toward Tiny, and kept hold of her while Tiny also took possession of her mouth. Cruz heard her whimper once while being ravaged by Tiny.

Finally, when the man leaned back, Roach said in her ear, "We know you're Ransom's. We don't disrespect our president. We don't take what's his without permission. But if you're gonna be his, you gotta know he likes to share."

Roach finally let go of her chin and Cruz watched as she turned slowly to look at Roach. He ran his hand down her cheek gently, as if he hadn't just been holding her chin hostage in his grip. Cruz could see the fading white spots on her skin as the blood made its way back into it.

Angel smiled shyly at Roach. "I'll see you guys next week at the party?"

"Yeah, Angel, you'll see us next week at the party. Make sure you only invite the cool girls that can handle it. Yeah?"

"Yeah, Roach. I'll make sure. I've had a good time today. Thank you for coming with me. Is Ransom gonna come see me? I really want him."

Cruz knew marijuana could make some people horny; Angel was obviously one of those people.

"I don't know, Angel. But I'll tell him how good you were today."

"Yeah, tell him that. I was a good girl for him."

For the second time that day, Cruz felt the bile creep up his throat. Time to get this show on the road.

"Come on, Angel. Let's get you inside."

Cruz came around the side and opened the van door and helped

Angel out. She wobbled on her feet and leaned into him. "You gonna kiss me too, Smoke?" she asked with a smile.

"Nope. I think you've had enough. Time to go inside and take a nap."

Cruz lifted his chin at Roach and Tiny, telling them he had this, and he carried Angel's bags, and held her around the waist as he got her to her door. He had to unlock it for her and practically carry her inside.

He dropped the bags just inside the door and helped Angel sit on her couch. As soon as he let go, she toppled over sideways. Cruz shook his head. He could do anything to her and she'd have no idea. It was a good thing he'd walked her up, and not Roach or Tiny. Cruz knew they wouldn't have hesitated to take advantage of her, their prospect status be damned.

Cruz squatted next to the couch and shook Angel's shoulder. When she opened her eyes and looked blearily up at him, he told her sternly, "Call your sister, Angel. Let her know you're home and you're okay."

"She's a fuddy-duddy."

"She loves you. Call her."

"Oh, all right."

Angel closed her eyes and rested her head back down on the cushion. Cruz had no idea if she'd do as he asked, but he hoped so. He'd done what he could. It wasn't nearly enough.

He stepped out and closed Angel's apartment door behind him, making sure it was locked from the inside before shutting it. Cruz went back to the van and climbed into the driver's seat once more.

Tiny and Roach hadn't moved. They sat in their seats, smirking at Cruz.

"She all tucked in safe and sound?"

Cruz nodded curtly. "You were pushing your luck there, Roach."

"Pffft. That bitch was squirming in our hands. She wanted it."

"She's Ransom's."

"Yeah, for now. But he doesn't give a shit about her except when he wants some pussy and to get her friends hooked. Once he's done with her, she'll need some comforting."

"Ransom doesn't like to share, that was bullshit."

"Yeah, but what Ransom doesn't know won't hurt him. It's not like I'm gonna bring her to the club and fuck her. Ransom has the right idea, keeping her on the side. I'll do the same shit. Once he's tired of her, I'll move in. Rich fucking pussy whenever I want it. Can't pass that up. When I'm done with her, I'll move on to her rich-ass friends. They're all dying for MC dick. I'm happy to oblige. Having them start coming to our parties was the best idea Ransom ever had."

Cruz shook his head but didn't say anything. He knew he'd never change their minds, and protesting any more would be suspicious. They'd been getting away with whatever they wanted for a long time. He vowed to protect Angel as much as he could and do whatever was necessary to prevent any of her friends from getting hooked on drugs, like Sophie had.

Cruz knew he should break things off with Mickie. Today proved that all the more. But he couldn't. For one, she was the only bright spot in his life at the moment, and two, Cruz had a feeling Ransom was going to act on his threats against her, and he wanted to be sure she was safe from the club and all the crap that went down there. He knew it'd be a miracle if Mickie would forgive him for his role in what was happening to her sister. He knew he was treading a thin line, but Cruz wasn't going to stop courting her. He couldn't.

Chapter Six

CRUZ PULLED UP in front of Mickie's apartment and took a deep breath. She'd texted him thirty minutes ago and asked if he'd be able to help her. When he'd learned why she needed his help, he'd been furious.

Apparently Ransom was sick of Mickie butting into Angel's business and had ordered Tick to make a statement. Thankfully Tick had only slashed her tires. It could've been a lot worse. Cruz had told Ransom he was keeping a close eye on Mickie, but after Angel told Ransom about how Mickie was still on her case, especially after her trip to the mall, Ransom had apparently lost whatever patience he'd been holding on to.

Cruz saw Mickie standing by her car, staring down at her phone. She looked sexy in a pair of jeans and a T-shirt. She glanced up and saw him striding toward her. She put her phone in her pocket and greeted him.

"Hey. Thanks for coming. I wasn't sure who else to call. I mean, I have other friends, but they're either working or busy. Not to say you weren't doing either, but I figured—"

"I'm glad you got ahold of me. How did this happen?" he asked, gesturing to her car. Cruz could see the muscle in her jaw flex as she ground her teeth together.

"Honestly? If I had to guess, I'd say it has something to with that damn motorcycle club."

Cruz was impressed with Mickie's intuition, but asked anyway.

"Why?"

"Because I was pissed at my sister the other day and let her have it. I tried once again to get her to see that the man she's dating is a thug. I'm sure that conversation got passed along and this is the result."

"That's a pretty big leap."

Mickie looked up at Cruz and cocked her head as she observed him silently for a moment. Finally, she said in an even tone that somehow conveyed anger, frustration, and irritation all at the same time, "I work at a car dealership, Cruz. I'm a divorced thirty-four-year-old woman who minds her own business. I don't go clubbing. I don't hang out on any street corners. I go to the movies with my friends; I sit at home and read books. The biggest law I've broken is not returning my library books on time. I *might* have a VHS tape that I never returned to the video store down the block that went out of business ten years ago. The only people I know who might do anything like this are connected to my sister. I irritated my sister recently, so it only follows that someone might want to get back at me."

"You think your sister did this?"

Mickie rolled her eyes and put both hands on her hips. "My sister wouldn't know the first thing about how to slash a tire...but that guy she's dating? Yeah. I can imagine this would be his very mature way of dealing with his girlfriend being harassed by her sister."

Cruz couldn't help it, the grin formed on his face before he could beat it back.

"You think this is funny?"

Cruz got serious. "Your tires being slashed by someone in a motorcycle club? Absolutely, one-hundred-percent no. But you? Yeah. I've got to say, you've either had a lot of practice, or you're a natural. That sarcastic tone conveys just a hint of snark with a bit of sassy thrown in for good measure."

Mickie smiled for the first time. "How can I be laughing when I'm so pissed?"

"Because sometimes it's better to laugh than to cry."

"You've got that right."

"So," Cruz stated, getting down to business. "You got any extra tires hanging around?"

"Yeah, one. The spare."

"Don't think that's gonna cut it here."

"Didn't think so."

"You know you're gonna have to replace all of them, right?"

Mickie sighed. "Yeah."

"Can you cover it? I know you said you had some cash from your folks, but this could end up being expensive."

"Yeah. It's fine. Besides, it's not like I can decide it's not worth the cost."

"I'm afraid you're right."

"Can you drive me to the shop? I'll buy the tires and see if they'll get a tow truck out here to get my car."

"No problem. But I'll be happy to bring you back here and change the tires for you."

"I can't ask you to do that."

"You didn't. I offered."

Mickie studied Cruz for another moment. She honestly would never have contacted him if she hadn't been desperate. She had a million things to do that she'd been putting off, and it just figured that this weekend of all weekends would be the one when Angel's boyfriend would choose to make his point. "If you're sure you're not busy..."

"I'm sure."

"Then thank you. I'd be very grateful if you could help me. But this isn't a date."

"What?"

"This isn't a date," Mickie repeated. "There are rules for dates."

"Rules." It wasn't a question, but Mickie saw the smirk on Cruz's face.

"Yes. First rule, the woman gets all dressed up so she can impress her date." She gestured to her outfit. "I'm not dressed up and there's no way I'm impressing anyone dressed like this. Second rule, the woman always offers to pay, to be polite. But I'm not offering—I'm paying. Period. Third rule, there's absolutely no drama allowed on the date. I think this constitutes as drama. Hence…this isn't a date."

Cruz's smile lit up his face and made him look years younger. "Deal. I'm still fixing you dinner later this week. We'll call this a friend doing another friend a favor then…all right?"

Mickie beamed at him. "Deal."

"Come on, friend. You've got some tires to purchase."

The trip to the tire shop was relatively painless, except for the cost of the new tires, which was absolutely ridiculous, considering there was a good chance her sister's boyfriend would just ruin this set as well.

On the way back to her apartment, Mickie asked, "Do you think I should make a police report? I mean, I figure you probably know more about it than I do."

Cruz glanced at her before sighing. "If you don't have any proof it was your sister's boyfriend, or that he asked one of his friends to do it, I'm not sure what good it will do."

Mickie nodded. "Yeah, that's what I figured. I even called the main office to ask about security cameras, but they don't have any that were pointed toward my car since it was parked at the back of the lot."

When Cruz opened his mouth, Mickie hurried on. "I know, I know. I shouldn't park back there, it's not safe, but I wanted to get my steps in for the day." At the blank look on his face, she explained further. "Steps. You know, you're supposed to get ten thousand steps in every day to stay healthy. It's good exercise."

"It might be good exercise, but it's not safe," Cruz returned.

"Obviously," Mickie grumbled. "But now I'll park nearer to my building because the lady in the office said the cameras are pointing at the buildings, and the cars that are nearest to them are on the tapes."

He nodded, satisfied with her answer.

As they pulled back into the lot of the apartment complex, Mickie pointed out unnecessarily, "At least you have room to work out here. If I'd parked closer you would've had to work around the other vehicles in the lot."

Cruz didn't answer, merely shook his head in mock exasperation. He popped his trunk and hefted out one of the tires, leaning it against the car. He got the jack out of the back and went to work on the first tire.

Cruz worked quickly and efficiently. It was warm out, as it usually was in Texas, but he showed no discomfort. He removed the lug nuts and jacked up the car. Before she knew it, the first tire was on her car and Cruz had moved to the second one.

"Can you talk and work?"

Cruz looked up briefly at that, surprised. "Yeah, why wouldn't I be able to?"

Mickie shrugged. "I don't know. My ex could never do two things at once. He had to concentrate on one thing at a time." She saw Cruz's lips twitch, but her opinion of him grew when he declined to comment on what would've been a great opening for a sexual innuendo.

"I can talk while I do this, Mickie. No problem."

"I just figured, even though this isn't a date, that maybe we could still get to know each other better. How'd you learn to change a tire so quickly?"

"My dad taught me when I was around ten. We were driving

across the country, moving to somewhere, I forget where now, but the tire on the car blew out on the highway. He stayed calm and pulled over on the side of the road. He got my stepmom out and safely out of the way, then he walked me through how to change the tire."

"Have you had much practice? It doesn't seem the kind of thing you'd do all the time, but you're obviously very good at it."

Cruz looked up at Mickie. She was sitting next to him, watching his hands as he worked on the tire. He'd never had a woman sit next to him when he changed their tire. Usually they were either inside a building or standing well away from him. She was refreshingly different from any other woman he'd met.

"Dad made sure I didn't forget. One day I went outside to go to school, and he'd taken one of my tires completely off my car. I remember I was so mad, but he simply shrugged and told me that tires didn't need changing only on the weekends when nothing else was going on. I needed to learn how to change it as fast as I could."

"Were you late for school?"

"Twenty minutes. Missed a quiz too."

Mickie smiled at him. "You've gotten faster at it."

They moved to the other side of the car so he could start on the third tire.

"Yeah. Anytime anyone in the neighborhood needed a tire changed, I got roped into it. It was annoying as all get-out at the time, but I'm grateful to him now."

"Me too."

"You want to learn?"

"Yes." Mickie's answer was quick and eager and Cruz couldn't help the chuckle that escaped.

"Cool. Watch me on this one and you can do the last one on your own."

"Can I ask something else?"

"Sure."

"How come you didn't become a cop when you graduated if you really wanted to help people?"

If Cruz had been eating or drinking anything he probably would've spit it out at her question, but other than a slight pause in what he was doing, he was proud of his non-reaction. "I didn't want to write tickets for people speeding and I didn't like all the politics that go on in police departments." It wasn't a lie. He'd thought about joining the force, but decided the FBI appealed much more to him in the long run.

Cruz knew he needed to turn the questioning around before she asked him something he'd have to outright lie about. "What's your favorite dessert?"

"What?"

"You asked a question, I get to as well...don't I?"

"Yeah. Of course. I just didn't expect that. My favorite dessert? I'd have to say cookie dough."

"Just the dough? Not the cookie itself?"

"Nope. I buy the bags of the ready-made cookies from the freezer section. You know, the little frozen blobs you're supposed to stick on a cookie sheet and cook? Yeah, I eat them raw. They're so yummy."

Mickie looked at Cruz. He'd stopped tightening the lug nuts on the tire and was looking at her in a way she couldn't decipher.

"What?"

"I was going to do my best to impress you by making sure I had whatever you told me was your favorite on hand later this week. But I'm not sure putting frozen cookie dough blobs on a plate is all that impressive."

Mickie couldn't help the giggles that exploded out of her mouth at the look on Cruz's face. And that only made her giggle harder. She held her stomach and giggled until tears rolled out of her eyes. Finally, when she had a bit more control, she choked out, "I'm so sorry, Cruz, but if you could only see your face… If it makes you feel better, I also like brownies."

One of Cruz's hands reached for her, but stopped short of actually touching her.

Cruz looked down at his filthy hands and resisted brushing away the wetness on her cheek. Watching as she'd laughed herself silly at his expense should've irritated him, but instead he found himself wanting to make her laugh again so he could see her unabashed zeal for life. He didn't often see that kind of pure joy in his line of work.

"I admit it wasn't what I was expecting, but I'll see what I can do to make sure I've got something you'll enjoy for dessert next week." He hadn't meant his words to be a sexual innuendo, but when Mickie started giggling again, he simply shook his head. God, she was funny.

"Come on, I'm done with this one, you ready to give it a try?" Cruz held a hand out to her and helped Mickie to her feet.

"I'm game if you are, but I can't promise to be as quick at it as you."

"Practice makes perfect."

"Let's hope I won't need to practice again anytime soon," Mickie mumbled as she stood and reached for the tire wrench. "Let's do this then."

Twenty minutes and lots of swear words later, Mickie's car had four bright and shiny new tires on it. Mickie was dirty and sweaty, but strangely enough, she'd actually had a good time. She felt good about finally learning how to change a tire, and Cruz had been very patient with her as she'd asked a million questions while changing the last tire.

"Thanks for coming over today. I appreciate it."

"Anytime. I mean that, Mickie. If you need anything, you can call me."

She nodded and then asked a bit uncertainly, "Are we still on for

Friday?" She wanted to see him again, enjoyed being around him, but she felt like she'd forced him into helping her today and didn't want to presume he wanted to spend any more time with her.

"Absolutely. I'm looking forward to it."

"Me too."

"Are you good here now? I hate to say it, but I have to get going," Cruz told her.

"Yeah, I'm good. Again, I do appreciate your help."

"No problem. I'll talk to you later. Okay?"

Mickie nodded and watched as Cruz climbed into his car and waved once, then drove away. She was looking forward to dinner, even though she tried not to get her hopes up for anything. It was one thing to spend a few hours together hanging out like friends would, it was another thing altogether to get together with the expectation of seeing if a relationship was possible.

CRUZ ENTERED HIS apartment and went straight to his kitchen where he washed his hands, scrubbing off the dirt and grease from Mickie's tires. He then headed into his small living room and sat on the couch. He let out a breath, rested his head on the cushion behind him and thought about the afternoon.

He liked Mickie. Oh, he'd thought she was nice after their dinner the other day, but seeing her today made him look at her in a new way. She wasn't afraid to laugh at herself...or him. She'd dealt with the stress of having her tires slashed and having to pay for four new ones without any drama. She was genuinely interested in learning how to do something new. And perhaps more importantly, she was down to earth and seemed very easygoing.

He loved those traits in Mackenzie, his friend Dax's girlfriend, but never thought he'd be able to find a woman like her. But watching as Mickie giggled, and the fact that she didn't care that she was sitting on the ground in the middle of a parking lot, made his interest in her notch up a level.

His plan had been to make sure she was safe from Ransom and the rest of the motorcycle club, and while he'd still be keeping her from harm, now he was interested in her for another reason as well. Knowing if she ever found out why he'd originally spoken to her in the café, that all he wanted to do was keep her safe until his undercover mission was completed, he'd probably lose any opportunity to have anything long-term with her, he still made the decision right then and there to do whatever he could to get to know her better.

Hopefully she'd understand that while his initial motives weren't a hundred percent honest, what he was feeling for her had nothing, absolutely nothing, to do with her sister, Ransom, or the damn Red Brothers. It was all her.

Chapter Seven

———— • ◆ • ————

MICKIE KNOCKED ON the door of apartment number sixteen. Cruz had given her directions when he'd called last night to confirm she was still coming over. The conversation had been short, and he'd apologized, saying he was in the middle of something.

She was nervous because Cruz had sounded weird. She didn't know what kind of weird, just that he hadn't sounded like the easygoing open guy she'd spent the afternoon with the other day.

She shook her head at herself in disgust. Mickie wasn't the type of woman to lust over anyone, but she thought she just might be in lust with Cruz. There was so much she didn't know about him, and Mickie knew it wasn't smart, but she couldn't help herself. She just plain liked him, not to mention the chemistry they had with each other was off the charts. She had no idea if he felt it too, but figured he must on some level. She wasn't ready to move in with him or marry him, but she wasn't ruling out jumping his bones.

The door opened in front of her, stopping her musings.

"Mickie, I'm so glad you're here. Please, come in."

Mickie stepped into the apartment and stared at Cruz. Jeez, he looked good. He was wearing a green polo shirt and a pair of khaki pants. Once again she could see part of his tattoo peeking out from the sleeve of his shirt. Mickie swore to herself she'd get a look at that tattoo sooner rather than later.

Cruz locked the door after she got in and turned to her. He put both hands on her upper arms and leaned down and kissed her on the cheek, then pulled back and held out his arm. "This way, milady. I've got some wine if you're interested."

Cruz tried to keep his voice level. Mickie was beautiful. He had no idea how anyone could've let her go. If she was his—

He broke off his thoughts. She wasn't his, most likely wouldn't be.

She was wearing a pair of black slacks and a pink short-sleeve shirt. It had a V-neck that plunged deeper than a regular T-shirt would. Cruz could see a slight bit of cleavage, but not enough to be indecent. The differences between her and her sister were striking.

Mickie's black hair was smoothed down and elegant while the other day it looked a bit chaotic. It fit her. One day she was casual and natural, and the next she was trendy and polished.

When Cruz had leaned over to kiss her cheek, her scent struck him hard and fast. She smelled...clean. He'd been buried in filth for way too long and her fresh scent had him hard before he'd even been able to try to control it.

Mickie looked around nervously as she made her way into his apartment. Cruz tried to see his place as she might. There was an entryway that held only a small table. It emptied into an open area. There was a couch separating the living area from the kitchen. He had a table up against one wall; he mostly used it when he was researching on his computer. The kitchen had granite countertops and there was a built-in bar with three stools in front of it. If he had company, they could sit at the counter and watch him cook.

Cruz helped Mickie sit on one of the barstools and poured a glass of red wine and placed it in front of her. She played with the stem of the glass and watched as he walked over to the table. He saw how uncomfortable she seemed and made a split-second decision to help her relax a bit. Even though they'd gotten to know each other a little the previous weekend, this was a date...and she was obviously nervous.

Cruz picked up his real cell phone and dialed. Without saying a word to Mickie, he began speaking.

"Hey, Mack. How are you? Yeah, it's really me. I know, I'll call again soon to touch base, but for now I need a favor. I've got a date over at my place and I want to reassure her that I'm not a serial killer."

Cruz held the phone away from his ear and smiled at Mickie. They could both clearly hear the woman on the other end of the line screeching in delight.

He put the phone back to his ear and tried again. "Mack, chill! You're going to scare Mickie away. She knows I work in security, and I'd prefer you not give her a blow-by-blow of my employment history. If you think you can keep that on the down-low, can you please reassure her that I'm one of the good guys...for real? Okay, hang on."

Cruz held his phone to his stomach and took a deep breath. Mackenzie wasn't stupid. She knew he was undercover and with her reassurance, he knew she wouldn't say anything to give him away.

He looked at Mickie. "Mackenzie is my friend's girlfriend. Remember when I told you we all went out recently and celebrated her life? Yeah, this is her. I just want you to be comfortable around me. You went out on a limb meeting me here and I don't blame you for being nervous, but I swear to you that I'm not going to hurt you. I thought maybe talking to a woman who knows me would put you at ease a bit."

Mickie about melted in her seat. Not only had Cruz realized how nervous she was, but he'd found the perfect way to reassure her. She held out her hand without a word.

Cruz reached out and grabbed it. He brought her hand up to his lips and kissed the back before looking up at her without letting go. "Mack is going to be a bit over the top and probably a bit crazy. I'd appreciate it if you just went with it. She also has a tendency to ramble when she's excited or nervous…and she's definitely excited right now." He smiled, knowing excited was an understatement.

"It's fine, Cruz." Mickie pulled her hand out of his grasp and wiggled her fingers. She realized he was worried she'd somehow think less of his friend. It made him seem more…human. She didn't think anyone with nefarious intentions would not only try to make her feel more comfortable around him, but also be concerned about his friend as well. "Give me the phone."

He held it out and Mickie took it and put the phone up to her ear.

"Hello?"

"Hi! I'm Mack."

"I'm Michelle…Mickie."

"Mickie. I like that name. So you're there with Cruz? Isn't he a hunk? I mean, I have my own hunk, but if I didn't have Daxton, I'd totally go for Cruz. Okay, well maybe TJ… Oh hell. All the guys he hangs around with are to die for. Just wait until you meet them. I *hope* you'll get to meet them. I don't know how long you've been with Cruz, but seriously, they're all great people. And Cruz? You *so* don't have anything to worry about. Okay, maybe spontaneously combusting around him, but that's not necessarily a bad thing. Do you have any questions for me about him?"

"Only about a million."

Mackenzie laughed out loud. "Yeah, I know the feeling. I don't know what he really wants me to say, but I swear on all the chocolate Easter bunnies in the world that Cruz is one of the good guys. I mean, he's a guy, so he's bound to fuck something up, they all do, but his heart is in the right place. You don't have to worry about him. I know his ex treated him like crap though. Oh shit, has he told you about his divorce? I didn't mean to bring it up if you haven't heard about it. Such a horrible situation all the way around, but seriously, Cruz is sexy as hell and I have firsthand knowledge of the fact that he's loyal to his friends. He'd do anything for them."

Mickie broke in before Mack could continue. "I appreciate the reassurance."

"No problem. When Daxton came over to my house for the first time, I made him give me not only his driver's license but his work ID as well. Then he insisted that I call his boss and make sure he wasn't carrying around fake IDs. Oh shit, I don't think Cruz wanted me to share that much with you, but I swear he's a good guy. Okay?"

"Okay. Thanks. I appreciate it. I *was* a bit nervous." Mickie looked at Cruz as she said the last words, knowing he was listening intently to their conversation.

"Good. I hope this works out with you guys. My best friend, Laine, and I try to have a girls' night out at least once a month, and we'd love to get some more girls to hang with us. I'll see if you're interested the next time we get together."

"That sounds good, but I don't know if—"

"Yeah, I know. But Cruz hasn't been out with anyone in ages. So if he's out with you, he has to be serious about it."

"Uh, I—"

"Yeah, sorry. I don't want to freak you out. You have a good night. Give him the benefit of the doubt. He might be guarded, but it's for a good reason. But that reason isn't to deceive you. All right?

"Yeah."

"Good, give me back to Cruz. Talk to you later!"

Mickie held out the phone to Cruz and said a bit dazedly, "She wants to talk to you again."

Cruz took the phone. "Thanks, Mack." He didn't take it away from his ear, but hooked his other hand around Mickie's neck and brought her into him. He kissed her forehead then let her go, taking a step away to give her some space. Mickie could hear Mack babbling in Cruz's ear as he moved to stand next to her. She took a sip of her wine as they finished saying their goodbyes.

"Yeah. Tell Dax I'll call him soon. Thanks again, sweetheart. I'll talk to you later. Bye."

Cruz clicked the phone off and placed it on the counter next to them. He met Mickie's eyes with his own and asked, "Do you feel better? I know we spent some time together, but you didn't look comfortable when you got here."

Mickie nodded.

"Sure?"

"Yeah, Cruz. Thank you."

Cruz's intense gaze didn't leave hers. "I'd like for you to meet my friends sometime."

"Okay."

"They're a bit crazy, but I trust them with my life. I'd do anything for them and I know they'd do anything for me too."

"I'm glad you have friends like that."

"You hungry?"

Relieved he was changing the subject—he was pretty intense normally, but seemed more so tonight—Mickie nodded and asked, "Are we having green beans or corn?"

"Corn, of course. It's what you said you liked."

"Just making sure."

Cruz smiled at her and stepped away. He snagged the phone off the counter and shoved it in a drawer in the kitchen as he walked by. It looked exactly like the phone he used at the club, but since it was his personal cell, he never carried it.

"I've got two steaks on the grill, as well as the corn on the cob and a salad. I thought I'd keep it simple tonight."

"I'm a vegetarian."

Cruz froze and looked over at Mickie. *Oh shit.* He'd screwed up right out of the gate. He'd asked her about what vegetable she wanted, but didn't think to ask her about the main course. Just as he got himself all worked up, he saw her smile.

"Gotcha!"

Cruz laughed and put a hand to his chest. "Don't do that to me, woman!"

"I have to keep you on your toes. Don't want you making any assumptions about me."

"I like that you can tease me."

"I like that I can tease you too."

They smiled at each other until Cruz turned to go out to the small deck off of the living room to get the steaks. The balcony wasn't huge, only big enough to hold the small grill and two chairs, but it was one reason he'd chosen this apartment over the others. Cruz loved to grill and wanted to make sure he had a space to do it.

After dinner, and after he'd brought out a tray with both brownies and cookie dough blobs on it, they relaxed on the couch. They'd talked about their favorite movies, foods, states, books, and even animals. The conversation stayed light and easy as they got to know each other.

They agreed that a night spent watching a movie on television was better than a night out on the town. Mickie admitted that since assuming responsibility for her sister, she hadn't made a lot of friends. When she was in college, she was too busy with school and Angel to bother making lasting relationships, and by the time she'd graduated, she'd lost the opportunity to make those close, lifelong bonds that most people made while in their early twenties.

Cruz told Mickie more about Dax and Mackenzie and even touched on some of his other friends, leaving out their professions in the various law enforcement agencies around the city.

It was approximately ten when Mickie looked down at her watch. "I can't believe how quickly time has gone by tonight."

"Do you need to go?"

"I should…" She let the words hang between them.

Cruz moved closer to Mickie on the couch and reached out to

play with the hair around her ears. "Stay. For a bit longer."

Mickie hesitated, then nodded.

Cruz didn't say anything, but took his time really looking at Mickie. His eyes went from her eyes to her nose, to her lips, up to her forehead and then to her ears. They were constantly moving, and each time they landed back at her eyes, Mickie wanted to melt.

"You're beautiful, Mickie," Cruz said softly.

Mickie shook her head.

"You are. I don't know why you can't see it, but you are." His other hand came up and his thumb brushed over an eyebrow. It then moved down to caress the apple of her cheek. As it bloomed with heat, Mickie saw him smile. "So responsive to my touch. I wonder if you're this responsive everywhere."

His words weren't a question, more of a statement. He ran his index finger over her top lip, then her bottom one.

Mickie knew she was pushing it, but she opened her lips and sucked his finger into her mouth, smiling at the groan that escaped Cruz's lips.

"I want to kiss you," Cruz stated in a husky tone. He leaned into her, and Mickie could feel his hot breath against her lips. "May I?"

"Yes. God, yes."

Before the last syllable left her mouth, Cruz's mouth was on hers. The hand that had been at her ear moved to the back of her neck and held her to him. Mickie's hands came up to rest on Cruz's chest. They flexed as his tongue caressed her lips, teasing. Mickie opened wider and licked at him in return. Their tongues met and she felt Cruz shift her in his grasp.

The hand that had been resting at her nape, playing with her hair, was suddenly gripping it, and the hand at her waist was now pulling her into him. Mickie gave as good as she got. Not backing down, or shying away from the carnality of the kiss, she participated fully. One of her own hands crept up to his neck and she dug her nails in lightly. The other rested low on Cruz's belly and she could feel his muscles contracting as he moved her against him.

Cruz tasted like the coffee they'd been drinking and Mickie tilted her head to get deeper. She heard him groan and smiled against his lips. She, Mickie Kaiser, made Cruz groan. She felt powerful and, yes, beautiful.

She didn't realize Cruz was tilting her until she was under him on the couch. One of her feet still rested on the ground, and the other leg was against the back of the couch. Mickie shifted so Cruz could settle even deeper in the vee of her legs. He hadn't taken his mouth off of hers as they'd moved, and even now, as they got more comfortable, he refused to separate them.

Finally, Cruz lifted his head, pushing his hardness into her with his movement. "God, Mickie. You taste so fucking good."

Mickie could feel the blush consume her face as she looked up at Cruz. "Thanks."

"That didn't come out right—" he started to say, but Mickie brought her finger up to his face and put it over his lips.

"It came out exactly right. It was what I was thinking about you."

Cruz lowered his head and kissed Mickie hard. He didn't linger, but Mickie found herself totally consumed anyway. Finally, he pulled back again and sat up, bringing Mickie upright as he went. He kept one arm around her waist and pulled her into him. She put her head on his shoulder and closed her eyes.

Neither said anything for a moment. Finally, Cruz said, "It's late. You probably need to get going."

She did, but Mickie hated to leave. She sighed. "Yeah, I have to work in the morning."

"All right. We'll get together later this week?"

"Yeah, I'd like that."

Cruz smiled at her. "Good. Come on, up you go. If I don't let you go now, I might not ever." He stood, pulling Mickie up with him as he went.

Mickie gathered her purse and headed to the door with Cruz at her heels. "You don't have to walk me out."

"The hell I don't. I'm walking you to your car to make sure you get there safely. Then you'll call me when you get home to let me know you made it there without any issues."

"I will?"

"Yes."

Mickie smiled at Cruz. "Okay. Thank you."

"Thank you?"

"Yeah. For giving a shit if I get home all right or not."

"I give a shit."

"Yeah, so thank you."

Cruz smiled at Mickie. "Let's get you home before you turn into a pumpkin." Cruz took Mickie's hand and walked her out of his apartment to her little Honda Civic. He opened her door after she unlocked it. He crouched next to her as she got her seat belt on. "I'll talk to you in a bit. Okay?"

"Yeah, I'll text you when I get home. Thanks for a great night. Next time, my treat, okay?"

Cruz leaned in and kissed Mickie on the forehead before pulling back. "Okay, sweetness. Good night."

"Good night, Cruz."

Cruz stood and closed her door. He waved at her as she drove out of the parking lot. He sighed and ran his hand over the back of his neck as he looked down at his feet. Cruz hadn't lied to Mickie tonight. He knew he was riding a fine line with her, knew from the bottom of his soul it could go bad, but he couldn't stop. Being with Mickie was so refreshing after dealing with the MC and the crap that went on there. The more time he spent with her the more he *wanted* to spend with her.

It wasn't about keeping her safe from Ransom anymore, although that was still a concern—it was about a man spending time with a woman who he was interested in.

Chapter Eight

————◆————

THE NEXT FEW weeks went by quickly for Cruz. Neither he nor Mickie had been able to get together after their date, but he was keeping a close eye on her.

Ransom had come into the club one night ranting about how he was going to kill Angel's "motherfucking sister" if she didn't butt out of his business. From what Cruz was able to understand, she'd had another conversation with her sister about all the parties she'd been going to and had actually threatened to call the cops on the club.

Knowing Mickie could really be in danger, Cruz had stepped up. "I'll keep my eye on her, Ransom."

The president eyed Cruz for a moment before responding. "Fine. She's yours. If she so much as *thinks* about calling the fuzz, I'm holding you responsible."

Cruz knew what that meant. *He* was as good as dead if Mickie followed through on her threat. "I'll be so far up her ass she won't have time to think about her sister *or* the cops," he reassured the president.

"I'll bet you'll be up her ass all right," Roach commented slyly.

Cruz had slugged him in the stomach hard, but hadn't said a word.

The club had upped its partying and were including Angel and her friends almost every night. They'd established somewhat of a routine, where the women would sit on one side of the room, smoking joints and drinking, while several members of the club entertained them. The other side of the room was more hard-core...and Ransom had slowly been allowing a few of the club whores and strippers to attend. He still wasn't allowing any full-out orgies, but Cruz had been there a few nights where it was obvious the couples weren't merely making out.

Angel was loving being the center of attention at the parties. Her friends were all very impressed she was dating the president of the club and were happy to shell out as much money as Ransom demanded in return for the unending joints.

The more parties they attended, the looser they got with the money—and their inhibitions. Cruz had hoped that the women would be smart and see what was going on, but so far no one had clued in. It even seemed a few of the women now thought they were "dating" some of the club members.

Bridgette and Cissy had even tried cocaine the other night at the party. Ransom was a first-class asshole, but he obviously knew what he was doing with the women. Cruz knew there was a party being planned where the women would be fully introduced to what it meant to be a "member" of the club.

They weren't old ladies, so that meant they were all being groomed to be club whores. Granted, the club had never had any whores who could actually afford to buy the drugs they were given, rather than earning it between their legs, but there was a first time for everything.

The nights Cruz got to speak to Mickie were the highlights of his existence at the moment. They might not have been able to get together, but the two-hour phone calls and the hilarious texts were almost worth the wait. Almost.

Cruz remembered the phone call that had really made him admit he was continuing his relationship with Mickie not to keep her safe...but because he honestly liked her. He'd called one night late after getting home from yet another party at the club. He'd never been a partier, and the constant loud music and half-naked whores, along with the stress of making sure he blended in with the uncouth club members, was exhausting.

He'd picked up his phone and dialed Mickie's number before he'd really even thought about it.

"Hello?"

Cruz could hear the sleepiness in her voice and cursed. "Hey, Mickie. It's Cruz. Sorry, I didn't realize how late it was."

"Everything okay?"

"Yeah. I just wanted to hear your voice." Cruz heard her stifle a yawn before she spoke again.

"I'm glad to hear from you too. How was your day?"

"Long. Yours?"

"Actually really good."

"Yeah?"

"Uh-huh. This woman came in, obviously stressed out. She had three kids with her and her car was acting up. She didn't have a sitter and had to bring them all with her. It was supposed to be a quick check-up, but the mechanic told her that it was most likely going to take all day. She looked like she was going to cry. I don't work the front, but I couldn't just sit there. I mean, haven't we all had days like that?"

"What'd you do?"

"I may or may not have kidnapped one of her kids."

Cruz almost spit out the water he'd just swallowed. "Uh, you do know that's illegal, right?"

Mickie giggled, and Cruz was reminded of when she'd lost it while he was changing her tire. He smiled remembering the look of pure and utter joy on her face then, and could almost envision it now.

"Okay, I might not have actually kidnapped her, but I asked the woman if she'd mind if I took her five-year-old and kept her busy for a while. I reassured her we weren't going to leave the building and that I'd be right around the corner. She was relieved, but still worried. She checked on us at least five times before she left us alone."

"Are you allowed to have kids working with you?"

"Well, no, but my boss was out today, so I just went with it. I got her some crayons from the waiting room and let her go to town. I made up scenes for her to color and we actually made an entire book."

"A book?"

"Yeah. I told her a story and she drew the pictures. I swear, Cruz, it was the cutest thing ever."

"I bet." Cruz could almost picture Mickie laughing and helping entertain a stressed-out mom's child.

"Luckily, the mechanics also had pity on the woman and they were able to get her car done before their estimated time. I was sad to see Rachel go, but her mom was super happy I'd entertained her for a few hours."

"Do you want kids?" The question came out before Cruz could think about it. They'd talked quite a bit, but it wasn't exactly the kind of question you really asked someone when you were first dating.

"Yeah. I didn't think I was really mom material. I mean, look how Angel turned out." Mickie sighed, but continued before Cruz could refute her words. "But I've been able to look back now and see that my own parents had a big hand in what happened. And now I know what *not* to do. I suppose I should be thankful to them for that at least."

"I think you'll be a great mother," Cruz told her honestly. "You saw how stressed that woman was today and didn't hesitate to jump in and help. And if you were able to keep that little girl entertained with only paper and crayons for several hours, you're going to be the most popular mom on the block."

"Thanks. I have no idea if it'll ever happen, but I'm not ruling anything out. What about you? Do you want kids?"

Cruz thought about it for a moment before answering. "I didn't think so until I saw Dax and Mack's relationship grow."

"What do you mean?"

"You know about my first marriage, it was a disaster, and I never wanted to bring a child into a situation where he or she wouldn't be the most important thing in my life. And I always thought having a kid would act as a dividing line between two people. That all the attention and love would be showered on the child, instead of the relationship. But seeing how Dax puts Mack first in his life, and in return she puts him first in hers, I got it. Having a child wouldn't tear that attention apart; it would only bring it together more."

"But your dad loves his wife, right?"

Cruz could hear the confusion in Mickie's voice, and he tried to explain. "He does. Barb is the best thing that could've happened to my dad after my mom died. But they don't...it's not an all-consuming love. They both loved me, but I also felt like an outsider around them as I got older. I never wanted any child I might have to feel like that. So I figured I'd be a better uncle to my friends' kids one day."

"I'd love to meet your friends someday, they sound like awesome people. And Mack was really funny on the phone."

I'd love to meet your friends someday. Her words settled into his psyche as if she herself burrowed into him. But they also scared the crap out of him. One part of him wanted her to meet Dax and all of his other buddies, but the other part of him knew that meeting his friends was just another step to this woman burrowing her way closer and closer to his heart. And the further in she got, the more it would hurt when she dumped him after finding out all his secrets.

Cruz had no idea when he'd be done with his undercover assignment, and there was no way he could let Mickie meet all the guys and

Hayden before then. She'd know for sure he'd been lying to her. But he wanted it. He wanted to bring her around to the group barbecues. He wanted to put his arm around her and stand next to her and laugh with her at the things that came out of Mack's mouth. He wanted it all.

"I'd like that, Mickie." The words sounded inadequate to his ears, but they were completely heartfelt. He heard her yawn again. "I should let you go."

"Yeah." She agreed with him, but her tone was reluctant.

"I hate that our schedules aren't meshing. I want to see you."

"Me too."

"Okay, I'm going to do my best to see what I can do to make that happen, yeah?" Cruz asked.

"Yeah. I'm off this coming weekend."

Cruz sighed, thinking about the big party Ransom had planned for that Saturday. Now that Angel and her friends were regulars at the club, he was raising the stakes. He hadn't expounded on what "raising the stakes" meant, but Cruz had a bad feeling about it. Ransom was getting impatient with the paltry amount of money he'd been making off the women with the pot, and wanted to up the ante. It was likely he was going to officially push Angel and the others to start paying for the harder stuff.

"This weekend isn't good for me, dammit."

"You work too hard," Mickie told him sincerely.

If only she knew. "You should know that while I'm working, I'm usually thinking about you."

"Hummmm, interestingly enough, it's the same with me."

Cruz smiled. "I'll text you. We'll figure it out even if it's just for a quick lunch during your break."

"Cool. Be safe this weekend."

Cruz was startled by her choice of words. "Safe?"

"Yeah. With whatever security thing you've got going."

"Ah. I will. Sleep well, sweetness. I'll talk to you later."

"Later, Cruz."

Cruz had sat on the couch for a long while after hanging up with Mickie. She hadn't lambasted him for calling so late and waking her up. She was empathetic and did her best to help others around her. She wanted kids. The more he learned about her, the more Cruz was determined to keep her safe from the shit her sister had gotten involved with…and the more he wanted to keep her for himself.

Chapter Nine

"LISTEN UP, ASSHOLES. We've got two things happening tonight. One, there's a big shipment coming in around eight. Bubba, Kitty, Knife, Dirt, Smoke, and Tiny, you'll head out to pick it up. Don't fuck this up. The other thing that's going on is Angel is coming over again tonight with her rich-bitch posse. Some of them have been getting nervous with all the whores that have been around. Tonight there will be *no* fucking on the floor in front of the rich-bitches. I'll allow that slut, Dixie, to be here tonight, but that's it. I don't give a shit if you take Dixie into the back and fuck her there, but absolutely not out here. Am I clear?"

There was a chorus of agreement from the members. Cruz was torn. He wanted to be at the club to watch out for Angel, he felt as if he owed it to Mickie, but he had no idea what he'd actually do if something went wrong. It wasn't as if he could risk his cover for her. And that was the horrible dilemma he faced, the moral conundrum he found himself in.

But ultimately, Cruz knew he needed to be at the drop-off. He needed to know who Ransom got his drugs from. That was one step to stopping the increase of all the shit into the city *and* ending his assignment. God knew the drugs would never stop, but if Cruz could cut off this one big supply, it'd make a huge difference, at least maybe for a while.

Ransom continued with his commands to his men. "I'm gonna push the bitch tonight. It's time to step it up a bit. I'll get her relaxed with the weed then bring out the blow. Nobody fucks with her tonight. Got it?"

"What about her friends?" Tick yelled out.

"I don't give a flying fuck about her friends. Just don't scare them away. We've got them almost where we want them. We've had too many lame parties with them to fuck it up now. Feel free to make them feel good, but no fucking on the floor. Feel them up, get them off, whatever, but don't screw this up for the club."

"Rich pussy. My fucking favorite," Donkey exclaimed, rubbing his hands together. Donkey had gotten his nickname because he liked taking women up the ass. He was a big man, all over, and Cruz felt extremely sorry for any woman who Donkey got his hands on. He wasn't gentle; he just took what he wanted.

Cruz glanced over at Roach; he could tell the man was jonesing for Ransom to be done with Angel so he could make his move. The way Roach had had his tongue in her ear when they were in the van was enough of a clue. So much for the 'loyalty to one' all the prospects were supposed to have.

If Ransom knew Roach had touched Angel, and what the man had said to her, he'd lose his shit, not because it was Angel but because for now, she was his property. Cruz knew better than to tattle. That was the quickest way to lose his standing in the club.

"All right, get the fuck out of here."

The members slowly made their way out of the room. Cruz strode over to where Bubba was standing with the others.

"Let's get the hell out of here, Smoke. We got shit to do."

FOUR HOURS LATER, Cruz walked back into the clubhouse with the other members who'd been tasked to pick up the drugs. The pickup was tremendously helpful for Cruz's mission, but he knew it wasn't over yet. They'd met with Axel, an extremely violent and dangerous gang member who Cruz knew worked hand in hand with some corrupt government officials in a small Mexican city just over the border.

The Mexican government had been working hard on battling corruption in their members and the police force, but so far the lure of the money drugs brought in was winning over doing the right thing.

Thankfully, Cruz hadn't had any interaction with Axel in the past, so his cover was safe for now. He just knew *of* him from Conor and TJ, both of whose agencies, Texas Parks & Wildlife Department and Texas Highway Patrol, had dealt with him extensively.

Bubba had met with Axel around Lackland Air Force Base, west of the city. They'd talked for a bit then they'd all gotten back into their vehicles and driven even farther west. Bubba had handed Axel a bag full of hundred dollar bills, and Axel tossed Bubba the keys to a truck and directions as to where the truck would be. They'd driven back into the city and found the truck sitting in the parking lot of a fast food restaurant.

Cruz was disgusted by how easy and simple the transaction seemed to be. Eighty feet away, inside the restaurant, kids were screaming and laughing and playing on the playground equipment. And here they were, driving away with almost two hundred thousand dollars in cocaine and weed. It was insane.

Bubba had driven the truck back to the MC hangout and now the guys were ready to party. Ransom had taken Bubba aside and they'd had a short conversation. Obviously satisfied with how the drop had gone down, Ransom clapped Bubba on the back and the two men had disappeared into a back room.

The party at the compound was in full swing. The music was loud, there were women everywhere, who the hell knew where they all came from, because they certainly weren't all strippers, whores, and old ladies, and the MC members were living it up. Cruz could tell they were holding themselves back because of Angel's friends, but they were still partying a hell of a lot more hard-core than most normal people would, and harder than when the women had been there in the past.

Cruz could spot Angel's friends easily. They were dressed as they always were when they came to the parties, as if they were at a fancy New Year's Eve party or something. Short skirts, high heels, glittery skimpy tops. They were sitting in a cluster around a table, laughing uncontrollably. It was obvious the first part of Ransom's plan was already in play. They were high from the joints they'd recently smoked and were having the time of their lives.

Donkey, Tick, Camel, and Roach were standing around the group of women, obviously waiting for their chance to make a move, while across the room, a crazy bastard named Vodka—because he'd once guzzled an entire bottle of the stuff and stayed standing throughout the night—and another guy who Cruz thought was named Steel, were sitting with Dixie. They were following Ransom's decree—barely.

Dixie was a club whore who'd do just about anything to score some coke. Vodka and Steel were sitting side by side on the disgusting, beat-up old couch, and Dixie was draped over Steel's lap, sucking Vodka's dick. Cruz could see Steel's hand moving rapidly under her skirt, fingering her as she serviced Vodka. His hand was on the back of Dixie's head, controlling the speed and the depth with which she took his dick down her throat.

Cruz turned away in revulsion. Jesus.

Just then, Ransom came into the room with Angel, who must've been waiting for him in one of the many backrooms. She made her way over to her friends, her hand a death grip on Ransom's arm. Cruz could tell he was tolerating it only because she was a part of his plan.

"Hey everyone! You remember my boyfriend, right? The *president* of the club." Angel winked ridiculously at her friends. They all tittered in response and greeted Ransom.

Angel continued, "He said he's got a surprise for us tonight."

Cruz winced, knowing what was coming.

"You ladies having a nice time?" Ransom asked. When all the girls nodded, he continued. "Good. Thank you for your generous donations to the party tonight, I'll personally make sure you're all rewarded. But let me know when you're ready for some *real* fun, and you've had enough of this pansy joint shit."

With that, Ransom peeled Angel's hand off his arm and stalked back through the crowded room, leaving Angel standing in front of her friends, embarrassed as hell. She looked around, confused about what had just happened, then slid over to stand uncomfortably next to a tall Asian woman named Li.

"What's he mean, Angel?" Li asked, brow crinkled in confusion. "We always have fun when we're here. We love partying with him and his friends."

As if they'd rehearsed it, Camel answered for Angel. "Coke, pretty lady."

The other women looked at him in surprise. Camel continued as if he hadn't just shocked the shit out of the country-club set. "And I'm not talking the fizzy-soda-pop kind. Those joints you've been smoking are fun, yeah, but they aren't anything compared to the high you get from snorting some coke. It makes you feel fucking invincible. You think the weed makes you feel good, shit, you have to try this. If you're scared to try it, no big deal, but I can personally guaran-damn-tee it makes orgasms stronger, longer, and for the ladies, makes you able to come all night long."

Cruz knew Camel didn't know what the hell he was talking about, but Angel's friends didn't know that. Cocaine did make the user feel euphoric and could make someone more energetic and talkative, but increasing their ability to orgasm? No. It *could* make the person using it have an increased reaction to touch, sight, and sound, which, Cruz figured, was where Camel was going with his orgasm comment.

Ransom didn't allow his MC members to use cocaine. He knew how addictive it was, and that having drugged-out members around the merchandise wasn't a good combination. Cruz had personally witnessed Bubba beating the shit out of a prospect when he'd first joined the club for stealing the cocaine he was supposed to be selling. That didn't mean the guys hadn't ever used before. Camel obviously knew what it felt like to be high on the drug.

There was silence around the table for a moment, then as Cruz could have predicted, Angel spoke up. "I'm in. Who else?"

When no one said anything, Angel sighed dramatically. "Fine. Y'all are pussies. I'll get Ransom to bring some over here and you can watch me. I'll show you I won't drop dead from it and then you can do whatever you want. It's not like using at parties is gonna make me into a drug addict." And with those words, she stormed away.

The mood in the room had changed a bit, though slowly but surely, the MC members moved in and worked their magic. Camel dropped his hand to Cissy's stomach and stroked her while talking into her ear. Donkey put his mouth to Kelly's neck and sucked hard, while at the same time holding onto her thigh and caressing her. Tick picked Li up off her chair and sat down in her place, holding her across his lap and against his erection as he ran his hands up and down her back, soothing, placating, and arousing.

While the other men were doing the same things to the other women, Roach was the most aggressive. He'd turned Bridgette's chair around so it was facing Vodka and Steel—and Dixie—on the couch. He stood behind her, whispering in her ear while running his hands over her chest, pausing every now and then to pinch her erect nipples. Bridgette's eyes were locked on the scene across the room as she squirmed in Roach's grip. It was obvious she was torn between embarrassment, and being turned on by what Roach was doing to her and what she was watching.

The men were using the women's altered states against them. The marijuana coursing through their systems was making them mellow and receptive to the guys' advances. They likely didn't feel any danger because they'd been coming to the club for nights on end. They knew the men, even if they didn't *know* them. Not to mention, Angel was encouraging the deviant behavior. It was a classic case of peer pressure. If Cruz didn't hate Ransom so much, he'd be impressed with the man. He was a master manipulator. Mickie would have a field day analyzing him with her psychology degree.

Cruz stopped his thoughts in their tracks. No way was he thinking about Mickie while he was standing in this pit of hell.

Angel came stomping back across the room with Ransom in tow. Ever the drama queen, she cleared the table nearest to her with one sweep of her arm. The glasses and bottles that had been sitting there crashed and broke as they landed on the floor. The women giggled nervously at her actions, but they must've been used to her over-the-top performances because they simply sat up straighter to get a better view of the drama that was about to happen.

Ransom smirked and set up the lines of cocaine on the tabletop. He tamped them down and held his hand out to Angel.

"Give me a hundred."

Angel reached into her purse and brought out a hundred dollar bill with no argument. They all watched as Ransom tightly rolled it up. He then handed it back to Angel and gestured toward the table. "Go for it. Show 'em how it's fucking done."

Cruz could see Angel was apprehensive, but Ransom didn't give her a chance to back down. He moved behind her and put his hands on her waist. He leaned in. Cruz only heard him because he was standing nearby.

"Go on. Fucking do it already. Any bitch of mine wouldn't be scared of this shit. You've done it before with the old ladies, what's the difference now? You a part of my MC or what?"

Angel squared her shoulders and put the rolled-up bill to her nose and bent over. She stood up and coughed and ran her hand under her nose, wiping away any white powder that might be clinging there.

"That's my good girl," Ransom told her. "Again." He put his hand on her back and pushed. Angel almost fell on the table, but caught herself at the last second. Ransom pulled her hips back and pushed his dick against her ass. His hands went to the bottom of her dress and he slowly ran them up her sides, pushing her dress up as he went.

As Angel leaned down to snort the second line Ransom had set out for her, he brought her dress all the way up and over her ass. Angel was wearing a black thong, her ass now visible to everyone in the room. Ransom ran his hands over her tan cheeks and then leaned into her.

When she was done, he pulled her up against him and gave her another joint to smoke. Ten minutes later, when Ransom knew the drug would most likely have taken effect, he addressed the women sitting around the table, who were now watching Angel and Ransom with fascination.

"Listen closely, ladies. Watch and fucking learn." He turned his head and spoke in a normal voice to Angel. "How do you feel, Angel? Can you feel it coursing through your veins?"

"Uh-huh." Angel vigorously nodded.

Ransom ran his hands down her sides and held Angel closer. One of his arms went around her chest, holding her against the front of him. His other hand went down and cupped her pussy. Her skirt was still rucked up around her waist. He was hiding her from her friends, but it was obvious what he was doing.

"And this? What does this feel like? Does it feel different?"

"God, Ransom!"

"Answer my fucking question. Now."

"Yeah, it feels different."

"How?"

Angel's head rested back on Ransom's shoulder and she rolled it back and forth. She grabbed his arm around her chest and the other hand went down to where he was now rubbing against her clit.

"Hands off, Angel. Don't even think about fucking stopping me."

Angel immediately retreated, putting her hand back on his arm.

"You want me to make you come? Right here in front of your friends?"

Angel simply moaned.

"I won't say it again. Give me a fucking answer."

"Oh God, Ransom, Please."

"Please what, bitch?"

Angel's hips were now thrusting against Ransom's hand. Cruz couldn't help but stare in morbid fascination as Ransom manipulated not only Angel, but her friends as well. Each rub over Angel's clit was meant to show her friends how wonderful the cocaine high was...even though the two really had nothing to do with each other.

Every one of the other women sitting around the table was silent and still, watching intently. The other MC members were *not* still. They were in various stages of caressing Angel's friends. Some nonchalantly and others more blatantly, but none as overtly sexually as Ransom.

"Please, let me come."

Ransom abruptly removed his hand from Angel's crotch and brought it up to her mouth. "Suck it."

Angel opened and Ransom shoved the three fingers he'd been fucking her with into her mouth roughly. Angel kept her eyes closed as she licked and sucked her juices off his fingers with no complaint as he worked them in and out.

"Now, finish the last line and then you'll tell me how it fucking feels when I ask, without hesitating, and I'll think about letting you come."

Angel obediently leaned over the table and quickly snorted the last line of white powder. Ransom snagged the rolled-up bill from her hand and shoved it into his back pocket, not missing a beat and never missing a chance to pocket easy money.

"Please, Ransom. You promised, please."

"You don't call the shots here, whore. You know that."

"I'm sorry. Please…"

Ransom brought her back against his chest again. "Put your hands up around my neck."

Angel did as he asked, once again resting her head on Ransom's shoulder.

Ransom inched one hand back down to her pussy and grabbed her throat with the other. He forced her head back farther as he squeezed her neck tightly. Angel coughed and gagged, but didn't otherwise try to remove his hands; she just kept undulating against him and trying to get herself off.

"Now, tell me what I want to know, bitch. Describe how this feels. Tell all your friends how it's different. How it's better."

Angel started slowly, but picked up speed as she described what she was feeling. Her voice was raspy and low, because her air was being restricted, but her friends could still hear her. "I'm wet. Really wet. I can feel every slide of your fingers inside me. Your fingernails scraping against my walls. It's heightened, as if I can feel every molecule of your fingers. They feel big. Huge, almost like it's your cock."

Ransom smirked. "You see, ladies? There's no better aphrodisiac than a bit of blow. It's completely harmless. As your friend here will demonstrate, it can make you multi-orgasmic. You think she cares you're all watching her? No. All she cares about is getting off. And I can guarantee it'll be the best orgasm she's ever had. Right, whore?"

His hand went to work between Angel's thighs. He smacked her pussy three times, making Angel twitch in his grasp. She started to move her hands from behind his head and Ransom tightened his grip on her neck and growled, "Leave them there, cunt."

Angel moaned and obeyed, squirming in Ransom's grasp.

Ransom reached up and lowered Angel's dress so that one breast was exposed to the group, who now stared as if hypnotized by the show before them.

He pinched her nipple between his thumb and forefinger until Angel was standing on her tiptoes groaning.

Ransom was smirking as he continued his demonstration. "The increased blood flow to her extremities is making everything I do to her feel twice as good as it would without the coke. There's no other feeling in the world like this."

Ransom's hand went back down to her crotch, holding Angel tightly against him as he delved under her thong once more. It didn't take long, only ten or so seconds, and Angel was howling and everyone watched as she orgasmed in Ransom's arms. Without letting her recover, he continued his assault on her clit.

"Now, she just came, but watch—I can make her come again and again, something she can't do without the blow. I know, I've fucking tried."

Angel screamed again and lost the battle to stand fully upright. Only Ransom's arm around her neck kept her standing.

"One more, bitch. Give me one more."

"I can't, Ransom, please, stop, it hurts!"

"Shut the fuck up. I'm in control here. You *will*. Put your fucking foot up."

When Angel didn't move, Ransom nodded at Camel, who was standing next to them. Camel leaned over and grabbed Angel's leg roughly and forcefully hooked the heel of her shoe on the bottom spindle of the nearest stool. The action opened her up to Ransom even more. He increased the speed of his thrusts inside her pussy and rolled her clit roughly with his thumb, her thong no barrier to his fingers.

He shifted and finally took his hand off her neck, only to snake it down to pinch her exposed nipple. They could all see the tip begin to slowly turn red from the pressure. He then pulled it away from her chest. Angel whimpered in his arms, but didn't otherwise fight his rough handling of her body.

"See girls? She's loving this. She doesn't care where she is or what I do to her. This could be you. All it takes is a bit of blow." He took Angel's earlobe between his teeth. "Come again, bitch. Come now." He let go of her nipple and as the blood rushed back into the nub, he grabbed her entire breast in his hand and squeezed hard enough that Angel would have bruises in the morning.

That was all it took. Angel came again with a screech, yelping Ransom's name.

Cruz observed the display with disgust. It was obvious Ransom didn't give a shit about Angel, he was just using her. Well, it was obvious to *him*. Hell, Cruz could tell the president wasn't even hard. He wasn't getting off on what he was doing. It was all a show, a ploy, and Angel and her friends were playing right into his hands.

When Angel had calmed somewhat, Ransom pulled her dress down and her bra up to re-cover her breast and removed his fingers from between her legs. He wiped his hand on her dress with what Cruz could see was barely concealed disgust.

"Now, who's in?"

The women around the table didn't immediately agree, but eventually the alcohol and weed they'd ingested made them lose enough of their inhibitions that they all decided to try it.

Ransom twisted with a smirk and slapped Angel on the ass. As he turned away, he said, "Thanks, bitch."

Angel hadn't recovered her equilibrium from the orgasms and didn't respond. Her hands were on the table in front of her and she leaned over it, trying to catch her breath. Bubba pulled out several small baggies of coke from his pocket and started making the rounds to Angel's friends, pocketing money, giving instructions, and handing them his business card so they could get in touch with him when they wanted more.

Cruz turned away. He didn't want to hang around and watch all the club members get these naïve women off. They had no clue they'd been played by a master.

As Cruz walked to the other end of the warehouse to get away from the depravity, he thought about how he could stop Ransom and his club from getting the rest of the drugs onto the streets, and how he was going to explain to Mickie that he'd stood around and watched as her little sister had been so crudely put on display for Ransom and all his club buddies. It was one thing to know she was having sex with the man, but if Mickie had seen what had just happened, she'd be as horrified as he was. He knew it.

Chapter Ten

———◆———

Good morning.

Good morning, Cruz.

All ok there? No more incidents?

CRUZ HAD STARTED texting Mickie each morning to make sure none of the other club members had taken it upon themselves to send her another message. If that happened, he'd have to make a stand, but so far they'd all stayed away from her.

Nope. All was good this morning. How'd the job go last night?

Cruz had told her he had to work a private party at the Alamo the night before. He hated lying to her, but telling her he was hanging out at a party thrown by the same motorcycle club she was trying to convince her sister to ditch, obviously wasn't going to work.

Good. No problems.

See any ghosts?

He laughed out loud at that. He recalled another conversation they'd had about how fascinated she was with the history of the Alamo and the downtown area, particularly regarding the spirits that had to still be around.

Not this time, only real people.

Darn.

Have a good day at work. I'll talk to you later?

Sounds good. Later Cruz.

Bye

An hour or so later, his personal phone rang.

"Cruz."

"Hey, it's Dax. How're you holding up?" Daxton Chambers asked, sounding concerned even over the phone line.

"I've been better."

"It's been almost two months. You doing okay?"

Cruz ran his hand over the top of his head. "I'm getting there. I've been reporting what I've seen and heard back to the field office. They say another couple of weeks and I'm out."

"A couple of weeks? Come on, man, you know they don't need you in there while they're doing the paperwork to shut them down."

"I can't leave right now." When Dax didn't say anything, Cruz reluctantly repeated, "It's personal. I can't leave now."

"I don't like it, man, but I understand. You know I'm here if you need me. Just say the word and I'm there."

"I know, and I appreciate it."

Changing the subject, Dax said, "So, Mack tells me she was your wingman when it came to a certain woman…" He let the sentence hang.

Cruz laughed. "Yeah, she was great. Thank her again for me."

"That's it? That's all you're giving me?"

Cruz chuckled at the disappointment he heard in his friend's voice. "She's amazing, Dax, but it's not going to go anywhere."

"Why do you say that?"

"Because. I'm fucking undercover. There's no way."

"Don't say that. I didn't expect to find Mack, yet, here we are."

"That's different."

"How?"

"For one, you weren't pretending to be someone you aren't with her."

"When you're with this woman, are you pretending?"

"Not really, but there's no way she's gonna forgive me when she finds out what I'm doing and that I'm not *just* in security."

Dax chuckled at that, but sobered quickly and said, "If there's something between you, you never know."

Cruz sighed and sat on a chair at his kitchen table. He'd spoken with Mickie several times since their last date, and every time he talked to her, he swore she just got better and better.

"I'm not sure I can forgive *myself* for what I've had to do this time, Dax."

"Take the afternoon off and come and visit with me and Mack."

"Thanks, but I can't."

"You know the offer is always open."

"I know, and I appreciate it."

"All right. You take care. I'll make sure Mack's around the next time I call, I know she'll want to talk to you."

"Sounds good, talk to you later. Bye."

"Bye, Cruz."

Cruz clicked off his phone and put it on the table. He thought back to the last week. After Ransom had gotten Angel off in front of her friends, and they'd bought a shitload of coke, the party had disintegrated into a disgusting display of the club members getting the ladies completely shitfaced with the drugs. The guys had then taken the women to different parts of the warehouse and gotten them off, much as Ransom had done to Angel.

Cruz had finally left, to the jeers of the club members because he didn't have any pussy to play with. It'd been three days since he'd spoken to Mickie because he'd felt guilty as hell about what had happened to her sister. If he was honest with himself, it was also because he felt dirty.

He put his head in his hands and let out a deep breath. He was being an idiot. This was a job. That's all.

But he knew he was lying to himself. Mickie had become very important to him in a short amount of time and he hated the double life he was living.

He hated being in the club, but he was happy that being there gave him a reason to talk to Mickie, and to see her more often than he probably would've been able to swing if he wasn't supposed to be keeping his eye on her. He hated when Ransom asked for updates on the "sister situation," as he called it, but enjoyed being able to be around her.

Later that morning, the phone on the counter rang and Cruz stood up to answer it. It was "Smoke's" phone that was ringing. Without bothering to check who it was, he turned on his MC persona as he answered.

"Yo."

"Hi, Cruz?"

Fuck. "Hey, Mickie." He immediately gentled his voice.

"Hey. Whatcha doing?"

"Sitting around thinking about making something to eat. You?"

"Feeling sorry for myself. Want to go grab something together?"

"Everything all right?"

"No."

"Mickie? Talk to me."

Cruz heard a big sigh on the other end of the line.

"It's nothing new, Cruz. It's Angel. We had another big fight today. I'm losing her and it's freaking me out."

Instead of asking more questions, Cruz suggested, "Want to meet at the pancake place on Timberhill and Grissom?"

"Yeah, I'd like that. Thirty minutes?"

"Perfect. Drive safe. I'll see you soon."

"See you. And thanks, Cruz. Bye."

Cruz hung up and immediately turned toward his bedroom.

It was obvious Mickie was feeling down and had called him to try to cheer herself up. He couldn't deny that it made him feel good inside that *he* was the one she wanted to talk to when she was sad. She was so open and trusting. Just being around her made Cruz feel calm.

But the thing that made him recognize he'd completely fallen for her was the realization that the second it dawned on him that she was feeling down, he'd done whatever he could to cheer her up.

He'd never felt that way about Sophie. He didn't like it when she wasn't happy, but he didn't feel this all-consuming need to see to her. Cruz knew he should go into the club and see what Ransom had planned for later, but Mickie came first. It wasn't until after he had hung up that he realized he'd already put Mickie before everything else in his life. His job, his friends…and he'd continue to, if it came to that.

Cruz pulled up to the restaurant in his little car and entered. He saw Mickie sitting at a booth in the back of the small room and made his way to her. The second she saw him, her face lit up in greeting.

Mickie had been nursing her cup of coffee for a few minutes when she saw Cruz come through the door. She waved him over and smiled as he arrived at the table.

"Hey, Cruz. Thanks for coming."

"The pleasure's all mine, believe me." Cruz scooted into her side of the booth and leaned over and kissed Mickie on the side of the head. "Are you okay?"

"As okay as I can be, knowing my sister is making the biggest mistake of her life."

"What's she done now?"

Before Mickie could answer, the waitress came over to their table. Cruz didn't have to look at the menu to know what he wanted to eat. He told her what he wanted and Mickie also ordered. Mickie picked up their conversation as if they hadn't been interrupted.

"I called Angel this morning and she sounded completely out of it when she answered. I asked how her job was going and she told me she'd quit. *Quit*, Cruz. It's not like she was working her dream job or anything, but what the hell does she think she's going to live on?"

"I was under the impression she had some money."

"She does. We do, but it's not enough for her to live on forever. I mean, I know I took Troy for half of everything he had, but I actually like working. Angel has to do *something*. She can't just sit around and eat bon-bons for the rest of her life. The thing of it is, she didn't sound like herself. She was totally unconcerned she was sleeping at ten in the morning. In the past, she always got up by eight so she could go to the gym and work out when all the hotties were there. Her words, not mine."

Cruz put his hand over Mickie's on the table. "Is she still seeing that guy?"

"I think so. I mean, she didn't say specifically, but when I asked about him, she told me to butt out and hung up on me. I swear if I didn't know better, I'd say she was high or something. Angel's done some pot before, when she was in high school, but this was different I think." Mickie sipped her coffee.

"What's going on behind those pretty eyes?"

Mickie looked at him. "She's my sister. I have to help her, whether she wants it or not."

"Mickie—"

"Don't take that tone with me, Cruz. I'm an adult."

"So is Angel."

"Yeah, but—"

"No buts about it, Mickie."

"Is that how you felt about your wife?"

Mickie wished she could take back the words as soon as they were out of her mouth. It was a shitty thing to say.

She put her hand on Cruz's arm and immediately apologized, "I'm sorry, Cruz. That was uncalled for. I just...I thought about following her one night to see where she went with that asshole Ransom. If I can take some pictures of him doing something illegal, get her to see that he's not a good guy—"

Cruz took Mickie by the arms and turned her toward him. "Ab-so-fucking-lutely not. Terrible idea, Mickie. No way."

"What am I supposed to do then?"

He spoke without thinking. "Let me ask some of the guys I work with. Some work as private investigators on the side. I'll see what they know about the MC."

"You'd do that for her?"

"No, I'd do it for *you*." Cruz stared into Mickie's eyes as they teared up.

Mickie leaned forward and put her arms around Cruz. "Thank you. Having you ask your coworkers if they know anything makes me feel like I'm not so alone in trying to look out for Angel. You have no idea how much this means to me. She's my only sister. I don't know what I'd do if something happened to her."

"Don't get your hopes up; I'm not sure what I'll find out. It'll probably be nothing, and even if they do know about the club, I don't know what good it'll do you." Cruz felt like he had to warn her. He had no idea what information he could give to Mickie that would satisfy her, but there was no way he wanted Mickie *anywhere* near Ransom and his fucking compound.

"I appreciate you even seeing what you can find out. I'm not sure it'll do any good, because I think Angel already knows Ransom isn't exactly on the up and up, but she doesn't seem to care. But maybe if he's doing something *really* bad, I can call the cops and turn him in. That would get him out of her life."

The waitress arrived with their food and Mickie sat back. They ate their meal with no more mention of Angel. Mickie seemed contemplative, but Cruz thought it was only natural with all she had going on in her life.

When they were done, Cruz paid the bill and they left the restaurant.

"What are you doing for the rest of the day, Mickie?" Cruz knew he would have to show up in the evening because of a job Ransom had for him and some of the other members, but he didn't want to let Mickie go. He loved spending time with her; she made him feel like a better person, even if it wasn't true.

Cruz had no idea what Ransom had in store for Angel or her friends that night, but he hoped now that Ransom had introduced them to cocaine, he'd lay off having parties almost every night and concentrate on supplying them with drugs individually.

The club members were headed out to pick up another shipment of drugs later that evening though, and Cruz knew he couldn't miss it. Bubba was in charge again, and he'd already tasked Cruz and some of the other members to go with him to do the pickup. Cruz was hoping to finally get enough information on the suppliers of the drugs to pass along to his boss so he could get the hell out of the op.

"I was gonna go home and wallow in my uneasiness about Angel...got something that could compete with that?" Mickie joked, holding onto Cruz's arm as they walked to their cars.

"How about spending it with me?"

Mickie stopped, causing Cruz to stop as well.

"I'd love to."

Cruz smiled, loving that Mickie didn't play games with him. If she wanted something, she said it. If she was hungry, she ate. If she was in a bad mood, she didn't pretend she wasn't.

"Great. Is it okay if we just go back to my place and hang?" he asked as they continued walking.

"You don't want to go to the mall?" Mickie teased.

Jesus, the last place he wanted to go to with her was the fucking mall. "No way."

She laughed. "I was joking. Got any good movies?"

"Yeah, I have a whole collection you can look through."

"I get to choose?"

"Sure."

"Not scared of what I'll pick?"

Cruz guided Mickie to her car and waited as she unlocked the doors. Once she clicked the locks, Cruz backed her against the car and caged her in with his arms. "Mickie, it's my place. It's not like I have a secret stash of romantic comedies for you to choose from."

Mickie giggled.

Cruz leaned in and smirked as her giggling stopped. "I hope you like action flicks. I'm not sure I've got anything else." He put his head to Mickie's neck and nuzzled her ear.

"I-I like them."

Cruz felt Mickie's hands go to his waist and hold on to his shirt. He purposely breathed in her ear before saying softly, "Good."

"On one condition…"

Cruz pulled back and looked at her. She was smirking at him. "One condition, huh? Okay, shoot."

"I want to see your tattoo." Mickie ran her fingertips over the edge of his T-shirt, right above the tattoo that snaked up his upper left arm.

"You like tattoos?"

"Never really thought about it before, but on you? Yeah, I think so."

"Deal. You can pick the movie and I'll let you see my tattoo."

"Cool," Mickie breathed as she looked up at him.

He drew back, knowing he was a second away from kissing the hell out of her. He put his hands on Mickie's face, tilting her head so she was looking up at him. "You want to follow me?"

"Uh-huh."

Cruz smiled; she was so fucking cute when she was flustered. "Okay then, let's get you ready to go." He kissed her on the lips briefly, wishing more than he could say that he could linger, and drew back. He turned her and put one hand on her back and waited for her to open her door.

She sat and Cruz held on to the car door. When she was belted in, he leaned his forearm on the roof and said, "Drive safe, I'll see you in a bit."

"Okay. You too." Mickie breathed out a sigh of relief once Cruz headed toward his car. Jeez, he was absolutely lethal. Over the last few weeks she'd gotten to know him pretty well—at least she thought she had. Every time she saw him, he took her breath away. He was just so freaking good-looking, and he was interested in *her*. It was crazy.

She wasn't one to believe in insta-love, but she'd taken her time with Troy, been very cautious, and look how that turned out. It wasn't as if she'd jumped into bed with Cruz on that first date, but she was definitely moving faster with him than any other relationship she'd had.

But the difference this time was that they were talking more. On the phone, via texts…without face-to-face contact, they'd had to rely on getting to know each other by *talking*. She liked it. She knew more about Cruz than she ultimately knew about Troy. But that really wasn't saying anything since apparently she knew nothing *real* about Troy.

Mickie would've been over the moon, if only it hadn't been for her sister. She knew she'd have to confront Angel, sooner rather than later. Something major was up with her and Mickie knew in her gut it wasn't anything good. She needed to get to the bottom of it, if only she knew how.

But first, Mickie had an afternoon to spend with Cruz. She shivered in delight. Maybe she'd be able to convince him to take their physical relationship a bit further than they'd taken it in the past. Mickie was ready—more than ready.

Chapter Eleven

C RUZ'S GAZE SWEPT from the road in front of him to his rearview mirror. Mickie was a good driver, and kept his car in her sights. Seeing her trusting him, following him wherever he wanted her to go, made him come to a decision. He was simply going to go with it with Mickie. As Dax had said, he had no idea how this would all play out in the end, but Cruz knew he'd never forgive himself if he gave up on whatever was starting between them without at least giving it a chance.

He wanted Mickie. She was cute, funny, and down-to-earth. She cared about her sister even when Angel was being hurtful, and was about as normal as any woman he'd ever dated…and that appealed to him more than he thought it would. He wanted someone who would love him as much as he loved her back. He wasn't sure if Mickie was that woman yet, but he'd be an idiot to let her go. She was the first woman since Sophie who he could even *imagine* himself in a long-term relationship with.

Soon they were pulling up in front of Cruz's apartment complex. He got out of his car and headed over to Mickie's Honda. He met her at the front of the car and took her hand in his as they headed to his door.

It seemed natural to hold on to her. Cruz had no idea why this woman made him feel this way, but it was what it was, and reiterating his thoughts on the way to his place, he wasn't going to fight it anymore.

Their quirky courtship, which thus far had mostly existed via phone, was completely different from anything he'd ever had before. As much as he'd thought he loved Sophie, he'd never felt anticipation when his phone vibrated. He'd never woken up wanting nothing more than to talk to her, and he never went to sleep hoping her voice would be the first thing he heard in the morning.

The more Cruz got to know Mickie, the more he realized what he had with Sophie hadn't been true love. He thought about Dax and Mack. Their love was what he wanted. After what Dax had been through, watching Mack literally die in front of his eyes at the hands of a serial killer, and how it'd affected him, Cruz knew *that* was what he wanted. Not the dying part, but the love part. He hadn't understood it…until now. Until Mickie. He wasn't sure he loved her yet, but he certainly cared a whole lot about her.

Cruz unlocked his apartment door and held it open for Mickie. She walked in and put her purse on the table by the door.

"Go on and choose what you want to watch. Movies are in the cabinet by the television."

Mickie headed over to his entertainment center and squatted down next to the cabinet with the DVDs. He went into the kitchen and got two cans of soda. Cruz went back into the living room and settled on the sofa.

Mickie held up *Beverly Hills Cop*. "Too cliché?"

Cruz laughed and stood up to put the movie into the DVD player. "Hell no. I love this movie." He scrunched up his face and raised his voice, mimicking Eddie Murphy, "Disturbing the peace? I got thrown out a window!"

Mickie immediately finished the quote. "What's the charge for getting pushed out of a car? Jaywalking?"

Cruz gawked at Mickie, not believing she could actually quote *Beverly Hills Cop*.

Mickie laughed. "I love it too. Eddie Murphy's the bomb."

"Will you marry me?"

Mickie laughed again, even as her heart beat wildly in her chest at his words. "Shut up."

Cruz sat on the couch next to Mickie and took her hand as the music started. They sat watching the movie for a while, Cruz smiling at Mickie mouthing various lines as Eddie Murphy said them. "At the risk of interrupting you, I just wanna say, thanks for coming over today."

Mickie looked over at Cruz. "I think that's my line. I was stressed about Angel and you offered to help me pull my head out of my ass."

Cruz lifted the hand not holding hers and brushed it over the side of her head. "I'm sorry about your sister. Seriously."

"I know."

"You'll figure it out."

"I hope so."

"Are you hungry?"

Mickie looked surprised at his change of subject. "No. We just ate."

"Thirsty?"

Motioning to her drink on the table next to the couch, Mickie shook her head.

"Comfortable? Need anything?"

"Cruz? I'm fine. What's up with you?"

"I just want to make sure you're comfortable and all's good."

"I'm fine."

"How into this movie are you?"

"Uh, it's good, but if you need to do something else, it's okay, I can go."

"I don't want you to go. I can't hold back anymore. The more I learn about you, the more I have to have you. You're loyal to your sister. You work hard, you're not selfish or spoiled. You're sexy as hell and I can't get you out of my head. I'm done waiting. I want to taste you. I want to feel your curvy body under mine. I need it. If you don't want that, please, tell me. Otherwise, this is happening. Right now."

Mickie swallowed hard. Cruz was dead serious. He wasn't smiling, he wasn't teasing her. She could feel her nipples harden under her cotton bra. Dear Lord. This handsome man wanted her. She didn't have to think about it. She'd decided earlier that she hoped Cruz wanted to move their physical relationship forward. "I want it."

"Thank fuck. Come here." Cruz hooked his arm around her back and tugged her into him as he fell sideways onto the couch.

Mickie tried to prop herself up so she didn't squish him as she looked down into his eyes.

"Relax, Mickie. I need to feel you against me."

"I'll squash you."

"Hardly. Mickie, you weigh nothing compared to me. Put your legs on either side of my hips. Straddle me. I like feeling you against me. That's it…" Cruz put his hands on her hips and held her to him. She was astride his stomach, which was probably good; he didn't want to scare her with how hard he was.

He ran his hands up from her hips to her sides, then back down. Then he did it again, going higher this time, until they were just under her breasts. Cruz kept his hands on her, soothing her, gentling her. "Relax into me. You won't hurt me."

Cruz felt when Mickie put her full weight on him. Her legs relaxed and he could feel the warmth of her core against his stomach. Her hands were braced on his chest and she was looking down at him as if she was starving and he was her last meal. It was a good look on her.

Wanting to move their lovemaking along, Cruz said, "You want to see my tattoo now?"

"God, yes. Please."

Cruz took his hands off her and put them up by his head. "Take off my shirt."

Mickie looked down at the exquisite man underneath her. She'd been nervous about sitting on him, but as he'd run his hands over her body, she relaxed more and more. Now she lifted her hips and reached under her to grasp his T-shirt and ease it up his chest. She teased them both by removing it slowly.

As she revealed his abs, Mickie gasped. "Wow, Cruz. You're built." She scooted backwards until she rested on top of his erection. She leaned down and kissed his stomach as she continued to ease his shirt upward. She kissed his belly button and then each of the defined muscles she revealed as she raised his shirt. Mickie felt him inhale at the first brush of her lips against his stomach. She usually wasn't this forward or fast with men, but there was something about Cruz that made her lose her inhibitions.

"That's not where my tattoo is," Cruz teased, breathing deeply to try to control himself. The feel of Mickie rubbing against his erection and her lips so close to his waistband was playing hell with his good intentions.

Mickie raised her head and watched as Cruz lifted his arms straight up so she could push his shirt completely off. Her eyes were glued to his left biceps and shoulder as he brought his arms back down, hauling her hips back up so she was straddling his stomach again.

She pouted at him. "I was comfortable where I was."

"Yeah, but if you want this to last for more than two minutes, I need you here right now."

Mickie smirked. "Two minutes?"

Cruz chuckled at himself. "Yeah, you've got me so hard if you'd ground yourself against me any longer, that's how long I would've lasted."

Mickie blushed and covered her cheeks with her hands when he laughed at her. "I don't think anyone's wanted me like that before."

"Well, rest assured, I do. You wanna take a look at this now or later?" Cruz asked seriously, gesturing to his shoulder with his head.

Mickie brought her hands down from her face and leaned into Cruz. "Now. Definitely now." She smoothed her right hand up his arm and over his tattoo to his shoulder. His tattoo was of a large bird with its wings spread. She wasn't sure what kind, maybe an eagle, maybe a hawk, but whatever it was, it was big, spanning the width of his muscular biceps. It was done in shades of black, which made the intricate artwork all the more beautiful. The initials AR were under the tattoo in curly feminine writing, a direct contrast to the hard, masculine lines of the tattoo. Mickie ran her fingertip over the letters, guessing their meaning. "Avery's initials?"

Cruz looked up into Mickie's eyes as she examined his ink. "Yeah." She leaned down and kissed his biceps, right in the middle of the tattoo. He'd been nervous to show her, as the eagle on his arm was the exact same eagle that was depicted on his FBI badge. He wasn't sure she'd understand why he'd felt the need to put Avery's initials on his arm, but he shouldn't have been surprised.

"She'd be honored."

"That's not why I got her inked on me."

"Why then?" Mickie sat up and braced one forearm on Cruz's chest, looking him in the eyes as she did, running her fingertips over his arm. She obviously approved and that made his stomach clench in relief. Not everyone understood tattoos, and while he wasn't covered in them, this one meant everything. It was who he was, what he stood for. She might not understand that right now, but it still touched him that she seemed to understand the tattoo had a deep significance for him.

Cruz realized she'd asked a question. He smoothed her hair behind her ear as he answered.

"To remind myself that behind every victim, there's a family. There are people who love and miss their loved ones. I saw what

Avery's family went through. Her brother Sam spent years trying to find whoever killed her. There wasn't anything the police could do for Avery, but they owed it to her family to investigate and find the person who'd killed her, not make her brother spend a lot of his life doing it. That's why I have her initials there. To remember. I might only be in security, but I try to remember that what I do can make a difference in people's lives." Cruz tacked the last part on...feeling it was lame, but trying to link it to what Mickie thought he did for a living.

"I have something to say, but it's inappropriate as hell."

Cruz blinked at Mickie's seemingly abrupt change in topic. "Okay. Go for it."

"Even knowing why it's there and what it represents...I gotta say, all it makes me want to do is rip the rest of your clothes off and fuck you right here, right now."

Cruz felt himself grow even harder, if that was possible, at Mickie's words. "Yeah?"

"Uh huh. I typically don't like tattoos. But yours? Combined with your body? Oh yeah. It works for you, Cruz. It most definitely works."

Cruz smiled and tightened his hold on her hips. "I've showed you mine. Gonna show me yours?"

Misinterpreting him on purpose, Mickie said, "I don't have any tattoos."

"You've got other things I wanna see. Better things."

Thinking about what he would see when her shirt and pants came off, Mickie bit her lip nervously.

"Don't even, Mickie." It was as if Cruz could read her mind. He brought one hand up and tugged her lip out of her teeth. Then he ran his fingers down her chest, not lingering at the hard nipple he could feel as he went, until he reached her hip again. He ground her against his stomach and sat up, bringing her with him.

Mickie slipped down so she was straddling his lap again. Cruz held her hard against him, making sure she felt how much he needed her.

"Hang on, I'm moving this to my bed."

Mickie squealed as Cruz stood and she grabbed his shoulders, tightening her legs around his waist so she wouldn't fall.

Cruz stalked down the hall, groaning as he felt Mickie's heat against his erection. She squirmed against him as he walked. He kicked open his bedroom door and made a beeline for his bed. He dropped Mickie on her back and immediately caged her in as he came down over her.

"Scoot up."

Mickie did as he asked and he continued, "Don't be nervous, Mickie. You have no idea how much I've wanted this, wanted *you*. Ever since I sat across from you in that restaurant that first day, I've dreamed of seeing you naked and getting my hands on you. I admit, I've thought about your nipples...I can already see they're extremely sensitive."

Mickie glanced down and clearly saw the outline of her nipples against her shirt, even through her bra. She'd always cursed her big nipples and how they were continuously embarrassing her, but now, seeing Cruz look down at her as if he couldn't wait to lick her all over, she wasn't embarrassed at all. She arched her back, urging Cruz on.

Cruz swallowed hard and ran the tip of his finger lightly over her nipple, feeling it bead even more at his touch. "Your curves are sexy as hell. I can't wait to dig my fingers into your hips as you take me. I'm hard everywhere. I want a woman who's soft and can take what I have to give. Can you take it, Mickie? Can you take me as I am?"

"I can take you, Cruz. God, can I take you."

"Thank God. I've jerked off to the thought of you more than I did when I was a teenager. Don't make me wait. Please. Show me what you've got under there, Mickie."

Chapter Twelve

————◆————

MICKIE HAD NO idea what had come over her, but she wanted nothing more than to rip off her clothes and be naked for Cruz. The thought of him masturbating when he imagined what she looked like was overwhelming. She reached down to her pants and undid the button of her jeans.

Cruz caught her hands in his, stopping her.

"I thought—"

"Oh, I want you naked, have no doubt, but I want to do it my way."

"Then hurry up, Cruz!"

"Slow. My way is slow."

"I hate slow," Mickie complained with a pout.

Cruz chuckled, somehow knowing she'd say something like that. "You'll love it by the time I get done with you."

Mickie groaned and put both hands above her head and sighed dramatically. "Let me know when you're done down there."

Cruz laughed again, not remembering the last time he'd had this much fun while making love to a woman. "Much obliged, ma'am. Just close your eyes and forget I'm here then." Not looking up to see if she'd done what he asked, Cruz leaned in and put his nose against her belly, nudging her shirt up until he was nuzzling against her skin. He inhaled deeply.

"What are you doing?" Mickie asked nervously, shifting under him.

Cruz held her hips tightly with his hands, silently asking her to be still. "You smell amazing. You're so wet for me. I can smell your arousal. That, along with whatever soap or lotion you've used, is a fucking aphrodisiac."

"Cruz—"

Whatever Mickie was going to say was cut off when Cruz moved quickly and unzipped her jeans. He shifted his head down until his nose was right over her mound. His hand pressed against her panties once, then his nose was there again.

"Cruz!" Mickie exclaimed, trying to push his head away.

"Easy, Mickie," Cruz murmured. "It's okay. I'm going to spend quite a bit of time here, you might as well get used to it."

Mickie giggled nervously and lay back again. "I still say fast is better."

Cruz did pick up his head at that. "You'll change your tune, sweetness, just give me some time."

Mickie just shook her head at him.

Cruz lowered himself and inhaled her unique scent once more. He hadn't been lying to her earlier. He'd jacked off to the thought of her body, of having her under him, of her scent, more often than even Cruz was comfortable admitting. It wasn't just lust, although there was a healthy dose of that; it was more. He admired her, and he knew, just *knew* she wouldn't want to be anywhere near him once she learned everything about his assignment. She was too loyal to her family, to Angel, to be able to forgive him. He might only get one shot at this, at having her, and he wasn't unselfish enough to do the right thing, to let her go.

He'd debated over and over whether he should pursue anything with her, even after his pep-talk to himself in the car. But sitting next to her on the couch, listening to her giggle and quote *Beverly Hills Cop*, had tipped the scales for good. He couldn't stay away from her. Cruz needed her.

He moved his hands until they were under her and lifted her pelvis into the air. "Push your pants down, Mickie. My hands are busy."

Obviously thinking he was getting on with it, Mickie hurried to do as he asked. She pushed her jeans down as far as she could reach. After she toed off her sneakers, Cruz lowered her hips back to the bed and finished taking her jeans off. She lay under him now in her panties, still covered from the waist up.

Cruz looked down at her. She was wearing a pair of gray cotton undies.

Seeing Cruz eyeing her underwear, Mickie apologized. "I'm sorry they aren't sexy, I didn't—"

"Not sexy?" Cruz interrupted, looking up at Mickie incredulously. "Are you kidding me? I've never seen anything sexier."

"Cruz, I'm a sure thing here. You don't have to lie."

"I'm not fucking lying, Mickie. Jesus, you have no idea." Cruz shifted and ran the index finger of his right hand down from her belly button to her anus, over her panties, and then back up. With the other hand, he pulled the cotton tight until it outlined her crease.

Mickie could feel herself grow even wetter at his actions. She clenched her inner muscles, wanting and needing more.

"No, you aren't wearing silk, and it's not a thong, but what I've got in front of me is a hell of a lot sexier than anything I've *ever* seen before." Cruz leaned down as if inspecting her, and he inhaled deeply. "Your panties are light gray. That means as they get wet, they turn dark gray." He ran his fingertip over her folds once more. "And right here, right now, they are so dark gray, they're almost black. You're soaked, Mickie. And getting wetter right in front of my eyes. There is nothing, and I mean nothing, sexier than that. Knowing you want me? That you're enjoying my touch and my words? Nothing. Fucking. Sexier."

Mickie whimpered. "Oh my God, Cruz. Seriously. Please, I need you."

"And you'll get me, Mickie. You think I'm not taking you after seeing how wet you are for me? Smelling how excited you are? No fucking way. But you'll get me on my time, not yours."

"I had no idea you were this sadistic."

"Oh, this isn't sadistic, Mickie. This is worship."

"I wish you'd worship faster then."

Cruz couldn't help it, he laughed. "After this, you'll get fast. Guarantee it. But I want to savor you. I want to unwrap you slowly, learn exactly what you like and how you like it. There'll never be another first time for us. I want to savor it. Now, lay back and enjoy."

Mickie lay back with a huff and Cruz smiled up at her. "You won't regret this, Mickie. Whatever happens in the future, I hope to Christ you don't regret this."

"I won't."

"Promise?"

"Promise."

With that, Cruz bent his head and got to work. He nipped and licked and stroked until Mickie was begging mindlessly. Finally Cruz moved her soaked panties to the side and ran his finger up her folds, with nothing between them.

"Oh my God."

"You have no idea how good you feel." Cruz didn't know if Mickie was really hearing him. She had a light sheen of sweat covering her from his teasing and her panties were literally soaked with her excitement.

"Let's get your shirt off, yeah?"

Mickie sat up so fast and had her shirt off before Cruz could even help. He laughed as she reached behind her to undo her bra clasp.

Mickie looked into Cruz's laughing eyes and smiled sheepishly. No longer embarrassed about what she might look like because she was so turned on, she told him, "I figured if I didn't get this off before you took over, you'd take another year to get to it."

Cruz didn't bother to respond, his eyes were locked on her chest. "Jesus, Mickie. Your tits are more beautiful than I could have imagined."

Mickie blushed at his crude words, loving them all the same. Having had enough of his slow pace, she brought her hands up to her breasts and lifted them, as if offering them to Cruz. "Large areolas, hard nipples."

Cruz ran his index finger around her right areola, and when she began to drop her hands, he ordered, "Keep them there. I like you offering yourself to me." Cruz looked up at her face when she moved her hands back under her breasts. "And I like that blush too."

Mickie knew she was breathing fast, but she'd never had a sexual encounter like this. With Troy, he'd just climbed on, did his thing, and rolled over. He'd never taken the time to really look at her before. None of the other men she'd been with had ever been this…intense, either. Mickie wasn't sure she liked it, but she certainly didn't hate it.

"Cruz…"

"And I like that pleading tone of your voice too. Hold them there." Not giving her time to say anything else, Cruz leaned over and put one hand under hers on her breast and lifted it higher. He put his mouth over it and sucked. When he heard Mickie's swift intake of breath, he took her nipple between his teeth and nipped. Loving how it got even harder under his teeth, he worked it with his tongue as he sucked harder. It wasn't until Mickie squirmed that he gave in and released her.

He brought his hand up and rubbed her breast soothingly. "You are amazing. I've never seen such big nipples before. It's as if they're begging for me to lick and suck them."

"Please, Cruz."

"Take off your panties," Cruz ordered in a guttural voice. "I thought I could make this last longer, but I have to have you."

Mickie scrambled to do as Cruz asked. He was just as busy getting rid of his own pants. He stood next to the bed, gazing at her. Mickie licked her lips as she stared at his body. His erection was long and hard. He was big—bigger than anyone she'd ever taken before.

She refused to get nervous. She could take him; women's bodies were meant to stretch around a man's. She reached out for Cruz.

Cruz forced himself to stay still as Mickie's hand gripped his cock. A bead of semen appeared on the head of his cock and almost fell to the floor. Mickie's hand caught it and rubbed it into his skin as she caressed him. Withstanding her touch for a beat, Cruz took a deep breath. Then, knowing he couldn't handle it much longer, he took her wrist in his hand and put a knee to the bed. He grabbed the other wrist and brought it above her head and pinned her hands there.

"As much as I crave your touch, this would cease to be slow and move quickly to Mach-10 if I let you continue to touch me."

"But—"

"No, not this time. Later, yes. I'll let you explore. I'll even beg you to touch me, to lick and suck me, but not now. Not this first time. Keep them there." When she nodded, he released her and ran his palms down her forearms to her biceps, over her shoulders, over her breasts, tweaking both nipples as he passed them, over her soft stomach and down to her hips. Cruz could see Mickie was breathing hard, and her eyes were firmly on his body as he moved.

Cruz shifted until his weeping dick brushed against her thigh.

"You're wet for me too." Mickie's voice was soft and incredulous.

"Yeah, there's nowhere I want to be more than buried deep inside your body, feeling you snug against me as I take you."

"Then do it already, Cruz. Jesus."

"Soon, Mickie. I'm enjoying myself here."

"Can't you enjoy yourself faster?" Mickie whined, squirming against him as he moved his fingers closer to her core.

"Nope. Not until I taste you."

Cruz reached up suddenly to his pillows and grabbed one, shoving it under Mickie's hips. "That's better. I can see you easier."

"Cruz…"

He ignored the pleading sound of Mickie's voice and scooted down the bed. He took her bottom into his hands again and tilted her up farther, until his head was directly over her weeping center. He blew against her folds and watched in fascination as she clenched in his grip. "Fucking beautiful, Mickie. I swear I can see you throbbing. Here's the deal—I'm going to make you come for me at least a couple of times before I make my way inside you. I want you nice and wet. If I'm going to take you without hurting you, you have to be soaked and ready for me."

"I'm ready now, Cruz."

"No, you're not. You're wet, but not wet enough. I want to see you dripping for me before I take you. Literally. I want to see your juices coming out of you before I push inside your hot body. Now hush and let me concentrate." Ignoring her cute groan, Cruz didn't mess around, he concentrated on her clit, licking it with a steady pace, then increasing his speed as she shifted under him. Cruz held her close, not letting her squirm out of his grasp and away from his rapidly flicking tongue.

It was only about three minutes later when he felt Mickie come for the first time. He quickly pushed one finger inside her, feeling her inner muscles clench around him. She threw her head back, lifted her hips, and moaned out his name. Cruz didn't let up, but instead kept at her. He lapped at her clit remorselessly, sliding a second finger inside her and curling them upwards so he stroked against her G-spot as he continued his assault on her clit.

"Too sensitive, please, Cruz. Oh my God…"

Cruz ignored her and kept going. Finally after her third or fourth orgasm—it was hard to tell as they were practically nonstop—he eased away from her body. He turned his head and kissed her inner thigh, enjoying her breathy pants and her still-shaking muscles. "*Now* you're wet. You're so wet you're leaking down your ass. You're soaking my pillow. I don't think I'm ever washing it. I want to sleep with my nose buried in it, remembering this vision right now."

"Please, for the love of God, Cruz. Shut the hell up and fuck me already."

Cruz kissed her rosy clit once more, enjoying the jolt of her body as he made contact with the sensitive bundle of nerves, before sliding up Mickie's body. He reached over to the table next to the bed and snagged a condom from the drawer. He hadn't brought a woman to his place in a very long time, but even though he'd never been a boy scout, he was always prepared.

He quickly rolled the latex down his erection and placed the tip against the shiny lips of her sex. "Slow and steady, Mickie," Cruz told her, not looking away from where he was about to take her. "If I hurt you, let me know. But I'm not stopping. No fucking way. I'll slow down and let you get used to me, but I'm coming inside." He looked up finally.

Mickie looked completely wrung out. The short hair on her forehead was sticking to her with the sweat that had accumulated there. Her face was red and she had a rosy blush on her upper chest. Her nipples were hard and reaching toward his ceiling. And her hands. Jesus, her hands. They were still where he'd placed them. She hadn't moved. Even during the orgasms he'd forced her through, she'd had the presence of mind to keep them right where he'd put them.

Cruz suddenly wanted her hands on him. Wanted to feel her clutching him to her.

"You can touch me, Mickie. Please put your hands on me."

Her hands immediately came down from over her head and rested on his biceps. She dug her fingernails in lightly, holding on, and nodded at him. "Fuck me, Cruz."

At her words, Cruz pushed in. The angle the pillow put her hips at allowed him to drag himself along the top wall of her sex. He pushed in an inch, then withdrew. Then he pushed in two inches, and pulled back out until she only had the tip of him.

Mickie raised her hips on her own and took the two inches back. Cruz pulled away again and followed her down as her hips lowered. He gained another inch and waited. When she pushed up impatiently, he pulled back, teasing her.

"Cruz, for God's sake—"

Before she could finish her words, Cruz pushed in until he couldn't any more. Then he pulled her hips up, and gained another half an inch. Cruz could feel his balls flush against her backside. They both groaned.

"Okay?" he managed to ground out, not knowing what he'd do if she said no.

"Oh yeah, more than okay." Mickie's fingernails were digging into his upper arms harder now. "I've never been this full before."

Cruz couldn't help but flex against her at her words. God, she was sexy. Cruz had never regretted wearing a condom before in his life. It was automatic to glove up before having sex, but this, this was something different. He wanted to fill her up with his juices. He wanted to watch it slowly leak out of her after they were done. He wanted to soak his pillow, which was still under her ass, and his sheets with their juices.

He shook his head. Jesus, this wasn't permanent. He had to keep reminding himself of that.

He pulled out then slammed back in, loving hearing her moan under him. "Hang on to me, Mickie. You wanted fast? You're about to get fast."

"Oh yeah. Finally. Thank God."

Realizing he hadn't kissed her since he'd brought her into his bedroom, Cruz leaned over, letting go of her hips so he could brace himself over her. He shoved in as far as he could go then brought his mouth down to hers.

He delved into Mickie's mouth, learning what she liked and what she didn't. Cruz sucked her tongue into his mouth and scraped it with his teeth. Then he took her lip and sucked on that. Finally, he thrust his tongue into her mouth and rocked his hips into hers. Kissing Mickie while she took all of him into her was insanely intimate. He'd kissed and he'd fucked, but something about this moment, right now, was more than just kissing and fucking.

Cruz broke contact with her lips and sat up, continuing his assault on Mickie. She smiled up at him. Cruz looked down and saw her breasts undulating with each of his thrusts. His Mickie was all natural and he loved it. He palmed one of her breasts and squeezed as he took her. Knowing she'd need more stimulation if she was going to come again, Cruz ordered, "Touch yourself."

"Wh-what?" she asked in confusion.

"Your clit. Make yourself come one more time. I want to feel you suck my cock in. Do it, Mickie. I'm hanging on by a thread here. I want you to come one more time before I lose it."

Mickie immediately took her right hand away from his arm and snaked it between them until she was touching herself. She rubbed her clit then moved her fingers down until they were caressing his shaft as he thrust in and out of her.

"Oh my God, Cruz. That is so hot."

"Stop fucking around, Mickie. I'll let you watch some other time, but for now, please, do it. Make yourself come."

Mickie didn't break eye contact as she moved her finger up and harshly stroked herself. Cruz could feel her orgasm getting closer and closer. He took her nipple between his fingers again and squeezed it…hard. Harder than he would've if she hadn't already come several times and if she wasn't about to come again. "Now, sweetness. Oh yeah, I can feel it. Squeeze me, yeah. Oh yeah. Fuck!"

Cruz felt Mickie lose it right before he did. He thrust once more and ground himself inside her as far as he could. He saw spots in front of his eyes as he emptied himself into the latex surrounding his cock.

When he finally came back to his senses, he realized he was lying on top of Mickie and she was stroking his back calmly. He immediately rolled over, taking Mickie with him, holding her hips against his own, making sure she didn't lose him in the process of them moving. She ended up sitting astride him. She pushed up and looked down, blushing.

"Wow."

"Yeah, Wow. That was amazing, Mickie. *You* were amazing."

"I think you did all the work."

"No way, it was all you."

Mickie giggled and Cruz groaned.

"When you laugh, I can feel you clench around me."

Mickie stopped laughing and blushed again. "Uh, don't you have to get up and…you know, get rid of the condom or something?"

"Yeah, but I'm comfortable where I am."

"Yeah, but—"

"And you might not realize this, sweetheart, but I can feel how wet you are because it's dripping down my cock and covering my balls and the sheet underneath us."

"That's gross, Cruz."

Cruz reached up and brought Mickie down onto him. He linked his hands at the small of her back and she cuddled into his chest and he thought about what she'd said. Had hanging around the MC made him cruder and more demanding in bed? Cruz didn't think so. It was Mickie. She brought out all sorts of things in him, the biggest being the ability to be his true self in bed.

"It's not gross, hon. It's us. Sex is raw and dirty and nasty…and completely wonderful. We can wash ourselves and the sheets. We can clean up and be back to normal in a heartbeat. But sharing this with you, sharing our bodies' natural reactions to each other and what we did together? That's fucking beautiful, not gross."

Cruz felt Mickie snuggle deeper, as if she were trying to burrow into him, and it made his heart clench. He tried to memorize the feeling of her in his arms, knowing as soon as she found out what he'd done—or not done, in the case of her sister—she'd look at him with disgust instead of the soft, sated eyes she was wearing now.

Cruz felt her sigh against his chest. "Tired?"

"Mmmm."

"Take a nap then. I don't have to be anywhere for a while."

Mickie began to move, and Cruz held her tightly to him. "Right there, Mickie. I like the feel of you on me."

"I like the feel of you *in* me."

Cruz chuckled when he felt her stiffen. "Didn't mean to say that, did you?"

"No," Mickie said, disgruntled.

"I like the feel of me in you too. Sleep."

"Has anyone told you that you're awfully bossy?"

"No."

"Well, you are."

Cruz merely smiled. He was content. For someone who had spent the last two months in the underbelly of the worst MC the city of San Antonio had ever seen, he was pretty damn happy at the moment.

He hadn't lied. He could feel his come leaking out of the condom and onto his skin and the sheet under him, but he wasn't about to move. He'd get up later. For now he wanted to cherish the feel of Mickie in his arms, sated and warm.

He couldn't remember ever feeling like this after being with a woman. He was usually antsy to get up and out of bed. Not with Mickie. He laughed lightly, hearing Mickie's soft snores. She was adorable, even when asleep.

Cruz tightened his arms and leaned up and buried his nose into her hair. He tried to memorize her smell, knowing he'd be back in the pit of hell soon enough.

Chapter Thirteen

B UBBA SHOOK HANDS with Axel as he delivered another shipment of drugs. Cruz, Kitty, Camel, Vodka, and Roach stood next to them as they discussed their future business.

"We down for another delivery next week?" Bubba asked.

"So soon? Fuck, man. Not sure I can make that happen," Axel told him, running his hand over his head.

"Fucking make it happen. Ransom wants that shipment."

"He better watch himself, you know Chico Malo won't like Ransom overstepping."

"Fuck that. If Chico Malo isn't enough of a bad fucking boy to deal with a little competition, then he doesn't deserve to be in the business."

Axel shook his head. "Dios mío, Bubba. You have no idea what he can do."

"Doesn't matter, man. If Ransom wants his shipments, he's getting his shipments. We can do business with *you* or find someone else."

Axel put up his hands. "Calm the fuck down, man. I'll see what I can do. I'll talk with Chico Malo. You know he only supplies who he wants, when he wants, and if he thinks you're trying to take over this area, it's not going to go well."

"You talk to him then. Ransom will be waiting, but tell him not to take too long." Bubba turned his back on Axel, a serious diss, and headed for the van.

"Fucker," Axel murmured under his breath.

Without a word, Vodka took a gun out of his back waistband and pistol whipped Axel. The man was on the ground, bleeding and disoriented, before anyone could move.

Bubba turned around, nodded at Vodka's action, spit on the ground and continued to the van. Camel and Kitty followed him, unconcerned about Axel. Cruz and Roach approached Axel, who was now sitting up—Cruz because it was expected, and Roach because he wanted to get his licks in as well.

Roach coldcocked Axel with his fist and Cruz could tell he'd broken the man's nose. Blood poured out and dripped down Axel's face. Everyone knew if Axel wasn't half conscious he'd be using the pistol they could see in the waistband of his pants, but he currently made for an easy target.

Roach laughed as Vodka leaned down to Axel. "There is no 'see what you can do' when it comes to what Ransom wants, motherfucker. If Ransom says he wants more drugs, you'll fucking get him more drugs. Got it? You don't want to be on Ransom's bad side."

Roach kicked the man, aiming for his kidneys. Knowing it'd look weird for him just to stand there and watch, Cruz aimed a kick at the man as well, trying to avoid anything vulnerable. Vodka watched as Cruz and Roach beat the man on the ground until he wasn't even flinching from their blows.

"That's enough. Let's get the fuck out of here." Vodka spit on Axel's bloody body as he passed, and Roach and Cruz did the same thing.

As the group traveled back to the clubhouse, Cruz thought about what he'd just found out. Chico Malo was the man in charge of a large criminal empire in Mexico. He was on the FBI's most wanted list for the amount of drugs he was importing into the States, as well as for the alarming number of bodies that were found in his part of Mexico.

The Mexican drug lords sometimes gave themselves innocuous nicknames, knowing the dichotomy between the cutesy names and what they did would freak people the hell out. In Chico Malo's case, it definitely worked. He might be called the "Bad Boy," but everyone knew he was no boy. He was one bad motherfucker, and no one had the guts to go against him. Ransom was insane for drawing a line in the sand and getting the attention of the notorious, dangerous, drug dealer.

But this could be the proof the FBI needed to nail Chico Malo. He'd had no idea Axel was dealing directly with the notorious Mexican drug lord. Oh, he and the FBI had had Chico Malo in their sights for years, but if they could catch him in the act and get proof, it'd go a long way toward trying to get the "legitimate" Mexican officials to do something.

If Axel was scared of the man, that was saying something. Axel was a dangerous drug dealer in his own right. If Ransom thought he could take over Chico Malo's empire and become a big fish in the drug world, Cruz knew he was sadly mistaken. Ransom was a big fish in his own small pond here in San Antonio. He wouldn't last a day in the Bad Boy's sandbox.

Cruz needed to get the intel to his boss as soon as possible. He had no idea when a confrontation was going to happen between Chico Malo and Ransom, but he knew it was coming. There was no way the Mexican drug lord would take the threat from Ransom lightly. Iron control, it was how all drug lords kept on top…that, and killing off their competition.

Cruz felt his phone vibrate in his pocket at the same time the ring tone sounded. He was loath to take it out in front of the others, but he had to. It could be Ransom or any of the other MC guys. It'd be suspicious if he didn't answer.

He pulled the phone out of his pocket and felt his stomach drop when he saw it was Mickie calling. She hardly ever called him. She usually texted.

He began to put the phone back into his pocket so he could call her back later when Roach said, "Why don't you answer it, Smoke?"

Not having a ready excuse and knowing it'd look weird if he didn't answer, Cruz merely shrugged. "Didn't want to bother you all with a conversation with my latest pussy, that's all."

Realizing he was making a mistake and there was no way this call could go well, but feeling pressured to answer, Cruz clicked to pick up the call.

"Yo."

"Hey, Cruz. I was wondering if you wanted to get together to-morrow? I have to work, but we could meet for lunch."

"Can't."

"Oh, okay. Tomorrow night maybe?"

Cruz could hear the confusion in Mickie's voice. She'd gone from happy and bubbly to uncertain, and all it took was one word from him. Cruz wished he could fucking kill all four men who were now openly listening to his conversation.

"Nope. Can't then either." Cruz tried to keep his part of the con-versation short, in the hopes Mickie would end the call before he said something she couldn't forgive him for.

Before Mickie could say anything else, Camel called out, loud enough for Mickie to hear, "You need some dick, baby? I've got some, say the word, *beg* for it, and I'll be right over!"

The other men laughed, loudly.

"Uh…I guess I called at a bad time."

"Yeah, I guess you did."

"He's fucking busy, bitch! Leave him the fuck alone. If he wants your pussy again, he'll come to you. Now hang the fuck up already." That was Vodka. He was a hard bastard and never pulled any punch-es.

Cruz heard Mickie's inhalation. Her voice was wobbly as she said softly, "I just wanted to let you know how much I enjoyed today. That's all. Sorry to have bothered you."

Cruz clicked off the phone at hearing the dial tone. Fuck. Double fuck. He knew Mickie was probably remembering how she'd begged him to fuck her and most likely thought he'd blabbed about it to his "friends."

He didn't have to fake the scowl on his face as he turned to Vodka. "Thanks a lot, asshole. Now I'll have to work double-time to get back in there."

"Fuck it, man. No pussy's worth that."

"It is when I'm not allowed to have club pussy." Cruz knew he was treading on a thin line with that statement, but he couldn't let Vodka think he could push him around.

"I could talk to Ransom about that."

"Whatever, man. Ransom isn't going to let prospects fuck club pussy, and you and I both know it. Just shut the fuck up about it already."

Bubba laughed. "I'm sure you can make it up to the bitch later. After we get back and let Ransom know what went down tonight you can go to her, make her suck your cock and she'll be begging for you to give it to her again."

Cruz hated that he grew hard at Bubba's words. It wasn't his words, *making* someone take him in her mouth didn't do anything for him...at all, but remembering how Mickie *had* begged him to fuck her that got to him; that and the thought of her on her knees sucking him off. And that made him remember her smell, the feel of her clenched around him, and how she'd blushed when they'd finally gotten out of bed that afternoon and she'd looked at the huge wet spot they'd left on the sheets.

Seeing his erection and misinterpreting the cause, Bubba sneered, "Liked that, huh? There's hope for you yet, Smoke."

Cruz just lifted his chin in response and kept quiet. He tried to think about anything but Mickie in his bed, at least until he could get the hell out of the MC clubhouse that night. Then all bets were off.

They pulled into the warehouse district and climbed out of the van after Kitty stopped at the back loading dock. They all headed inside to report back to Ransom about Chico Malo and Axel.

The only thing Ransom said when Bubba told him what Axel had warned was, "He's not the only supplier around here. If he wants to get into a war on my turf, he'll get a fucking war."

Cruz mentally shook his head. What a conceited asshole. There was no way Ransom would win a war against Chico Malo and his thugs.

"Oh, and Smoke here wants a piece of club pussy," Roach teased.

"No fucking way," Ransom growled. "Club pussy is just that, *club* pussy. When you've proven you're a part of this MC, you can have club pussy. Until then, keep your dick in your pants."

Everyone laughed and Cruz scowled at Roach.

"He's just pissed because the bitch he's screwing called and got upset," Bubba explained after they'd stopped laughing.

Cruz's gut clenched at Bubba's words. He didn't like to hear Mickie referred to as "the bitch," even if Bubba didn't know who he was talking about.

"I got it, Smoke," Ransom said seriously. "Angel's bitch-face sister is still on her case. Why don't you fuck *her* to get her off her sister's back? We need that money to expand business. I'm not going to lose it at this stage in the game to some cunt who has mommy issues."

If Cruz thought he was tense before, it was nothing to how he felt now. Every muscle in his body clenched and it took everything he had not to jump the man and beat the shit out of him. Luckily, before he could do something stupid, Roach chimed in.

"Yeah, although you'll have to close your eyes. Heard she's short and fat. But I guess pussy is pussy, right? You could always do her doggy style, then you wouldn't have to look at her."

"I'm not fucking the sister because you want to get her out of the way," Cruz said shortly, forgetting for a second the role he was playing.

Ransom was out of the chair he'd been sitting in and had punched Cruz in the face before he could defend himself.

Cruz immediately picked himself off the floor, ignoring the throbbing coming from his face. Ransom threw a mean punch.

Knowing hitting the president of the club back was tantamount to suicide, Cruz controlled himself...barely. He clenched his teeth and bit back the angry response on the tip of his tongue.

Ransom sat back down as if he hadn't just punched Cruz. He calmly said, "If I tell you to fuck someone, you'll do it. Loyalty to One, or have you forgotten already? Don't think for a second, Smoke, I don't have my eyes on you. You're new here. I don't care if one of Snake's boys vouched for you. I don't trust anyone, and that goes double for prospects. I was only half kidding anyway. I don't think that bitch of a sister of Angel's even *likes* cock. She's probably a muffer."

Cruz forced himself to stay calm and not lose his shit. It was better Ransom thought Mickie was a lesbian. Maybe that way he wouldn't order any of the other members to get it on with her to keep her out of Angel's business. Cruz knew, as well as everyone standing around, that if Ransom ordered someone to fuck Mickie, they would, no questions asked, whether she was willing or not.

"I'm loyal, Ransom, but I'll find my own pussy, thank you very much."

"Just remember what I said, Smoke. You're loyal to *me*, or you'll be loyal to no one ever again."

Cruz nodded once and turned and left. As a threat, it was pretty impressive. Cruz knew that however this went down, he'd have to make damn sure Ransom and the rest of the club had no idea he was undercover. They'd spend the rest of their lives trying to take him down, along with anyone he cared about.

He couldn't handle being around anyone in the club anymore. Each day it was getting harder and harder, and now that he had the information he needed, Cruz hoped like hell his stint with the MC would be coming to an end.

After he spoke with his boss, he had to figure out how to make it up to Mickie. They'd had an incredible afternoon, and he prayed it hadn't been ruined with one short phone call.

Chapter Fourteen

————◆————

MICKIE BLEW HER nose and tried to think objectively about what had happened yesterday. She'd called in sick today, knowing there was no way she'd be able to deal with disgruntled customers complaining about how much it cost to fix their cars.

When she'd heard his friends during their call yesterday, it was obvious he'd told them all about what they'd done. Intellectually she knew men talked with each other about stuff…especially sex. But she hadn't expected Cruz to be as crude as he'd been.

The short conversation didn't make any sense with what she knew about him. He was in security. He had the initials of a long-ago murdered little girl on his arm. He told her he wanted to do what was right for the families of crime victims. It all was a confusing mash of memories in her brain. The man she'd spent the afternoon with didn't mesh with the one she'd talked to on the phone. Who would hang out with the kind of men who'd use such harsh language and brag about…fucking…loud enough for someone they didn't know on the other end of a phone line to hear? Were those the coworkers he was going to talk to about the MC?

But ultimately, it was Cruz's behavior that hurt her more than any words the other men had said. She'd thought they'd made an honest connection. She'd never been so uninhibited and passionate— and he'd gone and bragged about it.

He'd sounded so different, ugly. Mickie had never heard him talk to her in that tone of voice before. It made her feel…small.

Well, fuck him. She wasn't going to sit home and sniffle over him anymore. She wasn't taking any crap from a man ever again. She was worth more than that.

Mickie sighed. She knew it would take more than an internal pep-talk for her to get over Cruz. She'd really been falling for him. It was everything about him. He was funny, and interesting, and she'd never known a man so…amazing in bed. That wasn't really the word she was looking for, but it'd do. He'd been concerned about her, and only her. At least until the end and his own orgasm. But to have him make her explode that many times in one go? Incredible, and something she thought only happened in romance novels.

To be honest, she wasn't sure she'd liked Cruz's intensity at first. One orgasm was fine, great actually, but when he wouldn't let up, even when she'd told him she was too sensitive…it had been pleasurable, but in a somewhat painful way. She'd seen a video online once where a woman had been strapped down and her boyfriend, or whoever he was, had forced her to orgasm over and over with a vibrator. It had looked painful…and exhilarating. Mickie understood for the first time how that woman must've felt. Luckily, Cruz had stopped after four for her, but she had no illusions. He could've gone on all day.

No. She had to stop.

Mickie got up and took a deep breath. Then another. Fine. She could do this. She'd take a shower then go see Angel. She hadn't talked to her in a few days, so she'd stop in, find out what she was up to, and see if she'd found another job.

An hour later, Mickie was ready to go. She grabbed her purse and opened her door—and stopped dead in her tracks.

Seeing the box on her doorstep took her aback. She nudged it with her toe and felt that it wasn't heavy.

Mickie looked up and down the hallway to the apartment. No one was there. She sighed. It could be another way for the MC to try to scare her, she imagined a dead rat or something being inside, but since it had a large pink bow on it she figured it was most likely from Cruz. Mickie had no idea who else would leave her a present. She picked it up and brought it back inside her apartment. She debated about opening it before going to see Angel. Knowing she'd never been good at waiting, Mickie reached for the bow and pulled and tugged on the top of the box.

It came off easily and she looked inside. Sitting at the bottom was a metal police car. It wasn't anything special, and Mickie was more confused than ever. She picked up the note that was in the box and cautiously opened it.

I ain't fallin' for no banana in my tailpipe!
   I'm sorry. If you're willing to listen, I'd like to explain.
Cruz

Mickie looked back down at the police car. She picked it up and turned it around and laughed out loud. Cruz had stuck a rolled-up piece of yellow paper into the little tailpipe on the toy car. *Beverly Hills Cop.* The man was quoting "their" movie. Mickie held the car to her chest and squeezed her eyes shut. She would not cry. She would not cry. Taking a deep breath, Mickie opened her eyes and placed the car carefully back into the box. She read the note one more time and sighed.

She wanted more than anything to hear what explanation Cruz had for what had happened and what she'd heard, but first, she needed to check on Angel. After that, maybe she'd see what Cruz had to say.

Who was she kidding? Of course she'd hear what Cruz had to say about how he'd treated her and about the men he was hanging around with. She wanted, and deserved, an explanation. She might be an idiot for wanting to give him a second chance, but she'd never felt about anyone, even Troy, the way she felt about Cruz.

Mickie pulled up to her sister's apartment, got out of her car and walked up the outdoor stairs to her door, knocked once, and didn't get a response. Concerned, Mickie went to the end of the walkway and looked down into the parking lot. Angel's car was there, so she should be home. It was possible she'd been picked up by one of her friends to go shopping or something, but this early in the morning, it was unlikely.

She went back and knocked on the door again. Finally, after getting no response, she dug into her purse and pulled out an extra key to Angel's apartment. She'd almost forgotten she had it. She and Angel had exchanged keys a year or so ago, just in case.

Mickie pushed the door open and almost gagged at the stench of the apartment. She waved her hand in front of her face. Pot. Mickie would recognize the smell anywhere. She'd learned really quickly when Angel had been in high school what it smelled like.

Even more concerned now, Mickie walked quickly through the apartment, calling out for her sister. Mickie pushed open Angel's bedroom door and gasped at what she found.

Angel was on her bed, dressed in a black skirt so short it barely covered her womanly bits. She wasn't wearing a shirt, but instead had on a bra that covered almost nothing. She had bruises on her sides and around her breasts.

Mickie went to her sister's side and shook her shoulder, relieved beyond belief when she moaned and turned away from her touch.

"Angel, wake up. Are you okay?"

"Mickie? What the hell are you doing here?"

"I was worried about you. Come on, sit up."

"Leave me alone."

"No, now come on, let's get you up and at least dressed."

"I am dressed."

"Uh, no you aren't. You're missing your shirt."

"This *is* my shirt."

Mickie was horrified. "What?"

"This is what I wore last night at the club."

"Oh my God, Angel. What club let you in half dressed?"

"Ransom's."

"Okay, that's it. No fucking way. Come on, we're having this conversation now whether you want to or not. Get up, get a shower and we'll talk afterwards."

Instead of getting pissed, as Mickie completely thought would happen, Angel simply snorted. "You're so pathetic, Mickie. You're such a prude. Swear to fucking God. Okay, fine. I'll get up, take a shower, then we'll talk. Now leave me the fuck alone. I'll see you in the kitchen."

Mickie took a step back. Ouch. Okay, she knew Angel didn't have a lot of love for her, and she'd heard worse, but still. There was a part inside Mickie that hoped one day they could have a sisterly relationship, but as the years went by that was looking more and more unlikely.

"Okay, Angel. I'll wait in the other room."

"Whatever. Get the fuck out."

Mickie went.

Half an hour later, Angel came into the kitchen looking somewhat better than when Mickie had found her. She was wearing a tight pair of jeans and a white tank top. Her bra was black and Mickie could see it easily through the thin material of her tank. It was skanky and a bit slutty, but knowing she had to pick her battles carefully, Mickie ignored it for now.

Angel crossed the room and went straight to the pot of coffee Mickie had brewed and poured herself a cup. She sat in the chair across the table from Mickie and huffed belligerently while crossing her legs.

"So, you wanted to talk? Talk."

"I'm worried about you, Angel."

"Yeah? What's new? You never think I can do anything, you think I'm an idiot, and you don't trust me."

"That's not true."

"Yes. It is. But I'll tell you something, Mickie. I don't give a fuck anymore."

"Angel—"

"No. You came over here today to talk me out of seeing Ransom again. I know you did. I *like* Ransom. He makes me feel good. He's a good person. He does a lot of things for the community. He donates to charities for little kids and he even dresses up as Santa for the hospital. He's a lot of fun and he likes my friends. Not only that, but he fucks me hard and I *love* it."

"Angel!"

"What? You're a prude, Mickie. You're in your mid-thirties and you're way past your sexual prime. You have no idea what someone my age likes or wants."

"And you want to dress like a whore and hang out in strip clubs? Is that it? And smoking marijuana, Angel? That's what you want? You want to be a drug addict for the rest of your life? For the last time, Ransom is *not* into you. Let me guess, he's supplying you with weed, right? He keeps you high so you'll do stuff to him sexually? Oh, and let me go even further and guess that he's brought your friends into it too, right?"

Seeing the look on her sister's face, Mickie knew she was on the right track.

"That's it, isn't it? He used you to get to your friends. They're probably shelling out a ton of money to get weed, aren't they?" Mickie laughed with no humor. "I wonder when he's going to get enough of you...huh? Once he has all your friends hooked, he'll probably dump you. He won't need you anymore."

Angel suddenly stood up, knocking her chair backwards in the process. "Shut the fuck up! You don't know anything!"

Mickie sipped her coffee, trying to look unfazed on the outside, but internally she was freaking out. "I don't? How often have you seen him since your friends have been buying weed from him?"

Mickie wasn't happy with the look that crossed her sister's face. It was one thing to be right, and another to hurt your only sister in the process.

"For your information, I saw him last night, at his club. And tomorrow night he's invited me to his clubhouse for a big party."

"Uh-huh." Mickie's voice dripped with antagonism.

"And because you asked, smartass, he might have sold us weed and coke but that's not why he's still with me."

"What the *hell*, Angel?"

As if she didn't hear Mickie, Angel continued, "He's with me because I can suck his dick so good it makes his eyes roll back in his head. He taught me to deep throat him and he told me no one has ever been able to take him so deep before."

In a horrified voice, ignoring her last statement, Mickie whispered, "Coke, as in cocaine?"

"Yeah, as in cocaine. It's fucking awesome. It makes everything so much…more. If you didn't have such a stick up your ass I'd let you try it, but I know it'd be a waste of good blow."

"Are you even listening to yourself? My God, Angel. We weren't raised this way. You're using drugs, for God's sake!"

"Yeah, and I *like* it. You have no idea how it feels to have a man look at you like you're the best thing that's ever happened to him. To know that *you* were the one who satisfied him."

"I do know how it feels, Angel, and it didn't take drugs to make it happen."

"Bullshit. There's no way you felt with Troy anything like what me and Ransom have."

Mickie didn't even argue or try to explain that it wasn't Troy she'd felt it with, she had more important things to worry about.

"Angel, please, you know taking drugs isn't good. Let me help you."

"Help me? Jesus, Mickie. Get over yourself. I don't want your help, or *anyone's* help. I *like* the drugs. I *like* how I feel on them. Nothing you can say will change my mind."

"How about the effects of cocaine on your body then? Hallucinations, depression, psychosis, heart attacks, destruction of the lining of your nose, your teeth falling out, infertility or brain damage. That's just to name the things I can think of off the top of my head."

"Whatever. You've been watching too many public service announcements or something. I'm *fine*, sister of mine. I can stop whenever I want."

"That's what everyone says," Mickie said sadly.

"Well, I mean it. Now, get the fuck out. Oh, but give me your key first. I don't need any more surprise visits like this one. I feel like shit and I want to go back to sleep. There's that party tomorrow night that I want to make sure I'm in top shape for."

"Party?"

"Yeah, I told you. At the clubhouse. Shit, see? You don't listen to anything I say."

"Angel, you can't go."

Angel laughed in an incredibly mean way. "Watch me. Now give me my fucking key and get out. I don't want to see you again."

Mickie knew Angel well enough to know there was no use talking to her when she was like this. She sadly put the key to Angel's apartment on the table in front of her and stood up. "I love you, Angel. You're my only sister and I practically raised you. I only want what's best for you. I worry about you and I'd give my life for yours, no questions asked. But I can't stand watching you throw your life away. You're smarter than this. I know deep down you know what you're doing is not only wrong, but dangerous as well. Ransom is *not* a good guy. I'm sorry you can't see that, and I hope like hell you will before it's too late. But if not, even if it takes you years, I'm here for you. That's what family does."

"Oh for God's sake, seriously, get the fuck *out*. Don't pull that family bullshit with me. You've always thought you were better than me, and I'm sick of it."

Mickie shook her head sadly and turned to leave. She paused at the front door, hoping Angel would somehow come to her senses.

"Why aren't you gone yet?" Angel walked over to Mickie and pushed her...hard.

Mickie stumbled out the door and almost fell on her ass. When she regained her balance, she looked up at the pissed-off face of her sister. Mickie didn't even recognize the little girl she used to play Barbies with anymore. That girl was gone, and in her place was an out-of-control woman on the path to destruction.

Mickie winced at the loud bang of the door as it slammed shut. She heard the deadbolt click into place and the chain being put on.

Not willing to give up on Angel altogether, no matter that she'd just shoved her hard enough that if she'd fallen it would've really hurt, Mickie thought about what she could do to help her sister as she walked toward her car.

She stopped suddenly in the middle of the parking lot.

If she could get proof of how much of an asshole Ransom was, Angel would have to at least *listen* to her. She wouldn't like it, but maybe, just maybe it would work. It was a long shot, but Mickie didn't know of anything else she could do to get through to Angel.

She walked quickly to her car, trying to think through what she could do. It was dangerous; it wasn't like she was a secret agent. She knew she was acting a bit stupid, but it was either risk it or lose her sister altogether.

Mickie knew Angel was at a crossroads. She'd been serious when she'd told her sister that she'd die for her. She loved Angel. No matter how many harsh words she threw at her, Mickie knew deep down Angel loved her too.

She was betting on it.

Chapter Fifteen

————◆————

MICKIE READ THE text on her phone and sighed. It was the second time Cruz had texted her and she wasn't sure she was in the right frame of mind to listen to his excuses. Angel's words were still rattling around in her head. Her sister could always find just the right, or wrong, thing to say to hurt her the most. Mickie looked down at her phone.

I know you're still mad. Plze let me explain.

She quickly typed in a response to Cruz and threw the phone on the coffee table in front of her.

Today sucked. Can it wait until tomorrow?

Mickie closed her eyes and thought through her plan for tomorrow night. It was risky, but then again, so was what Angel was doing. She sighed as her cell vibrated with another text, most likely from Cruz.

Mickie leaned forward and snagged the phone, looking at the text. It was long, Mickie knew it would've taken Cruz forever to type it all out with the way he hunted and pecked on the keyboard screen.

Yeah. It can wait. But know this, I didn't talk about what we did with anyone. There's no way I could even come up with the words to even try to tell someone else what we did, how I felt with you in my arms. I know it's fast, and we still have a lot to learn about each other, but please don't doubt that yesterday was the most intense, beautiful experience of my entire life. I'll call you tomorrow. Sweet dreams.

"Oh my God." Mickie simply stared down at the screen of her phone in disbelief. Still whispering, she declared to the room, "He did not just say that."

Just when Mickie was ready to completely break things off with Cruz, he went and said something that had her wishing he was there with her right now. Was she being as blind as Angel? Was Cruz playing her as she thought Ransom was playing her sister? She honestly didn't think so, but she supposed it was possible. She hadn't met any of his friends, had only talked to the one woman on the phone during their first date at his place. And how did she even know Mack was really Mack? Maybe it was some skank he'd put up to it. Maybe everything he'd told her was made up…

Mickie sighed and put her phone down next to her hip and rested her head on the back of the couch. It was too much to think about right now. She hated doubting herself. She hated doubting Cruz. She so badly wanted him to be a good guy, but she was confused, and yes, still hurt by what she'd overheard. She'd let his words sink in and call him tomorrow.

As much as she was disappointed in what had happened last night, she wanted to hear what Cruz had to say. She sure hoped he had a good explanation. Even with all her confusion and doubt, she didn't want to give him up.

AFTER A RESTLESS night's sleep, which was full of erotic dreams about Cruz, and nightmares about Angel, Mickie got up and showered. She had to go to work, which sucked, but she'd taken the day before off and knew her boss would be pissed if she called off too many days in a row.

She went into the parking lot, relieved to see her car still had four functional tires, and drove to work, thinking all the way about what her next step was with Angel. Mickie headed for her desk, calling out greetings to the mechanics and other administrative employees as she went.

Generally, Mickie liked her job and her boss, but she had a ton of stuff she needed to do, and working wasn't one of them. Sometimes it sucked to be a responsible adult.

Mickie wished Cruz was at the top of her list, but he wasn't. She had to figure out how to show Angel that Ransom was an asshole. Then she had to figure out how to convince Angel that she needed to get off of the drugs she was using and get her into rehab, if she needed it. Once she had that worked out, she could concentrate on Cruz and their relationship.

And that was the thing…Mickie had thought they *had* a relationship, but now she wasn't so sure. Was she a one-night stand to Cruz? Did he really care about seeing her again, or did he merely want to explain why he'd been so cold on the phone the other night and move on? Mickie sighed. She had no idea.

She settled into her chair at her desk while her mind was going a million miles an hour. Mickie started jotting her ideas down on a sticky note from her desk on what she was going to do that night. Angel was going to the Red Brothers' clubhouse for a party? Then so was she. It was a free country. If Angel could party with the MC, so could Mickie.

The phone rang. Mickie took a deep breath to get back into the proper head space for work, and answered.

OKAY, MICKIE KNEW she was officially crazy. She was standing in her apartment, looking at herself in the mirror. After work, she'd gone straight to the mall and to one of the stores she normally wouldn't ever think about shopping in. It had leather and spikes and all sorts of other clothing that teenagers might wear. Mickie knew if she was going to crash a party at a motorcycle club, she'd better at least try to look like she fit in.

She decided on a pair of jeans that were too tight, but she'd managed to squeeze herself into a size ten. The denim hugged her ass and her thighs and actually didn't look too bad, if Mickie did say so herself. The jeans were cut so that the extra weight she carried around her waist didn't spill over the top. They were so low, Mickie kept looking back to make sure her ass crack wasn't showing. It wasn't. Barely.

The top was harder to decide on. Mickie figured black was the safest color to wear, and so she'd bought a push-up bra that literally squeezed her boobs together higher than they'd ever been squeezed before, and a short-sleeved shirt that had mesh on the upper part and was solid below.

Mickie tilted her head and eyed herself critically. This was the most provocative thing she'd ever worn, and to think she was going to wear it to a party where there were drugs, bikers and, most likely, prostitutes, was completely unbelievable.

She wiped her sweaty hands down her thighs. The deep vee of the shirt's plunging neckline showcased her breasts in the tight bra. The mesh was actually really sexy and allowed her to show off her boobs, while the regular material hid her less-than-flat belly.

Mickie snorted. As if anyone would be able to look at anything other than her boobs. They were hard to ignore in the outfit. Her C-cup breasts were looking more like double D's.

Mickie took a deep breath and immediately regretted it. She actually watched in the mirror as her nipple popped over the top of the bra and got stuck in the mesh that was covering it. She giggled nervously, and adjusted herself so she was adequately covered again. She made a mental note. *No deep breathing.*

Mickie had spiked her short hair up and even added a streak of pink along the side with temporary dye. She had no desire to walk around looking like a punk rocker after the night was over. She felt like enough of an abnormality as it was, but if she came to work with that bright-pink streak, her boss would have a heart attack.

She had applied makeup to her eyes with a heavy hand. Her mascara and eyeliner were caked on and she had eye shadow up to her eyebrows. Hating lipstick, but knowing it'd complete the look, Mickie had chosen a dark-red shade that even she had to admit made her look mysterious, and yes, sexy even. Mickie thought she looked about as ready as she was going to.

The last thing she needed was her phone. Mickie didn't have any kind of special recording devices that women always seemed to have access to in the movies and television shows. It'd be handy to have a pin or something she could wear that would record everything she saw, but since she was flying by the seat of her pants here, and not dating James Bond, she'd have to rely on her cell phone, which was kind of a crapshoot.

She set it to the camera mode and clicked it to video. She'd practiced the best place to stash it and finally settled on her back pocket. The jeans were so tight it would keep the phone still, and Mickie could put it halfway in her pocket and it would stick up enough so the lens cleared the material. Then all she had to do was turn around and face away from whatever she wanted to film and voila!

Mickie's phone vibrated in her hand, scaring the shit out of her. She laughed nervously and saw it was another text from Cruz. He'd been texting her all day, and Mickie had mostly ignored him. She could tell he was getting impatient with her though.

You gonna call?

Mickie's fingers flew over the screen in response.

Tomorrow

Why not now?

I've got something I have to do

What?

Something

Mickie, I hate this

Mickie closed her eyes. She hated it too. But she had to get through tonight. At first she thought showing up at one of the motorcycle club parties and getting evidence for Angel that Ransom wasn't a good person, would convince Angel to break up with him once and for all. But almost as soon as she had the thought, she dismissed it. Angel knew he was doing things he shouldn't be, and unfortunately Mickie knew in her heart Angel was doing some of those bad things right along with him.

So her plan to "save her sister" morphed into something different. If she could get evidence of Ransom doing drugs, or selling it, or hell, even soliciting a prostitute, maybe she could get him arrested. If he was in jail, he couldn't be around her sister. He'd get out eventually, but maybe it would be a while and in the meantime she could get Angel away from the club and the lifestyle. Mickie was afraid she was losing her sister too.

I'll call you tomorrow

Ok. I have a thing I have to do tonight, but I'll call you in the morning and we'll talk. I'll tell you everything.

A thing?

Yeah. A security job. I'll call you early. Maybe we can get some lunch or something.

Ok

There was so much more Mickie wanted to ask, but she didn't

have the time and didn't want to do it over text anyway.

Her phone vibrated once more, but it wasn't a text from Cruz this time. It was Li. Mickie had called her and gotten Angel's friend to agree to take her to the party that night. She had to pretend to be interested in the MC lifestyle and the drugs she'd be able to get in order for Li to finally agree to take her, but Mickie was apparently a better actress than she'd thought, because after only a short while, Li had agreed. Even though Mickie had never hung out with Li before, she'd seen her several times and Li had been pleasant to her. Whatever Angel's faults were, she obviously wasn't constantly talking about her annoying older sister to her friends. Which worked well in Mickie's favor at the moment.

Here

Be right down

Remembering not to take a deep breath, Mickie once more turned to her reflection in the mirror. She almost didn't recognize herself. Angel would be pissed when she saw her there tonight, but it was for her sister's own good.

Mickie ran her index finger over the metal police car she'd put on her kitchen counter and smiled at the fake banana in the tailpipe. Cruz had a good sense of humor and she hoped they'd get to further explore what they had together.

She gripped her phone in her hand, stuffed her license and some bills into her back left pocket and headed out. She locked her door and then looked up and down the hall. Seeing no one, she awkwardly knelt in her tight jeans and put her key under her mat. Not the safest thing to do, but it'd work for tonight. Better than trying to keep track of a purse or putting the key in her pocket and risking losing it.

Mickie stood up and headed to Li's car. This would work. It *had* to work.

CRUZ RAN HIS hand over his head and cursed. Mickie was still pissed at him and he hadn't been able to talk to her yet. He'd wanted to talk to her before the party tonight, but she'd been at work for most of the day, and then she'd flatly refused to let him explain after. Cruz knew something was up, but he had too much other shit going down to be able to devote his complete attention to Mickie. As much as he hated that, it was true.

After the meeting with Axel the other night, and learning Chico Malo was the supplier behind Axel and the Red Brothers, Cruz had contacted his boss at the FBI. Knowing there was another large party at the clubhouse, which would be a great distraction, the takedown was planned for that night.

After the party got started, the FBI, with assistance from the Texas Rangers and SAPD, would surround the warehouse and take down Ransom and the rest of the members of the club. It was a huge operation, especially because of the amount of MC members that would be at the party and the danger involved.

Cruz didn't like it. He knew Angel would be there tonight, along with her friends, not to mention the old ladies and club whores. There were so many things that could go wrong; it was almost a suicide mission to try to take down the club as quickly as the FBI was moving, but it was out of Cruz's hands. He was somewhat surprised at the speed of the operation, but also secretly thrilled. The FBI had been after Chico Malo for a long time, and the connection between the Red Brothers and the Mexican drug lord was an added bonus to the op.

Cruz didn't care why they were mobilizing so quickly, just that they were. The sooner he could end this mission, the faster he could come clean with Mickie and see if she'd be able to forgive him. He hoped they could continue their relationship after everything was out in the open, but he'd even be willing to start from scratch if that's what she needed.

The plan was for the agency to take Cruz into custody along with the rest of the club, to try to alleviate suspicion that he was undercover. Once the dust had settled and everyone had been hauled off for interrogation and incarceration, Cruz would be able to sneak out and disappear.

This was the biggest party Ransom had thrown with Angel and her friends since he'd started playing her. Bubba had been busy supplying all of her friends with both weed and cocaine. The women had begun to contact Bubba themselves, instead of going through Angel. Ransom's plan had worked like a charm, and he no longer needed to keep stringing Angel along. He had her friends right where he wanted them, and she wasn't necessary anymore.

Cruz knew Ransom was planning on getting rid of Angel at some point during the party that night. He'd had enough of her "hanging on him" and was cutting her loose. He planned to make it very clear if she retaliated by taking her friends with her when she left, she'd regret it.

He was glad, on one hand, that Ransom was going to finally make the break with Angel, but didn't like to think about what Roach or any of the other members would do afterwards. Cruz was sure they were all dying to get their hands on her. If she was high on cocaine when Ransom scraped her off, there was no telling what she'd do to try to get back at him.

Cruz sighed. His "simple" undercover operation was anything but. It was fucked up ten ways to Sunday and all he wanted to do was hide in his apartment, in his bed, with Mickie.

"What's up your ass, Smoke?" Camel demanded, walking into the large room. "Still pissed you can't tap any of that?" He gestured to the other side of the room where Ransom was currently taking one of the club whores—Cruz thought her name was Billie—up the ass while several other members stood around with their gazes locked on the tableau in front of them, waiting for their president to finish so they could take their turn with the coked-out whore.

"Fuck no. Just ready for the party to start." Cruz took a swig of the beer he'd been nursing for a while and waited for Camel's response.

"Word is some of the prospects will be voted in tonight."

Cruz knew Camel was fucking with him. He simply nodded.

"What? Not curious if it's gonna be you? Don't you want it?"

Playing his part, Cruz answered, "Fuck yeah, I want it. Wouldn't fucking be here if I didn't. But me wanting it means dick. Ransom'll let me in when he wants to and not a second before."

Camel nodded in agreement and approval. "Got that shit right."

"When're the bitches getting here?" Cruz was hoping Angel's friends would be late and wouldn't get caught in the raid.

"Around an hour I think. You hear we have a special guest tonight?"

Cruz turned to him. He didn't know what the man was talking about. "Nope." Hoping his lack of questioning would make Camel open up more, Cruz held his breath.

"Yeah, the fucking Bad Boy himself will be here tonight."

Fucking hell. "Chico Malo?"

"Yup. Heard he was all pissed off at Ransom and his demands. They had some words and the prick decided to head up here himself to see what the fuss was all about. Apparently he and Ransom had a heart-to-heart and they're all buddy-buddy now. Ransom invited him to check out the new rich pussy we've got and to show him why we need more blow."

It was the most Cruz had heard Camel say at one time. He needed to get ahold of Dax and let him know the shit had just hit the fan, big time. It was quicker and easier to contact his friend, and Cruz knew Dax would pass the information on to the FBI and the rest of the team. Having Chico Malo at the compound when they were just expecting to take down Ransom and the club members was fucking huge. It upped the danger factor by a hundred and ten percent—but it would also make their job a hell of a lot easier if Chico Malo was indeed here in their territory and not hiding behind his evil minions across the border. Of course, it'd only be easier if Chico didn't bring his army of thugs with him to the party though.

"Fuckin' A. It's gonna be a hell of a party." Cruz lifted his bottle to Camel in a toast.

"Fuck yeah, it is," Camel responded, then drifted off toward the gang bang that was now happening in the corner of the warehouse.

Cruz stood leaning against the makeshift bar, trying to look as nonchalant as possible. He had a bit of time before the task force would be heading out. He couldn't bring attention to himself. He had to hang out and wait. Discreetly pulling out his undercover cell, he shot off a text to Dax. No one seemed to notice or care what he was doing, since a cheer went up in the corner of the room as Billie whipped off her bra and did an impromptu strip tease.

Cruz observed more people entering the large room. Slowly but surely it was getting more and more crowded. It looked like the entire MC had shown up for the special party. Dixie and Bambi were there, along with some of the stripper whores from the club. The alcohol was flowing and, at least for the old ladies and the whores, the drugs were as well.

He couldn't help but watch Dixie swallow Ransom's cock as soon as she was led to him. She knew the score. To get drugs, she had to service the president, but she wasn't able to get him off before he threw her away from him and ordered Bambi to bend over the arm of the couch.

Cruz had to give the man one thing, he was always able to get hard. He had no idea how he did it, but he watched for the second time that night as Ransom fucked a whore in front of his MC as they cheered him on.

Finally, Ransom pulled out and jacked himself off all over Bambi's back. She looked at him and smirked. Cruz observed Ransom slapping her on the ass then reaching into his pocket. He pulled out a small baggie and threw it onto the cushion in front of her.

Bambi didn't bother pulling her skirt over her naked ass before she snatched up the bag of drugs. She hurried over to a small table, fell to her knees in front of it and opened the bag. She poured the white powder out on the glass tabletop and immediately leaned over to snort it. She pushed away another one of the women who had come in with her when she tried to horn in on her stash. The woman fell back on her ass as the club members laughed.

Vodka hauled the second woman up with a hand on her neck. He leaned down and said something to her, most likely promising her own stash of drugs if she took him. She nodded enthusiastically, turned away from him, bent and grabbed her ankles, readying herself to be taken.

Meanwhile, as Vodka unzipped his pants, preparing himself to take her right there, Bambi was getting screwed by Tick as she leaned over to snort another line of the cocaine Ransom had given her, not even caring who was behind her fucking her.

Apparently the party had officially started.

Another hour passed and the members got rowdier and rowdier. The old ladies weren't passed around as the whores were, but the members had no problem taking their women in the main room in front of everyone. Even though the old ladies were respected, mostly, by the members of the club, they weren't treated well by any stretch of the imagination. They were expected to fetch drinks for the men, clean up, take the club whores to task when the men decided they needed it, and to service their men whenever and however they wanted.

Eventually, Angel's friends started arriving. Each time one walked into the room, one of the club members would intercept her and take her to the other side of the warehouse, away from the gang bangs, and get her to snort a few lines of coke. It was obviously all planned out in advance. They'd then pass her a joint and a shot of tequila and settle her into a tamer part of the clubhouse, away from the orgy but still in sight of it.

The club needed the money from the women, but they weren't willing to tone down their lifestyle in the long run. There was a better chance of the women accepting it if they were high than if they weren't. Ransom was hoping the high they got from the drugs was enough for them to overlook the harsher aspects of club life.

Cruz kept Angel's friends in his sights as they started floating from all the drugs and alcohol they'd ingested in such a short period of time. The looks in their eyes reminded him too much of Sophie and how she'd looked at him the last time he'd seen her. He'd gone down to the police station after his friend, Quint, had called him and let him know she'd been arrested for prostitution, again.

He'd wanted to try one more time to get her some help. She'd looked up at him and smirked. "Hey, Cruzie. You here to get me out? Want to party?"

He'd simply shaken his head, asked Quint not to tell him when she was arrested again, and left.

Cruz was sipping his beer when the door to the warehouse opened. He saw Angel's Asian friend—he couldn't remember her name—enter the space, along with another woman, one he hadn't seen before. She was curvy and sexy as all get out. Cruz's gaze went from her hips and chest, up to her face—and he almost choked on the beer he'd been about to swallow.

Roach and Steel sauntered over to the duo and each took hold of their arms and steered them to the other side of the room, as the other members had done with all of Angel's friends.

Cruz's feet were moving before his brain could fully comprehend what he was seeing. He recognized the sway of those hips, the short black hair that brushed against her neck, now with a pink streak along the side...the wide-eyed look of innocence in her eyes.

Fuck. It was Mickie, and she'd just walked straight into hell. They were both fucked.

Chapter Sixteen

MICKIE TRIED NOT to hyperventilate as the meanest man she'd ever seen took hold of her arm in a grasp she knew she couldn't break, and steered her toward a corner of the large room. She'd only been able to catch a glimpse of the area before she'd been hauled off, but she knew what she'd seen would haunt her forever.

There were women bent over pieces of furniture all over the left side of the room. Most were completely naked, while some were still wearing some sort of top, but all were being fucked. None were struggling, but none were actually participating either. They just lay there, or stood there, as someone pumped into them. Mickie also noticed, in the quick glimpse she'd had, that there were men waiting to take their turn with the women. They had their dicks out and were cheering their buddies on as they waited.

The music was loud, and the stench in the room was eye-watering. Body odor, alcohol, weed, smoke, and who the hell knew what else.

Mickie had regretted her stupid decision to come as soon as they'd pulled up. Li had tried to reassure her, but Mickie knew in her gut she'd made a horrible mistake. There was no way she'd be able to covertly film whatever was going on inside the warehouse. She was an idiot.

She'd tried to get Li to let her take her car home, promising to come back and get her whenever she was ready, but Li refused, saying that no one was allowed to drive her car, but her.

Li had driven them to a part of San Antonio Mickie had always avoided like the plague. It was industrial and notorious for always being on the nightly news because of the area's high crime rate. The music was loud even outside the building, and there were no lights on. The parking lot had been pitch-black, and only the light from the small flashlight on Li's keychain had illuminated the concrete as they'd walked to the side entrance of the building.

Mickie tried to wrench her arm out of the hold of the man who was propelling her forward, with no luck. She started panicking—but then heard the last voice she ever thought she'd hear in this hellhole.

"Let the fuck go, Roach, I got this one."

"Fuck off, Smoke. I got to her first. She's mine. When I'm done with her, you can take your turn."

"I said, let go."

"Fuck you. These tits and ass are all mine tonight."

Cruz didn't bother arguing, he simply hit Roach in the face with everything he had.

Roach fell with a thud, and didn't move. Cruz had knocked him out with one punch. No one put their hands on Mickie except for him.

"Wh—"

With the punch, Cruz knew he now had the attention of most of the club members so he had to play the next few minutes exactly right or they'd both be dead. Cruz cut Mickie off and grabbed her arm in the same place Roach had. "Shut the fuck up. Let's go."

Mickie kept her mouth shut. Cruz was pissed and she was scared out of her mind. She had no idea why the other man had called him Smoke, but she knew she was in deep shit. But when all was said and done, she'd rather Cruz have a hold of her than any other man in the place.

Cruz hauled Mickie over to a table covered in white powder. He had no idea how he was going to get through the next few minutes, but knew it was critical they both keep their cool. He couldn't screw this up now. Not when they were so close to shutting everything down.

Dax and the FBI knew Chico Malo was in play and they'd be at the compound within the hour, as planned.

Cruz brought them to a halt in front of one of two small tables and held his hand out to Steel. "Bag."

"Never known you to take such a liking to pussy before."

"Yeah, well, look at it." Cruz gestured to Mickie's tits crudely. "You blame me?"

Apparently it was the right thing to say, because Steel laughed. "Fuck no. I, myself, like Asian pussy." He put his hand over Li's crotch and stroked harshly, ignoring her nervous giggle. "It's smaller and tighter…but can't deny your taste is good."

"Thank you," Cruz ground out. "Bag," he demanded again.

Steel pulled a small bag filled with coke out of his back pocket and tossed it to Cruz. He caught it with one hand and kept the other tightly around Mickie's arm. He felt her squirm next to him and try to pull away from his grasp. "Stay still," he ordered gruffly, opening the bag with one hand.

Cruz could feel the sweat beading at his temple. Fuck. He kept Steel in his peripheral vision; he was bent over Angel's friend, his hand at her breast and his mouth at her ear. Cruz didn't waste any time. He stepped so that he was between the two small tables and, more importantly, blocking Steel's view of Mickie.

Mickie's heart was racing a million miles an hour. She couldn't believe Cruz was here, and had spoken about her so crudely to the other biker. She almost didn't recognize him. He had on boots with enough chains on them to set up a swing set. His chest was bare and he was wearing a leather vest that was open in the front. He was frowning and had at least a day-old beard that made him look scary as hell and Mickie was quickly putting two and two together.

All the times he'd asked about Angel, how he'd magically shown up right after Mickie had argued with her sister. He'd played her. Apparently he was a member of the same MC she'd bitched about all those times they were together. He wasn't going to talk to his coworkers about the club…he was a *part* of it.

She was the dumbest woman on the face of the earth and she was going to pay for her stupidity big time.

Cruz's voice interrupted her mental flogging. It was only slightly less harsh than a few seconds ago. "I'm going to put two lines on the table. When I push you down, breathe out slowly and blow lightly without pursing your lips. It'll spread the powder out to look like you snorted it. Whatever you do, don't inhale."

Cruz didn't wait for her acquiescence. He poured two short, thin lines of cocaine on the table and closed the baggie and tucked it into his pocket. He put his hand on the back of Mickie's neck and forced her over the table roughly, or at least what he hoped looked rough to Steel and anyone else who might be watching.

He'd put his free hand against her hip, and when he pushed her against the table, he moved the hand just enough so the table bit into his hand instead of her skin. "Snort it, bitch. That's it. You know you came here just for that shit."

Cruz let out a relieved breath when he saw Mickie doing just as he'd demanded. She didn't struggle against him, simply breathed gently on the line of cocaine and it dissipated amongst the other powder residue on the table. She put on a good show, moving her head and cupping her hand as if she was actually snorting the drug. If Cruz hadn't been watching carefully, he would've been fooled.

He wrenched her upward when the lines were gone and hooked her around the neck and backwards, until she was clutching his biceps, much as she'd done the other night as he'd pounded into her. She was arched over his arm, completely at his mercy. Cruz didn't give her a chance to say anything, but covered her lips with his and drove his tongue into her mouth roughly. With the way he was feeling, there was no way he could be gentle.

Cruz kissed Mickie with all the pent-up frustration, worry, and stress he had within him. Even with their situation, and how pissed he was at her for putting herself in the middle of a fucked-up motorcycle club party that was about to get raided by no less than three different state and federal agencies, the kiss quickly turned carnal. Mickie didn't lie in his arms docilely, she gave as good as she got. It was as if the danger surrounding them gave their attraction an extra edge. Their tongues intertwined and they sucked and nipped at each other as they relearned the taste and texture of each other's mouths.

Hearing Steel clapping behind him, and coming to his senses, Cruz finally lifted his head and stared into Mickie's eyes, keeping her immobile in his arms, hanging backwards. There was so much he wanted to say to her, so many things he needed to say, but now wasn't the time or the place. All it would take was one wrong word and they'd both be fucked.

Cruz finally whipped Mickie upright. Keeping his arm around her neck, Cruz turned to Steel. "Fuck yeah," was all he said.

Steel laughed and looked at Mickie's chest as he roughly grabbed Li's breast and squeezed. "When you're done with those titties, I'll take a taste for myself. I might like Asian pussy, but their tits leave something to be desired."

Cruz looked down and cursed under his breath. Mickie's nipples had popped over the top of her low-cut bra and were poking through the mesh tank top she had on. The sight was erotic, and Cruz wanted to gut Steel for looking at what was his.

Mickie looked at herself and gasped. Obviously being held over Cruz's arm had been too much for the miniscule material of her bra. She was totally flashing the scary man standing with Li, and everyone else for that matter. She brought a hand up to cover herself, but Cruz grabbed it and squeezed her fingers tightly. She held back a gasp.

"I don't think I'll be done with these tits for a while, Steel. Sorry." Cruz held Mickie's hand in his own and turned her away from Steel and his fucking eyes.

"I know, Mickie. I know. Hang on, I'll cover you in a second," Cruz whispered the words as he leaned down to her chest to put on a show for the guys sitting in the corner with the other women. He licked up the side of Mickie's neck and nibbled on her earlobe.

"Throw your head back and put one of your hands on the back of my head."

When Mickie hesitated, Cruz ordered curtly, "For Christ's sake, Mickie. If you want to fucking live to see another day, do it. I'm not going to hurt you."

Cruz felt her hand timidly rest on the back of his head, and he died inside as he felt her fingers trembling against him. Deciding to cut this little tête-à-tête short, he moved his head to her chest. Pretending to nuzzle against her, he grabbed the edge of her bra through the mesh with his teeth and pulled it up and over her nipple, covering her again. He did the same to the other side, making her at least mostly decent once again.

He lifted his head and refused to look at her. Cruz couldn't bear to see the disgust in Mickie's eyes. If he could get her out of this fucked-up situation in one piece, he'd take her hatred. He should've prepared for this. He'd known Mickie was scared for her sister. She'd even flat-out suggested that she do something crazy to help Angel...this was certainly that. Fucking hell.

Mickie tried to control her breathing. From the second she'd entered the warehouse, she'd been off kilter. From the sounds and what she'd seen on the other side of the room, to the big scary man grabbing her, then seeing Cruz there and him acting so weird...it was all so overwhelming.

Just when she'd thought she'd been completely wrong about Cruz, she'd finally figured it out.

She'd thought he was going to force her to snort the drugs on the table, but he hadn't. Then when he'd cushioned her against the table with his hand as he'd shoved her, and finally just now, when he'd covered her so she wasn't flashing everyone, she understood what was really going on. At least she thought she did.

No matter what she heard, Cruz's actions toward her were telling. Cruz was in security, he had a "thing" that night, he hated drugs… While she might not like the words he was using, or how he outwardly treated her, she got it. He *had* to be undercover—and Mickie swore not to do anything to fuck it up for him.

If he wasn't undercover, he was actually a member of this club, but thinking back to everything she'd learned about him…after seeing where he lived…she didn't think that was the case. She didn't like that he'd obviously lied to her, but at the moment, all she cared about was getting out of there in one piece. She'd talk to him later and learn just how much he'd lied about. But as of right now, he was the only thing standing between her and her worst nightmare. She'd keep her mouth shut no matter how awful things got.

For the first time since entering the building, Mickie relaxed. Cruz was here. He'd make sure nothing happened to her. He was one of the good guys, she was betting her life on it.

She glanced around quickly, inwardly wincing at the actions on the other side of the room. She didn't see Angel anywhere, which relieved her, but also freaked her out as well. What if she was in a backroom doing something worse than what was happening out here in the open? No, she refused to believe that. Angel always liked to make a grand entrance, she was most likely trying to be fashionably late or something.

Cruz led Mickie over to the tamer side of the room. He kept his arm around her neck and put one hand low on her ass. There were no open seats, so he simply leaned against the wall and pulled Mickie into his side. He kept her head pushed against his chest. He knew she'd be able to hear his heart beating way too fast, but Cruz didn't give a shit.

"Hey, Smoke," Tiny called from a nearby chair. "Didn't think you were into club pussy, man. Wanna swap when you're done? I'd love to bury myself between those fat thighs—"

"Shut the fuck up, Tiny," Cruz growled, tightening his arm around Mickie's waist. "I'm not fucking swapping. She's mine until I'm done with her, and I don't fucking share."

Tiny just smirked. "All right, but when you get sick of that, you can have some of this." Tiny pulled down the shirt of the woman who was sitting on his lap until her breast was exposed, and he squeezed so hard everyone could see his fingers turn white with the pressure. The woman yelped and squirmed against him futilely.

Cruz felt Mickie shift uneasily next to him. "Turn your head, hon. Don't look." His words were muffled and gruff...and tortured.

They all looked to the door when it opened once more. Angel strode into the room as if she were the Queen of England and there wasn't a drug-filled orgy going on in front of her eyes. No one stepped up to greet her and she looked around for Ransom.

Mickie tried to pull out of Cruz's arms, but he tightened his hold on her. He wouldn't let her look up at him. "Stay the fuck still. If she recognizes you, we're both fucked."

Mickie held her breath and stared at the scene unfolding in front of her, her heart breaking.

Angel kept searching the room until she found Ransom. He was on the other side of the space, where his club members were screwing the strippers and whores. He was sitting on a couch with two women kneeling in front of him. His pants were around his thighs and the women were taking turns sucking him off, as they, in turn, were being hammered from behind by two other men.

Ransom smirked at Angel and lifted a hand and crooked his finger at her. As if planned, and it probably was, the music abruptly stopped. Besides the sound of sex echoing around the room, it was fairly quiet.

Angel hesitantly walked over to Ransom.

"You want this? On your knees, bitch. Suck me."

"But, Ransom…I don't understand."

"What don't you understand?"

"I thought, we…you… I'm your girlfriend."

"Girlfriend?" Ransom threw his head back and laughed. He held one of the women down over his cock as she deep-throated him. She began to gag, but he still held her. "I don't have fucking girlfriends. What do you think this is, high school?"

He let up on the woman and she pulled her head off him with a gasp, saliva and pre-come dripping from her mouth. Ransom pushed her away and reached for the other woman's neck. He forced her head down on his cock and held her there as he had the first woman.

Angel continued to stand in front of him as if in a trance. It was as though she couldn't believe what she was seeing.

"Why would I want to tie myself to one woman when I can have all of this?" Ransom flung out a hand to encompass the room. "You were a nice change of pace for me, but you were just a fuck, Angel. You'll always be just a fuck. Now be a good girl and go join your friends. Snort some coke, but don't forget to pay for it first, then see if you can find one of my brothers willing to fuck you. I'm sure they'll line up for the chance. After all, they've heard from me what a tight cunt you have."

Ransom allowed the second woman to come up and off his dick, and she coughed harshly as she too gulped in air. Ransom gestured to Angel, "Unless you want to come sit on my dick and get me off first? I'll take that pussy any day of the week."

"Are you kidding me? I'm not going to fuck you after you've probably had your dick in these whores' cunts." Angel's words were acidic.

Ransom laughed mercilessly. "Bitch, there's no 'probably' about it. If you think yours was the only pussy I was getting, you're delusional. I fuck whoever I want, whenever I want, and don't give a shit what *you* want. I like your money. I like your rich friends' money. I like your pussy, ass, and throat around my cock, but honestly, I don't give a shit whose hole my cock is in as long as I get off."

The music started up again after Ransom's harsh words and people went back to what they were doing before his little show.

Everyone laughed as Angel spun away from Ransom and headed to the other side of the room as if she didn't know where she was going. Roach had picked himself up off the floor where he'd landed when Cruz had punched him, and was quick to get to Angel's side to comfort her. Ransom merely leaned back on the couch, smiling as one of the completely naked strippers came up to him and offered to sit on his dick and finish him off.

Mickie mumbled into Cruz's chest, "I need to go to her." She really didn't want to go anywhere at the moment. Cruz's arms made her feel safe in a definitely unsafe world. Even if he agreed, Mickie wasn't sure her feet would be able to move.

"Fuck no."

Mickie squirmed against Cruz, thankful for his answer but feeling guilty nonetheless. "Please?"

"No."

"Problem, Smoke?" Steel asked from a chair nearby. He had Li on his lap and his hand was buried under her skirt. Her eyes were closed and her head was thrown back, obviously enjoying Steel's attention.

"No problem. Bitch just needs a firm hand." Cruz grabbed the back of Mickie's neck and let go of her waist enough so he could bend her over. He held her there with his hand holding her still and the other planted in the middle of her back. He pushed his foot between her legs and spread them so they were shoulder-width apart.

She was completely helpless in his grasp. Her head was parallel with the ground now and Cruz leaned over to furiously whisper in her ear.

"Stop it right fucking now. In case you haven't noticed, we're in deep shit here. Keep your mouth shut. Angel can take care of herself. *You're* my concern right now, not your sister. You can help her tomorrow. Do what I tell you, *when* I fucking tell you, and don't bring any more attention to us. Got it?"

Mickie tried to nod, but couldn't. She sobbed once, but ruthlessly held it back. Even though Cruz had a tight hold on her, he wasn't hurting her. His words were mean and harsh, but he was exactly right. Mickie held no illusions about what would happen if someone, anyone, figured out what Cruz was doing there.

Cruz whipped her upright and pulled her into his embrace again, her head shoved against the top of his chest. He held her against him with a hand on the back of her neck and his fingers digging into her side.

"You need any help with that, just let me know," Steel commented dryly. "But it seems you have a good handle on her."

"Yeah. I got this. She's just got to learn to do what I fucking want her to do."

The other MC members laughed, high-fived, and agreed.

When the attention of most of the members went back to the women they were fondling or to their drinks, Cruz relaxed a fraction. Fuck, that had been close. He didn't know what time it was, but watching Ransom push the naked woman off his lap after he came, and pull up his pants, Cruz figured it was about time Chico Malo showed. There was no other reason for Ransom to make himself presentable.

Roach had steered Angel over to the tables covered in coke residue and encouraged her to snort six lines of the stuff. It was way too much, but Angel obviously wanted to forget what she'd just seen and heard, and was just stubborn enough not to leave the party altogether. After she'd snorted the drugs, and downed two shots of tequila, Roach took her to the other side of the room, away from her friends. Cruz figured she went with it because she was trying, unsuccessfully, to make Ransom jealous. The second they were seated, Roach had one hand on her crotch and the other on her breast, but Angel's eyes never left Ransom.

Just as Cruz was working through his head how he could get Mickie the hell out of there before everything went down, the door opened. A tall, slender Hispanic man entered the room, followed by at least ten other men.

Chico Malo had arrived—and all hopes of safely getting Mickie out of the middle of a turf war between a pissed-off Mexican drug lord and a cocky motorcycle club president disappeared like a puff of smoke.

As the door shut behind Chico Malo and his thugs, Cruz could only silently pray Dax and the rest of the task force would get there sooner rather than later.

Chapter Seventeen

———— ♦ ————

"**W**ELCOME TO MY club!" Ransom boomed, striding to greet Chico Malo before he made it too far into the room.

Three men moved so they were standing in front of their boss, preventing Ransom from getting too close to him.

"What's all this? Can't I greet a friend in my own club?"

"Stay back," one of the bodyguards growled, putting his hand on the butt of the gun in his waistband.

"Come on, Chico! Look around. Look at how much fun is being had. You want a woman? A smoke? A drink? Name it and it's yours."

Taking Ransom at his word, the drug kingpin slowly looked around the room. The music had been turned down after his arrival, but the strippers were still undulating against the poles that had been erected for the party, their eyes glassy, and bodies moving to the music. There were a few MC members passed out around the room and more not even bothering to pause their screwing of the club whores to greet the newcomer.

Chico Malo's gaze roamed to the other side of the room where Angel's friends were huddled with various members of the club. His eyes went to each woman, and Cruz's stomach clenched when they stayed on Mickie's ass a bit too long for his taste.

"¿Qué es esto?" Chico Malo asked, gesturing toward the right side of the room, obviously noticing the difference in the caliber of women on that side.

"Glad you asked," Ransom smirked. "That's the high-class pussy side of the room. See, this here's the reason we need to up our stakes in the market. These bitches have money to spend, and they want to spend it on my cocaine. You like what you see? Help yourself. My brothers would be glad to share."

Chico Malo looked back to Ransom and raised an eyebrow.

"Yeah, take your pick. It's the least I can do for a gentleman like yourself. And you know what, if we continue to do business together, you can have all the high-class pussy you want, whenever you want it."

"You don't think I can get it on my own?" Chico Malo growled. "You don't think we have high-class Mexican pussy?" His words were ground out in obvious irritation, his accent making the words seem caustic and biting.

"No, no, I didn't mean that. I just thought that maybe you'd like to partake in American high-class pussy, to break it up a bit. You know, for variety."

Chico Malo seemed to consider Ransom's words. He smiled and then turned and stared right at Cruz. "I want that one. The curvy one in black."

Cruz tightened his arms around Mickie as she gasped in horror. "No. Oh God."

"No. She's *my* fuck." Cruz bit the words out, his heart hammering in his chest. Dammit all to hell. A bad situation just got a hundred times worse.

"Prospect, you fucking know better than that. You don't *get* club pussy, remember? And any woman who steps foot in my clubhouse becomes club pussy unless she's an old lady." Ransom's words were hard. He waved his hand at Bubba, who strode across the room toward Cruz, determined to do his president's bidding.

"Mickie? What the *fuck*?"

Angel's words rang out across the room. She'd pulled herself away from Roach and was standing near Ransom, on the other side of the group of Mexican men. Her bra had been undone under her tank top and her short skirt was askew, though still covering the important bits. Her voice came out slurred, but still understandable. "Are you spying on me?"

Ransom turned toward Angel for a moment, then looked back at Cruz. "Well, well, well. The prodigal fucking sister has entered the lion's den. Looks like you were doing just as I asked and keeping a close eye on her after all. Bring her here, Bubba. I think we need to give her a proper Hermanos Rojos welcome."

"I said no," Cruz ground out, his teeth clenched. He'd seen what Ransom and the club did to the whores who wanted to be "regulars."

"You don't fucking *get* to say no, Smoke. Everyone in this club belongs to me. What I say goes. If I want to bend the bitch over and fuck her up the ass right here in front of everyone, I'll fucking do it. In fact, now we're *all* going to do it. Give her to Bubba and back the fuck away."

"No way! No fucking way!" Angel screeched at her sister, stomping her feet as if she were ten years old. "Ransom is mine. *Mine*! I'm the one who sucks his cock. *Me*! He sticks his dick in *me*! I'm the one he wants. Why would he want *you*? You're a fat, stuck-up, prissy little nobody! You're just here to fucking babysit me." The drugs and alcohol in Angel's system had clearly made her lose any filter she might have had.

"Angel, shut the fuck up and get out."

Angel, obviously high enough that she didn't care what her former boyfriend was saying, refused. "No!" She stomped her foot again for dramatic effect. "I found the club first. It's mine! Not hers. You can't want *her*. You like fucking *me*."

She turned to the scum of humanity who was standing amongst his henchmen smirking. "And you, fucking Hispanic jerk. You can't have her either. If you want your cock sucked, *I'll* do it. I'm better than she is! She's a fucking prude. Her own husband didn't want to fuck her, he kept his real love on the side and couldn't wait to fucking divorce her ass so he could be with her. Hell, Mickie probably called the cops before she even got here! She hates this MC. She hates *you*," Angel said, looking at Ransom. She turned back to Chico Malo, "And she doesn't even know you, but she probably hates you too."

Cruz swore under his breath. This was quickly getting out of control. The only thing he knew was that he wasn't going to hand Mickie over to fucking Ransom or a Mexican drug lord. He'd have to kill them first. His mind whirred with every scenario he could think of to get them out of this.

"You can't control your women very well, Ransom. *This* is the example you show me of high-class pussy?" Chico Malo growled, clearly annoyed at Angel's words, and Cruz's refusal to hand over the woman of his choice.

"I'll deal with this, Chico, no worries. Give me a second." Ransom stepped close to the still-fuming Angel. She smiled nastily, obviously thinking she'd won and had gotten what she wanted.

Ransom reached into the back of his jeans and pulled out a large knife. Without a word, he pulled the sharp blade across her neck from ear to ear, with a slow, methodical swipe.

Angel made one startled gurgling noise, then fell heavily to the floor.

Cruz spun Mickie around so that she was facing the wall as she gasped in shock. He stood next to her, holding her tightly with his left hand and partially blocking her with his body. He quickly growled, "Whatever the fuck happens, do *not* turn around. You got me, Mickie? I'll protect you, but you stay right here and don't watch."

"Angel—"

"You can't do anything for her right now. We'll be lucky if *we* get out of here in one piece."

Cruz didn't wait for her agreement, but turned his attention back to the clusterfuck happening right in front of him.

Angel twitched a couple of times on the ground as the pool of blood around her grew larger and larger. The men standing around were laughing as her body convulsed on the floor at their feet.

"Very nice, Ransom. Didn't think you had it in you." Chico Malo grinned. "Maybe this partnership will work out after all."

"Feel free to fuck her if you want...her pussy'll be warm for at least another thirty minutes."

It was as if Ransom's words broke through whatever spell was on Angel's friends. They suddenly completely freaked out, jumping away from the hands of the MC members who had been holding them and shrieking at the vision of their friend dying on the floor and bleeding out.

Ransom was yelling at his club members to control them while Chico Malo's goons looked on with humor, enjoying the chaos that had erupted around them.

Through the shrieking and crying of Angel's friends, Cruz heard Ransom call out, "Bring the fucking sister over here, Bubba. Now."

Cruz could feel Mickie trembling as she huddled against the wall. No way in fuck was Bubba, or anyone, getting their hands on his woman.

Just as the thought went through his head and Cruz readied to fight Bubba for Mickie, all hell broke loose in the room.

Flashbang grenades went off all around them, and even though Cruz had training on how to lessen the effects of them, his ears rang and his vision went dark from the unexpected explosions. He leaned against Mickie, covering her ears with his hands and crowding her, trying to cover her as much as he could.

The cavalry had finally arrived.

Cruz didn't relax. Even though Dax and the FBI task force had finally made their entrance, he and Mickie still weren't safe. Ransom and Bubba were gunning for Mickie, and probably him too, now that he'd refused to give her up. The MC members had knives and most likely a stash of illegal weapons. The Mexican drug lords obviously didn't want to get caught either, and they were certainly armed to the teeth.

"Crouch down, sweetness. Come on, that's it." Cruz urged Mickie to get as low to the ground as possible. He knew she probably couldn't hear him because of the loud percussion of the flashbang grenades, and was most likely in shock with what she'd seen and what was going on around them now.

He knelt with her and engulfed her in his arms, protecting her as best he could. It killed him not to be out in the fray, helping his friends and brothers in arms ferret out the bad guys and keep them contained, but at the moment all he could think about was Mickie, and keeping her safe. Now that Ransom knew she was Angel's sister, who knew what he'd do to get to her.

There were gunshots and shouts all around them. Cruz knew if they didn't get struck by a stray bullet, it'd be a miracle. He kept his arms around Mickie even as he put his hand on her head to push it farther down, to make her as small a target as possible. He literally put himself between her and the bullets that were flying around the room in the chaos.

When the commotion died down a bit, Cruz took stock, trying to get his bearings. There were several MC members on the ground with their hands on their heads being guarded by officers in riot gear. The women in the room, in various stages of undress, were being herded to a corner. The old ladies right along with the naked strippers and whores.

Most of Chico Malo's men were lying on the ground bleeding. Chico Malo himself was lying motionless on the floor with a bullet hole in the middle of his forehead.

Fuck. The FBI had wanted to take him alive. Cruz had no idea how he'd been killed, but his death would set off a power struggle in the drug world, most likely on both sides of the border, the likes of which hadn't been seen in quite a while.

Cruz could see three officers lying on the ground bleeding as well. Dammit. Although casualties were usually in the back of every police officer's mind, it was always a dark day when it actually happened. Cruz was relieved none of the injured men were Dax or Quint or anyone else he knew.

He looked around the room again—but didn't see Ransom anywhere.

It seemed quiet enough over where Angel's friends were all huddled together, sobbing. There were no MC members around them, but there weren't any officers with them either. It was a crap shoot on whether Mickie would be safe with them, but he didn't have many options at the moment. Cruz put his hand on her head and leaned close. "Go over to the other women. I'll be back." Before letting go, he took her chin in his hand and brought her lips to his. He kissed her once more, regretting everything that had happened.

Finally, without another word and ignoring the pleading look in her eyes, Cruz helped Mickie stand and gave her a slight push in the right direction. She took a stumbling step, then another, before she gathered her strength and headed straight for the relative safety of the group of Angel's friends, crying in each other's arms.

Cruz headed purposefully for the backrooms of the clubhouse, ignoring the shout for him to stop from one of the officers. The officer was either playing his part well in keeping Cruz's undercover status intact, or he honestly had no idea who Cruz was in the chaos of the raid. He didn't have time to stop and figure it out now.

Ransom knew the warehouse like the back of his hand. There was no way, after everything that had happened and everything he'd done, Cruz was going to let him get away. Not now, no fucking way. He knew right where Ransom would be holed up.

It was time to show the president who was really in charge.

Chapter Eighteen

CRUZ PROWLED DOWN the hall behind the big open room of the warehouse, intent on finding and killing Ransom. The hell with his oath to protect and serve. The man had murdered Angel with no second thought and had threatened Mickie. Mickie would never be safe if Ransom got away. He knew who she was and he'd come after her. Cruz had no plan in mind other than making sure the man paid for what he'd done and could never hurt what Cruz now thought of as *his*.

He came to Ransom's office. Cruz could hear the officers on the task force continuing to search the building farther down the hall from where he was. Realizing they'd already looked in the office and had found it empty, Cruz eased in and shut the door behind him.

This showdown would be between Ransom and him.

"You can come out, Ransom, it's just you and me." Cruz waited, knowing the man wouldn't be able to stay in hiding. He was pissed off and had something to prove.

Within moments, Ransom pushed the heavy panel in the floor back and climbed out of the panic room he'd built into the office floor. Not expecting it, but not entirely surprised, Cruz watched as Bubba also appeared out of the hidden room. Bubba being there would make the fight a bit lopsided, but Cruz wasn't backing down now. He was ready and willing to take them both on.

"Hiding like a girl, huh? Figures," Cruz taunted.

"You're a pig, aren't you?" Ransom correctly guessed. "I should've known; you're too fucking pretty to be a real man. Mall cop my ass."

"Took you long enough to figure it out, asshole, but whoops, guess not quick enough I'd say, wouldn't you?"

Bubba growled. "Let me fucking stick him, Ransom."

Ransom held up his hand. "I don't think so. He wants a fight? He'll get one."

Cruz nodded. "You think you're so fucking smart, but your downfall was Chico Malo. Axel knew you were in over your head, he sung like a canary the second he was faced with jail time." Seeing Ransom look at him in surprise, Cruz smirked. "Yeah, we got Axel. He knew Chico Malo would never let him live after he'd been arrested. He wasn't scared of *you* at all, a small-time, wannabe MC president."

Cruz could see the vein in the side of Ransom's neck throbbing, but he continued, knowing he was getting to the man. "You just couldn't be satisfied with owning the drug market on this side of the city, could you? Your strip club, whores, old ladies…none of it was enough. You were too greedy, Ransom. Once you crossed the line to Angel and her friends, you were done for, you just didn't realize it."

"Angel was a fucking whore, just like all the rest. She took what I gave her and was glad for it. A whore's a whore, even if she's wearing nice clothes. Just like her sister. But Mickie cleans up well, doesn't she? All tits and ass. Guess I was wrong about her being a muffer, wasn't I?"

Cruz refused to rise to Ransom's bait. "You're done, Ransom. You think anyone's gonna do business with you ever again? Your name's been reduced to shit. The second you step foot outside this clubhouse you'll be a giant target for every Mexican drug lord, not to mention your local rivals as well. You're finished."

"I had it all and you fucked it up!" Ransom yelled, finally losing his cool. "Loyalty to One. That *One* is fucking *me*! I was gonna rule this town and you fucked it up. You're gonna pay, Smoke! You're gonna fucking pay!"

"Come on then." Cruz egged Ransom on. It might not be professional, but he'd had enough of this asshole. Cruz felt as if he'd somehow allowed Mickie's sister to be killed. He didn't protect her and he couldn't bring her back now. He hadn't saved her, just as he hadn't saved Sophie. Oh, his ex wasn't dead, but she might as well be.

On top of that, Cruz knew Mickie would never forgive him. After what she'd seen and what Cruz had said to her, about her, that night. He might have lost the best thing that ever happened to him. If he could take down one more drug dealer in the process, all the better.

Ransom leaped forward, a knife materializing in his hand as he attacked. Cruz grabbed the wrist that held the knife and wrestled Ransom to the ground. They flipped each other over, and as Ransom frantically tried to make contact with Cruz's face, or neck, or anywhere, Cruz used his fist to pummel the asshole's face, and wherever else he could get in some licks. He was gaining the upper hand, until Bubba grabbed him from behind and wrenched his arms behind his back.

Smirking, Ransom pulled himself off the ground and wiped his bleeding nose on his sleeve. He spit on the ground before turning to Cruz. "Now what're you gonna do, asshole?" Ransom ground out, throwing his knife from one hand to the other, taunting Cruz.

When Cruz didn't answer, but continued to fight Bubba's hold, Ransom went on, "I'm gonna cut you, pig. Won't kill you though. Just hurt you enough so you can't fight back. Then I'll disappear, but when she least expects it, I'm gonna find the fat sister and I'm gonna steal her ass away. I'm gonna tie her down and fuck her. I'll leave her tied up and I'll fuck her in every hole she's got until she's bleeding and begging me to stop. Then I'll let Bubba fuck her. Then I'll invite every asshole motherfucker I can find to come in and take her. Then

I'll leave her there, tied up and bleeding. But I'll film the entire thing and send it to you, so you can watch it over and over."

Ransom leaned in close to Cruz, who was struggling harder to get out of Bubba's grasp. "And you'll take your last breath knowing it was *you* who did it to her. Do you know why I'm called Ransom? Usually I ransom the girls off. Send videos back to their families, ask for money. And they give it. Every fucking time. It's what I do. Bet you and your pig friends didn't know that about me, did you?"

Ransom laughed. "Drugs aren't how I make my money. Fuck no. The *real* dough is in kidnapping and collecting ransom money. But I'm not ransoming the bitch sister. I'll send you the video, but I won't tell you where she is. I'll tell her you refused to give me the money I asked for to let her go. She'll lie there, bleeding out of every orifice, dying, knowing it was *you* that put her there, and that you didn't want her enough to pay to get her back."

Ransom drew his hand back when he stopped speaking and swung the knife forward as hard as he could.

Expecting it, knowing Ransom was careless in his arrogant belief that he had him right where he wanted him, Cruz lurched to the side—just enough so the blade cleared him, sinking into Bubba's fleshy belly instead.

Cruz easily wrenched out of Bubba's now-lax grip and punched Ransom as hard as he could. The first punch dazed the man; the second knocked him out altogether.

He then turned to Bubba, who was on his knees holding the knife that had been in his belly. He pulled it out and made a half-hearted lunge at Cruz, but fell unconscious next to the MC president when Cruz's boot made contact with his face.

Cruz leaned over, putting his hands on his knees and taking a deep breath. Then another. Then one more. His adrenaline was through the roof. Ransom's words echoed through his brain and he curled his lip in disgust. How many lives had the man ruined? Cruz had always wondered why he was called Ransom, but none of the men in the club had known. His evilness was bone-deep.

He'd been able to visualize what Ransom had taunted him with. He could all too easily picture the look on Mickie's face as she lay hurt and dying at the asshole's hands. It'd been close. Too close. If Cruz hadn't moved quickly enough, or if he hadn't been able to dodge out of the way of Ransom's knife, Mickie would've been right where Ransom had insinuated she'd be.

Ransom had to die, and Cruz was just the man to do it.

He'd taken a step toward the knife lying on the ground when the door behind him slammed open and Cruz spun around, ready and willing to do battle.

Realizing it was the cops, Cruz reluctantly put his hands on top of his head in surrender. The adrenaline coursing through his veins made him want to continue to fight, but these were his brothers in blue. He wouldn't fight another police officer.

"Yeah, turn around, asshole," the officer sneered, slamming Cruz up against the wall. As he wrenched his arms behind his back, he leaned in and whispered, "Hang tight, we'll get you out of these as soon as we can." Cruz was glad the large officer knew he was one of the good guys; he hadn't been particularly gentle as he'd sent him crashing into the wall.

Cruz kept an eye on Ransom as the other agents called for medical attention for the two men. He knew it was probably too late for Bubba; Ransom had obviously hit something vital, because the blood pooling under the man was way too large for a simple stab wound. He hoped he died a slow, painful death.

Cruz was shoved back into the main room of the warehouse and he'd been docile enough, following the directions of the officers to the letter. He had no doubt Dax and the FBI would get to him eventually.

As he was led toward the door, he looked around frantically for

Mickie. Where was she? Was she safe? He flexed his hands in the cuffs. Fuck, why'd he let them put the cuffs on him before he'd made sure Mickie was safe? He couldn't help her with his hands behind his back.

Cruz's eyes roamed from the weeping women in the corner of the room to Angel's body...and found Mickie. She was sitting on the ground next to her sister with one hand on her arm and the other clenched tightly at her side. She looked up as they went by and Cruz could see the tracks her tears had left on her cheeks. Her mascara had run down her face, but it was the look Mickie gave him as he passed that nearly made his knees buckle under him.

Devastation. Emptiness. Despair. Her emotions battered him as if she'd physically assaulted him.

"Keep moving, asshole," the officer griped, playing his part to the hilt, not understanding the gut-check Cruz had just been dealt.

Cruz looked away from Mickie, devastated. He'd done that to her. He'd failed her, just as he'd failed Sophie. Just as he'd failed Angel. He couldn't help any of them now. As much as he wanted to take Mickie into his arms and comfort her, he not only didn't have the right, but he was physically unable.

Cruz stumbled once and managed to right himself as the finality hit him. He'd never have another chance to sit next to Mickie and watch her eat. He'd never smell her again, never feel her hand clasp his as they walked. Never see her laugh as she sat next to him when they watched movies. Never read a text from her again. Never look down at her beautiful face as her warm, wet folds engulfed him.

The officer opened the back door of a cop car and roughly pushed him in. As the door slammed, locking him inside, Cruz turned his head and looked out the window of the cruiser.

It was a beautiful night. There wasn't a cloud in the sky; the stars were shining brightly over his head. As the police car pulled away from the warehouse, Cruz wondered how it wasn't raining. With the way his heart hurt, it should've been foggy and raining.

He closed his eyes and swallowed hard as a tear, the first he'd shed over a woman, ever, fell from each eye and dripped onto his leather vest and slid down the fabric. It wasn't manly, and it wasn't macho. But he couldn't stop those tears if his life depended on it.

Chapter Nineteen

————— ◆ —————

MICKIE SAT ON a bench under a large tree, watching as cemetery workers nearby lowered Angel's coffin into the ground and began filling the hole with dirt.

The last week had passed in a blur. After watching in shock as Cruz was led out of the warehouse in handcuffs, Mickie had been pried away from her sister's body by the EMTs who had been on the scene. They'd treated her for shock and had even given her a shirt to wear since she'd been shivering and was obviously not dressed appropriately.

She'd been extensively questioned by the police and the FBI for hours. Mickie had to call their parents and let them know about Angel. They hadn't shown a lot of emotion, but they'd at least had the decency to show up for the service and the funeral.

Angel's friends had been questioned as well, and Mickie hadn't heard from many of them. Li had texted her to let her know she'd started seeing a counselor and was in therapy. Most of the women weren't so hooked on the drugs that they'd needed in-patient treatment, but Mickie hoped like hell they were all getting some sort of help. It wasn't as easy as it might seem to wean yourself off of a drug like cocaine, even though they hadn't been using for a long time.

Mickie allowed herself to think about Cruz for the first time in a week. She'd been busy, too busy to really think about all that had happened. But now, sitting in the fresh air, on a beautiful day that wasn't too hot for Texas, watching her sister being put to rest, Mickie could think.

A part of her had expected Cruz to show up at either the memorial or the graveside service, but she hadn't seen him. Mickie lowered her head and stared at her hands. Cruz. She'd asked about him when she'd been questioned by the FBI and no one seemed to know of him, or at least they weren't admitting it to her. Even with evidence that might suggest otherwise, she refused to believe he was an actual part of the motorcycle club. He'd been too protective that night. Too concerned about making sure she was safe.

Mickie chuckled under her breath. Now she was acting like Angel. Refusing to see what was right in front of her eyes.

She pulled out her new phone and fiddled with it. She'd had to get a new one because the FBI had confiscated her old one due to the video she'd taken.

She'd turned on the video feature right before she'd entered the warehouse that night. It had recorded until her phone had run out of memory. It had caught most of Cruz's words as the night had progressed. The video was shaky and made her nauseous to watch, but if Mickie closed her eyes, she could still hear Cruz's words. Some had been harsh and crude, but it was the others that she clung to in her head.

"Hang on, I'll cover you in a second.

I'm not going to hurt you.

She's mine until I'm done with her, and I don't fucking share.

Turn your head, hon. Don't look.

We'll be lucky if we get out of here in one piece."

He'd tried to reassure her. He'd kept her safe.

Mickie was cried out. She felt like she'd been crying for a week straight, but her eyes welled up once again. Damn.

"Hey, Mickie, right? Can I sit?"

Mickie looked up in surprise to see a petite, shorter-than-she-was, brunette, gesturing to the concrete bench she was sitting on. "Uh…"

Mickie didn't want her to sit, didn't want to share a bench when there were several others in the cemetery this woman could sit on. She wanted to be alone.

"My name is Mackenzie Morgan. We talked on the phone..."

Mickie struggled to remember, then suddenly it came to her. "Mack?"

"Yeah. So...can I sit?"

Mickie moved over without thinking and nodded.

"Thanks."

They sat there in silence for a moment before Mack started to speak. "He asked me to check on you, you know."

Mickie knew exactly who "he" was. "Was anything he told me the truth?" Her voice was soft and hitched once, but she controlled it. She got right to the point, needing to know.

"I don't know what Cruz told you, but I'm guessing as much as possible was."

Mickie turned to look at the pretty woman sitting next to her. "I'm having a hard time with all of this. I mean, I like him. I do. But this has all been so...unreal. I'm just so confused."

Mack put her hand on Mickie's leg, showing her silent support. "I'm sorry all this happened to you. I'm not trying to be a pain in your ass. But I know Cruz, and if you could see him now... Okay, will you let me tell you what I know about him? Then you can decide if what you've learned over the last few weeks is a lie or not."

Mickie nodded and waited for Mack to begin.

"Cruz is FBI. He was undercover in the Hermanos Rojos MC. His ex-wife is a drugged-out prostitute, who he didn't know was a drugged-out prostitute until he caught her servicing three men in their bedroom. He feels like it was his fault he didn't realize it or recognize the signs in her. He volunteered for this assignment so he could try to get some of the drugs in San Antonio off the street. He was supposed to find out information from your sister, but instead he met you. He wanted to call the whole thing off. He told Dax, my boyfriend, that he wanted out, but didn't know how."

Mack took a breath and then continued. "He loves you, Mickie. I'm not sure he's told you, or if he even realizes it, but he does. I've never seen a man so broken in my life. I've only seen him once since that day, and he looked like shit. That was today. He knew you were burying your sister and wanted me to come and make sure you were all right. I don't know what happened last week. Dax won't tell me, and it's not in the papers, but whatever it was…it broke him. He's put in paperwork to be transferred out of Texas. He won't talk about it. Not to me, not to Dax, not to any of his friends. We've bugged him, begged him, annoyed him, and flat-out ordered him to tell us what's going on in his head, and he refuses."

"I don't know what you want me to say," Mickie said, confused. Cruz had been honest with her. Almost everything he'd told her had apparently been true. The security job thing was a bit of a stretch, but technically Mickie supposed being in the FBI *was* security.

"I don't know either. I guess I'm just letting you know how much this has torn him up. If you care, at all, maybe you'll try to do something about it." Mack changed the subject abruptly. "I'm sorry about your sister."

"Me too. I should've done more."

Mack laughed, a humorous sound that had Mickie turning to look at her in shock.

"I'm not laughing at you. I'm laughing because that's the exact same thing Cruz told Dax when he talked to him last. I picked up the other line in the house and listened in on their conversation."

At Mickie's incredulous look, she said, "I know, terrible, but I was worried about Cruz. He's my friend. I'd do anything for him. Did you know Cruz was the one who found me when I was kidnapped?"

Mickie's head spun with the change of subjects, but she shook it anyway.

"Yeah, he wouldn't tell you about that…typical. I'd died. Taken my last breath. Dead. As a doornail. Dax saw me take my last breath on video and there wasn't a damn thing he could do about it. They didn't know where I was. While Dax was watching me die, Cruz searched the house the bad guy was in, and found a coffin in the basement. The bastard had pretended to bury me alive, but really had me in the basement of his house so he could hook up cameras and watch me die a slow, horrible death. Cruz didn't just stand there while Dax was watching me die; he searched the house until he found me. They got me out and I'm here today as a result. What I'm telling you is that Cruz doesn't give up. Ever. But whatever happened last week has made him *want* to give up. He's leaving San Antonio and has asked to be transferred to Victim Assistance.

"Now, I'm not saying he wouldn't make a great advocate for people who have been assaulted, raped, or any victim of any other kind of crime, but it's not where his heart is. He's good at what he does, Mickie. And for him to think he was responsible for whatever happened to your sister, or you, is just wrong. That's why I was laughing. You think *you're* responsible, and he thinks *he* is."

"I miss him."

"He misses you too."

"I don't know what to say to him."

"Well then, I think you're perfectly matched because I don't think he has the first clue what to say to you either. But one of you is going to have to make the first move, and I don't think it's going to be him. Look, next week is the annual law enforcement versus firefighter softball tournament. I'd love it if you came with me."

"I don't know."

"Cruz is going to be playing, along with my boyfriend and the rest of their group. Won't you please come and keep me company while the boys and girls duke it out on the field? I love all the guys, and it's hysterical seeing the firefighters do their best to trip and otherwise cheat their way to a win. And while I will always support Daxton, I'll tell you right now those boys in blue aren't afraid to do some cheating of their own. But no pressure. Promise. But it might be a good place to start if you're serious about missing him."

Mickie bit her lip, she knew it was going to take some time to work through not only what had happened with her sister, but also to herself and what had happened with Cruz. But the bottom line was that she did miss him. She'd found herself checking her phone several times a day, just in case there was a text waiting for her. It was stupid, but she'd gotten so used to talking to him that way every day, it'd become a habit.

Realizing Mack was waiting for her answer, she quickly nodded. "Okay. I'll come."

"Great! I'll pick you up if you want. Daxton is going early—he says to warm up, but it's really to talk smack to all the firefighters. The whole thing is really actually hilarious. It's gonna be really fun."

"I'd like it if you picked me up. Are you sure you don't mind?"

"Not at all." Mack stood and her tone turned serious once again. "He has a personal phone—his real phone, not the one you were communicating with him on. He had to turn in the one he was using as Smoke to the FBI. They had a tracker on it so they could keep tabs on where he was."

Mickie looked up at that. "So all the texts I sent…"

"I hope you didn't send him any naughty pictures, 'cos if you did, the FBI has them now." Mack smiled.

"No, I didn't, but…"

Mack handed her a piece of paper. "Here's my phone number and Cruz's real number. Reach out. If nothing else, maybe you can convince him to stick around here. Cruz is important to me and my boyfriend. We don't want to lose him."

Mickie took the paper without a word and looked down at it.

"I'm really sorry about your sister, Mickie. I don't know what I'd do if I lost either of my brothers. They drive me crazy sometimes, but they're still my family. I'll text you soon to figure out the details about the game." Mack put her hand on Mickie's shoulder, then turned and walked out of the cemetery.

Mickie continued to sit beside her sister until the cemetery workers had tamped down the last of the dirt and put up the temporary marker. The one Mickie had ordered wouldn't be ready for another few weeks.

Finally, as the sun got low enough in the sky that Mickie couldn't clearly read the words on any of the gravestones around her anymore, she got up and left.

She never saw the man watching, and guarding, her from the other side of the cemetery. Never saw him put his fingers to his mouth and sadly blow her a kiss as she drove out of the fenced-in cemetery grounds toward home.

Chapter Twenty

—◆—

MICKIE SAT NERVOUSLY in the stands at the charity softball game between Mack and an officer she'd been introduced to, Hayden Yates. She worked for the sheriff's office and had told Mickie that she'd recently hurt her shoulder in an altercation with a drunk driver, so she wasn't playing that day.

She'd also been introduced to all of Cruz's friends. Mickie recognized their names from one of the many conversations she and Cruz had late one night. Daxton was the first to come up to her and Mack when they'd arrived. He'd given Mack the kind of kiss Mickie had only seen in the movies…full of passion, as if they hadn't seen each other in years, instead of merely hours.

Dax was a Texas Ranger, and Mickie recalled Mack's story of how she'd been buried alive and ultimately saved by Cruz and his other friends. Quint introduced himself next. He was a lieutenant for the San Antonio Police Department. He'd taken her shoulders in his hands and gazed into her eyes for a long time before finally speaking.

"It's very nice to meet you, Mickie Kaiser. Whatever you do, don't give up on him."

"I'm not sure—"

"He's spoken of nothing else but you since that night. How brave you were. How sorry he was that you had to see what you did. How he hoped he'd be able to patch things up with you. I get that what you went through was horrible. I wouldn't blame you for wanting to forget everything about that night…for wanting to forget *him*…but if you care anything about him, please give him another chance. You'll never find another man more willing to move heaven and earth to keep you safe."

Mickie was surprised at the sentiment. She wasn't used to such deep speeches from men she'd just met. All she could do was nod, and hang on to him when he gave her another long hug.

They were interrupted by another man, who Mack introduced as TJ. Apparently he was a highway patrolman and the joker of the group. The introductions came in quick succession after that, luckily with no more deep speeches. She met Calder, a medical examiner, and Conor, a game warden, and of course, Hayden.

Cruz was also there, but didn't talk to her for long.

"Hello, Mickie. You look good."

"Thanks. You too."

He'd given her a quick hug and a brief kiss on the cheek, before joining his friends back on the field.

Mickie's head was spinning, but she couldn't deny the bubbly feeling deep inside at seeing him again.

"So, you gonna put that man out of his misery or what?" Hayden asked, not unkindly.

Mickie looked over at the small woman next to her. Hayden was built and obviously strong. She had the most beautiful auburn hair and her skin was pale, with freckles spattered across her nose. She looked fragile, but she spoke with the confidence that comes with many years of being in law enforcement.

"Look at him," Hayden said, gesturing toward the field with her head. "He can't keep his eyes off of you."

Mickie didn't need Hayden to point it out. She hadn't been able to keep her eyes off of him either. "A lot happened."

"I know. But you have to decide if what happened was too much to come back from."

"What do you mean?"

"I've seen it time and time again. Couples who go through extreme situations, as you and Cruz did, sometimes can't work through it to stay together. I'm not saying you guys can't get past this, but it takes a lot of effort. I wouldn't be a good friend to Cruz if I didn't make sure you were willing to put in that work."

Mickie looked away from the woman and back to the field. Her eyes blurred with tears as she thought about everything that had happened. Hayden was right. If she wanted to make whatever it was she and Cruz had successful, they'd both have to wrestle their own demons. She had no doubt that Cruz had them, just as she did.

Her voice came out just above a whisper. "I don't want everything that happened that night to have been too much."

"Good. Then you have my support."

"Mine too," Mack chimed in. She put her hand on Mickie's leg. "Welcome to the family."

Mickie glanced over at Mack. "What family?"

"This family," Mack replied instantly, throwing an arm out, encompassing the field. "This big, crazy law enforcement family. They're outrageous, they work too hard, they'll make you insane, but you've not only got me and Hayden as sisters, you've got all of them as brothers."

"But I just met them today," Mickie protested.

"I'm not talking about just Dax, Calder, and the others," Mack told her, laughing. "All of them. See all those firefighters out there?" At Mickie's nod, Mack continued. "They might treat this game as if it's the last battle of Waterloo, but everyone's actually on the same team. Moose, Sledge, Crash, Squirrel, Chief, Taco, and Driftwood are from Station 7, and if asked, they'll drop everything and come to your aid. To any of the guys' aid. Sometimes it can be annoying to have to share Daxton with them, but honestly? It's wonderful. I love seeing how well they all get along.

"But I have one word of advice…when you want an uninterrupted night, and Cruz isn't on call...turn off the phone. The guys have the uncanny ability to know when we're about to have sexy times. They've interrupted us more than once."

Mickie laughed, as she supposed Mack meant her to. It was nice to lighten the mood a bit. The rest of the afternoon went by quickly and Mickie only had the chance to briefly speak with Cruz once more before she left.

She'd been waiting for Mack to say goodbye to Dax—the guys were going out with the group of firefighters Mack had pointed out earlier—when Cruz came up beside her.

"How are you doing?"

"I'm good."

"I'm glad. For what it's worth...I'm sorry about your sister."

"Thanks."

"I'll talk to you later?"

Mickie had nodded and watched sadly as Cruz walked back toward the other men. She wasn't brave enough to say anything right then, there was too much going on around them anyway, but she'd made the decision to reach out to Cruz to see if they could salvage their relationship. She just had to figure out how to do it.

Chapter Twenty-One

MICKIE STARED DOWN at her new phone. The FBI had allowed her to write down any contact information she'd wanted from her old phone before they'd confiscated it. She was one of the holdouts and had never set up her stupid Cloud, but as soon as she had time, she was going to make sure she did it. It was a pain to have to re-enter all the settings and contacts.

They'd said she would get her old phone back eventually, not that she cared too much. There were some pictures on there that she wanted to keep, but it wasn't as if she could complain about them taking it. If the video she took would put some of the MC members away, she wouldn't put up a fuss.

She'd saved Cruz's new number Mack had given her into her contacts two weeks ago at her sister's funeral, and was now debating whether or not she should hit send on the text she'd written. She hadn't lied to Mack; she missed Cruz. She missed texting him, she missed talking to him, and she certainly missed the feel of him holding her.

Spending time at the softball game with Mack and Hayden, and seeing how well all the men had gotten along and how close they were, had solidified Mickie's desire to try to work through all that had happened with Cruz. He'd been giving her space, which she appreciated, but she'd finally decided it was time to reach out to him.

She'd thought about what Mack had told her at the funeral; in fact, hadn't slept that great as a result of not being able to *stop* thinking about it. Cruz believed he was to blame, but when Mickie really examined everything that happened, the person responsible for Angel's death was Angel. And Ransom, and all the other assholes in the motorcycle club. Cruz was there to do good, and he'd done what he could to protect Mickie.

She had been stupid enough to put herself in danger. Mickie never should've gone to the party that night, and in turn had put Cruz in danger. It was obvious he knew the club was going to be busted, but he did what he could to shield her from the worst of it. He'd protected her and risked having his cover blown as a result. She'd been terrified out of her mind when the crazy drug lord had decided he wanted *her*, but not once did she think Cruz would hand her over. Even with everything going on around them, she knew he would protect her and somehow get them out of there.

It was that bone-deep realization—that when the shit hit the fan, Cruz would protect her—that had made her type out the text in the first place.

The whole situation was fucked up and it killed Mickie to know Cruz blamed himself. It wasn't his fault; *none* of it was his fault.

She pushed the send button on the phone before she could analyze what she'd written anymore. Heck, Cruz probably wouldn't even know what the hell she was talking about. Probably wouldn't even know it was her.

She sat on her couch clutching her phone and trying not to hyperventilate.

CRUZ LAY ON his bed with one hand under his head and the other resting on his stomach. This was where he came when he needed to feel...something. He'd been numb for the last few weeks. Nothing seemed to be able to penetrate. But here, in his bed, where he could still smell Mickie, *here* he could feel. It hurt, but it was something.

He shifted onto his side and turned his head into his pillow. Yup, he could still smell her, barely. He hadn't washed his pillowcase, which he knew was probably disgusting, but if he had, he wouldn't be able to smell Mickie. He'd be empty again.

He thought about the raid. Cruz had been taken to the police station and the officer removed his cuffs when Quint met him at the door. Cruz had turned and shaken the officer's hand and thanked him.

He'd been debriefed by the SAPD and his boss at the FBI. They'd informed him Mickie had taken an audio recording, and a very crappy video, of most of what had happened at the warehouse. They now had that video and audio in their possession and were going to use it against as many people as they could.

Cruz had had to sit down upon hearing that. Apparently she'd gone to the party in the hopes she'd be able to gather proof that Ransom wasn't a good guy that she could bring to the cops, to get him away from her sister. Well, she'd certainly gotten more than she'd bargained for.

Bubba *hadn't* survived the knife wound Ransom had given him by accident and Ransom had been arrested. He'd only been in the county jail for three days before he'd been found dead in his cell. It was ruled a suicide, but Cruz had his doubts. Ransom was too conceited, too in love with himself, to do something so final as to take his own life.

Chico Malo might be dead, but whoever his successor was had found a way to take down his competition with a vengeance. At least Cruz didn't have to worry about his or Mickie's safety anymore. The other MC members were either dead or sitting in jail. And since no one but Ransom and Bubba had known Cruz was undercover, his identity was safe.

Cruz should feel glad. He'd gotten the Red Brothers MC shut down and had a part in dismantling a major international drug supplier. But he couldn't stop thinking about Mickie. He'd give it all back if he could have her in his life again.

Realizing that was impossible, Cruz knew he couldn't live in the same city as Mickie and not completely lose his mind. He didn't think she hated him, not after the softball game where he'd noticed she'd kept her eyes on him, but her not hating him and them being able to have a relationship were two completely different things. Not sure he could handle seeing her and not having her for himself, Cruz had put in for a transfer. He didn't care where, as long as it wasn't in Texas. He'd volunteered to work in Victim Assistance. He could still honor Avery, and now Angel, and their memories by helping victims of crime get their lives back.

Cruz's phone buzzed. He was tempted to ignore it. Mack and Dax had been on his ass to get back into the land of the living. Not to mention the other guys. TJ and Quint typically called him once a day, and even Calder and Conor tried to convince him to go out to dinner one night with them. Hayden, the lone woman in their circle of friends, had attempted to sweet talk him into taking her to see the latest action movie in the theaters. He'd turned them all down.

Quint had sat him down and had a long talk with him after the softball game the other day. Cruz had been surprised to see Mickie there, but should've known Mack wouldn't let a chance to throw him together with Mickie go. She was his biggest fan, other than Dax, and he knew she wanted him to be happy.

He and Quint had had a long talk about what it was they wanted out of their lives, and Cruz was surprised to learn that Quint felt much as he did, especially after seeing how happy Dax and Mack were. Quint had flat-out said he didn't care if the woman meant to be his wasn't perfect...as long as she loved him as much as Mack loved Dax, it wouldn't matter.

Thinking about that conversation, as well as the look of longing in Mickie's eyes at the game, made him want to grab ahold of her and never let go.

He made the decision to reach out to her. If he didn't try, he knew he'd always regret it. And she'd shown up at the game...that had to mean something.

Cruz reached for the vibrating phone, knowing if he didn't respond, whichever of his friends it was, wouldn't leave him alone.

He read the text in confusion. It made no sense.

I remember you used to drive that crappy blue Chevy Nova. What do you drive now?

Cruz didn't drive a Chevy. He had a Harley and a black Toyota. It wasn't in the best shape, but it wasn't crappy by any stretch. Cruz was about to ignore the text, assuming it was a wrong number, when something niggled at his brain.

He sat up and stared at the number. It was local, but not a number he recognized. Cruz struggled to remember what he needed to in order to respond. Finally, it came to him. He hoped like hell he wasn't wrong about who'd sent the text. He could feel his heart literally leap in his chest. Cruz painstakingly typed out a response.

The same crappy blue Chevy Nova.

He held his breath.

You want to accidently be at the same place at the same time tomorrow to feed ourselves?

Cruz closed his eyes and choked back the emotion crawling up his throat. Mickie. Thank God.

She'd reached out with a line from *Beverly Hills Cop*, then asked him the same thing he'd asked her all those weeks ago when he'd asked her out for the first time. He suddenly felt stronger and more with it than he'd felt in a few weeks.

Yeah. I'd like that.

I know a good Mexican place on the River Walk :)

Cruz tried to smile, but couldn't quite make it.

How about my place? I make a mean BLT.

It was several minutes before Mickie texted back, and Cruz could swear his heart stopped beating until she did.

What time?

One?

Okay. See you then.

I've missed you.

Cruz wasn't going to go there, but couldn't help himself.

I've missed you too. See you tomorrow.

Bye.

Cruz clicked off his phone and lay back on the bed, holding the phone to his chest. He had one more chance with Mickie. He didn't want to fuck it up. The depression that had settled on his shoulders seemed to disappear as if by magic.

He got up off the bed. He had a ton of shit to do. Mickie wasn't just going to accept him back without him working for it, so he was going to do whatever he could to convince her to give him another chance. She apparently had more gumption than he'd expected. He hoped like hell her reaching out meant she was considering giving him another shot. Her text was just what Cruz needed to get his head out of his ass.

He wanted Mickie. He wanted his life in Texas...with Mickie. He was going to do everything in his power to make her realize how good they were together. Even if it took months, he was up to the challenge. She was worth it.

Chapter Twenty-Two

MICKIE NERVOUSLY WIPED her hands on her thighs as she waited for Cruz to open his door. She wasn't sure why she was so nervous, except she really wanted this to work out. She knocked softly.

Cruz opened the door almost immediately. "Hey, Mickie."

"Hey, Cruz."

"Come in. Please."

Mickie brushed past Cruz into his apartment. She heard him close and lock the door behind her and she continued walking into his living room.

"Want to sit at the table to eat? Or the couch?"

"Either."

"Couch okay then?"

"Yeah." Mickie hated the stifled conversation between them, but didn't know how to fix it. "Need any help?"

"Sure, if you want to grab the drinks, I'll get the plates."

Mickie grabbed the two soft drinks and brought them over to the coffee table as Cruz followed with their sandwiches. They both sat down, and Cruz turned sideways with one leg hiked up on the couch, facing her.

Mickie sat straight forward, feeling awkward. She grabbed her sandwich and took a bite. She put it back on the plate and rested her head against the cushions. She turned her head to see Cruz watching her intently. She swallowed hard. "Cruz—"

"Thank you for coming over today, Mickie. I've said it before, and I'll say it again. I'm very sorry about Angel."

Mickie nodded. "Yeah...thanks."

"I was going to sit next to you and make small talk while we ate. Then I was going to suggest a movie, maybe *Beverly Hills Cop 2.* Then I was going to ask if you wanted to go out again...soon."

"You *were* going to do all of those things?" Mickie asked, clearing her throat nervously.

"Yeah, but now I'm not."

"You're not?" Mickie felt like a parrot, repeating back everything Cruz said to her.

"No. I can't." Cruz held up a hand between them. "Look, I'm shaking. I'm so afraid you only came over today to tell me what an asshole I am. And I *know* I'm an asshole, I know what I did was wrong, but I—"

He stopped speaking abruptly when Mickie reached up and took his shaking hand between both of hers. She lowered their hands to his knee and rested them there. "You aren't an asshole, Cruz."

"Mickie—"

"Seriously. Listen to me for a sec. I was hurt after that phone call. I'd just had the most amazing experience with you and thought you felt the same. When I heard what those guys were saying, I couldn't understand how you could go and cheapen what we had by telling them about us."

"I didn't tell anyone anything."

"I know that *now*, Cruz, but I didn't at the time. And it hurt. And then I saw you at that party. I was scared and confused and when you talked about me like you did to that first guy, I was completely freaked out. But then you protected me. You didn't make me do the drugs, you covered me back up when I inadvertently exposed myself, and when push came to shove, when the cops came and the bullets flew, you shoved me against that wall and made sure not one inch of my body was vulnerable. You literally put yourself between me and stray bullets."

"Mickie—"

"I'm not done."

"Sorry, go ahead." Cruz couldn't help but smile. She was so cute.

"I have a question for you. If you answer it right, I…I want to see where this can go between us."

"And if I don't?"

Mickie shrugged. "Then you'll get transferred and we'll both go on with our lives."

Cruz turned his hand within hers and brought it up to his face. He rested his forehead against the back of Mickie's hand and nodded once. He took a deep breath and looked into her eyes. "Ask."

"Was it all a lie? Were you using me to try to get information about Angel, and thus about the MC?"

Cruz didn't even think. "No. It wasn't all a lie. I had thoughts about trying to get in with Angel, to find out what she knew, to see if she knew anything about how the drugs got into the club in the first place, but I found out pretty quickly she was an innocent bystander. Ransom was using her. I had no intention of getting involved with you, but when Ransom got pissed at you for trying to butt in with Angel, I wanted to protect you.

"You were right about the tires. Ransom ordered one of the club members to do that. I didn't know about it until you called me though. But the thing is…once I started protecting you, it stopped being about the club and the job, and started being about you. I should've gotten the hell away from you, but I couldn't. I knew from the first time I saw you that you were an open book. Not only that, I knew what else you were."

When he didn't continue, Mickie tentatively asked, "And what was I?"

"Mine."

"What?"

"Mine. I know that sounds terribly chauvinistic, but it's what I thought. Sitting across from you, talking to you, touching your hand. A part of me knew you were what I'd waited my entire life for. You were the reason why I'd been married to Sophie. If I hadn't been married to her and experienced what I did with her, I wouldn't have been driven to take this undercover assignment. And if I hadn't taken the assignment, I never would've met you. I never would've smelled you, tasted you, felt what you feel like when I was deep inside you. I might not have been there when you went to try to save your sister. Who the hell knows what would've happened to you. I'm pretty sure I'm in love with you, Mickie."

"Cruz…"

"You'll never know how scared I was when I realized you'd walked into that warehouse. There were men having full-out gang bangs, people snorting cocaine, and me—me being an asshole. You were in danger and there wasn't a damn thing I could do about it and keep my cover. But you should know, I'd already made the decision that I didn't give a shit about my job, or my cover. I was going to do whatever it took to make sure you got out of there in one piece. You will always be more important to me than my job. Always."

"I'm sorry, Cruz. I never should've done it. You told me not to do anything crazy and you were right. I was an idiot and I can swear to you that it'll never happen again."

"Damn right."

Mickie smiled for the first time that night. Cruz sounded so disgruntled.

"The thing is, Mickie, for the first time in my career, the job wasn't important. I'd been undercover for almost three months and the only thing I cared about was your safety. I wasn't going to let Roach, or Vodka, Chico Malo, or even Bubba touch you. I didn't care if I blew my cover, but they weren't going to fucking touch you.

I would've died getting you out of there untouched, Mickie. You're mine." Cruz's voice broke, but he continued on.

"I'll do whatever it takes to have you trust me again. I'll quit and see if I can get hired on at the SAPD. I'll tell you anything you want to know. I have no secrets from you, never again. We'll honor Angel's memory somehow, however you want…"

"Will you have to go undercover again?"

"No."

"You sound sure."

"I'm sure. Most of the time, we don't get sent undercover, sweetness. Agents volunteer for that shit. If I have you, I don't ever want to go undercover again. I wouldn't want to be separated from you and I certainly wouldn't want to put myself in danger like that again."

"I don't want you to quit the FBI. You're good at what you do. I think I love you back."

"Me going undercover could put you in danger as well, and I won't do it. I'll even—wait…what?"

"I love you."

Cruz could only stare at Mickie in bewilderment. His badassness was gone. This woman was his world and she had him completely under her thumb. "But, Mickie… I killed your sister."

Mickie sighed and scooted closer to Cruz, until he had to drop his leg and turn so he was sitting correctly on the cushion. She pulled her feet up and lay her head on his shoulder. Her left arm went around his chest and she pushed until her right arm was between his back and the couch. She smiled when Cruz tentatively put his arm around her shoulder and pulled her close.

"You didn't kill Angel. Ransom killed Angel."

"But if I—"

"*No.* Ransom killed her. There's enough blame to go around to everyone. Ransom, Angel herself, me, you, her friends, my parents…I could go on and on, but the bottom line is, the only person responsible for taking her life is Ransom."

They were both quiet for a heartbeat. "The service was beautiful, hon."

Mickie lifted her head. "You were there?"

"Yeah, I was there."

"Mack said you sent her to make sure I was all right."

"I did. But I was there too. I hung out at the back of the church and I was there at the cemetery until you left that evening."

"I didn't see you."

"I know. I want us to work. I want to get back to where we were, but this time, I want you to hang out with me and my friends. I want to be able to talk to you about my job, at least what I can. I know it's going to take some work, on both our parts, to get completely past what happened. But I'm willing to try. I'm hoping you are too."

"I am," she replied immediately. "I was thinking the same thing. I'm sorry for what happened, I'm sorry you had to worry about me and Angel in the middle of having to worry about keeping your cover and staying safe while everything was happening. I'm happier than I can say to be here with you." Mickie put her head back down and buried it in Cruz's neck. She inhaled deeply. "I've missed you, Cruz. So much."

"I've missed you too. Are we good?"

"Yeah, I think so, why?"

"Because I've spent the last few weeks missing you more than I thought I'd ever miss anyone in my entire life. I've thought of nothing but you. My friends are ready to disown me and I'm completely useless at work."

Cruz disengaged himself from Mickie and stood up. He held his hand out to her. "Let me show you how much I've missed you. I'm in love with you, Mickie. I want to take you to my bed and not get up for days. I need you. Will you come with me?"

Mickie didn't hesitate. She put her hand in his and squealed when he pulled her upright forcefully and bent so she was sailing over his shoulder. He caught her and wrapped his arm around the back of her legs. He turned and headed down the hall to his bedroom.

He dumped her on the mattress and she laughed as she bounced.

"I think we've done this before," Mickie exclaimed, referring to the last time he'd dropped her on his bed.

"No, this is gonna be something completely different. I know we went slow before, but I can't this time. I came too close to losing you and it's been too long since I've held you in my arms. Tonight will be fast, at least the first time, but I promise to make it good for you."

"Cruz...God."

"I love you, Mickie. It has to be love. I've spent my whole life waiting for you. I might not be able to take it slow this time, but you'll love everything I do, I promise."

Mickie sat up, propping herself up with one hand and reaching for Cruz's face with the other. "I will, because it's you doing it to me." She fell back and arched, anticipating his touch. "Do your worst."

"One question before we get started and I can't think about anything but your scent and your body..."

"Yes?"

"Will you wear that outfit for me sometime? Just for me?"

Mickie smiled up at the man she loved, knowing exactly what outfit he was talking about. "I *did* enjoy the way you got creative with your teeth when you covered me back up..."

"I'll take it that's a yes?"

"It's a yes."

Cruz looked into her eyes. "I promise to show you every day how much you mean to me. I won't lie to you again. We'll work through any issues that come up."

"I'll do the same, Cruz. The thought of losing you was eating me alive."

"I'm here now. Let me show you how much you mean to me. Take off your shirt. I've got to see you."

Mickie eased her shirt over her head and gazed at Cruz. She loved the look of adoration in his eyes. "Yours too?"

"Of course. I've got to feel you against me."

Mickie quickly stripped off her pants and shed her bra and panties and scooted up on the bed as Cruz took off his clothes. Before even a minute had passed, she felt Cruz's heart thumping against her chest. She figured he could feel hers too, as it felt like it was beating out of her chest.

"You're beautiful, and I swear I feel like the luckiest guy in all the world that you're here with me."

"I think I'm the luckiest girl for being here with *you*," Mickie countered, smiling.

Cruz didn't bother to argue with her, he simply dropped his head and covered her lips with his. His hands moved over her body as he devoured her mouth, relearning her taste. He flipped them over and held onto Mickie's hips as she got her balance on top of him.

"Take me, Mickie. I'm yours. As fast or as slow as you want."

Mickie looked down and saw that he'd put on a condom before coming to her on the bed. She'd been worrying about her own clothes so much she'd missed it. "Are you ready?"

He laughed as if she'd said the funniest thing he'd ever heard. "Sweetheart, I took one look at those nipples of yours and I was ready."

Mickie smiled shyly down at him and rose up on her knees. Her smile grew as he groaned at the first touch of her hand on his cock. She stroked him once before fitting him to her, then sank down on him inch by inch, groaning along with him as her hot, wet body engulfed his hard length.

She stayed motionless when he was inside her as deep as he could go. She felt his thumbs caressing her hips, but otherwise neither of them moved.

"Are you okay?" he asked in a quiet voice.

"Never better." Mickie lifted up an inch, then dropped back onto Cruz. His hands tightened on her hips, letting her set the pace.

"That's it. Move on me. Do what feels good."

"Everything feels good."

They looked into each other's eyes as she continued riding him. Mickie braced her hands on his chest as she increased her thrusts against him. She knew when Cruz lost his battle to let her have control when he held her in place above him and rocked his hips up and into her.

Sensing he was close, Mickie quickly moved one hand from his chest down to her clit and frantically rubbed herself as Cruz fucked her. She threw her head back and shuddered over him, in the midst of a monster orgasm when Cruz pumped into her one more time and held her on top of him as he exploded.

Several moments later, when Mickie's muscles felt like Jell-O and she lay on top of Cruz, just as they had after the first time they'd made love, connected in the most intimate way two people could be connected, Cruz cleared his throat and Mickie expected to hear something romantic or sexy come out of his mouth.

"By the time the average American is fifty years old, he has five pounds of undigested red meat in his bowels."

Mickie had watched *Beverly Hills Cop* five times in the last couple of weeks, simply trying to be closer to Cruz. She giggled as she responded appropriately, "And why are you telling me that, Cruz? What makes you think I have any interest in it at all?"

Cruz nuzzled the top of Mickie's hair and whispered, "Well, you eat a lot of red meat."

"I love you, Cruz Livingston."

"And I love you, Michelle Kaiser."

Epilogue

—————◆—————

M ICKIE GRINNED AT the group around the table. They were having lunch on a Saturday, almost three months after Cruz's undercover mission had come to a screeching halt. All of his friends were there, and Mack was trying to convince the guys and Hayden that they needed to do a sexy calendar photo shoot to raise money for her nonprofit group.

Not surprisingly, no one was very keen on the idea.

"Come on, you guys. It'll be awesome. It's not like you have to get naked or anything. And we can even invite your firefighter friends. Think you can get Squirrel or Chief...hell, *any* of them to say yes? It'll be epic if you can get everyone to agree!" Mack tried pouting, hoping it'd get her what she wanted, but everyone just laughed at her.

Mickie put her hand on Cruz's knee and smiled when he immediately covered it with his own.

The last three months had been wonderful. She and Cruz had moved into a new condo together last month. They both knew they were moving their relationship along very quickly, but it felt right. Marriage wasn't in the plans yet, but it was definitely a possibility in the future.

Mickie thought back to this morning. She'd been dreaming the most wonderful dream, that Cruz was making slow, sweet love to her, and had woken up to the reality of Cruz running his fingers up and down her chest and nuzzling against her neck.

"I love you."

"I love you too."

"I want you."

Mickie had smiled and her nipples tightened in his grasp. "Then take me." She'd thought he'd pounce on her, but instead he took his time. He worked his way from her chest, down her belly, until he'd made himself comfortable between her legs. He'd grabbed a pillow and shoved it under her butt until she was just where he wanted her. He'd feasted on her folds until she was begging for mercy. Then, and only then, had he crawled up her body and entered her slowly. As much as Mickie had begged, he'd taken her at his own pace, whispering words of love and adoration the entire time.

Finally, when Mickie had exploded again, he put both hands on the mattress at her shoulders and lost control. He'd pounded into her, not taking his eyes away from hers. He'd pushed in one last time and held himself as far inside her as he could go and filled her with his come.

They'd lain in bed for another long while, simply enjoying being alive and connected. While they'd made love countless times since everything had happened, that morning was one of the most memorable...besides their first time.

Mickie was brought out of her semi-dazed state when Cruz leaned over and nuzzled behind her ear as the good-natured ribbing continued around them. "I'll pose for Mack's calendar if you pose with me in your biker-babe outfit."

She turned her head and kissed Cruz quickly before pulling back. "As if you'd allow me out of the house with that on."

"Who said anything about 'out of the house'?"

Mickie smacked Cruz lightly on the arm. "You're so bad." They grinned at each other and Mickie soothed Cruz's arm where she'd smacked him. She looked down and grinned at the addition Cruz had made to his tattoo. Alongside Avery's initials was now a large AK, in tribute to Angel. She hadn't been very nice to Mickie, especially at the end, but she was Mickie's family, and a victim. She deserved to be remembered and honored.

"I love you, Cruz. Not only that, I'm very proud of you."

"I love you too, Mickie. And while there are times I know I'll probably do things that will piss you off, I'm going to try to live every day to make you proud to be by my side."

Mickie leaned her head against his arm and closed her eyes. She had no idea how she'd gotten so lucky, but she wasn't going to give Cruz up. No way, no how.

A large crash rang out through the restaurant and made Mickie jump away from Cruz in surprise and a little bit of fright.

"Easy, sweetness. You're okay."

Mickie nodded and she looked over to where the sound had come from.

A woman was standing in the middle of the restaurant apologizing profusely to the man she'd just run into. It was a busboy and he'd dropped an entire tub of dirty dishes.

"Jesus Christ, are you blind? Watch where you're walking, why don't you?" The man was standing with his hands on his hips, glaring at the tall, slender woman in front of him. "How would you like it if I came to your workplace and made you look like a schmuck in front of everyone?"

Quint scooted his chair back and stalked quickly over to the duo, intent on preventing the situation from escalating. Most of the time, just the sight of his SAPD uniform could chill out the angriest individual.

"As a matter of fact, I *am* blind," the woman said, sounding a bit peeved. "I already apologized for running into you, but if you'd been paying attention as well, you would've seen me and you could've gone around me."

"Everyone all right here?" Quint asked, making his presence

known to the two angry people.

"Hunky-dory," the busboy groused, dropping his attitude after seeing Quint's uniform, and squatting down to start cleaning up the mess.

"Miss? Why don't you just step over here out of the way." Quint put his hand on the woman's elbow and led her away from the shattered plates and water spilled from the cups. "Are you okay? You didn't get hit by any flying glass or anything?"

"No, I think I'm all right. Thank you."

"Can I help you—"

"I'm not an invalid, no matter what you might think of blind people."

"I didn't—"

"Yes, you did, most people do." Her voice was partly resigned, as if she was used to being thought less of because of her disability, but there was also a bit of irritation not quite hidden beneath her words.

Quint couldn't remember the last time someone had spoken to him with such disdain.

"I really just wanted to make sure you wouldn't slip on the water on the floor."

"Why? Because I can't see it? Because I'm an idiot and I'd go tromping through the middle of the spilled stuff to prove a point?"

"Well, no, because I'm trying to be a gentleman."

The woman snorted. "A gentleman. Yeah, like there are any of those left in the world today."

Smiling, not offended in the least, Quint looked down at the stressed-out, prickly woman in front of him. She was tall, only a few inches shorter than his six foot two. She had long blonde hair that was pulled back into a messy ponytail and eyes so blue they didn't look natural. They were almost more turquoise than blue. As he looked closer, if he had to guess, he'd say they were most likely contacts or prosthetics.

She had wisps of hair that were escaping the tight confines of the band that held it and she wore no makeup. She was wearing a T-shirt that fit her like a glove and a pair of jean shorts that were neither too short nor too long. On her feet were tennis shoes and a cute pair of pink socks. She had a long white cane with a red tip hooked around her arm.

Quint reached out and touched her hand briefly, not knowing the protocol for wanting to shake someone's hand when they were blind and couldn't see the gesture. "My name is Quint Axton, I'm happy to meet you."

She didn't hesitate, but reached her hand out to him. "Corrie Madison."

"Are you meeting someone here, Corrie?"

"Yeah, he should be here any moment. So you can just leave the poor blind woman here against the wall and he'll be along to take care of me soon." Her voice was still laced with a bit of irritation.

"Maybe I should start us off again." Quint brought Corrie's hand up so it rested over the badge sitting on his chest. "My name is Officer Quint Axton with the San Antonio Police Department, and I'm pleased to meet you."

"Oh my God," Corrie whispered, her tone of voice immediately changing to one of chagrin and snatching her hand back after moving it over his badge and realizing what she was feeling. "Uh, yeah, sorry. I didn't mean any disrespect, I mean…"

Quint laughed and put her out of her misery. "I just wanted to make sure you knew before you said something you might really regret."

"I really am sorry. I'm not usually like this. I've had a really really *really* bad week."

Quint chuckled, remembering the story of how Mackenzie had said the same thing after TJ had pulled her over all those months ago. "It's okay. Now, are you *sure* you're all right here? The person you're waiting for will be here soon?"

"Yeah, he's my lawyer."

"Your lawyer?" Quint scrunched his eyes together in concern.

"Yeah." Corrie continued in a low voice, "I heard a murder. I think someone's trying to shut me up, and I have to figure out what's going to happen next."

Read on for the next book in the series:
Justice for Corrie.

JUSTICE FOR CORRIE

BADGE OF HONOR

TEXAS HEROES
BOOK 3

By Susan Stoker

Acknowledgements

Thank you to Christie M. for helping me make sure I did justice to Corrie's character. For the blind, it's not easy living in a sighted world and your suggestions helped make Corrie more "real". Thank you!

Also, thank you to Diana C. for your help with finding me a good restaurant in San Antonio. Your hometown perspective is always welcome.

And as always thanks to Rosie, Henry, and Annie for your unflagging support.

Chapter One

————— ◆ —————

"HELLO, MR. TREADAWAY. How are you today?"

"Hi, Corrie. I'm okay."

"It's been a while since you've been in for an adjustment."

"I know, I've pushed it a bit too far."

"You've been in a lot of pain?"

"Yeah."

"Okay, go ahead and get ready. You know the drill. I'll be back in as soon as I go over your most recent X-rays with my assistant. When I come back, I'll do an exam and you can tell me where you're hurting the most. We'll do the adjustment and I'll expect you to return to see me sooner next time. All right?"

"Yes, ma'am."

Corrie could hear the humor in the older man's voice. Jake Treadaway was in his early fifties. He had a low voice that was pleasing to her ears. He had an average build, not overly muscular, but not overweight either. He was taller than her five-nine, but not by much.

As a blind chiropractor, Corrie had to rely on her hands and her sense of touch to be able to correctly diagnose her patients and to adjust them properly. She knew there were a lot of people who still didn't believe she could do the job, but Corrie was comforted by the fact that she had a lot of clients who *did* believe in her; patients who had no issue with her disability.

After graduating with her degree, she'd applied and met with the majority of chiropractors in San Antonio, and the only person who would give her a chance was Dr. Garza. He hadn't blown her off immediately upon finding out she was blind, and after she'd shown him she knew what she was doing, he'd given her a trial run. It had worked out and they were both thrilled. Dr. Garza had wanted to spend more time with his family and was happy to take on a partner. They usually alternated work days, so they could both have some time off.

There were several clients who were uncomfortable with her disability, and had refused to let her adjust them, but Dr. Garza had no problem taking on those less-than-open-minded clients.

Corrie wouldn't apologize for who she was and what she did. She'd worked hard, damn hard, to get through chiropractic college. Luckily, there'd been a few other blind students who had blazed the trail before her, forcing colleges to provide reasonable accommodations for blind students so she was able to complete the rigorous training.

Her parents had fought for her right to attend "normal" schools her entire life. She was an only child, and Chad and Shelley Madison had taught her that she was just as capable as any sighted person. She'd been born with anophthalmia, a condition where her eyes didn't form during pregnancy. She'd worn sunglasses for most of her elementary school years, but once she'd been old enough, and after a lot of begging, she'd started wearing prosthetics.

She'd painstakingly learned to clean and care for her "bionic eyes" as her best friend, Emily, called them. It had only taken one infection because of her laziness and the resulting hospital stay, for Corrie to learn it could be a life-or-death situation if she didn't properly clean and disinfect the prosthetics on a regular basis.

Corrie closed the exam door behind her and turned right to walk down the short hallway to her office. She knew exactly how many steps it was from the exam room she always used to the office, how many strides she had to take to reach her desk, and exactly where her chair would be. The cleaning service employees had learned not to move any of her things even one inch after an incident where her trash can hadn't been put back in its spot and Corrie had fallen over it one morning.

Corrie eased into her chair and thumbed through the files sitting on her desk. Their administrative assistant, Cayley, always placed the files of the clients she'd see each day in the center of her desk in the mornings. The tabs had the names of each patient written on them, but Corrie had also printed out labels of their names in Braille and placed them on the front of each folder.

Corrie reached out and grabbed her mouse, it was right where it always was, and clicked. A female voice talked Corrie through maneuvering within Mr. Treadaway's online file and medical history. She made some notes in a recorder she kept on her desk. Cayley took the device and typed up her notes on each person at the end of every day.

Finished with her preparations for Mr. Treadaway's adjustment, Corrie stood up and walked back to her office door. Her assistant, Shaun, should've been in her office by now. He would know by now that Mr. Treadaway had arrived. They always went over his radiographs so Corrie would know which vertebrae she needed to concentrate on. She'd never work on a patient without the review. She didn't want to hurt someone or, God forbid, paralyze them by adjusting the wrong place on their spine.

Shaun was about her age, thirty-two, and married with two kids. His younger child had been in a swimming accident a year and a half ago. Five-year-old Robert fell into their neighbor's pool and wasn't missed for approximately ten minutes. By the time they found him and fished him out of the water, he'd been clinically dead for eight of those minutes. The doctors had been able to revive him, but he'd never have a normal life again. The lack of oxygen had reduced the little boy to a shell of who he'd once been, and Corrie knew Shaun and his wife, Abigail, were going through financial issues trying to pay his medical bills from that time, as well as paying to keep him home with full-time medical assistance.

Corrie felt terrible for Shaun. He'd worked with her for about six months before Robert's accident, and she knew he wasn't the same man since it had happened. Lately though, his performance at work was suffering, and Corrie dreaded the talk she'd have to have with him. He'd been showing up late for work more and more often, and he seemed sullen and even borderline paranoid, always asking who was sitting out in the small waiting area and if anyone ever called for him at work.

Just as Corrie reached for the doorknob to see if she could find Shaun—he usually hung out in the makeshift break room toward the back of the clinic—she heard angry voices in the reception area, followed by a weird popping noise. She froze in her tracks and tilted her head to the side, trying to figure out what was going on.

It wasn't until she heard Cayley's scream cut short that Corrie figured out something horrible was happening.

Knowing better than to open her door and try to stop whatever was going on, Corrie stepped quickly away from the door and imagined her office layout in her head. As the popping noises and the screams continued—and got closer to her office—she frantically thought about where she could hide.

Her desk was large, and sat perpendicular to the doorway. She could walk from the door straight to the chair at her desk without having to swerve around any furniture. She kept her office purposely free of extraneous chairs and tables so she didn't have to worry about tripping over them. She could hide under the desk, but wasn't that where everyone always hid—and died doing it? If she was a crazy person hell-bent on killing everyone around her, that's the first place she'd look for stragglers who might be hiding.

The exam door down the hall was opened and Corrie heard Mr. Treadaway ask, "Who are you?" before the awful popping sound came again.

Knowing time was running out, the gunman would be at her office within moments, Corrie made the split-second decision to see if she could fit in the small area under the sink. There was no other place she could hide.

When she'd been hired, there hadn't been any extra space for her to have an office in the small clinic. A small break room had been converted for her, and the sink and cabinets still lined one wall. It would be a tight fit, an *extremely* tight fit, but Corrie didn't hesitate.

Hearing the unsteady gait of someone walking down the hall, Corrie raced over to the sink and opened the cabinet underneath. She shoved her butt in first and wiggled it around, knocking over a few odds and ends that were stored under there in the process. She drew her knees up as close to her chest as she could get them and sighed in relief as she realized she fit, barely. Her neck was bent down at an awkward angle and she couldn't breathe very well, but Corrie quickly, and quietly, closed one door, then the other, praying whoever was shooting wouldn't think to look under the sink for anyone.

At the same moment Corrie heard the soft click of the cabinet door to her hiding place engage with the small magnet that kept it shut, she heard her office door burst open.

Because Corrie was blind, her other senses had always been more acute than a sighted person's. She seemed to hear, smell, and taste what people with no disabilities couldn't. The man who'd entered her office walked straight to her desk. Corrie heard her desk chair being pulled away. Yup, he'd immediately checked under there to see if someone was hiding from him. She heard him walk to the small window and held her breath.

Corrie nearly jumped out of her skin when she heard the man's cell phone ring. He answered it and paced around her office as he spoke to whomever was on the other end.

"Yeah? Just about. No trouble whatsoever. Easiest job I've had in a long time. Haven't seen the asshole yet. Yeah, he was supposed to be here. I've got one more room to check. No, no witnesses. Yes, I'm fucking sure. He'll wish he paid what he owes us once he sees what happened to his coworkers. Fuck off. You'll hear from me when you hear from me."

Corrie breathed shallowly, trying not to make a sound. She knew she was one cough, one muscle twitch, one wrong move away from death.

The shooter sounded mean. She couldn't tell what he looked like, of course, but his voice had a unique accent. She couldn't place it, but Corrie was pretty sure if she ever heard it again, she'd recognize it. She listened as he walked around the room one more time. It sounded as if he was limping; there was a light pause between his footsteps, as if he dragged one leg a bit more than the other.

She almost had a heart attack when he came over to the sink and turned on the water above her. Corrie heard it gurgling through the pipes her knees were jammed against and even felt the pipe warm as the liquid coming out of the faucet heated up. The water turned off and she heard the killer grab a paper towel from the stack next to the sink.

As she sat under the sink, wondering if the man would somehow realize she was there and shoot her in the head, Corrie could smell the cologne he was wearing. She'd never smelled anything like it before. If she'd met a man out at a party or a club, she might find the scent attractive, but because of her circumstance, and the knowledge that she was two inches away from death, she almost gagged at the stench of him. The smell of gunpowder also clung to the man, as if he were cloaked in it. Corrie knew she'd never forget the scent of his cologne mixed with that horrible smell of gunpowder.

Finally the man limped to the end of the row of cabinets and must've thrown away the wet paper towel he'd used to dry his hands. Such a polite murderer, not leaving any trash around. She heard him open the first upper cabinet and rummage through it.

What in God's name was he doing? Shouldn't he want to get away? He'd just shot and probably killed people—was he looking for condiments now? Why wouldn't he just *leave* already?

She almost whimpered in relief when she heard the faint sound of sirens. Either someone in the clinic must've called 911 before they were killed or someone nearby heard the shots. It took the man another few beats to hear them and he'd opened another cabinet in the meantime. When he finally heard the wailing of the police sirens, he turned away from the cabinets and walked quickly to the door to the office with his uneven gait.

Corrie didn't hear the door to her office close, and listened as the man walked to the last room he hadn't checked yet. It was the small break room. Shaun obviously wasn't there, because Corrie didn't hear any more gunshots. The mystery man then walked back up the hall the way he'd arrived, and not too much later, Corrie heard nothing but silence.

The quietness rang in her ears. It wasn't normal for her work-place. Usually she heard the sounds of keyboard keys clacking as Cayley worked on her computer. She'd hear Shaun talking with Cayley, or on the phone, or with a client. Clients sometimes spoke on their phones while they waited for their appointments, or talked to each other. Hiding under the sink, Corrie couldn't even hear the hum of the air conditioner that usually drove her crazy by the end of each day. It had a high-pitched squeak that no one but her seemed able to hear.

Corrie's legs were cramping, but she was too scared to move. She couldn't see what was going on, if the man was really and truly gone, or if he had an accomplice. Maybe he was waiting to see if any witnesses, like herself, crawled out of their hidey-holes, so he could blow them away as well. She'd never been so scared in her entire life, and that was saying something.

Growing up blind hadn't been a walk in the park. She'd made it through too many terrifying situations to count, including being lost in the middle of a large shopping mall. Or the time she went out with friends in college and got separated from them when a fight broke out in the bar they were in. Corrie could hear grunting and fists hitting bodies, but had no idea which way to go to escape the danger all around her.

But this—this was a whole new kind of scary.

Corrie stayed huddled under the sink, listening as several people finally entered the clinic area. They didn't say a word, but Corrie could hear them methodically making their way through each room, saying "clear" as they entered each one. It was obviously the police, and she'd never been so glad to hear anything in her entire life.

Not wanting to get shot, she didn't dare pop open the cabinet doors to crawl out. When she heard two people enter her office, she took a chance and tentatively called out, "Don't shoot! I'm a chiropractor. I'm hiding under the sink."

"Come out with your hands up."

"Okay, I'm coming, but please, don't shoot me." Corrie's voice wobbled as she answered. She leaned against the cabinet door with her shoulder and as she expected, the small magnet holding it shut popped open easily. She tried to keep her hands in full view of whoever was in the room. She stuck them out first and swung her legs out.

"Slowly."

She nodded at the terse order. Corrie heard a shuffling sound to her right and to her left. There were at least two officers in the room. She ducked her head and emerged from the small space with a relieved sigh, staying on the ground, knowing her legs wouldn't be able to hold her up just yet anyway.

"Put your hands on your head and don't move."

She did as instructed, intertwining her fingers together on the back of her head, knowing the officers were probably jacked-up on adrenaline, and she didn't want to survive the workplace shooting only to make a wrong move and be accidently shot by the good guys. She felt her wrists being forcibly grasped and held in place. She stayed sitting, waiting for more instructions. She felt another pair of hands patting down her sides, obviously looking for a weapon. After they found nothing, Corrie felt her hands being released.

"Who are you? What's your name?"

"Corrie Madison. I'm a chiropractor here."

"Can you tell us what happened?"

"I can tell you what I know, but please…is Cayley okay? What about Mr. Treadaway? I think there were others waiting for their appointments…" Her voice drifted off as she waited for reassurance that wouldn't ever come.

"I'm sorry, Ms. Madison, they didn't make it. Now, what can you tell us? What did you see?"

Corrie turned toward the demanding voice. Sometimes she forgot people couldn't tell she was blind. It was refreshing, usually, but she'd give anything, absolutely *anything* at this point, to be able to tell this officer that she could identify who had killed her coworkers. She tried to hold back her tears. This was no time to lose it.

"I'm blind, officer. I didn't *see* anything."

Chapter Two

CORRIE TRIED TO follow the hostess as she led her to a table in the crowded restaurant. She tapped her cane on the ground in front of her, making sure she didn't run into any chairs or tables. People didn't necessarily take the easy way when leading her places, and Corrie had banged her shins too many times to risk not using her cane.

Besides that, Corrie wasn't at her best. She was stressed-out, jumpy, and definitely out of sorts. In the six days since the shooting, she'd experienced extreme highs and lows, and today was definitely a low.

Immediately after the massacre, she'd been brought to the police station to be questioned. She'd told the detective everything she knew about the man who'd murdered Cayley and the other innocent people. She'd told them about the shooter's cologne and how she thought he had a funny walk. Knowing her observations probably weren't very helpful, she tried to tell the detective everything she could think of anyway.

After she was allowed to leave, she'd called her best friend, Emily, and her partner, Bethany, to come get her. She'd stayed at their house that night, but refused to stay any longer than that. She was tough; she had to get back to her life.

Corrie had thought she was handling everything that had happened pretty well...at least until the funerals had started. Emily had taken her to Cayley's service and subsequent funeral, and it'd been one of the worst experiences of her life. All she'd wanted to do was mourn her friend and coworker, but the reporters wouldn't leave anyone alone. Thank God they didn't know she was the lone survivor of the actual shooting. So far, at least, the police had managed to keep her name out of the media for her safety, but Corrie knew it was only a matter of time before her name was leaked.

She hadn't slept well the first couple of nights back in her apartment, but Corrie had expected that. She kept hearing the shooter's voice in her head and she swore the smell of him was somehow stuck in her nostrils.

She thought she was finally getting back to normal, although she hadn't been able to step foot back into the clinic yet. Dr. Garza was being very patient with her. He'd hired a company to clean the small office from top to bottom and was hoping to re-open the following week. Corrie had no idea if they'd be able to make it in the same space...who would want to come and get their spine adjusted at a place where some crazy person had come in and killed a bunch of people? Dr. Garza *had* made some security changes to the front reception area. Hopefully that would make clients feel safer.

They still hadn't heard from Shaun, and it wasn't until after her initial police interview that Corrie remembered what the killer had said on his phone to somebody, that he'd been specifically looking for someone who wasn't there. It had to have been Shaun, and now no one could find him. Corrie had tried calling his wife, but the woman had been distraught because she hadn't heard from him since the massacre either.

She'd immediately called the detective who had done her initial interview and let him know what she'd remembered.

Corrie hadn't been planning on meeting with her lawyer again— she'd retained the services of one with Emily's urging—until there was more information about the case, but she'd received a threatening phone call yesterday. She remembered every word...there weren't very many to remember.

"Keep your mouth shut and you'll live."

It seemed as though her name had somehow been leaked after all.

Corrie realized the person on the phone wasn't the same man who had killed everyone in the clinic; she didn't recognize the voice. It was deep and menacing and she knew he meant every word. It pissed her off and scared her a bit at the same time.

She wasn't paying as much attention to her surroundings as she should've been as she made her way to her table in the restaurant, because she was thinking about all that had happened in the last day and trying to figure out what the hell she was going to do. She was wrenched back to her surroundings when she bounced off of someone and heard a loud crash as whatever he was carrying fell to the floor, shattering around them.

"Oh my, I'm so sorry!"

"Jesus Christ, are you fucking blind? Watch where you're walking, why don't you? How'd you like it if I came to your workplace and made you look like a schmuck in front of everyone?"

Corrie didn't like to bring attention to her disability, but this guy's words rubbed against her raw nerves. "As a matter of fact, I *am* blind," she retorted "I already apologized for running into you, but if you'd been paying attention as well, you would've seen me and you could've gone around me."

She heard the man huff and take in a breath to respond when another voice cut in suddenly. It was muted and gruff, and Corrie felt goose bumps race down her arms as he spoke.

"Everyone all right here?"

Before Corrie could pull herself together enough to respond, the busboy groused, "Hunky-dory."

"Miss? Why don't you just step over here out of the way."

Corrie gasped a bit as she felt the man who'd asked if they were okay take her elbow in his large hand and steer her off to her left. His hand was warm on her elbow. She could feel each finger wrap around her bare arm, and the feeling of safety and protection she experienced almost made her jerk away in confusion. She'd never, in her entire life, felt anything like it. She didn't understand it, and that freaked her out.

"Are you okay? You didn't get hit by any flying glass or anything?" The man's voice was soothing and calm.

"No, I think I'm all right. Thank you."

"Can I help you—"

"I'm not an invalid, no matter what you might think of blind people."

"I didn't—"

"Yes, you did, most people do." Corrie didn't know what had come over her. She usually blew off people's concerns and went on her way. She'd never, not once, been as snarky to someone who was clearly just trying to be polite and helpful as she was to this man. But after her crap week, and not liking the feeling of vulnerability that came with his touch, she was unusually gruff.

"I really just wanted to make sure you wouldn't slip on the water on the floor."

"Why? Because I can't see it? Because I'm an idiot and I'd purposely go tromping through the middle of the spilled stuff to prove a point?" Corrie breathed hard. She really wanted to stop the words that were vomiting out of her mouth, but she was so stressed, she just couldn't. She wouldn't blame the man if he turned around and left her standing there...*she* would've if their roles had been reversed.

"Well, no, because I'm trying to be a gentleman."

"A gentleman. Yeah, like there are any of those left in the world today."

Corrie felt a light touch on her hand, and heard the humor in the man's voice as he said, "My name is Quint Axton, I'm happy to meet you."

Reacting on instinct, Corrie lifted her hand in greeting. "Corrie Madison."

"Are you meeting someone here, Corrie?" He hadn't let her hand go and Corrie was irritated with herself for noticing how large it was and how small she felt standing there with her hand in his. And she wasn't a short woman. At five feet nine, she was generally the same size, or taller, than most people, but Corrie could tell this man was a bit taller than she was. He smelled good, like soap and the coffee he'd obviously drunk sometime recently. She could hear his clothes rustling and creaking as he stood in front of her. She had no idea what in the world he was wearing that would make him creak, but she had other things to worry about right then.

"Yeah, he should be here any minute. So you can just leave the poor blind woman here against the wall and he'll be along to take care of me soon." The words came out without thought, Corrie forgetting the hostess was probably lurking nearby to guide her to her table. She just wanted this man to go. He was disturbing her on a personal level and she didn't have time to be attracted to anyone. Her life was way too up in the air right now. She mentally kicked herself for not taking Emily up on the offer to accompany her today.

"Maybe I should start us off again." The man brought the hand he was still holding up to his chest. Corrie fingered the cold metal under her fingertips, even as she was aware he hadn't completely let go of her hand. His fingers were resting on the back of it, running his thumb over the bones there as if trying to gentle her, as she tried to figure out what it was she was touching.

"My name is Officer Quint Axton with the San Antonio Police Department, and I'm pleased to meet you," he said formally.

"Oh my God," Corrie whispered, her tone of voice immediately changing to one of chagrin. She snatched her hand back after realizing what she was feeling. "Uh, yeah, sorry. I didn't mean any disrespect, I mean..."

The man laughed, and Corrie sighed in relief. The last thing she wanted to do was piss off a cop. She had enough on her plate at the moment.

"I just wanted to make sure you knew before you said something you might really regret."

"I am so sorry. I'm not usually like this. I've had a really really *really* bad week."

The officer, Quint, chuckled. "It's okay. Now, are you *sure* you're all right here? The person you're waiting for will be here soon?"

"Yeah, he's my lawyer."

"Your lawyer?" Quint's voice dropped in concern. A concern Corrie could somehow physically feel. She ran her hands up and down her arms, trying to get warm, feeling her cane bump against her leg as it dangled from her wrist.

"Yeah," Corrie said in a soft voice. "I heard a murder. I think someone's trying to shut me up, and I have to figure out what's going to happen next."

Corrie felt herself being moved again. Quint had taken her elbow in his hand and shuffled her farther to the side.

"We're here at the booth. Do you need help scooting in?"

Corrie put her hand out and felt the back of the seat. "I've got it. Thanks."

She knew she should be freaking out right now, but she just didn't have it in her. After everything that had happened, it felt good to have a police officer take control. She had no idea if this was the table the hostess was going to lead her to or not, but at the moment, she didn't care. She couldn't help but remember the relief she'd felt when she heard the officers come into the clinic, knowing they'd be able to help her.

Corrie felt the cold plastic through her jeans and swiveled her hips until her legs were under the table. She folded her cane without thought, having done it more times in her life than she'd ever be able to count, and stuffed it into her purse at her side. Corrie moved over and heard Quint sit on the other side of the table. She didn't say anything, figuring she'd probably already said too much. It wasn't like her to blurt out her personal history to anyone, even if he *was* a police officer.

"Corrie...right?"

"Uh-huh."

"Why don't you start at the beginning."

"No."

"No?" He sounded surprised.

Corrie sighed. "Look, I'm not trying to be difficult here. But I don't know you. You could be the guy after me." She knew he wasn't, he didn't smell anything like the shooter and didn't sound like the other man on the phone, but she went with it anyway. "Anyone can go out and buy a badge and pretend to be a cop."

"Cruz!"

Corrie jerked in her seat. He wasn't talking to her, but his voice had been loud, nevertheless. He'd turned his head and barked the name in the opposite direction from where she was sitting. He'd obviously been shouting at someone across the restaurant. It wasn't fifteen seconds later when Corrie heard two sets of footsteps coming up to their table.

"Yeah, what's up?"

Quint answered the man without giving her a chance to speak. "This is Corrie Madison. She can't see, and doesn't believe I'm a cop. Would you please reassure her?" His words were not pitying, just stating the facts.

Corrie burst in without thinking. "Okay, yeah, that won't work either. If he's your friend, you guys could've planned this in advance...pick up some unsuspecting woman who will buy your story, and if she doesn't, bring in the friend to validate you are who you say you are. And the fact that I'm blind is just icing on the cake, making your entire scam that much easier."

A feminine chuckle rang out through the silence that followed her somewhat foolish statement. Corrie had forgotten there were two people who'd come up to the table. "You tell 'em. And for the record, I like you, Corrie."

"Mickie…" The voice was teasingly warning the woman to shush.

"Sorry…just pretend I'm not here…carry on," she commented, but with a hint of humor in her voice, as if she was used to her boyfriend's demanding ways.

Corrie could just imagine the man standing by their table rolling his eyes. His voice was calm and reassuring when he spoke. "Yeah, you're right. We *could* be running a scam here, but we're not. The man sitting across from you *is* Quint Axton. He's six foot two, has dark hair, thirty-six years old, and has worked for the San Antonio PD for about ten years. I could tell you a lot more, but I'm trying to be brief. I'm Cruz Livingston, FBI. My girlfriend here is Mickie Kaiser. If it's not enough validation for you, I could call our other friend, Dax, who is a Texas Ranger. I understand why you're being careful, but Quint *is* who he says he is. I'd swear on Mickie's life."

Those pesky goose bumps rose on Corrie's arms again. She could tell the man was being one-hundred percent earnest. She'd gotten pretty good at reading people's voices, since she couldn't see any nonverbal cues. The fact that this man swore on the life of the woman standing next to him was about as honest as she'd ever heard from anyone before.

She held out her hand in the direction of the man standing at the side of the booth. "Corrie Madison. It's nice to meet you."

Her hand was gripped in a strong but not crushing grasp. "Nice to meet you too, Corrie." He dropped her hand and they all stayed silent for a moment. It felt awkward to Corrie, but she didn't know if it was just her or not.

She couldn't see Cruz raise his eyebrows at Quint, and she didn't see Quint motioning his friend to go back to his table with his head.

"Hopefully I'll see you around, Corrie. Trust Quint. He's one of the best officers the SAPD has. He'll do right by you."

With those words, Corrie heard Cruz and Mickie step away from the booth and head back across the restaurant.

"Okay?"

Corrie really wasn't okay. She had no idea what the hell she was doing. Would she be able to go back to work? Was the threatening phone call for real? What would her lawyer suggest? She had no idea what was going on and she felt as though her life was spinning out of control. Before she could open her mouth to spill her guts and say something wussy and out of character for her, such as "no, I'm not okay, but I think if you held me it might go a long way toward making me feel better," Corrie heard another set of footsteps approach the table.

"Ms. Kaiser? Oh! Lieutenant Axton, I didn't realize you'd be here too. This situation is a mess. I'm glad you're here."

Corrie's heart leapt in response to Mr. Herrington's words. He knew the officer by sight, so he had to be legit. She'd already pretty much believed it after Cruz's words, but it was nice for it to be validated again.

"The shit's hit the fan," Mr. Herrington continued, obviously assuming Corrie and the lieutenant were friends, and easing into the seat next to her, "and Corrie here is gonna need all the help she can get to stay one step ahead of this asshole."

Chapter Three

CORRIE'S HEART SANK at her lawyer's comment. Lord, what now?

"Talk to me." Quint's words were terse and grumbly...that was the only way Corrie could describe them.

"Corrie? I'm assuming you're okay with him being here and hearing our conversation? I didn't realize you knew Lieutenant Axton."

"I—"

"She knows me." Quint cut off her words, and Corrie tilted her head at him, wondering what he was doing. Technically he wasn't lying, she'd just met him so she guessed that meant she knew him, but he was obviously implying that they'd known each other for a while...longer than ten minutes or so.

"This is a bit unusual. Are you here on or off the record?"

"Off."

"Corrie?" Mr. Herrington's question lay between them.

Corrie was confused. She didn't know Quint, didn't know why he was there—other than to help her not slip in the spilled water from the busboy she'd run into—didn't know why he *wanted* to be there. Had no idea why he'd said things were off the record. She trembled in confusion, wanting to have someone else help her make some scary decisions about what she was supposed to do now, but was Quint the man to help her? She honestly didn't know.

She heard the creak of Quint's clothes, realizing now it was probably the utility belt around his waist and possibly even a bulletproof vest making the creaking noises, as he leaned toward her. He put one of his warm hands over both of her cold ones. She was clenching them together in front of her. She could feel the heat from his large hand seep into her skin. When his thumb brushed back and forth over the back of her hand again, reassuring her without words, she took a deep breath and made her decision.

"Yeah, I want him here." Her decision went back to that time long ago when she'd been lost in the mall. The first person to stop and help her had been a police officer. He'd picked her up and let her play with his badge until her parents had found her again. That memory had stuck with her throughout her life, and went a long way toward making her soften toward Quint.

Not even hesitating, Mr. Herrington started in. Corrie heard him lift his bag into his lap and rummage through it as he spoke.

"Okay, here's the thing…I got the case file from the detective and your description of the guy that came into your clinic is probably not enough to identify him definitively; it's not like you can have a smell-o-vision lineup even if they catch the guy, but that doesn't really matter. If he thinks you can identify him, you could be in danger."

"Not enough to identify him? I know I could pick him out if I heard him talk or walk, I wouldn't have to smell him."

"Right, but he could always alter those things. I hate to sound pessimistic, but a blind witness is a tricky thing and many lawyers won't take the chance on the testimony being thrown out. I'm sorry if that sounds harsh, but juries would have to one-hundred percent buy into the idea that you knew who it was without seeing him. No one wants to convict an innocent person. Reasonable doubt and all that. His lawyer would tear you apart on the stand. It'd be a hard sell."

"So…what? He gets away with it? With killing Cayley? Mr. Treadaway? All the others?" Corrie's voice rose in her agitation. "That's not fair or right. What happened to justice?" she hissed, frustrated and pissed at the same time.

It wasn't her lawyer who responded, but Quint.

"Easy, Corrie."

She took a deep breath and tried not to cry. She never cried. She hadn't asked for any of this, didn't know if she could even deal with it.

"The jerk had the nerve to call and threaten me yesterday."

"What? Did you call the cops?"

"Not yet, but it's on my agenda for today. I wanted to let you know first hoping that it would help persuade someone that I could testify."

The lawyer sighed loudly. "I don't know that it will, but it puts a different spin on your safety. I'm thinking whoever did this is scared you *will* testify and that you *can* identify the shooter. Do you have anywhere you can go until the detectives have time to dig deeper into the investigation and find more clues?"

Ignoring his question for the time being, Corrie asked, "Are they any closer? Have they figured out who did it?"

"No. Not from what I've heard. I don't get all the up-to-the-minute information though. Lieutenant, do you know more?"

"I didn't know this was Corrie's case until today…"

Man, he's good, Corrie thought to herself. He hadn't even known *her* until today, of course he didn't know about the case.

"…but I know the detective investigating the case. We've all heard about it, of course, and been briefed on what to be on the lookout for. I'll touch base with him when I get back to the station and see what I can find out."

Corrie turned to Quint in confusion. Her head spun with all that had happened this morning.

"Okay, Corrie, do you have any more to add to what you've already told me?" her lawyer asked.

"Yeah, I think so. It might not be anything, but I thought about it last night." She paused, not wanting to throw Shaun under the proverbial bus, but knowing anything she might be able to tell her lawyer, and the police, might help catch whoever killed Cayley and the others. She felt Quint squeeze her clenched hands in support. He hadn't let go of them while they'd been talking.

"Shaun, my assistant. He wasn't there. He was *supposed* to be there helping me with the radiographs. We go over them together before I meet with the clients. Mr. Treadaway…" Her voice cracked, remembering what had happened, and she forced herself to continue. "Mr. Treadaway was waiting for me to get back in there and make his adjustments. I was upset because Shaun hadn't come to get me yet; I was on my way to see where he was when I heard the man come into the clinic."

"Have you talked to him since?" Quint asked the question this time.

Knowing he was talking about Shaun, and not about poor Mr. Treadaway, Corrie shook her head. "No, and that's really weird. We aren't buddy-buddy or anything, it's not like we phone each other on the weekends, but I called his wife and she hasn't heard from him in a couple of days either."

"Corrie, the cops know about Shaun. They've been looking for him too," Mr. Herrington told her, sounding almost impatient. "Go over with me again exactly what you overheard the shooter saying on the phone."

"He was bragging that it was an easy job and he also talked about not seeing someone and that they thought he was supposed to be there. The last thing he said when he hung up was something about whoever this guy was, he would wish he'd paid what he owed after seeing what had been done to his coworkers."

Neither man said anything for a moment after her statement. Finally, Mr. Herrington spoke out loud, obviously not asking her a question, but contemplating what she'd said. "So they were specifically looking for someone and Shaun just happened to not be there."

Quint asked, "Do you know of any reason why this Shaun person would need to borrow money?"

"Unfortunately, yes. His little boy nearly drowned a year or so ago and he's got huge medical bills. He doesn't talk about it much, but Shaun told me once he felt like a failure to his wife and his other child because they were probably going to lose the house in foreclosure since he couldn't afford to pay all the medical bills that were piling up."

Corrie turned to her lawyer. "That's what I wanted to tell you today. If they're looking for Shaun, the police need to find him before the bad guys do." Corrie supposed she should be pissed at Shaun, or at least upset at the entire situation, but at the moment she was more worried about what he'd gotten himself into. She didn't want Shaun killed on top of everyone else she'd lost.

"You need to go to the station and tell the detective this on the record, Corrie," Quint said seriously.

"Will they protect Shaun and the rest of his family? Oh my God!" Corrie suddenly thought of something she hadn't thought of before. She turned her hand over in Quint's, and looked his way earnestly. "What if they go after his wife? Or his kids?"

Quint tightened his hold on Corrie's hands. "I don't think they will. Now, I don't know who's behind this, but typically loan sharks don't go after family. They make their point with whoever owes them the money. But again, that's just typically...nothing about this case feels normal to me."

"You have to figure out what you're going to do, Corrie," Mr. Herrington told her seriously. "I'm with the lieutenant, this feels off and especially after that phone call, it's obvious that you aren't safe."

"But you just said I couldn't testify because I'm blind; that I couldn't identify the killer."

"I did say that, but I also suggested that *they* didn't know that. These aren't honor students, Corrie. If they think there's even a smidgen of a possibility you can help the police figure out who they are, and get them arrested, you're in danger."

Corrie felt her heart rate increase, but she tried to hide her trepidation. She had no idea what she was going to do, but first things first. She had to go to the police station and tell the detectives as much about Shaun as she could. Then she'd worry about what she was going to do next. She'd always been practical; her blindness forced her to be. She'd work through things one at a time. Baby steps. It was all she could do.

"Okay, if you'll call me a cab, I'll talk to them, then I'll figure out where I'll stay and I'll let you know."

Mr. Herrington put his hand on Corrie's forearm. His hand was hot and sweaty, and it felt stifling. Corrie knew the older man wanted what was best for her, but she felt suffocated, trapped inside the booth all of a sudden. She didn't know what to do and his pushing was just making it worse.

"You keep your head down and stay safe. Keep in touch with me and let me know where you'll be so I can keep you up-to-date on what's going on."

Corrie nodded quickly. "I will." She sighed in relief when he removed his arm. Surprisingly, she heard Quint shift across from her and felt him move so that his other hand came to hers. He covered her hand with both of his and squeezed, as if he knew she'd disliked the feel of her lawyer's hand on her arm. The friction and warmth of his soothing touch wiped away the clammy feel of Mr. Herrington's fingers.

"I'll take her. I have to get back anyway. My lunch hour is over."

"Great. I'd appreciate that. I have another appointment in thirty minutes. I'll be in touch." He leaned over and patted Corrie's shoulder. Corrie could hear the plastic squeak as he eased out of the booth next to her and she heard his fading footsteps over the din of the restaurant.

"You okay?" Quint asked softly, not letting go of her hand.

Corrie pulled back, knowing she couldn't get used to this man's touch, and he immediately let go. She heard him sit back in his seat. "Of course. I'm always all right. You don't have to take me to the station, you know. I can get there on my own."

"Of course you can. You're a grown woman. But it doesn't make sense for you to pay for a cab when I'm going to the same place you are."

"It just seems...I don't know...weird. I don't know you."

He ignored her statement and said instead, "I'll even let you sit in front in my squad car if you want."

Corrie laughed, as she figured he'd meant for her to. "You mean you'd actually make me get in the back where the criminals have to sit?"

"Well....it's very nice back there. A nice hard plastic bench, top-of-the-line seat restraints, and of course the nice shatterproof plastic to keep you from flying into the front seat in case of an accident or from shanking me as I'm driving."

Corrie just shook her head in exasperation. Quint was funny. She liked that. "Okay, you convinced me. Who can pass up a ride in a cop car? If I'm good, maybe you'll let me turn on the siren or something." She smiled so he'd know she was kidding. "Can you give me a moment to stop at the restroom before we go, or will that make you late?"

"It won't make me late, come on, I'll steer you in the right direction."

Corrie stood up and held out her hand so Quint could take it, loop it around his elbow and help her find her way. She was surprised when he ignored her obvious prompt and instead took her hand in his. No one had ever held her hand while leading her. She'd had men hook her hand over their arm and press themselves into her sexually, but most people were awkward and only held on to her with their fingertips, not knowing exactly how they were supposed to help her.

Quint not only took her hand in his as if they were dating or something, but he put his other hand on her upper arm as they walked through the restaurant when someone got too close and jostled them.

"Go straight about fifteen paces. It's the first door on your left. Pull it toward you to open it. Are you sure you don't need help?"

Corrie chuckled. This she could deal with. "I'm fine. I've been in enough public bathrooms to know what to do. And if I do need help, I'll ask someone who is in there." She pulled out her cane from her purse and unfolded it even as she spoke.

Quint didn't make it awkward, he simply said, "Okay, I'll be right here waiting for you. Take your time."

Chapter Four

—————◆—————

CORRIE MADE HER way down the hall and disappeared into the women's restroom. Quint pulled out his phone and sent a quick text to Cruz, letting him know he was headed back to the station and he'd talk to him later. He knew Cruz would ask him a million questions about Corrie and what was going on, and Quint would be happy to answer them...after *he* figured out exactly what was going on.

After reading Cruz's affirmative response, Quint put his phone back into his pocket and thought about Corrie. She intrigued him, and he wasn't usually so captivated by a woman after knowing her for such a short period of time. He'd seen a lot throughout his career as an officer with the San Antonio Police Department. People usually fit into stereotypical molds he'd formed in his mind, especially women.

Flirty, scared, victimized, angry, entitled...the list went on and on, but he couldn't for the life of him place Corrie into any of the items on that list. He'd been amused at her feisty reaction to the busboy and even her rejection of him at first was cute.

Then when he'd figured out exactly who she was and why she was at the restaurant in the first place, she'd stunned him with the matter-of-fact way she seemed to be dealing with everything that had happened to her over the last week or so. Oh, she was unsure and shaken about the phone call, but she wasn't outwardly freaking out or crying uncontrollably, and that went a long way toward raising his opinion about her.

Of course he'd heard about the shooting that had happened. All the officers had been briefed on the incident and were told to be on the lookout for anything suspicious. The detectives didn't have a lot to go on in finding the killer, and the media had been putting a lot of pressure on the chief and the department to find who had killed all those people.

Quint had even been aware there was a witness, but he'd had no idea the "witness" was blind. He still hadn't heard everything Corrie had gone through while the man was killing her friends and workers, but he would.

He realized suddenly that he wanted to know everything about Corrie. Why was she blind? Was it an accident? How had she survived? Was she seeing anyone?

His last thought brought him up short. Seeing someone? He wasn't one to have relationships with women. He wasn't a man-whore, but he'd never found anyone who he felt like he'd want to spend the rest of his life with. He'd dated women, he'd had a couple of one-night stands, he'd even thought he was in love once, but it wasn't until recently he'd decided he was missing out by being single. After watching Cruz and his other friend, Dax, find the loves of their lives, he'd seen firsthand that having someone to love, and being loved in return, could be an amazing thing.

Not only that, but he genuinely liked both Mackenzie and Mickie. They were tough women who seemed to bring out the best in both Dax and Cruz. They lightened up their gatherings and for some reason he could totally see Corrie fitting in with them. Of course he was getting ahead of himself, he'd just met the woman after all, but the thought was there nonetheless.

Quint used to think that having a serious girlfriend would be a handicap, especially for him. Being a police officer wasn't an easy job. It involved lots of long hours, including overtime, and he was in danger more often than not. Over the last year or so, there had been a lot of highly publicized cases of what the public was calling unnecessary roughness against citizens. It was tough to be a police officer today, but Quint wouldn't want to do anything else.

Quint had wanted to be a cop since he was a little kid. Most children grew out of their first dreams of occupation, but not Quint. As soon as he was old enough, he'd asked for cop toys. His mom had bought him curtains with police cars on them. His bedding was blue and white. Quint knew his parents had thought it was cute at first and that he'd grow out of it. But he'd joined the junior officer league when he was in high school and hadn't looked back. He'd gone to college and earned his Criminal Justice degree and had been hired not long after his graduation.

Quint smiled, thinking back to the green cop he'd once been. Luckily he'd started his career in the town of Bowling Green, Ohio. It was a small Midwestern college town. It was close to Toledo, but not so close that they had murders and other extreme crimes all the time. The college kids used to call it "Boring Green" because not much exciting ever happened there…other than the annual tractor-pull championships.

In time he'd needed more of a challenge, and while Quint knew his parents wanted him to stay in Ohio, he'd eventually moved south to Texas.

Quint loved San Antonio and truly felt he'd found his ideal job and police department. He had close friends and enjoyed the way the other law enforcement agencies in the city worked together. The feeling of comradery between him and Cruz, Dax, Calder, TJ, Hayden, and Conor were unique. Not to mention the group of firefighters they hung out with on a regular basis. Having so many friends who were involved with serving the city was rewarding. They worked hard, and played hard, and got along amazingly well. He knew he'd never find a better group of friends than the firefighters at Station 7 and the law enforcement officers he hung around with.

Not only that, but Quint felt a deep satisfaction in being able to find and arrest people who were a danger to society...and unfortunately there were a lot of people who were a danger to others in the southern Texas city he called home.

He'd recognized that same urge, that urge for justice, in Corrie today. She'd been disturbed to realize her testimony, because of her blindness, would be discounted. She so badly wanted justice for her friends, and wanted to be a part of that justice, he could almost feel her disappointment.

Quint hadn't been around many blind people—hell, really *any* blind people—but Corrie oozed competence and independence out of every pore. If she hadn't spoken up, and hadn't been carrying a cane, he wouldn't have known she couldn't see.

His thoughts turned to her situation. He had no idea what she planned to do after seeing the detective, but hopefully she had somewhere she could go where'd she be safe.

QUINT KEPT HIS eye on the door to the interrogation room. After leaving the restaurant, he'd taken Corrie to the station and released her to the care of Detective Algood. Matt was an excellent cop who'd treat her with care and make sure she was comfortable while telling him all she remembered.

He shook his head. Since when did he care if Matt treated someone with care?

Since Corrie. She'd been friendly and funny on the way to the station. He'd given her the "tour" of his cruiser when they'd first gotten in. She'd asked if she could touch the things he was explaining to her. He'd agreed and helped her find and run her fingers over things like the switches for the lights and siren, the laptop, the shotgun safely locked in its holder. The bright smile she flashed him when he let her flick on the siren for a moment lit up her face. Even in the midst of all the shit going on in her life, she didn't hesitate to show her pleasure in something as simple as riding in a squad car for the first time.

Quint supposed it was because she couldn't see the world passing by as they drove, but she'd kept her head turned toward him, and had concentrated on him, the entire trip to the station. He'd had her complete attention as he explained proper protocol of things like when to use lights and sirens, and how he'd use the laptop as he hurried his way to a call.

They'd arrived at the station and Quint had asked Corrie to wait in the car and he'd gone around to her side and helped her out, not letting go of her hand as he walked them into the back door of the station. Her hand felt small and fragile in his, although he knew that was a lie. She was strong, if not physically, mentally. After what had happened to both Mackenzie, Dax's woman, and Mickie, Quint knew being mentally strong was sometimes a better trait to have than simple physical strength.

Luckily, Quint had some paperwork he had to catch up on, so he was able to stay at the station and finish it while Matt spoke with Corrie. He could watch and wait for her to be done and he could help her get to where she was going next. He didn't even bother to analyze *why* he wanted to be there when Corrie was finished. He wouldn't be able to sleep well without talking to her and finding out what her future plans were.

Finally, after a long two hours, the door opened and Matt and Corrie walked out. Matt looked stressed, running his hand though his hair as he looped Corrie's hand over his elbow and led her down the hall toward Quint.

Quint closed down the report he was working on, knowing he'd easily be able to finish it in the morning, and stood. He met them before they reached his desk.

"Hey, Matt. Corrie."

"Hey, Quint," Matt returned. "Thanks for bringing Corrie back in."

"You get what you need?"

"Maybe. It's more than we had to start with. I'm going to see what more we can do to find Shaun. We'd already been looking for him, but knowing he was most likely the reason that guy was there puts things in a different perspective. I have a feeling he can shed a lot of light on this case."

Quint looked at Corrie. He'd thought she was good when she and Matt walked toward his desk, but up close, he could now see the furrows in her brow and the pinched look around her lips.

"You okay, Corrie?"

She nodded, but didn't say anything.

Quint looked at Matt and raised his chin, asking what was up.

Matt just gazed back at him with a frustrated look on his face and shrugged his shoulders. Quint shook his head at his friend.

"What? I know you guys are talking with that nonverbal man-speak crap. I'm standing right here. It's rude. I *hate* when people do that." Corrie's voice was a mixture of pissed off and sad at the same time.

Quint immediately felt bad. "Sorry, Corrie. Really. I'm worried about you. I was simply trying to ask my buddy here what was up."

"You could've asked me directly." Corrie dropped Matt's elbow and put her arms around her stomach defensively. Her stance made her look uncomfortable and vulnerable.

"You're right. I should've. I'm sorry. Come on, let's go sit over here." Quint didn't bother trying to defend himself. Corrie was right. It *was* rude. He hadn't thought so at the time but looking at it from her perspective, he knew he had to change his thinking.

There were a lot of ways he had to change his thinking, he suddenly realized. Just because Corrie was blind didn't mean she was helpless or clueless. Trying to talk about her, in front of her, when she couldn't see, was like talking about someone who didn't speak English in front of them…they'd know you were talking about them but wouldn't be able to understand what you were saying.

Quint took Corrie's hand again and led her into a small room. "There's a chair to your left." He dropped her right hand and took her left in his and guided it to the arm of the chair. "There's a desk in front of you and I'm going to go and close the door. It's private in here, no one can overhear us."

Corrie nodded and eased herself into the chair. Once she got her bearings, she didn't fumble or fidget, she just sat and waited for him to return.

Quint closed the door and pulled a seat over so he could sit next to Corrie, and not behind the desk. He didn't want to be that far away from her.

"So…what's up? Are you okay? What did Matt have to say?"

Corrie couldn't stay mad at Quint. She'd been furious when she'd realized he and Matt were "talking" right there in front of her. She'd called him on it and he'd immediately apologized. Most people, when she confronted them on the same thing, tried to make excuses or lied and said they weren't talking about her right in front of her face. Quint got points for that.

"I'm fine. I told Detective Algood about the threatening phone call. We went over everything that happened that day ad nauseam and here I am. He's going to see if he can find Shaun and figure out what in tarnation is going on."

"What about the threat you received?"

"What about it?"

Quint clenched his teeth. He'd never met such a stubborn woman before. This was almost as bad as interrogating someone. "What is he doing about that?"

Corrie shrugged. "There's not much he *can* do about it. He's going to tap my phone; if the guy calls back, it'll be recorded and we'll go from there."

"Where are you staying then?"

Corrie squirmed uncomfortably in her chair for the first time. The detective had asked the same thing and she'd tried to explain. She'd known he hadn't liked it, and Corrie knew in her gut, Quint wouldn't either.

"Home. I'm staying at my apartment."

"Corrie—"

"Really, Quint, it's fine. Look, I'm sure once whoever it is finds out I'm not allowed to testify, they'll be appeased. I'll make sure to lock my door, and I'd already decided to call a security company to install some sort of alarm."

"Can't you go somewhere to stay?"

"Like where?"

"I don't know…a friend's house? Your parents'?"

"If you were me, would you go to your friend's or parents' house if you thought for a second it might put them in danger?" Knowing the answer, Corrie continued. "No, you freaking wouldn't. My best friend, Emily, and her partner, Bethany, have a little boy. There's no way in heck I'd put either of them in danger, and I'd rather die myself than bring a killer to their doorstep who might possibly hurt Ethan. He's only six months old, for goodness sake. He can't protect himself."

Corrie was working herself into a full tizzy, and couldn't see the tender look on Quint's face.

"And my parents? Are you crazy? After all they've done for me…after they helped make me independent, you think I'd go running back and ask to hide behind them? No freaking way. I'm fine. Detective Algood is going to figure this out, and everything will go back to normal."

Corrie was startled out of her angsty ramblings when Quint put his hand on her cheek and turned her head toward him.

"I don't like it." His tone didn't match the words. He sounded amused.

"What's so funny?" Corrie asked, exasperated.

"Not what you think, obviously."

"Darn it, Quint."

"I was just sitting here thinking how endearing you are."

"What?"

"Yeah, you worked yourself up into a frenzy, but not once did you slip and swear."

Startled at his words, Corrie could only mumble, "Huh?"

"I swear all the time. I know I shouldn't, but I can't help it. Must be the company I keep. I hope that's not going to bother you." Quint knew the words coming out of his mouth were some sort of commitment to this woman he'd just met, but he wasn't sorry. "I know finding you funny is inappropriate as hell, because the reason you're saying what you said is anything but humorous, but I thought it was cute and hilarious at the same time."

Quint's tone changed with his next words. He got serious and all humor was gone. "But that's not to say I like your plan. I don't. Not one bit." He gently squeezed Corrie's hand when she opened her mouth to speak.

"That being said—I get it. I do. I wouldn't want to put my parents at risk either. And you certainly shouldn't put Emily, Bethany, or Ethan in danger. Have you told your friend what's going on?"

Corrie shook her head. Oh, Emily knew about the shooting and what had happened of course, she'd stayed at her house right after it happened, but Corrie hadn't told her about the phone call yet.

"She's going to insist you stay with her."

"I know, but I'm going to insist I don't in return."

Quint sighed. He didn't like it. He *really* didn't like it. But what could he do? They weren't dating; he'd just met this woman today. He didn't have any say in what she did in her life. None. And he found himself hating that.

"Do you have a cell?"

Corrie looked at him as if he had two heads. "Uh, yeah. Everyone has a cell."

Quint chuckled again. Damn, she was so fucking cute. "I wasn't sure."

"Oh, because I can't see?"

"Yeah."

"Look, Mr. Cop. I'm going easy on you because I don't think you're trying to be discriminatory or a jerk about this. I'm normal. I'm as normal as you. I cook, I clean, I talk on the phone, I even use a computer. I can read, I can tell time, I can pay for my own stuff with real money, I dress myself every morning and manage to color coordinate my clothes with the help of Braille labels. I can play specialized board games and figure out what socks go with which, except if the dryer monster eats them like it always seems to somehow. I'm just like you, Quint. I eat the same, brush my teeth the same, make love the same, orgasm the same, cry, smile, and get pissed…just like you."

"Will you go to dinner with me later this week?"

"What?" Corrie shook her head. Had she heard him right? She'd just gotten done haranguing him, and he was asking her out?

"Will you go to dinner with me?" When Corrie didn't immediately answer, he added, "Please?"

"I don't know…"

"I've been attracted to you since I saw you from across the restaurant today. I don't like doormats, so when you stood up for yourself with that guy who ran into you, I was impressed. I'm even more impressed now. You don't take crap from me, you'll protect your friends with everything you have, and you have a slight sarcastic streak. You're beautiful, you're a perfect height for me, you call me out on my idiotic bullshit, even when I say it out of a lack of knowledge and not malicious intent. Call me a masochist, but I like the fact you can stand up for yourself with me. You're not afraid of me, and that's very refreshing, you have no idea. I want to take you out and get to know more about you. I want to know about all the idiots who you put in their place for acting stupid. I want to know how you can do all those things you just threw in my face. I like you, Corrie. Please let me take you out."

"Oh. After that passionate speech, I'd be a horrible person if I refused." Corrie couldn't think of anything else to say after all that.

Quint smiled, for once glad she couldn't see his amusement. God, she was so refreshing. She didn't play games, and he'd never been so attracted to anyone before. "Give me your phone."

Corrie reached down and grabbed her purse that she'd placed next to the chair when she'd sat and plucked her cell out of the side pocket she always put it in. She held her thumb to the button at the bottom for a few beats to unlock it, then handed it over to Quint.

He didn't say a word, but Corrie could hear him clicking some buttons on her phone.

"I'm assuming you use the voice feature on here to call people?"

"Uh-huh."

"Okay, I put myself in as simply 'Quint' to make it easy when you want to call me."

Feeling a bit of her inner snarkiness coming back, Corrie quipped, "I'm going to want to call you?"

She could hear the laughter in Quint's voice when he responded. "I sure as shit hope so."

He fiddled a bit more with the phone and she heard his own cell vibrate in the room. "I hope you don't mind, but I called my cell so I'd have your number too. I'll program it in later. Here ya go, your phone."

Corrie held out her hand and Quint put it into her palm. He brought his other hand under hers and clasped her hand with both of his. "I'm worried about you, Corrie."

She inhaled. She hadn't been sure if he was going to let it drop or not. Apparently he wasn't. But it'd been so long since anyone had worried about her, Corrie had almost forgotten what it felt like. She hadn't lied; her parents had brought her up to be self-sufficient and they hadn't coddled her at all. Oh, they loved her fiercely, but they wanted her to be independent and able to live on her own. They'd done the best they could for her, and Corrie was thankful as all get out. She wouldn't be where she was today if her parents hadn't been so awesome.

Corrie knew Emily worried about her as well, but it was somehow different, especially since Bethany had given birth to their son. They had someone else to worry about now. Their first concern was Ethan, and should always be Ethan.

"I'll be okay."

Quint hadn't let go of her hand. "You'll call if something doesn't seem right?"

"Call *you*? No. I'll call 9-1-1."

"Okay, I'll give you that, but you'll call me if you're uneasy, or if you just need someone to talk to?"

"I don't know you, Quint. Why would I call you?"

"I don't really know you either, but I'm trying to. I can't help this worry that's sitting in the pit of my stomach when it comes to you and this situation. I think about you unable to see, sitting in your apartment, and someone breaking in."

Corrie started getting mad again and tried to tug her hand out of his grasp. "I told you, I'm not helpless."

"I *know* that, Jesus. I *do*. But I can't turn this off. My gut is screaming at me that there's more to this than what we've been able to figure out as of yet. I wouldn't like it if you were a man who was six foot five and a bodybuilder. I'd like to say it has nothing to do with your eyesight, but we'd both know I'd be lying. Corrie, I've been a cop for a long time. I've learned to listen to my gut. If I honestly didn't think you could take care of yourself, I'd insist on you going to a motel, or to someone's house, anyone's place other than your own. But I can see how self-sufficient you are. That competency practically oozes out of your pores. But that niggling feeling is still there. So please, for the love of God, call me if something seems off. I can check it out without embarrassing you. Then if it's nothing, you haven't felt like you've bothered anyone else. Yeah?"

Corrie ran his words over and over in her head. He was right. This was a messed-up situation, and she didn't like it either. He'd said he was worried about her. It felt good. And she liked him. He wanted to take her on a date. Why the heck was she fighting him about this?

"Okay."

"Just okay? No other commentary?"

"I don't think so."

"Thank Christ."

She giggled a bit at his response. Quint finally let go of her hand and she turned and put her cell back into the small pocket in her purse.

"Come on, I'm off duty. I'll take you home."

Corrie fought the automatic refusal that almost came out of her mouth. She was independent, yes, but it was stupid to refuse a ride. Why shouldn't she let Quint take her home? She wouldn't have to call Emily to come pick her up now or take a taxi. She usually didn't mind using cabs to get around, but with everything that had happened she knew she'd feel safer with him. Besides, she told herself, he'd need to know where she lived if she was going to go on a date with him.

"Okay, I'd appreciate that." She stood up and held out her hand, smiling at the now familiar feel of Quint's big hand wrapping around her own. It really was amazing that after thirty-two years, she'd never felt so normal when she was being helped around as she did with Quint. The simple act of taking her hand rather than letting her grab on to his elbow, even though he had no idea he was doing it "wrong," made her feel as though she was on an actual date, rather than feeling helpless. She liked it. A lot.

Chapter Five

————————◆————————

D *ING*
The loud noise from her phone made Corrie jump what seemed like ten feet. She reached over and pushed the button on her alarm clock to see what time it was. The mechanical voice announced that it was eleven forty-three.

She hadn't been sleeping well the past few nights because of everything that had happened and every little sound now made her jump. She was hyperaware and hated it. Even the normal sounds of her apartment now frightened her. The ice maker in the refrigerator making ice, the sound of the air conditioning turning on and off, even the sound of the automated voice of her clock made her jump. Every sound made her wonder if someone was in the apartment. She'd conditioned herself over the years to almost not even hear the sounds, but not now. Corrie despised it.

She pushed a button on the phone and heard the computerized voice read the text that had woken her up moments ago.

Quint- Hey. Just wanted to check in. Just got off shift. I hate the new-and-improved shifts the chief is trying out...the hours are constantly changing. Anyway...everything ok with you?

It was a little annoying that the program read the name of the person sending the text every single time, but Corrie hadn't had a chance to get the upgrade yet. Quint had been texting her intermittingly since he'd dropped her off earlier in the week. He'd come up to her apartment and checked it out for her, declaring it "bad-guy free." She'd laughed at the time, but occasionally wished over the last few days that he'd been there to check it out for her again and simply to keep her company.

She clicked on a button and spoke into the phone, knowing the program would turn her words into a text automatically. All she had to say was send after she was done speaking, and her text would go through.

I'm ok. Your shift go ok?

Quint- Typical. Seriously, you all right?

As all right as I can be. Nights are the worst. I swear every time an ice cube falls in the fridge, it scares me to death.

Quint didn't respond for a few minutes and Corrie sat up in bed nervously. Shoot. She knew she should've kept her mouth shut. She'd always kept their conversations light and easy in the past, not even wanting to admit to herself that she was frightened, let alone Quint. She had no idea why she'd decided to let him know how she really felt tonight.

The ding of the incoming text scared Corrie again. Crap.

Quint- I have a confession.

Okay.

Quint- I've been driving past your place after my shifts this week to make sure everything looked okay.

And?

Quint- That's it.

That's your confession? Corrie didn't see what the issue was.

Quint- Yeah.

Okay.

Quint- Okay? You don't have an issue with me driving by?

No. Why would I? You're a police officer, you have a gun, you're ob-
viously a lot more equipped to deal with bad guys than I am.

Quint- True. Now I have another confession.

Corrie smiled now. She forgot all about how she'd been scared
and concentrated on the pleasure coursing through her that Quint
had wanted to check on her.

Another? You like to put on women's underwear at night and
prance around your house?

Quint- Good Lord, woman. No! Jeez.

Corrie giggled, waiting for him to tell her his next confession.

Quint- I'm outside your apartment now. I didn't want to text and
drive so I pulled over to check on you. Would you feel better if I
came up to make sure there's nothing to be afraid of in your
apartment?

Corrie struggled to get her thoughts in order. On one hand, she
loved that Quint had been thinking about her and wanted to make
sure she was safe. But on the other hand, she didn't want to rely on
him. He wouldn't always be around. She knew being in a relationship
with her wasn't easy. She'd had several boyfriends and even one who
had moved in for a while. But he hadn't been able to deal with her
"quirks," as he'd called them.

Living with someone who couldn't see could be tough. The furniture couldn't be moved, everything had its place. There were assistive
technologies throughout her house, helping her function on her own.
Almost everything could "talk" and her last serious boyfriend even
complained about her knowledge of Braille, wondering out loud what
she was typing and saying about him that he couldn't understand.

Even after a week, Corrie knew letting Quint into her life could
be dangerous to her heart. He seemed like the kind of man who went

all in whatever it was he was doing. If he went "all in" with her then decided she wasn't worth the effort, it'd hurt. Bad.

She knew he was still waiting for her response. She thought long and hard. Was it creepy he was there or not? Corrie thought about it…and decided it was a bit weird, but Quint *was* a cop. He'd told her time and time again he didn't like it that she was staying in her apartment alone, so she decided that he wasn't being stalkerish, he was being protective. She spoke into her phone and waited.

> I'd like that. Thank you.
>
> Quint- I'll be up in a few minutes. I'll knock twice, pause, then twice more, so you'll know it's me.
>
> Okay. I'll be waiting.

Corrie put the phone down on her nightstand where she was always careful to place it. Emily had bought her one of those things that were usually used to hold remote controls for the television to put her cell in each night. She'd "lost" her phone too many times in the past by putting it down in random places. She'd learned to always put it in exactly the same place so she could find it when she needed it.

She reached for her comfy terry-cloth robe that was over the back of the easy chair in the corner of her room and pulled it around her, making sure to tie it closed tightly. She wasn't wearing anything sexy, a long-sleeved sleep shirt and a pair of sleep shorts, but it seemed prudent to cover up. Corrie ran her hands over her hair, trying to decide if she should go and get a scrunchie and put it up, but finally decided against it. She combed it with her fingers and shrugged. Oh well. It would have to do.

Corrie padded down the hall to the living room and went straight to her front door to wait. She didn't wait long. She heard two knocks, then two more.

"Quint?" she asked through the closed door.

"Yeah."

Corrie keyed in the security code on the panel next to the door, then twisted the bolt and unlocked the doorknob before opening the door a crack, keeping the security chain in place.

She once again asked tentatively, "Quint?"

"Yeah, it's me."

"Okay, hang on." Corrie closed the door and undid the security chain, then opened the door fully.

She stepped back and Quint came into her apartment, shutting the door behind him. Corrie took a deep breath. He smelled wonderful. She could tell he was still in his uniform because she could once again hear the telltale creaking of the leather belt around his waist. He smelled like leather and teakwood cologne of some sort. She could also smell a slight odor of sweat. Whatever he'd been doing tonight had obviously made him perspire at some point.

She startled a bit when she felt Quint's hand at her shoulder.

"You look exhausted. You're really not sleeping well, are you?"

Corrie shrugged, careful not to shrug off the comforting hand at her shoulder. "I'll sleep when I'm dead," she quipped, expecting Quint to laugh. He didn't.

"That's not funny. I'm being serious."

Corrie sighed and turned to walk into her living room, only cringing a little inside at losing his touch. "I'll be fine, Quint. You're right, I'm not sleeping that well right now, but this will pass eventually. I heard from Detective Algood today and he said they're getting closer to finding Shaun. Once they do, he'll tell them what they need to know to catch this guy and I'll go back to sleeping a full seven hours a night. I'd love it if you could look around and make sure all is safe and secure. Then I'll be able to sleep better, I'm sure. I'll just sit over here on the couch while you look around…okay?"

Quint looked at Corrie's retreating back. He was frustrated. He hated that she wasn't sleeping at night, but there wasn't much he could do about it. He had no idea what it was about her that made him feel so much, but it was something. Something that he couldn't walk away from.

He forced himself to tear his eyes off of Corrie and look around. Quint had been in her apartment once before, the first time he'd taken her home, and just as he'd been then, he was amazed at how neat everything was. Some people might say her apartment looked institutional, it was so pristine, but when he looked closer, he could see her little touches everywhere.

There were no pictures on the walls, nor were there any bookshelves. She wouldn't have any reason to have either of those things around since she couldn't see them. There was a large television set up against one wall. She had a remote control holder thing on her coffee table and the remotes were lined up precisely from tallest to shortest within it. She was sitting on a comfortable-looking leather couch and there was a big easy chair sitting at a right angle next to the sofa. A coffee table was sitting on a tan rug in front of the couch.

He turned his attention to the kitchen and noticed there were no papers lying around on the counter but there was a stack of mail sitting in a basket.

Quint strolled over to it and looked in. It seemed as if there was several days' worth of mail in the basket. "How do you read your mail?" The question came out without him thinking. Quint winced, hoping it wasn't insensitive.

"Emily comes over once a week and goes through it for me."

Her answer was congenial enough. Appeared as if she didn't take offense to his question.

As if she had mind-reading abilities, she said, "Quint, you can ask whatever you want. Despite evidence to the contrary, I'm usually hard to offend, especially when it comes to someone asking genuine questions about assistive technologies."

"Thank you, I will. I find everything about you fascinating."

Quint noticed she didn't turn his way, but thought he saw a sheen of red bloom over her cheeks. He continued checking her place out. The kitchen appliances seemed normal at first glance, but he didn't know much about what appliances in a blind person's kitchen would look like. Like most men, he lived on microwave meals and whatever he could make on the stovetop and in the crockpot. Of course, he could also grill a mean steak.

Quint looked around the rest of the living room and kitchen, and seeing nothing out of place, went down the hall to the bedrooms. He opened the first door he came to, remembering from the last time it was the linen closet. The sheets and towels were stacked neatly, and impressively, the towels were stacked by color and the sheets were all in sets. He closed the door and went into the guestroom.

The area reminded him of a hotel room. There was a double-size bed with a black dresser against the opposite wall. There was a small window with forest-green curtains and not much else in the room. Again, there were no pictures on the walls or any extra decorations. Quint briefly lifted the comforter and looked under the bed. Nothing but a few dust bunnies. Neat as a pin.

He then went into the small guest bathroom. The shower curtain on the single shower was pulled back, showing a completely empty stall. The single sink and toilet were off-white and the entire place smelled fresh, as if it'd recently been cleaned.

Quint then continued into the master bedroom. This room, at least, looked a bit more lived in. Corrie's bed covers were mussed and he could tell how she'd thrown back the quilt as she'd gotten out of bed. Her cell phone was on a little table next to the queen-size bed in another remote control holder. There was a comfortable-looking easy chair in the corner of the room and a four-drawer dresser next to the chair. The window was large and had dark blue curtains, which were tied back. He looked under the bed, and again saw that it was empty and clean, not even a dust bunny to be seen this time.

He peeked into her bathroom and smiled. It was definitely a woman's bathroom. There were two sinks and a row of lotions lined up next to one of them. There was even a tray filled with makeup in the bathroom as well. He hadn't thought about it before, but now that he saw Corrie's personal space, he realized that she'd always been wearing a bit of makeup when he'd seen her before tonight. She'd somehow learned how to apply it…and it looked good on her.

Quint took the time to glance into the shower and, seeing it empty, headed back down the hall to Corrie.

"All clear?" she asked as he came back into the room.

"All clear," Quint confirmed as he sat on the other end of the sofa. When she smiled, he asked what she was thinking about.

"Every time you move, I can hear all your equipment moving and creaking. I think I'd know in a heartbeat if I was in the same room as another cop based on the sounds of your stuff as you move around."

Her words brought home to Quint just how observant Corrie really was. It fascinated him. "What else?"

"What do you mean, 'What else'?"

"What else can you tell about me from listening?"

"Is this a test?"

"No. I'm just curious. No, that's not exactly right. It amazes me. *You* amaze me. I'm in awe of you, Corrie."

Her cheeks pinked and she bit her lip, thinking about his question as if no one had ever taken the time to get to know her in this way before. Finally she answered. "Let's see…I can smell your shampoo, at least I think it's your shampoo. It's faint, but it smells like teakwood?"

"You're good. Go on."

"And you've eaten a peppermint recently."

"Yup, right before I came up."

Corrie nodded as if she'd known she was right all along. "And I can tell you've been sweating. It's not bad, but you must've done something tonight that made you exert some energy."

Quint scooted over to sit closer to Corrie and took hold of the edge of her robe which was lying on the cushion next to him. "Had a drunk man resist arrest. I had to subdue him." Quint said the words easily, but he was blown away by Corrie. Seriously, she was fucking amazing.

"I'm sorry my apartment isn't very fancy."

"What?" Quint hadn't been paying attention really. He'd been watching his fingers play with the edge of her comfortable-looking robe.

"My apartment. I don't have any knick-knacks or anything around. There's no point."

"It's fine, Corrie. Why would you have that crap around when you couldn't see it?"

"Emily tells me all the time that she's willing to help me spruce it up. Even if I can't see the stuff, apparently she thinks it'd make me look more approachable or less boring or something."

Quint felt his teeth clenching. "You aren't boring, not at all. And you're very approachable, Corrie. You're so approachable it's taking all I have to behave myself here."

She turned her head in his direction. Quint had to remind himself, again, that she couldn't see him. It sometimes seemed as if she looked straight into his soul. Her robe was gaping a bit at her chest and he could see her pink sleep shirt underneath. It was cotton, but for some reason, on her, it was very tantalizing. It wasn't cut so low that he could see any cleavage, but he *could* see that her nipples were hard and pointed under her nightclothes.

"Oh." The word was breathy and unsure.

"Come on, sweetheart. You need to get back to bed. You're exhausted, I'm tired, it's been a long day. Come lock the door behind me and set the alarm after I go." Quint knew if he didn't get out of her apartment, he'd do something he might regret. He felt as if he was seventeen again, getting hard at the sight of her erect nipples. It was definitely time to go.

They walked to her front door and Quint opened it, but turned around to face Corrie. She looked up at him expectantly. It even looked as though she was holding her breath.

"Corrie—"

"Are you going to kiss me? I'm only asking because I can't see any nonverbal cues you might be giving off, and honestly, I'd hate to miss it, or to have you misinterpret my actions if I didn't reciprocate because I can't see you."

Quint smiled. She was so fucking cute. He loved that she was brave enough to ask, even if she flushed as she did. "No." He ran his finger over the frown lines on her forehead. "I want to wait until I drop you off at your door after our date. It's not that I don't want to right now, but I want to kiss you as your date, not as the police officer who came to check on you."

"But you're the same person," Corrie protested, lifting a hand to lightly rest it on his chest.

Quint couldn't feel her touch because of the protective vest he wore under his shirt, but he imagined what her fingers would feel like on him and it almost broke his resolve...almost. He closed his eyes for a moment, relieved that she somehow seemed to see him, the real him, even with everything she'd been through.

"I'm glad you think so, sweetheart. Now, close and lock this behind me. I'll see you in two days. Yeah?"

Corrie nodded. "Yeah."

Quint leaned forward and kissed Corrie's forehead, then drew back far enough for her hand to fall from his chest. "Goodnight, Corrie. Talk to you soon."

"Night, Quint. Thank you for checking things out for me."

Quint stood at her door, waiting until he heard the click of the deadbolt and the slide of the metal chain engaging. He hoped she'd be able to get some sleep tonight. By the looks of her, she needed it.

He practically flew down the stairs and back out to his cruiser. He couldn't believe how excited he was for his date with her. It was almost pathetic.

His phone made a noise, notifying him of a text as he unlocked his car and got in. He looked down at his phone and smiled at the text from Corrie.

Just so you know, I want to kiss both the police officer and my date. Make it happen, would ya?

Quint smiled as he typed in his response.

Count on it. See you soon. I'll text with the details.

Quint looked around as he drove out of the parking lot, not seeing anything out of place.

A MAN SMOKING a cigarette observed as the cop car left the parking lot. He then looked up to the apartment on the second floor that he'd been watching for the last week. The time was coming to give another warning. If she wanted to ignore the first two…so be it.

Chapter Six

— ◆ —

"**A**RE YOU SURE I look okay?" Corrie asked Emily for what seemed like the hundredth time.

"*Yes*! You look awesome!" Emily responded enthusiastically.

Corrie ran her hands down her thighs and tried to stop worrying but it was impossible. She'd asked Emily to come over and help her get ready. For the first time in a long time, she wanted to look as nice as possible for a date. It was kinda stupid because Quint had already seen her "normal" self, but she wanted to primp for him...wanted him to know this was important to her.

Emily had helped pick her outfit. Corrie was wearing jeans...of course; she rarely wore anything else outside of work. She'd paired it with a pink sleeveless top. Emily had done her makeup for her, as Corrie could only really manage blush, mascara, and lipstick. She could feel when the mascara wand touched her eyelashes and lipstick was easy enough. For blush, she used a brush and counted swirls to avoid using too much, but she never wanted to mess with foundation because it could be a disaster since she couldn't see how much was too much.

She was wearing a pair of gold hoops in her ears and a charm bracelet with some of the charms Emily had given her over the years. Corrie knew it'd make her feel better to have something her best friend had given her when she got nervous.

The outfit was topped off with a pair of cute cowboy boots. Corrie thought they probably looked silly and was going to wear some sandals, but Emily convinced her they looked great.

"Why am I so nervous, Em?"

"Because you like him."

"I do, but…"

"Cor, you *like* him. From what you've told me this week, he's been great. He's been over here and seen how bare it is…relax. He's into you. Just go with it."

"What if I knock over my glass? Or drop food in my lap or—"

"Jesus, Corrie. Get over it. He knows about you. I think he'll be cool. Take a deep breath."

"You're right. Did you feel this way when you went out with Bethany for the first time?"

"No. I actually thought she was a bitch. You know this story…we met at that Gay Pride event in Austin and her girlfriend at the time badmouthed me. I thought Bethany agreed with her and I was pissed. But later, she met back up with me and told me she had no idea her girlfriend was such a bitch, and she'd dumped her. We spent the rest of the weekend hanging out together and realized we had sparks. The rest is history."

Corrie hugged her friend. "I'm so happy for you guys. Seriously, Bethany and you make a great couple. I know you were worried that you're ten years older than her, but I'm glad you both got over that. You're perfect for each other."

Emily hugged her back. "I know, you tell me practically every time you see me."

They both laughed. "Come on, Cor. Let's go through your mail before Quint gets here. I'm sorry I haven't had the time to come over before now and help you with it."

"Not a big deal. Let me grab my checkbook so we can take care of any bills that aren't paid electronically."

Corrie grabbed a light jacket from the hook in her closet where she kept it and followed Emily into the kitchen. She eased herself onto a stool and waited for Emily to shuffle through the envelopes.

"Trash, trash, ad flier—oooh, this looks interesting!"

"What is it?"

Emily laughed. "A catalog for sex toys."

Corrie shook her head at her friend. "Whatevs, come on, hurry up."

"In a hurry, Cor?"

"What time is it anyway?"

"You've got a bit before he's supposed to be here. Relax. Okay, let's see…cell phone auto payment notification, same for the electric and cable…when are you going to cancel your cable? Seriously, you never watch TV, it's a waste."

"I like the background noise sometimes."

"Oh…what's this?"

"What?"

"It's a letter."

"Well, no crap, Emily. They're all letters."

"No, I mean, it's a personal letter. You usually don't get letters from people."

Corrie didn't take offense. Emily was right. Anyone who knew her wouldn't write her a letter, and very few of her friends and family knew Braille, and none were proficient enough to write her an entire letter in the language. They stuck to the computer for their correspondence. "Who's it from?"

"I don't know, there's no return address."

"Fine, would you open it already then?"

She heard Emily tearing open the letter and then silence as she read it.

"Oh my God."

Corrie had never heard that tone of voice from her friend before. "What? What is it?" Corrie felt Emily's hand at her elbow, gently tugging her off the stool and out of the kitchen. "What? Emily, you're freaking me out."

"Quint's gonna be here soon, let's wait out here."

"Emily Brooks, you tell me right now what the heck is going on." Corrie dug her heels in and refused to take another step.

"It was a threatening letter."

"Threatening? What did it say?"

Before Emily could respond, there were two knocks on the door, a pause, then two more.

"It's Quint," Corrie said softly. "That's his special knock to let me know it's him." She walked over to the door and went through the same process she did the other night to verify his identity. It was better to be safe than sorry. When Quint confirmed it was him, Corrie opened the door.

"Hey, you look beautiful."

"Thanks." Her voice was reverent when she told him, "You smell divine."

He chuckled. "Is that your way of telling me I look nice?"

"Yeah, smell is kinda a big thing for me, for obvious reasons." When Corrie heard a throat being cleared behind her, she said, "Oh, sorry. This is Emily," and gestured to where she'd left her friend standing.

"Hi, Emily, it's nice to meet you. Corrie has talked a lot about you."

"Hi. Uh, Corrie, we need to tell him."

"Tell me what?"

"I don't think—"

Emily interrupted her. "She got a threatening letter."

Corrie thought she could actually feel the air around her change. She really hadn't wanted to do this now. She wanted to go on her date and put all the scary crap behind her for the night.

She sighed, knowing it was too late now. Darn it.

"Show me." Quint's words were clipped and urgent.

They all walked back into the kitchen. Corrie could hear Quint head over to the counter where they'd been going through her mail.

"I dropped it as soon as I realized what it was. It was toward the bottom of the stack, so it probably came earlier this week. I haven't been able to get over here to help Corrie in about seven or so days. I'm so sorry, I should've been here sooner, I—"

"This isn't your fault, Emily. Don't blame yourself. I was over here the other night. I should've at least thumbed through it."

"Both of you, stop it," Corrie said firmly. "The only fault here is with the jerk who sent it. And Quint, if you'd started pilfering through my mail, I wouldn't have been happy."

Corrie could hear the humor in Quint's voice as he asked Emily, "Does she ever swear?"

"No. It's annoying as hell too. I keep telling her Ethan's too young to pick up on any bad words, but she still refuses to use adult words when she's pissed."

"Okay, you two. Quit. Quint, what should I do with it?"

"You don't need to do anything with it. I'll take care of it. Can you give me a few minutes to call my friend Dax and let him know what's up?"

"Uh, Dax... That's not the guy who was at the restaurant was it?"

"No, that was Cruz. Dax is with the Texas Rangers."

"But, I thought the police department was working the case?"

"They are, but we call in the Rangers when we need assistance in investigating cases. Because of the nature of what we're dealing with, and the fact we haven't been able to locate Shaun yet, Matt...err...Detective Algood, asked for assistance from the Rangers."

"Oh, okay. I guess we'll have to reschedule anyway."

Corrie heard Quint take a step toward her and then felt his hands on her shoulders. She looked up to where his face should be.

"This isn't going to end our date, Corrie. As soon as I take care of this, we're still going out," he said in an earnest voice. "I told you I wanted to take you on a date, so that's what I'm going to do."

"Okay, but just so you know, if it gets too late, I'm fine with doing it another day."

"It's not going to take very long, promise." He kissed her forehead, then stepped back, taking his hand with him. "Emily, I know we just met, but can I ask a huge favor?"

"Of course."

"Once Dax gets here, can you stay until he's done? I want to take my girl out."

"Of course. No problem."

"Emily," Corrie protested, "don't you have to get home to Bethany and Ethan?"

"No. They'll be fine. You've been looking forward to this date all week. I got this."

Corrie groaned in embarrassment. Please God, let the earth open and swallow her up. She heard Quint chuckle and knew she was turning red.

She felt his breath against her cheek then her ear as he leaned into her and whispered so only she could hear him, "Don't be embarrassed, I've been looking forward to taking you out all week too."

He then backed away and Corrie heard him walk to the other side of the kitchen.

"Holy hell, girlfriend. I'm sorrier than you'll ever know that you're going through this, but wow. That is one hunk of a man you've got there," Emily whispered.

"Really?" Corrie turned her back to Quint and kept her voice low so he couldn't hear their conversation.

"Really. If I wasn't in love with Bethany, you might have a fight on your hands."

"Whatever, you're so stupid in love with her you wouldn't look at anyone else, even if you *were* attracted to men. Can you describe him for me?"

Emily didn't even hesitate, having done this for her friend many times over the years. "He's taller than you are, with dark hair. It's got a bit of a wave in it and I'm sure it probably sticks up all over the place when he runs his hand through it. His dark against your blonde looks amazing. He's as muscular as anyone I've ever seen, except on TV, and he has some sort of kickass tattoo sticking out from under the right sleeve of his shirt." Emily wrapped it up. "He's got prominent cheekbones and a square jaw. Brown eyes, full lips, no piercings that I can see. In short? I might pitch for the other team, but I'm telling you, he's fucking *hot*."

Corrie chuckled and shook her head at her friend. She couldn't help but be pleased that Quint was good-looking. It wasn't that she put a lot of stock into a person's looks, because honestly, there were a lot of other factors that were way more important to her considering she couldn't even see him to appreciate what he looked like, but even without her sight, she could easily imagine how good-looking Quint was. Emily's description matched his voice to a T. She tried to play it down. "Whatever." Corrie's voice got sincere. "Thanks for being here for me, Em. Seriously. I love you."

"You're welcome. We're here for each *other*. Always. Never forget it. Whatever you need, whenever you need it."

"Come here." Corrie held out her arms and smiled as Emily wrapped hers around her. They embraced and held on until Quint came back across the room to them. "You guys okay?"

Corrie pulled away, smiling. "Yeah. We're good."

"Okay. Emily, Dax should be here pretty quickly. He was already out finishing up an investigation. He said he'd swing by here and collect the letter. I know you know this, but don't touch the envelope again. We'll probably need you to come down to the station and give your fingerprints so we can exclude yours when examining it."

"No problem."

"Oh, but Em, what about that warrant for your arrest back in New York?" Corrie's voice was serious and urgent—and she waited a beat before succumbing to the smile she'd been holding back.

Emily burst into laughter and choked out, "Oh my God, Cor, you should've seen his face."

Corrie laughed along with her friend. It felt good to laugh and tease Quint. She and Emily used to play tricks on people all the time. Corrie knew she should probably be freaking out about the letter and the threat that obviously came with it, but she couldn't work up the energy. Her impending date with Quint was first and foremost in her thoughts at the moment. Later that night she'd probably freak out about the letter, but for now she was more excited about spending some time with Quint.

Frustrated that she probably wasn't going to have the luxury to not think about what it said, she resigned herself to seeing if she could get Quint or Emily to read it to her before they left. At least that way she'd get the worst of it over with. Then maybe, if the date went well, she could think about that rather than whatever the contents of the stupid note were.

"You'll pay for that, sweetheart," Quint mock threatened, putting his arms around her from behind.

Corrie leaned back against him, loving the feel of him along the length of her body. He was a few inches taller than she was, and because he wasn't wearing his uniform or bulletproof vest, she could feel his hard strength, so different from her own. She didn't dare back all the way into him, it was too soon for an intimacy like that, but she couldn't help but wonder if she aroused him at all.

Stopping those kinds of thoughts before they could strengthen, she asked, "Will you read me the letter, Quint?"

"No."

Corrie turned around and put her hands on her hips, not expecting his quick, blunt response. "What? Why not?"

"You don't need to hear it."

"Yes, I do. It was addressed to *me*. And how can I keep myself safe if I don't know what I'm up against?"

"First of all, you won't have to keep yourself safe…you've got me, and the department, and all of my friends at your back. Secondly, I don't *want* you to hear it."

Corrie nodded. "I know you don't, I'm not doing cartwheels about it myself, but I'm not five years old. It's not like I'm going to lose any *more* sleep over it. I'm already not sleeping, imagining the worst. In some way, maybe this'll make me feel better. Make me feel like I'm not making up the creepy feeling crawling up the back of my neck each night. Please, Quint."

She heard him sigh. "I don't want to…but okay. We'll get it over with, but as soon as Dax gets here, I'm taking you out and we're going to forget all this for a night."

"Thank you."

Quint ground his teeth together as he walked back to the counter and to the letter lying there. It was written on a piece of lined paper torn from a notebook. The lettering was overdone, obviously camouflaged. It was short and to the point. He'd used a napkin earlier to turn the letter over so he could read it.

He looked at Corrie. She was standing tall, not looking worried at all, while her friend Emily looked completely freaked the hell out. The two women were holding hands, and with a second glance, Quint could tell that Corrie wasn't as calm as she might appear. Her hand was clutching Emily's so hard her knuckles were white.

Fuck. He hated this. He might as well get it over with.

"It says, '*We told you to keep quiet. You didn't. Hope your affairs are in order. Too bad you'll never see us coming.*'"

"It's a little dramatic isn't it?"

"Damn it, Corrie. This isn't a laughing matter."

Quint could see Corrie's mood shift.

"I know it's not. Darn it, Quint. I was in that room stuffed under the sink wondering if I'd live to see another minute. I heard my friends being killed. I was *there*. I know this isn't funny, no matter if whoever sent that thinks *they* are, with their little dig about my eyesight. But I can't lose it. If I lose it, they win. Whoever 'they' are. I have to be smart, use my head. They're trying to scare me, and it's working, but I can't let them get to me. I just can't."

Quint had her in his arms before she got the last word out. "You won't let them get to you. *I* won't let them get to you."

He absently heard Emily puttering around the apartment, obviously trying to stay out of their way. Finally he drew back and looked at Corrie. He ran one of his thumbs under her eye. "Dry. You don't cry easily, do you, sweetheart?"

She shook her head. "I just...I cried a lot as a child. I don't know why I don't now. It's hard to get completely worked up over things knowing how bad life can really be sometimes. Stubbing my toe hurts, or listening to a sad book or movie...but I have a hard time crying over those things when they're honestly superficial in my life."

"I'm going to do what I can to keep you safe," Quint told her, breezing over her comment about her lack of tears.

"Okay."

"I am."

"Can we talk about this later?"

Just as the words left Corrie's mouth, there was a knock at the door.

Emily rushed over to answer it as Quint stepped back from Corrie.

"Yeah, we'll talk about this later," he promised. He turned, keeping one hand on the small of Corrie's back. "Come on, that'll be my buddy. I want you to meet Dax. Someday I'll tell you the story of what happened to him and his girlfriend, Mackenzie."

After the introductions were over, Dax pulled on a pair of gloves and put the letter and envelope into a plastic bag and headed back to the door to leave.

"That's it?" Corrie asked incredulously. "You're not going to take fingerprints, or ask me any questions, or otherwise grill me about anything?"

"Yup, that's it…unless you've got any more notes stashed somewhere or have anything else pressing you want to tell me right this second?"

"Don't you want to hear what happened?"

His friend laughed. "Ms. Madison, it's clear you and Quint are on your way out. I'm happy to stand here and discuss this letter all night, but it looks like you have other plans. My buddy hasn't been on a date for a *very* long time and I'm fucking thrilled he's managed to get someone as pretty as you to agree to be seen in public with his ugly self."

Corrie could hear the affection for his friend in Dax's voice. She smiled as he continued, "I've also been working all day and I'd like to get home to Mack, my girlfriend. I'll catch up with you tomorrow, by phone if that's easier for you, or I'll get in touch with Detective Algood, if you're more comfortable talking to him. Either way, you both look too pretty to be cooped up in this apartment gabbing about something none of us can do anything about at the moment. Go out. Have fun."

Corrie looked up at where Quint was. "Is he always like that?"

"Fuck no. He's usually a pain in the ass and all about protocol. But I'm not looking a gift horse in the mouth. If he says to get out of here, I'm all for it."

"Okay, let me grab my jacket and purse."

"Here you go, Cor." Emily was there with her stuff. "I'm going too. This works out great. I can get home to Bethany and our son and eat with them."

The foursome walked out of the apartment and Corrie reset the alarm and locked her door. As soon as the door was locked and Corrie had put her key away, Quint took her hand in his to lead her to the car. They all walked down to the parking lot together. Quint gave Dax a chin lift and he returned it before heading to his vehicle and easing out of the lot.

"Call me tomorrow, Cor. I need to know what's going on and what we're doing next."

"*We* aren't doing anything, Em. I already told you, I'm not involving you any more than you already are."

"But—"

It was Quint who interrupted her this time. "I'll be in touch, Emily. I agree with Corrie, though. You shouldn't be involved in this. I'll take care of your friend."

"Swear?"

"Swear."

"Okay...don't do anything I wouldn't do tonight then."

Corrie laughed out loud. "I don't think that's the best advice, knowing how much you love Bethany."

Quint watched the banter between Corrie and Emily with a grin. It was obvious that the two women were close. And the fact that Corrie wasn't prejudiced made him like her all the more. Every scrap of information he picked up about the woman standing next to him, seemingly content to hold his hand, solidified the warm feeling in his belly that she was meant to be his.

After Emily had gotten in her car and driven off, Quint returned his hand to the small of Corrie's back. He felt her arch against him just a bit and he smiled. "Come on, sweetheart. I have a dinner to take you to."

Chapter Seven

—————◆—————

CORRIE NERVOUSLY UNLOCKED her door, somehow managing not to drop her keys in the process. She could feel Quint standing at her side. He had one hand on her hip and she could feel his thumb caressing her side as he stood patiently, letting her unlock her apartment by herself.

It was one of the four hundred twenty-three thousand things she found herself mentally calculating that she liked about the man. Holding her hand as he helped her navigate? Check. Asking her if she read Braille, then requesting a Braille menu from the hostess? Check. After the waiter put down their drinks, moving hers until it touched her hand so she'd know where it was? Check. Calmly and without fanfare explaining, by using a typical clock face, where the food was on her plate? Check.

Even now, he could've been overbearing and asked for her keys so he could open her door for her, but he didn't. He got it. He really seemed to understand that she wasn't helpless because she couldn't see.

They'd talked a lot throughout dinner about how she got around and what assistive technologies she used in her everyday life. She promised to show him some of them when they got back to her place.

Now they were here. Corrie's heart beat quickly. He'd been touching her all night, and it was driving her crazy.

She finally got the door open and she keyed in the code to the alarm.

"Wait here while I go and check things out."

Without giving her a chance to argue, Quint was gone. If Corrie was honest with herself, she was glad he was here. She would've been very nervous to come back to her apartment by herself, especially after receiving that darn letter.

Quint was back within minutes. "It's all clear. Let me take your jacket."

Corrie turned and shrugged out of her jacket and felt Quint take it. "Where does it go?"

"What?"

"Where does it go?" Quint repeated easily.

"Just put it anywhere."

"No. Tell me where it goes. I'm not an idiot, Corrie. I can tell that every single thing in your apartment has its place. If I put it down somewhere, you won't find it as easily. Tell me where you'd put it if you came home alone."

Darn, she kept forgetting how observant he was. "In my closet in my room. The third hook on the right when you walk in."

"Be right back."

Corrie wandered into the kitchen as she heard Quint head down the hall to her bedroom. She fought a blush, thinking about him in her room. She'd just pulled the coffeepot to the edge of the counter when he returned.

"Do you want coffee?"

"Sure, if you'll have some with me."

Corrie nodded and reached for the water faucet. She held the carafe under the faucet until it was nearly full. Then she turned to the pot and opened the top and poured it into the reservoir. She put the now-empty glass pot on the burner on the machine and lifted out the little basket with used grounds in it. She opened the cabinet under the sink and dumped the grounds into the trash can.

Next, Corrie turned the water back on and ran the basket under it, rinsing the old grounds away. Then she placed it back into the coffeemaker and grabbed the plastic bin of coffee grounds.

"I hope vanilla is okay?"

"It's perfect."

Corrie screeched in surprise as Quint's voice came from right beside her. "Holy cow, you scared me! I didn't realize you were right there." She laughed shakily. "That doesn't happen often, you know, I always hear people when they approach me."

"You were distracted. And I must say, you are absolutely fascinating to watch."

"What do you mean?" Corrie turned back to the coffee. She pulled out a spoon that she kept inside the plastic jug and scooped out a large spoonful. She managed not to jerk in surprise when she felt Quint's arms snake around her waist to rest right under her breasts. He held her loosely, but with control. The contradiction was arousing as hell.

"You know exactly where everything is. You didn't fill the pot too full, you got it right to the ten-cup line. You didn't hesitate to pour it into the right place on the coffeemaker. If I didn't know better, I'd think you were pulling my leg this entire time and you can see as well as I can."

Corrie tried to ignore the huge compliment Quint had given her without realizing it, but couldn't. "Thank you. Seriously. You have no idea what it means to someone like me when people don't realize I can't see." She continued with what she was doing, a little hesitantly now that she knew Quint was scrutinizing her so closely. She managed to get three scoops of the coffee grounds into the basket. She flipped the lid closed and turned the machine on. She soon heard the gurgling of the water making its way through the machine and the alluring smell of vanilla coffee wafted through the air.

"Show me some of the other assistive technologies you have in the kitchen," Quint demanded as he stepped back, giving her some room.

"Seriously?"

"Yeah. Everything about you amazes me."

Not knowing how to respond to that, Corrie reached over and opened a cabinet. She pointed to where she knew her measuring set was. "I have a Braille label maker. I've marked all of the measuring spoons and cups with their sizes. I really don't need them much anymore, I can tell by touch which cup is which.

"My salt and pepper shakers have Braille marks on the ridges so I know which is which without having to taste them. I have a boil alert disk that I put in the bottom of the pan when I'm boiling water. It rattles when the water starts boiling so I know it's time to put in the pasta or rice or whatever. I have talking meat thermometers; my kitchen timer, as you can see, has raised bumps for minutes and larger markings at five minutes and a big raised bar at an hour."

Corrie pointed to her right. "Even my microwave talks to me. And as you noticed, everything has its place, especially in the kitchen. Emily helps me when I need it, but I try to do most things myself. I order lots of food online so I don't have to worry about the grocery store, I label everything. Every now and then I'll open a can thinking I'm eating soup to find something else entirely." She laughed at herself. "The fridge is organized so I know what's in there and where it is. I sometimes forget about the expiration dates, but I've learned to sniff everything before I use it, just in case."

"Did I say you were amazing?"

"Uh, yeah, but it's not that big of a deal."

"I was wrong." Quint ignored her and kept on. "You're *fucking* amazing."

Corrie giggled a bit. "Actually, I'm probably considered on the extreme side of anal to most people."

"No. Not at all."

Corrie sobered a bit as she looked up at Quint. He'd taken her in his arms as she was explaining some of the things in her kitchen that helped her be independent. He'd clasped his hands at the small of her back and held her to him. Corrie could feel his hard thighs against hers and, if she wasn't mistaken, his hard length as well.

"I realize this isn't a normal way to live, Quint. No sighted person could live this way."

"Why not?"

"Why not? Because. Look at it. It's crazy. I know it is."

"Someone told you that, didn't they?"

Corrie paused before nodding in agreement.

"Come on." Quint took her hand and led her to her couch. Corrie didn't have the gumption at the moment to tell him he didn't need to lead her to her own couch, she knew where it was, but she enjoyed the feel of her hand in his. He pulled her to the couch, then sat. Corrie stood awkwardly for a moment before he pulled her down next to him. He settled her into his side as if they sat like that all the time.

Corrie could feel the beat of his heart under her hand. She resisted the urge to explore. She hadn't "seen" this man yet, the time hadn't been right to ask him if she could run her hands over him to see what he looked like. But now…it seemed right. Before she could ask, he spoke.

"Tell me."

"Tell you what?" Corrie was confused. What were they talking about?

"Tell me about the asshole who told you he couldn't live this way."

Corrie froze. How had he figured out that it was a *man* who'd told her that? When she'd agreed with him, she figured he'd think it was her parents or a friend who'd made the insinuation. She sighed softly. Damn Quint's observation abilities. She was silent for a moment, not knowing where to start.

"I don't bite. Go on."

"I know you don't. I was just trying to figure out where to start this sad tale of woe." Her voice came out just this side of snarky.

Quint laughed. "I love when you get like this. Go on then, take your time."

Corrie shook her head at the crazy man currently holding her in his arms. She could feel one of his arms around her back, resting on her hip. The other hand was resting over her own palm on his chest. He rubbed the back of her hand with his thumb. He smelled so damn good, and Corrie just wanted to bury her face in his neck and never come up for air, but he'd asked her a question. She wanted to tell him, to make him understand what life was like living with a blind person. Well, at least living with *her*. She supposed every person was different. Other people might not be as anal as she was. She didn't know. All she knew was that she wanted whatever it was they were doing to continue. She'd never felt so comfortable with someone so quickly before.

Corrie took a deep breath and started. The sooner she told him, the sooner it'd be over. "I was dating Ian for several months. We got along great. He was attentive, but not smothering. We used to play cards almost all night—"

"How do you play cards?"

"Are you going to let me tell this story or what?"

"Yeah, after you tell me how you play cards."

Corrie lifted her head and looked up where his voice was. "You're kinda annoying, you know that?"

"Yeah, so my friends tell me. Cards?"

"And persistent," Corrie grumbled, but gave in with a smile. "I ordered a couple decks of special cards off the Internet. They have both Braille and regular print on them so I can play with a sighted person without any issues. They're plastic and actually waterproof and are really cool. Not that I'd play cards in the shower or tub or anything, I just thought it was neat to have cards that could get wet and wouldn't get ruined."

"Huh, I never knew anything like that existed either. Strip poker in the rain…who knew. Okay, go on. Ian," Quint sneered his name, "was attentive, but not smothering."

Ignoring the obvious disdain in Quint's voice, Corrie continued her story. "Yeah, as I said, we got along well. I thought he loved me. I thought I loved him. He asked me to move in with him, I told him I couldn't, I was way too comfortable in my space, but I wouldn't mind if he moved in with me. He agreed. He moved in, was here about two weeks before leaving. We tried to keep dating after he moved out, but it wasn't the same. He admitted to me that he'd had no idea living with a blind person was so…'exhausting' was the word I think he used."

"Exhausting? What the fuck does that mean?"

"I think he meant what I showed you. Everything has a place. The kitchen drove him especially crazy. He told me once it reminded him of that movie with Julia Roberts where she's being stalked by a crazy ex…*Sleeping with the Enemy*. He hated that all my food was lined up precisely and I'd spend at least an hour after shopping labeling it all. He'd leave his shoes in the middle of our bedroom and I'd trip over them. I once hit my head on the corner of my little table and Em told me I had a huge bruise for days."

Quint growled, and Corrie felt the rumble under her hand resting on his chest, but he didn't say anything, so she tried to finish up her story quickly. "I tried to show Ian where I'd made room in my closet for his shoes and things to go. He whined that he was tired and it was hard to put everything in a specific place every single time. The last straw was the time I accidently started a small grease fire. I heard the whoosh of the flames and felt the heat on my face, and reached for the baking soda, but he'd moved it the last time he was in the kitchen when he was doing something else. I was yelling at him to come and help me because I couldn't find the darn stuff and the fire almost got out of control. I kinda lost my temper and told him off. I told him how important it was that he not move things without telling me. He got pissed, we said some unforgivable things to each other, and he left that day."

"Prick."

"What?"

"I said he was a prick."

Corrie sighed sadly. "No, he really wasn't. It's mostly my fault, honestly. It's impossible for someone who can see to understand the importance of needing to know where things are."

"Corrie, you're wrong. If he'd come to you and said, 'Hey, I bought some spices and I'd like to put them in the cabinet where the baking soda is, can you come help me figure out how to organize everything so you know where it is,' would you have gotten mad and refused?"

"What kind of question is that?" Corrie questioned testily. "No, of course not. I don't really care *where* things are, as long as I can find them when I need them. I don't want to put sugar in my food when I think it's really salt."

"Exactly."

"Quint, you're confusing the ever-loving daylights out of me. Exactly what?" Corrie felt Quint lean in closer to her. She could feel his breath on her face as he spoke earnestly.

"It's not that you're opposed to moving things around, you just want to know where they are."

"Yeah, that's what I said."

"So, if I said, 'Hey, I want to move the couch so it's under the window and put the chair in the other corner'...what would you say?"

"Sure. Whatever. It's not like I can say it doesn't look as good where you want it. I can't see it anyway. It's knowing where it is that's important."

Corrie startled as Quint eased her backward until she was lying on her back on the couch. She could feel him crouched over her. "Quint! What are you doing?" She reached up and found his chest. She put both hands against it and held on.

"You're not anal, Corrie."

She snorted at him.

"You're not. You don't care where things are. You don't care what's in here. You just care *where* it is so you don't run into it or so you can find it again."

"That's what I've been telling you," Corrie told him, confused, wondering where he was going with his observations and feeling like they were talking in circles.

"Living with you wouldn't be exhausting. It would simply mean communication, compromise and, the caveman part of me wants to say, protection as well."

Corrie didn't know what to say, so she kept quiet. Quint didn't seem to mind as he continued.

"If you were mine, and I was living here with you, I'd see it as my duty to put things back where they belonged. It would be my way of protecting you. How much of a selfish bastard would I be to move furniture without telling you, or to leave my shit in the middle of the floor where you could trip over it and get hurt? I'm not saying it wouldn't take some getting used to, but I honestly don't see it as that big of a deal."

Corrie felt Quint's hand on her cheek. "You're normal, Corrie. As normal as anyone else. Just because you can't see doesn't mean you're anal or 'exhausting.' You're just you. You deserve love as much as anyone else."

"I don't know what to say," Corrie told him honestly after digesting his words.

"That's a first."

Corrie huffed out a laugh, then got serious again. "Can I touch you?"

"Touch me?" Quint's voice deepened as he said the words.

Corrie laughed nervously. "I didn't mean that...exactly. I don't know what you look like. I mean, Emily described you a little to me tonight, but I'd like to see for myself. I know what you smell like, how tall you are, that you have this wonderful, deep growly voice and that you're muscular, but I have no idea what you *look* like."

"Is this a deal breaker?"

"Are you nervous?" Corrie couldn't believe Quint could be sensitive about his looks.

"A little. I mean, you're gorgeous. I'm not in your league at all. You might take one look at my crooked nose and kick me to the curb."

Corrie giggled. "As if. Emily told me you were freaking hot."

"I bet she didn't say 'freaking.'"

Corrie laughed then inhaled sharply as Quint rolled, careful to keep a firm grasp on her waist so she didn't fall off the couch. He held her to him until he'd switched their positions. He lay under her and Corrie straddled his hips. There was no way he could hide his erection from her, as she was currently perched right on top of it, but he didn't think she'd mind. At least he hoped not. He stretched his arms up and put them under his head. "Have at it, sweetheart."

Chapter Eight

————◆————

CORRIE DIDN'T HESITATE in case Quint changed his mind. She loved getting to know people this way, but didn't often get the chance. It wasn't like she could put her hands all over people when they first met.

She put her hands on Quint's chest and ran them down to his waistline, then back up to his neck. She splayed her fingers and did it again. She then ran her hands over his shoulders and down his arms, gripping his muscles as she explored.

"You're very muscular."

"Um-hummm."

Corrie didn't pause in her perusal, but noted his lack of response vaguely. She squeezed his biceps and barely held back a groan. His arms were huge…and immensely sexy.

"Emily told me you have a tattoo. What's it of?"

"It's not that exciting."

Corrie smiled and teased, "A naked woman? A naked man? A giant octopus wrapping its tentacles around your arm and down your back?"

Quint laughed and Corrie could feel his chest rumbling under her hands. "It's an American Flag with writing on it."

"There has to be more to it than that," Corrie groused. "I'll never be able to see it. Please describe it for me. I want to picture it in my head."

"It's big, about six inches long. It goes from the top of my arm to the middle of my bicep. Some of it can be seen when I wear a short-sleeve shirt, like right now. On the red stripes, I had the artist add in cursive a phrase I wrote when I graduated from the police academy: Honor those who have fallen. Protect those who are weak. Serve those who need help. Always remember those less fortunate."

Corrie pictured it in her head. It was probably sexy as all get out…patriotic and hot at the same time. She was sorry she'd never see it. "You said you wrote that? It's beautiful. Does it have a deeper meaning?"

"Deeper meaning?"

"Yeah, I mean, I get that it's about your service to our country and all…but I have a feeling there's more to it."

Quint brought his hands down from his head and rested them on her hips. He ran his thumbs over the skin under the hem of her top as he spoke. "I told you that I'd always wanted to be a cop. From the time I was a little boy until I decided to major in Criminal Justice in college, it was the only thing I ever wanted to do. Graduating from the police academy was one of the most monumental things I'd ever done in my life. I felt like my true life was just starting. I wanted to commemorate it, to wear ink that would always remind me of why I'm in this profession. I doodled those words on a napkin one night and they stuck with me. It's my mantra, so to speak."

His words gave Corrie goose bumps. She'd never felt that strongly about anything before. She was impressed and honored Quint had shared the story behind his tattoo with her. "I love it. I bet it's beautiful." She rubbed up and down his biceps, enjoying the feel of his muscles flexing under his shirt below her hands.

"Want me to take off my shirt?" Quint tried to change the topic…and get to the good stuff.

"Yeah, but I thought it might be weird if I asked this soon. I mean, we just had our first date tonight."

"We might've had our first date tonight, but we've been talking a lot before that."

"You wouldn't mind, then?"

"Hell no, sweetheart. I wouldn't mind."

Corrie felt Quint shift under her as he removed his T-shirt and then she felt his warm, muscular skin under her hands. "How are you always warm?" She'd asked it as a rhetorical question, but he answered her anyway.

"My body temperature has always run a bit warmer than ninety-eight point six."

"Interesting, mine has always run a bit cold."

"We're a good match."

"Maybe so." Corrie was fascinated with the ridges and muscles of Quint's chest. She ran her hands over his pectoral muscles again and grinned when his nipples peaked under her fingers. "You like that." It wasn't a question.

"Sweetheart, having your hands on me is beyond exciting. I feel I should warn you…if you keep that up you might bite off more than you can chew here."

"Sorry," Corrie said, not meaning it at all. She couldn't hold back the smile on her face. She felt the back of Quint's finger trail down her cheek.

"I like to see you smile."

"It's you. You make me smile."

"Good."

Corrie scooted forward a bit until she was straddling Quint's lower stomach instead of his hips, so she could more easily reach his face. She brought her hands up to where she thought his head was and paused.

"Don't stop now, Corrie. Go on. See me."

She did as Quint requested. Her fingertips feathered over his cheekbones, then up to his eyebrows. She felt him close his eyes and she learned the shape of them. She brought her fingers down to his nose and felt the bump he'd mentioned earlier. "It's not so bad...I'm sure it makes you look...rugged or something."

Corrie felt his lips curl up into a smile, but he didn't say anything. She continued her exploration at his lips. She traced his upper, then his lower lip with the tip of her finger, laughing when he pretended to bite at her. Bringing both hands back into play, she brought them up each side of his face and traced both ears, then ran them though the hair on his head.

Finally, after she'd explored and traced every inch of his face and head, he drawled, "So...do I pass inspection?"

"Yeah, you're cute."

"Cute?" he mock grumbled, bringing his hands up from her hips and tickling her sides. She screeched and tried to buck off him, but Quint had a tight hold on her. Finally he stopped torturing her and they both lay on the couch smiling.

"Can I massage your back?"

"Huh?" That wasn't what Quint expected Corrie to say at all.

"Can I give you a massage?"

"Really?"

"Yeah. You know I'm a chiropractor, I'm good at it. I promise."

"Sweetheart, anytime you want to rub my back, I'll be all for it."

"Good, we need to get on the floor though. The sofa is too soft."

Corrie stood up, giving Quint room to get up as well.

"I'm going to move the coffee table up against the wall, giving us more room. It'll be about four feet farther back than where it is now. You okay with that?"

Corrie smiled at Quint, loving how he tried to keep her safe from hurting herself. "That's great. Thanks."

Corrie heard Quint move the table, then lie on the ground. "I'll be right back, okay? I'm going to go get some lotion."

"Sure, I'll be riiiiight here where you left me."

Corrie giggled, knowing she sounded like a silly schoolgirl. She rushed off toward her bedroom and grabbed her vanilla lotion, knowing it was the least girly smelling stuff she had. She came back to the living room and to Quint's side. She popped open the top of the bottle. "You ready for this?"

"Give it your best shot."

Corrie grinned and got to work.

Thirty minutes and two sore hands later, Quint was a pile of goo under her. She'd worked his back muscles, massaging out all the kinks and knots she could find. She was glad she could help ease some of his pain, but if she was being honest with herself, she enjoyed having her hands all over him just as much.

"Feel good?"

"I might never move again. I'll just take up residence here on your floor and you can throw me a hotdog every now and then to keep me alive."

"I take it you enjoyed it."

Quint turned suddenly until he was on his back and Corrie was straddling his hips again. She felt his hard erection under her and gasped.

"As you can tell, I enjoyed it. Probably too much." He brought one of Corrie's hands up to his face and nuzzled into it. "I'd like to thank you properly."

Corrie's heart leapt as if she'd just run a two-mile race. She wasn't sure what he had in mind, but whatever it was…she wanted it.

She nodded, figuring he'd see her. She felt his hands cup her cheeks and draw her down onto him. She caught herself with her hands on the floor by his shoulders and eagerly leaned down.

Quint looked at the beautiful woman over him. Her blond hair had partly come out of the clip that was holding it back and her face was flushed. He could smell the vanilla lotion she'd used on him. It permeated the air around them.

He gripped the sides of her neck with his hands and brought her slowly down toward him. He didn't want to rush her if she wasn't ready, but when she came down to him eagerly, he smiled. Thank God.

"I'm going to kiss you, Corrie. In light of our conversation the other night at your door, I wanted to make sure I didn't surprise you."

"Please, Quint."

His lips settled on hers and he heard a small gasp leave her mouth. Quint took advantage and plunged his tongue between her lips. He licked and sucked and learned her taste. Needing some air, he paused to take a breath. Corrie began to pull back, probably thinking the kiss was over, but Quint knew he'd not had enough of her yet. He turned them until Corrie was under him. She didn't stiffen in his embrace at all, but eagerly strained upward toward him.

Quint ran one hand down her neck, between her breasts and to her belly, then back up. He continued the dual assault, one hand on her body and his lips on her mouth, until she moaned under him. He lifted his mouth off hers. He needed to talk to her, or else he'd end up taking her right there on the floor...and he wanted more than that for both of them.

"Will you teach me to read Braille?"

"What?" Her confusion was adorable. Quint knew he'd lobbed that one at her out of left field, but he suddenly wanted to know everything about her. It probably wasn't fair to break off the hottest kiss he'd had in a long time to blurt it out, but being around Corrie made him want to be a better person...for *her*. He wanted to belong in her world as much as he was beginning to feel as if she belonged in his.

"I want to learn to read Braille. I know I'll never be as good at it as you are, but I want to do this with you."

"No one has ever asked me that before," she said with a hitch in her voice, obviously still lost in their kiss.

Quint waited until she'd worked though his request in her brain.

Finally she nodded, "Okay, if you really want to, I'll teach you Grade 1 Braille."

"What's Grade 1? Is that like first-grade Braille for kids?" he asked, genuinely confused.

"You really want to talk about this now?"

Quint smiled at the frustration in her voice. It wasn't the best time or place, but he felt the need to be as close to her as possible, and this was one way to do it. He ran his hand over her hair and tucked a piece behind her ear. "Humor me."

"Grade 1 isn't an elementary school grade; it's where every letter of the alphabet is expressed in a Braille pattern. Like, one dot is an A, two is a B, and so on. But I have to warn you, there aren't a lot of books or stuff written in Grade 1 because it's kinda tedious. Grade 2 is when some cells of Braille are used individually or in combination with other cells to form words or phrases."

"Can you give me an example?"

"It's hard to tell you and not show you, but for example, the Grade 1 cell for the letter Y is also the word 'you' in Grade 2 Braille."

"I get it. So it's kinda shorthand. I can learn the individual letters, but in more advanced Braille, a letter might represent a full word in Grade 2. Cool."

Corrie chuckled under him. "You say that now—"

Her words were cut off as Quint's mouth came down on hers again. He didn't warn her it was coming or tease this time, but tilted her face to what he deemed was a perfect angle and devoured her. Their tongues tangled together and he alternated thrusting in and out, and then drawing back and nipping and caressing her lips.

Between kisses, Corrie begged, "Close your eyes."

"Why? I want to see you, you're beautiful." Quint hated the sadness that crossed her face for a split second before she blanked it. "Oh shit, that was insensitive of me. I'm sorry, Corrie."

"Don't be sorry. I'm glad you like the way I look. I don't want you to constantly watch what you say around me. I've been blind my whole life, Quint, I'm not going to get offended or burst into flames if you say 'I see' around me."

Ignoring her words, Quint told her evenly, "My eyes are closed."

"What?"

Quint brought her hand up to his face and drew it over his now closed eyes. "My eyes are closed. Talk to me."

Corrie cleared her throat and tried to hold back the tears she claimed she never shed anymore. He was so sweet to humor her. "What do you smell?"

"You."

"Be more specific."

Quint leaned into her and buried his nose in her neck and inhaled loudly. He smiled when Corrie giggled. "I smell vanilla. The lotion you used to massage my back."

"Anything else?"

"Lavender."

"That's my shampoo. Good job. Now kiss me."

"Gladly."

Quint kept his eyes shut and leaned down. He missed her lips the first time and they both giggled. He quickly righted his aim and kissed her hard again. It was different somehow this time. More intense. He'd certainly kissed women with his eyes closed before, but this time he actually thought about using his other senses while he did it. Without sight, everything seemed...more. He could taste the coffee she'd had after dinner, and the smell of the vanilla lotion filled his nose and made her even taste like vanilla, if that was possible. It was weird...and completely awesome.

He lifted his head and felt Corrie's hand on his face.

"Your eyes are still closed," she whispered, as if she'd expected him to cheat.

"Yeah."

"So?"

"It was more intense. I had to use all my other senses to experience the kiss."

"All those shows and books on BDSM know what they're talking about when they discuss the use of blindfolds."

Quint chuckled and finally opened his eyes. "I can't say I've read many romances about BDSM, and while I do admit to watching some porn, that's not really my thing. But it certainly makes for a more intense experience."

They were quiet for a moment and Quint ran his fingers over Corrie's face one more time. "We should get off the floor."

"Probably."

It was obvious Corrie wasn't going to move, so Quint eased himself up until he was on his knees and grabbed her hands. He helped her sit, then moved them both up and back onto the couch. He pulled her into his arms, loving the feel of her against his bare chest, and held her tight.

"For the record, Corrie Madison, I like you."

She smiled against his shoulder. "I like you too, Quint Axton."

"Glad we have that covered."

They sat in silence, until the automated voice from the clock in Corrie's room announced it was eleven o'clock.

"I have to get going," Quint said reluctantly.

"Do you want to stay?"

Quint almost groaned. Did he want to stay? Oh yeah, but he couldn't. He didn't want to rush her. He was enjoying the dating game they were playing. He hadn't played it since he was in high school. The one step forward, two steps backward dance they were doing was much more interesting and intense than most of the adult relationships he'd had. The women he'd been dating didn't bother playing games, but instead told him outright they wanted to sleep with him. But the dating game with Corrie was fun, different. Besides that, she looked almost embarrassed she'd said the words, and the last thing he wanted was for her to regret anything they did together.

"Yes, I want to stay, but I'm not."

"You're not?" Corrie sat up against him.

"Retract your claws, woman," he said with a laugh.

Corrie gasped and unclenched her hands, which had fisted into his chest when he'd said he wasn't staying. "Sorry."

Quint flattened his hand over hers and rubbed her with this thumb. "There's nothing more that I want to do than take you to your bed, strip you naked, and taste you from your toes to your luscious lips..." He heard her inhale sharply, and he smiled. "But I don't want to rush you."

"Rush me, Quint. I'm okay with that."

He kissed her hard, forcing her head back until she gasped and surrendered against him. He lifted his head and ran a fingertip over her plump just-kissed lips. "I don't want to rush this because I want it to last. I want *us* to last. I want you to get to know me. I want to get to know you better. I want to fall in like with you before I take you to bed and fall in love with you."

"F-fall in love with me?"

"Yeah, 'cos I can see it happening. I'm not there yet, but I don't want to rush what we're doing and not get the chance to see what we could become."

"I think I'm already falling in like with you, Quint."

He smiled down at her. "Good. Then my master plan is working. Come on, walk me to the door then lock up behind me."

"Okay."

Quint put his shirt back on and pulled the table back to where it was when he'd arrived. He looked around, making sure nothing else was out of place.

"What are you doing?" Corrie asked, standing by the kitchen

counter.

"I'm making sure everything's put away." Quint finished examining her space and came up to where Corrie was and saw a weird look on her face. "What's wrong now?"

"You were really trying to see if anything was out of place?"

"Of course. I don't want to leave anything out where you could get hurt if you ran into it."

"I think Emily and Bethany are the only ones that have done that before…but usually it's because they've brought over all of Ethan's baby stuff and the place is a disaster area by the time they're ready to leave."

Quint leaned down and kissed her hard again. "I'm glad to help."

She smiled up at him. "Thanks for making me forget everything for a night."

"You're welcome, sweetheart. Text me tomorrow? Let me know what you're up to?"

"I will. I'll call the station in the morning about the letter and see what's up."

"Good. Why don't you come with Emily when she comes in to give her fingerprints? Let me know when you'll be there and I'll try to come and meet you. We can talk about what the detective found out and perhaps come up with a plan. Maybe we can do lunch afterwards?"

"I'd like that."

"Will Bethany come too? She's more than welcome."

"Probably not. She's been staying at home and watching Ethan while Emily is at work. She's taking some time off of work to be with him. I'm not sure they'll want to bring him to a police station. They're a little overprotective. Especially Bethany. I swear she wouldn't even let me hold him if she thought she'd get away with it."

Quint chuckled. "Okay, I'm sure I'll meet her at some point."

"You want to?"

"Of course I do. She's your friend's partner. Why wouldn't I?"

"I've told you that I liked you tonight, haven't I?"

He smiled. "Yeah, but you can tell me again."

"I like you."

Quint brought Corrie into his arms and hugged her tightly. "Stay safe, Corrie. Don't let anyone in this apartment if you don't know who they are."

"I won't."

"Okay. I'll see you tomorrow." Quint kissed Corrie on the forehead, not trusting himself to stop if he touched his lips to hers again.

"Bye, sweetheart."

"Bye, Quint."

For the third time, Quint listened as Corrie locked herself into her apartment. He only wished he could stay there and keep her safe. He hadn't earned the right yet, but he hoped it'd be soon.

THE MAN KEPT a keen eye on the door from his hiding spot as the cop left the blind bitch's apartment. He pulled out his cell and made a call.

"He's gone."

"I want that whore eliminated," the voice on the other end of the phone growled.

"The pig is becoming an issue. We need to wait."

"You know what? It's not about the cops or the fucking FBI. She's a pain in my ass and I *want* her eliminated," the other man insisted.

The man in the parking lot took another drag off his cigarette before speaking. "She's got a security system and is dating a fucking cop. I told you that letter was a bad idea. She's got more protection now than she had right after I did the job. We need to back the fuck off and let everyone chill. I can get to her a lot easier if everyone thinks the threat is over."

"I thought you wanted to grab her now and fuck her up?"

"I *did*, I *do*, but there's too much heat on her now. And when they don't find Shaun, they're gonna step up their game and there will be even more heat on her...and you and your operation."

"No, there won't. That asshole will be just another missing person. No one is ever gonna find his body. You made sure of that."

The man in the parking lot sighed quietly. He'd made his case. He could probably get to the blind chick if the boss insisted, but he hoped he'd see it his way.

He wanted her, all right. She wasn't fat, her tits would squeeze nicely in his hands, and he'd love to stick his cock inside her, but at the moment there was just too much attention around her. He didn't say anything and the boss man on the other end of the line continued.

"Fine, we'll do it your way...for now. But you stay on her. If it looks like they're closing in on my operation, end her. Got it?"

"Yes, sir."

The man stubbed out his cigarette under his boot and pocketed his phone after ending the call. Good. His way. He fucking liked his way. The poor little blind girl didn't have a chance in hell of getting away from him. He just needed to keep watch and figure out the best way to get to her...without causing her to alert anyone. He'd be patient. When it came to killing, he was always patient as long as, in the end, people ended up with their brains blown out. If he played with her a bit before he killed her...no one would be the wiser. Besides, he'd never fucked a blind chick.

He adjusted his pants over his erection and faded back into the shadows.

Chapter Nine

CORRIE HELD ON to Emily's elbow as they walked to the table in the small restaurant. Her cane dangled by her side just in case, but she usually didn't need it when she was with Emily and Bethany.

They loved Kona Grill. It was an eclectic restaurant that had everything from sushi to burgers. It'd been about a week and a half since her date with Quint, and Emily couldn't wait to give her the third degree anymore. They'd talked about Quint over the phone and after their first date, but Corrie knew she'd be grilled tonight by both Emily and Bethany. Which was okay; it meant they cared about her...and that they were simply nosy. They'd planned it so they'd have time for some girl talk before Quint got there.

Corrie was nervous for Quint to meet Emily and Bethany together. Oh, he'd already met Emily on the night of their first date, but for some reason it seemed different since he'd be meeting and talking with them together as a couple. Corrie didn't care about the fact that they were *together*-together, but this was Texas. Not exactly the most progressive state.

Emily was her best friend. She'd always been there for her. If Quint didn't get along with Emily—or Bethany—their relationship would be over before it began. And she really *really* wanted their relationship to continue.

The other night she and Quint had spent two hours talking about nothing in particular on the phone. It was nice to get to know him and ask him things that she would've felt embarrassed asking about face-to-face. He, in turn, felt comfortable to question her about her blindness. Corrie had no problem whatsoever telling him whatever he wanted to know, even if his questions weren't necessarily politically correct. It was obvious he was asking because he was curious and not out of maliciousness.

Quint had gotten off work in the afternoon then was doing some shooting practice with some of the other officers in the department and wouldn't be able to get to the restaurant until around six-thirty. Emily had picked her up at the clinic at five and the plan was for them to go to the restaurant, and meet Bethany there. Since Quint was meeting them later, he'd told them to go ahead and order and not to wait for him; he'd grab something as soon as he got there.

"Hey! Em! Over here!"

Corrie heard Bethany's voice carry over the din of the other diners. Emily steered them toward her. Corrie dropped her friend's arm when she stopped at their table and listened as Emily and Bethany greeted each other.

"How's my little man?" Emily cooed to Ethan.

Corrie smiled. She loved how gushy Emily got whenever she was around her son.

"How was he today?" Emily asked her partner.

"Good," Bethany preened. "He really is a perfect baby. He did his normal baby stuff today…ate, slept, and pooped."

They all laughed. Corrie settled into the chair Emily had stopped her beside and put her elbows on the table.

"So…" Bethany started. "Corrie, Em tells me you've snagged yourself one hot hunk of a man."

"I don't know about that, but so far he seems pretty darn near perfect."

"We'll see." Her tone was skeptical.

"Bethany!" Emily scolded. "Don't go chasing him off tonight. He really did seem like a good guy when I met him."

"I know, but again, I'm reserving judgment. I don't care if he seems to be as nice as Mr. Rogers himself...I have to see it for myself. You know I'm protective of those I love, Em."

Corrie smiled as she heard her friends kiss briefly.

"So...how's he in bed?" Bethany asked nonchalantly.

Corrie about choked on the water she'd just picked up. "I don't know...yet. But if he makes love as well as he kisses, I'm sure it'll be fantastic."

"You haven't slept with him yet?" Emily asked.

"Uh, no," Corrie said in a drawled incredulous voice. "It's only been a week and a half since our date. And besides, he's kinda in on my case. You know, the whole bad-guy-threatening-me thing."

"Pbsst."

Corrie could picture Emily waving her hand in the air as she airily dismissed her words. "The looks that man was giving you as you left for dinner last week were smokin' hot. I can't believe he hasn't locked you in his room and made passionate love to you all night long."

"Emily!"

"What?" Her voice was amused.

Corrie shook her head. "You're impossible. Please don't embarrass me tonight."

"Would I do that?"

"Yes!"

They all laughed.

The waitress chose that moment to come up to the table. The trio had been to the restaurant so many times they didn't even need to see the menu anymore.

"I'd like the jambalaya, please." Emily always ordered the spicy seafood dish.

"Lobster mac and cheese."

Corrie smiled. Bethany's weakness was carbohydrates, and she always splurged whenever they went out. She was still trying to lose some of the baby weight she'd gained while carrying Ethan, but she'd probably run about ten miles tomorrow to take care of the extra calories she'd consume tonight. She'd never seen anyone able to eat and drink as much as Bethany did, and still be able to retain her slim figure.

"I'll take the big kahuna cheeseburger."

"I have no idea how you manage to eat that thing without getting it all over you," Emily complained good-naturedly. "Seriously, that thing is huge and drips with all the condiments they put on it. You're the neatest blind person I've ever met. It's annoying."

"You love me and you know it."

Corrie felt Emily lightly punch her in her arm teasingly. "I do, you crazy bitch."

They all laughed and fell into a comfortable conversation about work, catching up with their lives in general, and even Ethan's bowel movements and eating habits.

"I can't believe we're sitting here talking about poop and what the best way to pulverize food into infant-sized chunks is. What happened to us? We used to be cool!" Corrie teased her friends. When they started to defend themselves, Corrie held up a hand. "Okay, maybe we were never really cool in the first place. But seriously, I'm so happy for you two. With all that's stacked up against not only you having a relationship together, but also the prejudice against raising your son in today's society, I'm thrilled to be in both your lives. And I know I've told you this before, but I'll never do anything to put any of you in danger. I'd rather die than lead the guy who killed Cayley and the others to your door."

Corrie felt a hand on her own. "I might give you crap, but Corrie, I know how much you love Emily and Ethan." Bethany's words were heartfelt and as serious as Corrie had ever heard. "I never dreamed I'd find a woman to love like Emily. And as sure as I stand here, I never thought I'd be a mother. Ethan means everything to me.

I'd do whatever it took to keep him safe. If Satan himself walked into our house and told me to choose between my life and Ethan's, I'd choose Ethan every time. So I get what you're saying, and as Emily's wife, and as Ethan's mom, and as your friend…thank you. Seriously."

Corrie knew she had the goofiest grin on her face, but she couldn't help it. "We're so sappy, aren't we? What happened to us being cool?"

"We were never cool," Emily laughed. "You said it yourself!"

"True!"

The three women ate their meals when they arrived and ordered a round of some frou-frou drink the waitress recommended. They were laughing and reminiscing over stories when Bethany said in a quiet voice, "Don't look now, but there's a hottie coming straight for the table, and he can't take his eyes off of you, Corrie. I'm assuming your Quint has arrived."

Corrie turned in the direction from which she'd arrived at the table in and smiled. She felt a hand on her upper back, right before she smelled Quint's unique scent. His lips touched her temple then he spoke in his deep voice, which never failed to send a shiver down her spine. "Emily. Good to see you again. And you must be Bethany."

Corrie could picture in her head Quint holding out his hand for Bethany to shake.

"Hi. We've heard a lot about you."

"And I've heard nothing but good things about you, Bethany. And this little guy too."

Corrie lost the feel of Quint's hand as he went over to Ethan and cooed at him. Before too long he was back at her side, and Corrie heard the empty chair next to her being pulled out from the table and then Quint settle in beside her.

"Hi, sweetheart. Did you have a good day?" Quint's voice was breathy and intimate right next to her ear.

Corrie turned to face Quint. "Yeah. It feels good to get back into the swing of things at the clinic."

"All was quiet?"

Corrie knew what he meant. They'd talked at length regarding the reservations she had about returning to the clinic. He'd played devil's advocate and had given her lots of reasons not to return to work, but in the end told her he'd support her no matter what she decided as long as she was careful about her security.

She nodded at his question. "Yeah, nothing out of the ordinary happened. No calls, no letters, no firebombs." She smiled when she said the last and she felt Quint's finger stroke down her cheek.

"Good, that's good."

"How was your day?"

"Same old, same old. Two reports of burglaries, one cat stuck in a tree, and twelve speeding tickets."

"Only twelve? You're slipping."

Corrie heard Quint chuckle before Bethany interrupted them.

"Oh my Lord, you guys are so fucking cute it's almost sickening."

"Bethany! You can't swear in front of Ethan!" Corrie turned and scolded in what was a recurring argument between them.

"Just because *you* gave up swearing, doesn't mean I did."

"But you're his mom," Corrie said, appalled. "You can't swear around him either! You're supposed to be peeved when other people do."

"Cor, I think a few swear words are gonna be the least of this kid's issues as he grows up. And you know it."

Corrie knew what Bethany was talking about. Society was changing, but it didn't mean it'd be easy growing up in an unconventional family environment. "Yeah, well, regardless, he shouldn't grow up to be a potty-mouth...so his Aunt Corrie will be swear-free around him."

The others all laughed at her righteous indignation.

"So...Quint..."

Corrie groaned, knowing Bethany was starting her inquisition.

"What're you doing about this asshole who's threatening our Corrie? You got any more leads on the case? 'Cos I'll tell ya right now, me and Emily are not likin' it one bit."

"I'm right there with you, Bethany. What I'm doing is working with the detective on the case to dig up as much as we can on this Shaun guy. My friend on the Texas Rangers and my other friend in the FBI are also working as hard as they can to shut this shit down. We're not there yet, but I'll tell you this, I'll do everything I can to keep Corrie safe. You have my word."

There was silence around the table for a moment and Corrie just knew Bethany was giving Quint her "bitch face." She was about to open her mouth to try to say something...anything to break the tension, when Bethany spoke.

"Okay then. Good."

Introductions had been made, the tension had eased, and Corrie was able to relax as her friends continued to chat about nothing in particular and get to know Quint.

He was amazing. Corrie felt his hand on the back of her chair as they talked. He'd occasionally play with a strand of her hair and rub his thumb on the back of her neck. Even though he wasn't talking to her specifically, Corrie knew Quint's attention was on her.

She tried to imagine what Quint saw in her friends. Emily was thirty-four and Bethany was twenty-five. Emily sometimes complained that she felt like a cougar when people gave them weird looks. They were about the same height, five-six or so, but very different in looks. Emily had crazy curly black hair that she was always complaining about being in her way, but Corrie knew was probably beautiful and lush. Bethany was slender and blonde. Even though she looked harmless and cute and kinda like a pixie, Corrie knew firsthand she could be a complete hardass. She might have gotten past being the one to start fights, but if someone else did, she was one-hundred percent in. Corrie loved them both. They were as good friends as anyone could ever have.

"Okay, kids. I hate to break this party up, but Ethan's getting restless and we need to get him home," Emily stated during a lull in the conversation. "Corrie? You coming with us? We can drop you off."

"I'll take her." Quint's voice was lazy, but firm.

"It's not a big deal," Emily said. "Her place is on our way home."

"It's fine. I'm happy to drop her off. You guys need to get that little guy home."

Corrie could hear Ethan kicking and gurgling in his carrier. When Emily started to protest again, Corrie kicked where she thought her leg might be under the table to shut her up.

"Ow! Shit, Corrie. I have no idea how you always know right where my leg is!"

Corrie knew she was blushing. Darn Em for calling her out.

Quint laughed. "Come on, sweetheart. I'm sure you have to be tired."

They all packed up their stuff and stood from the table. Corrie felt Quint's arm go around her waist as he steered her through the tables to the front of the restaurant. When they got to the door, he shifted and took her hand in his, as he always did. Corrie squeezed his hand lightly in thanks.

"It was good meeting you, Quint," Bethany said seriously. "You seem like a nice guy. You weren't awkward with me or Emily at all. That means a lot to us. And because Corrie is one of our best friends, you'll probably be seeing us again. Treat her right, would ya? Otherwise you'll have to deal with *us*."

Corrie winced, but she should've known Quint would handle Bethany with grace.

"I like Corrie. Any friend of hers is gladly a friend of mine. I couldn't care less if you were male, female, tall, short, purple, or yellow. As long as you treat her as a friend should, I have no issues whatsoever. Good friends are hard to find. She, and I, would be stupid to care about all that other shit."

"Good answer." That was Emily. She hadn't said a lot, letting Bethany take the lead, but Corrie could tell she was impressed.

"And just so you know, I'd love if you guys could get together with me and Corrie and my friends sometime. I think you'd like Mackenzie and Mickie. They're girlfriends of two of my friends. You guys seem like the kind of people they'd like."

"Sure, that'd be great. Can't have too many friends. Thanks," Emily told Quint enthusiastically.

Corrie let go of Quint's hand and turned to Emily and held out her arms. She gave her a big hug, and then Emily passed her to Bethany. She repeated the gesture and then leaned down to kiss Ethan on the forehead.

"Good night, you guys. Drive safe. Emily, text me when you get home."

"Will do. You too, please."

"Of course."

"It was nice to meet you, Quint."

"You too."

Their goodbyes said, Emily and Bethany headed for their car. Corrie felt Quint once more take her hand in his and they walked to his car and climbed inside. He started it up without a word and pulled out into the night.

They'd been driving for a while before Corrie spoke up. "Thanks for tonight, Quint."

"For what?"

"For treating my friends like people. For not judging them. For being awesome. I think they really liked you."

"You don't have to thank me for that, Corrie. I was being honest with them when I said I didn't care about their sexual orientation. I've met a lot of horrible people in my line of work and it's what's inside someone that matters, not the superficial stuff. I can tell you're really close with them. I couldn't care less about any of that other societal crap." His voice changed from serious to teasing. "So are you dead set on getting home right this second? Or do you wanna do something fun?"

Corrie allowed him to change the subject. "I don't have any plans. I could use some fun."

"How about a driving lesson?"

"What? Quint! I can't drive!"

"Sure you can. I'll be right here to guide you."

"My seeing eye cop?"

He laughed. "Sure. That works."

"You're serious?"

"Yup."

Corrie was silent as Quint drove. Really? Drive? It was crazy. But if she admitted it to herself, it sounded like fun too. "If you won't get in trouble, I'd love to. Where are we going?"

"Someplace safe."

"I *hope* so," Corrie teased.

Corrie felt the car slow down about ten minutes later.

"Okay, we're here."

"Where's here?"

"The middle of nowhere." Quint laughed at the bewildered look that Corrie knew was on her face. "It's a random rural road. No one is out here. It's dark, the road is mostly straight. Come on, hop out and we'll change places."

Corrie got out, suddenly nervous. She couldn't believe he was crazy enough to let her drive his car. She kept her hand on the car as she made her way around the back. She ran into Quint and he grabbed her shoulders to keep her from falling. She looked up at him. "I'm not sure about this. You really won't get in trouble, will you?"

He kissed her hard. "It'll be fine. I won't get in trouble and I won't let anything happen to you. Trust me."

Corrie could only nod. He took her hand and led her the rest of the way to the driver's seat. He got her seated, fastened her seat belt, closed the door, and jogged around to the passenger's side.

"Okay, put your right foot on the brake pedal on the left."

Corrie did as he said.

"Good. Now hold on a sec." He adjusted something on the steering column. "Now, very slowly, ease your foot up off the brake."

Corrie did and felt the vehicle shift under her. She stomped her foot back on the brake and grunted as her seat belt kept her in place as she flew forward.

Quint didn't scold her, he merely laughed and told her, "Good. Do it again."

Corrie did as he instructed and felt the car move forward again. This time she kept her foot ready to brake again, but didn't immediately push it. "Holy crud, Quint. It's moving!"

"Yeah, sweetheart. You're driving."

"Not really."

"Okay then, let's drive. Keep your hands on the wheel at the ten and two positions. For now, just keep your foot off the brake, don't push on the gas pedal to the right of the brake yet. I'll tell you to ease right or ease left on the steering wheel. Okay?"

Corrie nodded enthusiastically. "Okay. Yeah. Quint?"

"Yeah?"

"If I forget to tell you later...thank you. Most people treat me as if I'm totally helpless," Corrie told him breathlessly, loving that he was giving this to her.

She felt him lean into her and kiss her temple. "You're welcome. Just don't steer us into a ditch. I'm not sure I'd be able to explain it to the insurance company."

Corrie laughed and eased up on the brake pedal again. She smiled broadly as she followed Quint's directions.

He talked her through actually turning onto another street and then she got brave enough to even use the gas pedal. Heck, Corrie knew she wasn't going fast at all. Probably no faster than ten miles an hour, but it was exhilarating and exciting, and something she wouldn't have been able to do with just anyone. She trusted him not to let her steer the car into a ditch.

Finally, Corrie braked and turned to Quint with what she knew was probably a goofy look on her face.

"Had enough?"

"Yeah, I think so. I'll never be Mario Andretti, but seriously, that was awesome, Quint."

He leaned over and moved the gear shift into park, explaining what it was to her this time. "You can take your foot off the brake now. It won't go anywhere. Come on, hop out and I'll get you home before your chariot turns back into a pumpkin."

Corrie giggled and undid her belt. She got out and started around the front of the car this time, keeping her hand on the metal to guide her. Once again, Quint met her halfway. This time he pulled her to him with a hand behind her neck. The other went around her waist and he drew her against him.

"You're beautiful." His words were whispered and reverent. Without giving her a chance to respond, he kissed her. It was a deep kiss, one that if they were anywhere but standing in the dark in the middle of a random rural road, would've led to more. As it was, it took a vehicle driving by and honking to bring them back to their surroundings.

Corrie realized she'd put both hands under his shirt and had been clawing at his back, trying to get closer. Quint's hands had also moved, one to her breast and the other to her ass.

Corrie put her head against his chest and laughed weakly. "We have to stop meeting like this." She loved the unrestrained snort that rumbled up through Quint's chest and out his mouth.

He didn't answer, but kissed her hard once more, and reluctantly pulled away. He grabbed her hand. "Come on, let's get you home."

They traveled back to her apartment in a comfortable silence. Quint pulled into a parking spot and asked Corrie to stay put. He came around to open her door and helped her out and, as usual, took hold of her hand and walked her to her apartment.

After she unlocked her door and entered the security code, she stood inside the door as he did a quick walk-through to make sure all was well. "All clear."

"Thanks for a good time tonight, Quint. I'm glad you like my friends, and I loved driving!"

"I've created a monster," he kidded her.

"You have no idea what being treated as if I'm not blind means to me. Most people wouldn't have even had the *thought* to let me do that tonight."

"I'll see what else I can come up with for you later. If there's something you've always wanted to do, or if there's something you want to experience, just let me know and I'll find a way to make it happen."

Corrie didn't answer, knowing her voice would probably break if she did. Instead, she stood on tiptoes to initiate a kiss and he cooperated by lowering his head and touching his lips to hers. He wouldn't let her deepen the kiss, and pulled back way too soon for her liking.

"I'd like nothing more than to make out in your front hall, then take you into your bedroom and get to know you even better, but it feels too soon."

Corrie nodded reluctantly, knowing he was right. She'd loved making out with him on her couch, and she'd loved giving him a massage, but that was then, this was now.

"Lock up behind me, sweetheart, and I'll talk to you later. We'll get together soon. Yeah?"

"Yeah. I'd like that."

"Don't forget to text Emily and let her know you got home all right."

Corrie's heart melted just a bit more. She would've forgotten if he hadn't reminded her. "Thanks for the reminder. I will."

He kissed her on her forehead and squeezed her hand one more time. "Good night, Corrie. See you soon."

"Night."

Corrie set her security system when the door shut behind Quint. She listened as he walked away from her door. She turned her back to the wall and put her hands around her stomach...and smiled a contended smile.

Things were looking good. Very good. She'd never been happier.

Chapter Ten

CORRIE SMILED WHEN her phone rang and the electronic voice told her it was Quint calling. It was about a month and a half after their first date, and they'd had a handful of other dates since then...including the date he'd let her drive. Corrie was realizing that Quint was about as perfect as she'd thought back on date one.

He certainly wasn't completely perfect...he swore too much and tended to be a bit too protective for her comfort level, but he was a generous tipper, liked her friends, and somehow seemed to understand her better than anyone ever had, other than maybe Emily and her parents.

Quint had also apparently been serious about learning Braille. Corrie had grappled with deciding if she wanted to start out with Braille 1 or Braille 2, finally deciding while it was more difficult, and not as widely used, having him start out by learning individual letters and numbers would help him more in the long run.

They'd sat at her table one night and started. Corrie had used her label maker to type out the alphabet. Braille wasn't easy to learn, even for a blind person. Quint was having a hard time, but Corrie was proud of his persistence.

"And here I thought English was a difficult language," he'd complained while struggling to be able to tell the difference between some of the letters.

"Close your eyes. I think it'll make it easier."

He had, and Corrie had put her fingers over his while he traced the dots. "Visualize what the dots look like on the page and memorize how they feel under your fingers. You'll have to move slowly at first, so you can understand what they say. If you move too quickly they'll all run together."

They must've sat at the table for three hours that first night while he'd attempted to get the basics down. The numbers seemed to be easy for him; he'd quickly picked those up, even was able to figure out simple math problems. He'd been so proud of himself and Corrie hadn't been able to resist giving him some positive reinforcement in the way of kisses every time he'd gotten an equation right.

They'd worked on his lessons here and there over the last three weeks, and while he'd probably never be fluent, and it was slow going, Corrie was impressed with his tenacity and his honest desire to learn.

Since she and Dr. Garza had reopened the clinic, they weren't getting the business they'd had before the shooting, but they were bouncing back…slowly. They'd had an open house, and invited the media, showing off their new security measures. They'd wanted to show the public they'd taken the extra steps to try to make sure something like what had happened before, would never happen again.

The media attention had, for the most part been successful, and Corrie was back to working every other day. She'd been reluctant to go back by herself at first, and Dr. Garza understood completely. They worked together for the first week they were back in business. Corrie would always be thankful to him for understanding her fears.

Shaun was still nowhere to be found and Dr. Garza had hired a new assistant for Corrie. Samantha was competent and Corrie liked her, but she still missed and worried about Shaun. No matter what horrible things he might have done, he'd been good to her and she missed him.

Not to mention, Corrie knew his wife was struggling. Robert's medical care was too much for her to deal with alone, never mind pay for. Her husband was missing and was a possible accomplice in a workplace shooting. Corrie felt horrible for her and their children.

Corrie closed her office door and answered her phone.

"Hello?"

"Hey, it's Quint."

"I know."

He didn't tease her like he usually did, but got right down to business. "Matt needs you to come down to the station today."

"Why?" Corrie whispered the word, not liking Quint's tone.

"I can't talk about it over the phone, sweetheart."

"I still have four patients to see today."

"I think that'll be all right. I'll talk to Matt. I can pick you up around three-thirty. Will that work?"

"Yeah, I think so. My last appointment is supposed to end at three. That'll give me time to record my notes before I leave." Corrie paused, biting her lip in consternation. "Is everything okay?"

Quint's voice dropped to the low, rumbly tone he used when he was trying to be gentle with her. It made Corrie's stomach clench. As much as she loved the sound, she hated knowing whatever he was going to say was going to be stressful.

"They found Shaun."

"Thank God! What'd he say? Where's he been? Did he explain everything that's been going on?"

"Sweetheart…"

It was the tone that clued her in. "Oh God."

"I'll pick you up at three-thirty. We'll talk then. In the meantime, be safe."

"I will. See you later, Quint."

"Bye."

"Bye." Corrie clicked off the phone and put her head on her desk. Crap. It was good they found Shaun, but she could tell by the seriousness of the conversation she'd had with Quint, whatever happened was bad. Crap crap crap. She'd wanted to ask a million other questions, but it was obvious Quint wasn't going to tell her anything sensitive or concerning over the phone.

She lifted her head, took a deep breath and got herself together. She had four more patients to see today, she had to give them her utmost attention. She didn't want to hurt them. The last thing the clinic needed was a lawsuit on top of everything else.

At three-twenty, Lori, their new administrative assistant, came to tell Corrie there was a gorgeous police officer in the lobby asking for her. Corrie smiled at her description. She might be blind, but she'd "seen" him in her many explorations, and would have to agree. Corrie hadn't been able to convince Quint she was ready to do more than explore each other from the waist up…yet. She'd been hoping tonight would be the night she'd finally get him out of his pants, but now with everything that was going on with Shaun, she wasn't so sure.

"Thanks, Lori. Tell him I'll be right out."

Corrie heard Lori leave her office and head back to the front of the clinic. She hurried to complete her notes on her last client and then pack up her stuff. She grabbed her cane, loving the fact that she only had to use it when she wasn't around Quint. She never felt the need to have it when she was with him because he always, every single time they'd been out, helped her get around by holding her hand. It'd become second nature to them both. Corrie felt more connected to him as a result. When she was holding his hand, she could pretend they were like every other couple on the street. She almost felt normal. Almost.

She headed out of her office and down the hall, looking forward to being with Quint, no matter the circumstances. She opened the door to the waiting area and stopped, knowing Quint would come to her. Corrie felt a hand at her elbow.

"Hey, sweetheart. You look good."

Corrie smiled, knowing he was lying, but enjoying his words all the same. "Thanks, but I know better. I've been working all day and my hair is probably a mess and I can smell the medicinal lotion on my hands and clothes."

She felt Quint lean close and whisper in her ear as he ran a hand lightly over her hair. "You look delightfully mussed...it makes me wonder what you'll look like first thing in the morning. And I've grown addicted to whatever lotion you use while you work; one sniff and my body recognizes it as you...and reacts accordingly."

He moved slightly so she was flush against his side, and even with him wearing his utility belt with all his equipment, Corrie could feel what he meant. She blushed.

Quint chuckled. "Come on, sweetheart. Let's get this done. I have plans for tonight."

"You mean moving up to the next Braille primer?" she teased cheekily. Corrie loved the sound of his laughter.

"Yeah, that's what I meant," he drawled sarcastically.

Corrie waved goodbye to Lori and they headed out the door, her hand firmly grasped in Quint's as they headed for his patrol car.

"HE'S DEAD."

Corrie tried not to react, but knew she failed when she heard Quint growl from somewhere behind her. They'd arrived at the police station and had immediately been whisked into a room, where she'd been informed Detective Algood and another man called Conor Paxton had been waiting for them. Quint introduced everyone and he'd settled her into a chair at a small metal desk.

Detective Algood continued. "Conor is a game warden with Texas Parks and Wildlife, and was the one who received the tip about a body being found in Medina Lake. It's a miracle the body was even discovered; it looks like he was weighted down with plenty of cinderblocks, but he was dumped too close to shore. As you all know, we're way down in rainfall this year, and someone noticed something dark in the lake. When they investigated more, they saw a foot sticking up out of the water and called the Parks and Wildlife office. Conor went to check it out. Body's with Calder Stonewall in the medical examiner's office at the moment; it's unrecognizable, but it's looking pretty good that it's Shaun."

Corrie inhaled sharply. God, unrecognizable? She felt a comforting hand on her shoulder.

"Jesus, Matt. Remember who you're talking to," Quint groused.

"Sorry, ma'am. No offense."

"How can you know it's Shaun? I mean, if he'd been in the water that long…" Corrie asked tentatively.

"His clothes. His wife told us what she remembered him wearing the last time she saw him, and it matches perfectly."

"How did he die?"

Conor shared a look above Corrie's head with Quint. There was no way they'd want to share the horrible details with her. While the body had been decomposed beyond all recognition, it was missing its hands and there were several bullet holes throughout the body—nonlethal holes. One in the knee, one in each bicep, and two through the calves. The fatal bullet was the one in the middle of the man's forehead. It was obvious he'd been tortured before finally being executed.

"We're not sure yet, but Calder will figure it out," Conor said in a soothing, easy voice.

"So what does this mean?" Corrie couldn't understand why they'd felt it necessary to bring her in to tell her about Shaun.

Detective Algood spoke again. "It means whoever did this never wanted him found. If it wasn't for the drought in the area it would've been a very long time, if ever, before we found the body. It means you could be in danger."

"But I've been in danger since it happened, haven't I? So what's different now?"

Quint knew Corrie was smart. He wasn't happy she'd mostly figured it out so quickly, but he was impressed nevertheless. He knelt down by her side and put a finger under her chin and turned her face toward him. He hated seeing the worried look on her face.

"We assumed Shaun was probably dead, sweetheart. We also assumed the lack of any more threats against you meant they were backing off and leaving you alone. We're afraid since we found Shaun's body, and possibly clues, they'll once again turn their sights to you to try to make sure anything we *do* find can't be traced to them. The possibility of you being able to identify them is just another reason for them to be rattled...and pissed off."

Corrie tried to think through what Quint was telling her. "I still don't get it. If I can't testify, and didn't actually *see* anyone that night, why would they care about me?"

This was the part Quint had been holding back. "The district attorney hasn't ruled out you testifying."

Corrie inhaled sharply. "What? Really?"

"Yeah. With the shooting being on the national news, there's been a lot of attention focused on the department and the city. She wants to catch whoever did it, and after she heard everything you told Matt about how you could recognize the shooter, she's contemplating allowing your testimony."

"Oh my God. Quint..." Corrie reached out a hand. It landed on his chest and she slid it to his bicep. "That's great news! I wanted to testify from the very start. I know I can pick him out. I just know it."

Quint didn't even smile. He was pleased Corrie wasn't shying away from doing her duty and that she was eager to put the man behind bars who'd killed her friend and the others, but as the man, and cop, who was coming to care for her a great deal, he didn't like it one bit.

"I know you can too, sweetheart. And so do the bad guys." He let that sink in. He knew it had when her forehead crinkled in concentration.

"Oh." She turned to the direction she'd last heard Detective Algood. "So now they'll want to shut me up too, won't they?"

Matt nodded, forgetting Corrie couldn't see him.

Conor answered her question. "Yeah, we think so."

Quint watched as Corrie literally pulled herself up by her bootstraps and blithely commented, "Okay then. I'll just have to be more careful."

He shook his head and half smiled. Jesus, she was cute, but totally clueless. He caught Conor's gaze and shook his head. Quint would break the news to Corrie.

Conor nodded at him and gave a head tilt to Matt, letting him know it was time to leave.

"I know you guys are talking without talking again," Corrie said peevishly, crossing her arms over her chest. Then, mumbling under her breath, continued, "I hate that."

Quint waited until the men had left the room. He pulled the chair sitting on the other side of the table around so it was next to hers. He physically turned the metal chair Corrie was sitting in, wincing as it screeched against the floor, until they were sitting face-to-face, knees touching. He picked up her hands and held them in his own.

"What is it, Quint? Tell me."

"I don't think you should stay at your place."

Panic crossed Corrie's face before she banked it.

"But I don't have anywhere to go. I already told you I won't stay with Emily and Bethany."

"What about your parents?" Quint knew what her answer would be, but asked anyway. He was purposefully leading her right where he wanted her.

"You know I won't do that either. Besides, they live up in Fort Worth. I can't leave Dr. Garza in a lurch like that. I can go to a hotel."

"There's no security in a hotel, Corrie. And what about all the other people there?"

"Crud. You're right. Darn it, Quint. What am I going to do?"

Bingo.

"Stay with me." Quint held his breath as Corrie absorbed his words.

"But...I don't..."

"I have a security system. I live in a house in a subdivision. If there are unknown cars in the area, my seventy-seven-year-old neighbor will let me know. She's a one-woman crime-stopper team." While Corrie bit her lip, Quint continued. "I have two extra bedrooms, sweetheart. I have lots of space. I'm not saying I *want* you to stay in either of those bedrooms, but I'm not going to pressure you. You can stay with me and let me protect you. Once this is over, if you want, we can see where this chemistry between us goes. No pressure. Honestly."

"I don't do so good in unfamiliar places."

Quint sighed in relief. Her hesitancy wasn't because of him, but because of her nervousness about her lack of sight and his house. He took her hands in his and rubbed the backs of them with his thumbs as he spoke. "I know. You said as much when you told me Ian moved in with you rather than you going to his place. Sweetheart, I'm a bachelor. Have been for a long time. I don't have a lot of stuff. I'll walk you through my house as many times as you need to learn the layout. We'll bring over as much of your assistive things as you want. Hell, you can redo my kitchen however you need to. Trust me to take care of you, Corrie. I'm not that douchebag Ian. Trust that I'll make my home as comfortable for you as yours is. I swear I'll do whatever it takes."

"I'm not easy to live with."

"It'll be an adjustment for both of us."

"You have an extra bedroom?"

Quint's heart dropped, but he forced himself to say normally, "Yup."

"I want to stay with you."

"Thank God." Quint breathed the words. Not caring that they were in an interrogation room with a two-way mirror, he leaned forward, listening to his gear creak as he moved, and brought Corrie's mouth to his. He kissed her long and deep, putting the things he hadn't yet said into his kiss. He finally drew back and looked at her.

Corrie's hands were on his chest and she had a rosy glow on her face. Even with all that was happening, she was levelheaded and so gorgeous he almost couldn't believe she was here with him.

"On one hand, I hate this vest you're wearing because I can't feel *you*…but since I know you have it on to protect yourself, I can't *really* hate it."

Quint chuckled. Corrie constantly surprised him.

"Come on, sweetheart. Let's go tell Detective Algood where you'll be staying and we'll go to your place to gather your stuff."

"This doesn't mean you're getting out of your lesson today, buddy."

Quint pulled Corrie into his side and kissed her temple gently. "I didn't think it would." He shifted until he had her hand in his and headed for the door.

"Thank you, Quint."

He stopped. "For what?"

"For being you. For liking me as I am. For understanding I'm not like other women. For just…everything."

"You don't have to thank me for liking you and as far as you not being like other women…I thank my lucky stars every day for that. Come on. We have a lot of stuff to do tonight."

Chapter Eleven

---◆---

CORRIE SAT NERVOUSLY on the couch in Quint's house. He'd been very patient with her as she'd decided what she needed to bring to his place, even going so far as to reassure her that if she realized she needed something she'd left behind, he'd be sure to collect it for her as soon as he could.

His house smelled good. Corrie didn't know what she'd expected it to smell like, but cinnamon wasn't it. He obviously had air fresheners strewn about to make it so fragrant, but Corrie wasn't complaining.

He'd held her hand and brought her straight to his sofa and told her to hang tight there while he brought in the rest of her things. She'd been all too ready to stay where he'd put her, because she didn't want to look like an idiot fumbling around his house trying to find her way. He'd said he'd show her around, and she was taking him at his word.

Corrie heard him go out to his garage a few times and walk down a hall into the back of the house. He'd puttered around in the kitchen a bit, most likely putting down the box of her kitchen doohickeys she'd decided she'd need immediately.

Finally she heard his footsteps coming closer to where she was in his family room. She felt the couch dip as he sat next to her and she sighed in relief when he took her hand.

"Relax, sweetheart. I promise you'll get through this."

"I'm just nervous. I don't like new places."

"I know you don't, but soon this will feel like your home too. I swear I'll do whatever you need in order to make you comfortable."

"I'm being silly, I know, I—"

Quint cut her off with a kiss. He pulled back and whispered against her lips, "You're not being silly. I'd feel the same way as you in your shoes. Just please, trust me to fix this for you."

Corrie took a deep breath. He was right. "Okay."

"Okay, first a tour. Then we'll decide where to put some of your things. Yeah?"

Corrie nodded and gripped Quint's hand tightly when they stood up. "Lead on, oh brave warrior." She tried to lighten the mood.

Quint laughed as she hoped he would.

They spent the next hour touring his house several times. Quint never lost patience with her as he told her where his furniture was. He held her hand while they explored and she used her cane to gauge the distance between pieces of furniture and the width of halls and doorways. She felt more at ease after using it to figure out where things were and having Quint there to explain what everything was as she touched it.

After she'd been through every room twice, she began to feel comfortable enough to suggest moving some of the furniture here and there. She wouldn't have been so bold, but Quint had repeatedly told her it was fine and encouraged her until she made some suggestions. Of course he immediately agreed and they worked together to find the best layout of his stuff.

When they'd entered his bedroom for the first time, Corrie was extremely nervous, but Quint kept his tour clinical and she only caught a brief innuendo or two. He was trying to be on his best behavior.

Finally, after she'd walked through the house without holding onto his hand twice, and she was confident that she'd remember where she was and how it was all set out, she called it quits for the night. Corrie knew there'd be times she'd forget, she was too used to her own place, but she appreciated Quint's patience more than he'd ever know.

"How come you don't have a seeing eye dog?"

Corrie figured he'd ask at some point, since most people did, but she wasn't offended. "A dog is a lot of responsibility for someone who lives alone. I'm not opposed to one, heck, I love dogs, but knowing myself, I'd probably worry about its health, and what it was getting into that I couldn't see. For now, my cane gets me around just fine, and if I need help, I'm never afraid to ask people around me for assistance."

"Have you ever had one?"

"A dog? Unfortunately, no. My parents were allergic, and even once I moved out, I'd just gotten comfortable in my routine."

"You're off tomorrow, right?" Quint asked, changing the subject abruptly, as he was sometimes wont to do. It was as if once he got the answer he wanted, his brain was constantly in motion and he moved on to the next question.

Corrie smiled and did what she usually did, just went along with his change in conversation. "Yeah. It's Dr. Garza's day tomorrow."

"I've asked for the day off as well. We'll start on the kitchen and you can tell me the best place for everything. We can try to set up the pantry and fridge the same way you've done it at your place."

"You're too good to be true, you know. Are you a cyborg? Something out of the future?"

Quint chuckled. "Nope. I'm just me."

"I like 'just you.'"

"I'm glad. I like you too."

Corrie knew she was smiling like an idiot, but couldn't seem to stop. "We're still going to hit the books tonight, though. I hope you know that."

Quint burst out with a short laugh. "Of course, slave driver. Let's do this." He pulled over the papers she'd printed out and concentrated on what she'd set up for him tonight. He reviewed the alphabet and only made a few mistakes.

"Okay, tonight we're going to start working on Grade 2 Braille. You ready?"

"Yup, sock it to me, woman."

Corrie shook her head and continued. "Okay, try this."

"I, L, Y."

"Right," Corrie praised, "but remember, this is Grade 2, the dots don't necessarily represent letters, but actually words.

"So the I might not be an I, it could be a word instead."

"Yup."

"How do I know the difference?"

"Most things nowadays are written in Grade 2, so it's a good bet if you come across something, it's actually a word and not the letter. You've got a short sentence in front of you in Grade 2. If I'd written it out in Grade 1 Braille, it'd be eight letters. But since it's in Grade 2, it's only three."

Corrie held her hand over Quint's as he traced the dots with his fingertips again. "What does it say?"

"I like you."

He traced the dots again. "Okay, so the I is really just an I. The L represents the word like, and the Y the word you. Cool. But I have a question."

Corrie could tell Quint was looking at her. His hand was motionless under hers.

"Shoot."

"How do I know the L represents the word like, and not loathe, or lick, or," he paused and his voice lowered seductively, "love?"

Corrie's heartrate jumped. "Practice, really. You have to figure out the context of what you're reading."

"Ummmm, so if *you* were sending me a letter in Braille it could be love, but if I got one from a scumbag prisoner, it would probably be loathe."

Corrie felt Quint put his free hand on her neck. She knew he could feel her heart beating extremely fast. She nodded. "Yup, that's it."

"Got it." He paused and they sat there without saying a word for a moment. "I think study time is over. It's late. You have to be tired. Come to bed with me?"

He'd asked the question, but Corrie could tell he wasn't really asking if she was tired. It was finally time. She nodded enthusiastically.

Quint leaned toward Corrie and kissed her. He couldn't hold back. Jesus, having her here in his space, having her stuff all around his house, made it seem more like a home. He'd only brought one or two women to his house before, and it hadn't made him feel as comfortable as he was with Corrie here.

He couldn't wait to put her things away in his kitchen, to arrange it so it would work for her. Quint wanted to watch her making coffee in his kitchen. Wanted to see her cooking and being comfortable in her own skin in his space. He wanted her clothes hanging in his closet, her stuff on his bathroom counter and her sexy body in his bed, on his sheets. He had it bad.

He licked her lip as he pulled away and scooted back his chair suddenly. "Come on, sweetheart." Feeling like a bull in a china shop, he towed her quickly down the hall to his room, not bothering to turn off the lights as he went. Not wanting to let go of her, feeling as if he did, she'd disappear, Quint forced himself to drop her hand and turn her toward his bathroom.

"Go on, sweetheart. Bathroom is straight ahead, maybe five steps. Do what you need to do. I'll use the guest bathroom."

Corrie nodded and headed off to the bathroom, her arms held out in front of her cautiously so she didn't run into anything, as her cane was sitting on the kitchen table where she'd left it. Quint watched her backside sway as she headed for the bathroom and shook his head when she disappeared inside. He had to get himself together.

He quickly stripped off his clothes and carefully put them in the hamper in his closet. Usually he just threw them in the general direction of the plastic container, but he had a new reality now and couldn't afford to be careless anymore. He kept his boxers on and strode out of the room toward the guest bathroom to get ready for bed.

He got back to his room a few minutes later to see Corrie standing uncertainly by the edge of his bed. She had one hand on the mattress and was standing with her legs crossed, one foot on top of the other. He inhaled deeply at seeing her. She was wearing a long T-shirt, and he couldn't see anything else. He had no idea if she was naked underneath it or not, but her long legs about made his heart stop.

"Hey," she greeted nervously. "I didn't know which side you slept on."

Quint quickly came to Corrie's side and lifted her hand to his mouth. He kissed the palm and engulfed it in his own. "I don't really have a side. I'm usually in the middle."

She smiled at that. "Figures."

"Go on, climb in. Whatever side you're most comfortable in, you can have."

Quint almost groaned when Corrie lifted the comforter and scooted into the bed over to the far side, leaving room for him. He followed her in and gathered her close.

"Your heart is beating a hundred miles an hour. Are you that nervous? We don't have to do anything, sweetheart. We can just lie here. Sleeping with you in my arms is something I've dreamed about a lot over the last month."

Quint heard and felt Corrie sigh. "I am nervous, I can't deny it.

But not for the reasons you may think."

"Just relax. You're fine."

"I know you probably have never thought about this, but you always smell so good. Your bed smells so good."

"My bed?"

"Yeah, your sheets smell clean, but it's mixed with you. The cologne you sometimes wear, the soap you use in your shower, the detergent you use...*you*. It smells like you."

"And that's a good thing?"

"Oh heck yeah." She paused, then continued, "I know I haven't seen you...there yet. And it's taking all my self-control not to push you over and rip off those boxers and examine the hard length I've been feeling against me every time we've made out."

Quint gurgled deep in his throat. It was a cross between a gasp and a laugh. "The feeling is definitely mutual, sweetheart. I don't know what you're wearing under that T-shirt, but my palms are actually itching to slowly ease it up your body until you're as naked as the day you were born. I know this is a he-man macho thing to say...but you have no idea what the sight of you on my sheets is doing to me. I've dreamed about it. I've even got myself off right here in this bed thinking about it. I think between the two of us, our first time is going to be pretty damn quick."

"Are you complaining?"

Quint could hear the smile in her voice. "Hell no."

"Did you turn off the lights?"

Quint took a moment to respond, not understanding her change of topic. "No."

"Good."

"Good?" Most women Quint had been with had asked him to turn the light off before they'd bared themselves to him.

"Yeah, I want you to have your fantasy. I can't wait to lie here naked, imaging your eyes on me. But I'll warn you, there'll be a time when I'll want the light off, simply so you can experience us together as I do."

"Jesus, Corrie. Every time you open your mouth I get harder."

"I can think of something *else* I can do with my mouth that will make you harder."

Quint couldn't think straight. He swore his vision went a bit gray at her words. He knew Corrie could speak her mind, and usually wasn't shy, but this…this was beyond his fondest fantasy. He'd always been annoyed when women hemmed and hawed about their looks. It wasn't as if he didn't understand, the media was murder on a woman's self-esteem, but maybe that was why Corrie was so self-assured and okay with her body. She couldn't see any of the pictures of the stick-thin women in Hollywood that were constantly on television, magazines and the Internet. It was refreshing as all get out to be with a woman who liked her body.

Quint grabbed the bottom of Corrie's T-shirt and forcefully drew it up. He didn't ask, and she didn't protest. She merely lifted her arms to help him. He saw her dusky pink nipples briefly before leaning down to devour them.

He took one in his mouth and sucked hard, while his fingers found the other and tweaked it playfully. Corrie moaned in his arms and grabbed hold of his biceps while he played.

He wasn't nearly done when he felt one of her hands snake down his body between them. Quint helpfully pulled his hips away to give her room. She found his cock with no issues and squeezed him through the cotton of his boxers.

He lifted his head and gasped.

"God, Quint. You feel amazing."

"I think that's *my* line."

"We'll share it."

Quint tolerated her hand on him for another moment before rolling to his back and lifting his hips to remove the offending material.

The sooner Corrie's hand was on his bare skin, the better. Before he could roll back over, Corrie was there. He looked up at her and grinned. She was so fucking sexy and she had no clue. No clue at all.

Her blonde hair was mussed and falling around her face. She brought one hand up and absently smoothed it behind one ear before putting her hand back on his body. Her cheeks were flushed and she alternated between licking her lips sensuously then biting the bottom one.

Her thighs were full, but muscular. He could see her quads flexing as she moved into place next to him. Quint knew they'd be soft under his hands.

Her breasts were perfect. They weren't small, but they weren't huge either. He could fit them in the palms of his hands easily. Her stomach was softly rounded and she had small love handles. Quint couldn't resist her, not that he had to hold himself back anymore. He'd seen glimpses of her before when they'd made out on her couch, but he'd never seen her like this. Naked, straddling his body, and all his.

He ran his hand over her breast and down to her stomach. Quint played with her belly button for a moment before moving his hand. He gripped her side, squeezing her skin until she shifted in his grasp.

"You are so soft. God, Corrie. You're amazing."

She didn't answer, but scooted back on his legs, breaking his hold on her and bringing her hands to his hips to explore. Quint drew in a quick breath as one hand cupped his balls and the other grasped his erection just under the head.

"You like that."

"Yeah."

Corrie didn't say more, simply continued running her hands over him. She learned his shape and texture. She used her fingertip to trace the head of his cock, smearing his pre-cum over him and massaging it into his skin.

Finally she spoke again. "Does it hurt?"

"Does what hurt?"

"This." She squeezed him lightly. "I can feel the veins sticking out and throbbing. It feels like it should hurt. Your balls are tight, I'm not sure I've ever felt anything like it before."

Quint didn't like being compared to anyone else, but ignored that for the time being. He ran his hand over her head, not offended in the least that she seemed to be staring off into the room. It didn't matter if her head was tilted down toward his cock or up at his face, she couldn't see him, at least not with her eyes. She was doing all the "seeing" she needed to with her hands at the moment, and it felt fucking awesome.

"It doesn't hurt...exactly. It's painful in a way because I'm so turned on, but it's a good hurt. I know that I'll soon be buried inside your hot, wet body and that it'll feel so damn good...it's worth any hurt I'm going through right now."

Without a word, Corrie leaned down and licked the head of his dick. He groaned when she squeezed him and did it again.

Corrie's head came up and looked to where his face should be. "I want you."

Her words gave him the push he needed to take control. "Lay back." As good as her mouth felt against him, he knew he'd never last if he let her continue. There'd be time for that later...hopefully. If she wanted to.

She did as he asked and Quint pulled the sheet down until no part of her body was obstructed. He put one hand on her belly so she'd know he was there. He looked down at his tan hand against the pale skin of her stomach. It was so erotic, Quint knew if she touched him now, he'd explode.

As he looked at her, she stretched and arched her back. She put her hands up over her head and Quint swore she looked just like the pictures of Marilyn Monroe he used to drool over when he was young.

"Is it like you imagined?" Her voice was husky and sultry and slightly teasing.

"No." Quint clipped the word out without thinking. It wasn't until he saw Corrie frown and start to put her hands down that he realized what he'd said. He put his hands on her wrists and forced them back up over her head and leaned down to whisper in her ear. "It's so much fucking better, I'm about a second away from coming all over your pretty tits. Keep your hands there. Don't move. If you touch me, I'll lose it, and I have a lot I want to do before that happens."

The smile crept back over Corrie's face and Quint relaxed. He never in a million years wanted her to feel awkward in his bed...or anywhere for that matter. Quint eased down her body, licking here, nipping there, until he reached his final destination. He sat on his haunches between her legs. "Open wider for me, sweetheart." She did and Quint could feel his mouth watering. Oh fuck yeah.

Her folds were pink and glistening with her arousal. He eased down until he was on his belly between her legs. He put one hand under her ass and lifted her up. The other hand he used to spread her open for him.

"I hope you're comfortable, Corrie, because I have a feeling I'll be down here for a while." Quint smiled at the moan that escaped her mouth, but he didn't look away from his prize. He licked once, from bottom to top, paying attention to her clit when he reached the summit of her folds. As she jerked in his grasp he murmured more to himself than Corrie, "Oh yeah, a good long while."

Chapter Twelve

CORRIE HELD HER breath as she felt Quint's tongue on her. Holy cripes, his touch was perfect. She desperately wanted to put her hands on his head, but she kept them where they were. She'd had a couple of men go down on her before, but it had been more of a "let's get this done so we can get to the good part" kind of thing.

But with Quint, he made *this* feel like the good part. He made it seem as if he truly was enjoying what he was doing. Corrie could hear his low moans and the sounds he made in the back of this throat. His grip on her butt was strong and every now and then his fingers flexed against her. She could feel his shoulders rub against her inner thighs as he concentrated on giving her pleasure. Corrie heard the sound of licking and the sound of her juices against his fingers as he used them to stroke inside her. It should've embarrassed her, but right now, it turned her on more.

Everything about what he was doing was hot as hell…and that was without being able to actually see it. She could only imagine what she looked like through Quint's eyes as he was up close and personal with her womanly bits. Corrie blushed, hoping Quint would be too busy to notice.

Quint loved Corrie's taste. If asked, he wouldn't be able to describe what she tasted like, but it was arousing as anything he'd ever experienced in his life. He moved his hips against the bed as he continued to lick and suck at Corrie's folds. He was so hard he knew the second he got inside her he'd lose all control.

He eased two fingers into her hot sheath and concentrated his attention on her clit. Quint could feel Corrie shaking as he pushed her closer and closer to the edge. He rubbed against her inner walls, trying to find her G-spot. When she jumped in his arms as he felt a small spongy spot inside her, he knew he'd found it.

"That's it, come for me, Corrie. Come all over my fingers. I want to feel it." He lowered his head and threw her over the edge with his dual assault on her bundles of nerves.

Quint struggled to keep his mouth on her clit as Corrie bucked in his hold. He smiled and his eyes stayed glued to her face as she thrashed in his arms. She moaned and he could feel her hands in his hair. He mentally smirked, realizing in the throes of passion she couldn't keep them above her head as he'd asked. Just as she was coming down, he used his fingers, which were still inside her, to stroke hard against the weeping walls of her sex one more time.

He lifted his head and watched as she shook uncontrollably in his arms once more. He'd seen other women come apart, but this was different. She wasn't moaning and carrying on. In fact, she wasn't really making much noise at all, other than a slight purr here and there. Her reactions to his ministrations were genuine and honest and somehow a hundred times sexier than anyone he'd ever been with. Corrie seemed to feel her orgasm from the tips of her toes to the top of her head. It was fucking awesome.

Quint pulled his fingers out of her body slowly, even as she continued to jerk and pump her hips into the air, appreciating how her body gripped him tightly, trying to prevent him from leaving her. He sucked his come-covered digits into his mouth, enjoying her strong musky taste. He pulled himself onto all fours and crawled up Corrie's body until he was hovering over her.

Her arms were lying limp at her sides and the cutest smile was on her lips. She looked completely sated and absolutely undone.

"Hey. You okay?"

"Shhhhhh."

Quint grinned. He didn't say anything, but leaned down and began kissing her neck. He nipped her collarbone and worked his way up to her ear. He took the lobe in his mouth and tongued it, then bit down gently.

Corrie moaned under him and finally moved her hands, bringing them up to his sides to grip him tightly. "Not fair," she mock complained even as she tilted her head to give him more access to her sensitive neck and ears.

"Don't mind me, sweetheart. Just lie there and ignore me."

"I couldn't ignore you if I tried."

Quint smiled again. She was so much fun. He'd never smiled this much while in bed with a woman before. In the past he'd been all about getting them off, then getting off himself. He'd never wanted to play and tease. He'd never known what he was missing.

"I want you, Corrie." Quint's words were serious now. He pulled away and looked down into Corrie's face. She looked up. Her bright blue prosthetic eyes gazed where she calculated he was. Quint swore they could see right into his soul somehow.

"I want you too, Quint. I want to feel you inside me, filling me up."

"God." Quint gritted his teeth as his cock flexed against Corrie's stomach. He leaned over to the drawer next to his bed and pulled out the brand new box of condoms. He'd bought it last week in the hopes he'd get Corrie in his bed at some point. At the time he hadn't cared if that was months or days...although he was hoping for closer to the day timetable.

He tore at the box, cursing himself for not having the foresight to open it before now. In his rush to get it open, the condoms went flying everywhere as he jerked the cardboard top. Corrie threw her head back and laughed as she obviously felt the vinyl packets land on her body and around them.

She grabbed one that had alighted on her breast and held it up. "Looking for one of these?"

Quint leaned down and kissed Corrie hard and fast before taking the condom from her grasp. "Yeah, thanks."

He ripped open the foil, ignoring the other condoms now strewn over his bed, and leaned up on his knees to roll it down his eager cock. Quint inhaled as Corrie's hands knocked his away and finished the job.

Breathing through his arousal, he clenched his teeth and asked, "How'd you get so good at that?"

"Not how you might think," Corrie quipped as she pinched the tip of the condom and ever so slowly slid it down his cock.

"I didn't mean...sweet Jesus, woman...I meant..."

Quint's voice trailed off and Corrie answered what he was so badly trying to ask. "Hey, I might not be able to see, but I practiced right along with the rest of my health class in high school when it came to putting one of these babies on a banana."

"Did that really happen?"

"Yup. Can't imagine parents would allow it in the public schools today, but it was extremely enlightening for me and my friends. All done." She caressed his now-covered erection and tugged, encouraging him to finish what he'd started.

Trying to ignore how good her hands felt on him so he wouldn't go off before he'd even gotten inside her, Quint leaned back over her. "Hold on to my arms, sweetheart. This is gonna be hard and fast. I'm sorry. Next time I'll make it better for you."

"If this was any better, I'd be dead. I want you. I want to feel you inside me. Take me, Quint. Do it."

He waited until her hands gripped his upper arms before bracing himself on one hand by her head. Then he reached down and grabbed hold of the base of his dick with his other hand. He felt Corrie spread her legs even farther apart to give him room. He ran the head of his cock over her clit once, twice, then eased lower and pushed in. Quint groaned as he slowly drove himself into her hot, wet folds.

"Shit, Corrie. Jesus, you feel good."

Quint's hand came back up next to her shoulder on the bed to support himself as he pushed inside her warm body as far as he could go. He felt Corrie's knees bend and her legs wrap around his hips. She crossed her feet at the ankles and squeezed him. She tilted her hips and Quint swore he sank in another inch.

"God," Quint pulled out to the tip, then pushed in again slowly, "you feel," again he pulled out, then pushed in, "so fucking good."

Quint stopped talking; he couldn't get any other words out. His thrusts sped up as he powered in and out of Corrie. She felt like heaven.

"I can't...shit...hold on, sweetheart. Let me know if I'm hurting you...okay?"

Corrie groaned and pulled him closer. Quint fell onto his elbows over her.

"You're not hurting me. Do it. Please." Her voice was soft and breathy next to his ear. He felt her warm inhalations as she panted against his neck.

Quint let go of his restraint and pounded into Corrie as if his life depended on it. Amazingly, he felt her quake under him just as he lost control. He'd lasted longer than he thought he would...but only about two strokes longer. He held himself inside Corrie as he threw his head back and groaned.

Not able to hold himself up anymore, Quint eased down and to Corrie's side, making sure to keep one of her legs over his hip so his length stayed inside her for as long as possible. They lay there, both breathing hard, Corrie snuggled into his chest as Quint tried to catch his breath.

"Holy shit, woman."

Corrie giggled in his ear and Quint thought it was the most beautiful sound he'd ever heard.

They held each other for a few minutes, enjoying the aftermath of their orgasms. Finally, Quint pulled away reluctantly. "I have to take care of this condom, don't move."

Her leg eased off of him and Quint reached down and held on to the latex as he slipped out of her warm body, secretly loving the disappointed groan that came from Corrie's mouth. He leaned over, kissed her on the lips and whispered, "I'll be right back."

Corrie rolled to her back and smiled up in his general direction as she nodded. Quint went into the bathroom and took care of the condom. He turned on the water until it ran warm, and then wet a washcloth. He walked back into his bedroom and stopped, once more enjoying the sight of Corrie on his bed, naked. She'd turned on her side and was facing his direction. She had one arm under the pillow under her head, and the other was draped over her waist. Her legs were bent and she looked like a pinup model. Quint thanked his lucky stars she was all his.

He walked over to his bed and sat on the side. "Roll over on your back, sweetheart."

"Why?"

"I have a washcloth, I want to clean you up."

Corrie blushed and held out her hand. "I can do it."

"I want to." Quint held the wet towel out of her reach. "Please."

Without a word, Corrie rolled over, but kept her head turned toward the ceiling.

"You can't be embarrassed about this." Quint made small talk as he went about the extremely pleasant task of soothing her well-used folds and cleaning away the evidence of her arousal.

"I am."

Quint chuckled and finished what he was doing. "I enjoy it. I like making sure you're comfortable and have what you need."

She didn't say anything and Quint let it go. She'd get used to him. He hoped.

He didn't bother taking the washcloth back to the bathroom. He just dumped it on the floor by the bed, making a mental note to pick it up right when he got out of bed in the morning so Corrie didn't step on it. He couldn't imagine how gross it would be to step on a cold wet towel first thing in the morning.

Quint did his best to brush the condoms that had been scattered across the bed in their hurry off the mattress and then snuggled back into bed and pulled up the sheet, then the comforter. Something in his chest squeezed when Corrie didn't hesitate, but wrapped herself around him without a word. He felt her hand on his chest, tapping.

"What are you doing?"

"I'm writing in Braille with my fingertip."

Quint concentrated on what she was "writing." He smiled widely when he recognized the letters. He buried his face in her neck, crushing her fingers between them. "I like you too, sweetheart."

CORRIE ROLLED OVER and groaned. She was deliciously sore. It'd been a while since she'd had sex, and Quint wasn't a small man...anywhere.

She blinked—then stilled at the almost painful sensation. Crud. Every month she had to remove her prosthetics and give them a thorough cleaning. She hadn't done it this month yet, and with the pain she was feeling, it was obvious she'd put it off too long. She really didn't want to do it in front of Quint, but they were supposed to spend the day together getting his kitchen set up for her, so she wouldn't be able to avoid it. Her eyes really felt crusty and she knew it had to be done.

Corrie remembered when she'd put off the deep cleaning before. She'd gotten a terrible infection and had received a long lecture by her doctors. But she was embarrassed to take her eyes out in front of Quint. She'd once asked Emily what she looked like without them and her friend had been honest and told her it was a bit creepy looking. Emily had laughed and told her she looked like a character from a horror movie with the two blank holes where her eyes should've been. The last thing Corrie wanted was to look creepy in front of Quint, especially after the delicious night they'd had. They were still getting to know each other and she didn't want to look like a horror-show zombie in front of him.

Her prosthetics had to sit in the cleansing fluid for at least two hours, and really should be in there longer to give them the deep cleanse they needed. Shoot, Corrie knew she should've done it last night. They would've been done and ready to go by now if she had.

"What's wrong?" Quint's voice was sleepy by her ear.

"Nothing, go back to sleep." Corrie gave it a shot. She still felt Quint's head come off the pillow behind her where he'd been spooning her.

"I'm not tired. What's wrong? Are you having second thoughts about us?"

"No. Jeez, why do you have to be so observant?" Corrie complained a little petulantly.

"Because. Corrie, if it's not us, then what. Is. Wrong?"

He enunciated each word clearly. She could tell he was both irritated and worried by the tense way he held her in his arms.

It wasn't a big deal. Right? If she was going to be with him, she'd have to tell him sooner or later. "Ihavetocleanmyprosthetics."

"Okay...and?"

Darn. "And I have to take them out in order to do it."

"Yeah..." He drew the word out, beginning to sound confused as well as annoyed now.

Corrie turned in his arms and buried her face in his chest. He smelled so good, like him...and sex. It comforted her. "It's gross. I don't want you to see me without my eyes in."

She felt Quint pulling away. She sighed. She pulled back and looked up to where his face would be. She felt his hands on the side of her head, holding her still.

"You have to take them all the way out?"

"Uh-huh."

"Cool! Can I watch?"

Corrie drew back in confusion. "What?"

"I've never seen anything like it before. Does it hurt? How do you get them out? I didn't know they *came* out. I mean, of course they come out, they're prosthetics, but how do you clean them? Are they round?" He almost sounded like a little boy, excited for his first trip to see Santa or something.

Corrie reached up and blindly tried to find Quint's mouth. She missed at first, covering his chin, but readjusted her hand until it covered his mouth. She smiled at him weakly.

"I'll answer your questions if you really want to know, but I want you to understand, without my prosthetics in, I'm weird-looking. Emily told me."

Quint moved her hand away from his mouth and leaned in until he could kiss both eyelids. "You'll never be weird-looking, Corrie. You're different. Yeah. So what? What we look like doesn't make us who we are inside. And you, sweetheart, are beautiful. You could have two heads and I'd still think so. I'm in like with you, and I'm quickly falling in love with you. Not with your eyes, or with your body, but with *you*. And this is a part of who you are. I want to know everything about you, this included. Okay?"

"Okay." It was the only thing she could think of to say. She wanted to screech like a little kid and bury her head into her pillow. He was falling in love with her? Holy crapola! She didn't have time to process it though, because Quint was herding her out of bed.

"Cool, let's go. I can't wait to see this."

Corrie just shook her head and followed Quint. He'd grabbed her hand and dragged her into his bathroom.

"Can I have a minute?" Corrie asked shyly.

"Shit, yeah, sorry. I'll go down the hall to use the other bathroom. Don't start without me."

Corrie laughed as she heard Quint hurrying out of the room and jogging down the hallway. She went back out into the bedroom and found her T-shirt that Quint had taken off the night before. Before they'd fallen asleep, Quint had sleepily leaned over, found it on the floor and told her he put it on the end of the bed so she could find it when she needed it in the morning.

Corrie went back into the bathroom and quickly took care of her morning routine and waited for Quint to return.

Quint breezed back into the bathroom and came up behind her. "Okay, carry on. I'm ready. Just pretend I'm not here."

Corrie shook her head and smiled nervously. As if. But she tried. She got out the supplies from her bathroom kit. She asked Quint for a clean towel and when he gave it to her, she covered up the sink in front of her. If she popped her eye out, she didn't want it to land in the hard sink and get chipped. She'd learned that the hard way too.

She pulled out the extractor from her cleaning kit and pulled her lower lid down until she could get the small edge of the plastic piece under the edge of the prosthetic. She pried it up until it cleared her lid and caught it in her other hand as it popped free of her eye socket.

The prosthetic wasn't round, as most people assumed. It was kinda oval shaped and hollow on the other side. It sat like a cup in her eye socket, rounding it out to make it look more like a normal eye.

Trying to ignore the fact Quint stood silently behind her, most likely watching everything she did with that observant way he had, Corrie continued with her cleaning ritual.

She used a wet cotton ball to clean away any dirt and discharge around her empty eye socket. Then she filled the eye bath with the special saline she made up at home and tipped her head back to wash out the socket of her eye.

Corrie then took the prosthetic and ran it under warm water in the sink, using the non-scented soap she carried with her to scrub it clean. She put it into a special container to let it soak in a bath of the saline solution. Some people didn't bother with this step, but she always felt it cleaned the eye better than simply running water and soap over it.

She put that eye to the side and started all over again with her other prosthetic. When she finished and both eyes were in the cleansing solution, Quint spoke for the first time. "How long do you soak them?"

"It depends. I usually keep them in the solution overnight, but today, two hours should do it."

Corrie felt Quint turning her in his arms. She resisted for a moment but gave in. This was a part of who she was. He was right. If she wanted this to work, he had to see her without her prosthetics. She hated it, but it was better to do it now than later, when she was even more connected to him.

She felt Quint put his finger under her chin. Corrie lifted her head and waited, trying not to hyperventilate. She felt Quint's lips against her forehead, then her nose, then her lips, then she closed her eyes and felt him gently kiss both eyelids.

"You are beautiful, Corrie. Seriously. You are no less beautiful to me now, without your prosthetics, than you were lying naked on my bed waiting for me. And I have to say, and this is my inner geekiness coming out, that was the coolest thing I've seen in a long time."

Corrie snorted.

"Seriously. And sweetheart, I honestly don't see any difference in what you just did and what someone who wears contacts does every night. I don't want you to feel weird about that with me. If you need to take them out and clean them before we go to bed, do it. If you think that's gonna make me not want to bury myself deep inside your hot body, you're way wrong."

Corrie stumbled into him as Quint tugged her into his embrace. She could feel his cock, hard against her belly. "Having you here in my arms, in my bathroom, wearing nothing but that shirt, is almost as good as having you naked in my bed. Two hours, huh? Good. Plenty of time for me to make up for last night."

"Make up for it?"

"Yeah, I was a minuteman. I need to prove my virility to you so you don't think I'm always that quick."

Corrie giggled. "Don't we have stuff to do today?"

"Yeah, but it can wait. This is more important."

"Okay, I'm in. Show me what you can do." Corrie was more relieved than she'd ever be able to say. She'd been so afraid that he'd take one look at her empty eye sockets and be disgusted.

She laughed and grabbed hold of Quint's neck as he hoisted her up into his arms and headed out of the bathroom to his bed. Oh yeah, she was in like with this man. Definitely.

✑

THE MAN USED his foot to crush out the cigarette he'd been smoking. So, the bitch had finally moved in with the pig cop. It made his plans harder, but not impossible. He'd finally learned the best way to get to her. It had taken two weeks, but he knew just how it'd go down now.

The boss was pissed the cops had already found Shaun's body. That wasn't supposed to happen. He'd been careful, but the fucking Texas heat had done him in. If there hadn't been a drought, no one would've ever found that fucker.

The man gritted his teeth when thinking about his boss. He was the most successful loan shark in the city, but he got that way because he was a complete asshole. He didn't trust anyone. He had no other staff...they'd all disappeared over the years.

The man wasn't stupid; he knew if he pissed the boss off, he'd disappear too, but for now the money was good and he enjoyed the side benefits of getting to kill and torture people and getting to screw whatever pussy he could get.

That thought brought him back to the present. He just had to wait a bit longer. The boss was securing a new place to take the blind bitch once she was grabbed. They had to figure out what she'd told the police and use her to set an example for others around the city who might be thinking about squealing about their business. The boss wasn't putting anything past her, though. They'd bring her somewhere she'd never be able to get away, and where her screams wouldn't be heard by anyone...and he'd get to have some fun.

The man reached down and adjusted his cock. He loved when he got to play with women. They were so much more fun to torture than men. When he shoved his cock up their pussy right off the bat, they usually cooperated much better.

The bitch was blind, which was weird, but he could work with it. No problem. She'd better enjoy fucking that cop while she could. Soon she'd be his to do with as he pleased. He couldn't wait.

Chapter Thirteen

————◆•————

CORRIE LAY IN bed and listened to Quint get ready for work. He had an early shift and she was more than happy to go back to sleep for a couple of hours. They'd been up late the night before because they couldn't keep their hands off each other. The last time they'd made love, Quint had kept his eyes closed the entire time at her request. He'd told her it was the most intense experience he'd ever had. Corrie smiled at the memory.

He'd started by caressing her from her head to her feet, and then after he'd teased her unmercifully until her toes curled, Corrie pushed him to his back and returned the favor. She'd enjoyed his moans and groans as she'd run her hands and lips all over his body. She'd taken him deep within her mouth and Quint had told her how incredible, how much…*more*…it had felt like when he could only imagine what she was doing and couldn't watch.

He'd pulled her off his cock before he'd exploded and turned her over. He'd urged her to her hands and knees and had taken her from behind. After rolling on a condom, Quint had powered in and out of her with a slow and steady rhythm, keeping up a running conversation about how good she felt, how soft she was, how he loved feeling her skin ripple and shake under his hands. He'd even smacked her ass lightly and marveled at the feel of her ass heating up under his ministrations.

It finally took Corrie snaking a hand under them and caressing his balls as he slowly entered her to get him to lose his iron control.

He'd taken hold of her hips in his hands and had slammed himself inside her. Corrie had lost her balance and fell to her forearms on the bed, but the change in angle simply seemed to make him lose even more of his control. They'd both moaned and groaned until first Corrie, then Quint, had exploded.

He had eased himself down to the bed and held Corrie to him and they'd lain there without words for what seemed like forever. Finally, Quint had eased out of her and headed to the bathroom to dispose of the condom. He'd returned with a warm washcloth, as he always did, and after cleaning them both up, he'd snuggled in behind her again and whispered all sorts of amazing things while kissing her neck and shoulder.

It had been incredible…but then again, each time Quint made love to her, it was mind-blowing.

It'd been seven days since Corrie had essentially moved in with Quint, and he'd kept his promise and done everything possible to make her comfortable in his home. She'd been extremely worried about it, but so far it was working out.

Corrie knew she was moving way quicker with Quint than she probably should, but she couldn't help it. He worked hard, was attentive to her without being smothering, was loyal to his friends to a fault, was romantic, and the chemistry between them was off the charts.

As she'd noticed before, Quint wasn't perfect. He had a habit of throwing f-bombs around a little too much and sometimes when he slept on his back he'd snore loud enough to wake the dead. She also had a feeling he still tended to think of her as fragile because of her blindness…but for now, their relationship was working well. She'd have plenty of time to work on that other stuff with him. She hoped.

She listened as the shower turned off and Quint wandered around the room getting dressed. There was something very intimate about listening to him put on his clothes. Corrie never would've guessed.

She hadn't felt this way about Ian, not even close.

Corrie heard the creaking of Quint's equipment belt as he walked toward her, and felt the bed dip as he sat down next to her hip.

"You gonna sleep for a while?"

"Um-hum."

"Okay. You have to be at the clinic at nine?"

"Yeah, my first appointment isn't until nine-thirty so I get to go in a bit later today."

"Emily is picking you up?"

They'd argued about this the night before as well. Quint had been taking her to work every day, but since he had to go in so early, she didn't want to inconvenience him by having him come back to the house during his shift. She was also being selfish by wanting to sleep in, and not get to work as early as she would if he took her in when his shift started. Emily had never minded picking her up, and when she'd asked, her friend had agreed immediately. It'd been a while since she'd had her Emily fix and they were both looking forward to catching up.

Corrie knew she had to think about rescheduling the car service she'd been using before everything had happened. She'd temporarily canceled it after the shooting, but she hated always relying on Emily and Bethany, and now Quint, to take her everywhere she wanted to go.

Realizing Quint was waiting for her answer to his question, she quickly said, "Yes, she'll be here around eight-thirty. We'll talk a bit, catch up, then we'll go. It's fine."

"Okay. Want to have lunch together?"

Corrie mock frowned up toward Quint. "You've taken off for lunch every day of the last week. Aren't you going to get in trouble?"

She felt his hand smooth over her head and tuck her hair behind her ear. "No. We *are* allowed to eat while on shift you know."

"Okay then, yes. I'd love to have lunch. I'd never turn down spending time with you."

Quint leaned into her and brushed his lips over Corrie's forehead. "As much as I'd rather crawl back into bed with you, I gotta get going."

Corrie brought her hand up to the back of Quint's neck and pulled him down to her mouth. She kissed him long and hard before pulling back. "Okay, go on then. I'll see you later."

"Jesus, sweetheart. Now I have to go to work with a hard-on."

Corrie giggled. "You'll live. Now go. I'll see you at lunch."

"Maybe if I play my cards right I can get a lunchtime quickie," he teased playfully. He kissed her one more time quickly and backed away. "I'll set the alarm and lock up as I leave. Stay in bed, enjoy your lazy morning."

"Okay, thanks."

"Bye, sweetheart. See you later."

"Bye, Quint."

Corrie smiled and snuggled deeper into bed as she listened to Quint walk through the house, fiddle around in the kitchen, and walk out the door. God, she loved him.

Wait. What?

Corrie thought about it. Yup. It hadn't been that long, but she could admit it, to herself at least. She loved him.

He'd shown her in a million ways how much she meant to him…from putting all his clothes in the guest-room closet—and then arranging all her stuff in the master closet so it was exactly as it had been at her own house—to putting some of his furniture in storage so there would be more room to walk around and less chance of her hurting herself.

They'd also painstakingly rearranged the kitchen together, making sure she could reach all the plates and cups and cooking utensils. He'd added a shelf to one of the cabinets so all of her cooking spices could go there in the same order they'd been in at her own apartment.

And not once—not one single time—had she tripped over something he'd accidentally left out. He was super conscientious about putting his things away. Everything had its place, and so far he'd stuck to it. Corrie knew it couldn't last forever; it was inevitable that he'd forget something, but with as much effort as he'd been putting into trying to make sure he didn't leave anything out of place, Corrie knew it would devastate him when it did eventually happen.

Quint was attentive to all her needs in bed, he was sexy as all get out, and he was trying so hard to learn Braille, it almost made her heart hurt. Even her parents hadn't tried this hard to be able to read and write the way she did. They'd made a halfhearted attempt when she was younger, but with the escalation of technology, and the ability for her to "read" the computer and emails, they'd given up.

Corrie thought back to the day before when Quint had shyly handed her a note he'd meticulously used her Braille label maker to write. It was awkward, and he'd mixed both Grade 1 and 2 Braille, but she was able to read it. It'd said: *You make me happy. The luckiest day of my life was when you ran into that busboy.*

It was the first time she'd cried in front of him, and Corrie thought he was going to lose it. He'd been horrified that he'd made her cry, until she went down to her knees and had taken him in her mouth as a thank you.

She grinned at the memory. God, she loved how he smelled...and tasted. Corrie turned on her side and pushed a button on her specialty clock.

Alarm set for seven-thirty, the monotone computerized voice said.

Corrie snuggled back down into the blankets, satisfied that she had another hour and a half to sleep. She fell asleep immediately, dreaming of Quint.

∽

CORRIE WOKE UP with a start. Someone was ringing the doorbell to Quint's house. The loud *ding-dong* echoed around the room, then faded. She reached over and pushed the button on the clock.

Seven-thirteen a.m., the mechanized voice announced.

Corrie threw her legs over the side of the bed and reached for her T-shirt as the doorbell pealed again. She threw the shirt over her head and hurried to the closet. She went to the shelf and felt for her sweatpants. She didn't bother looking for the Braille tag that would tell her what color they were, but simply pulled the first pair she touched up her legs. She kneeled down and felt for her shoes, and grabbed the pair of flip-flops that was on the end of the row.

"Coming!" Corrie called out as the doorbell rang again. Maybe Emily was early. It wasn't like her to be early for anything though. Typically she was right on time. Corrie had made fun of her more times than she could remember for having an annoying habit of being right where she was supposed to be at the exact time she was supposed to be there.

Corrie stopped at the front door. "Who is it?" she remembered to ask before simply opening the door.

"It's Bethany."

Corrie frowned. What the hell was Bethany doing there?

Oh Lord—Emily or Ethan. Something had to be wrong!

Corrie turned to the alarm panel next to the front door and punched in the numbers to disarm it. She unlocked and opened the door. "Bethany? Where's Emily? And Ethan? Are they okay?"

Corrie heard Bethany whisper, "I'm so sorry," before the strike to her head rendered her unconscious.

QUINT SAT ACROSS the desk from his friend Calder Stonewall, the medical examiner who'd been responsible for the autopsy on Shaun's body. San Antonio wasn't a huge city and they'd crossed paths so much in the past, they'd become close. They had a law enforcement clique of sorts, with five others in various law enforcement agencies.

"Talk to me, Calder. What sort of sick fuck are we dealing with?"

"You're not going to like it, Quint."

"I know I'm not. Sock it to me."

"I don't have the hands to be able to tell, but based on the fact that each of his toes were cut off, I'd bet they did the same to his fingers before cutting off his hands altogether."

"Christ. Go on."

"Lots of typical shit. Cigarette burns, broken ribs, bruises, and petechial hemorrhaging."

"They strangled him?"

"Probably repeatedly. They most likely cut off his air until he passed out, then waited until he wasn't unconscious anymore to do it again."

"Fuck."

"What did they want, Quint? This isn't normal shit. This is highly sadistic behavior and not the sort of thing criminals around here are usually into. If the man didn't have any money, what would torturing him do? It's unlikely he was hiding money from them, he was legitimately broke. Whoever did this is unstable and *enjoys* what he's doing, and does it extremely well. I'd expect to see this sort of thing with the mob or something, not here in San Antonio."

"Detective Algood wasn't able to find out a lot, but after we called in Cruz and the FBI, they were able to piece together some of what Shaun had gotten himself into."

Calder nodded for Quint to continue.

"Since Shaun's son had his accident, they were hemorrhaging money. It costs a fuck of a lot of money to keep that kid alive. First the hospital bills on the day of the accident, then the medical bills to keep him alive and functioning. Catheters, breathing machines, feeding tubes, mechanical beds, prescriptions, round-the-clock medical care…you name it, that kid needs it. There's no way a normal family can afford all that shit."

"He made a deal with the devil then?" Calder asked.

"Yup. Specifically, a Mr. Dimitri Prandini."

"Holy shit, he had a death wish, didn't he?"

"I'm assuming he had no idea what he was getting into." Quint and Calder both knew Dimitri because he was a local loan shark…one who wasn't known for his touchy-feely ways. "Apparently he borrowed more than a hundred thousand dollars and when Dimitri wanted to collect, with interest, Shaun couldn't pay. He sent his henchman, Isaac Sampson, after him to collect."

"How does a man with only one employee get to be such a success?"

Quint grimaced and nodded in agreement. "I know. By all accounts, the other sharks around here should've gobbled him up by now. But Dimitri is especially vicious. I heard from Cruz, the FBI has been keeping their eye on him, and would love to arrest him, but they don't have enough hard evidence yet. When he first started in the business he had about a dozen 'helpers.' They'd troll the city looking for schmucks who were stupid enough to gamble away money they didn't have. Dimitri also ordered hits on the other loan sharks for no fucking reason. His henchmen would just ambush them and kill them outright."

"But, Quint, that doesn't make any sense. Didn't the other sharks band together against him or something?"

"Yeah," Quint agreed grimly. "They did. And Dimitri changed tactics from ambushing the sharks, to ambushing their women."

"Jesus."

"Yeah, Dimitri has no soul. None. He ordered his men to kidnap, rape and torture the wives and girlfriends of anyone who publically spoke out against him. There were still some rumblings of the sharks ganging up and putting an end to Dimitri's reign once and for all, until he went after an entire family."

Calder didn't say anything, just growled.

"Needless to say, it wasn't pretty. The man had three daughters...ages three to twelve. Dimitri's thugs started with the oldest daughter and worked their way down. Then they started on his wife, and finally killed the guy. After that, no one has dared to go against him."

"And his posse of henchmen?"

"No one knows for sure, but rumor has it Dimitri's paranoid and decided one day that they were all out to get him, and he disposed of them all."

"Jesus fucking Christ. And this guy ordered the hit on Shaun at the chiropractor office?"

"Yeah."

"And he's now gunning for your woman."

Quint hadn't told any of his friends how serious he was about Corrie, but apparently he didn't have to. It was obvious enough. "Yeah."

"But how does your Corrie fit into all this?"

Quint couldn't deny the words "your Corrie" settled right into his soul as if they belonged there. "They're trying to tie up loose ends. Dimitri isn't the smartest tool in the shed, and Isaac isn't much better. He's the last of his henchmen, and known to be the most sadistic. I'm assuming they think if they can get to Corrie and shut her up, they'll get away with the murder of both Shaun and all those people from her clinic, scot-free."

"Dumbasses."

"Yeah."

Before Quint could say anything else, the phone on his desk rang. He leaned over and picked it up.

"Axton here. What? Yeah, she knew. She was planning on getting there around nine. Are you sure? Okay, I'll give her a call. She might have overslept. Thanks, Dr. Garza."

Quint hung up the phone and swore.

"Everything all right?" Calder had picked up on the urgency in Quint's tone.

"Not sure. That was Corrie's partner. She was supposed to be at work at nine, but Dr. Garza just heard from Lori, their new admin, and she hasn't shown up yet." Quint looked at his watch. Nine forty-five.

He dialed Corrie's number and waited. She didn't pick up. He dialed it again, and once again it went to voice mail after four rings. The hair on the back of his neck stood straight up and goose bumps sprung up all over his arms. "Fuck. Calder, I gotta go. Let me know if you find anything else out."

"Want me to call Cruz and the others?"

Quint didn't hesitate. "Yes. Something's wrong. I feel it."

"On it. Go."

Quint didn't wait, thankful he could rely on Calder to get him some backup. He strode from his desk straight to his deputy chief's office. He had to get SAPD rolling. He didn't have an extra second to spare. Corrie might not have that extra second. He had a bad fucking feeling about this, and it didn't help that he'd just recounted what horrible human beings Isaac and Dimitri were. Calder's description of what Shaun had gone through raced through his mind on repeat.

Fucking hell.

Quint raced through his neighborhood with his lights and sirens blaring. He didn't know how he knew this was bad, he just did. Two other patrol cars followed behind him with their lights on, but no sirens. Cruz was meeting them at his house as soon as he could get there.

All looked quiet at the house as Quint screeched to a halt, skidding up onto his lawn as he fought to control his car. Without bothering to take the keys with him, although he did flip off the siren, Quint crouched and ran, gun drawn, toward his front door.

The door was closed—but Quint could hear the screaming of an infant clearly though the thick oak.

What the holy fuck?

He noticed with detachment that his hands were shaking as he pulled out his house keys and put them in the lock. It was stealthier to open the door with the keys than to kick it in. And if anyone was in the house, he didn't want to give them a head's up he was inside.

The door swung open and Quint looked at the alarm panel.

Off. *Fuck.*

The wail of the baby crying was louder now that they were inside the house. The infant was clearly in distress. It wasn't a "give me food, I'm hungry" cry, it was a "if I don't get attention immediately, I might die," kind of screaming.

As they'd been trained, the officers ignored the distressed cries coming from the back of the house as they concentrated on making sure the area was safe. In an active-shooter scenario, the scene had to be cleared before any wounded victims could be taken care of. It was one of the hardest things to have to do…ignoring the pleading and cries from any injured persons begging for help, and to step over them, if necessary, to make sure the scene was safe for the first responders and the rest of the potential victims.

Quint gestured one officer to the right and the other to the left, to take his back. They methodically went through the kitchen and the living room. Both were empty. The baby's screams were coming from down the hall. They cleared both guestrooms and the bathroom.

The last room was the master bedroom.

The door was shut. Quint put his hand on the knob and looked to both the officers. They nodded at him, indicating they were ready, and he twisted the door handle and brought his hand back up to his pistol. Quint had no idea what they'd find, but he prayed harder than he ever had in his life that it wouldn't be Corrie, bleeding and possibly dead.

They surged into the room—and Quint's stomach dropped to his toes.

Jesus fucking Christ.

Bethany was on his bed.

He was surprised to see Corrie's friend, and not Corrie, but it was how they found her that really shook him to his very soul. She'd been crucified to the wooden headboard with a knife through each of her palms.

She was conscious, which greatly relieved Quint, but she was obviously in a lot of pain and moving with agitation on the bed.

Ignoring the woman for the moment, the three officers continued to clear the room. It was empty, with no sign of Corrie, Emily, or any bad guys. Quint headed to the bathroom, not stopping to reassure Bethany as she pleaded with him to help her son.

Inside the bathroom, Quint immediately saw that Ethan's life was in extreme danger. He was on his back in the bathtub. The stopper had been put in the bottom and the water had been turned on. It wasn't dripping, but it wasn't gushing either. It was a sluggish stream that was slowly filling up the tub, with Ethan in it, helpless on his back.

The baby was naked and screaming. His face was bright red and he was flailing his arms wildly. The water had filled the tub enough that most of Ethan's body was under it. The water was halfway up his chest and quickly getting higher and higher. If they'd been even an hour later—hell, thirty minutes—the water would've covered his face completely and Ethan would've drowned.

Quint holstered his gun without thought and reached for the frightened baby. The water was ice cold. No wonder Ethan was screaming. He grabbed a towel off the rack and swaddled the infant up as best he could before cradling him against his chest and rubbing his back soothingly. Frigid water dripped from the wet towel onto Quint's shirt and the vest underneath, but he didn't even feel it.

Quint heard the second officer calling for an ambulance and the crime scene techs. He turned back into the bedroom. Ethan was still crying, but it had changed from a terrified wail, to more hiccupping sobs. He'd burrowed into Quint's chest and lay against him, almost unmoving, except for his little chest heaving with his sobs.

Quint walked over to his bed where Bethany lay, tears streaming down her own face. He could tell she'd struggled, but she hadn't been able to stomach the pain it would have taken to release herself from the knives through her palms.

"He's okay, Bethany. He's fine. Cold, but fine." He watched as she tried to control her crying. "The ambulance is on the way, you're both going to be just fine. I swear. Can you tell me what the fuck is going on? Where's Corrie? Where's Emily? What happened here?"

"A guy showed up at the house this morning." Bethany's voice was agonized. "He broke in and grabbed Emily. He told me he'd kill her if I didn't do exactly what he told me to. He looked crazy. I believed him."

Quint nodded and urged her to continue.

She spoke through her sobs, understanding how important it was to get as much information to Quint as possible. "He told me to hold Ethan, then he tied Em up and beat the ever-loving shit out of her. He told us we were dykes and not fit to walk around on the planet. He said if I tried to stop him, he'd kill Emily with a bullet in her brain right there in front of me. That if I got away, he'd rape and then kill her. She looked at me as he was beating her, with pleading eyes. I knew she was begging me to take care of Ethan and not worry about her."

"Bethany, I know you're in pain, and help is coming, but I need you to tell me your address so we can get help for Emily," Quint ordered as gently as he could.

Quint turned to the officer standing behind him, looking on helplessly. They both knew if they tried to take the knives out of Bethany's palms, it could kill her. She'd already lost too much blood. Her face was deathly pale. He really didn't have to tell the officer, but immediately after Bethany whispered her address in a pained voice, he ordered, "Call it in."

The officer nodded and turned away, already keying his mic. Quint heard him telling dispatch about the other woman. They'd get units to Emily's house and make sure she was okay.

Quint turned back to Bethany. Corrie was his concern now. He kept rocking Ethan and rubbing his back, trying to calm him down. "We've got officers headed to your house to check on Emily. Please, what happened here? Where's Corrie?"

"After he beat Em into unconsciousness, he forced me into his car. I wanted to leave Ethan at the house, but he grabbed him from me. He drove here with Ethan on his lap, ranting the entire time about how he was an evil child, that Ethan would be better off if he just killed him now instead of letting him grow up as the son of a lesbian couple. I wanted to do something, but I didn't know what. I thought about bailing out of the car, but that'd leave him with Ethan. I couldn't leave my baby. He would've killed him on the spot."

"Shhhh, I know you couldn't. You did the right thing. Then what?" Quint tried not to lose his patience, just put a soothing hand on her leg.

"He held a knife to Ethan's throat and forced me to knock on your door. Corrie answered and I told her it was me. She opened the door and he hit her hard enough to knock her out."

Quint saw red and squeezed the baby a bit too hard. Ethan cried out, but settled again when Quint bounced him in his arms soothingly.

Bethany continued, her voice growing weaker. "He left her on the floor and forced me in here. He threw me on the bed and pulled the knives out. He told me I had a choice…either I lay still and let him do…this, or he could do it to Ethan." Bethany gasped and Quint saw the tears fall from her eyes again.

"He swore he'd put him on the floor and leave him alone if I did it. So I lay still and let him stab me. I never knew anything could hurt so damn bad. As I lay there screaming, he took Ethan into the bathroom, telling me all the while what he was doing and how Ethan was going to die anyway. I yelled at him to leave him alone, that he promised, and he only laughed at me. Then he left. I tried to get up but I couldn't. It hurts, Quint. It hurts so damn bad."

Quint moved his hand from her leg to her forehead to try to console her. It was a safe place he felt he could touch and not hurt her further. "Did he tell you where he was going? Anything that will help us find Corrie?"

"No."

"*Think*, Bethany. Anything you can remember, even if it seems as if it's nothing, will help us at this point."

Quint held his breath as Bethany closed her eyes and thought back through what had happened that morning.

Her eyes opened and Quint could see her mentally straighten her shoulders. He'd never been so relieved. She looked up at Quint. "He mumbled something while we were driving through rush-hour traffic about how he hated the city and couldn't wait to get out to the cabin."

Quint closed his eyes briefly in thanks. Bingo. It had to be enough. It was a long shot, but knowing they were in a cabin outside the city was more than they would've had to go on without Bethany. He leaned over her and kissed her forehead, much as he did with Corrie when he was trying to comfort her. "Thank you." Quint could hear the ambulance arrive and the EMTs enter his house. "You're going to be fine. Ethan's okay, and they'll get to Emily as well."

Her eyes stared up at him, glassy with pain, but clear. She was one tough chick. Quint was glad Corrie had her as a friend. "You'll find her? You'll keep that asshole from hurting Corrie?"

"I'm going to do my damnedest."

Bethany nodded and the medical personnel came into the room. Quint handed Ethan off to one of the men, leaving the explanations about what had happened to the other officers. They'd been standing behind him when Bethany told him what happened.

Quint stepped into his living room to find Cruz there, along with Dax, their friend TJ, and even Hayden Yates. TJ was a Highway Patrolman, but he'd never shied away from helping wherever he was needed. He'd been there when Dax had confronted the serial killer who had buried Mackenzie alive. Hayden was a sheriff's deputy, and she was one of the toughest law enforcement officers Quint had ever met, male or female. He'd take all the help he could get right now.

He quickly explained what Bethany told him had gone down that morning.

"So she's been gone about three and a half hours now," Cruz calculated. "Do you think she has her cell on her?"

Quint looked over to see Corrie's purse on a hook by the front hall table. He strode over to it and held his breath. He reached into the small pocket and pulled out her phone where she always kept it and showed it to the others. Damn.

"Okay, so we can't use that to track her. What else we got?"

"Cruz, who do you know that can dig deep and find us information?" Quint asked, desperate.

He shrugged. "The guys at the bureau are good, but are somewhat limited because of…you know….laws."

"Fuck." Quint spat out the word. "This all needs to be on the up and up so it doesn't get fucked up. I know this is Dimitri and Isaac. It's the only thing that makes sense. But going through proper channels is going to take too long."

"I might know someone," TJ said quietly.

Four sets of eyes swung to the Highway Patrolman. He spoke before anyone could ask. "You guys all know I used to be Delta Force. There were times we relied on an outside guy to get us some intel on our marks or to give us some extra recon before we went on missions. He's totally legit...works for the government, but I'm fairly certain how he gets his information isn't always completely legal."

"Call him," Quint said immediately. He didn't care how the man got his information, as long as it led them to Corrie.

"If he comes through, we'll need a cover story on how we found her," TJ warned.

Quint looked around at the best friends he'd ever had. The only two missing were Conor and Calder. "If it was Mackenzie, would you do it?" he asked Daxton.

"In a heartbeat," was his immediate response.

"Please, TJ, call your guy. I'll take the rap for this if it comes to it. Corrie means more to me than anything, even my job."

TJ didn't say another word to try to dissuade his friend; he clicked on a contact in his phone and put the phone up to his ear. After only a moment, he began speaking to whomever it was who answered. "Ghost. It's Rock. Yeah, I know, it's been too long. I need Tex. Yeah, C-Red." He held his hand over the speaker and interpreted for his friends, "Code-Red." His attention was brought back to the phone as the mysterious Ghost continued to ask questions. "We need intel immediately. Kidnapped. Thanks, I appreciate it. We totally need to get together soon. I heard you snagged yourself a woman." He chuckled at something the man on the other end of the phone said, then got serious again. "Thanks, I appreciate it. I'll let you know how it goes. Later." TJ clicked off the phone.

"Well?" Quint asked impatiently.

"Give him a moment. He'll call. Ghost is going to get a hold of him."

"Why don't you have this guy's direct number?" Hayden asked.

"Tex is…eccentric. He knows everyone, and those of us who have worked with him understand that while he can find us at a moment's notice, he doesn't want his contact information spread across all the groups and men he works with. Only the team leaders have his direct line, and even that changes almost monthly. Look, the man could disappear with his family and no one would ever find him, he's that good. He makes himself and his computer abilities available to us in emergencies."

"What does he want in return?"

"A marker. He'd never take money for anything he does. He claims the government pays him more than enough for him and his family to live on. But he lives and breathes information. If he needs us, he'll let us know."

"Whatever he wants, whenever he wants," Quint vowed. "If he can get us to Corrie, I don't give a rat's ass what he requires of me."

"And that right there is why Tex is the best," TJ said in a solemn tone. "He's collected markers from a country full of men who are just like you, Quint. But honestly, I know he'd do it just because it's the right thing to do."

TJ's phone vibrated and he quickly tapped it and brought it up to his ear. "Tex…I know, it's been a long time…Corrie Madison, she's blind…Dimitri Prandini, P-r-a-n-d-i-n-i, and Isaac Sampson… Near as we can tell over three hours… Witness says whoever it was that forced her to go to Corrie's house talked about a cabin…Yeah…We'll be waiting." TJ clicked the phone off and turned to his friends.

"Well?"

"He's going to call me back."

"This is ridiculous," Quint barked out, turning to Cruz. "I can't just stand here waiting for some mysterious fucking guy named Tex to find out where Corrie is after a thirty-second phone conversation. Cruz, call your guy at the bureau. Have him search for properties that trace back to Dimitri or Isaac. It's a long shot, but they might be arrogant enough to have taken her to one of their own damn houses."

"Give Tex five minutes, Cruz," TJ ordered. Everyone looked at him in surprise. TJ was the happy-go-lucky one of their group. It was surprising enough that the man had been Delta, he just didn't seem to have the disposition, but one look at his demeanor and countenance at the moment and no one doubted the man was a lethal killer.

"Tex will find her. He's a fucking hacker. I didn't give him much information, but he'll do his magic computer shit and tell us where they are. It'll take Cruz's FBI guy three hours to do what it'll take Tex five minutes to find."

"I can't lose her," Quint said, heartbroken.

"You won't," Daxton assured him with conviction. "These guys are too cocky. They think they're invincible. They've left a trail that this computer geek'll find. Believe it."

No one said anything for several minutes. Quint paced as the other SAPD officers and medical personnel gave the quintet a wide berth. They were obviously putting out some intense vibes because no one bothered them.

Finally, after seven minutes had passed, TJ's phone vibrated with an incoming call. He immediately clicked it on and listened before saying, "All right, give us a second."

TJ motioned for the others to follow him outside. Without asking why, everyone followed the Highway Patrolman until they arrived next to his car, out of the way of others who might overhear their conversation. He clicked the speaker icon on the phone and held it out in the middle of the tight circle of lawmen.

"Okay, go ahead, Tex. We're all here."

"First, I'm sorry as I could be that these assholes got ahold of your woman," Tex said with a hint of a southern drawl. "But the good news is that they aren't very smart. Prandini has several aliases. Prado, Prandino, Prandima…as I said…not very smart. Anyway, looks like the man held a marker for a down-home country boy named Chaz

Willis. Chaz had a bit of a gambling problem, but also had some issues on the side with not one, but two ex-wives. He somehow conned his sister-in-law into purchasing a house for him in her name, so his current wife wouldn't be able to find him when he was hooking up with his first ex or his current girlfriend."

"Jesus, is there a point?" Quint asked, stressed beyond control.

"I have a point," Tex said, not seeming to be ruffled at all by Quint's outburst. "It's that Chaz owed Prandini money. Money he didn't have. All of a sudden our friend Chaz hasn't made any trips out to his little hunting cabin at the lake in over a year. Cell phone and credit card records show he's living a perfectly miserable life right there in the heart of San Antonio. There haven't been any 'hunting trips' for the man in all of that time. Oh, and his third divorce is pending."

"Prandini?" Cruz demanded.

"Yup. He's the proud new owner of a small, out-of-the-way cabin on Medina Lake. He's been switching up his credit cards, but there have been gas and food charges awfully close to that area. I have a feeling the man isn't the outdoorsy type."

"Fuck me. Medina Lake," Quint breathed incredulously. "I should've thought of that."

"What's the connection?" Hayden asked.

"Shaun's body was found there," Quint informed the group matter-of-factly.

"Address?" Cruz asked, a pad of paper in his hand, ready to write it down.

"The cabin has a half-mile dirt road leading to it and is surrounded by trees and scrub. As you all know, this has been a warm year for Texas, but there are still lots of places to hide out there. You'll need to go in quiet and sneak up on them."

"Fuck, Tex. Who the hell do you think you're talkin' to here?" Quint groused. "Address?"

"South side. Take PR 2670 off of route 265. Go one-point-two miles north and there's a dirt road on your left. It's down that road. I'll send the coordinates to Rock."

"Let's go, it's at least thirty minutes to get out there," Quint said, turning to head to his truck.

"Quint," Tex called out.

He paused and waited for the man to continue. He was itching to get the hell out of there and get to Corrie, but he owed Tex another couple seconds of his time. If he was right and this is where Corrie was...Quint knew he owed him a lot more than mere time.

"From what I could tell in the five minutes I had to research her, your woman is intelligent. If there's a way out of this, she'll find it."

"Thanks. I'm counting on it." And with that, Quint strode toward Hayden's vehicle. It was a four-wheel drive and they'd decided while they were waiting for Tex to call back, that if needed, they'd take hers since it was more maneuverable in the backcountry of Texas.

He blanked out the others getting into their cars and even his phone vibrating with a text with the coordinates from TJ. All Quint could think about was Corrie. Had too much time passed? Was she all right? What were those pricks doing to her?

Never in his life had he wanted to be a knight in shining armor as badly as he wanted to be one today. It had never been as vital to his well-being as now.

"Hang on, sweetheart. I'm coming for you," he whispered as Hayden pulled away from the curb. "I'm on my way."

Chapter Fourteen

CORRIE LAY ON the floor where the man had thrown her. She'd awoken in his car. She was disoriented and dizzy, but knew she was in big trouble. She remembered Bethany being at her house, then nothing. Was she okay? Emily? Ethan? Dang it, she hated not knowing, but she'd be damned if she asked her captors.

She'd known the second she woke up that she was in the presence of the man who'd killed Cayley and all the others at the clinic. She recognized his voice, and his nasty smell. That stench was stuck in her nose. She felt a little vindicated, because no matter what the DA thought, even if the woman was thinking about allowing her testimony, she'd *known* she'd be able to pick him out. But vindication at this point wouldn't help her.

The man, Isaac—he'd actually introduced himself to her as if they were at a fancy party—had talked the entire time they'd been in the car. He'd talked in great detail about what he'd done with Shaun, he'd even bragged about his and his boss's plan to bring her out to the middle of nowhere to torture and kill her.

Corrie had wanted to ask about Bethany and Emily, but kept her mouth shut. It seemed to piss him off that he couldn't get her to talk to him, but no matter what vile thing he said, she refused to open her mouth.

They'd driven for what seemed like forever until he'd pulled off on a gravel road. Corrie could tell the difference in the texture of the road under the car's tires. He really was bringing her to the middle of nowhere. She smelled pine trees all around, and dust. It was dry, wherever they were.

Corrie felt a panic attack coming on, but held on to her sanity by the skin of her teeth. She couldn't lose it now. Her parents had trained her to use her senses when she got turned around. This was the same thing. She just had to concentrate.

Isaac had pulled her roughly from the car and hauled her forward, laughing as she tripped over objects in her path. She had no idea where they were or where they were going, but Corrie played up her helplessness as much as she could. She wanted Isaac and his boss to think she was completely unable to help herself in any way.

Isaac had thrown her into a room and slammed the door. Corrie heard the lock being engaged from the other side. She got up and carefully made her way to the door, arms out in front of her to try to keep from running into anything, feeling good about only hitting one chair. She leaned her ear against the wooden door and listened.

"What now, Dimitri?"

"Now we figure out what she knows and what the cops know."

"Then what?"

Corrie heard a smacking sound and Isaac cried out.

"Calm the fuck down. You'll get to stick your dick in her as soon as I know what I want to know."

Corrie didn't like the sound of any of that.

She heard the two men coming back down the hall. Corrie hurried back to the middle of the floor where she'd been thrown and held back a sob. *Where are you, Quint? I need you.*

❦

QUINT HELD ON to the safety bar and gritted his teeth. Hayden drove like a bat out of hell. She didn't even slow down going around corners. The SUV she'd commandeered from her department groaned and made all sorts of god-awful noises as she pushed it to its limit.

All Quint could think about was how scared Corrie probably was. She hadn't even wanted to move into his house because she wasn't sure where all his furniture was. How scared would she have to be now? In the middle of a fucking forest with two psychotic assholes doing who knows what to her? She didn't even have her cane...he'd seen it folded in her purse when he'd gotten her cell phone out.

He ground his teeth together. He'd kill the motherfuckers if they'd touched so much as a hair on her head.

"We're gonna get to her, Quint. Not only us, but I think most of Station 7 is on their way too. You know those firefighters would do anything for you." Hayden said calmly from next to him. He looked over at her. She seemed to be calm, cool, and collected, even as she drove like she was competing in the Indianapolis 500.

"Yeah," was all Quint could squeeze out between his clenched teeth. He was happy the EMTs were on their way too, Corrie might need them, but he hated the thought of her even having a papercut. This was torture. They'd get to her all right. It was what they'd find when they got there that worried him.

CORRIE TRIED TO ignore the adrenaline coursing through her body and pretended as if she was a helpless female. "I don't know what you're talking about. I didn't see anything! I didn't hear anything but gunshots. I don't know why the cops think I can tell one person from another. I'm bliiiiind." She whined the word, trying to sound even more pathetic. "I didn't see *anyone*."

"Jesus fucking Christ," Dimitri bitched, pacing back and forth in front of the chair they'd plunked her in. "She doesn't know shit. We've spent all this time and money for nothing."

Corrie shook her head, trying to clear the ringing from her ears. Her face hurt from where Isaac had clocked her earlier at the house, and again from where both Dimitri and Isaac had taken turns slapping and hitting her to try to figure out what she knew. The idiots hadn't even bothered to tie her to the chair, thinking she was a pitiful, helpless, blind female—thank God.

"Can I have her now then?"

Corrie heard Dimitri's fist hitting Isaac's face again. "You are such a fucking horn-dog. We have damage control to do first, asshole. Leave her alone. You'll get your fuck later, then you can get rid of her. And this time, you'll do it right. Not like that fucker Shaun."

Isaac laughed and Corrie flinched and cried out involuntarily as a foot made contact with her knee. Darn, that hurt. She leaned over and wailed excessively, trying to show both men she was out of it, emotionally and physically.

"Come on, we have shit to do," Dimitri said, walking to the door to her room.

Corrie held her breath. *Please don't leave me alone with Isaac. Please don't leave me alone with Isaac.*

"I'll be back, bitch. Hope you're ready for me to shove my big cock up your asshole. I like to start there because it hurts the most. Then I'll move on to your cunt and your face. I love watching as I shove my dick down a chick's throat. Did you know the last woman I killed, I did it by strangling her with my dick? She looked up at me while my cock was down her throat, she couldn't breathe and she died with my jizz coating her stomach. I can't fucking wait."

Isaac slammed the door behind him and Corrie heard him lock it.

Lord. Her hands trembled imagining every horrible thing he wanted to do to her. She held her hand over her mouth, trying not to throw up. She couldn't lose it now. She took a couple of deep breaths. Thank God he'd left her alone and thank God they hadn't tied her up. She had to get out of here. She couldn't wait for Quint to find her; she didn't think he was going to make it in time. Isaac was way too determined to rape and kill her. It was up to her to save herself.

She heard Isaac and Dimitri arguing in the next room, and it gave her even more incentive to try to escape while they were preoccupied.

Corrie got up, wincing as her knee almost gave out on her. Darn it. One of the men had kicked her harder than she'd thought. The tears that came to her eyes were real this time, not faked. Corrie refused to let them fall and hobbled around the room, hands out in front of her, trying not to run into anything and bring attention to herself.

Her shin hit a table, then a chair, then a bed, but she kept going. The small pains didn't matter, it was better than being dead or brutally violated.

She felt along the wall, breathing a sigh of relief when she found what she was looking for. A window. It was about three feet by three feet, plenty big enough for her to squeeze through. It was around five feet off the floor, which would make it tricky to get up and out of, but she tried to open it.

It didn't budge.

Panic set in and Corrie wasted a bit of time huffing and puffing and straining helplessly to push the window open. Finally she stopped to think and felt for a lock. There! She turned the knob at the top of the window and tried again, pushing slowly.

It moved. Oh my God, it freaking moved.

Corrie continued to push open the window slowly in case it made any noise. It didn't. Thank goodness for owners who took care of their properties. Corrie could hear Isaac and Dimitri still arguing in the other room, so she continued making her escape. Finally the window wouldn't go up any more. Corrie felt with her hands. It wasn't open all the way, but it'd have to do. Remembering the chair, she bent over and shuffled back to where she thought it was.

Bingo. Her fingers made contact with the back and she almost knocked it over. She panted through her terror, knowing if Isaac heard anything suspicious, he'd be back in the room in a heartbeat and she'd lose her chance to get out of there. She carefully picked up the chair, thankful it was a flimsy wooden piece of crap.

Carrying it carefully back to the window, Corrie put it down and climbed up. Hopefully she'd have enough of a head start before Isaac came back to rape her.

Pausing, Corrie took a few precious seconds to draw seventeen dots on the wall next to the window before she escaped her prison. She'd found and pocketed a pen when she was searching the room earlier, and while she knew she was taking a chance—a big chance that she'd take too long—she had to do it.

Finished, she put the pen inside the window sill, and stuck her head out of the little window and waited. She tilted her head, listening. She could hear the wind blowing, smell pine and decaying leaves, but nothing else. It was now or never.

Corrie pulled herself through the window head first. She lay on her stomach on the sill and put her hands out. She couldn't touch the ground. Darn. She'd hoped that maybe she'd get lucky and there'd be some sort of hill or the ground would be built up next to the house. She had no idea how far it was to the grass below, but since she hadn't gone up any stairs when Isaac was dragging her into the house, she hoped she didn't have too far to fall.

She put her hands on the sill again and wiggled until she was precariously balanced on her hipbones. Corrie put her hands out again and wiggled one more time. Gravity did the rest of the work for her. She fell out of the window and landed hard on her hands. Her elbows gave out and she hit her head as her body crashed to the ground.

Corrie didn't wait to take stock. She picked herself up and started walking quickly toward the smell of the trees. She kept her hands in front of her, used exaggerated steps to walk, and stayed hunched over, trying not to trip over anything in her way. She knew she probably looked ridiculous, but without her cane, it was really hard to walk in unfamiliar places. She knew she was moving way too slowly, but it wasn't like she could just run off. She had to be smart and careful. She only had one chance. If they caught her, she was as good as dead.

No matter what, she had to keep going. No matter how many times she fell, no matter how many times she ran into things…the key to staying alive was putting one foot in front of the other. All she had to do was picture what Isaac wanted to do to her, and it gave her the motivation she needed to keep going.

She was scared to death, this was not fun, and she'd once had nightmares about this exact situation…being lost in the woods.

But Corrie kept going. Step by painfully slow step. Once she got away from the house, she'd figure out what to do next. Corrie knew she just had to stay away from Isaac. Quint would find her eventually. She just had to find the perfect hiding spot. She knew what she was looking for, but it was a crapshoot as to whether she could actually find it.

She stumbled on, hoping just once that luck was on her side.

"NO MATTER WHAT, you can't lose your shit," Hayden warned as they closed in on the cabin. They'd turned off onto a gravel road. Hayden slowed down only enough so they wouldn't lose a wheel on the deep ruts in the road.

"I'm not going to lose my shit."

"I've read the file on this Isaac guy. We both know what we might find."

Quint ground his teeth together and didn't respond.

"If she's been raped, you have to keep it together," Hayden said stubbornly. "She might not want to be touched. Sometimes even the slightest touch can drive a woman deep into her mind. Just let me see where her head's at before you grab her. If needed, Penelope can help her rather than one of the other male firefighters."

"Shut up."

"Quint, I'm not saying this to hurt you, but you might have to treat her with care."

Quint turned to Hayden. His voice was low and even and only cracked once. "I know exactly what I might find. I might find her scared out of her mind and so far into herself I can't get in. I could find her beaten unconscious, or crucified to a fucking wall. I'm hoping she's still alive. I can deal with anything but that. There's no telling what those assholes could've done to her by now. She's fragile and I'm hanging on by a thread here. So you telling me that asshole might have stuck his cock inside what's mine is *not* helping. I know you mean well, and I appreciate it. I do. But I'd appreciate it more if you could get us the fuck there so I can find my woman and take care of her. Okay?"

"Okay. But Quint?"

He grunted in response.

"I think you're underestimating her. I don't know Corrie, but from what you've told me, I don't think she's all that fragile. She's lived her entire life blind. This isn't new for her. She's been in scary situations before."

"Not like this."

"You're absolutely right, not like this. But you're talking about her as if she sits at home scared to leave the house every day. She has a career. From what you tell me, one she fought like hell to have. She had the presence of mind to hide from Sampson when he shot up her clinic. Remember what Penelope went through over in Turkey. Women are a lot tougher than we seem. Don't sell Corrie short."

Quint could feel his throat closing up. He didn't answer, merely nodded. He hoped Hayden was right. He hoped like hell she was right.

The cab of the SUV was silent the rest of the way to the cabin.

CORRIE'S HANDS HURT. She knew they were scraped up, and she'd hit her head, hard, on a low branch, but she kept going. Her knee was still throbbing from where she'd been kicked, but she kept hobbling on. She was probably covered in dirt and blood. From the injuries Isaac and Dimitri had given her before she'd gotten out of the cabin, to now, she knew she had to look like an escaped inmate from Laurel Ridge, the psychiatric hospital in San Antonio.

She stopped every now and then and cocked her head to listen, to see if Isaac or Dimitri had realized she was gone yet. So far it was quiet behind her. She had no idea how far she'd gotten, only that it wasn't far enough. It'd probably never be far enough. She had to find what she was looking for soon, otherwise it'd be too late.

She started forward again and before she'd gone a dozen steps, she stopped abruptly. She heard yelling from back the way she'd come. Crap. They'd figured out she was gone.

Corrie walked faster, her heart beating hard. She had to hide. She needed to find the perfect place to hide…*now.*

Corrie bounced off what felt like the fiftieth tree since she'd left the cabin and hit the ground hard. She panted for a moment. Why in the world did she think she'd be able to pull this off? Fuck, she wasn't comfortable negotiating herself in a strange room, nevertheless in the middle of a fucking forest.

She sobbed once. Great. Just great. Now she was swearing *and* crying. She got to her feet and put her hands out in front of her again. She just had to keep going. One step at a time. She wasn't going to make it easy for those assholes. If they wanted her, they'd have to fight for her.

She stepped forward another dozen steps and ran into something. Darn it. Another freaking tree.

Wait… She felt this one.

Oh my God, it seemed perfect.

There was a limb close enough to the ground that she could grab it. That had been her plan from the second she'd decided to crawl out the window, and this was the first tree that it seemed might work. She grabbed the first branch, which was around shoulder height, and put her knee on the trunk to help her climb. She pulled herself up, trying not to grunt with the effort it took. Her arms shook, but she didn't give up. Finally she managed to haul herself up on top of that first limb. Corrie put one hand above her head, thanking God there was another branch there, and slowly pulled herself up. She only got to a crouch before she hit another limb. Bingo.

She felt around her and stepped up to the next branch. She continued climbing. Slowly but surely. She could feel the tree she was in swaying gently in the breeze, but she didn't stop. She had no idea how high she'd climbed, but she knew she had to keep going. She had to get high enough that Isaac and Dimitri couldn't see her. She prayed there were leaves on this tree to hide her; she thought there were because she could hear the rustling in the air that blew around her. Even if they saw her, they'd have to climb up to get her. Dying from falling out of this tree would be better than whatever Isaac had in store for her.

Finally, when the limbs seemed too skinny and frail to be able to hold her weight if she stepped on them, she halted her frantic upward climb. She hugged the trunk of the tree tightly and tried to calm her breathing. It wouldn't be much of a hiding place if she gave herself away by panting too loud.

Corrie knew she was high. The sound of leaves rustling made her feel hopeful that she was sufficiently covered. The trunk she was gripping wasn't that wide this high up, her arms fit all the way around it with room to spare. Even though it made no difference, she squeezed her eyes shut, praying she couldn't be seen from the ground.

She wasn't sure how long she'd been clinging to the tree like a frightened monkey, but all of a sudden the silence around her was broken by Isaac and Dimitri's voices as they made their way toward her. They were moving much quicker than she had.

"Come out, come out, wherever you are," Isaac taunted in a sing-song voice that would surely give children nightmares rather than soothe them. "You might as well come out now. We know you came this way because we saw your fucking footprints leading right into the woods. If you give yourself up now, I promise to go easy on you."

Corrie stayed silent.

"Come on, sweet cheeks. You're not going to get away from us. You're fucking blind. You're gonna lose. If you yell out now, I'll kill you quickly."

Dimitri's voice cut through Isaac's fake pleasant tone. "Get out here, bitch! You're gonna fucking pay for this. No one makes a fool out of Dimitri Prandini."

Corrie shivered at the hate and insanity in his voice. She trembled as she adjusted her grip. She held her breath as the men seemed to stop right below the tree she was hiding in. She felt exactly like she had that day so many weeks ago when she knew if she made one wrong move, or one wrong sound, she'd die.

Exactly like that.

"We don't have time for this shit, Dimitri."

"We aren't leaving her. She could ruin everything."

"They're not going to take a blind bitch's word that I was the one who shot those fucking people."

"I don't give a fuck about you taking the rap for that! I care about her getting away and being charged with attempted murder, kidnapping, and you being a pussy in interrogation and fingering me for Shaun's death as well."

"I wouldn't turn against you, Dimitri."

"The fuck you wouldn't."

"Look, you know I want that bitch more than anyone. Not only did she manage to hide from me, but I'll be dammed if I go to jail because of some handicapped blonde whore. I agree that we need to find her, but we can't stay out here all night. She can't have gone far. She's blind, for Christ's sake. Where else would she go out here? Let's keep looking for a bit longer. She's bound to trip over something and hurt herself badly enough so she can't get up. We'll bring her back to the house, I'll fuck her, you'll torture her, then we'll kill her. I'll be sure to dispose of her body so that no one will ever find any trace of her."

"You fucked this up, Isaac! Leaving her in a room with a damn window. I think she's more resourceful than you gave her credit for! Her ass needs to die. Maybe she could've identified you, maybe she couldn't, but she most certainly can *now*. She's heard us talk; she knows what we were planning. We can't let her escape now. No fucking way."

"Dammit. Fucking bitch. It's getting dark. We've got those high-powered flashlights in the car...let's go back and get them. There's no way she'll be able to spend the night out here alone. She'll most likely try to make her way toward the road. If she gets there and is able to flag down a car, we're screwed."

Corrie heard the two men walking back toward the way they came, but she didn't dare move. She let out her breath slowly as the men's voices got softer as they headed back to get their lights so they could continue to search for her. She had no idea what she'd do if they found her, or how they would get her out of the tree. Corrie wasn't planning on coming down anytime soon, they'd have to climb up and get her, or chop the tree down. She wasn't moving. No way, no how.

As the adrenaline in her body receded, she began to shake. Soon, she couldn't tell what was the wind, and what was her trembling muscles. It didn't matter. She wasn't budging. She'd stay right where she was until Quint found her, even if she had to spend the night out there. She had no doubt Quint would come for her. No doubt at all.

QUINT, DAX, HAYDEN, TJ, Cruz, and six other officers from both the SAPD and the FBI crept through the trees toward the cabin. They'd left their vehicles about half a mile down the gravel road so as not to alert Isaac and Dimitri they were coming. There were two trucks from Station 7 firestation on stand-by as well as an ambulance.

There was a black SUV parked in front of the cabin, so hopefully that meant the men were still there. The group of law enforcement officers split up and surrounded the house. Isaac and Dimitri weren't going to get away. No fucking way.

Quint wanted to rush the cabin and get to Corrie, but knew they had to move slowly and carefully. One wrong move could force either of the men to kill her outright before they could get to her. He wouldn't put it past them.

"Window open on the west side," Quint heard Cruz say in a deep voice through his earpiece.

"Front door standing open," Hayden replied in a steady voice from the other side of the cabin.

Quint and TJ turned together when they heard voices coming from behind them. They rushed to the other side of the SUV to conceal themselves and watched incredulously as Isaac and Dimitri came walking out of the woods—as if they'd been on a nice leisurely stroll through the trees and hadn't just kidnapped a woman and almost killed two others.

"Hurry up and get them. We need to take care of this once and for all. We're one step ahead of the pig cops right now, and need to keep them off our asses as much as possible. After she's disposed of, we'll hit up some of our other clients and get the fuck out of here. We can lay low and re-group. A blind woman isn't going to be the end of my business. No fucking way!" Dimitri bitched as he sauntered next to Isaac.

The men were almost to the SUV when TJ popped up from around the front of their car, his pistol pointed at Dimitri. "Sorry, guys, the pig cops are all *over* your asses."

Quint would've rolled his eyes at the corny joke, but he couldn't muster the wherewithal to do it. Where were these assholes coming from and where was Corrie?

Isaac and Dimitri turned to run back into the woods, and came face-to-face with four more officers with guns. They were completely surrounded.

Isaac, obviously the more impulsive of the two, decided to make a grand gesture and pulled a pistol out of the holster at his side.

Several shots rang out through the clearing despite Quint's demand to hold fire. Within seconds, neither Isaac nor Dimitri would ever collect another dime from anyone again.

Quint didn't give a fuck whose bullets actually ended the slimeballs' lives, except for the fact that they might have been the only two people on the earth who knew where Corrie was. They'd been talking about disposing her body, and that alone almost destroyed him. He tried to stay positive and hope that they hadn't gotten around to killing her yet.

Hayden put her pistol back into her holster. She shrugged her shoulders at Quint before they turned to run toward the house to look for Corrie. "Two less cockroaches to worry about." She really was hard-core, right down to her bones.

Quint holstered his own smoking service pistol as he sprinted toward the open door to the cabin.

He walked briskly through the small cabin. Every room was empty. Standing in one of the small bedrooms, he turned to TJ, who'd followed him inside.

"Quint..." TJ shook his head sadly.

Quint held up his palm to his friend. "No. Fucking no. I won't believe she's dead until I see it with my own eyes."

"Buddy, they were coming back from the woods."

Suddenly Dax was there. He put his hand on TJ's shoulder. "No. Quint's right. Until we see her, she's not dead. Remember Mack? I watched her die, but she's still with me today. We continue on until there's absolutely no hope, then we continue on some more."

TJ nodded solemnly. "Fuck. Yeah, you're right. Let's re-search. There has to be something here."

The men split up. Dax and TJ went back to the main part of the house and Quint looked around the rooms in the back. He searched the first room with no luck, but as he headed toward the second room, he took another glance at the door.

Yes! There was a brand-new knob on the door, but it was installed backwards. The lock was on the outside, not the inside of the room. He went in and looked around. How the fuck had he missed it the first time?

He'd been looking for Corrie, not clues, that's how.

This was the room with the open window. There was a chair sitting under it. Quint scanned the room. It seemed to be nothing out of the ordinary. A twin bed, a dresser, a small closet, and that chair. He looked more carefully.

A pen. There was a pen in the windowsill.

Adrenaline coursed through Quint's body. "Dax!" he yelled, even as he walked to the window to take a closer look. Just as Dax was striding into the room, Quint saw it.

Small dots on the wall.

She'd left him a fucking message.

"What is it?" Dax asked, coming up beside Quint.

"Braille."

"What's it say?"

Quint ran his fingers over the dots. They weren't raised like Braille was, but he couldn't stop himself from touching them. His

Corrie had been there and left them for him. He tried to concentrate on the message she'd left for him.

"Well?" Dax asked impatiently.

"Give me a second. I'm new at this. O, V, T...no, wait...U. O, U, T. Out."

"Out? Okay, with the chair sitting right there it's obvious she went out the window. Is that it?"

"No, there's more." Quint tilted his head to look at the last two letters. She'd used Grade 1 Braille to spell out the letters. She probably knew he was still trying to get the hang of Grade 2 and didn't want to risk him not understanding what she wanted to tell him.

U and...P. Up.

"Out and Up. She went out and we need to look up."

"Did your blind girlfriend really jump out a window in the middle of a forest after being kidnapped and head off to try to find a fucking tree to climb?"

Quint smiled at Dax's words. Hayden had been right. Women *were* tough as shit. It was the first time he'd allowed himself to relax since he'd heard Corrie was missing. "Yeah. I think she did."

"Damn, I like her, Quint. Anyone who can rescue herself is totally worthy of you."

"Yeah, I like her too. Now, can we go and find my woman and get the fuck out of here?" Quint was already on the move as he said the words. Dax was right behind him. They collected TJ, Cruz, and Hayden on their way out.

The five officers gathered next to the cabin under the open window. Quint looked around. He closed his eyes, put his arms out and started walking.

He didn't get ten feet before he opened his eyes. He couldn't do it. He had no idea how Corrie had found the strength and courage to walk, literally blind into the forest. He couldn't make it past ten steps.

Hayden had been completely right in chastising him for underestimating Corrie. She wasn't fragile, not in the way he'd been thinking. He had no doubt everything that had happened today would traumatize her, but he'd be damned if he ever disparaged her again by thinking she was weak.

He continued walking forward, alternating between looking down and looking up. He'd be the first person to tell her how proud he was of her…as soon as he found her.

Chapter Fifteen

CORRIE SHIVERED. SHE didn't think it was cold outside, but she couldn't really tell. She couldn't feel her feet; the thin branch she was standing on had cut off her circulation. Climbing a tree in flip-flops wasn't the smartest thing she'd ever done, but it wasn't as if she'd had a choice.

Her head and knee hurt where Isaac and Dimitri had hit her. She felt dizzy, but wasn't sure if it was because of the swaying of the tree she was in, or something else. She shivered and hugged the tree tighter. The last thing she needed was to fall out before Quint found her. She just wished he'd hurry up.

She dozed off for a bit, but she woke up with a start and convulsively grabbed at the tree. She sighed in relief when she didn't fall. She leaned her forehead against the scratchy bark and tried not to cry.

"Cooooooorrie!"

Corrie lifted her head and tilted it in the hopes of hearing better.

"Cooooooorrie. Where are you?"

Her heart started beating like a jackrabbit again. Was Isaac back already? Darn it, she hoped maybe they'd give up the idea of looking for her when they got back to their car. Maybe the batteries in the flashlights would be dead or something. She kept her mouth shut and tried to slow her breathing.

"Corrie? Are you out here?"

The voice was female. Corrie didn't understand what was going on. Had Dimitri and Isaac come back with reinforcements? Did they kidnap another woman? She was so confused.

She could hear more voices now. They were muted so she couldn't catch their words.

"Corrie, sweetheart…can you hear me? It's Quint. You're safe."

Quint? Quint was finally here! His voice echoed around the trees and blew into the wind.

Corrie looked toward the ground. It was silly; it wasn't as if she could see anything. She waited. The voices got closer and closer.

What if it was a trap? What if Dimitri had a gun to Quint's head or something? He could be using Quint to flush her out.

For the first time in a really long time, Corrie wished she could see. She used to pray to God to give her sight when she was little, but now she really *really* wished she could see what was going on because if she got Quint killed, she would hate herself for all eternity.

She had to take a chance. Would all those people be with him if Isaac had him? She hoped not. "Quint?" Her voice came out as a croak. She tried again, stronger this time. "Quint? I'm here."

"Corrie? Thank fucking God!"

Corrie almost laughed at the relief in his voice.

"Again, talk to me again so I can find you."

Corrie swallowed down the tears clogging her throat. "Here. I'm up in a tree."

"Keep talking, sweetheart. We'll find you."

We? She didn't care who was with him. She couldn't wait for him to hold her. "I'm up here. I climbed as high as I could so they couldn't see me. I have no idea how high I am though. Can you see me yet?" The last part came out way too pathetic-sounding for her peace of mind.

Quint stopped beneath the tall tree and stared up. He could barely see Corrie. Good God. He had no idea how she'd even gotten up that high. How in the hell was he going to get her down? "I see you, sweetheart. You just keep hanging on, okay?"

"Quint? Are you okay? They're not with you?"

He immediately understood. Figured she'd be worried about him and not herself. "No, Corrie. They're not here. I'm here with Cruz and some of my other friends. You're safe."

"Did you get them? Their names are Isaac and Dimitri, they killed Shaun. They were going to kill me too, but I got away. Did you get my message?"

Quint's heart hurt. Corrie sounded so sad and lost. He wanted nothing more than to grab hold of her and never let go. "We got them, sweetheart. They won't hurt you or anyone else again. They were shot and killed back at the cabin. And yes, I got your message." He tried to interject some humor into their conversation, even though he wasn't really feeling it. "And so you know, your U looks like a V."

"It does not," she protested weakly. "You just need more practice."

Quint snorted and started undoing his shirt. He'd need to take off his vest and belt in order to be able to get through the thick network of branches to get to her.

"I got this."

He turned to see Hayden had already taken off her gear and was reading to shimmy up the tree. He put a hand on her arm. "No, she's my responsibility, I'll go up."

"There's no way you'll fit, Quint, think about it. I grew up climbing trees like this. Besides, you weigh more than me or Corrie. You'll possibly break the branches and she'll be stuck up there. Trust me. I'll bring her to you safely."

Quint hated it with every fiber of his being, but Hayden was right, dammit. "Okay, but," he didn't take his eyes off of Hayden's, "be careful. She means the world to me."

Hayden simply nodded and demanded, "Give me a boost."

Quint put his hands together and held them down for her to step into. She did and he hoisted her easily up to the first branch. Looking at it, Quint had no idea how Corrie had managed to haul herself up there with no help. "Help's coming, Corrie. Hang on."

"You're coming up to get me?"

Quint could hear the hope in her voice and hated to disappoint her. "No, not me. I'm too big. But Hayden's coming. Remember me telling you about her? She's a sheriff's deputy and can outshoot and outrun most of the guys in my department. And whatever you do, don't challenge her to one-on-one combat. She's the only woman I know who can manage to flip me." Quint kept his words calm and soothing. He could tell Corrie was on the verge of freaking out. "Corrie?"

"Yeah, okay. I'm scared. I've been waiting for you, why'd you take so long?" Corrie hated the wobble in her voice, but she'd been brave for as long as she could be, and now that Quint was there, she allowed herself to fall apart…just a little. She'd added the last to try to keep herself from freaking out more.

"I know you are, but I'm so fucking proud of you. You have no idea." Quint kept his eye on Hayden as she shimmied up the tree as if she'd been born in one. "I set off to find you and closed my eyes for about two-point-three seconds before I had to open them again. I couldn't do it. But you did, sweetheart. You did it. You outsmarted those assholes and saved yourself. You didn't need me to do it."

"I—" Her voice cut off. Quint could see that Hayden had made her way to Corrie and was talking to her.

CORRIE JERKED AWAY from the touch on her calf, then relaxed when she heard the female voice.

"Easy, Corrie. It's me, Hayden Yates. I'm going to help you down. All right?"

Corrie nodded. "Okay, thank you. I had no idea how in the heck

I was gonna get out of here. How high am I?"

"You did a good job, and you don't want to know how far you climbed, but it was high enough that we almost couldn't see you from the ground. Even if those assholes stood right under you, they probably wouldn't have seen you."

"I think they *did* stand right under me."

"Ha, well fuck them then. Come on. I'm going to take hold of your sweats and guide your foot to a branch. Your shoes aren't going to make this easy, but we'll take this slow and steady. Take your time, there's absolutely no rush. No bad guys are waiting, only Quint, and he can just cool his jets down there…right?"

Corrie smiled, realizing Hayden was trying to relax her. She nodded again.

"Okay, this first step is easy. The branch is about six inches below your right foot. Just shift your hold on the trunk and ease your foot down. That's it."

Corrie followed Hayden's gentle pressure on her sweats and moved her foot carefully. The branch was exactly where she said it'd be.

"Good, now move your left foot the same way. It'll fit right next to your other one on the same branch."

Corrie did as directed and took a deep breath. Okay, she could do this.

They continued their slow and steady pace down the tree until they got to a tricky part. Corrie remembered this particular gap in the branches as she'd climbed up.

"Okay, this is the last of the hard parts, Corrie. It's about a four-foot gap between where you're standing now and where the next branch is below you. You're going to need to crouch down, leaving one foot on the branch and reaching down with your other one. It'll be a stretch, but your legs are long enough to reach. Promise. I'll help guide you so your foot will go right where it's supposed to."

Corrie nodded. She'd come this far. She circled the trunk of the tree with her arms and bent her legs. She moved her left foot until it dangled down. She felt Hayden's grip on her ankle.

"Just a bit more, that's it. Almost there…"

Just as Corrie thought she felt the branch under her foot, her right foot slipped off the branch it was on.

She screeched and knocked her forehead on a branch at her head level as she felt herself falling. Her shin whacked against the limb she'd been standing on and she gripped the broad trunk of the tree for dear life. "Shit!"

"Corrie!" Quint's voice was frantic.

Hayden's voice came below her. It was calm and even, as if she hadn't just watched her almost fall out of the stupid tree. Corrie could feel the strong and secure grip the other woman had on her ankle. Hayden held her steady as she knelt on the limb like an idiot.

"No problem, Corrie. Just a small slip. You're okay."

"That's the second time I've sworn today, darn it. That's not cool."

Hayden chuckled. "You're crackin' me up. I think you have a right to say a swear word or two."

Corrie shook her head. "No, I promised myself when Ethan, my friend's kid, was born that I'd stop. I was a complete potty mouth before. I had to go cold turkey or his first word was bound to be a swearword he learned from his Aunt Corrie."

"Come on, you're almost there. Trust me. Give me some of your weight and I'll guide your foot to the next branch."

Corrie took a deep breath and did as Hayden asked. She wanted out of this darn tree and the only way to do that was to get past this section. She eased off her shin and felt Hayden guide her foot, exactly as she'd promised. Corrie felt the sturdy limb under her foot and breathed a sigh of relief.

"Okay, I've got you, slide your other leg off and grab hold of the branch it was just resting on with your hands."

Corrie felt one of Hayden's hands on her lower back and the other on her calf. She shifted and Hayden moved the hand that was on her right calf to her hip. "There you go. Good. Piece of cake. We're only about eight feet from the ground, and Quint is waiting for you. Only about two more steps and he'll have his hands on you. Ready?"

Corrie nodded eagerly, more than ready.

They moved quickly past the next couple of branches and just as Hayden had said, Corrie felt large hands grasp her around her waist. She hadn't felt anything as wonderful as Quint's arms coming around her.

"Thank God," Corrie heard Quint mutter as he lifted her out of the tree and into his arms. She heard a thud as Hayley jumped out of the tree herself. She knew she should thank the deputy, but being in Quint's arms, smelling his unique smell, was more than she could take after everything that had happened.

Corrie burst into tears and buried her face in Quint's neck. She felt his hand cradle the back of her head as he held her against him.

Quint dipped his head and breathed into Corrie's hair as he hugged her. "You're okay, sweetheart. I've got you. You're good." He continued to whisper nonsense as he followed his friends back through the woods to their vehicles. Corrie vaguely realized she probably should've at least said hello to the other men who were with Quint, but she couldn't seem to stop crying long enough to manage it. She heard them talking as they walked, but couldn't concentrate on their words.

Their little group quickly reached the clearing and Quint didn't even pause to look at the dead bodies lying near the black SUV. Someone had collected the police and fire vehicles from down the road and they were lined up and waiting.

Quint kept Corrie's head against his neck and headed straight for Hayden's SUV. He leaned down and managed to open the door without letting go of Corrie. He sat on the seat sideways and propped his feet on the running board. His heart hurt as Corrie cried in his arms. After a few minutes, she hiccuped and he could tell she was trying to bring herself under control.

He looked down at her and grimaced in sympathy. She had a scrape on her forehead, probably from when she'd almost fallen out of the tree on her way down. There were bruises forming on her jaw and cheekbone. Her hair was a mess and she had dirt smeared from her nose to her ears.

She'd never looked more beautiful to him.

"I love you, Corrie Madison." Quint couldn't have kept the words back if his life depended on it. "I've never been so scared in all my life than when I realized you were gone. I don't want to go through this crazy life without you. I don't care how long it takes, I'm going to show you day in and day out how much you mean to me in the hopes that you'll eventually love me back. I…"

He paused. Corrie had lifted her hand to his neck and was tapping against him. Two diagonal taps, then three vertical taps, then five taps in a backward C shape. She did it again. Then again.

He smiled, and it was his turn to bury his nose in her neck. "You love me?" he mumbled against her.

"Yeah." Corrie sniffed. She knew she probably looked like death warmed over, but Quint didn't seem to care. "When I was stumbling blindly through the woods looking for a tree to climb, all I could think of was how much I loved you and how sad I was that I hadn't told you. But you know what else?"

She felt Quint raise his head. "What?"

"I knew you'd come for me. No matter what. I was going to hang on to the top of that darn tree forever if it took that long, because I knew you'd figure it out and find me."

"Lord, Corrie."

She thought about something suddenly. "Oh no! Bethany…is she okay? What about Emily and Ethan? I don't remember what happened."

Quint ran his hand over her hair again, soothing her. "They're fine. I'll tell you everything later, but they're fine."

"Promise?"

"Yeah. Promise."

Corrie snuggled into Quint, grumbling about the hard bullet-proof vest for the first time. She hadn't noticed it before, but now she wanted him. Just him.

"Corrie? My friends Sledge and Crash are here. They're firefighters and EMTs. They just want to take a quick look to make sure you're all right."

Corrie didn't even move from her position curled around Quint. "I'm fine."

"I know you are, but I'd still feel better if you'd let them check you over."

"We're not so bad, promise," a deep voice said from beside her.

A second voice chimed in as well, "Yeah, although I'm the good-looking one."

Corrie turned her head and tried to get herself back together. "Sledge and Crash?" she questioned.

"Long story. Does anything hurt?"

Ten minutes later, assured that Corrie really was okay, other than being scared and some minor scrapes and bruises that would fade and eventually heal, Quint stood up with Corrie in his arms. He nodded at Sledge and Crash, and gave a thankful chin lift to Penelope, Chief and Moose, other firefighters from Station 7 who were standing next to the trucks, in case they were needed.

"You guys ready to go?" Hayden asked as she opened the driver's side door.

"Yeah."

"Great, but you can't hold her like that, Quint. You know the law. Safety first."

Corrie laughed at the disgruntled noise that came from Quint's throat. "We have to sit in the back, don't we?"

Quint's answer was to stand up without letting go of Corrie. He shut the front door with his hip and opened the back door. He sat down, still holding on to her, and hauled Corrie over his lap and placed her in the seat next to him. He pulled the seat belt over her waist and then buckled his own. Ignoring the stretch of the material over his shoulder, he pulled Corrie into the crook of his arm and relaxed as she melted against him.

"Take us home, Hayden."

Chapter Sixteen

------- ◆ -------

"**A**RE YOU SURE you're all right?" Corrie asked Bethany for what seemed like the hundredth time.

Quint had Hayden take them straight to the hospital. Corrie had tried to insist she didn't need to see a doctor, especially since his friends had looked her over and said they thought she was fine, but Quint didn't care. He trusted Sledge and Crash, but they weren't doctors. He told Corrie she could have internal injuries that she simply didn't realize because of the adrenaline coursing through her body. It wasn't until he'd told her what had happened to Emily, Bethany, and Ethan that'd she'd agreed—hell, she insisted.

Quint had refused to let her see her friends until a doctor had checked her out. She sat still...barely...and answered the doctor's questions with ill-concealed impatience.

"Ms. Madison, besides some scrapes and bruises, I'd say you are one very lucky woman."

"Okay, great." Corrie had turned to where Quint was standing. "I told you so...and so did Crash and Sledge. Will you take me to see Bethany *now*?"

Quint had resisted chuckling, knowing it would irritate Corrie and probably put him in the dog house. "Yeah, sweetheart. Thanks, Dr. Davis. I appreciate you taking a look. I don't know what I'd do without her."

Corrie had squeezed Quint's arm, acknowledging his sweet words, but then ruined it by huffing, "If I could find her by myself,

I'd do it, but since I'd probably keep running into people and walls, I need you to show me where my friends are."

The doctor had nodded at Quint and smirked. Quint just ignored the older man and took Corrie's hand in his and set out to find her friends.

The second Corrie had walked into the hospital room where Bethany was recuperating, Emily, who was also visiting, burst into tears. Emily had rushed into Corrie's arms and they spent more than a few minutes enjoying the feel of each other alive and well.

Corrie put her hands on Emily's face and ran her fingers over it. "Does it hurt?"

Emily laughed a watery laugh. "About as much as yours does, I'd imagine."

Corrie grimaced in commiseration.

"Hey, you two, I'm the one in the hospital bed here."

Corrie rushed over and asked if she was okay.

"I'm good. Are you sure you don't hate me, Cor? I didn't want to do it…but he threatened Ethan."

"Lord, Bethany. Of *course* I don't hate you. God, I would've done the same thing. You did the right thing, and besides, it all turned out fine in the end. I'm just sorry you both got sucked into the entire thing. If it wasn't for me—"

Both Emily and Quint spoke at once, interrupting her.

"That's not—"

"Don't." Quint's word was louder. He spoke over whatever Emily was going to say. "This is not your fault. If you want to blame someone, blame Isaac. Or Dimitri, or even Shaun, but there's no way I'll let you blame yourself."

"But—"

Quint shut Corrie up the only way he knew how. He swooped down and covered her mouth with his own. He dimly heard both Emily and Bethany catcalling, but he didn't stop. He thrust his tongue into her mouth, more relieved than he was willing to admit out loud when she returned his kiss. He'd been afraid she'd be too scared with everything that had happened to return his passion. He should've known better.

He finally raised his head and nuzzled against the side of Corrie's neck as he tried to rein in the urgent need to get her alone and show her just how much she meant to him, and to relieve some of the stress he'd been feeling since finding out she'd been kidnapped.

"In case you're wondering, Ethan is fine."

Corrie spun at Emily's teasing words, almost clipping Quint's chin in the process. "Ethan! Where is he? He's really okay? I'm a horrible aunt for not even *asking* about him!"

Quint stood behind Corrie and put his hands around her waist. He pulled her into him, loving the way she trusted him to take her weight.

"Calm down, Cor. He's fine. He was checked out and didn't even have a scratch on him. Thank God Quint realized something was wrong and showed up when he did. He was a little cold, but otherwise fine." Bethany's words were strong and sure.

Emily sat down in the chair next to Bethany and stroked her forearm above the bandages covering her hand. Quint knew Bethany had a long road to recovery ahead of her...some of the nerves in her hand had been severed and there were lots of surgeries in her future.

"My mom came and took him home with her for the night," Emily explained.

"Your mom? But she doesn't approve—"

"I know. But apparently a psycho beating me up and almost killing my partner and son made her think twice about everything."

"It's about darn time."

Emily simply laughed. "So, now that you know we're fine, and we can see you're hunky-dory...go home."

"What?"

Emily repeated herself. "Go home, Cor. You look exhausted. If I'm not mistaken, your man is foaming at the mouth to get you home and taken care of."

Corrie tilted her head up, as if she was actually looking at him. "But...can we go home?"

Quint kissed the top of her head, knowing what she meant. "Yeah, Dax and Hayden called in reinforcements. After the crime scene techs did their thing, they managed to get us an all new bed. I didn't want any reminders of what happened to Bethany there. It's all good, sweetheart."

"Promise?"

"Yes. I wouldn't bring you back there if I wasn't one-hundred percent sure it was safe and clean for you to go back to."

Corrie turned to her friends. "I love you guys. So much. I'll come back up and see you tomorrow."

"Okay. You know we love you too. Thank God you were smarter than those assholes."

Corrie smiled. "I don't know about smarter, but maybe more determined."

"Good enough."

"Come on, sweetheart. You're dead on your feet. Let's go home."

"Home. That sounds good."

Quint smiled huge. She was right. It did sound good.

He waited patiently as Corrie hugged Emily one more time, and leaned over Bethany and gave her an abbreviated hug and kiss on the cheek. She came back to him and reached for his hand. "Love you guys. See you tomorrow."

Quint led Corrie out of the room and down the hall to the waiting area. He gave a few chin lifts to the doctors and nurses who waved as they went by. He couldn't wait to get Corrie home.

CORRIE WAS RELIEVED to be back in Quint's house. They were standing in his bedroom. He'd dragged her to his room the second they'd arrived.

"You aren't afraid to be back here?"

Corrie shook her head. "No. One, you're here with me. And two, Isaac knocked me out as soon as I opened the door. I don't remember anything that happened. I'm guessing Bethany isn't going to want to come over for a very long time, but me? I'm good."

Quint hugged Corrie to him, loving how she snuggled up against him without hesitation. He had a lot he wanted to say to her, but wanted to get her clean and comfortable first. "Good. Go ahead and shower. I want nothing more than to hold you against me as soon as I can."

"You want to shower with me?" Corrie asked shyly.

Quint kissed her forehead. "If I get in that shower, I won't be able to take my hands off of you."

"And that's bad because…"

"Because I want to hold you. To reassure myself that you're really okay. I've had a shit day, I wasn't sure if I'd ever hold you warm and breathing in my arms again. I need you in my bed, in my arms."

"Okay, Quint. I'll be quick. I need that too."

"I love you, Corrie."

"I love you too."

"Shower, I'll be waiting in our bed."

Corrie nodded and Quint kissed her once more before turning her toward the bathroom.

He stripped down to his boxers and waited for Corrie to emerge from the shower, which had quickly filled with steam as she cleaned off the dirt from the events of the day.

Within ten minutes, Corrie padded out of the bathroom with only a towel wrapped around her body. Quint had never seen anything so beautiful in all his life. And she was all his.

"Come here, sweetheart."

Corrie walked cautiously to the bed with one arm out in front of her, making sure she didn't run into anything. When her knees hit the mattress, she held out her hand toward where Quint's voice had been coming from. Quint took it in his and watched as she unhooked the towel and it dropped to the floor.

"Holy shit, Corrie. You are so fucking beautiful."

She smiled. "Scoot over."

He did and she crawled under the sheets and into his arms.

"It doesn't smell like you anymore."

"What?"

"The sheets. They don't smell like you anymore. I hate that."

"They will soon. Don't worry." Quint felt his heart clench as Corrie nuzzled into him. She put her nose into his neck and inhaled deeply.

"But *you* smell like you, so it'll have to do," she teased.

Quint rolled Corrie under him. He put his legs on either side of hers, pushing his hips into hers, and rested his elbows next to her shoulders. He knew he was probably squishing her, but he needed to feel every part of her under every part of him.

"I know I told you this today, but I am so proud of you. I've seen a lot of brave things in my life. Battered women having the guts to leave abusive husbands, single parents raising handicapped kids by themselves, inner-city kids resisting the lure of gangs and drugs, firefighters rushing into burning buildings as everyone else rushes out."

Corrie took a breath to interrupt, but Quint hurried on.

"Even Mackenzie and Mickie, Dax and Cruz's women, continually impress the hell out of me. But when I was on my way to you, I have to tell you, I wasn't sure what I'd find. I thought you'd be scared and, I'm ashamed to admit...broken."

"Quint..."

Quint ignored her attempt to stop him again and forged ahead. "Hayden was the one who told me that I was underestimating you. And she was right. She was so fucking right. You didn't need me to save you. You saved yourself. Blind, scared, hurting, and having no idea where the fuck you were...you still figured out a way to help yourself." He shook his head in amazement. "I'll never underestimate or doubt you again. You can do anything you want. And I love you for it."

"Can I talk now?" Corrie's voice was soft and serious.

Quint kissed the tip of her nose. "Yeah, you can talk."

"The only reason I was brave is because I knew you were on your way to me."

"Damn straight."

"Hey, it's my turn." Her hands rested on Quint's biceps, and she stroked the words inked on his arm unknowingly.

"Sorry, sweetheart. Continue."

"Thank you. As I said. The only reason I even tried to get away was to give you time to get to me. I know what he wanted to do to me. He took great pleasure in telling me how he was going to kill me and what he was going to do to me before he blew my brains out. But I wanted to live with every fiber of my being. For the first time in my life, I loved a man, and I wanted to experience that. I got mad. I didn't want them to take that from me. I wasn't brave, Quint. I was scared out of my mind every second I was out there."

"But you did it anyway."

Corrie nodded. "I did it anyway, because I knew you were on your way. If I could find a way to stay alive, you'd take care of Isaac and Dimitri."

"Of course. I'll always take care of you, sweetheart. All you ever have to do is wait, and whenever you need help, I'll be there."

"I know."

"When are we moving the rest of your stuff over here?"

"What?"

"The rest of your things. We need to talk to your landlord and put in your notice. You're moving in with me as soon as you can."

Corrie wanted to argue with him, but it was hard when there was nothing that would make her happier than living permanently with Quint. Knowing he was just as anxious for it was a heady feeling. "I'm already here. I have no desire to go anywhere."

Quint rested his forehead against hers. "I love you."

"I love you."

When Quint didn't move, Corrie ran her hand over the back of his head and leaned up to whisper where she thought his ear was. "Are you going to make love to me or what?"

Quint didn't budge an inch, but she felt him smile against her. "Yeah, I'm going to make love to you. Then I'm going to fuck you. Then eat you out, then fuck you again. That meet with your approval?"

"Oh yeah, as long as I can return the favor."

Quint eased off Corrie just long enough to push his boxers down and off, then he was back. "Lay back and let me show you how appreciative I am that you're a brave, badass woman. *My* brave, badass woman."

Corrie stretched her hands over her head and arched her back. "Have at it. I'm all yours."

Epilogue

——————◆——————

"**W**HAT I DID is no more amazing than what you went through, Mackenzie," Corrie insisted. A couple of weeks had passed since Dimitri and Isaac had kidnapped her, and Quint had introduced her to Mackenzie and Mickie, Dax and Cruz's girlfriends. She'd gotten to know both men fairly well, since they'd made a point to come over to Quint's house to check on her when he was on shift and couldn't be home with her. Today they were all hanging out at a bar and reminiscing about the crappy things that happened to them, much to the chagrin of their men.

"That's not true. I can't believe you had the guts to wander outside of a house when you had no idea where you were and not only that, but you actually evaded tweedle-dee and tweedle-dum," Mackenzie enthused. "All I did was lie there and cry, hoping Dax would find me."

"You're both super women, all right?" Mickie said in exasperation.

Mackenzie turned to the other woman and teased, "You are the crazy one in the group though, Mickie. Getting all slutted up and marching into a motorcycle club as if you were the bionic woman or something. I swear I'll see you in that outfit I've heard so much about one of these days."

Mickie chuckled. "Yeah, not my finest moment for sure."

Corrie knew that Mickie's sister had been killed in the raid that had happened during the party Mickie had crashed. "I'm sorry about your sister, Mickie. Seriously."

"Thanks, Corrie. Me too. But looking back, I don't think she would've changed. I'm not saying I'm glad that she was killed, but I think her life would've continued to spiral downward if it didn't happen."

Because Corrie's hearing was so much better than everyone else's due to her blindness, she heard Cruz say to Mickie in a soft voice, trying to soothe her, "I love you, Mickie."

She turned to Quint before she heard Mickie's response, "Thank you for introducing me to your friends."

"You're welcome."

"I thought Penelope was going to be here tonight?" Corrie was intrigued with the petite firefighter. Quint had told her she was The Army Princess, the soldier who had been kidnapped while on a mission in Turkey. She remembered hearing the news stories about her, but hadn't realized Sledge was her brother, and the man behind all the intense media attention the case had gotten. It was almost unreal.

"She had planned on it, but she took a trip up to Fort Hood for something or other," Quint told her. "It's kinda crazy that this Tex character who TJ knows and who figured out where you had been taken, is the same person who helped coordinate her rescue, not once but twice." He shook his head, amazed at how things seemed to work out. "I'm sure you'll meet her soon. She's been dying to sit down with you too. She told me that if I was this head over heels in love, then you had to be amazing."

Corrie blushed. She didn't even know the woman, but she seemed like someone she'd get along with really well. Corrie leaned against Quint and listened to the conversation going on around her.

"Can you believe the calendar is actually going to happen?" Mackenzie asked her friend Laine, who had joined them at the bar.

"No. Actually I'm shocked you convinced your new boss to go

ahead with it," Laine told her best friend, taking a drink.

"Calendar?" Corrie asked with a tilt of her head.

"Yeah, a charity thing. Every year my company does something to raise money for the community, and now that we have all these hotties at our beck and call, we decided a calendar was a great idea! This year we're going to do law enforcement, and hopefully next year we'll do the firefighter thing. Of course we don't have all of the models yet." Mack looked up at Dax with big doe eyes, then continued, "But we're working on it. Even Hayden has agreed to pose for us."

"So it's not just men?" Corrie queried.

"Nope...well, mostly. Most of the women don't want to have anything to do with being in it, but we convinced Hayden."

Hayden rolled her eyes at Mackenzie. "You didn't 'convince' me, Mack. You threatened and blackmailed me."

Everyone laughed.

"What's she holding over your head?"

"Mack, if you answer Corrie, you'll die," Hayden threatened.

Mackenzie held up her hands in capitulation. "My lips are sealed, but we *do* need at least one other guy. I'm pretty sure I've got all the others lined up."

"I might know someone," Daxton told Mack.

Her head whipped around so quickly it was comical. "Really? Who?"

"There's a guy at work. His name is Wes and he works with me."

"A Texas Ranger?" Corrie asked.

"Yeah. And a cowboy."

"I vote yes," Laine chimed in.

"You don't even know what he looks like!" Mack exclaimed.

"I bet he's hot. Is he hot, Dax?"

"I'm not sure about that. I'm not an expert of what's hot and what's not as far as you ladies go, but he *is* always getting hit on when we go to calls."

"Oh yeah, he's hot," Corrie said decisively. "Hayden? Do you know him? Is he hot?"

"On a scale of one to ten? I'd say he's at least a twelve," the law enforcement officer sighed in a breathy voice.

Everyone laughed.

"Great, it's a done deal. Daxton, get me his number and I'll somehow get him on board. Laine, you'll go with me for the shoot right? We can totally use the cowboy angle because none of the other guys are into that. Does he have a ranch? Yeah, I bet he does. Laine, we can go together and scope him out and see if he's got any hot ranch hands. We need more eye candy in our life. I need to get with the photographer and set everyone's sessions up, then talk to the printer and find out what the final schedule is going to be, and—"

Dax put his hand over Mack's mouth and held up his glass. "Since we're here to celebrate Corrie's awesomeness and climbing-a-tree-like-a-monkey ability, I would like to propose a toast...to Corrie. You are an amazing woman who doesn't let anything get her down. I admire your stubbornness and resilience. You are one tough chick and a perfect match for Quint. Welcome to our family."

Corrie couldn't see the men and women sitting around the table, but she knew they were all looking at her and Quint and smiling. She'd surprised herself in the forest, but she supposed the motivation to stay alive for Quint had been strong. She raised her glass and said in return, "I didn't do it myself. I knew Quint...and you guys...were on your way. That you'd find me. That's what let me keep going even when I was scared." She took a breath and turned to where she knew Laine, Hayden, TJ, Conor, and Calder were sitting.

"I hope you guys find the person out there who was made just for you. Don't give up, he or she is out there somewhere, and you'll never know when you'll meet them."

"Lord is this getting mushy," Hayden complained good naturedly.

"Thank you for being brave. For not letting those assholes get you down," Quint said and leaned over and kissed Corrie on the side of the head. "I love you. You mean the world to me."

Everyone sighed in contentment at witnessing the love between Quint and Corrie. She'd shown them all that just because a person had a disability, it didn't mean they were helpless.

After clinking glasses and drinking their toast, talk turned back to the calendar, and other work related incidents.

Corrie snuggled into Quint and let the conversation roll over her head. She was content to sit with her new friends, and boyfriend, and soak in the goodness that surrounded them all. Life was good, and she was very very lucky.

Read on for the next book in the series:
Justice for Laine.

JUSTICE FOR LAINE

BADGE OF HONOR

TEXAS HEROES
BOOK 4

by Susan Stoker

Chapter One

———— ◆ ————

"**N**O. ABSOLUTELY NOT," Laine told Mackenzie emphatically. "Please?"

Laine Parker sighed in exasperation. Mack was her best friend, but sometimes she thought they shouldn't be friends at all. Mackenzie was curvy and outgoing and somehow seemed to light up a room the second she walked in. Laine was almost the exact opposite. She was tall and slender and would rather spend the night at home in her sweats than go out… but it was hard to meet a guy that way. Still, they were thick as thieves, went together like peanut butter and jelly, and were like blood sisters.

"I only said I'd come because *you* were going. I have no desire to go out to some random guy's ranch, watch as he takes his shirt off and poses for your charity calendar," Laine told Mack in an irritated tone of voice.

"I know," Mack whined, obviously stressed out. "But my new boss asked me to go with her today to check out the venue for our annual charity ball. I wouldn't normally agree, because it's not like she can't go and look at a ballroom herself, but I'm trying to make sure I stay in her good graces. After Nancy left, we floundered a bit before Loretta got here. I don't want to do anything to make her reconsider her employment choice. And, Laine, this isn't a random guy. Wes works with Daxton. He's a Texas Ranger. It's not like I'm sending you to a Chippendale club or something. Besides, Jack will be there."

Laine took a big gulp of her iced tea, wishing it was something stronger. Mackenzie had asked her to lunch today, and she'd thought it was so her friend could grill her on her lack of a love life. Ever since Mack had fallen in love with her hunky Texas Ranger, she'd been trying extra hard to find Laine a man as well.

"Jack being there isn't a positive in my book. I don't really know *him* either. I know I've met him a few times, but you were always with us. Look, you know I love you, but why do I need to go at all?"

"Seriously?" Mack asked, raising her eyebrows.

"Yeah, seriously."

"Okay, here's the thing. Jack is a great photographer. He's one of the best. We were lucky to get him to take the pictures for the calendar. But you know the kind of men Daxton and his friends are... they're manly-men. Alphas. Cops. They're not comfortable stripping and having their picture taken... especially for another man." She held up her hand to hold off Laine's protestation. "I know, I know, Jack isn't gay, but it doesn't matter. It's weird for them. Daxton told me straight out that if I wasn't there, he wouldn't have done it. So I *need* you to go so it's not just Wes and Jack. Please? Wes is the last model I need to finish this calendar. I don't have a backup guy, he's it."

Laine put her head on the table in front of her in defeat. It wasn't as if she didn't have the time. As a realtor, she had the luxury of setting her own schedule. She'd cleared her calendar so she could be there with Mack for the shoot. The Petersons had gladly moved the tour of the house they wanted to see until the next day, and the Whispersons had no issue moving their showing *up*. So she had the time blocked off to spend with her best friend.

Picking up her head, she acquiesced. "Okay, but you owe me, Mackenzie."

"Yay!" Mack clapped her hands softly in glee. "It'll be fun. I know how much you love seeing the old ranches. Wes's ranch has been in his family for at least a hundred years. Daxton said every second he's not working a case, he's out there doing what he loves. He's a true cowboy in every sense of the word. In high school and college, he was on the rodeo team. He did that roping thing."

"What roping thing?"

"You know, where they let a cow go and they ride out behind it on a horse and lasso it with a rope... mm hmm... that's next on our agenda," Mack exclaimed. "We need to go and check out a rodeo."

"We've *been* to a rodeo. We went to one last year," Laine reminded her friend.

"Oh, but we weren't really trying to understand anything, we were just there for the eye candy and so we had an excuse to wear our new boots. We need to go and check out what all the events are."

Laine shook her head. Mack was a goof. She tended to ramble too much and was clumsy as all get-out, but they'd been best friends since middle school. Laine would move heaven and earth for her if she asked, especially after almost losing her to a psycho serial killer. Knowing Mack had found the love of her life made Laine happy, even if she was a bit sad at the same time that she herself hadn't found someone yet.

For so long it'd been just the two of them. They'd make spur-of-the-moment plans, hang out all night at each other's houses, and they were confidants. But Laine could see the writing on the wall. Now that Mack had Dax, he was the center of her life... as it should be. They'd tried to find the right man for themselves all of their lives, and now that Mack had, Laine felt as though she was being left behind. It was a difficult thing to get used to.

"What time do I need to be out at his place?" Laine asked Mack, trying to get her back on track.

"Ten. I'm not sure what Jack has planned for the shoot, but he said he'd like to use a barn in a shot, if it works out when he gets there. He's been very good at being able to put the other guys at ease.

He can figure out the best place to pose them for the shots that show off their assets. Seriously, Laine, you should see some of the pictures so far. Daxton, of course, is hot, but you'd never guess that under his lab coat, Calder is totally ripped. And Quint? Hot damn. Seriously, they could all quit tomorrow, start their own strip club and make millions."

"What about Hayden?"

Mackenzie smiled an evil smile. "Oh, she didn't want to do it, but I bribed her."

"With what?"

"I promised I wouldn't ask her to go shopping with me for at least six months."

Laine giggled. "No wonder she agreed. The last time you dragged her out, she was traumatized for life."

"That's not true!" Mack protested. "Just because I thought she'd look good in that corset thing and the zipper broke and the manager of the store had to come in and cut her out of it, doesn't mean she was traumatized."

"Uh. Yeah. It does."

"Whatever." Mack waved off the incident.

Laine had heard all about the shopping trip from Hayden one night at the bar. The men had thought it was hysterical, but Hayden had glared daggers at everyone for the rest of the night. She wouldn't admit it out loud, but Laine would've paid big bucks to be a fly on the wall during that incident.

"Anyway, I swear you'd think Hayden was a model by looking at the pictures Jack took of her. They went to the shooting range and he somehow convinced her to take off her deputy's jacket, and the picture I think we're using of her is a profile shot where she's aiming downrange. She's wearing a white tank top and her red hair against it is absolutely beautiful. She wanted to keep it up in the bun she always wears it in, but Jack convinced her to take it down. It's a bit curly and the wind blew at exactly the right time for the shot. It's as if she had a fan in front of her, wafting her hair back perfectly. Seriously, I was jealous as all get-out of her hair. Even though she's the only woman in the calendar, I'm so glad we convinced her to do it. The rest of the guys are gonna crap their pants when they see her. She's usually so... mannish. Even I had no idea she was so beautiful. She hides it well."

Laine suddenly looked at her watch. "Crap, I gotta get going. I have an appointment in twenty minutes."

"You going to look at another ranch?" Mackenzie asked, knowing how much her friend loved showing the properties on the outskirts of San Antonio.

Laine wrinkled her nose. "Nope, this one is a plain ol' suburban three bedroom, two bath."

"Poor thing."

"I know, right?"

Mackenzie stood up with Laine and hugged her. "Thank you so much for doing this for me. I swear I wouldn't ask you to go if I didn't think it was important."

"Have you met this Wes guy?" Laine asked Mack, putting her purse strap over her shoulder.

"No, but Daxton says he's easy to work with and he respects him. I guess they're pretty close work friends."

Laine shrugged. "I guess that's as good of a recommendation as the man'll get."

"Damn straight."

They hugged again. "Be safe. I'll call you tomorrow night and you can tell me all about it," Mack said.

"I will. Love you."

"Love you too. Bye."

As Laine headed out to her car, she wondered just what in the world Mackenzie had gotten her into now.

Chapter Two

———— ◆ ————

LAINE PARKED NEXT to a large, black pickup truck and turned off her engine. Gazing at the house with her realtor hat on, she was impressed. It was big, two stories with a huge wraparound porch. She didn't know what it was about porches, but they seemed to make a house cozier and homier. She thought the house was probably at least three thousand square feet, maybe more if it went back farther than she could see from the front.

It was painted a steel-blue color, which stood out among the plains surrounding it. There was a large red barn off to the left and fences as far as she could see. A few horses grazed on the land around both the barn and the house. Overall, it looked idyllic, and Laine could almost imagine little kids running around while their mother sat on the porch swing watching them play.

She shook her head. At thirty-seven, she was too old to have mommy regrets. It wasn't that she *couldn't* have kids, she knew women were able to have them later and later nowadays, but she was at a point in her life where kids weren't high on her priority list anymore. It was interesting, however, that with all the houses she'd shown and sold over the years, none had made her think about what she might be missing in her life more than this one.

A knock on the window next to her head made her screech and duck to the right in fright.

Jack. The photographer was standing next to her car, grinning like a maniac. Laine put a hand to her chest and willed her heart to slow. Criminy, he'd scared her.

She opened the door and stepped out, smacking the large man on the shoulder as she stood next to him. "Not cool, Jack."

"Couldn't resist. You were sitting in your car like a zombie."

"Maybe I was thinking."

"Yeah, well, think on someone else's time. I need to get this done so I can go and take pictures of a Quinceañera."

"Have you seen Wes yet?" Laine asked, pocketing her keys. She'd dressed for comfort today, as she did most days, in a pair of well-worn jeans and her old brown cowboy boots. They were scuffed and not that pretty looking, but they were comfortable. She'd learned after her first trip to a ranch, years ago, that sandals or sneakers weren't the best footwear for the uneven ground of a working farm in Texas.

"Not yet, but one of his employees said he was in the barn and that he was expecting me."

"Let's get this over with, yeah?" Laine asked, already walking toward the large open doors to the spacious building. "Do you have a plan?"

"Not yet. I want to see what the inside of this monstrosity looks like... see if there's a decent place to take some shots. The light is good this morning, but if it's too dark inside, I'll need to find a more appropriate place outdoors instead."

"How many other cowboy shots have you done for the calendar?" Laine questioned as she matched the photographer's stride.

"Actually, none, they were all more law-enforcement based. The other guys and Hayden aren't exactly the cowboy types. That's why I'm excited about this one. Mackenzie told me this guy's the real deal. I'm thinking if I can get what I want, it might be a good cover picture. We *do* live in Texas, after all."

Laine didn't respond, withholding judgement. She'd known a lot of men in her life who wanted others to think they were stereotypical

Texan cowboys, but she could count on one hand the number who she'd actually classify that way. Wearing boots and a Stetson did not make a man a cowboy.

They stopped inside the sliding doors of the barn and waited for their eyes to adjust to the dimmer light. After a few seconds, when she could see clearly, Laine almost gasped at the sight that met them, but managed to refrain.

There were several stalls on either side of the space; most were empty, except for two. There was an obviously pregnant mare in one and a younger colt in another. The loft over their heads held hay bales stacked and ready for the colder months, and on the entire back wall hung various leather tack for the horses and other ranching tools.

But it was the man, who hadn't sensed their presence yet, who stole her breath. He was shirtless, and his jeans rode low on his hips, highlighting his flat, muscular stomach. He was tall, probably a few inches taller than her five-nine, and he wasn't a young guy either... which actually relieved Laine. She would've felt uncomfortable if she'd been attracted to someone in his twenties. There wasn't anything wrong with it, but she'd always preferred older men.

His profile was to them as he shoveled manure out of one of the stalls. The muscles in his back and side rolled and stretched as he scooped the waste out of the hay on the floor and into a wheelbarrow next to him. His biceps flexed as he turned back to the empty stall and continued with his chore.

Laine could've stood there all day doing nothing but watching this amazingly beautiful, rugged man work, but Jack was seemingly not as gobsmacked as she was, because he cleared his throat loudly and asked, "Westin King?"

The man at the other end of the barn lifted his head and nodded in greeting when he saw the two of them standing at the door. He rested the shovel against the wall and headed toward them. He grabbed a rag hanging off the rail of another stall and used it to wipe his hands as he walked.

Laine felt as if she was stuck to the floor. He'd obviously been in the barn working for a while, because even though it wasn't exactly hot yet, his chest was covered with a sheen of sweat. He had dark hair, and some strands were stuck to his forehead, and the hair on his neck was wet as well. With the way his jeans fit, Laine could clearly see the mysterious and sexy-as-hell V-muscles that she'd only seen a couple times in her life. Laine had no idea what they were really called, but whatever they were, this man's were highly defined and pointing toward the Promised Land.

His abs were equally as impressive and she could see a clear six-pack that flexed as he came toward her and Jack. Her eyes roamed down his legs, over his well-worn and dirty jeans to the tips of his brown, well-used boots.

"My eyes are up here," he drawled, clearly amused at her intense perusal of his body.

Laine knew she was blushing, and immediately looked up into his face. His eyes were a dark brown, the color of the mahogany desk she had at home, and he had laugh lines around them. His lips were full and pink and currently pulled up into a smile, as if he knew exactly what she was thinking. Which would be extremely embarrassing, since she'd undressed him and had her way with him in her mind during the few seconds it'd taken for him to get to them.

Thank God Jack was there to run interference before she asked the sexy cowboy to turn around so she could check out his ass.

"Jack Hendershot. It's great to meet you." He held out his hand and the men greeted each other.

"Wes King. Likewise." Then he turned to Laine. "You don't look like any photographer's assistant I've ever seen. Mackenzie?"

She shook her head. "Oh no, I'm Laine, spelled l-a-i-n-e. No y at the end. Laine Parker. Mackenzie is my best friend. She couldn't make it today. I was only coming to keep her company, but then she bailed on me and begged me to still come so you wouldn't feel weird about being half naked with Jack."

Laine froze and forced herself to stop talking. Oh my God. She sounded exactly like Mack. She'd obviously picked up some of the other woman's habit of vomiting out whatever she was thinking when she was nervous. She put her chin down and a hand on her forehead, refusing to look at the man who'd scrambled her brains. She'd never been so embarrassed in all her life.

Wes chuckled, and Laine couldn't help but notice his laugh was just as sexy as the rest of him. "I have to be honest and say I'm extremely glad you aren't Mack."

"You are?" Laine looked at Wes.

He nodded. "Yup. 'Cos I know Mackenzie is taken. It's good to meet you, Laine Parker."

Laine stared at his outstretched hand for a beat, trying to process what he'd just said. He was glad she wasn't Mack because she was taken? Did that mean he had the same immediate attraction to her that she'd had to him? She held out her hand automatically and inwardly groaned at the feel of his calloused hand against her smooth one. Jesus, even his hands were sexy.

Jack nudged her with his shoulder, almost knocking her over, before saying to Wes, "I think this'll work just fine. Do you have any objections to me setting up in here? I need to get my stuff from the car, but it'll just be a few lights to make sure the photos aren't too dark and a reflector disc. I think if we use one of the stalls, it'll be a great backdrop. Maybe afterward we can go outside and find one more location as well, just in case."

"No problem."

"Thanks, I'll be right back."

Laine's head whipped up and she was going to offer to help, so as not to be left alone with this man who made her feel way too much, but Jack was already out the door and headed to his car. She looked at Wes and stuffed both hands in her back pockets to try to prevent herself from doing something crazy, like running her palms up and down his glistening chest.

"So... you're a cowboy." She mentally smacked herself in the forehead. She was *such* a dork.

"Yup, among other things. You want to meet Star?"

Assuming he meant the pregnant mare, Laine nodded, thankful he wasn't going to bring up her inappropriate behavior, and that he was keeping whatever it was between them at a low simmer. She shouldn't have been surprised though, not really. This man was a Texas Ranger... not a twenty-two-year-old kid straight out of college. He was far too suave to say or do something either demeaning or juvenile.

Wes stood back with an arm out, obviously telling her to precede him. Not wanting to seem rude, Laine headed for the stall, all the while conscious that Wes was behind her. Was he looking at her ass? No. He wouldn't do that... would he? She looked back at him. Yup, he was totally checking out her butt.

The thought made her stumble and she would've fallen face first into the hay and dirt at her feet if Wes hadn't caught her elbow.

"Careful."

"Sorry. Wasn't watching where I was going."

Grateful he refrained from commenting further on her clumsiness, she arrived at the gate to Star's stall. Wes leaned up against the door and gestured for Laine to step up on the bottom rung so she could reach over the rails.

"How much longer does she have?" Laine asked, reaching out a hand to pet the beautiful chestnut-brown horse who eagerly came to the door of her stall to greet them.

"Anywhere from a month to a month and a half."

"That much? She looks huge."

"Yeah, but it's actually normal for a horse her size. Here, give her this." Wes held out a carrot he'd grabbed from a bucket behind him. "She'll be your friend for life. She's addicted to them."

Laine held out her hand and took the vegetable from Wes. She held it out to the mare and laughed as Star's horsey lips brushed against her palm when she took it from her. "She's beautiful."

"Yeah."

Laine looked over at Wes. He wasn't looking at the horse, but at her. She immediately felt as if she was fourteen again and Timmy James had told her he thought she was the prettiest girl in school.

"I'm thinking the last stall will work."

Jack's words broke through the spell weaving itself between Wes and Laine. She laughed nervously and stepped off the rail, brushing her palms against her jeans. "What can I do to help?" she asked Jack, hoping he had something for her to do that wouldn't entail her drooling over the man in front of her.

"Here, take this," Jack told her, handing her a silver reflector panel. "It'll only take me about five minutes to set up over here."

Laine grabbed the large, spherical reflector panel that looked like an oversize sun screen people used in their cars. She wandered over to the last stall, watching Jack as if it was the most interesting thing she'd ever seen.

She was completely tongue-tied and had no idea what to say to Wes. She'd been attracted to men before, but not like this. There was something about him that made her lady parts sit up and take notice.

The only thing that made her feel less guilty about the entire situation was that it seemed as though Wes was feeling some of the same things she was. Every time she glanced at him, he was watching her. She couldn't take her eyes off him, and apparently, it was a mutual thing.

Finally, Jack was ready.

"Okay, chicks dig the hat and rope thing, so I'm thinking that's the route we should go. Do you have a preference for if your face is shown in the picture or not?"

"Is that an option?" Wes asked seriously.

Jack shrugged. "Sure. I mean, I don't think any of the other guys cared if their faces were seen or not. The FBI guy said he wasn't going to be doing any more undercover gigs, and the others thought it might be good for their dating life or the image of their respective departments. But it's up to you."

"What do you think?" Wes asked Laine.

"Me?" The word came out as a squeak.

"Yeah, you. What do you find sexier? A faceless cowboy or one where you can see his eyes along with the rest of his body?"

"Um… well, it depends."

"On?"

Laine didn't really want to get into it, but both Wes and Jack were looking at her in expectation.

"On whether or not I was married or dating."

"Go on," Wes encouraged when she didn't elaborate.

"I don't know why it makes a difference, but if you must know… if I was with someone, I think I'd prefer to not see a model's face. It would allow me to put my own guy's face onto the model… so when I fantasized, I'd see the man I loved instead of a stranger."

"And if you were dating the model? Would you prefer single women who bought the calendar to fantasize about a random body or your boyfriend?"

Holy. Crap. Laine couldn't take her eyes away from the hot-as-all-get-out man in front of her. Was he serious? She wasn't sure. But she couldn't help but be honest with him. "If I was dating someone and they were having their picture taken for a sexy publication that I knew horny women of all ages were going to buy to drool over… I'd prefer his face to be hidden so he'd be anonymous. They could enjoy his body, but I'd want his face to be all mine."

Wes didn't respond to her, but turned to Jack and said nonchalantly, as if he wasn't rocking her world, "Faceless."

Jack grinned, but stayed professional. "No problem. Go ahead and pick up the rope that's hanging over there on the wall. We'll start with that looped over your shoulder. Do you have a Stetson in here? We'll definitely need that, especially since we're going the anonymous route."

Laine didn't say another word, but watched silently as Wes followed Jack's instructions, strode to the nearby wall and picked up the rope. She felt the goosebumps pop up on her arms as she thought about Wes's words. Unfortunately, she could feel her nipples harden in response as well. Her body was standing up and taking notice of the sexy-as-hell cowboy in front of her.

The next forty minutes were excruciating for Laine. She hadn't realized how difficult posing for pictures could be. She figured the model just stood around for a bit and that was it. But Jack was a tough taskmaster. He asked Wes to pose in all sorts of positions, most with his head tilted down, shielded by the wide brim of his cowboy hat.

It was the flexing, and the sight of his perspiring chest that made Laine shift where she stood. He was so amazingly sexy, she had a feeling if she was alone with Wes, she wouldn't have been able to control herself... and that wasn't like her at all.

What also wasn't like her was thinking about what the cowboy could do with the rope he posed with. She'd never been into bondage, but thinking about Wes lassoing her and tying her hands to one of the stalls as he bent her over and took her from behind, made her face flush with arousal.

Finally, Jack was satisfied with the pictures he'd gotten inside the barn. They moved outside, where the photographer decided that if Wes leaned against the fence, with the barn and horses grazing in the pasture in the background, it was perfect for a possible cover shot for the calendar. While he set up his cameras again, Wes ambled over to

Laine.

"So… you're friends with Mackenzie, who is Dax's girlfriend. What else?"

"What else, what?"

"I want to know more about you. How old you are, what you do for a living, favorite color, if you'll go out with me next weekend."

Laine bit her lip and looked up at the man next to her. He wasn't that much taller than her, probably four or five inches. His eyes were pinned to hers; he wasn't distracted by anything going on around them, which was heady. She was used to men—and women, for that matter—being distracted by their phones, other people, the houses they were looking at… all sorts of things, so being the recipient of all of Wes's male attention was a bit disconcerting.

"You're awfully forward," Laine said, crossing her arms over her ribcage, trying to act like she wasn't dying to jump in his arms, hook her legs around his waist, and kiss his luscious lips.

One side of those lips quirked up. "I'm no more forward than you, Ms. Parker. You were undressing me with your eyes the entire time I was posing back there… and I can tell you, if we were alone right now, you'd find out how appreciative I am of your eyes on me."

"Uh…" Laine was tongue-tied and had no idea how to respond.

"Just tell me you aren't attached," he demanded.

The hell with it. Laine was attracted to him and it seemed as if Wes was attracted right back. Why was she even trying to play coy? "I'm not attached. Thirty-seven—although you're not supposed to ask a woman how old she is—I'm a realtor, purple, and yes."

Her opinion of Wes rose when he followed the conversation easily. "I'm forty-two, you know what I do for a living, I don't have a favorite color, but I'm thinking I'm becoming partial to purple as well…" He nodded pointedly at the lilac blouse she was wearing.

Laine looked down and blushed when she could see her nipples showing through the cotton bra she'd worn under her tank top. Dang it. She'd thought she'd gotten herself under control. She usually didn't have a problem with spontaneous nipple hard-ons when she was out and about, but obviously this man was making her body stand up and take notice of him without even trying.

Wes continued, "I'll pick you up at your place Friday night." It was a statement and not a question.

Laine quirked an eyebrow. "You will?"

"Yup."

"And if I won't tell you where I live?"

"Mackenzie will."

Darn it. He was right. "Okay, but I'm only allowing it because you're a Texas Ranger. I typically don't let men know where I live before a first date."

"Smart."

"You ready?" Jack asked from a few steps away.

Once again, Laine was surprised by the other man. It seemed as though when she was with Wes, everything else faded away... which was good and bad.

Laine watched as Jack did his thing with Wes for another twenty minutes. The photographer seemed very pleased with Wes, and the shots he'd gotten, and finished up the shoot quickly. He held out his hand to the Ranger. "Thanks for allowing me to interrupt your morning. If you ever want to make some money out of this photo thing, please contact me. Real cowboys are in high demand in the romance novel cover market. You'd make a ton of money without even trying." He chuckled at the horrified look on Wes's face. "Okay, okay, but I had to throw it out there. I know you probably have a ton of stuff to do. I'll send over the best shots for your approval before the calendar goes to print."

"I'd appreciate that."

Jack shrugged. "I figure if you're volunteering your body for charity, it's only fair to allow you to say yes or no to the shots I pick out.

It'll probably be a month or so before you see them. I still have a couple more shoots to do for another project, and of course then I have to edit and put together the calendar."

The photographer turned to Laine. "You'll tell Mack that the shoot went well?"

"Yeah, I'll tell her."

"Great. Thanks for coming out today," Jack added.

"I don't think I was that much of a help," Laine countered honestly.

"Oh, I think you were more of an inspiration than anything else." Jack smirked, referring to the sparks flying between her and Wes.

"Whatever," Laine murmured, blushing.

"See you later, Laine. Drive safe going back into the city," Jack told her seriously as he turned to head back to his car.

"I will, you too," she called out behind him. Laine took a step toward her own car when she was stopped in her tracks by Wes's hand at her elbow.

"Hang on a second... please?"

Laine nodded, not sure why she was nervous to be alone with the charismatic man standing next to her, but she was. She waited for him to say something, but he stood silent until Jack's car was headed down his driveway.

Then, still without a word, Wes put one hand on the side of her neck and the other wrapped around her waist, pulling her close. Laine's hands rested on his chest in surprise as his head dropped down to hers. Her fingers flexed against his warm skin and she had two seconds to let it register that his chest was just as hard as she imagined it would be before he moved.

He didn't ask. He didn't hesitate. Wes took her lips as if it was the hundredth time rather than the first. When she gasped in surprise at the electricity she swore she felt as his lips touched hers, he took advantage and surged his tongue inside her mouth.

Tilting her head at his urging, Laine reciprocated enthusiastically, loving his aggressiveness as his tongue dueled with her own. When he sucked on her lower lip and nipped it gently with his teeth, she whimpered. Lord, the man could kiss.

He pulled away, not bothering to look around to see who might have seen them making out. As though pulled by an invisible force, he leaned down and kissed her once more, but with more tenderness than passion this time. His tongue lazily caressed hers, seemingly not in any rush and without making her feel it was merely a way to butter her up to get into her pants.

Finally, he took a step back, keeping his hand on her waist until she got her balance. "I'm looking forward to next weekend," he said in a husky voice.

"Where are we going?"

"It's a surprise."

"But I won't know what to wear."

"Ah, I should've thought of that. Okay, dress casually comfortable, but I'd love to see some skin." Wes's finger ran along the strap of the tank top over her shoulder.

Laine knew she should smack his hand away, but his touch felt so good, she knew she wouldn't.

"Okay, but you should know I get cold easily. I swear I don't know what it is about Texas that when the temperature goes above eighty, the people in charge of the air conditioning in buildings think they need to crank it down to fifty."

"I won't let you get cold."

Lord, it was as if they were having sex, but standing upright... and a foot from each other.

"Okay then. Skin, comfy, and casual. I think I can do that."

"Good. Drive safe, and I'll see you Friday around five-thirty."

Laine could only nod as she backed away from Wes. She kept eye contact with him until she reached her car. Fumbling into her pocket for her keys, she finally looked away as she got into the driver's seat.

Driving down the road away from the ranch, Laine looked in the rear-view mirror and saw Wes standing where she'd left him, his eyes on her car as she drove away.

Chapter Three

———◆———

"**Y**OU ARE IN big trouble, sister," Laine told Mackenzie that night when she called to tell her how the photo shoot went.

"Why? What happened?" Mack asked, alarmed.

"You didn't tell me how crazy hot that man was."

There was silence on the phone, which was telling, as Mackenzie was never at a loss for words. After a long moment, she seemed to come back to herself. "What? Are you kidding? I didn't *know*. I mean, we had that discussion in the bar after Quint's girlfriend, Corrie, was rescued. Everyone said he was good looking, but it's not like Daxton would tell me that one of his coworkers was *sexy* or anything. I take it the cowboy thing worked for him? Did you ask him out? Was it weird? How did he act with Jack?"

Used to her friend's nonstop questions, Laine waited until she wound down to speak. "First of all, yes, the cowboy thing worked *really* well for Wes. When we walked into the barn he was shoveling shit out of one of the stalls, shirtless. And let me tell you, I almost had a spontaneous orgasm right then and there."

Laine heard Mack laughing, but went on.

"Jack was cool. But I got sucked into a conversation about whether or not they should take shots that would show his face and Wes actually asked me," Laine's voice dropped, mimicking Wes's low, sexy voice, "'if you were dating the model, would you want your man's face to be shown or not'?"

"He. Did. *Not*!" Mackenzie exclaimed, almost hyperventilating.

"Oh, he did."

"And what did you say?"

"I said that if I was dating someone, I wouldn't want other women to fantasize over my man's face. That they could drool over his body, but his face was all mine. So Wes turned to Jack and told him 'faceless', and so he posed with his hat over his face."

"Holy shitballs."

Laine could understand Mack's reaction, because it was much the same as she'd had standing in front of Wes when he'd asked. "And he's taking me out next Friday."

"Really?"

"Really."

"Truly?"

"Yes, Mack. Truly." Laine heard her friend sniff. "Are you crying? What's wrong?"

"I'm just... I'm so happy. I love Daxton with all my heart, but a part of me was sad that you didn't have a man of your own. I've had friends who I've grown apart from because they got married and went on with their married life. I didn't want that ever to happen with us. And I'm just so happy. Because not only are you with Wes, but he's a Texas Ranger just like Daxton. It's like it was meant to be."

"Mack," Laine warned. "This is one date. Don't marry us off yet."

"I know, I know, but this is so *cool*. Where are you going?"

"I don't know. He wouldn't tell me."

"But how do you know what to wear?" Mackenzie asked.

Laine snorted. "I know, right? That's *exactly* what I said! He told me to dress casually, comfortable... and to show some skin."

"You know what this means, right?"

"No, what?"

"We get to go shopping!"

Laine laughed at her friend. Shopping wasn't usually her favorite thing to do, but Mackenzie was right, Laine wanted to look her best, and a new outfit that flattered her always made her feel good about herself and gave her a boost of confidence.

THE NEXT WEEK seemed to go by extremely slowly. Monday came quick enough, and Laine and Mack had spent Sunday afternoon at the mall, but between indecisive homebuyers and house inspections that didn't go the way the sellers wanted them to, it'd been a long week. Laine had only gotten to scope out one rural property as well, which was one of her favorite things to do.

But it was *finally* Friday. Laine had left work around noon so she could go home and get ready and try to get rid of her nerves. She'd taken a long bath to relax and dressed in the new pair of Lucky jeans she'd bought the previous weekend. She'd found the perfect blouse for her date as well… at least Mackenzie reassured her it was perfect.

It was a dark purple that looked black in low light. It was sleeveless, with a high neck in the front. It was made of a silky material that draped her flatteringly. It looked modest from the front, but the back scooped down to the middle of her spine, leaving most of her back bare. It wasn't so crass as to dip down to her butt crack, but a nice, modest—if you could call this shirt modest—mid-back drape. A regular bra wouldn't work with the shirt, but there was no way Laine was going without one. Her nipple hard-on fiasco was still fresh in her mind, so she'd made a detour to the lingerie shop in the mall and bought a bra that had one of those versatile straps to it.

Laine refused to get a push-up bra, not wanting to falsely advertise what she didn't have, but she made sure there was adequate padding in the lacy contraption so if (who was she kidding… *when*) her nipples peaked, she wouldn't advertise it to the world… or Wes. Been there, done that, got the T-shirt. The straps wound around the sides of her ribcage and her lower back, safely tucked away below the drape on the back of the shirt.

It felt sexy and daring... and way more aggressive than Laine would've worn in the past. There was something about Wes that made her feel at ease and safe. His profession had something to do with that, of course, but it was ultimately him. He'd obviously been attracted to her, but other than the stolen kiss, he'd controlled himself and hadn't acted like a hormone-driven asshole.

On her feet, she'd strapped a pair of open-toed sandals with a slight heel. Not high enough that she'd have to worry about tripping over her own feet, but enough to give her an extra inch or so. They had a thick block heel and a delicate strap that wound around her ankle.

She couldn't wait to see what Wes had in store for them tonight. Laine had spoken with Mack earlier, promising to call no matter what time she got home that night, as was their custom. It was five twenty-three when her doorbell rang. Laine was glad Wes was early; she couldn't stand when people were late. Her grandmother had been late for everything when Laine was little. They'd usually tell her something started fifteen minutes earlier than it did, just so they could get there on time.

Looking through the peephole to make sure it was Wes before she opened the door, Laine unlocked the deadbolt, opened the thick oak door and stared at the man standing on her stoop.

Wes looked every inch as delicious today as he had the week before. He was wearing a pair of black jeans and a western style shirt that had what looked like snaps up the front of it. It was a deep purple color... not as dark as her own shirt, but purple all the same. It figured they matched. They really were on the same wavelength.

The top two buttons of his shirt were open and Laine could see he was wearing a white tee under the button-up top. He had on a pair of what she would call "dress-up boots," as they looked shiny and pristine.

To top off his outfit, he was holding a black Stetson in one hand, and a single purple rose in the other. She had no idea where in the world he'd found a purple rose, but at the moment, she didn't care.

"Hi, you look amazing," Wes observed as she simply stood there staring at him.

His words shook her out of her holy-hell-is-this-man-hot daze. "Oh, yeah. You do too. You want to come in while I get my purse?"

"No. I'll wait here."

"Really?" Laine asked, somewhat confused. His answer wasn't what she'd expected.

"First, even though you invited me, I don't want to overstep my bounds. Second, if I come in, I'm not going to want to leave. So yeah, I'll wait here."

"Oh... okay." Somehow she'd forgotten how blunt the man could be.

He held out the rose to her. "Better take this and put it in some water though. Wouldn't want it to die while we're out and about."

Laine reached out and took hold of the rose, bringing it to her nose to smell before telling him, "Thank you. It's beautiful. I'll be right back." She whirled around, leaving the door open, to head back inside to fill a glass of water for the flower and grab her purse.

After a quick trip to the kitchen to fill up a large glass to put the rose in, she went back into the living room where she'd been pacing before Wes arrived, and over to the coffee table. She grabbed her purse and her sweater, which she'd put on the back of her suede couch so she wouldn't forget it, and headed back to her front porch and Wes.

He took a step back as she exited the house and waited patiently as she locked her front door. Laine put her keys in her purse and hooked it over her elbow as she turned back to him. Wes held out his hand, indicating that she precede him down the two stairs and to her front walk-way. She felt his hand on her bare back a split second before he spoke in an almost too-casual way.

"Mind you, I wasn't disappointed in the least when you opened the door, but I was a bit surprised at your choice of attire. I figured your interpretation of 'showing some skin' was different than mine… but I was okay with that." Laine felt his thumb caressing her spine as they walked toward his large black truck. "But it's a good thing I turned down your invitation to come into your house, because, darlin', if I'd have seen the back of this shirt before you asked me in, I would've taken you up on it and we wouldn't have left at all."

Laine smiled and looked over her shoulder at him. The compliment was awesome to hear and if she was being honest with herself, she would've been disappointed if he hadn't said anything about it at all. She'd chosen it to on purpose to try to make an impression. It was nice to have that validated. Wes was walking next to her, and she shivered once again as he shifted closer to her and his hand wrapped around her bare side under her shirt, not quite inappropriate-for-a-first-date territory… but close.

"We can still go back inside. We haven't left yet," Laine noted enthusiastically. She was all for the dating thing, but with the way she felt while around Wes, and with his warm palm on her side, she could totally do the sex thing first, then the dating thing.

She felt his hand squeeze her waist in reaction to her words, before he relaxed. "Nope. No can do. We're out, and we're staying that way… at least for a couple of hours. I've got plans, woman, and your seduction attempts will have to wait."

"*My* seduction attempts? *You* were the one who told me to show some skin," Laine protested weakly, loving his sense of humor.

"You're right, I did," Wes chuckled as he clicked the locks on his truck. He opened the passenger door without another word, finally easing his hand out from under her shirt to hold it out for her to grab on to as she hiked herself up and into the seat. When she was settled, Wes leaned in, resting one arm against the doorframe.

"I don't know what it is about you, Laine Parker. I gave myself a talk before I got out of the truck. I told myself I would keep my hands to myself and be a complete gentleman. But there's just something about you that makes me want to chuck all that away and take you down to the ground and ravish you. I don't know if it's the look in your eye that tells me you want to do the same thing to me, or if it's just some crazy 'it's been too long since I've held a sexy woman in my arms' thing. Whatever it is… rest assured, I like it. I like feeling this way. And just so you know, as much as I might want to, I'm not going to make love with you tonight. I find myself wanting to draw out this anticipation. I have a feeling the wait will be worth it. That *you'll* be worth it."

Laine didn't know what to say, she could only sit there with her mouth open in shock as Wes leaned back and shut the door, sealing her inside his truck. As he walked around to the driver's side, Laine muttered to herself, "Holy mother of God. I've hit the mother lode."

Chapter Four

—————◆—————

WES HELD ON to Laine's hand as they left the movie theater. He'd done the typical dinner and movie date for their entertainment that evening. It wasn't that unique, but he wanted to put her at ease before they headed back out to his ranch. She knew he was a Texas Ranger, but that didn't mean she should trust him immediately. Just being in law enforcement didn't mean a man was trustworthy, although it should. Nothing pissed him off more than a crooked cop.

He'd been completely bowled over by her tonight. First, standing on her doorstep and getting a look at her bare back as she'd turned away from him almost made him shoot off in his pants. Wes knew he wasn't a young man. While he'd seen his fair share of pretty women in his forty-two years, something about Laine was different, and she turned him on, big-time.

Her shirt, showing off her entire back, wasn't what he'd expected when she'd turned to lock her door, but it was a nice surprise. He'd grilled Dax earlier that week, wanting to know as much information as he could about Laine before their date. Dax didn't say a lot, it wasn't in his nature to gossip, but he did say enough for Wes to understand that she was a good person, and if he played with her emotions, Dax would kick his ass.

It was the implied threat that did the most to convince Wes that Laine was someone he wanted to get to know better. If Dax didn't seem to care if Wes wanted a one-night stand, it would mean Laine wasn't relationship material. It seemed like Laine was a woman who had a good head on her shoulders and she knew what she wanted... and as it turned out, it looked like she wanted him as much as he wanted her.

They'd gone to a local hole-in-the-wall steak place that Wes knew about. He'd assisted the owner with a robbery investigation a few years back, and the man hadn't ever forgotten. Wes made a point to eat there as often as possible, which wasn't a hardship since the food was delicious. Laine had laughed without being self-conscious, and had warmly greeted the owner as if he was a millionaire instead of just a humble local restauranteur.

She was good company, eating a hearty dinner and not counting calories, laughing at his stories, contributing to the conversation easily, not bragging about her career, and not acting over the top regarding his. In short, Laine was interesting, funny, sexy, and Wes couldn't wait to get his hands on her.

He hadn't lied to her earlier when he said they wouldn't make love that night. Oh, Wes wanted inside her more than he wanted a lot of things in life, but he was enjoying the heavy glances and the way she made his heart rate increase with every small touch. Wes wanted to draw it out because he knew when he finally got Laine in his bed, it was going to be mind-blowing.

The movie had been an action flick, her choice. The special effects were overdone, as was the acting, but they both knew they weren't really there for the movie. He sat next to Laine with his arm tucked around her waist, his hand under her shirt, as she cuddled into him. Thank goodness he'd had the foresight to choose one of the newer cineplexes that had the rocking seats with the armrests that could be folded up.

Her perfume distracted him from the movie and after it was over, if someone had asked what the plot was, Wes wasn't sure he would've been able to say anything about it with any conviction.

"Thank you for a wonderful night," Laine said as they headed toward his truck in the parking lot.

"Oh, the night isn't over yet. The best part is still to come."

"The best part? Even better than the fried Oreos at dinner? You'll have to try pretty hard to top that one, Ranger."

"Darlin', you haven't seen anything yet." Wes felt Laine shiver at his endearment, but was too much of a gentleman to say anything about it.

He drove them to his ranch, and to her credit, she didn't protest or otherwise tell him to take her home.

When they stopped, she commented dryly, "I thought we weren't going to have sex."

"We aren't. First of all, I said we weren't going to make love, not have sex. I have a feeling it will never be just sex between us. Secondly, I want to show you something... and no, it's not in my bedroom," Wes joked before she could comment. Her snarkiness was just one more thing he liked about her.

Wes grabbed her hand and relaxed when she didn't hesitate to squeeze his in return. "Lead on, oh fearless cowboy. But remember, I'm not wearing my boots."

"You don't have far to walk, just hold on to me and I'll make sure you don't fall." He led them to the barn, grabbing a canvas jacket that was hanging on a hook just inside the double doors. He helped Laine into it then continued, holding on to her hand, to the backside of the large structure, relieved to see the four-wheeler sitting just where he'd asked his foreman to put it when he was done with it for the day. He threw his leg over and looked back at Laine. "Climb on, darlin'."

"Really? Cool!"

Wes was relieved at her reaction. Once upon a time, he'd wanted to do this same thing with another woman he'd just begun to date, and she'd recoiled in horror at the thought of riding through his ranch on the back of an ATV.

He took a deep breath as Laine didn't even hesitate and got on behind him. She immediately wrapped her arms around him and snuggled into his back. Wes took a moment to enjoy the sensation of being in Laine's arms. He could feel her warmth soak into his skin and suddenly had a vision of them lying in bed snuggled together, just like this.

He sat up a bit straighter and put one hand on her thigh next to his, and with the other, he reached behind him and awkwardly wrapped it around her back. They sat like that for a moment, before Wes reached for the handlebars and started the machine.

Being careful not to go too fast so the ride wasn't as bumpy—and to make it last as long as possible—Wes finally pulled up to their destination and cut the engine. They were in the middle of his largest pasture, and once the light to the four-wheeler was cut, it was pitch dark.

"Wow, I didn't realize how dark it could get out here," Laine said with a nervous laugh.

Wes helped her stand, and kept her hand in his. He reached into the bag between the handlebars, pulled out a flashlight and clicked it on. "Yeah, without the moonlight or the city lights, it's tough to navigate. Here, watch your step, we don't have far to go."

Wes kept the light focused on the ground so they wouldn't step into a hole, any cow patties, or trip over any rocks or sticks. Cognizant of the sandals Laine was wearing, he'd wanted to get as close to their destination as possible with the four-wheeler, while still keeping it a secret until the last minute. After a few minutes, he raised the light and showed Laine where he'd been taking them.

"Oh my."

"Is that an 'oh my, this is neat' or an 'oh my, what in the world was he thinking'?" Wes teased.

"Definitely the former. This is amazing."

Wes shrugged. *This* was two plastic lawn chairs, the kind where you were mostly reclined when you sat in one, sitting side by side. Each had a throw blanket on the seat in case it got too chilly. There was a bottle of wine and two glasses sitting in a small basket next to them. It wasn't fancy, but it was something Wes thought Laine might like.

He'd never admit it, but when he'd talked to Dax about Laine, he'd quizzed him about what she liked to drink. He'd said that she was similar to Mackenzie. No-frills, down-to-earth, and fairly easy to please. He told him what kind of wine he'd see her drinking when she hung out with him and Mackenzie. The last thing Wes wanted to do was offer up a nice romantic gesture, and have it fall flat because she was a recovering alcoholic or she didn't like wine.

Wes walked Laine to the first chair and helped her get settled. He draped the blanket over her so she was comfortable. Then he poured them each a glass of the specialty wine from the Brennan Vineyards in Comanche, Texas. He clicked off the flashlight, leaving them sitting in the darkness of the evening. Wes waited for her to take a sip, and wasn't disappointed in her reaction.

"How in the world did you know this was one of my favorite wines?"

Wes took a sip of the fruity alcohol and sat back. "I have my ways."

Laine chuckled and sat back herself. "Whatever. You totally asked Mackenzie, didn't you?"

"Maybe."

"Anyway, I guess it doesn't really matter. Thank you. Seriously, this is the best ending to a great date."

"Look up."

"What?" Laine asked in surprise.

"Look up. You'll never find a more beautiful view of the stars than out here in the middle of nowhere."

Laine was silent for a moment as she took in the light show above her head. "Wow. I had no idea. I can see the Milky Way so easily."

"Um hum."

"And Orion's belt, and the big dipper."

Wes could hear her turning in her seat.

"And there, there's the little dipper. Holy cow. This is amazing."

Wes reached over, found her free hand in the darkness and wrapped his fingers around hers. They sat there in silence for quite a while, drinking wine, listening to the sounds of the crickets and other animals around them, and enjoying the serenity of the night.

"Why aren't you married?" Laine's question was whispered, as if she didn't want to break the beauty of the moment. "I mean, you seem like a decent guy." She chuckled to show him she was teasing him. "I don't get it."

"The same reason you're still single, I imagine," Wes told her honestly. "I never found the right woman at the right time. When I was younger, I focused on my career and I thought I'd have lots of time to find someone and start a family. Once I was accepted into the Rangers, I'd been an officer for quite a while, and I guess I'd become cynical. I hadn't run into many women who I could imagine spending the rest of my life with. They were either eager to sleep with a cop, just to say they did, or they weren't at a point in their lives that *they* wanted to settle down."

Laine murmured in agreement. "That's it exactly. I was all ready to pop out two-point-five kids when I was in my twenties, but all the men I met weren't eager to start a family. They wanted to sow their wild oats or some such thing. Then when Mack and I hit our thirties, it was all about our careers and spending time with each other. That sounds bad, but when she moved here leaving me in Houston, I was so lonely without her. We'd become as close as sisters and I was depressed. I'd go straight home from work and spend as much time as possible talking to her on the phone and over the Internet. I finally decided enough was enough and packed up my things and hightailed it down here. Then there was getting used to the new area and trying to get my feet under me and make a name for myself as a realtor here. Not the easiest thing to do, I'll have you know."

Wes squeezed her hand in commiseration. "How are you guys now that she has Dax?"

"Actually, good," Laine told him with no hesitation. "I thought it'd be weird. I mean, she has someone else full time in her life, but she's never, not once, made me feel like a third wheel. Maybe it's because we're older and understand how important friends are. Whatever it is, I'm very grateful."

"You don't resent him?"

"Dax? For what? Loving Mackenzie? Wanting the best for her? Saving her life? Hell no. I love that man as if he's my brother. As far as I'm concerned, I'm writing him into my will."

Wes chuckled and she continued, "Seriously, I'm too old to be jealous, and he gives me no reason to be. I talk to Mack all the time, almost every night still, we get together for girls' night out all the time and he has no issue with us having sleepovers."

They were quiet for a moment, before Wes broke the silence with what had been on his mind all night, certainly since after dinner. "I like you, Laine Parker. I'm not sure why it took so long for us to cross paths, but I swear when I turned around and saw you standing in the doorway to my barn, I wanted to get to know you better. You're easy to be around, you're beautiful and funny, and I just plain enjoy being in your company."

He fell silent, not sure what he was expecting the wonderful woman next to him to say, but he couldn't have held back the words if his life had depended on it. He was too old to play games.

"I thought it was only me. I mean, we obviously have this crazy chemistry, but I like being around you too... and not just because you're hot." Laine's words were soft and filled with awe.

"Nope."

"Thank God. But you know what this means, don't you?"

"What, darlin'?"

"I'm going to have to live the rest of my life with Mack gloating and saying she set us up."

Wes laughed and squeezed Laine's hand. "I can live with that."

"Yeah, me too."

They sat in their chairs, looking up at the stars and talking long into the night. Wes finally knew it was time to take Laine home when she didn't answer one of his questions and he looked over and she was sound asleep. He sat, watching her sleep for twenty minutes or so, barely able to make out the features of her face in the darkness, but thanking his lucky stars they'd somehow managed to find each other in the million or so people who lived in San Antonio.

Maybe it was luck. Maybe it was fate. Whatever it was, Wes was going to do what he could to see if they could make it work, because Laine was everything he'd looked for all his life.

Chapter Five

————— ◆ —————

LAINE LAY IN bed and shot off a quick text to Mack. It was late... or early, depending on how you looked at it, but she didn't want her friend to worry about her.

Just got home. A.M.A.Z.I.N.G. We'll talk later. Love you.

Laine yawned and put the phone on her nightstand. Mack was either asleep or busy gettin' it on with Dax, and probably wouldn't respond until the morning. She closed her eyes, exhausted, but running high on adrenaline and hormones at the same time.

The kiss Wes had given her at her door had made her wetter than some foreplay she'd had in the past. She'd left the light on before leaving earlier, but after she'd opened her door, Wes had reached around and turned it off, plunging them back into darkness, with only the light from her kitchen faintly illuminating the area around them.

He'd taken her into his arms and proceeded to make love to her mouth—that was the only way to describe how he'd kissed her. Wes's hands had roamed into dangerous territory, quickly learning the intricacies of how she was able to wear a bra with that shirt, but her own hands had wandered too, discovering that he was a briefs man instead of boxers.

Wes had been the one to pull away, regretfully. He'd rested his forehead on hers and moved his hands down to her waist, tucking them under the waistband of her jeans. "Lord, darlin'. You are somethin' else."

"I take it that's good?"

"Oh yeah, that's good. When can I see you again?" he'd asked, impatience clear in his voice.

"Depends."

"On?"

"On your thoughts on having sex on a second date as opposed to the first."

Laine laughed out loud, the sound echoing off the empty walls, remembering his response. His hands had tightened at her sides and he'd told her, "Dammit, woman. You're killin' me. Tomorrow we have one of those crazy softball games with the firefighters. I'm not on Dax's team, but the Rangers from Division 10 are as much a bunch of cheaters as Dax's firefighter friends from Station 7. After the game, I have to head down to Galveston to interview a witness. I'm not going to get back until late. Sunday night, I'm also working."

Laine had told him that she was extremely busy the next week with house showings and inspections. It seemed like every newlywed in the city wanted her to show them a house in the next seven days.

"Next Saturday," Wes had told her decisively. "Make it happen. You want me to pick you up, or will you meet me at my ranch?"

"I'll meet you there. What time?" Laine didn't even pretend to not want to see him again as much as it seemed he wanted to see *her* again.

"Whenever the fuck you want."

Laine had laughed. "Okay, Wes. I'm looking forward to it."

"It?"

She'd blushed and told him, "Yeah, spending the day with you. What did you think I meant?"

As usual, he didn't hold back his thoughts or his words. "Spending the day with me. Feeling me deep inside you as you come for me. My tongue on your pussy. My hands all over you."

"Wes!"

"Laine!"

"Lord have mercy."

He'd gotten serious. "You've unleashed a monster, darlin', I hope you know that. I can't wait to see you either. All of you. But yes, I enjoy talking to you and doing nothing with you as well. I do have to get some chores done around the ranch, but maybe you'd be interested in watching and helping with some of them?'

"Of course I would. I'm not just going to sit around while you do all the work."

"I never thought you would."

Wes had kissed her again, hard and brief before letting go and stepping back. "Be safe next week. I'll see you on Saturday."

Laine stretched in her bed and refused to touch herself. She could feel the anticipation building inside, but wanted to wait. The books and movies always said orgasms could be better when they were a long time in coming. She laughed out loud at that. Jeez, what a bad pun. But whatever, she'd hold off and see if the sex with one Wes King was as good in person as it was in her head. Lord help them both if it was.

THE NEXT DAY, Laine sat on Mack's couch, holding a pillow to her chest and trying to explain to Mack exactly how she was feeling about how fast things were moving with her and Wes.

"So there we were, sitting in the dark, looking up at the sky, and all I could think was that I could see myself sitting there forty years in the future, holding his hand and mulling over how great our life had been."

"And? What's wrong with that?" Mackenzie asked seriously.

"What's wrong with it? Mack, I met the man a week ago. That's what's wrong with that. How can I feel deep down that this man is meant to be mine when I just met him?"

"Do you love him?"

"No."

Mack didn't say anything and the silence stretched on, until Laine felt she had to clarify. "I mean, I don't really know him well enough to know if I love him or not."

"You're not fifteen. Or even twenty-two, Laine."

"I know."

"You've dated. You've been in love before."

"Yeah."

"So if you're imagining yourself being with him when you're old and gray, I think you owe it to yourself, and to Wes, to take it seriously. No one's asking you to run off and marry him tomorrow. But don't sell yourself short. Date him. Sleep with him. See how things go. But whatever you do, don't end things before they get started because you're scared you might actually be compatible and could live happily ever after."

"Why do you have to be so damn smart?"

"Because," Mack said smugly. "And you know what else?"

"What?"

"Just remember who set you up."

Laine rolled her eyes and threw the pillow she'd been clutching at Mackenzie. "I knew you were going to go there sooner or later. You didn't actually set us up. You backed out of your commitment and made me go by myself. If he would've been a serial killer, you'd be thinking differently right about now."

"Yeah, well, he wasn't and he's not. And you're gonna get some fantastic sex next weekend... so you should be buying me a present every year on that date for forcing you to go without me."

Laine laughed. "You know what? You're right. And I swear, if this ends up good, I'll send you a dozen roses every year on the anniversary of that damn calendar photo shoot in thanks."

"Deal."

The two friends smiled at each other for a beat before Mack leaned over and took Laine in her arms. "I love you. I always wished I had a blood sister, but even if I did, she wouldn't be as wonderful as you are."

"Ditto."

They hugged for a moment before Mackenzie pulled away. "Come on, I'm starved. I think we've got some leftovers we can dig into."

"Sounds good."

"Laine?"

"Yeah."

"You had better call me as soon as you come up for air next weekend."

"I will. You know I will."

Chapter Six

———•♦•———

"**Y**OU'RE COMING OVER tomorrow still, right?" Wes asked Laine the following Friday toward the end of their nightly phone call. Even though they'd both been extremely busy, they'd found the time to connect via the phone each night. One night they'd only been able to talk for ten minutes, but another they'd carved out a couple of hours.

"Of course. I thought I'd get there around eleven or so. Is that too early?"

"No. That'll give me enough time to get most of the chores knocked out. I'll talk to my foreman and make sure he's got everything under control, although I have no doubt he will. Want to take a ride with me?"

"A ride? On a horse?"

"Yes. On a horse." Wes laughed.

"Sure, but I should warn you, I'm not that good. I've been on a few trail rides and stuff, but I think the last nag I was on was about four hundred years old. The only thing it was interested in was getting back to the barn and eating some hay."

"I'll take care of you, Laine. I won't let you get hurt."

"Promise?"

"Promise."

"Okay then. But not a long one... okay? I don't want to be too sore."

"You got it. I wouldn't do that to you... or us. Just a short ride. I need to check the fence line to see if there're any holes or if it otherwise needs repairing, so we'll go nice and easy and take as many breaks as you need. How about we have a picnic lunch while we're out too?"

"You're too good to be true."

"Nah, I just know how hungry I get while I'm riding the fence."

Laine laughed. "Okay, if you say so."

"I'm looking forward to spending time with you. And I'm not just talking about in bed."

"Me too. It's been a long week."

"Very long. It's weird, the things that reminded me of you as I went through my days."

"Really? Like what?"

"Lots of things. A billboard for a winery. A news article about a meteorite shower coming up next week. I pulled over a woman and she was wearing a purple shirt... I even let her off with a warning because what she was wearing reminded me so much of you. Hearing one of my fellow Rangers talk about a rodeo."

"A rodeo made you think about me?"

"Yeah... rodeo... cowboys... rope... made me think about you eyeballin' me during my photo shoot."

"Whatever, smarty."

"I just wanted you to know that as much as I'm looking forward to seeing you naked on my sheets, I'm just as much looking forward to holding your hand, watching you enjoy your lunch, seeing you interact with Star... it's everything. I feel like a little kid who gets to spend all day at the amusement park. I feel like a teenager again, looking forward to a first date. The anticipation is killing me."

"I hope the reality is as good as your expectations," Laine said a bit nervously.

"I have absolutely no doubt it will be. So... eleven, right?"

"Yeah. That'll give me time to sleep in, have my three cups of coffee so I can wake up, and to pretty myself up for you."

"Bring an overnight bag."

"I'd planned on it," Laine told Wes without missing a beat.

"Shit. You're perfect."

"Not really, but I'll happily let you think it."

"Have a good rest of the night. I'll see you in the morning," Wes told her in a soft voice.

"You too. Later."

Laine clicked off the phone and smiled. She'd thought a lot about what Mack had told her the other day. It had been very insightful and deep, and she'd been exactly right. Laine decided that whatever happened tomorrow, she wasn't going to sweat it. She liked Wes a lot. He was handsome, sexy, and honorable, and she'd be an idiot to blow him off because she was afraid she liked him too much.

Eleven o'clock couldn't come fast enough.

IT WAS AFTER dinner on Saturday night and Laine lay in the circle of Wes's arms on his couch. She should've been tired after the long day, but she was wired and more than ready to take her relationship with Wes to the next level.

She'd arrived right at eleven that morning and was met by Wes in front of his house with a toe-curling kiss. He was wearing a tight T-shirt and a pair of jeans with his brown work boots. His ever-present cowboy hat on his head, shading his face from the sun. He'd taken her hand without a word and led her into the barn, where they had a bit more privacy, and proceeded to kiss her to within an inch of her life.

Reluctantly he'd pulled away, and had helped her mount a gentle mare. They'd ridden lazily along the fence line of his large property. Every now and then, he'd stop to make some adjustments to and reinforce parts of the fence. Each time, he'd helped Laine dismount and she'd assisted him where she could.

They'd stopped and had lunch under a few trees on the far north side of the pasture. They'd made out after they'd eaten and Wes had pulled back before they'd gone too far. He'd looked sheepishly at her and said, "I swear I had only planned for us to eat lunch."

He'd been so earnest, all Laine could do was laugh.

They'd arrived back to the barn and made their way into the house. They'd talked some more, eaten a light dinner, and watched a movie. The show had long since been over, but neither had the desire to get up and put in a new one, so they sat in each other's arms, enjoying being together.

"Tell me you feel it too," Wes said during a lull in the conversation.

"What? The anticipation? The electricity? Yeah, I feel it too," Laine reassured him.

"I keep telling myself that it's too soon. I haven't been this interested in a woman in a long time."

"I know. I feel like I should consider myself a slut for even contemplating going to bed with you tonight, but I don't. Not in the least. It feels right." Laine looked up at Wes and put her hand on his face. "Take me to bed?"

"With pleasure," Wes told her, standing up, grabbing hold of her hand as he did.

Laine stood up with him and followed him into his bedroom.

WES FELT THE adrenaline coursing through his veins. He was more hyped up to see Laine naked for the first time, to feel her skin next to his own, than he was when he tracked down a fugitive. He hadn't really thought about finding a woman he could spend the rest of his life with… figuring no one would really want to hole themselves up on his ranch and all that came with being married to a rancher. He wasn't ready to pull out a ring and ask Laine to marry him. But he liked her. A lot. He wanted to spend more time with her... not to mention, he really, *really* wanted to get her into his bed.

Reaching behind his neck, Wes pulled his T-shirt off with one quick tug. He smiled as Laine's eyes widened at the sight of his wide chest. Not feeling self-conscious in the least, Wes undid his jeans and pushed them down his legs until he was standing in his boxer-briefs, which left nothing to the imagination. He was way too excited at this point to hide his erection or even try to control it.

Laine reached for the hem of her own shirt and slowly drew it up and over her head. She bit her lip and paused in her disrobing.

Seeing her discomfort, Wes took over, not wanting to do anything to make her feel ill at ease. He soothed his hands from her shoulders to her wrists and back up. "You're beautiful, Laine. Never doubt that I find you attractive." He ran his palms over her breasts, still covered in her lacy bra. "I'll never forget the sight of you standing in front of me outside my barn, blushing when you realized how hard your nipples were as you'd been gawking at me."

She smiled up at him at that. "I was so embarrassed to know I was showing you a full nipple hard-on."

Wes chuckled. "Nipple hard-on?"

Laine nodded. "Yeah, me and Mack came up with that term in the tenth grade. We'd been at a football game and it was raining. We'd forgotten our jackets and were freezing. A freshman cymbal player looked at us and his eyes got huge. We didn't know what his problem was until we scrutinized each other. We decided our hard nipples were the equivalent to a guy getting a hard-on at an inconvenient time."

Wes smiled at Laine's story while he reached around her back, unhooked her bra, easing it down her arms and dropped it on the floor. He lifted her tits in his hands and gently squeezed, not taking his eyes away from her hard little nipples, amazed when they tightened further in front of his eyes.

"This moment will forever be engrained into my head." He glanced up and looked Laine in the eyes for a moment, before gazing down at his prize again. "My mouth is watering, I want to taste you so badly." He took a step closer to her so she could feel his erection against her lower stomach. "I feel like I could burst just from looking at you, from smelling your arousal." When she moaned, he added, "From listening to the sounds you make."

Wes ran his thumbs over her nipples once... then twice, before lowering his hands to her pants. "If I don't get your pants off, I might just do that." He deftly undid the button on her jeans and unzipped them, pushing them, along with her panties, down her legs without missing a beat. "Step out, darlin', then scoot back on the bed."

Wes took care of his own underwear as Laine moved onto his mattress. He noticed her eyes were taking in his body as much as he was taking in hers. She was all woman. Yes, she was tall and slender, but she had an hourglass shape, which made his hands itch to trace her slight curves, and she had a pair of tits that made him want to bury his head between them.

Laine licked her lips and she took her time taking him in as well. "My God, you are gorgeous, Wes. Seriously. I feel like the band geek who somehow managed to snare the quarterback."

Wes crawled over to Laine on his hands and knees and his legs almost gave out when she took his cock in her hand and caressed him.

"You wouldn't have liked me back in high school. I was a self-centered prick who probably wouldn't have taken a second glance at anyone outside my own circle. I know better now. When I see the sexiest realtor I've ever seen in my life, I'm not dumb enough to hesitate to make her mine."

Wes ran his hand from Laine's hip up to her chest, taking her breast in his hand again, pushing it up as he came down onto his elbow next to her. He licked the rosy nipple begging for his touch, watching as her pectoral muscle jumped under his ministrations, before stating, "And make no mistake, Laine, after tonight, you're mine. I'll never get enough of this body... of you."

Done talking, Wes leaned down to stake his claim once and for all. He engulfed her nipple in his mouth and sucked, hard, loving how her back arched into his touch. One of her hands came up to grab his naked ass, and the other landed on the back of his head and pushed him harder into her.

He took his time worshiping her breasts. First one nipple, then the other. He licked around the turgid bud then kissed along her collarbone. He nipped her earlobe and blew into her ear, loving how she shivered under him and goosebumps rose on her arms.

She tried several times to reciprocate, but Wes hadn't had nearly enough of her to let her take her turn yet. She apparently got impatient with him taking, but not letting her give anything in return, because she pushed against him hard, and Wes rolled over onto his back.

Laine immediately straddled his stomach and put her hands on his chest. "My turn," she demanded, waiting for him to argue.

The view Laine was giving him was heavenly and Wes had no desire to deny her. He put both hands on her hipbones, letting his thumbs rest in the creases where her legs met her groin... close to her folds, but not touching.

Without taking his eyes away from where she was weeping for him, Wes encouraged, "Knock yourself out. But I'm warning you, darlin', you've only got a couple of minutes before I take over again. I need you too much."

She didn't argue, or hesitate. Laine ran her hands down his chest to the hair above his cock, then brought them back up and pinched his nipples. She leaned down, blocking his view of her gorgeous pussy, and sucked one of his small buds into her mouth. The position might have obstructed his view of her, but it also pushed her hips farther down his body. She shifted until she was straddling one of his legs.

Wes swore his vision went black for a moment when she sucked hard on his nipple, snaked one hand down his body until she grasped his hard length, and ground herself against his leg, smearing her wetness on his thigh in the process.

Before he even thought about what he was doing, Wes had pushed Laine over until she was on her back again and he was hovering over her. "Goddamn, darlin', you make me lose my head. You're so fucking perfect I can't... shit, I can't even talk," he groused as he felt his balls pull up against his body.

"Bad timing, I know, we should've already talked about this," Laine ground out, "but I'm on the pill. I haven't had sex in a year and a half and I'm clean."

"Fuck. I have condoms in the drawer. I meant for this to go slower. It's been fourteen months for me. I'm clean too. Swear." Wes groaned as Laine arched into him and his cock brushed against the trimmed hair above where he wanted to bury himself. He cleared his throat and rushed his words, wanting to get this part over with so he could experience bliss. "The papers are in a drawer in my kitchen. I'd planned to discuss this with you like a civilized person while we relaxed after dinner."

"Fuck me, Wes. God, please. I've resisted the urge to get off this week because I wanted to wait and see if it made this better. I'm so damn horny I feel like my skin is on fire, and I need to come so bad. Please."

Before the last word was out of her mouth, Wes took hold of the base of his dick and guided his way inside her hot folds. He slipped in easily, her excitement coating his way. They both groaned at the feel of him coming inside. He caught himself on his hands on the mattress next to her shoulders. He closed his eyes, not moving, wanting to memorize the moment.

"Wes?"

"Shhhhhh."

"What are you doing?" Laine whispered.

"I'm imprinting this exact moment to memory." Wes opened his eyes and looked deep into Laine's. "The first time I am inside you. How perfect it feels. How amazingly, wonderfully perfect this is."

"Wes…" Laine's voice trailed off as he pulled almost all the way out and pushed his way back inside.

"As much as I want this to last forever, I'm afraid it's not going to," Wes warned as he continued to thrust in and out of her.

"It's okay, we can do it again."

"There'll never be another first time," Wes told her a bit sadly.

Laine brought her hands up to his face and held it lovingly. "But there'll be a second. And a third. And a fourth. And if we're lucky, a four thousand one hundred and sixty-eighth. Make me come, Wes. I need you."

Her words were all it took for him to let go of the iron control he'd been holding onto. He moved one hand down to where they were joined and used his thumb to press against her clit as he thrust harder into her. "I didn't get the chance to taste you, but I will. That's on my list… and you should know, my list of things I want to do with you is getting longer and longer. But for now I want to feel you come apart under me." His thumb was relentless, dipping down to where they were joined to gather her juices, and caressing, rubbing, and pressing down on her sensitive bundle of nerves.

Wes felt her clit swell until the tip peeked out from the hood that usually protected it as she writhed under him. Loving that he could turn her on that much, he sped up his efforts until Laine was shaking on the verge of her orgasm.

He thrust inside her and held himself still as he felt Laine's orgasm explode from the inside out. She gripped his cock so tightly, it was all Wes could do to hold off his own orgasm so he could fully appreciate her ecstasy.

Finally, Laine was only twitching in his grasp instead of out-and-out jerking. He pulled out then slammed back into her. Once. Twice. Then, knowing he was close, bit out, "I'm coming, darlin'. I'm coming." He thrust into her to the hilt and held her to him as his balls drew up close to his skin and he burst forth harder than he'd ever done before.

He vaguely felt Laine's hands running up and down his chest as she caressed him through his orgasm. Wes dropped down lightly onto her, pushing her legs open farther, forcing her to wrap them around him. He felt himself growing soft and mourned the end of their first lovemaking session.

"Don't be sad," Laine said, somehow reading his mind.

"I'm not sad, exactly."

"Then what, exactly?" Laine asked with a smile in her voice.

"Uh…" Wes couldn't think. "I guess I *am* sad. I wanted it to last longer."

Laine giggled, and they both groaned when her laughter pushed his flaccid length out of her body. Wes immediately rolled so Laine was resting on top of him.

"What are you doing?"

"Well, since we didn't use a condom, the gallons of jizz that you forced out of my body will, sooner or later, be making its way out of yours. I didn't think you wanted to sleep in the wet spot… so I'm trying to be a gentleman here."

"Oh, you goof. Let me up. I'll go take care of things and come back, then neither of us needs to sleep in the gross wet spot."

"I like you here," Wes whined.

Laine pushed up to her hands and knees then leaned down and kissed him, pulling away when he tried to deepen it. "I'll be right back, don't move."

Wes watched in the dim light of the room as Laine hopped off the bed and headed for the bathroom. He thought for the hundredth time that night how lucky he was and how pretty Laine was.

She was back within moments and snuggled into his side. Wes drew the sheet up and over them both and closed his eyes in appreciation for his life.

Chapter Seven

——◆——

L AINE SMILED DOWN at the text on her phone the next morning while she sat at the table waiting for Wes to finish making their breakfast. He'd insisted on making them both omelets, and Laine didn't argue. Why would she? She'd let Wes cook her every meal if he wanted to.

"What are you smiling about over there?" Wes asked as he carried two plates to the table, putting one down in front of her.

Laine turned her phone so Wes could see the text that Mack sent.

On a scale from 1-10?

Wes's brows furrowed in confusion. "What's that mean?"

Laine looked down at her phone as she typed out a reply. "She wants to know on a scale of one to ten how the sex was. I told her a seven point five."

Laine screeched as her phone was grabbed out of her hands. "Hey!"

Wes was looking at the screen. "You did not. A twenty?" He grabbed Laine around the torso and tilted her chair until it was resting on the back two legs.

Laine squealed again, holding on to Wes for all she was worth and laughing at the same time. "Wes! Let me up! Of course it was a twenty! Good Lord, man. You were there. Do you disagree?"

Wes kissed her until she couldn't breathe and finally brought her upright. "I would've told her at least a thirty."

Laine snatched her phone back up and read Mack's response.
You're welcome.

They both laughed. Laine relaxed as they ate their breakfast. She'd been a bit worried that the morning after they'd had such awesome sex would be awkward, but it hadn't been. Laine had opened her eyes that morning to find Wes up on an elbow, watching her. He'd smoothed a length of her hair behind her ear and smiled down at her.

"Good morning, sleep well?"

"Yeah. You?"

"Best I've slept in a long time. You make a good pillow."

They'd both laughed and Wes had told her to use the master bathroom and he'd use the guest one. Yes, they'd had sex, but it was still a bit weird to do normal morning stuff with him the morning after, and he'd somehow known it. So they'd taken showers in separate bathrooms and met in the kitchen.

"What are your plans for the day?" Wes asked her after they'd finished eating.

"I have a showing this afternoon. You?"

"I'm assisting in an interrogation of a suspect in a robbery, and I'm on call."

Laine wrinkled her nose.

Wes smiled at her and stood up. He kissed the top of her head and grabbed their dishes. "Such is life for two working adults. But know this, darlin', I'm going to make every effort to see you every time I can. When I've got time off, I want to spend it with you. When you've got the time, I'd love to meet you for lunch. As much as possible, I want to spend the night with you. I don't care if we're both dead on our feet and all we do is sleep, I like being around you."

Laine stood up, followed Wes into the kitchen, and watched as he nonchalantly rinsed off the dishes and put them into the dishwasher without having to be prompted. It hit her then. Wes wasn't a boy.

He was a responsible man, who'd lived on his own for a long time. He wouldn't expect her to cook all the time, or always do their laundry, or clean the dishes… he was used to doing those things for himself, just as she was. The perks of dating a man like him occurred to her again. She smiled and came up behind him, wrapping her arms around him and resting her head on his back.

"I'd like that."

"Like what?"

"All of what you just said. Meeting you for lunch. Sleeping with you. Hanging out with you. Spending time with you when we're both free… and when I'm not busy hanging out with Mack."

Wes turned in her arms. "I'd never make you choose between me and Mackenzie, Laine. I know how important she is to you."

"Thanks. I know I told you about our close relationship before, but wanted to make sure you really understood.

"Never be afraid to tell me how you feel. As we've said, we're not sixteen. Communication is the key to having a strong relationship."

"Agreed. So we're officially dating?"

"Absolutely." Wes beamed at her, showing off his perfect smile. "So… what time is this showing you have this afternoon?"

Laine grinned back at him mischievously. "What time do you have to go into work?"

"Not for a few hours."

"Same here."

Wes started backing her out of the kitchen toward his room. "Looks like we have a few hours on our hands then. Whatever shall we do to pass the time?"

"I might have some ideas," Laine said, then turned and sprinted down the hallway, laughing as she heard Wes pounding after her.

Chapter Eight

―――――◆―――――

I can't wait to see you tonight

LAINE'S LIPS TURNED upwards in a small smile at the text. Wes never failed to make her feel good. They'd been dating for a little over a month and everything about him made her happy. He was protective, but not stifling. He was responsible and polite, and he made her laugh. Oh, he'd pissed her off too, but because she immediately called him out on his actions, they worked their way through them when they did occur. Just as he did with her when she said or did something that he wasn't sure about or didn't like.

Me either. I'm going to check out a property then I'm headed to your place.
Be careful. See you soon.
I will. Later.

Laine turned off her cell to save the battery, which was only at twelve percent. She'd forgotten to bring her charger today and she wanted to make sure she had enough juice for her trip back to his place, just in case. Safety first. Wes had gotten upset with her the other week because he'd tried to call her and couldn't get through because her phone was dead. She'd tried to tell him how she was simply too busy to remember to keep her charger with her all the time, and he hadn't listened to her, rightly so. It wasn't a big deal to carry the stupid thing and she was trying to be better at keeping her phone charged. She didn't want to worry Wes and she'd be upset if the shoe was on the other foot and she couldn't get in touch with him if she needed him.

She put her cell back in her purse and climbed out of her car. The ranch took some doing to find, as it was way off the beaten path... but it was so worth it. The neglect was obvious, but the property was gorgeous. Laine could see through the neglect to the gem it could be once again. A porch swing was hanging by one chain on the wide screened-in porch on the front of the house. She could hear the banging of a door from somewhere; she assumed it was coming from the large barn off to her right.

The house was one story, a true ranch-style property. There was a large window in the front, which faced west. Laine could almost imagine the beautiful sunsets the previous occupants of the house had enjoyed over the years. The current owner was a ninety-two-year-old woman who'd long since been moved to the city and into a nursing home. She had one daughter who had no desire to live on the ranch. It was kinda sad, as the home had been in the Johnson family's possession since the 1800s. But since there weren't any relatives who wanted it, they had put it up for sale.

There had been several additions over the years and it now boasted five bedrooms and four full baths. The paperwork said it was forty-five hundred square feet, but Laine knew that when the guesthouse square footage was added in, it would easily top six thousand in living space.

It had been on the market for a couple of years, and the daughter was desperate to sell it. The woman had contacted her, wanting to switch to a different realty company, to see if that would breathe new life into the listing and hopefully to sell it.

Laine leaned into her car and grabbed her ever-present boots, remembering how she'd worn them the first time she'd been out to Wes's ranch. The memory made her smile as she tugged off her sandals and put on the socks and boots. She wanted to walk around the entire grounds to get a feel for it personally. She'd found the best way to represent a property someone wanted to sell was to find out all about it… pros and cons. If she was upfront with a potential buyer, or another realtor, it went a long way toward fostering trust that she wasn't trying to gouge someone or pull the wool over their eyes.

Appropriate footwear on, Laine headed out. She knew she probably looked silly, but no one would see her in her skirt, lacy top, and comfortable old boots. She normally wouldn't wear a skirt while touring a property, but she'd had lunch with new clients earlier, and had wanted to look professional.

She slowly circled the house, looking at the foundation, seeing if she noticed signs of termites or other critters, and even checked the wood in places to see if it had rotted away in the heat of the sun and the harsh Texas weather conditions.

As she rounded the side of the house, pleased so far with what she'd seen, Laine stopped dead in her tracks. Sitting in front of the large porch was the ugliest dog she'd ever seen. No, ugly wasn't fair… pathetic was a better description.

It had been a long time since the dog had seen any kind of gentle care. Her fur was filthy. It looked like some sort of pit bull mix. She was obviously female, as her teats hung low, as if she had puppies somewhere who relied on their mother for nourishment. As Laine took a step toward her, the dog's tail tucked between her legs and she backed up.

"Oh, you poor thing. I'm not gonna hurt you. Do you have babies somewhere? I don't blame you for being wary of me. Come here, baby." Laine knelt down in the dirt and held out her hand, trying to coax the dog to her.

When it was obvious the dog wasn't going to come near her, Laine said out loud, more to herself than the dog, "You look hungry. I bet I have something in my car that you'd like."

She stood up and the dog made a break for the barn at her sudden movement, keeping well out of her way.

Laine's heart broke. She wanted to hold the dog and reassure her that she'd never hurt her, but the dog wasn't going to let her get anywhere close.

The house forgotten for a moment, Laine opened her passenger-side door to see what she could scrounge up from her purse. Thankful that she always carried some sort of snack, Laine triumphantly pulled out a granola bar. Luckily, it had no chocolate in it, so the dog could safely eat it. It was some sort of protein thing, which tasted like shit, but Laine didn't think the dog would care. She peeled off the wrapper and dropped it onto her purse to throw away later before she shut the door.

Looking over at the barn, Laine saw the dog peering at her from the broken door. She walked slowly toward the barn, stopping when she was halfway there, figuring any farther would be pushing her luck. She broke the granola bar into pieces and placed them on the ground, knowing the poor dog wouldn't care about a little dirt on the snack.

"There ya go. See? It's just food. I'm sure you're hungry. You look hungry to me. I know it tastes horrible, but you need the fuel. Think of your puppies. They need you to stay healthy, I'm sure." She stepped back slowly, not taking her eyes off the dog. "Go on, it's safe. Promise. I'll stay out of your way while you check it out. It's all yours, I'm not gonna steal it back before you can get it."

Pleased when the dog slunk toward the food, Laine kept backing away. She stayed about twenty feet from the dog the entire time and smiled when she sniffed her offering and then wolfed it down, never taking her eyes from Laine.

Feeling as if she'd won a gold medal in the Olympics when the mangy mutt wagged her tail, Laine smiled and took a step toward her.

Startled anew at her movement, the dog whirled and took off around the side of house.

"Darn." Looking around—for what, Laine had no clue—she shrugged and followed where the dog had gone. There was no one out there. There were a few clumps of trees here and there, but for the most part the land was empty and desolate. There was no way she could just leave the dog and puppies. Even though she hadn't seen any signs of other dogs or of the puppies, there had to be some around. Most likely in the barn. Laine had no idea how she'd get the frightened animal, or any puppies she might find, in her car, but felt she had to try.

Rounding the back of the house, she saw the dog sitting about a hundred yards into a large pasture. She was sitting on her haunches now, as if she didn't have a care in the world. Laine ducked under the rail of an old wooden fence and climbed through after the dog. She spoke to her as she walked, keeping her eyes on her, trying to portray friendly vibes.

"It's okay. I'm not going to hurt you. You look like you need some help. Those mats can't feel good, right? I can bring you to a lady who can shave those things right off. You'll feel two hundred times better once they're gone, promise. And food. Oh, as much as you can eat. Your babies will get the care they need too. You're probably tired of them nursing, yeah? They'll get their own food and you can get healthy again. I don't know what kind of dog you are, but I bet you're beautiful under all that muck, aren't you? I might be able to find something else for you—"

Laine's words were cut off as the ground under her gave way and she screamed, terrified, as she fell. The pain radiating up from her ankles as she landed made her knees immediately buckle, and she fell onto her butt into about half a foot of water. The boards, which had been covering whatever she'd fallen into, bit into her skin and made her groan out in pain as she sat there for a moment trying to process exactly what had just happened.

Laine could feel the darkness creeping in at the sides of her eyes from the pain in her ankles, but she closed her eyes and tried to breathe deeply until the sensation passed. When she thought she was past the danger of fainting, she opened her eyes and looked up, needing to know just what the hell she'd gotten herself into now.

She could see the blue sky and the light fluffy clouds she'd thought so pretty ten minutes ago above her head... *way* above her head. She was probably around twenty feet down, with no way of climbing out. There were no hand holes or steps leading up. She was in some sort of shaft... if she had to guess, she thought maybe it was an old well.

It smelled musty, as if it'd been covered up for a long time. Laine sneezed three times in a row as the mold in the air tickled her nose. She put her hand on the side of her tomb to test the strength of the walls surrounding her. The dirt flaked off in her hand. It was more like clay, but Laine could see as the walls went upward, the clay made way to drier dirt. Hell, she was lucky she wasn't buried alive. She knew as well as anyone how dangerous these old wells were. With the droughts they'd had recently, many wells were drying up and even collapsing because of the lack of water in the soil.

Laine half sighed, half sobbed, not believing how stupid she'd been. All of her attention had been on the dog, and not on where she was walking. Laine knew better. She'd been trained on how to recognize the signs of abandoned wells on properties. Had to sit through an entire class for her realtor's license, in fact. Laine thought back to what she'd learned in the eight-hour course... pipes sticking up, depressions in the earth, windmills, or random pieces of lumber lying around. They were all signs that there might be a well or mine, and to beware.

Knowing she wasn't going to be able to get out, Laine climbed to her feet carefully, and turned her attention to her immediate surroundings. She was standing in about six inches of black, murky water; luckily it wasn't more. There were some sort of insects on the surface of the water and Laine couldn't help but think of snakes and leeches. Figuring she was safe from snakes, thank God, as she didn't immediately see any, her concern went to the bugs that decided she must've been sent by a higher power to feed them. They were on her legs and buzzing around her face. Laine waved a hand in front of her to try to keep them away.

Her ankles hurt. They'd taken the brunt of the landing from her fall. She cautiously moved one; it throbbed, but she didn't think it was broken. Somehow she must've used her hands to slow her fall on her way down. Whatever the reason, she was glad she wasn't more injured than she was. Laine didn't dare take her boots off to check her ankles, for fear if they started swelling, she'd never get them back on.

The wooden boards lay around her, mocking her decision to step on them. She shifted and piled them up. When they were stacked, they made somewhat of a seat, which was high enough to be out of the water. It wasn't comfortable, but at least she wouldn't have to have her butt in the water all the time. The diameter of the well was probably around three feet, not huge, but she could turn around. When she sat, her knees had a bit of room, but not a lot. There was certainly no way to lie down. Sleeping wouldn't be something that she'd be doing much of, that was obvious.

Laine shivered. The sunlight wasn't able to reach the bottom of the hole she was in because of the position of the sun, and she was wet from the water she'd landed in when she fell. As her situation sank in, Laine's heart sank with it, and she swallowed the bile that crept up her throat.

She was in deep shit. Her phone was sitting in her car... off. When she didn't show up at Wes's, he'd look for her. He was a Texas Ranger, he would use his connections to try to find her. The first thing he'd do was try to track her phone… but she'd turned it off to save the stupid battery.

She hadn't told anyone where she was going either. She'd never had reason to in the past. Rose, one of her friends at work, knew she had plans to tour a property, but not which one. Same with Wes. She'd texted him that she'd be at his place later, but she hadn't told one person the address of the ranch. She was a smart, independent woman—who made a dumb mistake not to share the details with anyone as to where she was headed alone. When she made it out, she'd not make that mistake again.

The first tear escaped her eye and Laine tried not to give in to the despair she was feeling. She wiped it away, knowing she was smearing dirt on her face, but not particularly caring at the moment.

Wes would find her. She had to believe that. He always bragged about his success rate with his cases so he wouldn't give up on her. The only question was—would he find her before she died of dehydration or infection or who the hell knew what else?

Laine looked at the water at her feet, trying to determine if it was drinkable. She shivered; it was gross. There were both dead and live bugs floating on top and it looked absolutely disgusting, but Laine knew she'd be drinking it later if she had to. She'd do whatever it took to give Wes, and even Dax, the time they needed to find her. She had no doubt they'd be looking.

Laine wanted to live. She was too young to die.

Hearing a noise, Laine's head whipped up to the opening of the hole, high above her… and she saw the stray dog. She bit back a hysterical laugh. Of course. *Now* the dog was curious. *Now* she came over to see what she was all about.

Resting her head on the dirt wall behind her, not caring in the least about how filthy she was going to be when she was finally hauled out of this tomb in the ground, she refused to think that this would be her final resting place. Laine did what any sane person would do… she talked to the dog as if she could understand her.

"Hey there. I'm pretty safe down here now, aren't I? I can't hit you, or kick you… or any other number of things, can I? Here's the deal… how about you go and get some help. Run to the road, flag down a motorist, preferably a trustworthy one and not a big, scary, hairy guy who would rescue me only to rape and torture me to death. And while I'm asking, make it a cop, would you? You've got all sorts to choose from. Let's see… SAPD, maybe a game warden, a sheriff's deputy, FBI or CIA agent, and I'd even take a medical examiner like Calder. Any of them will do. Oh, I know, you can pick a firefighter. If you can get one from Station 7, that'd be great. I've met most of them. Then lead him or her or them back here to this hole in the ground. There's a big juicy steak in it for you if you do."

The dog lay next to the hole and rested her head on her paws as she continued to look down into the deep hole. She didn't make a sound, only watched her with what seemed like curiosity.

The tears began again, and Laine felt her lip quiver as well. She wrapped her arms around her waist and continued to talk out loud. It made her feel better to hear her own voice. Made her feel not so alone. "Where's Lassie when you need him? I'm scared, dog. I fucked up and I'm scared I'm gonna die down here and no one will ever find my body. I need Wes. I'm usually pretty self-reliant, but I'd give anything to have his strong arms around me, telling me it'll all be okay."

The dog didn't answer; only lay at the mouth of the abandoned well as if trying to understand what the strange human was doing.

Chapter Nine

———— ◆ ————

WES PACED THE floor in agitation. Laine was late. Very late. Like three hours late. It was nine o'clock already and she was supposed to have been at his place at six. He'd texted and called her cell and gotten no answer. The call had gone straight to voice mail, as if her phone was turned off or dead.

They'd had a conversation about keeping her cell charged, so it could be she'd forgotten to charge it again. But he didn't think so. She'd been very apologetic when he'd explained why he was so upset with her, and seeing him distressed troubled her in return, and she'd sworn she wouldn't let it go dead again. That had only been a week and a half ago, and Wes didn't think she'd break that promise so soon after they'd had the discussion.

Wes had called Dax to see if Mackenzie had heard from her best friend. She hadn't. Dax and Mack had even driven over to Laine's house to see if she was there, and Mack had used her key to go inside to make sure she wasn't injured and not able to get to the door... but neither she nor her car were there and it didn't look like she'd been home that night after work.

The last thing Laine had told him via text was that she was going to check out a property.

All sorts of horrible scenarios ran through Wes's head. He couldn't turn off his Ranger brain, thinking about all of the scary things that could've happened to her. Someone could've followed her and accosted her while she was isolated. She could've gotten in a car accident. She could be lost, although that was unlikely since she had a map app on her phone.

She could simply be doing some errands and running late. But in the past, when she'd been running late, she'd called or texted him. He didn't want to embarrass her if nothing was wrong, but he was worried.

Deciding he'd waited long enough, Wes decided it was time to call in the cavalry.

Wes didn't have a close contact with anyone in the SAPD, so he called their general line. His position as a Texas Ranger went a long way toward getting him immediate attention and accelerating the investigation. Typically, people had to be missing for at least twenty-four hours before a report could be taken and the wheels of an investigation started, but thankfully in this case, things were moving quickly.

When Dax had heard about Wes's concerns, he'd called his friend, Cruz, in the FBI, as well as another friend, Lieutenant Quint Axton, who Wes didn't know, in the SAPD. It was all very confusing and Wes wasn't even sure how Dax was connected to everyone, but when Hayden Yates, from the Sheriff's Department, had called and said that Fire Station 7 had their paramedics on standby, just in case, and to let her know if she could do anything, he gave up trying to figure it out, relieved that at least things were happening quickly.

He'd seen his brothers and sisters in blue... and red... in action in the past, rallying around their own when they were in trouble, but he'd never had to rely on them for his own personal use before. But Wes knew he needed every single eye, every single brain, to figure out where Laine was. He was well aware that the first twenty-four hours of any missing persons case was critical. If Laine had been kidnapped, it was likely the person would either kill her outright, or would keep her to... do whatever... to her for at least a few hours. It was that "whatever" that Wes didn't want to think about.

He and Laine had been dating, and even though he saw the bad things that could happen to people, and even the awful things that humans could do to each other, through the course of his job, he still hadn't really thought anything would happen to either of *them*. They'd been enjoying getting to know each other, in and out of the bedroom. She was quickly becoming one of his best friends, which felt right. Wes never thought he'd lose her, not so soon after he'd found her, or that there might be a chance she'd disappear from his life in such a mysterious way.

He had a new respect and empathy for the families of missing persons he'd spoken to in the past. He'd felt bad for them, but hadn't really understood what they were going through... until now.

As Wes stood in his house, clutching his phone, willing Laine to call him and tell him with that nervous laugh she had that it was all a misunderstanding, it hit him.

He loved her.

He was devastated just *thinking* about never seeing her again. If she really was gone, he suddenly realized he would've lost one of the best things that had ever happened to him. He might've been telling himself they were just dating, but it was suddenly very obvious that wasn't the case.

He hadn't told her, they hadn't spoken of love to each other, but it was there nonetheless. Wes figured he'd loved her from the first time he saw her standing in his barn. From her nipple hard-ons, as she called them, to the blush on her face when she realized she'd been staring at him, he loved everything about her. She was his soul mate—and he didn't even want to think about how he might not get the chance to tell her.

As the night wore on, and his adrenaline spiked each time the phone rang, then plummeted when he realized it wasn't Laine on the other end, Wes's determination hardened. She was out there... somewhere. He'd spent his entire life investigating crimes and murders and missing persons. He was going to have to use every ounce of what he'd learned over the years in law enforcement to track her down. Somehow he knew Laine was waiting for him, counting on him to do his job and find her.

It was almost as if he could hear her words in his ear... whispering over and over, "Find me, Wes. I'm waiting for you to figure out what happened and come get me."

LAINE SHIVERED IN the narrow space, but kept her chin tilted up so she could see the sky. Seeing proof she wasn't buried alive kept the claustrophobia she was feeling at bay... for now. The night was clear and the stars out here in the middle of nowhere were shining just as bright as they were on her first date with Wes. Looking up at the same stars she'd gazed at with Wes made her feel closer to him. Was he out there right this second, looking up at the sky and thinking about her? If so, they were seeing the same stars... somehow that felt significant to her.

"I wonder if there are aliens out there, dog," she croaked out in a hoarse voice. She'd been talking to the dog for hours; it made her feel not quite so alone. "Maybe ET is out there now, lying on his back looking up at his purple sky and three moons and wondering what happened to his little friend he left behind on Earth."

The dog had been gone a while, but Laine kept speaking to her, nevertheless. She knew the mutt was probably gone for good... off to take care of her puppies, or to find something to eat. She certainly had no reason to continue to hang out at the top of a hole and stare down at her. She really wasn't that exciting.

Laine shuddered again and wrapped her arms around her waist even tighter. She'd tried to prop her heels up on the boards by her butt and pull her skirt over her bare legs to keep warm, but it didn't work. The boards were too short and her ankles throbbed when she kept them in that position too long. She was covered in bug bites, the mosquitos having a field day with her fresh blood. Laine had resorted to using the water to wet the dirt on the walls to smear all over her arms and legs. It was drying now, and she felt like an experiment at the spa gone wrong.

Thinking back to the missing dog, Laine knew that even though it was Texas, it was chilly in the fall at night, and the dog was probably curled around her babies, snug and warm, the strange human a long-forgotten memory.

"Maybe if I send up a quick prayer, a cyborg or alien will hear it in passing and send down a search team. They'll find me in this hole and beam me up, like on *Star Trek*. They'll fix up my ankles, and put me in that beautiful blue dress that Cinderella wore in the latest version of the movie. I'll twirl around and around and when I stop, Wes will be there in his Ranger uniform. He'll tip his Stetson to me and we'll dance off into the sunset."

When she stopped talking, Laine couldn't hear a thing other than the crickets and their incessant chirping. "Oh my God," she exclaimed to the night. "I really *have* turned into Mackenzie. Seriously, this is too much. I've made fun of her my entire life for babbling on and on, but look at me. I'm doing the same damn thing."

Laine closed her eyes and her chin fell to her chest in despair. Her words came out as a whisper this time, "I need you, Wes. Please, don't stop looking for me. I'm here. I'm right here."

AT SEVEN O'CLOCK the next morning, Wes met Rose, a realtor who worked with Laine, at their office. She showed him Laine's cubicle, and he got to work going through her files. He wasn't a computer geek, so he was out of luck on searching her computer, not able to even log in because he didn't know her password, but lucky for him, Laine was old school. She had a calendar sitting on her desk with doodles and appointments all over it. He found a drawer full of papers about various listings and notes on houses in the area.

It took him three hours to go through it all, but just when he was about to give up, he thought he just might have found a clue. On yesterday's date, she'd written, "Johnson." It was, unfortunately, a common name, but she'd also scribbled "Morningside."

Doing a quick Google search on his phone, Wes found that there was a Morningside Long-Term Care Facility in the city. The two weren't necessarily connected, but it was more than he had before he'd been to her office. He quickly dialed the number on their website.

"Good morning, Morningside Long-Term Care, where we care for your loved one as much as you do. How can I help you?"

"My name is Westin King. I'm a Texas Ranger investigating a missing persons case."

"Oh, how can I help you?" the lady on the other end of the line repeated, sounding more concerned rather than falsely chipper, as she had when she'd answered.

"Do you have any patients with the last name of Johnson?" As soon as he asked the question, he knew he was being too vague.

"Yes. But none of them are missing."

"Let me be more specific. The woman who has disappeared is a realtor. The last time anyone heard from her, she was going to look at a property. We don't know where the property is, or even whose it was. The only clue we have is the last name of Johnson written on her calendar yesterday, with Morningside written on the same date. I was hoping you might know of anyone who might be in your facility who's putting their house up for sale? Or maybe their relatives are?" Wes knew he sounded desperate, but he couldn't help it.

"I'm really sorry, I'm just the front desk person. I have a list of our patients, but I'm not close enough to them to know about their personal lives."

Wes gritted his teeth, knowing every second that went by was a second that Laine needed him, and he wasn't there for her. "Can you please ask around and call me back as soon as you can? The woman who's missing is my girlfriend. This is personal for me. Please. Anything you might be able to find out could mean the difference between life and death for her."

The sympathy Wes heard in the woman's voice, even over the phone, was palpable. "Of course. We can't tell you any medical information or anything, but I'll check the patient list and see if I can talk to the nurses who work with anyone with the last name of Johnson. Maybe they'll know more."

"Thank you." Wes gave the woman his number and clicked off the phone and tried to think. He'd asked Dax's friend in the FBI, Cruz, to use his connections to trace Laine's cell phone, but that hadn't exactly been the homerun they'd needed. The phone was now either turned off, dead, or destroyed. They had no way to tell, but the bottom line was that it wasn't transmitting a signal, so it couldn't be traced.

Cruz's FBI tech contact had been able to tell him that it had last pinged at a tower south of the city, but the area was very rural, and there was no guarantee she was anywhere near there now. Wes wanted more information before he organized a huge search party of the area, which might end up being a waste of time. He needed to narrow it down, or at least have more concrete evidence on where she might be first.

His phone rang and Wes put it up to his ear after clicking the green talk button. "King here."

"Have you found her?" Mack's frantic voice echoed though his brain.

"No."

"Where could she be? Daxton and I drove around a bit last night looking for her, with no luck. Cruz and Mickie got together with

Calder and Hayden and searched around her house. No one they talked to had seen her. Even the guys who weren't on duty at the fire station were out looking. Where's her car? If we find her car, I bet we'll find her. She has to be somewhere, Wes! Dammit! Where is she?"

Wes didn't get upset at Mackenzie. He'd been around her enough in the last month or so to know how she was. She wasn't accusing him and was obviously just as worried as he was about Laine. "I don't know. But I'm following up on a lead. I'm going to find her. There's no way I've gone forty-two years before finding my soul mate to lose her now."

When Mack didn't say anything, Wes said, "Mackenzie?"

Then he heard her sob. Shit. Dax's voice came over the line.

"What? Did you find her? Is she hurt?"

"I haven't found her, Dax."

"Then why is Mack crying?"

"Because I basically told her how much I love her friend. Because she's emotional. Because she wants to find her friend as much as I do." His voice dropped in anguish. "Because I have no fucking idea where Laine is and it's tearing me apart."

"Dammit, Wes. This doesn't make sense. Any leads on the BO-LO?"

Wes appreciated his friend not commenting on his break in professionalism, instead focusing on the "Be On The Lookout" Wes had put on Laine's car. He cleared his throat, got himself under control and answered. "No. Nothing. But that's not too surprising. If it's parked amongst other cars or otherwise doesn't stick out, it could take days or weeks to find."

They both knew her car could be anywhere. It could be at the bottom of a pond or lake... with Laine still inside. If she'd crashed, it could be years before anyone found it, or her. Or the car, and Laine, could be in Mexico... or another state. There were so many scary scenarios, it hurt Wes's heart to even think about what may have happened to her.

"I called in a favor from a friend of a friend of a friend," Dax told Wes in a serious voice. "Moose is a firefighter from Station 7 that I've worked with in the past. As you know, we've played Station 7 in those charity softball games for several years now. Anyway, one of his crew is the Army Princess—"

"The soldier who was rescued from the Middle East? The one held by ISIS?" Wes interrupted in surprise. He'd met the firefighters, but wasn't close with them. But now that he thought about it, Penelope, the female firefighter, did look familiar. He vaguely remembered all the press coverage on her when she'd been held as a prisoner over in Turkey.

"Yes, that's her. Anyway, somehow in all that went down with her, she met this man who's a former SEAL and some sort of techy geek. Penelope heard from Moose that Laine was missing, and she knows she's Mack's best friend, and since Mack is my girlfriend... shit, it's all so convoluted, but anyway, the bottom line is that this guy did some searching to try to help... and he came up blank."

"What?" Wes asked in surprise, sure Dax had been about to tell him that this mysterious hacker had found Laine.

"Yeah, I think it stunned him as much as it did us. He told us the same thing Cruz's guy did about the phone. He knows it pinged on that rural tower, but that doesn't give us enough information to organize a search party or head down there to start looking in any constructive way. He couldn't find any local surveillance cameras with her car or license on it. He's been up most of the night searching databases, with no luck. He says that he could probably find her if he had more time and information, but we're running low on both at the moment. I'm kinda at a loss."

Wes knew the connection between Laine and this mysterious guy was tenuous at best, but he wouldn't look a gift horse in the mouth.

"Ask him to look into a property owned by someone with the last name of Johnson in that area. Also, Morningside. Both names were written on yesterday's date on the calendar at Laine's desk. I've searched through all of the MLS listings in her files, without success. I'm waiting on a call back from someone at a long-term care facility named Morningside, here in San Antonio, but I have no idea when they'll get back to me, or if anyone will have anything that will be useful enough to find Laine. We know she was looking at a property, but not where or whose. I'm hoping this mysterious property owned by someone with the last name of Johnson was where she disappeared. If not… I have no idea where to go next."

"Will do. Let me see if I can get Moose to ask Penelope to contact him again. Jesus… this feels like the telephone game," Dax said in disgust.

"Give him my number. He can call me direct," Wes demanded, thinking much like Dax, that they needed to cut out the middlemen.

"I will. Don't give up, Wes. Remember, we found Mack when all the odds were against it. Laine comes from the same stock as Mack. She's tough and I know we'll find her."

"I know. Thanks, Dax. I appreciate it."

"Anytime. Not only because you're my friend, but because if anything happens to Laine, it'll devastate Mack."

"She still there?"

"No, I sent her to the other room to lie down. She didn't sleep at all last night and she's stressed out to her breaking point."

"Take care of her. I've come to like that woman of yours."

"I will. Call me the second you have a lead. I've got a whole team of people ready to move at a moment's notice. Firefighters, cops, paramedics… you name it."

Not for the first time, Wes thanked his lucky stars he was where he was and he'd made the type of friends he had. It was as if Fate had made him wait as long as she did to find the woman meant for him, until he had exactly the right combination of friends around him. If anyone could find and save Laine, it was the army of law enforcement and firefighter friends who were on his side. "I will. Thank you. Seriously, you have no idea how much that means to me. I'll be in touch."

"It's what Rangers do. And friends, Wes. Later."

"Later."

Wes was striding toward the front of the building before he'd finished speaking. He couldn't just sit around and wait for a phone call. He didn't know what he needed to do, but waiting idly was at the bottom of the list.

Chapter Ten

THE DOG WAS back. Laine looked up and saw her muzzle peeking over the edge of the hole, way above her head. "Hey, dog. You come back to laugh at me some more?" Sometime in the last two days, Laine decided that was really what the dog was doing. She was obviously wary of people and was probably thinking karma was getting back at the human race.

The first night hadn't been so bad... she'd been sure Wes, or Dax, or someone would realize she was missing and track her down, and she'd be sitting at Wes's house eating breakfast within hours. But as the second day came and went, she understood the trouble she was in.

Laine was thirsty. She couldn't remember exactly how long it was before someone died from a lack of water, but she thought she could probably hold out a few more days. The fact that she was thinking about how many *days* she might have to live was absolutely terrifying.

She'd stopped sweating the day before and she was dizzy most of the time now. Her mouth felt as though she'd been sucking on cotton balls, but it was the confusion that scared her most of all. Laine had woken up a while ago and had no idea where she was. She'd stood up and tried to take a step and ran her face into the dirt wall. She'd fallen on her butt on the boards and it'd taken her too many minutes to work through in her mind where she was and how she'd gotten there. She was terrified that her body was shutting down on her.

Her voice was still scratchy, but along with the chills, hunger, thirst, and all of her aches and pains, Laine could add shaking to her list of things that were just not going her way.

"You run off to get help yet?" she asked the dog, still staring down at her. "'Cos I could really use some here." Laine stood for a moment, and wished with all her heart she could lay down. The first night had been long, cold, and uncomfortable, but the second had been absolute misery. Her legs were cramping and her back was killing her from not being able to stretch it out properly. The bruises from her initial decent into hell were starting to make themselves known as well. She'd slept in spurts, sitting up. Her neck hurt, but not as much as her ankles. She'd started trying to stand for periods of time, ignoring the shooting pains in her legs. If she got a blood clot from sitting for too long, she'd die of that as easily as anything else.

Once, when she was completely miserable, she'd given climbing the walls of the abandoned well the ol' college try, and failed miserably. All she'd done was make her ankles ache more, and rip a large chunk of dirt from the wall of the shaft, further contaminating the murky water at her feet. She had to look like the monster from the black lagoon by now. Covered in dried mud from her attempts at using it for a bug repellant, and the additional dirt and mud that she'd gotten on her over the last forty hours or so.

The water had finally begun to seep through the weathered leather of her boots and Laine could feel her toes squishing in her socks. And she was thirsty. So damn thirsty. Now that the sun had come up again, the temperature had risen in her hole. It wasn't as bad as it could've been if she'd been in direct sunlight, or if it'd been the middle of summer, but the gnats and other insects had taken up residence with her again and were driving her crazy, along with all her other maladies.

The dog panted as she whined above her. "Now I know how you felt when I got here, girl. I hope that granola bar was good. I'd kill for one, although it'd make me even thirstier than I am now, which would totally suck. You see anyone up there? Anyone at all? Maybe someone will come look at this stupid house. It is on the market, after all. I know, I know," Laine continued the one-sided conversation, not expecting the dog to suddenly talk back, "it's been on the market for two years and hasn't had one contract on it… but you never know. Maybe today's the day. Maybe today, someone will decide they want to live on a real live ranch and take a tour."

Laine eased herself back to her makeshift seat on the rotten boards and fell silent. She was cried out, and didn't have any tears anymore anyway. She closed her eyes, feeling tired. So tired. She'd just close her eyes for a moment; she'd be okay, she was just resting her eyeballs.

As she fell into a fitful sleep, she didn't even notice the gnats settling on her face, or that the dog stayed by the hole high above her head, as if watching over her.

WES TRIED TO look around Laine's house with the eye of a detective, rather than the man who recently had an epiphany that he loved her. The first night had been bad, but he'd still held out hope that she was hunkered down somewhere and not really missing, but now that a second night had come and gone with no word from or about her, the feeling in his gut that she would die if he didn't locate her was eating away at him.

Dax's mysterious techie friend hadn't called him back yet, neither had anyone from Morningside, and he'd taken to driving the streets of San Antonio, trying to see if he could find Laine's car. In a last-ditch effort, he'd gone to visit Dax and Mack and had gotten the key to her apartment from Mackenzie, wanting to see for himself that she hadn't come home and packed to go on a spur-of-the-moment trip or something.

Not being able to find her, and not having any information com-ing in, was killing him. He should've found her by now. He felt like he was on the cusp of having all the information they needed, but hadn't been able to put the pieces together. It was incredibly frustrat-ing.

Everything at Laine's house looked in place, exactly as it'd been the last time he'd seen Laine. Nothing was knocked over, as if she'd been in a tussle with someone. Her boots and sandals were missing, which wasn't unusual, she usually had the boots in her car in case she needed to walk around a muddy or dangerous property. There wasn't any food left out on the counter. It was exactly as if she'd gotten ready for a day of work with every intention of returning. Dammit.

His phone rang, and Wes answered immediately with a terse, "King."

"My name is Tex, and I'm the friend of a friend of a friend who's been looking into your missing girlfriend." The man on the other end of the phone didn't bother beating around the bush.

Wes didn't care about introductions at this point, he was just glad to finally be hearing from Dax's friend. "Do you have anything?"

"Yes. I'm pretty sure I do. You were right on, and I don't think I would've found what I did without your help. I searched the MLS database for a property for sale by someone with the last name of Johnson. There were four hundred and thirty-two in and around San Antonio."

Wes's stomach dropped, but he didn't get a chance to say any-thing as Tex continued.

"But there's only one that's connected to Morningside Long-Term Care Facility *and* is south of the city. Ethel Johnson, age ninety-two. She's been there for four years. She has one daughter, who lives up in Austin. The ranch went on the market two years ago and the price has dropped three times. They own it outright, so there's no mortgage. I took the liberty of hacking into one of the government's satellites and checking it out with the best cameras available. Not that crap that Google uses. According to the DMV, Laine owns a 2012 Toyota Avalon. It's hard to be one hundred percent sure, but it looks like there's an Avalon sitting in front of the house at the property in question."

Wes didn't give a shit at the moment how many laws the man on the other end of the phone had just broken, or about the fact that he'd admitted as much to a law enforcement officer. All he cared about was Laine, and it looked like he was finally getting a viable lead. Sometimes it worked that way in his job. He'd work for days with nothing, and the most inconsequential thing could lead to solving the case.

"What's the address?" Wes's heart rate increased. He'd known it.

Tex gave it to him then warned, "I've already told Penelope, who's most likely informed the rest of her crew and Mackenzie by now. I'm sure *she's* told Daxton, so if you're heading out there, be ready for the cavalry to be at your heels."

"If she's there, I'm forever in your debt."

"No, you aren't. You'd do the same if it was my wife. And you have, not with me or mine, but with many, many other people. I've looked into your record. You're a hell of a Ranger. It's my honor to help you. Let me know if you ever need any other help. I've got your back, King. Good luck and godspeed."

Wes didn't bother saying goodbye, as the other man had already hung up. He closed and locked Laine's apartment door behind him and climbed into his vehicle, taking the extra seconds to put the address Tex had given him into his GPS. It sucked to take the time, but it would be even worse to be lost on the back roads of southern Texas, knowing he was close to Laine, but not getting there in time because he'd been a dumbass.

As he raced to the deserted ranch, his phone rang once again. Expecting it to be Dax or one of his other fellow Rangers, Wes answered brusquely, "Yeah?"

"Is this Texas Ranger Wes King?" The voice was hesitant after hearing the sharp way he'd answered.

"Sorry, yes, this is he. Can I help you?"

"My name is Mary. I work at Morningside. Our receptionist said you were interested in one of our patients with the last name of Johnson that was maybe selling a house?"

Wes was pretty sure he had the information he needed already, but he didn't tell Mary that. "Yes, do you know of anyone like that?"

"Yes. Ethel Johnson is in her nineties and the sweetest woman I know. I've spent many a night sitting up with her listening to the stories of her life in that house. Her husband died twenty years ago and she's been lonely ever since. Her daughter tried to help as much as she could, but since she lives in Austin, she couldn't be around all the time. A few years ago, Ethel fell and couldn't get up. Her daughter decided she needed to be in an assisted-living facility, and she's been here ever since."

"Can you tell me the address?"

"No, I'm sorry. I would if I could, but I don't know it. But I *do* know it was south of the city. Ethel sometimes talks about how she and her husband used to sit on the roof and gaze northward at the city lights."

Tex had been right. He was on the right track. The address he was racing toward *was* south of San Antonio. Wes was relieved, but not a hundred percent. He might have the address of the property Laine was going to look at, but that didn't mean she was there. But at least it was a place to start. "Thank you, Mary, I appreciate you calling me back."

"Do you think the missing woman might be out there?"

"I don't know, but I'm praying she is."

"Good luck. I hope she's okay."

"Me too. Please tell Ethel she'll have a visitor soon. I'd like to come and thank her myself once I find my girlfriend."

"Oh, she'll like that. Will you wear your uniform? She has a thing for cowboy hats, *and* the cowboys who wear them."

"I will. Thanks again."

"Bye, Ranger."

Wes clicked off the Bluetooth on his phone and gripped the steering wheel hard as he raced south. "Hold on, Laine, I'm coming for you." His words were whispered, but he hoped with all his heart that the man upstairs was listening and would keep the woman he loved safe until he could get there.

Chapter Eleven

———— ◆ ————

WES DROVE DOWN the rutted and badly in-need-of-repair dirt and gravel driveway at a speed much too fast than was safe, but he didn't care. Turning one last corner, he saw a house—but more importantly, Laine's car.

Daxton was already there, leaning into the driver's side.

Not bothering to pull the keys out of the ignition, Wes slammed his car into park and jumped out.

"What do you have?" he growled out at his friend in agitation.

"Nothing. Her keys aren't here. But her purse is. Her phone is in it."

Wes walked around to the other side of the Avalon and opened the door. Her purse was sitting on the passenger seat, with a granola bar wrapper and her phone resting on top, as if she'd thrown both there without much worry. It didn't look like anything was out of the ordinary with the car. The seat looked to be in the right position for her five-nine height. There was no blood or anything else that would be evidence of a struggle.

Using his shirt to pick up her phone, trying to preserve evidence if it was needed later, Wes turned it on. The charge was at twelve percent. "It's almost dead. I bet she turned it off to try to conserve it. We had a conversation about it and she was probably trying to make sure it didn't die altogether."

Dax nodded in agreement. "Her sandals are on the floorboard near the pedals. She took the time to change into her boots. It doesn't look like she was in distress, at least when she left her car."

They both looked around the car and could see Laine's footprints all over the dusty ground. They led toward the house as well as partway to the barn. They weren't spaced far enough apart for her to be running. She was just walking around. They didn't immediately see any other footprints indicating another person had been there and had possibly snatched Laine, but somehow it didn't make Wes feel better. She was still missing.

He looked around at the desolate property and the hair on his arms stood up. Laine was close. He could feel it.

Before they could split up to begin searching for her, a line of cars made their way up the long driveway. All of Dax's friends piled out. Quint, Hayden, Cruz, Calder, TJ, and even Conor, came up to them.

An ambulance bounced along the driveway next, as well as a brush truck from Station 7. A short woman who Wes now recognized as the infamous Penelope Turner, the Army Princess herself, popped out, along with five other firemen. Even though he'd met them in passing before, they were quickly re-introduced as Moose, Sledge, Chief, Squirrel, and Driftwood.

"Taco and Crash had to stay back in case we got any calls, and they're pissed. But they said if we needed anything, to call it in and they'd send anyone and everyone they could," the tall firefighter named Moose explained to the group.

Wes wasn't sure who Taco and Crash were, but he didn't care. He was feeling extremely emotional at the moment, thankful for the support of so many wonderful men and women.

He swallowed the knot in his throat and quickly organized a search. "Okay, everyone pair up. A firefighter with a cop. Don't be a hero. If you find her, call out, but be careful. We have no idea what the structural integrities of the buildings are. There might be a bad guy hiding out. The last thing we want is a shoot-out or a hostage situation. Be smart, stay alert. If you find anything, don't touch it. If there are fingerprints, we need to preserve them. Look down, you can see her footprints. She's wearing boots. Don't mess them up, if you can help it. They could help later. If you find, Laine," Wes's voice cracked, but he choked it down and continued with determination, "call out or whistle so the rest of us can get there to help. Any questions?"

When no one said a word, they all spread out, watching where they were walking, trying not to obliterate Laine's footsteps as they went.

Dax stayed with Wes as the other pairs headed out. Some went toward the barn, others toward the house. Squirrel and Calder headed up the driveway, looking for clues, and TJ and Driftwood walked around the back of the barn.

Neither Wes nor Dax said a word as they started around the house, following Laine's footprints. Noticing as she stopped here and there to look at the foundation or a gutter that was barely hanging on to the side of the house. They got all the way back around the house and hadn't found any sign of Laine.

Wes stopped and turned in a circle, looking for... something. He wasn't sure what, but his gut was screaming at him that they were missing something vital.

"What is it?" Dax asked, standing patiently by his side.

"I don't know. I'm trying to see this place through her eyes." They heard the other pairs of first responders talking to each other as they searched the house. Dax looked over to the barn and saw Quint and Moose coming out. Each was holding two puppies in their arms.

That was it. What was niggling at him finally clicked in his brain. He immediately went around to the back of the house again, knowing Dax followed him. Wes's eyes moved to the large pasture at the back side of the property. He'd glanced at it as they'd rounded the house the first time, but hadn't bothered to pay much attention, more concerned about watching Laine's footprints in the dirt.

He saw what had caught his attention, but hadn't really registered as anything important at the time. A dog.

The dog was sitting in the middle of the field, motionless. It was odd behavior for any dog... friendly or not. She should be either running toward them, if she was friendly, or away from them if she wasn't. And the fact that there were puppies in the barn meant that the dog should be trying to protect them. But she wasn't doing any of that. She was simply sitting on her haunches, head tilted, watching them.

He never would've looked twice in the large field if it wasn't for that dog. Nothing seemed out of place. It was simply a large, flat, open space, full of weeds.

Wes started for the wooden fence, not taking his eyes off the stray that seemed to be watching him with just as much intensity. He heard Dax following him and whistling for Squirrel and the other paramedics to be on standby.

The dog fidgeted a bit as Wes came closer, but didn't bolt. She was a mangy thing... had obviously been on her own out at the property for quite a while. She looked skinny, and had scars on her muzzle, as if she'd been in too many fights with other animals to count, but her teats were full of milk and almost dragging the ground, even as she sat still, observing him. Her fur was almost black with dirt. The dog looked extremely pathetic. But Wes didn't care about any of that.

It was the hole the dog was sitting in front of that concerned him the most. He didn't see it until he was almost on top of it.

"Easy. We're not gonna hurt you. Is Laine there? Is that why you're here? You guarding her? You're a good dog. Take it easy."

The dog half whined and half growled low in her throat and backed up as Wes continued his slow, cautious approach. "Keep the others back," Wes warned Dax as he heard the group gathering behind him.

He spoke in a calming voice as he eased to his knees about five feet from the dog… and the hole behind her. "She's down there, isn't she? Thank you for watching over her, for staying with her. I bet she was scared, wasn't she? I swear to God, you and your pups have a home for life with me if she's down there. I'll feed you steak every night if you want… although just a warning, that might make you get fat."

The dog cocked its head at Wes and her ears perked forward, as if she understood his words.

"Please don't run away, but can I see? Will you let me come closer so I can see if Laine's okay?"

Amazingly, the dog backed up and went to the other side of the jagged hole in the ground. She lay down with her muzzle resting on her paws, never taking her eyes off Wes.

"Thank you," he told the dog earnestly, putting his Stetson to the side and laying on his belly. Wes crept forward, using his elbows and knees to propel him, not knowing how stable the hole in the ground was. Old wells and mines were notorious for caving in if caution wasn't taken. The ground around it seemed solid, but knowing he was most likely this close to Laine made him not want to take any chances.

Wes eased toward the hole, not daring to breathe as he finally got close enough to look down. He couldn't see all the way to the bottom of the cavernous hole. "Give me a flashlight," he ordered, holding his hand back toward the others. Someone, Wes had no idea who, put a light in his palm and he brought it up and clicked it on.

Shining it down into the dark hole, Wes felt the bile crawl up his throat.

He'd found Laine, but he couldn't tell if he was too late or not.

Chapter Twelve

———◆———

LAINE'S HEAD WAS lying at an awkward angle and Wes could only see the top of it. She was covered in dirt and mud so he couldn't tell if she was bleeding from anywhere. Her legs were splayed apart, her skirt sitting at the tops of her knees. Her frilly blouse was ripped on one shoulder and her arms were hanging limply at her sides. The water in the bottom of the hole reflected back up at him from the light he shone downward. Most importantly and disconcerting, however, was that she wasn't moving.

"Laine? Can you hear me, darlin'?"

"Is she there? How far down is she?"

Wes thought it was Conor who asked.

Without moving from the side of the hole, Wes twisted his head and answered, "Yeah. She's here. I'm not sure, but I think she's about twenty feet down or so. She's hurt, though. I can't tell how badly and she's not answering me." He turned back, heartsick.

"Laine, I'm here. I'm gonna get you out of there. You hear me? Just hang on, I'm coming for you." With one last look at the woman who held his heart in her hand, he scooted back, needing to make a plan.

Wes saw four of the firefighters running toward the house and their truck, hopefully going to get supplies to get Laine out of the hole. Thank God they'd brought their truck. They'd have extraction equipment appropriate for this sort of rescue.

"What did you see?" Conor asked urgently.

"She's sitting at the bottom; again, I think it's about twenty to twenty-five feet down. There's water at the bottom, it reflected off my light, but I can't tell how deep it is. Her head was down, so I didn't get a look at her face. She has to be hurt though. By the looks of the broken boards up here, she most likely stepped on them without even knowing and fell through. I don't know if her neck is broken, or her back or what." Wes tried to keep his voice matter-of-fact, but it took everything he had.

"What was she doing out here in this field?" Penelope asked.

"I don't know, but at the moment, I don't really care," Wes told her, dismissing the question, but not harshly. At this point, it didn't matter if she was running away from someone, or if she'd been out for a little stroll to hunt for chupacabras. What mattered was getting her out and to the hospital and making sure she was okay. They'd deal with all the other stuff later.

Hopefully there'd *be* a later.

Wes and the others continued to strategize as they waited impatiently for the firefighters to make it back to them with their emergency equipment.

Laine groaned softly as she regained consciousness. She knew she was going in and out, but this time seemed different, she was hearing things. "Great, now I'm hallucinating," she tried to say, but all that came out was a faint croak. She opened her eyes and looked up, not sure what she hoped to see. But the sight that greeted her was the same thing she'd seen every time she'd opened her eyes since the sun had risen—the scruffy dog blinking down at her from high above.

She tried to swallow, but her mouth was completely dry and she had nothing *to* swallow. "Hey, mutt, what's new?" Laine whispered, shocked as hell when the dog let out a bark. It was the first time she'd heard the animal make any kind of noise except for a couple of whines when she'd first seen it.

Wes turned in surprise at the sound of the dog's bark. He'd been deep in conversation with the others about the best way to go about getting Laine out of the hole, especially if she had a spinal injury. The mutt was sitting up with her tongue out, panting. She looked at him and barked, then dropped down onto her belly and barked down into the hole.

Without thinking, Wes dropped onto his own stomach and inched his way back to the side of the hole. He felt someone grab hold of his ankles, just in case the hole opened up and collapsed under him. The last thing they needed was him falling into the well on top of Laine.

Peering over the edge, Wes shone the flashlight down into the darkness and almost stopped breathing at the sight that greeted him. Laine was awake and he could see the whites of her eyes in the darkness of the well. "Hey, darlin'." It wasn't what he'd planned to say, but the words popped out anyway.

"Wes? Did that mangy mutt actually pull a Lassie, or am I still hallucinating?" It didn't sound like her, but she managed to get the words out as best she could.

"Not only am I here, but everyone else is too."

"Everyone else?"

Wes winced at the sound of her voice. It was scratchy and he had to strain to hear her, but she was alive and talking, so it was the sweetest sound he'd ever heard.

"Yeah, Dax, Hayden, Cruz, Calder, TJ, Quint, Conor, and most of the crew from Station 7. Are you hurt?"

"Yeah."

When she didn't elaborate, Wes urged her to continue. "Okay, don't move, keep as still as you can. Where, darlin'? Where do you hurt?"

"My ankles. My arms where the planks scratched them. My stomach 'cos it's empty. My feet; they're soaked and probably permanently wrinkled. I've probably lost a size or two off them as a result, Mack might be happy to go shoe shopping with me. My head is pounding, probably because I'm so thirsty, but I refused to drink the sludge in the bottom of this hellhole, but if you'd taken any longer I might've resorted to it. I'm dizzy and my tongue feels like it's three sizes too big."

Her words sounded like they were coming from a ninety-year-old who smoked a pack of cigarettes a day, but they were understandable, and she was alive. Wes would take it.

"Wow, she sounds an awful lot like Mack right about now," Quint said from behind him. Wes had no idea how they could hear Laine with her voice the way it was, but that didn't matter at the moment. Reassuring the woman he loved did.

"There's an IV up here with your name all over it, Laine. Fresh, clean water all for you. Just hang on, as soon as we get you out of there and hook you up, you'll be needing to pee before you know it."

Laine giggled, and even though it was weak, it was still the sweetest sound Wes had heard in a long time. Just then, Chief and the other three firefighters arrived back from the brush truck and ambulance parked in front of the house. Wes glanced back and saw they had a ladder, as well as rope, a stretcher, a huge first-aid kit, and other rescue paraphernalia.

"Wes, back up. We're gonna hook Squirrel up and lower him down."

"No, I'll go down and get her," Wes argued resolutely.

"You won't fit," Dax told him firmly. "Look at Squirrel, Wes. He's tall and skinny and will be able to fit down there without an issue. He'll hold Laine to him in the harness as we haul them up. You're big; it'll be a better fit with Squirrel."

"Wes?" Laine's voice was still weak, but she'd obviously overheard the conversation.

"Yeah, darlin'?"

"Please let them get me out of here. I've had about enough of this place."

"Do it," Wes told Dax and Squirrel with no more questions. He scooted around to the other side of the hole, not willing to lose sight of Laine. Amazingly, the dog stayed where she was, only moving over a bit, as if giving Wes room.

The entire rescue took no more than ten minutes from start to finish. Squirrel was hooked up to the rappelling gear and was slowly lowered down into the abandoned well. Wes lost sight of Laine as soon as Squirrel blocked the passageway, but he still didn't move. Finally, the firefighter's head appeared at the mouth of the hole after the others pulled both Laine and him up and out.

Squirrel lay on his back and held Laine tightly to his chest, keeping her immobile as his crew tugged him backward and away from the hole. Wes shuffled alongside them, keeping his hand on Laine's back as they moved, needing the physical contact with her.

When they were safely out of the way, Wes let Moose take hold of Laine's head and hold her neck still as the others assisted in rolling her off Squirrel and onto the waiting stretcher, but he immediately grabbed her hand.

Her eyes were closed, and she looked serene, but her grip on his hand belied her peaceful demeanor. She was covered in dirt from head to toe. Mud was smeared on her legs and arms, her frilly pink blouse was now a dirty brown and her hair was caked with it.

Wes's eyes never strayed from her face as the firefighters worked around them, securing her to the backboard for the trip to the ambulance. She lifted her eyelids when she was finally safely strapped down. The whites of her eyes looked extremely bright against the mud covering her face and hair.

"You sure are a sight for sore eyes, darlin'," Wes whispered into her ear before Moose fit a C-collar on her.

"You have no idea how wonderful it feels to be flat on my back after all that time sitting up. I swear I can feel my spine lengthening… in a good way." She breathed out in ecstasy. "Do me a favor?" Laine whispered as the firefighters prepared to walk her to the ambulance.

"Anything," Wes told her immediately.

"See if you can get that damn dog to come to you. I've talked to her for two days straight now. I've become a tad bit attached. Besides, she's hungry and needs a home."

Wes smiled and vaguely heard some of the others chuckling above him. "I'd already planned to. I sort of promised her a big juicy steak."

"You too?"

Wes chuckled, not surprised they were on the same wavelength. "And you might be interested in knowing that the dog is a mommy four times over."

"Really?" Laine's eyes had closed as she was being carried across the field, but they opened to look up at him. Wes was quick to shield them from the harsh sunlight beating down on them. "I saw her when I got out here and figured she was hiding them somewhere. She was scared of me and took off across the field. Stupidly, I wasn't paying attention and stepped right on the boards. As soon as I did, I knew I'd screwed up. I thought she'd take the chance to get the hell away from me. But you know what? She stayed with me the whole time, other than a bit at night when she must've taken a break to feed her puppies. She let me babble to her. I think she kept me sane."

"I wouldn't have even thought to look out here if it wasn't for her sitting next to your hole," Wes told Laine, still holding her hand as the firefighters continued with their precious bundle across the field. "It looks like we have ourselves a dog."

"*If* you can catch her," Laine said with a hint of the snark he knew and loved.

"If I can catch her," Wes agreed.

They were silent for the rest of the trip to the ambulance and as

Moose and Sledge got her settled in the back.

Gesturing to the dog with his head, Wes silently asked Dax to take care of somehow getting the dog to come with him. He'd heard their conversation and nodded, telling Wes he'd get it done.

Watching in disbelief—as all it took was for the other Ranger to open the back door of his car, and the dog jumped right in, joining her puppies now sleeping together on the floor in the backseat—Wes smiled, happy it'd been so easy. Laine would've been devastated if they couldn't help her. Hell, *he* would've been upset about it. He owed the stray everything.

Knowing Dax would have two of the others take care of both his and Laine's vehicles, Wes settled on the bench next to Laine in the ambulance, keeping one hand on her forehead to make sure she didn't feel alone, not even for a moment.

When Sledge got the IV drip going and they were finally bumping their way back down the driveway, Wes blurted out, "I love you."

Laine couldn't turn her head, but her eyes widened as she looked up at him. "What?"

"I love you," he repeated. "When you never showed up at my house and no one knew where you were... I knew that my life would never be the same without you in it. We've been hanging out together a lot, and I just assumed we'd continue to do so. Eventually I would've told you how I felt and hopefully we would've gotten married and spent the rest of our lives together. At least that's what I assumed was what would happen.

"But instead, you scared the shit out of me and I never want to feel that way again, ever. I realized that I wouldn't be that frightened if I didn't care about you as much as I did. I love you, Laine. I don't want to wait. I'm one hundred percent sure that you're it for me. It took me forty-two years to find my other half, and now that I have, I'm not letting you go."

"I want to name her Chance."

"What?" Laine's comment was so far away from how he thought she'd respond to his declaration of love and sort-of marriage proposal, he had a hard time switching gears to follow her line of thinking.

"The dog. I want to name her Chance, because without her, we wouldn't have a chance to get married and live happily ever after."

"Okay, darlin'. Chance it is." Wes couldn't help the goofy smile that crept over his face.

"I love you too."

Wes sighed slightly in relief. He didn't think he'd care if she said it back or not, but he did. He cared a lot. He didn't know if she realized that *she* basically asked *him* to marry her, but he was going to hold her to it, no matter what she said later.

"When I was sitting at the bottom of that hole, all I could think of was that I'd never told you and I'd never get a *chance* to tell you. But then I looked up at our stars and knew you were out there somewhere... looking for me. And I had no doubt you'd track me down. Although... I was kinda hoping it wouldn't have taken so long."

Wes chuckled. "Sorry about that, darlin', it took an expert hacker to figure out the clues you left behind."

"How *did* you find me?"

"I went to your office and saw the names 'Johnson' and 'Morningside' scribbled on your calendar."

"And?"

"And what?"

"That's it?" Laine asked incredulously. "I knew you were good, but I didn't know you were that good."

Wes leaned over and kissed her forehead gently. "When you're feeling better, I'll tell you the whole story. But suffice it to say, you have a lot of friends who busted their asses to do everything they could to find you."

"Thank you." Her words were slurred as the painkillers Sledge pushed through her IV began to take effect.

"Close your eyes and rest now, Laine. I've got you. You're going to be fine."

Laine didn't say another word as she slipped into dreamland, but Wes wasn't expecting it. She was safe, and in relatively good shape for spending two days at the bottom of a well. He wouldn't complain.

Chapter Thirteen

————•◆•————

LAINE SAT ON the middle cushion of Wes's large couch surrounded by her friends. Mackenzie and Dax, Cruz and his girlfriend Mickie, Quint and Corrie, Conor, TJ, Hayden, Calder, and even Penelope and Cade from Station 7 were there. When Laine had found out that Sledge's name was Cade, she'd refused to call him by his horrible nickname, proclaiming it 'too silly for such a good looking man.'" Maybe because she wasn't quite up to par after her ordeal, he didn't complain.

Wes had backed away, giving her friends time to see for themselves that she was all right, but Laine knew it was only because he'd had her to himself for the last day. She'd spent twenty-four hours in the hospital for dehydration and for tests, but they'd let her go early the morning before. Her ankles hadn't been broken, only badly sprained, and she'd bounced back quickly after having two bags of IV fluids pushed through her body. Wes hadn't even asked, but had brought her straight to his house and got her settled in his bed, where he'd proceeded to pamper her.

Mack had been waiting at the hospital when they'd brought Laine in. Wes had heard an earful from her about how Dax hadn't let her come with him out to the property. He'd been scared about what they might find and had wanted to spare Mack the possible sight of her best friend dead. But he'd called as soon as Laine had been on the way to the hospital, so she could meet her there.

And she *had* been there. She'd browbeat and badgered the hospital staff enough that they'd let her say a quick few words when Laine had been wheeled in. Enough to satisfy Mack that her friend was indeed all right, and would be fine after everything that had happened.

After arriving back at his place, Wes had cooked a delicious lunch and dinner and brought both to her bedside. They'd watched a couple movies, but her favorite part of being with him was their conversations. She'd told him how she'd felt so alone at the bottom of the well, but that she'd never given up hope that he'd find her. Wes, in turn, admitted that in all his years of being a Texas Ranger, he'd never been so scared he'd screw up a case as much as he was while she'd been missing.

"It gave me a whole new perspective on what the families go through. I remember some of the things I've said to them and it makes me cringe."

"You didn't know." Laine had tried to soothe him.

"I didn't, but that doesn't mean I had the right to be condescending or rude, even if I didn't *know* I was being condescending."

The entire ordeal had brought them closer together, and while she wished it hadn't happened, Laine was pleased with the ultimate outcome.

"I can't believe how different Chance looks, now that you got her cleaned up," Mickie said, commenting on the dog who Wes had brought home while Laine had been in the hospital. She'd been to the groomer and had a thorough bath, her nails clipped, and her ears cleaned. A trip to the vet for a once-over and some shots, and the exhausted but obviously happy dog was currently sleeping in the corner of their bedroom with her puppies, away from the commotion of all the people.

"I know, right? I thought she was a mix when I first saw her, but I can see now she's probably mostly pit bull," Laine said, her voice still a bit lower than usual.

"Are you afraid to have her around?" It was Cade who asked.

"No," Laine said immediately. "I don't care what breed she is. That dog literally saved my life. She didn't show one ounce of aggression at the groomer or the vet, or even when we've been handling her puppies. I think she somehow knows that not only did we save her and her babies, but she saved me too."

Wes told the story only some of the people in his living room had heard. "We were searching the property and I'd begun to think Laine had been snatched away and we'd have to start the search from scratch, when I looked into the pasture and saw Chance sitting there. She wasn't moving, just sitting stock-still. It was unusual and it made me want to know why. If that dog hadn't been out there by that old well, we would've left and never known Laine was there."

Mackenzie put her arm around Laine and hugged her to her side. "I love you, Laine. Don't do that again."

Everyone laughed at the complete seriousness in Mack's voice.

"I won't. From now on, everyone is going to get a complete run-down of my plans for the day… every day. Getting up. Drinking coffee. About to shower. Driving to work. Going to X address for a showing. Driving home. Eating dinner."

All the women laughed, the men did not.

"I was kidding," Laine said with a smile, looking at the alpha men staring at her.

"Someday I'll tell you a story about people knowing where you are at all times," Penelope said, fingering the Maltese cross around her neck with a faraway look in her eyes.

"Actually, that's a good idea," Quint agreed with Laine, and she could see him squeeze Corrie's hand. Corrie had her own drama she'd been through… kidnapped by loan sharks, and she'd managed to save herself while waiting for Quint to find her. Of *course* he'd agree that it was a good idea to have her text with her whereabouts all day, every day.

"Yeah... no," Laine shot back. "Look, it was a freak thing. Just like Mack being buried in that coffin. Or Mickie being in the middle of a turf war between a motorcycle club and a drug lord. The same with Corrie and Penelope being kidnapped. It's not going to happen again."

"Did you hear what you just said?" Conor questioned. "Those things usually don't happen to most people, but the fact that they've happened to four of the most wonderful women—five, if I include you—I've met, who just happened to be dating some of my best friends? Yeah, I think all of you women should make a note of what your plans are every day... just in case."

Laine smiled, but hid it behind her hand when she yawned. She probably wouldn't make a list of every second of her day, but she *would* be a bit more careful in the future. She could've saved herself, and Wes, a lot of heartache if she'd only written down the address of the property she was going to, or at least told Rose or Mack where she was going. It had been careless and even a bit reckless on her part, and it wouldn't happen again.

"Laine's tired," Wes said in a firm voice over the din in the room as the women—except for Hayden, who was sitting with her arms crossed as if daring one of her colleagues to suggest she needed to broadcast where she was every second of the day—argued against giving a blow-by-blow of every minute of their plans for the day to their men.

Wes's words were the impetus to get everyone moving. One by one they said their goodbyes to Laine, every single person making sure she knew how happy they were that she was going to be okay.

Penelope gave Laine an extra-long hug when it was her turn. "I'm very glad you're okay. If you ever need to talk to anyone, please let me know. I'm in a group... it's for people who've been held hostage, and I know it's different from what happened to you, but it might help if you need it. It's nice to know there are others who are feeling a lot of the same things as you."

"You okay?" Laine asked. She wasn't that close to Penelope, but she'd met her a few times and really liked her. She was a firecracker and tough as a whip, but she somehow put out vulnerable vibes at the same time.

"Yeah. I'm okay. Some days are better than others. I was serious about the group. There are people who have gone through a lot of shit, and they're amazing. One of my best friends in the group has to attend electronically now, but she's working on her issues. It makes what you and I went through look like a walk in the park."

Laine's interest was piqued. "Worse than what you went through?"

"Yeah. She moved here from California. She'd been kidnapped by a serial killer. A SEAL team rescued her and another woman before the sicko could kill them, but he'd had her long enough to make her life a living hell. She has problems leaving her house now as a result. It all sucks. She was doing really well, but recently she's been having issues getting to the meetings in person, so I set it up so she could attend remotely."

Laine wanted to ask more, to get to know more about what the poor woman had gone through and how she was doing, but another yawn broke through before she could comment.

Penelope gave her another long hug then pulled back again. "Okay, I'll let you go. I'm glad you're all right, Laine."

"Thanks, Penelope. See you later?"

"Definitely."

Wes put his arm around Laine as they waved to everyone from the doorway. Finally, when they were all gone, he pulled them inside and closed and locked the door.

Feeling more tired than she thought she'd be, Laine didn't protest as Wes helped her walk into his bedroom. He got her settled and said, "Let me take Chance out, now that the coast is clear. I'll be back."

"Okay." Laine held out her hand and Chance came over to the side of the bed and licked at it, before she and her four puppies followed Wes out of the room.

Laine snuggled down into the covers and closed her eyes.

She felt when Wes returned and climbed in behind her. He was warm against her back and the arm around her waist held her tightly to him.

"I love you," Wes murmured as he kissed her ear.

Laine turned to her back and smiled up at the handsome man above her. "I love you too."

"Will you marry me?"

Laine wasn't all that surprised at the question. She'd basically already told him she wanted to spend the rest of her life with him while they were out at the Johnson property, after Squirrel had hauled her out of the hole, but it felt good to make it official. "Yes."

"Good. When?"

"Whenever you want."

"Really?"

"Really."

"Tomorrow?"

"Uh… excuse me?"

"Tomorrow. We can go to the courthouse and do it."

"Don't we have to get a license and sit out the waiting period and all of that?" Laine asked.

"Damn. Yeah, I think it's seventy-two hours or something."

"What's the hurry? I'm not going anywhere," Laine soothed, running her hand up and down his biceps.

"When I realized how much I love you and how precious life is, I recognized that our time here on earth is just too short. I want to spend every second of the time I have left with you."

"We can do that and not be married," Laine said reasonably. She wasn't trying to talk Wes out of it, but was trying to understand the urgency he was feeling.

"I want my ring on your finger, and I'm hoping you'll change your name to King. But I would totally understand if you didn't want to. It's kind of archaic that the woman has to be the one to change her name, but I can't help that it would make me feel good."

"Laine King. It sounds good," she mused.

"It sounds fucking fantastic," Wes agreed, then leaned down to kiss her.

"As soon as the three days go by, I'll marry you. Although... Mack is gonna lose her mind if she's not invited. And probably Mickie and Corrie too. And I wouldn't want to do it without your friends there. Oh, and Squirrel and Moose and Penelope, and all the others from the fire station too. We can't leave them out."

Wes laughed. "How about we have a nice quiet civil ceremony then have a big-ass party later?"

"Deal. I want to make love to you, Wes." When he opened his mouth to speak, Laine put her finger on his lips to shush him and continued, "But I'm still too sore. Just the *thought* of spreading my legs is enough to make me wanna hurl, imagining the pressure it'd put on my hips. But as soon as I'm feeling up to it, you had better watch out. I'm gonna jump you."

Wes chuckled. "I'll look forward to it, darlin'. I'm perfectly content to hold you close all night and every night until you're healed enough."

"Maybe in the barn... can we reenact that moment when we first saw each other? I'd love to act out my vivid dreams of running across the barn and taking you to the ground and having my way with you," Laine told Wes with a smirk. "That rope and your cowboy hat have played front and center in a lot of my fantasies as well. I swear to God, the first thing I thought when I saw you standing there without your shirt on and your V-muscles leading to my Promised Land, was that you were the most amazing specimen of a man I'd ever seen in my life."

"You too?" Wes asked with a grin. "That was *my* fantasy. Not my abs, but pulling you into my arms, stripping off your top so I could get a good look at those tits and the nipples that stood up to say hello to me, and taking you right there against the wall in my barn."

"I'm so glad I didn't back out of coming to watch that photography session that day. It changed my life… for the better."

"Mine too." Wes kissed Laine, making sure she kept still so as not to hurt herself. "I got the photos from that day back from Jack. I'm supposed to pick my favorite three. I forgot about it until now. Will you help me choose?"

"Oh, shit yeah. I want you to be the hottest man in that calendar, but I was serious when I told you back then that I'd prefer for you to be all mine. I'll let others drool over your body, but your face is all mine. My very own Texas Ranger cowboy. I love you, more than you'll ever know."

"I know, because I love you like that too. Sleep now. Tomorrow is the first day of the rest of our lives."

Look for the next book in the Badge of Honor Series:
Shelter for Elizabeth.

If you want to know more about Penelope, the Army Princess, and her ordeal of being kidnapped by ISIS, please check out
Protecting the Future.

Sign up for Susan's newsletter to be notified when all her books go on sale and for other information and prizes.

To sign up for Susan's Newsletter go to:
http://bit.ly/SusanStokerNewsletter

Or text: STOKER to 24587 for text alerts on your mobile device

Discover other titles by Susan Stoker

<u>Badge of Honor: Texas Heroes Series</u>
Justice for Mackenzie
Justice for Mickie
Justice for Corrie
Justice for Laine (novella)
Shelter for Elizabeth
Justice for Boone
Shelter for Adeline (Jan 2017)
Shelter for Sophie (Aug 2017)
Justice for Sidney (Oct 2017)
Shelter for Blythe (TBA)
Justice for Milena (TBA)
Justice for Kinley (TBA)
Shelter for Promise (TBA)
Shelter for Koren (TBA)
Shelter for Penelope (TBA)

<u>Unsung Heroes: Delta Force</u>
Rescuing Rayne
Assisting Aimee – Loosely related to DF
Rescuing Emily
Rescuing Harley (Nov 2016)
Marrying Emily (Spring 2017)
Rescuing Kassie (May 2017)
Rescuing Bryn (Nov 2017)
Rescuing Casey (TBA)
Rescuing Wendy (TBA)
Rescuing Mary (TBA)

Ace Security Series
Claiming Grace (Mar 2017)
Claiming Alexis (July 2017)
Claiming Bailey (TBA)

SEAL of Protection Series
Protecting Caroline
Protecting Alabama
Protecting Alabama's Kids
Protecting Fiona
Marrying Caroline (novella)
Protecting Summer
Protecting Cheyenne
Protecting Jessyka
Protecting Julie (novella)
Protecting Melody
Protecting the Future

Stand Alone:
The Guardian Mist

Beyond Reality Series
Outback Hearts
Flaming Hearts
Frozen Hearts

Writing as Annie George
Stepbrother Virgin (erotic novella)

Connect with Susan Online

Susan's Facebook Profile and Page:
www.facebook.com/authorsstoker
www.facebook.com/authorsusanstoker

Follow Susan on Twitter:
www.twitter.com/Susan_Stoker

Find Susan's Books on Goodreads:
www.goodreads.com/SusanStoker

Email: Susan@StokerAces.com

Website: www.StokerAces.com

To sign up for Susan's Newsletter go to:
http://bit.ly/SusanStokerNewsletter

Or text: STOKER to 24587 for text alerts on your mobile device

About the Author

New York Times, USA Today, and *Wall Street Journal* Bestselling Author Susan Stoker has a heart as big as the state of Texas, where she lives, but this all-American girl has also spent the last fourteen years living in Missouri, California, Colorado, and Indiana. She's married to a retired Army man who now gets to follow *her* around the country.

She debuted her first series in 2014 and quickly followed that up with the SEAL of Protection Series, which solidified her love of writing and creating stories readers can get lost in.

If you enjoyed this book, or any book, please consider leaving a review. It's appreciated by authors more than you'll know.

CPSIA information can be obtained
at www.ICGtesting.com
Printed in the USA
LVHW081553121119
637003LV00038B/853/P

9 781943 562